THE SECRET OF THE RAVENS

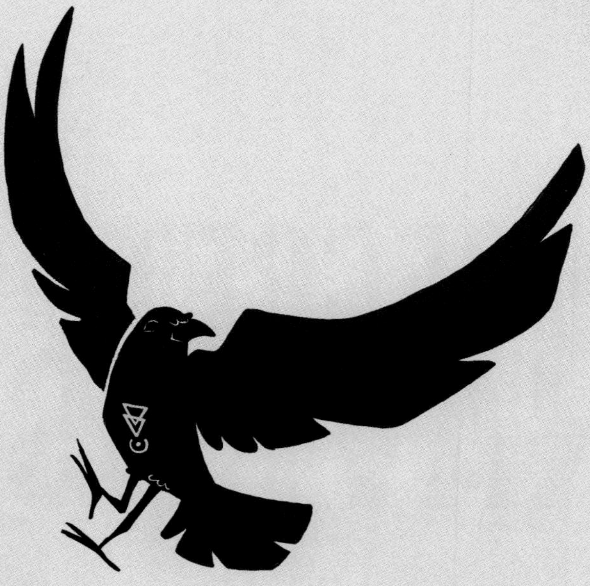
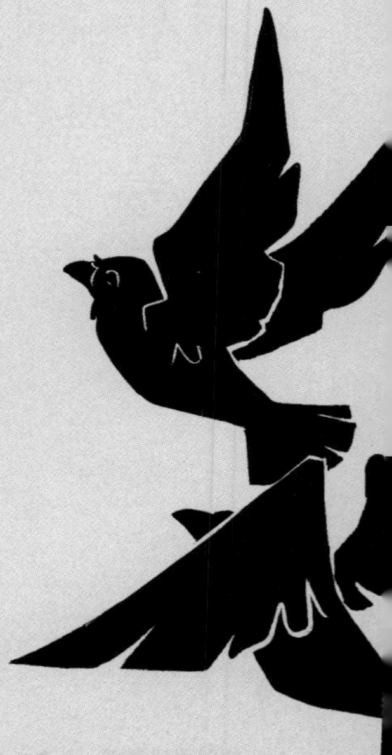

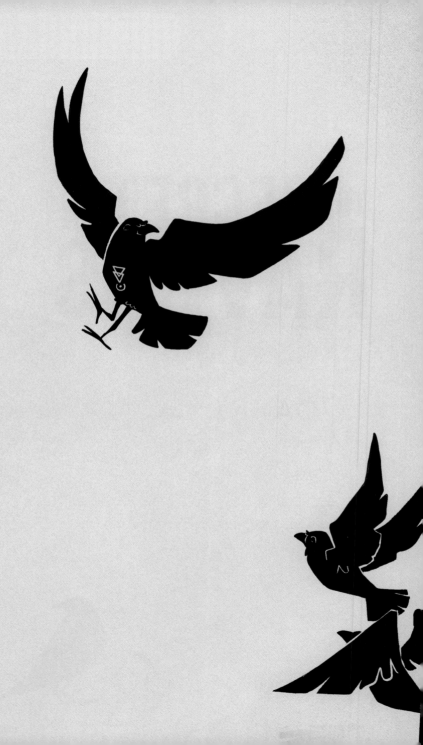

THE SECRET OF THE RAVENS

JOANNA CACAO

CLARION BOOKS
Imprints of HarperCollins*Publishers*

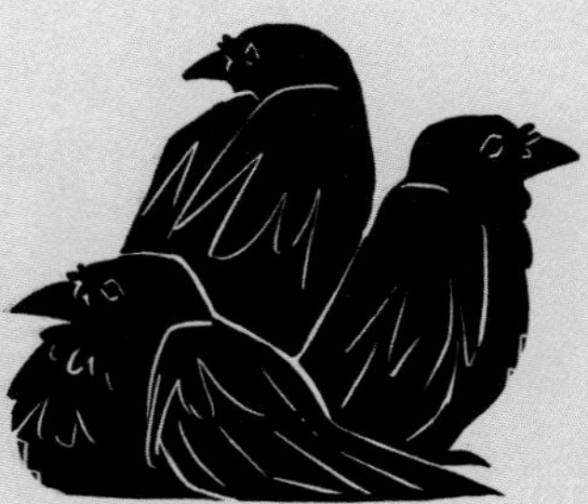

CLARION BOOKS IS AN IMPRINT OF HARPERCOLLINS PUBLISHERS.
HARPERALLEY IS AN IMPRINT OF HARPERCOLLINS PUBLISHERS.

THE SECRET OF THE RAVENS

FOR INFORMATION ADDRESS HARPERCOLLINS CHILDREN'S BOOKS, A DIVISION OF HARPERCOLLINS PUBLISHERS, 195 BROADWAY, NEW YORK, NY 10007.
WWW.HARPERALLEY.COM

ISBN 978-0-35-862944-3 — ISBN 978-0-35-865011-9 (PBK.)

THE ILLUSTRATIONS IN THIS BOOK WERE DONE IN PROCREATE ON AN IPAD PRO (2018 MODEL).
LETTERING BY KYLA AIKO
DESIGN BY CELESTE KNUDSEN

23 24 25 26 27 GPS 10 9 8 7 6 5 4 3 2 1

FIRST EDITION

TO ALL THOSE WHO DREAM OF CREATING STORIES FOR A
LIVING, MAY YOU FIND JOY IN WHAT YOU DO.

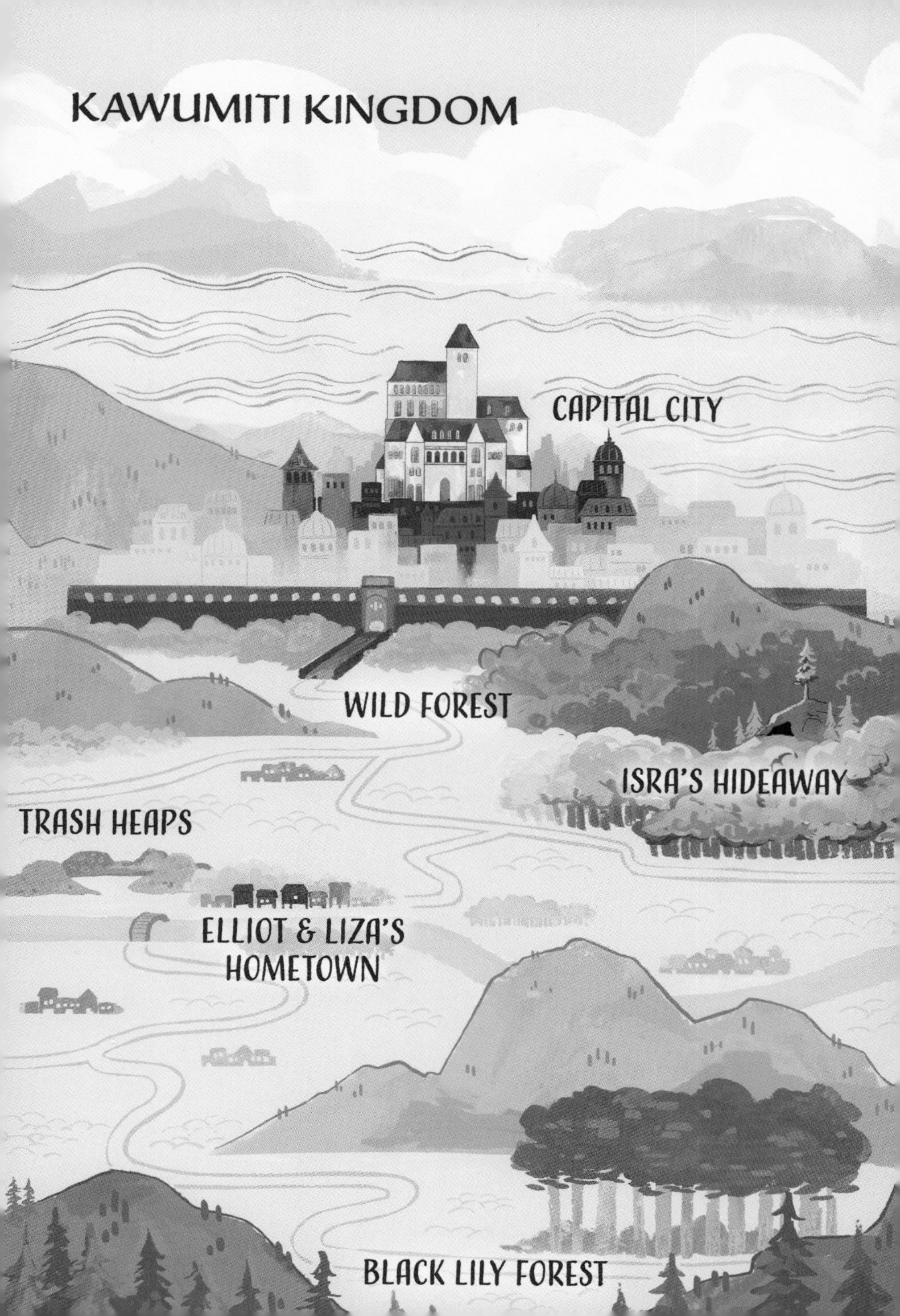
KAWUMITI KINGDOM
CAPITAL CITY
WILD FOREST
ISRA'S HIDEAWAY
TRASH HEAPS
ELLIOT & LIZA'S
HOMETOWN
BLACK LILY FOREST

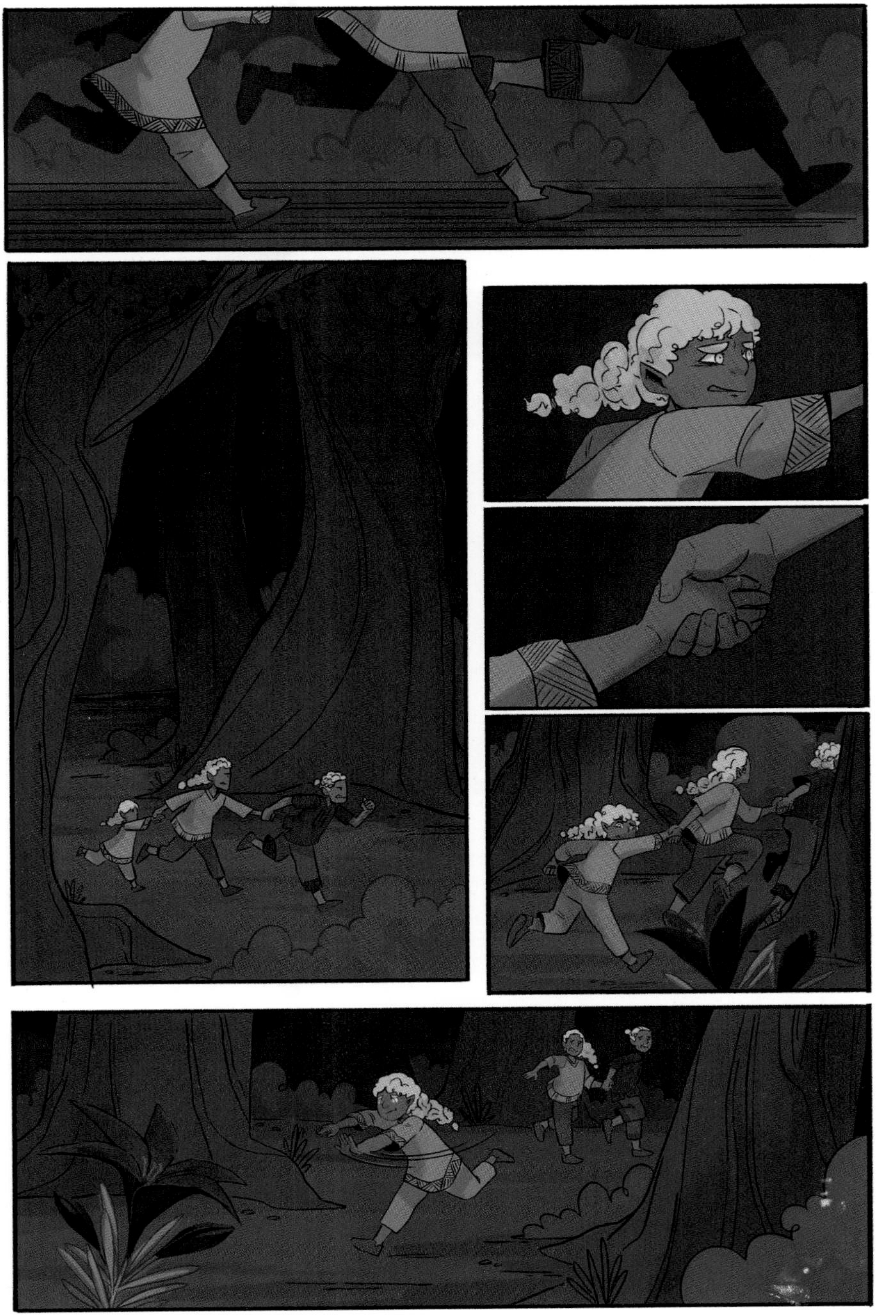

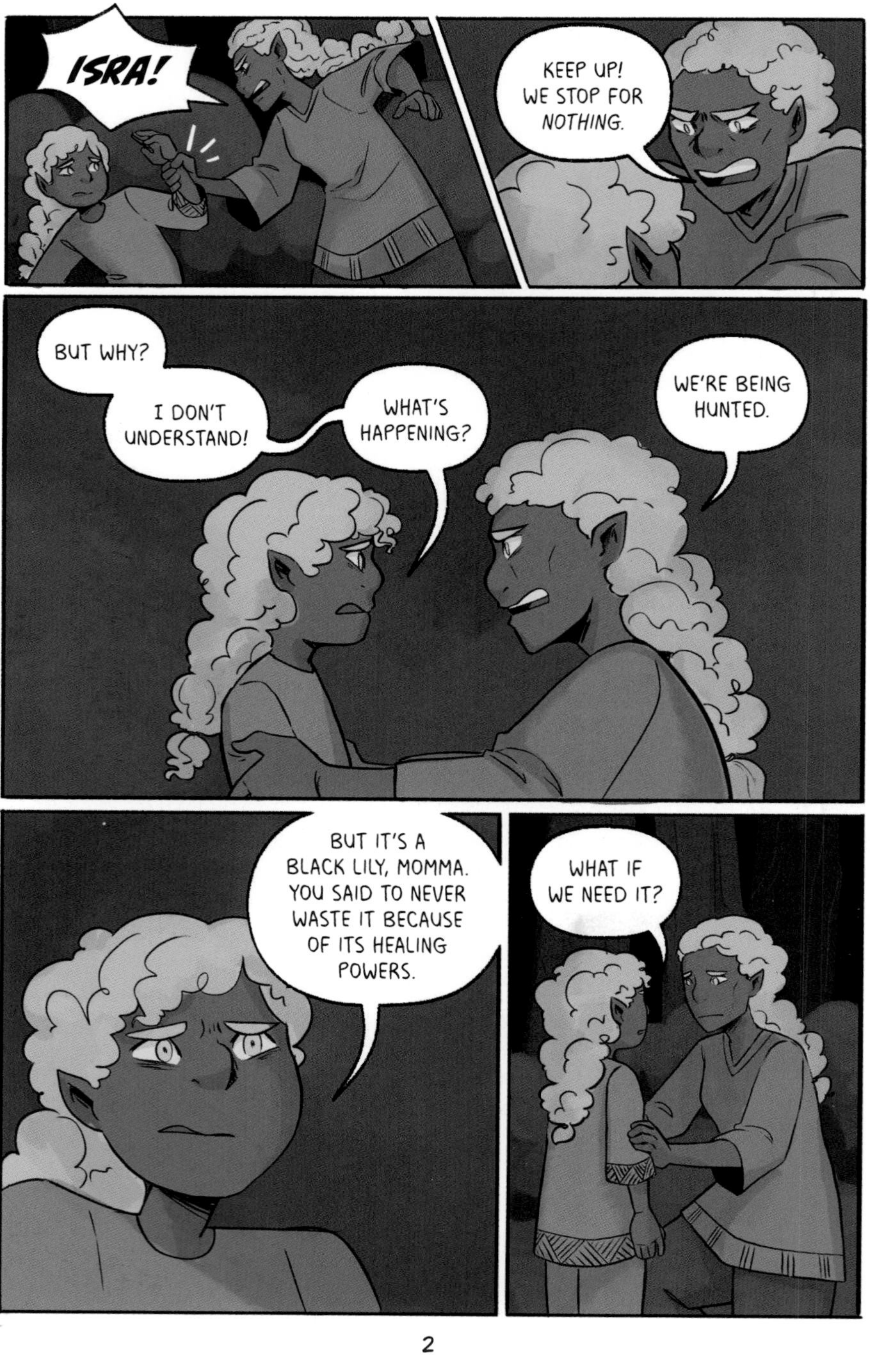
ISRA!
KEEP UP! WE STOP FOR NOTHING.
BUT WHY?
I DON'T UNDERSTAND!
WHAT'S HAPPENING?
WE'RE BEING HUNTED.
BUT IT'S A BLACK LILY, MOMMA. YOU SAID TO NEVER WASTE IT BECAUSE OF ITS HEALING POWERS.
WHAT IF WE NEED IT?

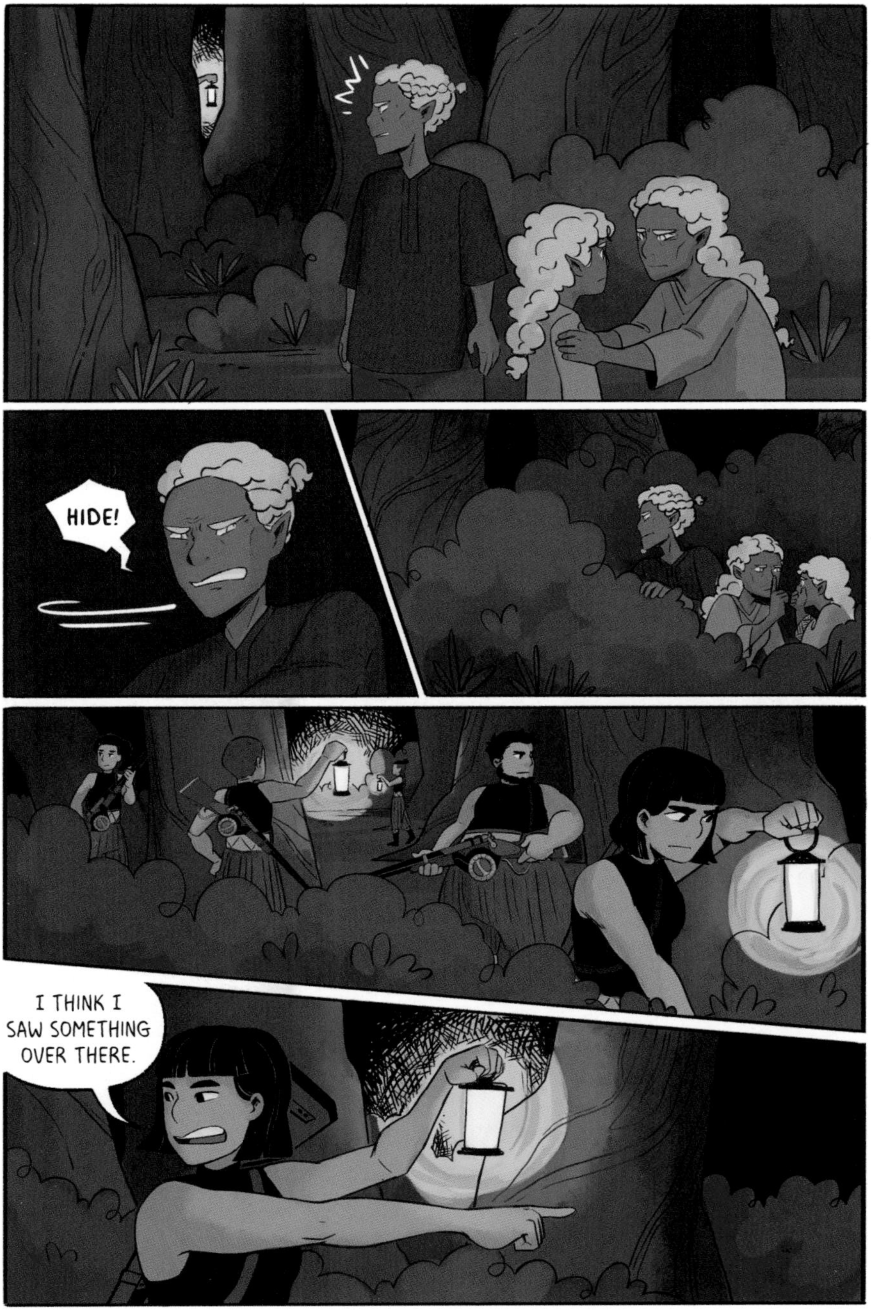
HIDE!
I THINK I SAW SOMETHING OVER THERE.

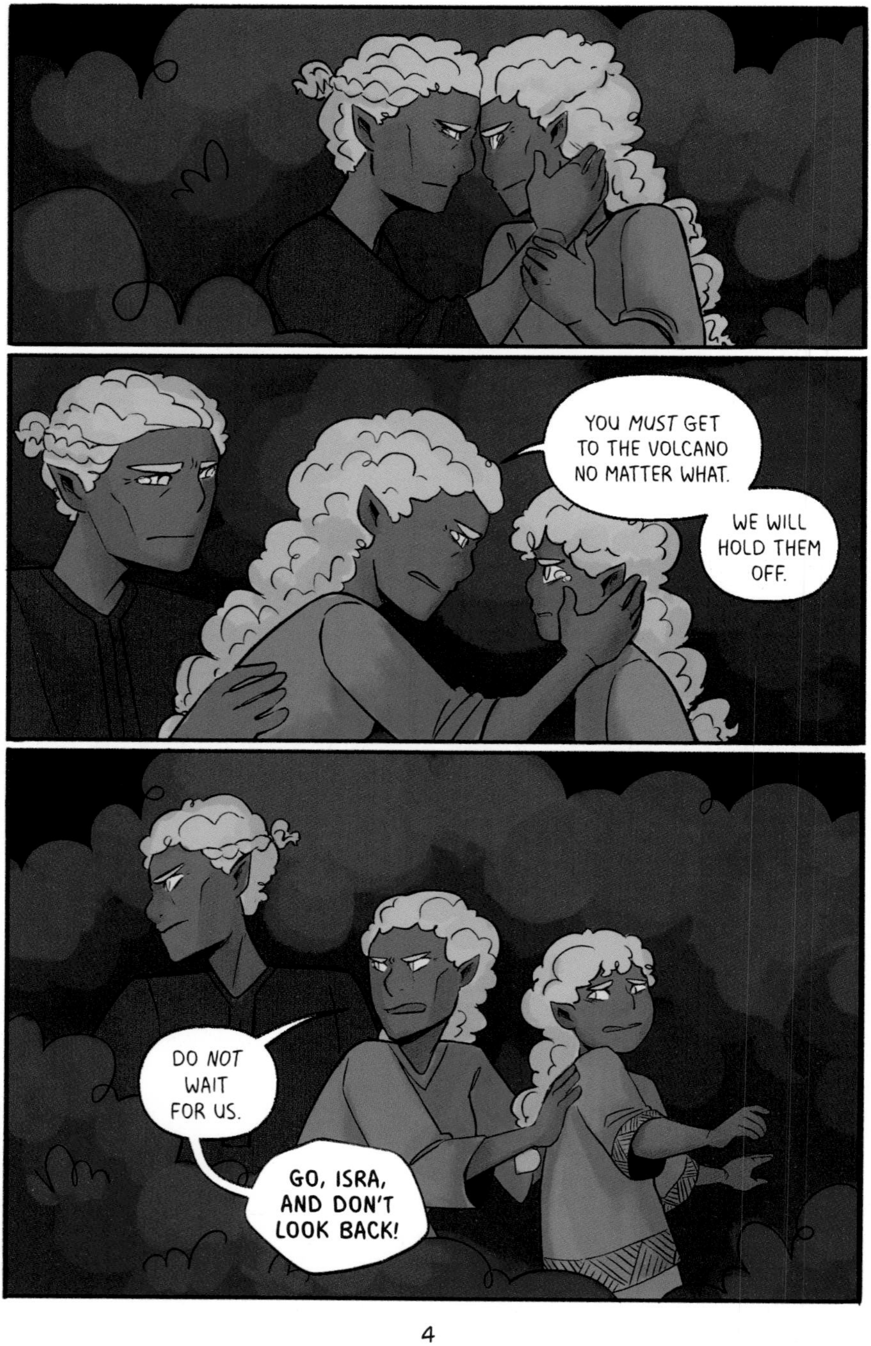
YOU *MUST* GET TO THE VOLCANO NO MATTER WHAT.
WE WILL HOLD THEM OFF.
DO *NOT* WAIT FOR US.
GO, ISRA, AND DON'T LOOK BACK!

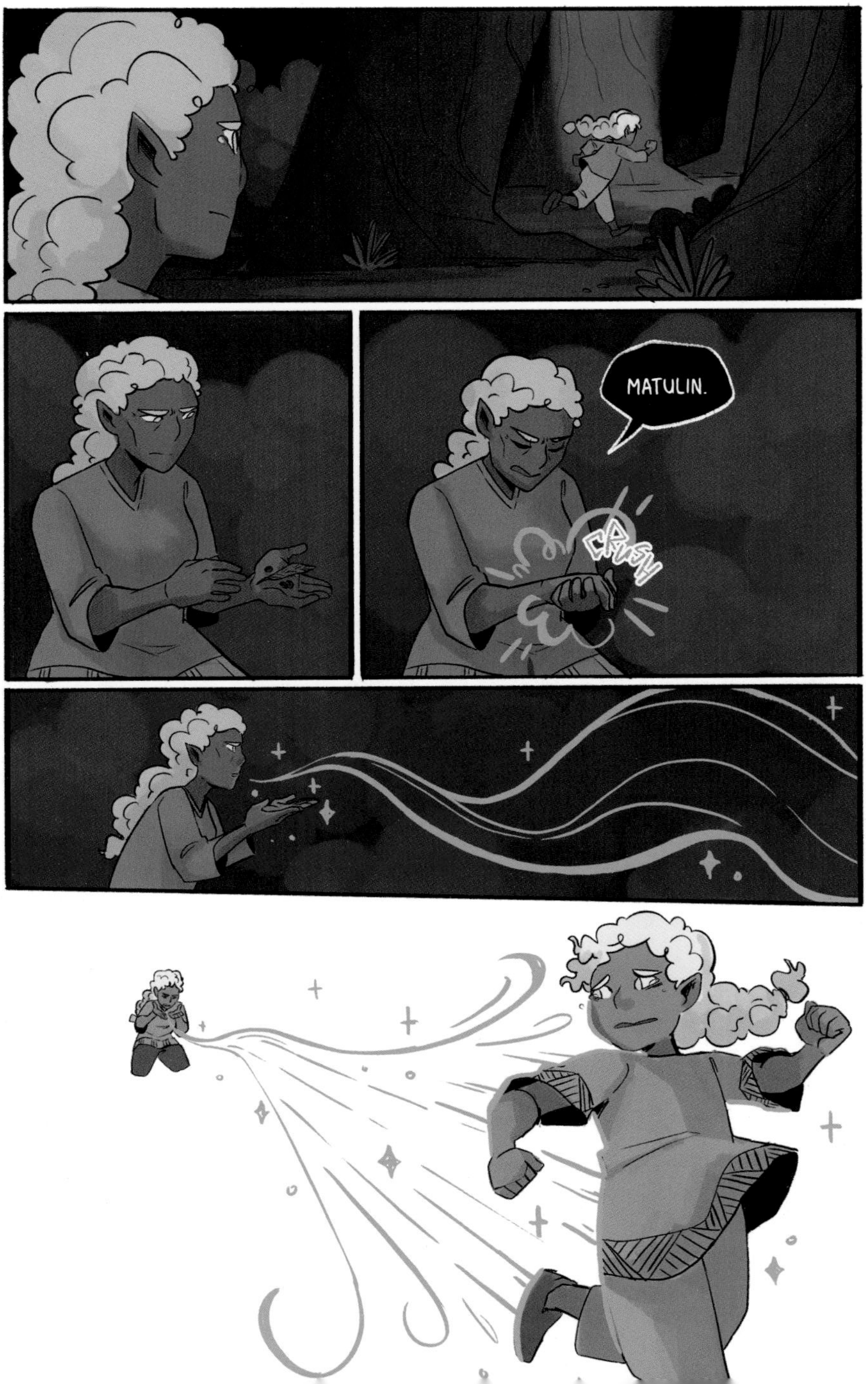
MATULIN.
CRUSH

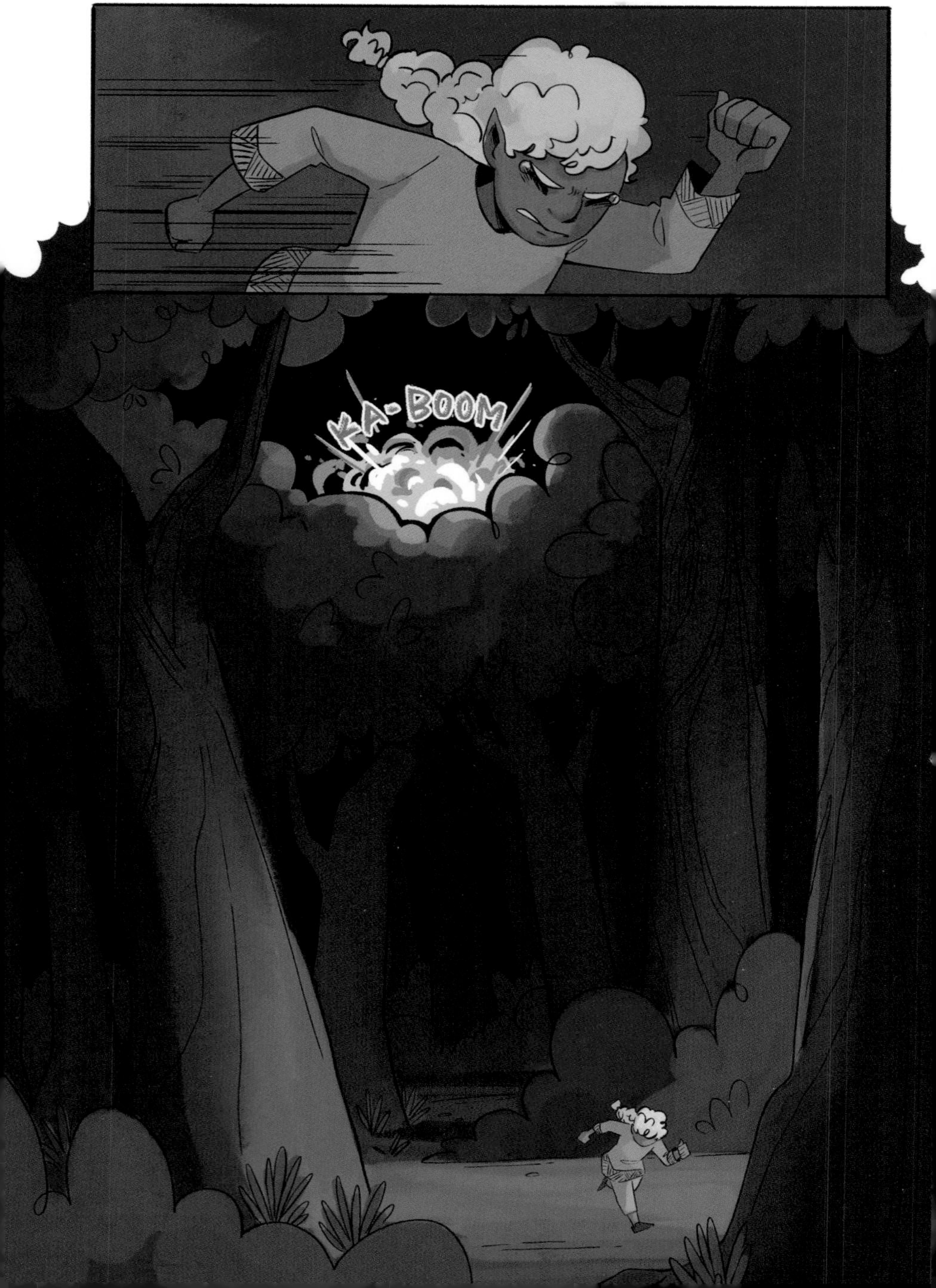
KA-BOOM

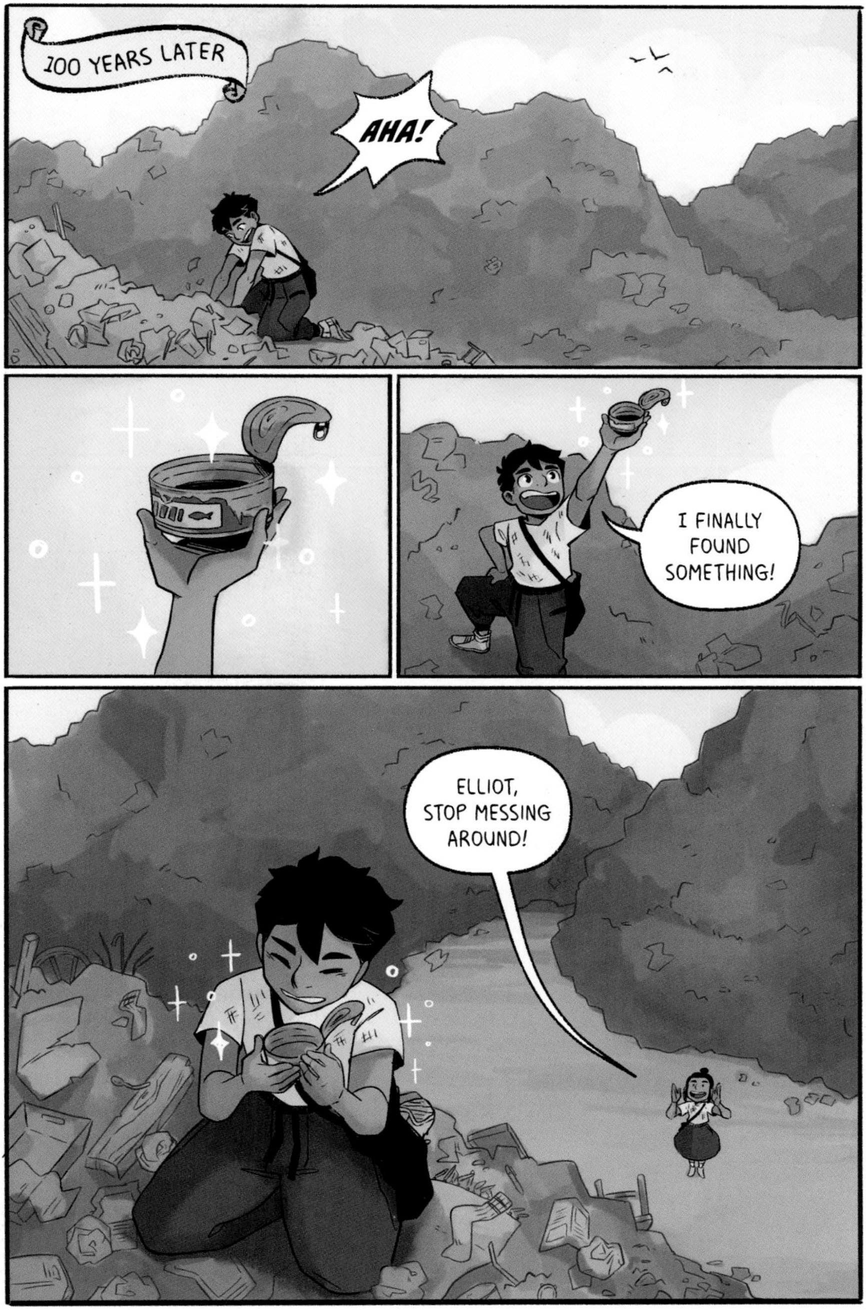
100 YEARS LATER
AHA!
I FINALLY FOUND SOMETHING!
ELLIOT, STOP MESSING AROUND!

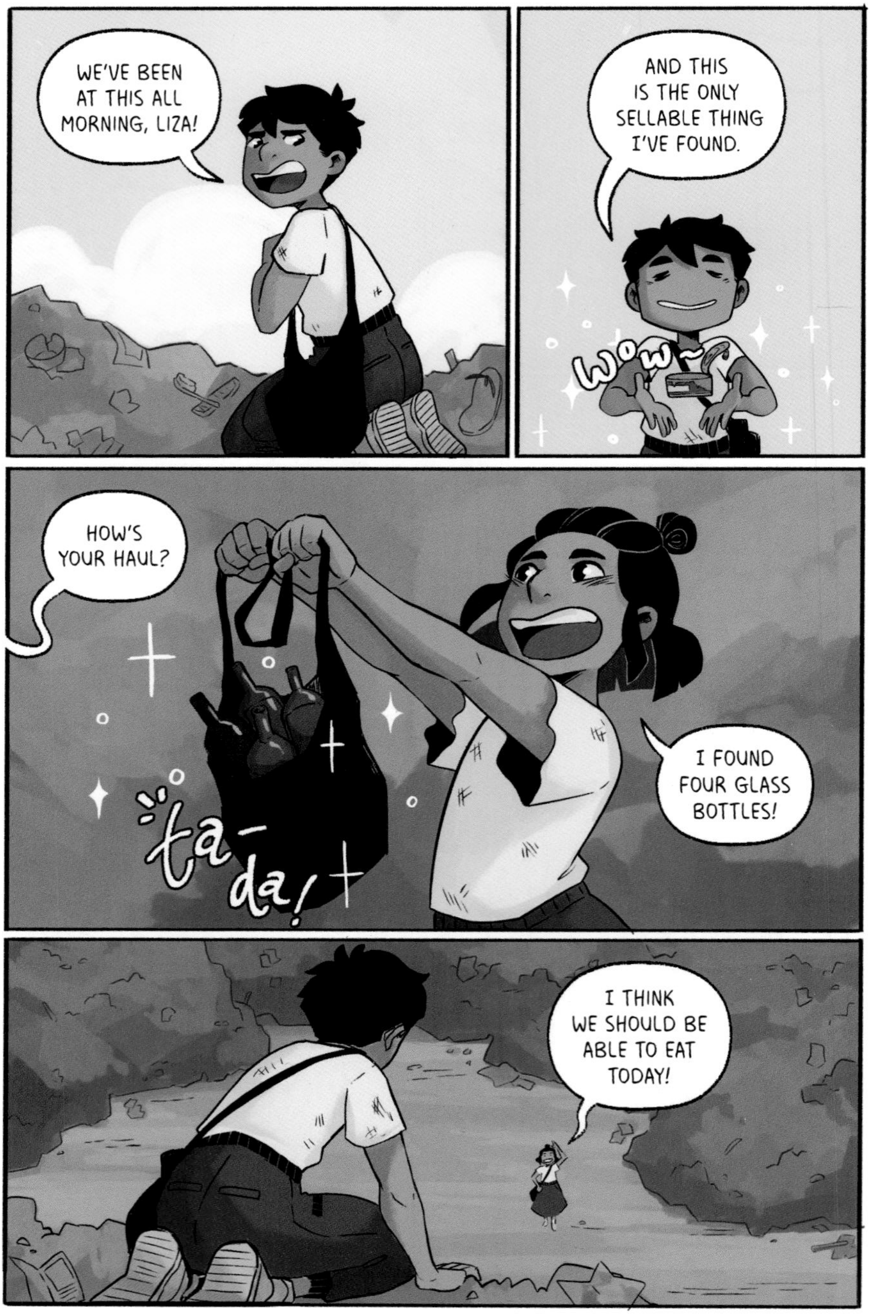
WE'VE BEEN AT THIS ALL MORNING, LIZA!
AND THIS IS THE ONLY SELLABLE THING I'VE FOUND.
wow~
HOW'S YOUR HAUL?
I FOUND FOUR GLASS BOTTLES!
ta-da!
I THINK WE SHOULD BE ABLE TO EAT TODAY!

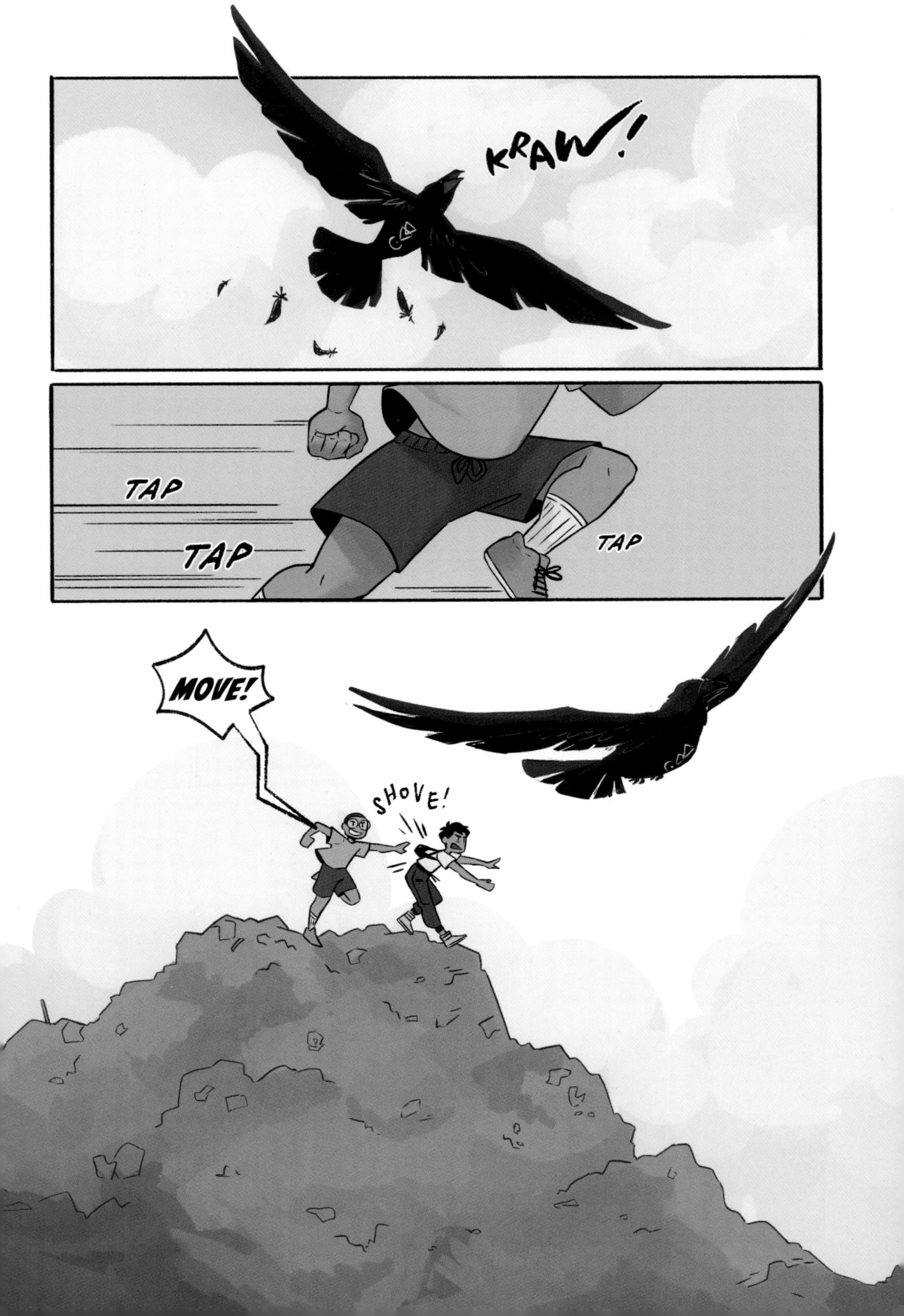
KRAW!
TAP
TAP
TAP
MOVE!
SHOVE!

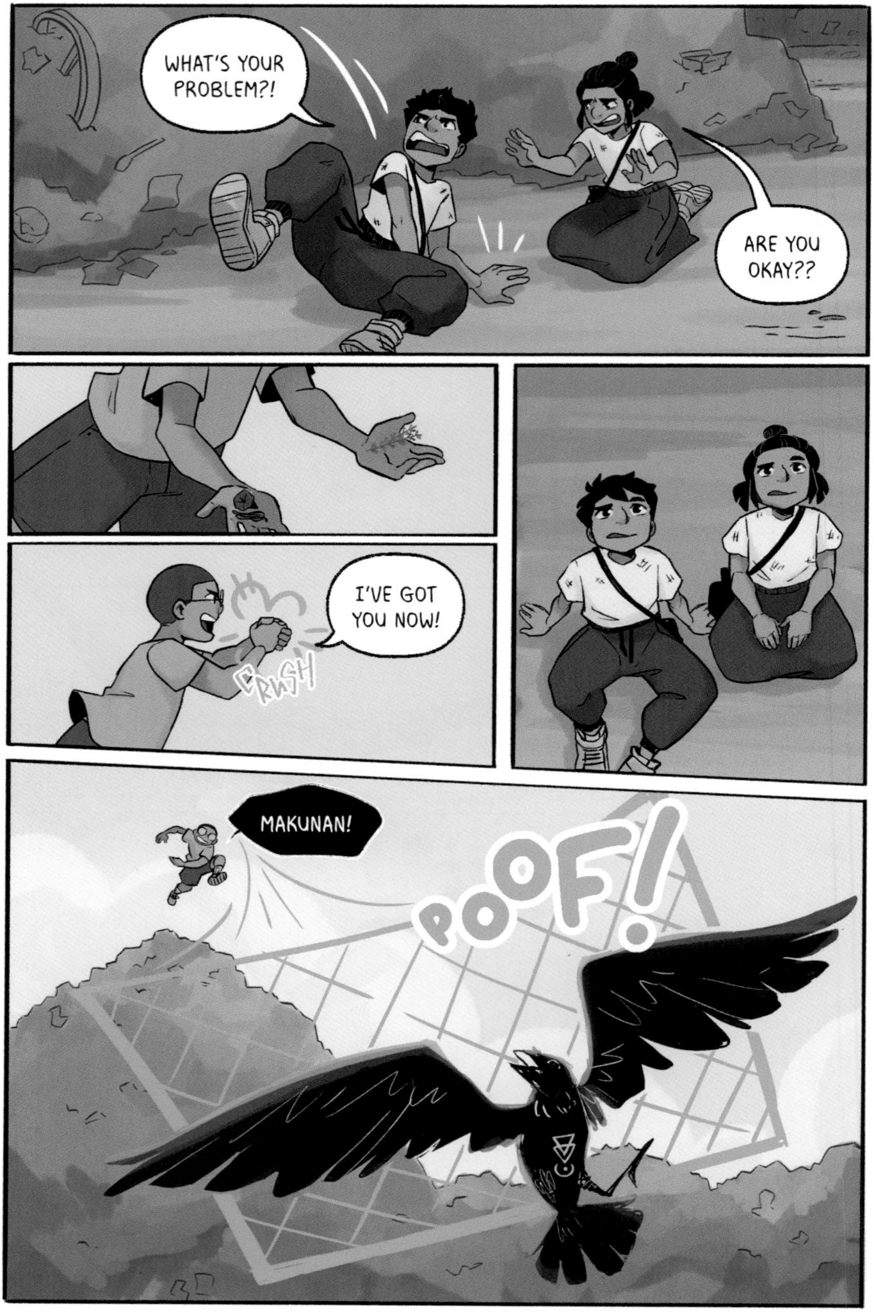
WHAT'S YOUR PROBLEM?!
ARE YOU OKAY??
I'VE GOT YOU NOW!
CRUSH
MAKUNAN!
POOF!

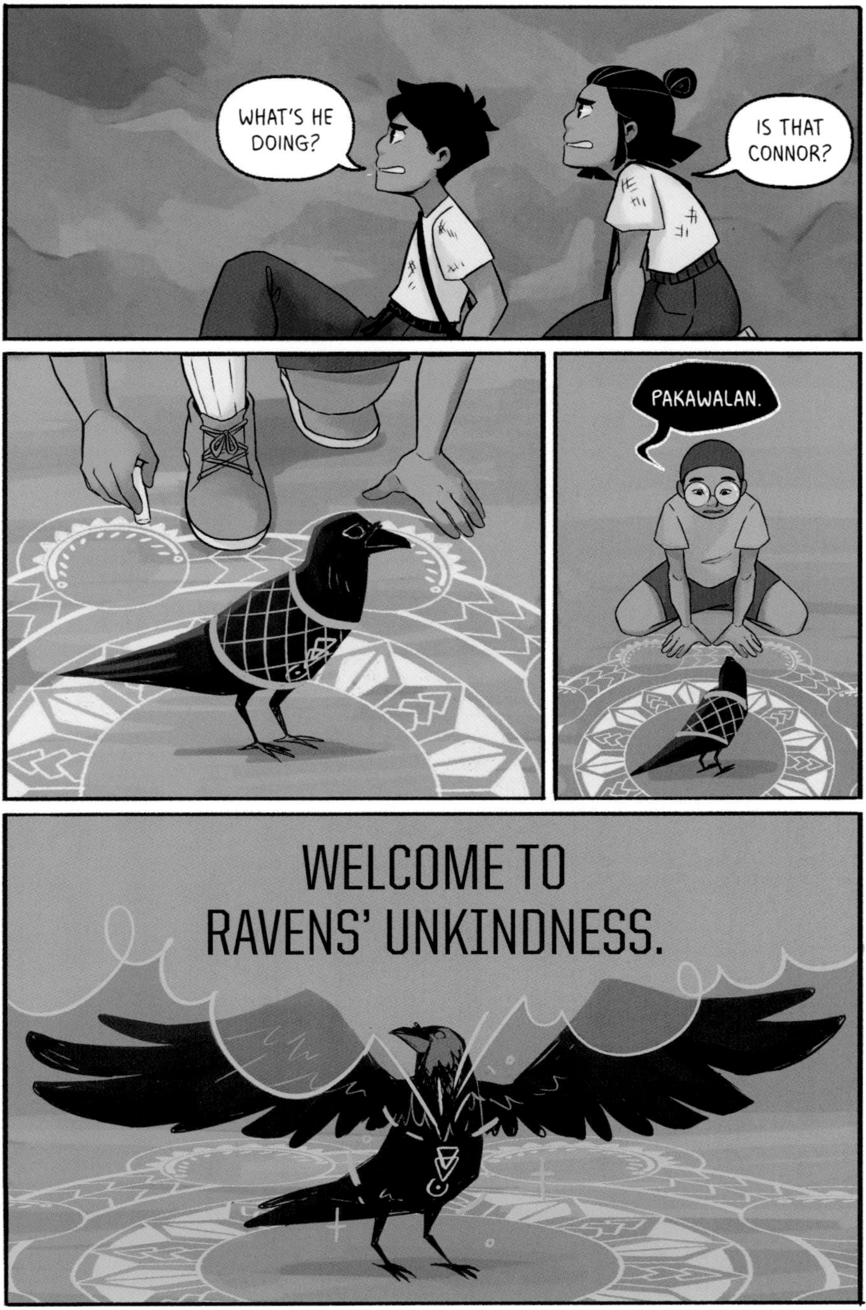
WHAT'S HE DOING?
IS THAT CONNOR?
PAKAWALAN.
WELCOME TO RAVENS' UNKINDNESS.

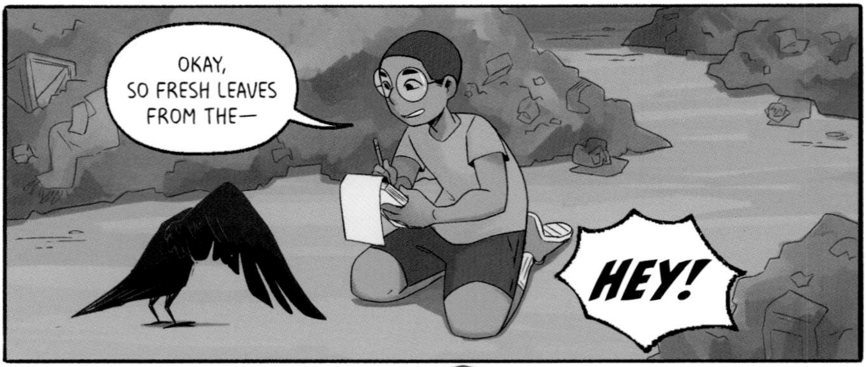
OKAY, SO FRESH LEAVES FROM THE—
HEY!

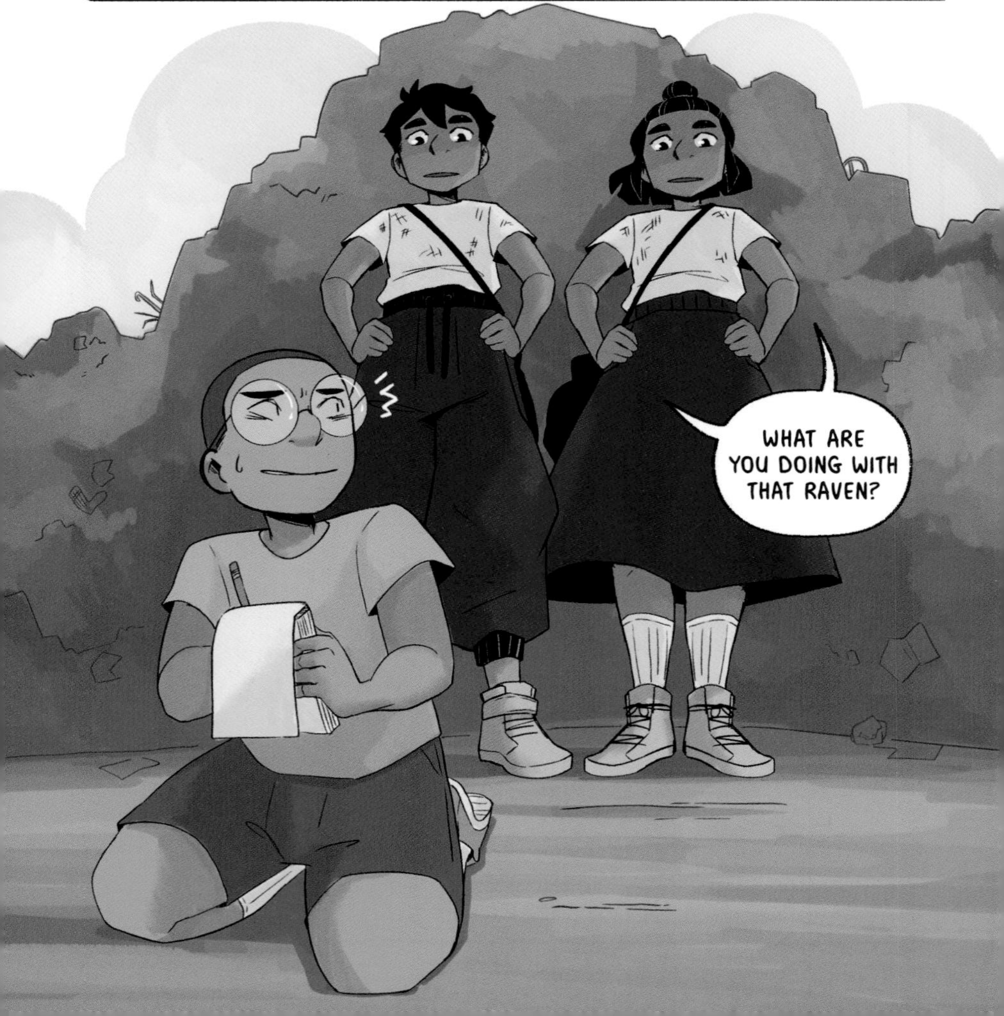
WHAT ARE YOU DOING WITH THAT RAVEN?

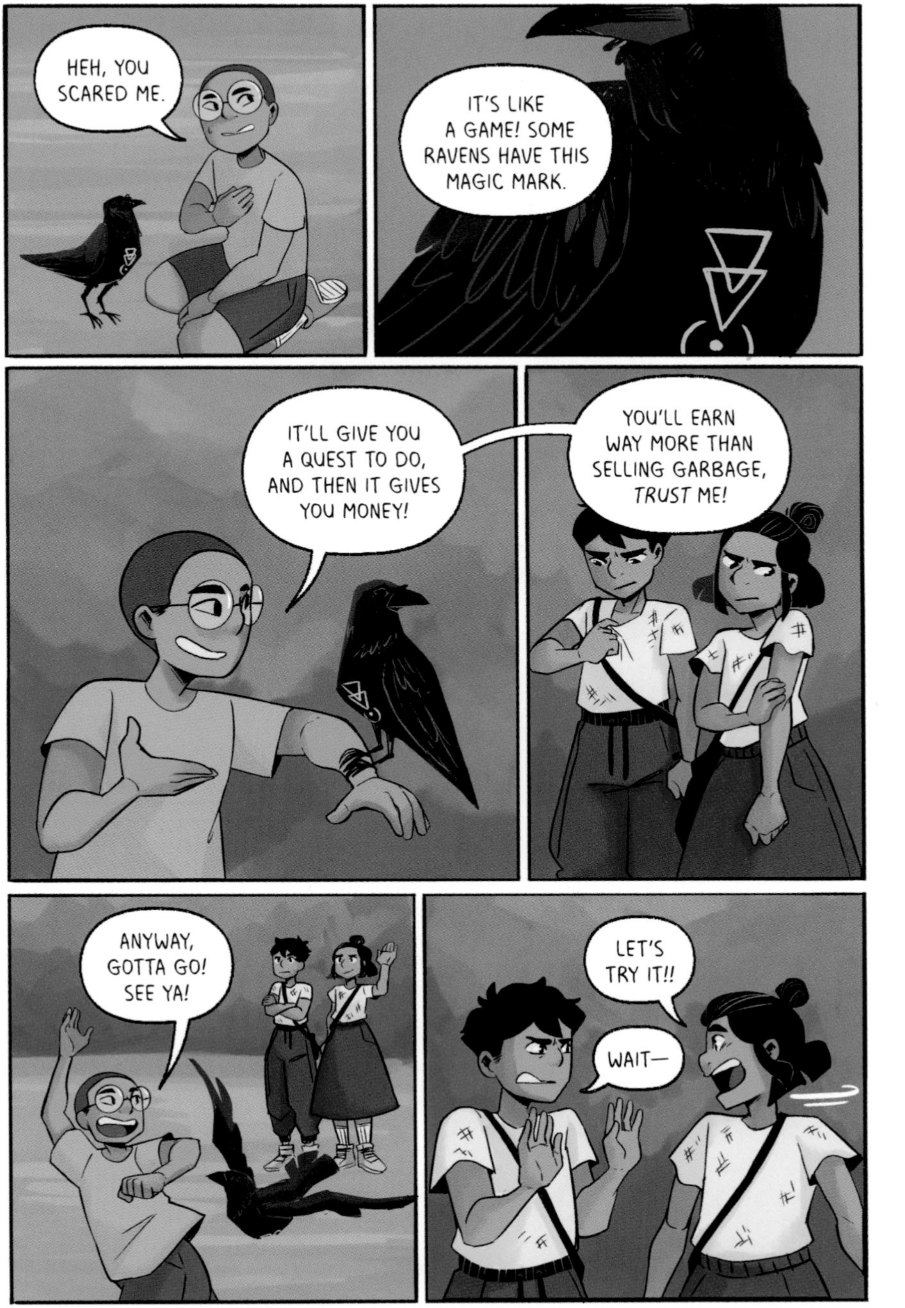

HEH, YOU SCARED ME.
IT'S LIKE A GAME! SOME RAVENS HAVE THIS MAGIC MARK.
IT'LL GIVE YOU A QUEST TO DO, AND THEN IT GIVES YOU MONEY!
YOU'LL EARN WAY MORE THAN SELLING GARBAGE, *TRUST* ME!
ANYWAY, GOTTA GO! SEE YA!
LET'S TRY IT!!
WAIT—

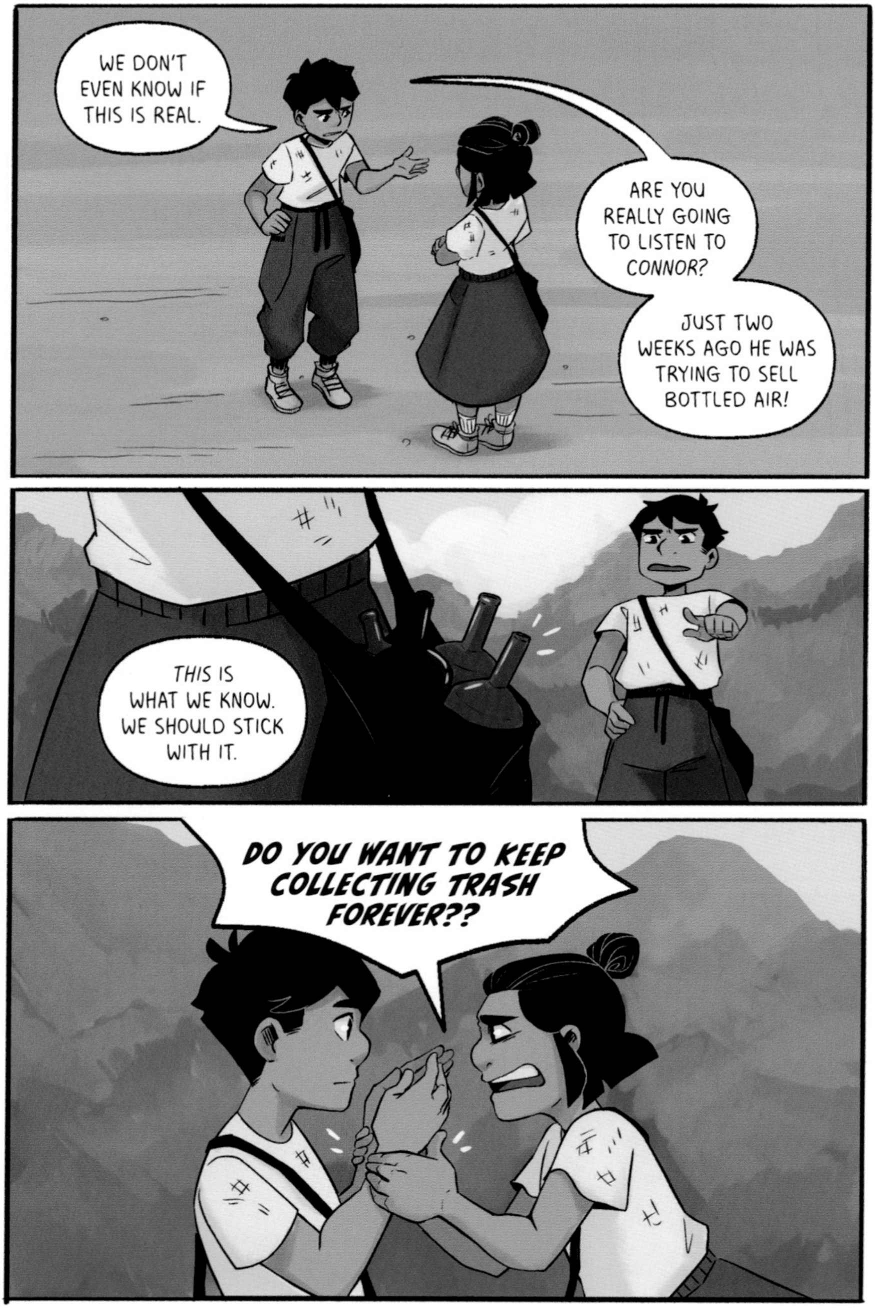
WE DON'T EVEN KNOW IF THIS IS REAL.
ARE YOU REALLY GOING TO LISTEN TO *CONNOR*?
JUST TWO WEEKS AGO HE WAS TRYING TO SELL BOTTLED AIR!
THIS IS WHAT WE KNOW. WE SHOULD STICK WITH IT.
DO YOU WANT TO KEEP COLLECTING TRASH FOREVER??

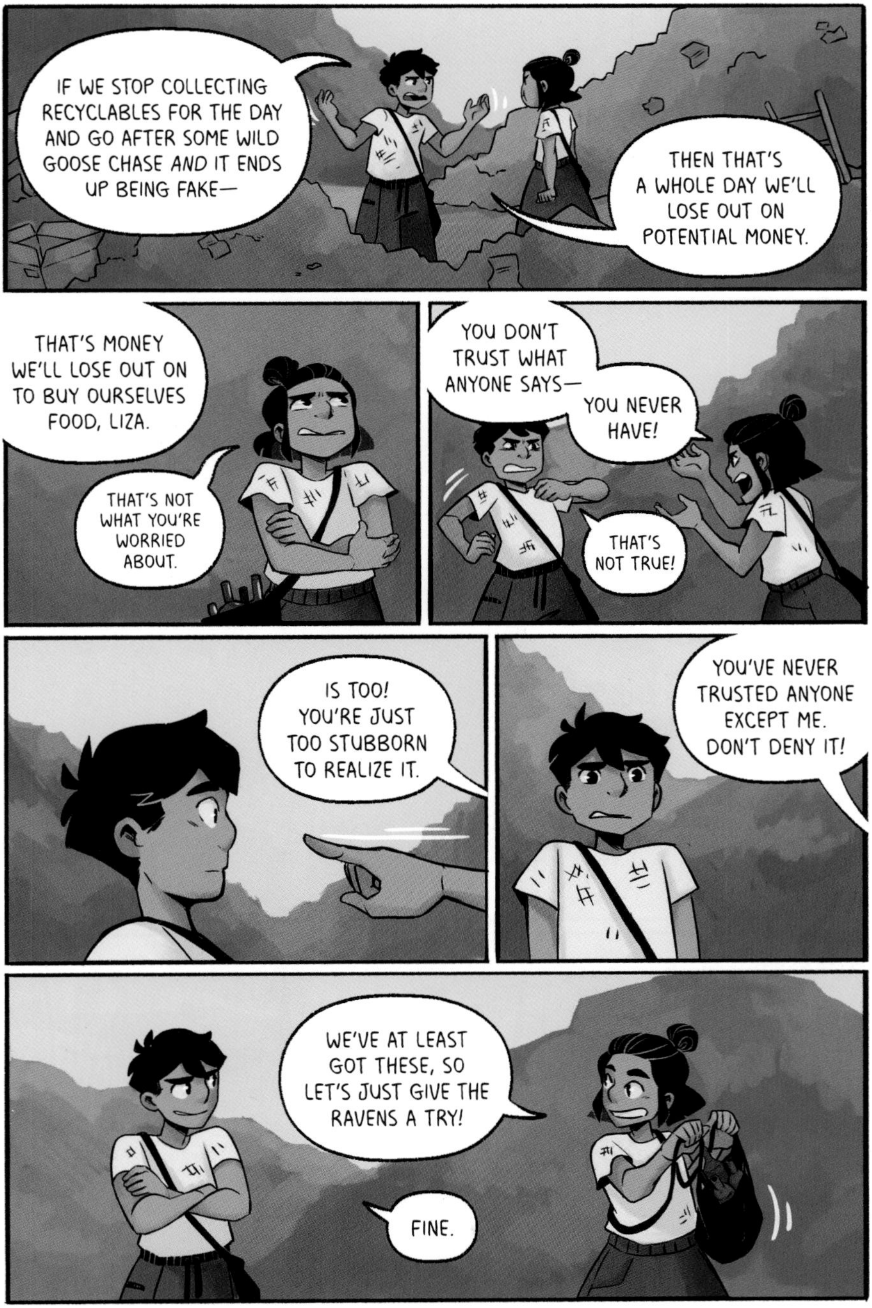
IF WE STOP COLLECTING RECYCLABLES FOR THE DAY AND GO AFTER SOME WILD GOOSE CHASE *AND* IT ENDS UP BEING FAKE—
THEN THAT'S A WHOLE DAY WE'LL LOSE OUT ON POTENTIAL MONEY.
THAT'S MONEY WE'LL LOSE OUT ON TO BUY OURSELVES FOOD, LIZA.
THAT'S NOT WHAT YOU'RE WORRIED ABOUT.
YOU DON'T TRUST WHAT ANYONE SAYS—
YOU NEVER HAVE!
THAT'S NOT TRUE!
IS TOO! YOU'RE JUST TOO STUBBORN TO REALIZE IT.
YOU'VE NEVER TRUSTED ANYONE EXCEPT ME. DON'T DENY IT!
WE'VE AT LEAST GOT THESE, SO LET'S JUST GIVE THE RAVENS A TRY!
FINE.

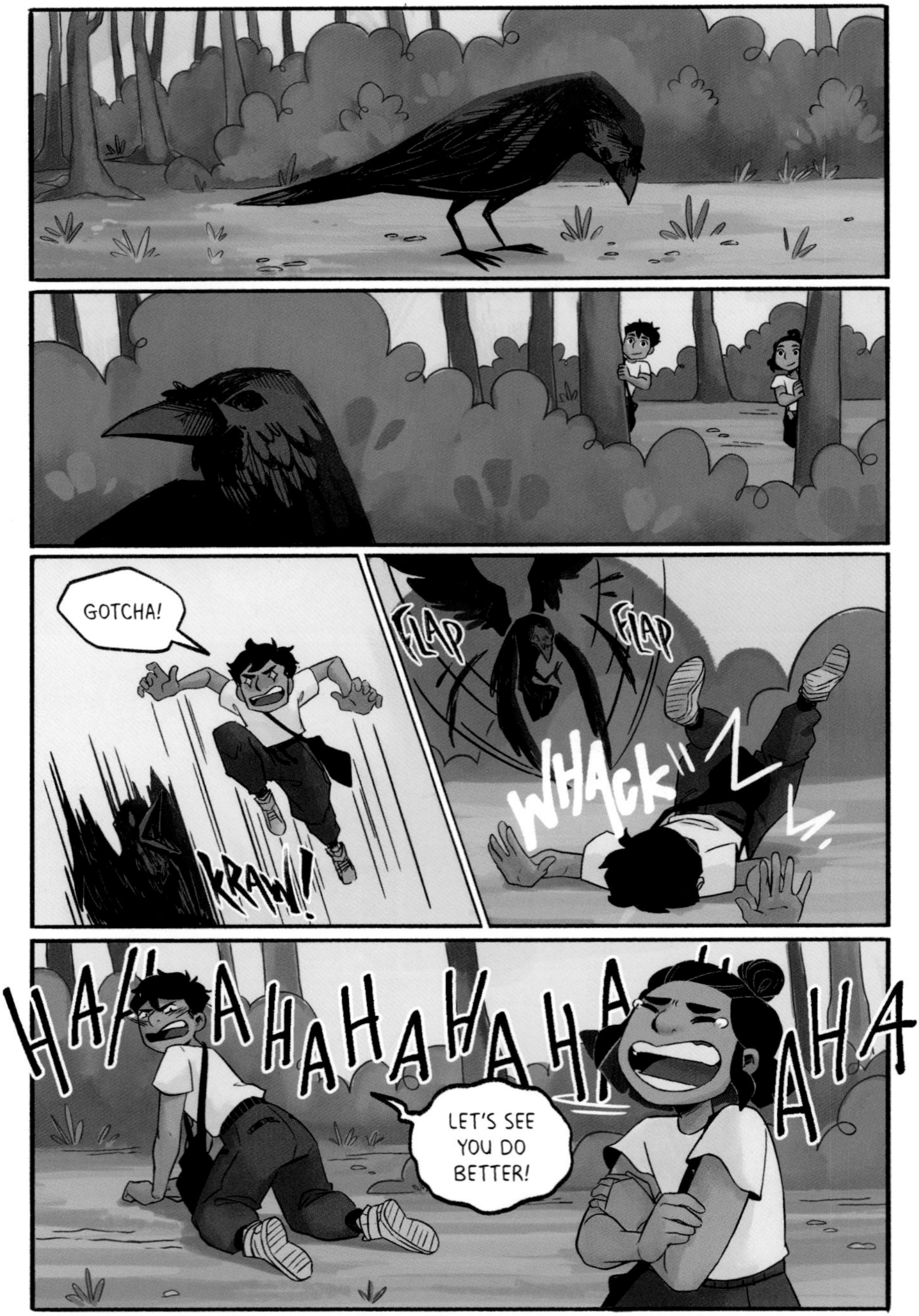
GOTCHA!
KRAW!
FLAP FLAP
WHACK
HAHAHAHAHAHAHAHAHAHA
LET'S SEE YOU DO BETTER!

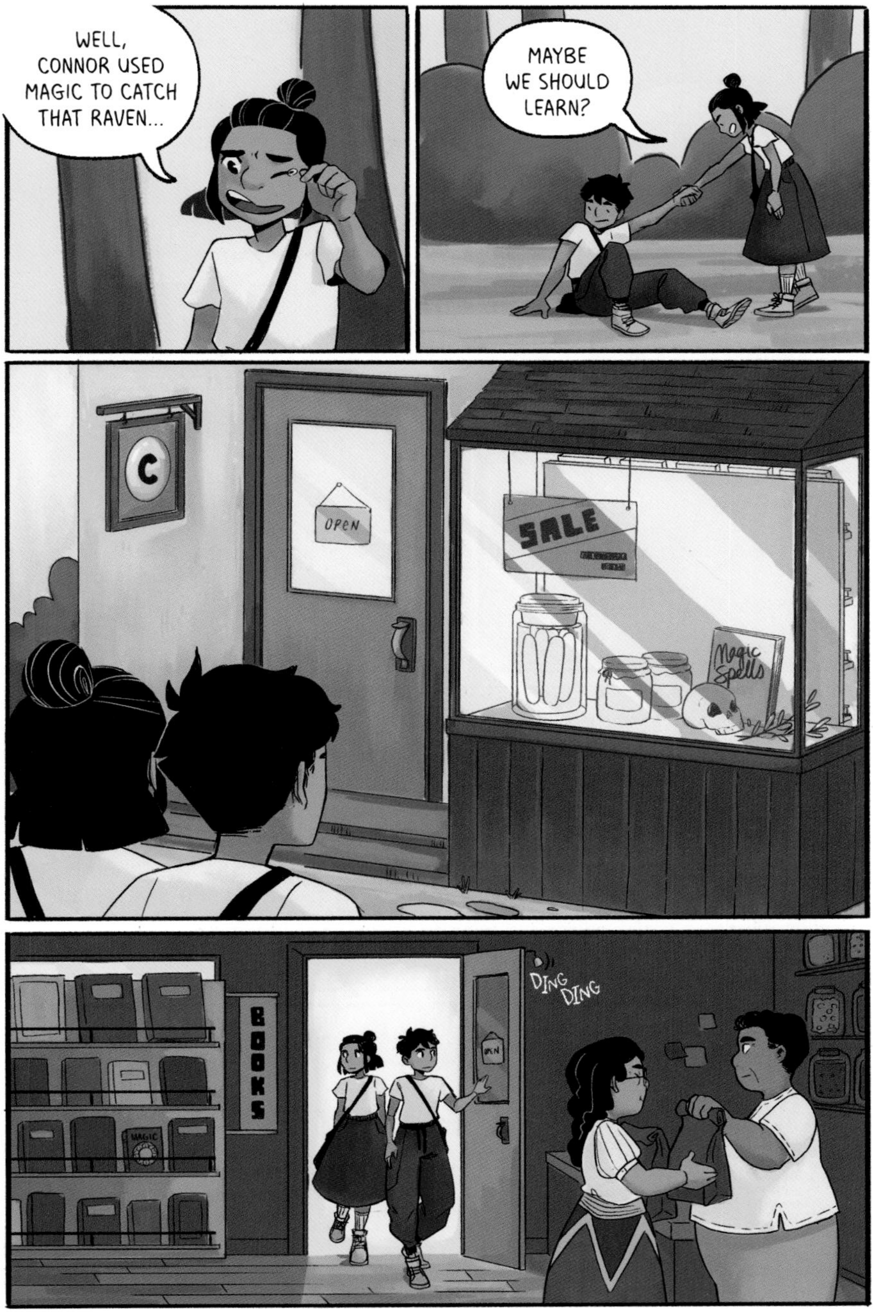
WELL, CONNOR USED MAGIC TO CATCH THAT RAVEN...
MAYBE WE SHOULD LEARN?
C
OPEN
SALE
Magic Spells
BOOKS
MAGIC
OPEN
DING DING

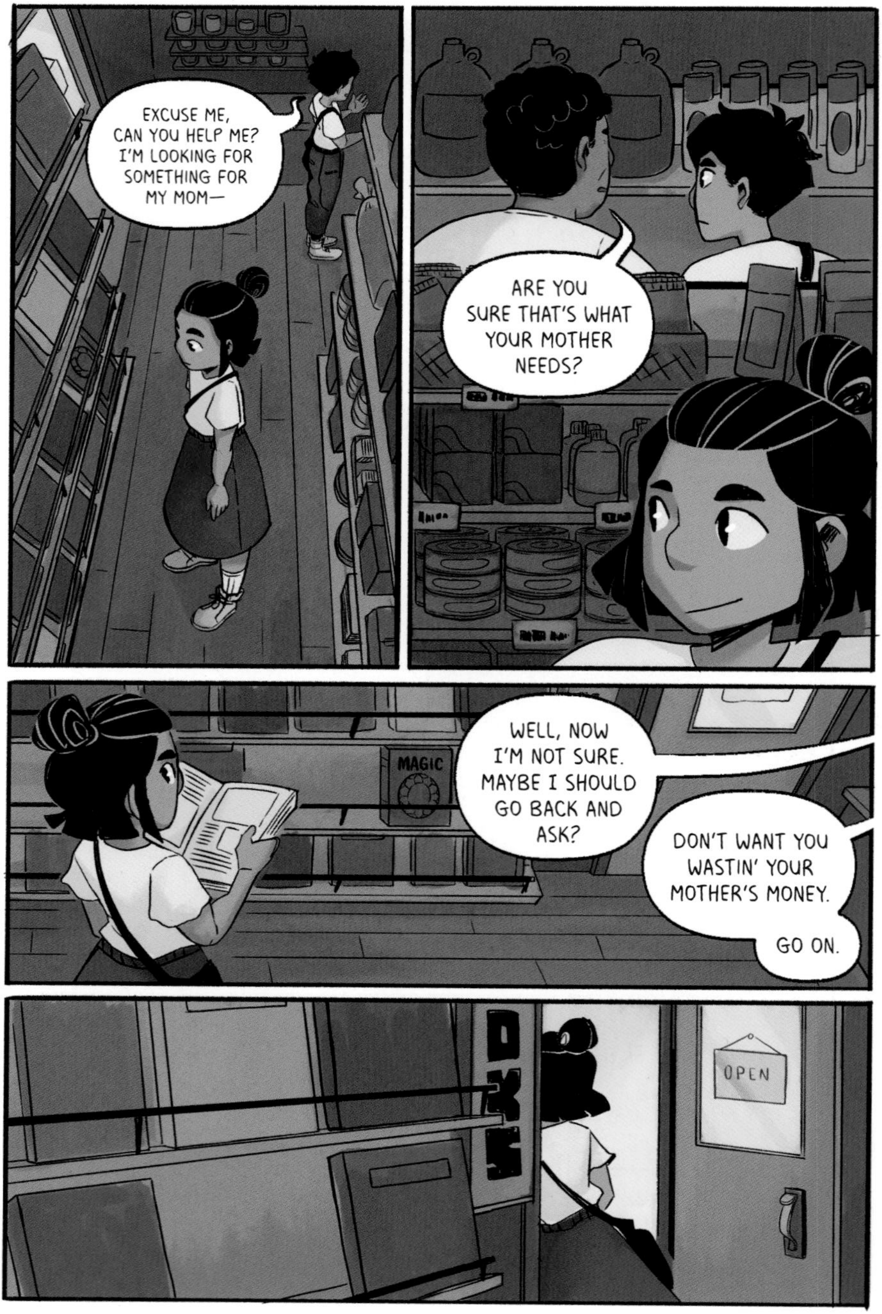
EXCUSE ME, CAN YOU HELP ME? I'M LOOKING FOR SOMETHING FOR MY MOM—
ARE YOU SURE THAT'S WHAT YOUR MOTHER NEEDS?
MAGIC
WELL, NOW I'M NOT SURE. MAYBE I SHOULD GO BACK AND ASK?
DON'T WANT YOU WASTIN' YOUR MOTHER'S MONEY.
GO ON.
OPEN

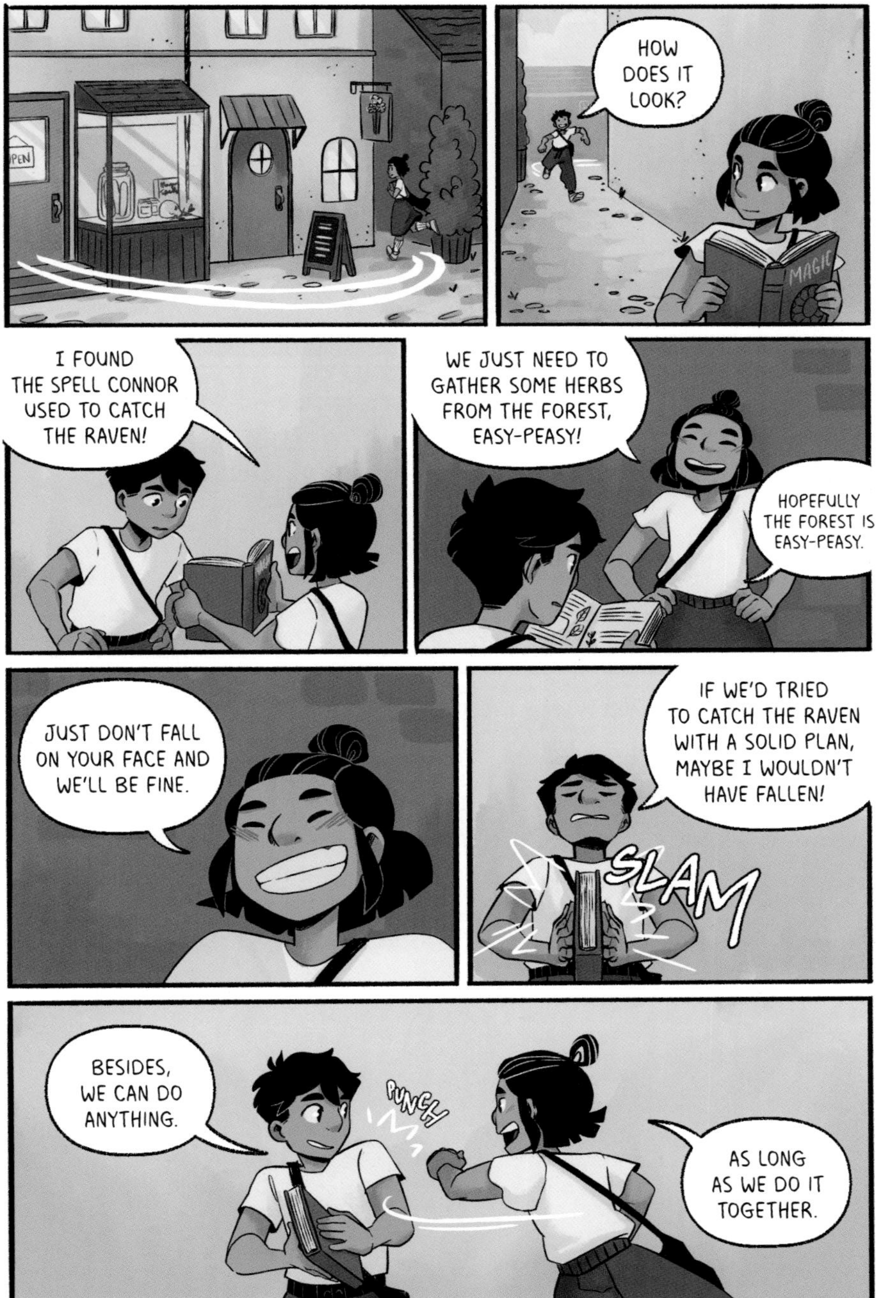
HOW DOES IT LOOK?
I FOUND THE SPELL CONNOR USED TO CATCH THE RAVEN!
WE JUST NEED TO GATHER SOME HERBS FROM THE FOREST, EASY-PEASY!
HOPEFULLY THE FOREST IS EASY-PEASY.
JUST DON'T FALL ON YOUR FACE AND WE'LL BE FINE.
IF WE'D TRIED TO CATCH THE RAVEN WITH A SOLID PLAN, MAYBE I WOULDN'T HAVE FALLEN!
SLAM
BESIDES, WE CAN DO ANYTHING.
PUNCH
AS LONG AS WE DO IT TOGETHER.

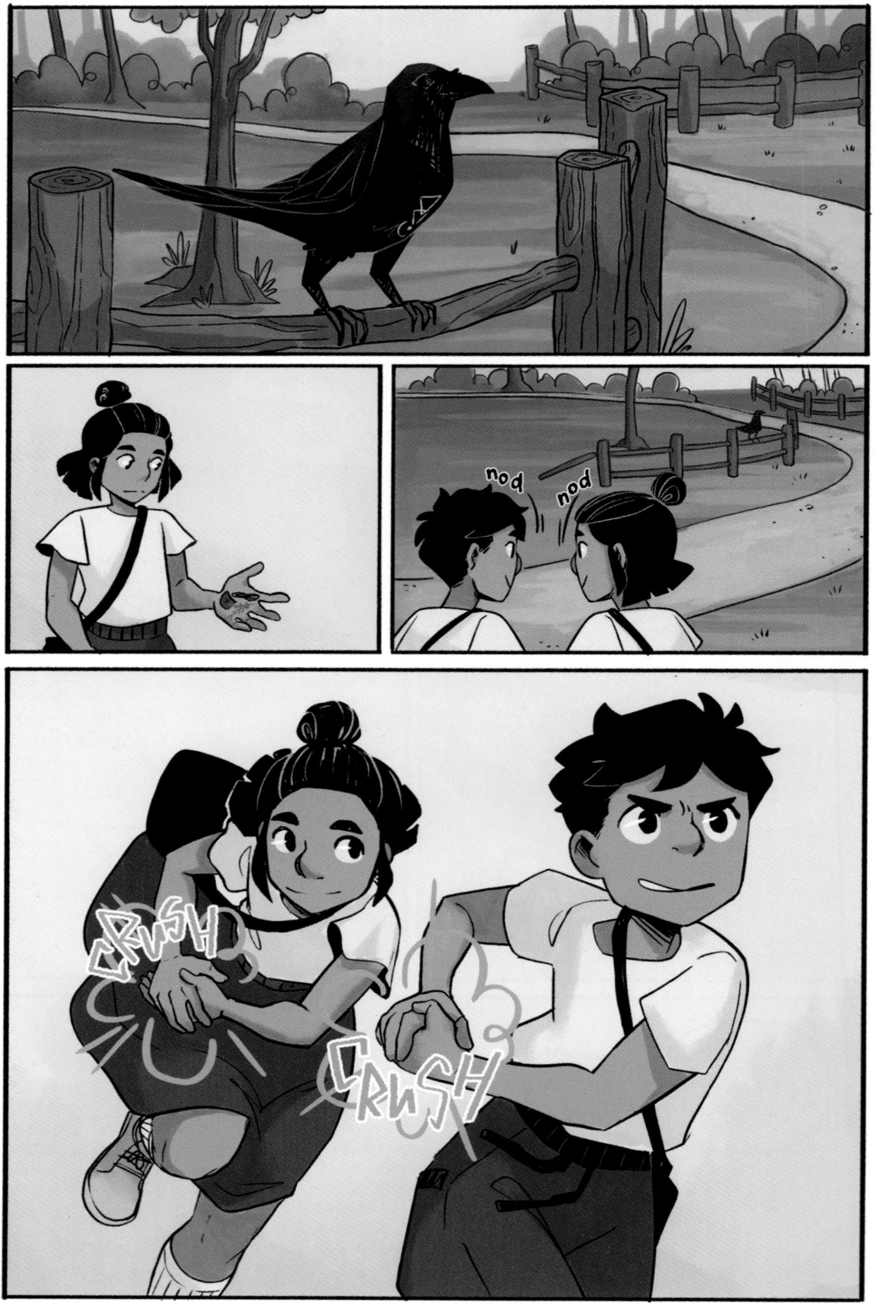

nod
nod
CRUSH
CRUSH

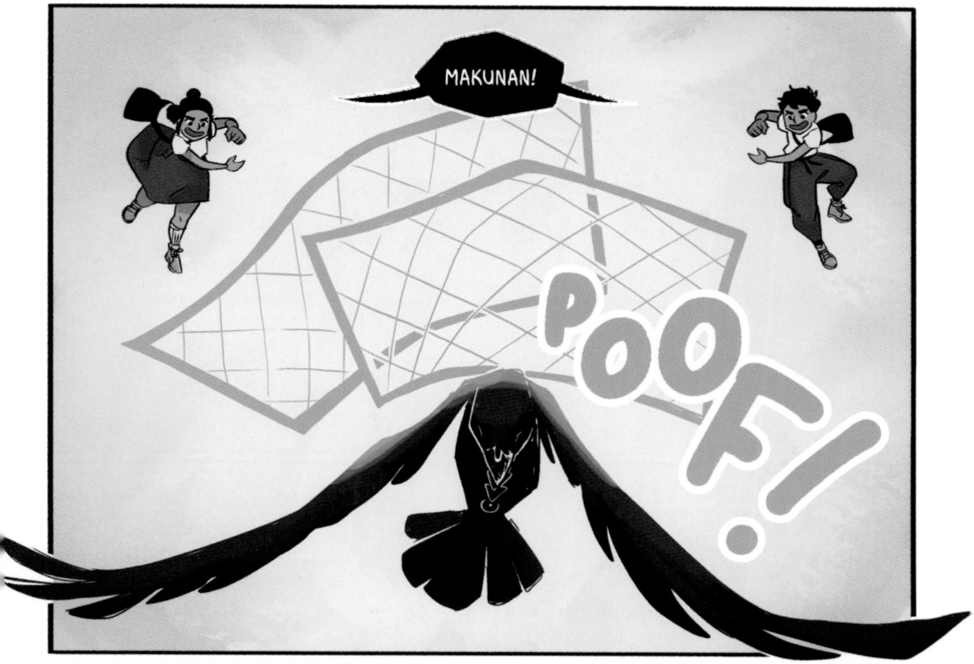
MAKUNAN!
POOF!

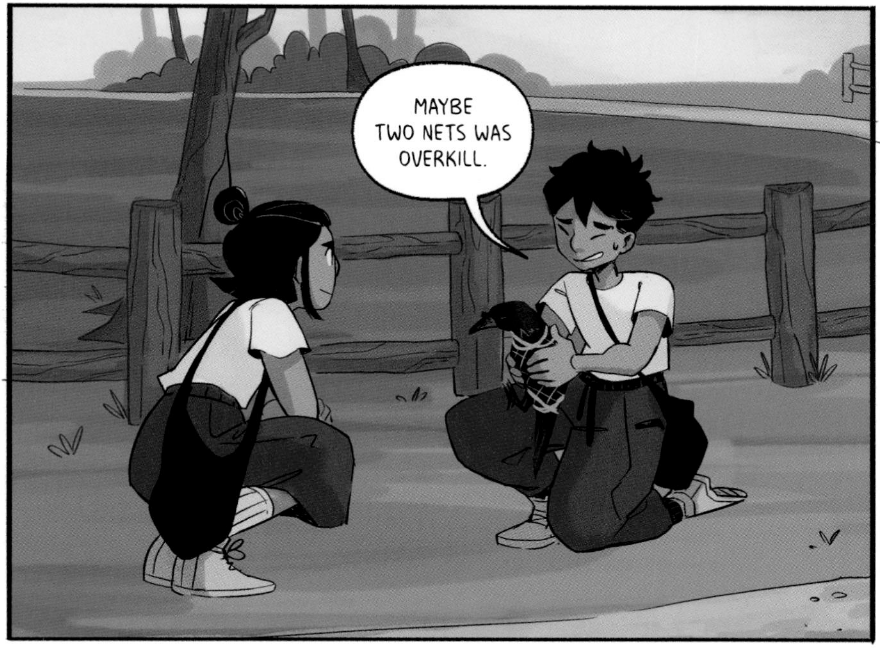
MAYBE TWO NETS WAS OVERKILL.

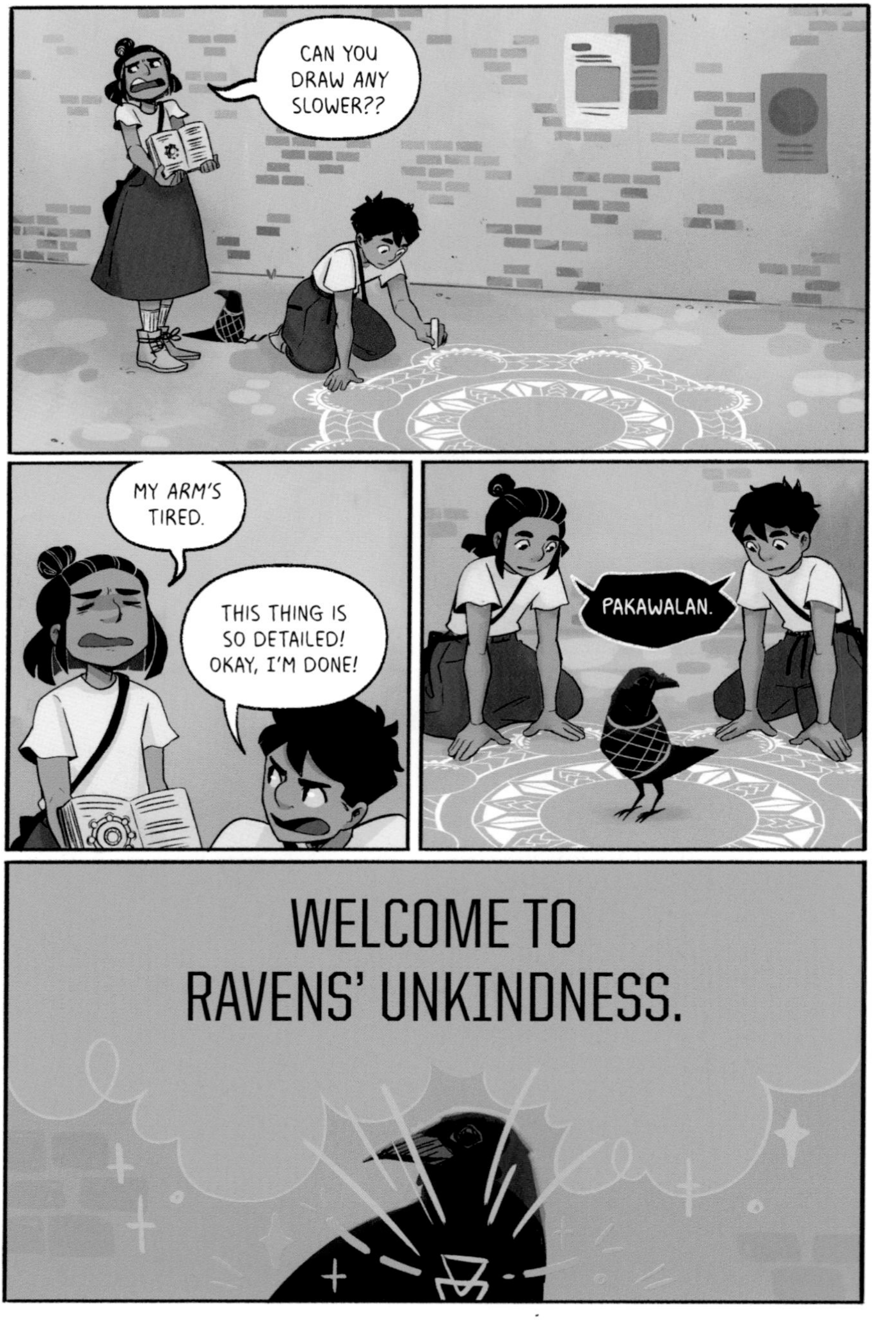
CAN YOU DRAW ANY SLOWER??
MY ARM'S TIRED.
THIS THING IS SO DETAILED! OKAY, I'M DONE!
PAKAWALAN.
WELCOME TO RAVENS' UNKINDNESS.

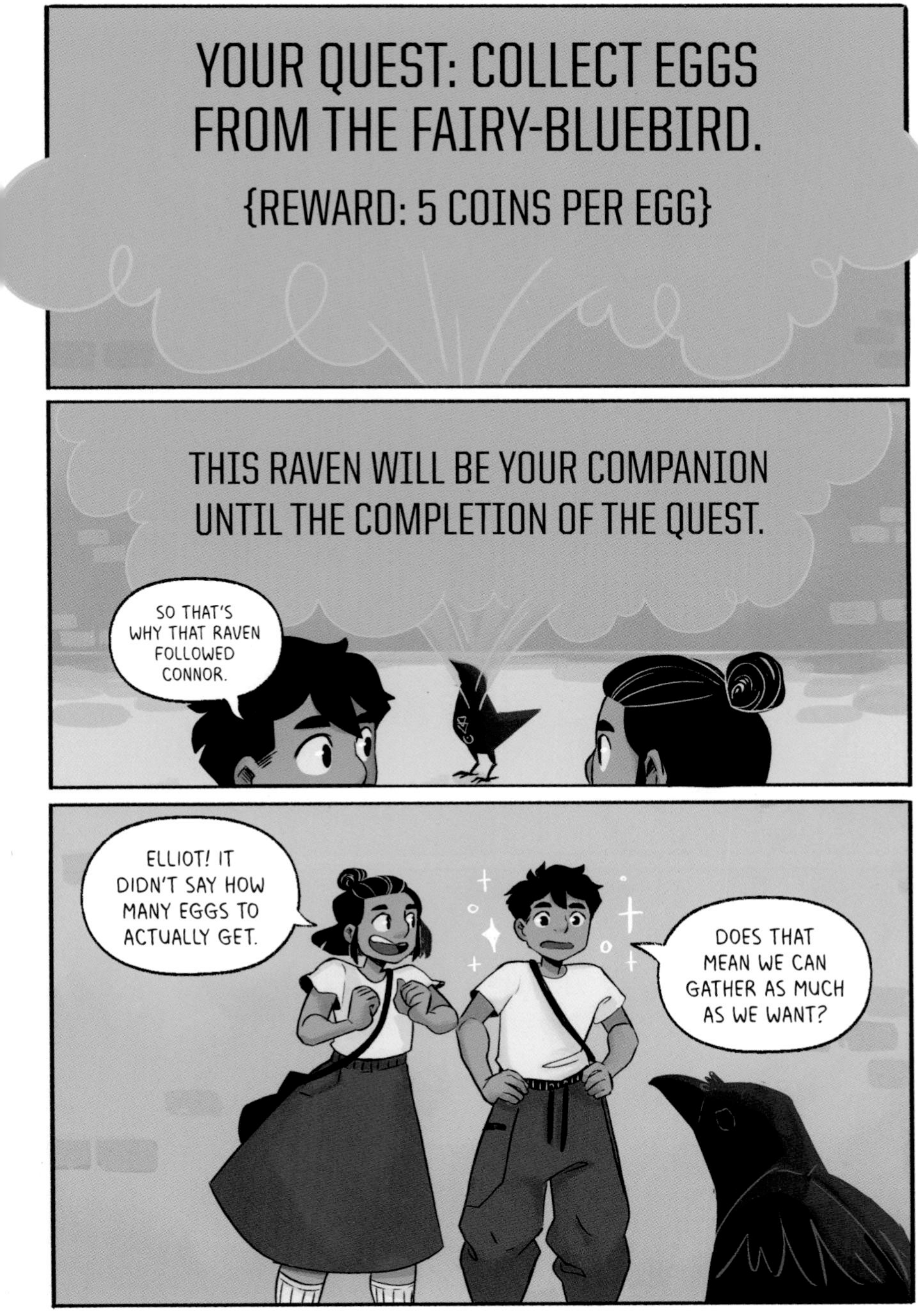
YOUR QUEST: COLLECT EGGS FROM THE FAIRY-BLUEBIRD.
{REWARD: 5 COINS PER EGG}
THIS RAVEN WILL BE YOUR COMPANION UNTIL THE COMPLETION OF THE QUEST.
SO THAT'S WHY THAT RAVEN FOLLOWED CONNOR.
ELLIOT! IT DIDN'T SAY HOW MANY EGGS TO ACTUALLY GET.
DOES THAT MEAN WE CAN GATHER AS MUCH AS WE WANT?

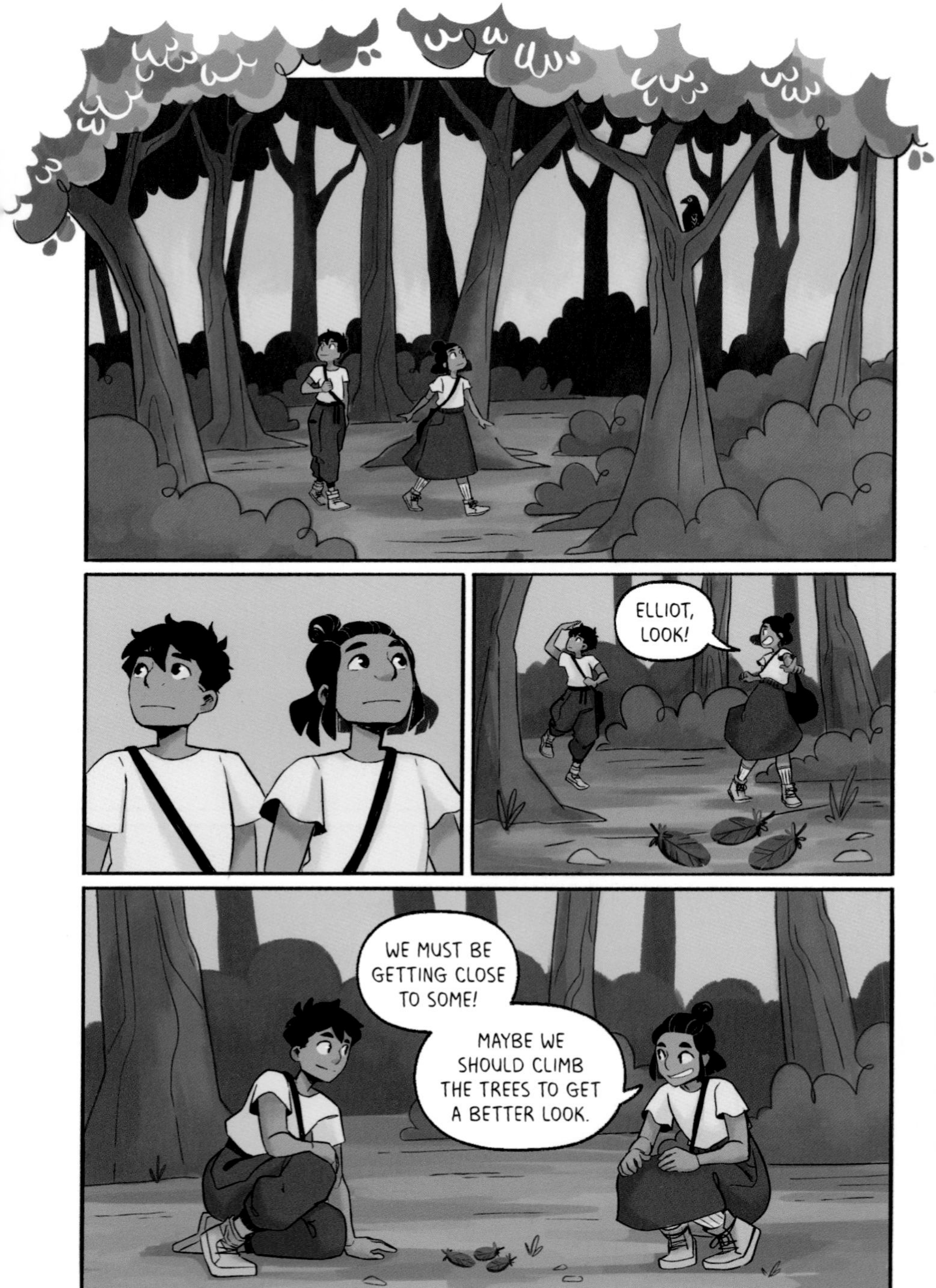
ELLIOT, LOOK!
WE MUST BE GETTING CLOSE TO SOME!
MAYBE WE SHOULD CLIMB THE TREES TO GET A BETTER LOOK.

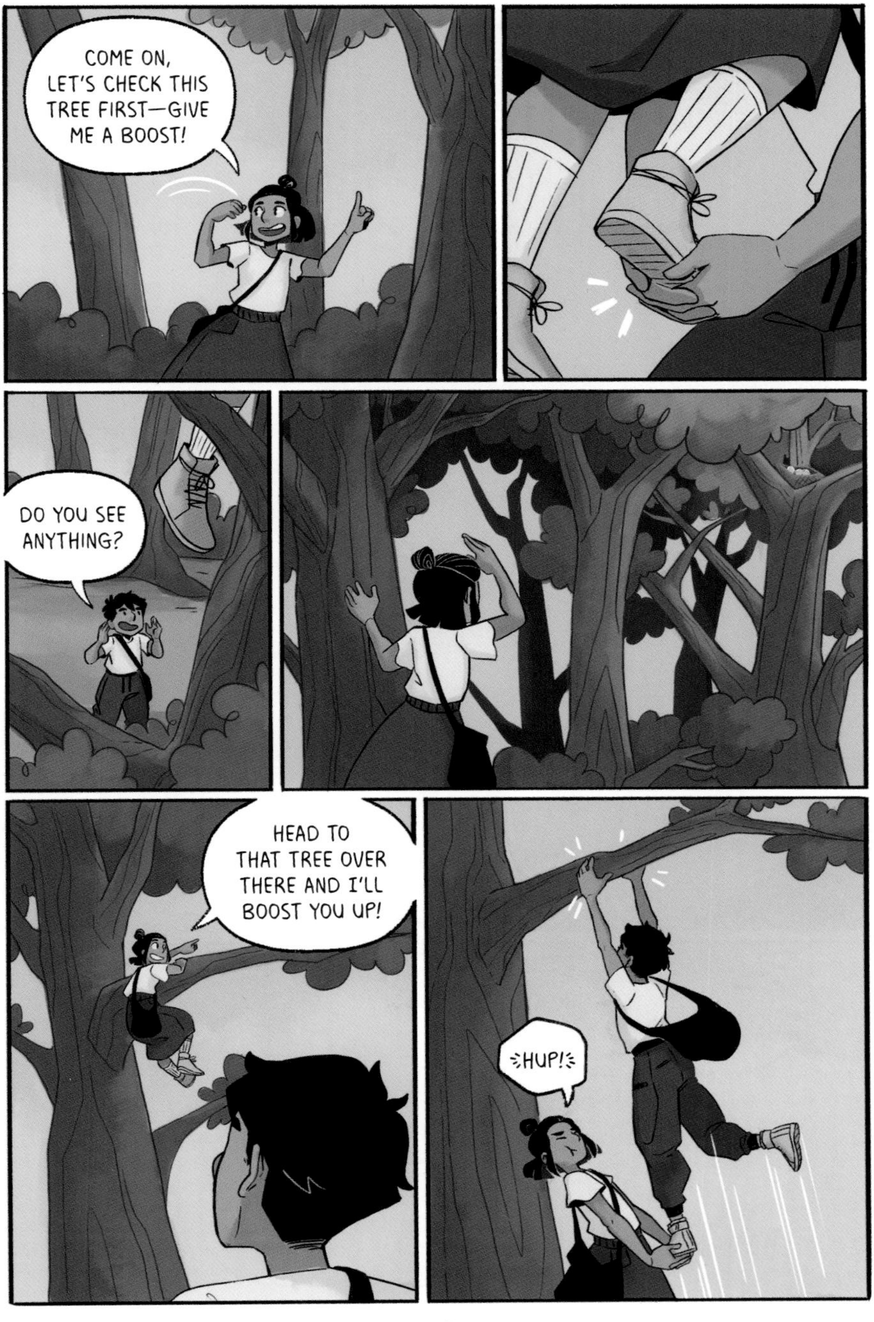
COME ON, LET'S CHECK THIS TREE FIRST—GIVE ME A BOOST!
DO YOU SEE ANYTHING?
HEAD TO THAT TREE OVER THERE AND I'LL BOOST YOU UP!
HUP!

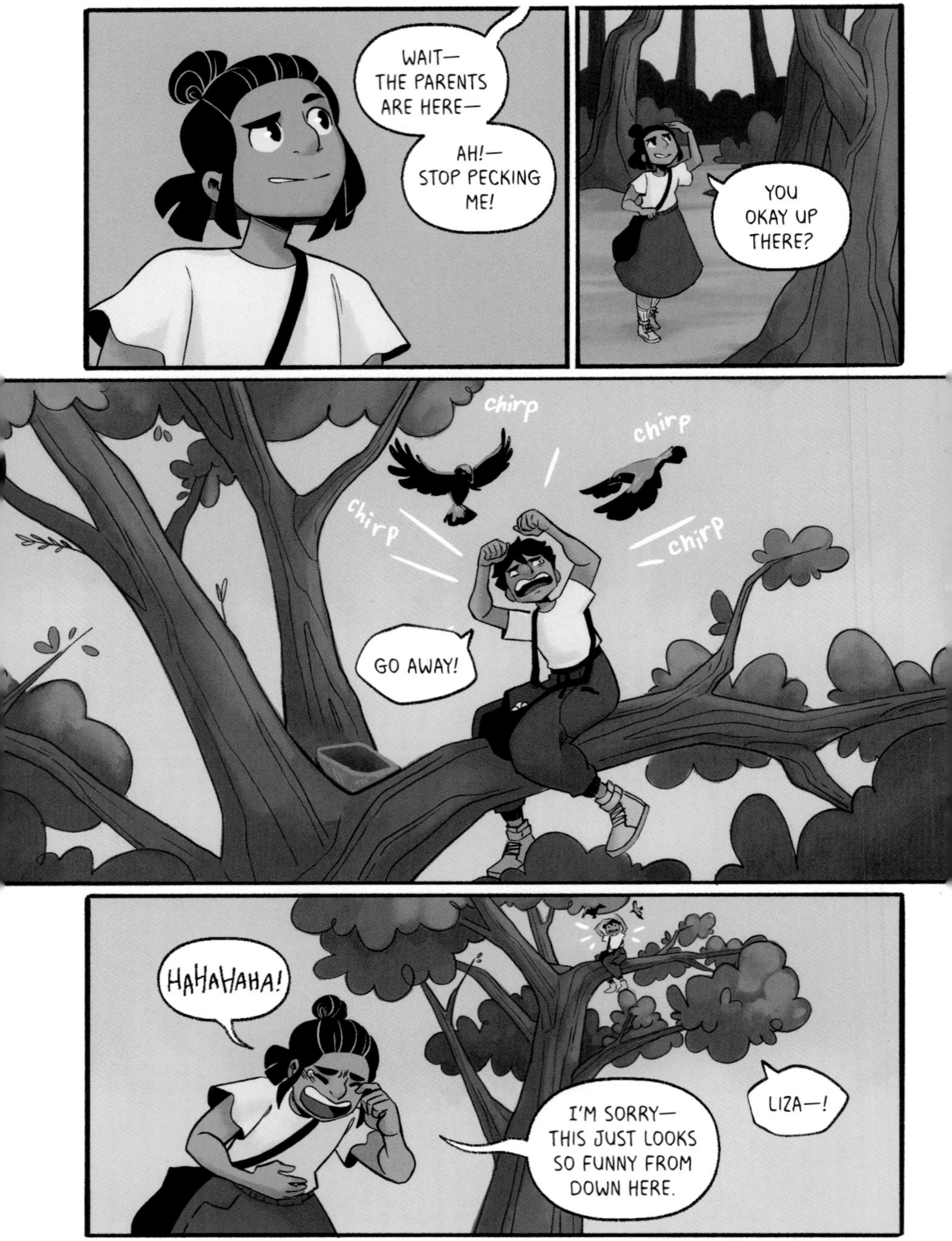
WAIT— THE PARENTS ARE HERE—
AH!— STOP PECKING ME!
YOU OKAY UP THERE?
chirp
chirp
chirp
chirp
GO AWAY!
HAHAHAHA!
I'M SORRY— THIS JUST LOOKS SO FUNNY FROM DOWN HERE.
LIZA—!

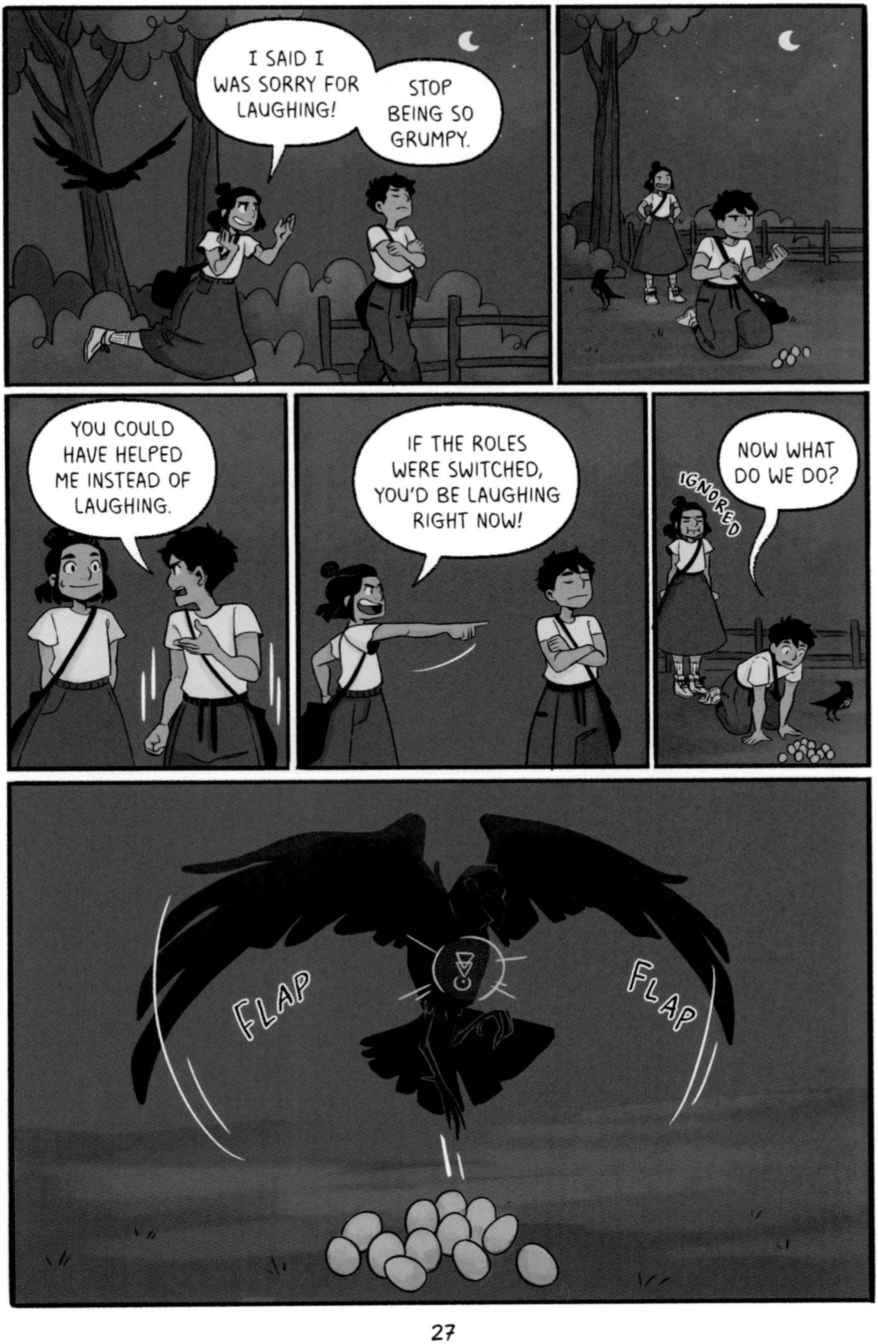
I SAID I WAS SORRY FOR LAUGHING!
STOP BEING SO GRUMPY.
YOU COULD HAVE HELPED ME INSTEAD OF LAUGHING.
IF THE ROLES WERE SWITCHED, YOU'D BE LAUGHING RIGHT NOW!
IGNORED
NOW WHAT DO WE DO?
FLAP
FLAP

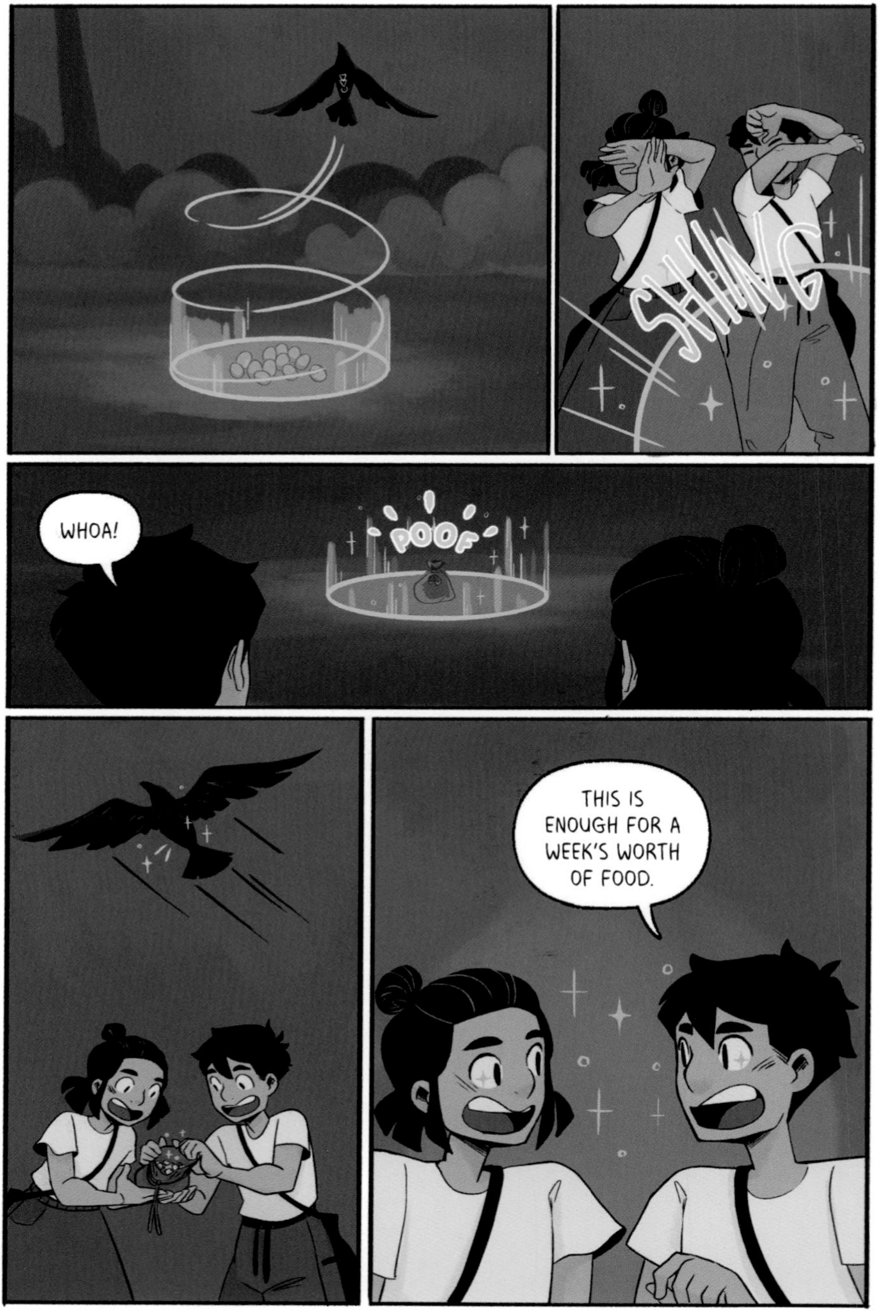
SHING
WHOA!
POOF
THIS IS ENOUGH FOR A WEEK'S WORTH OF FOOD.

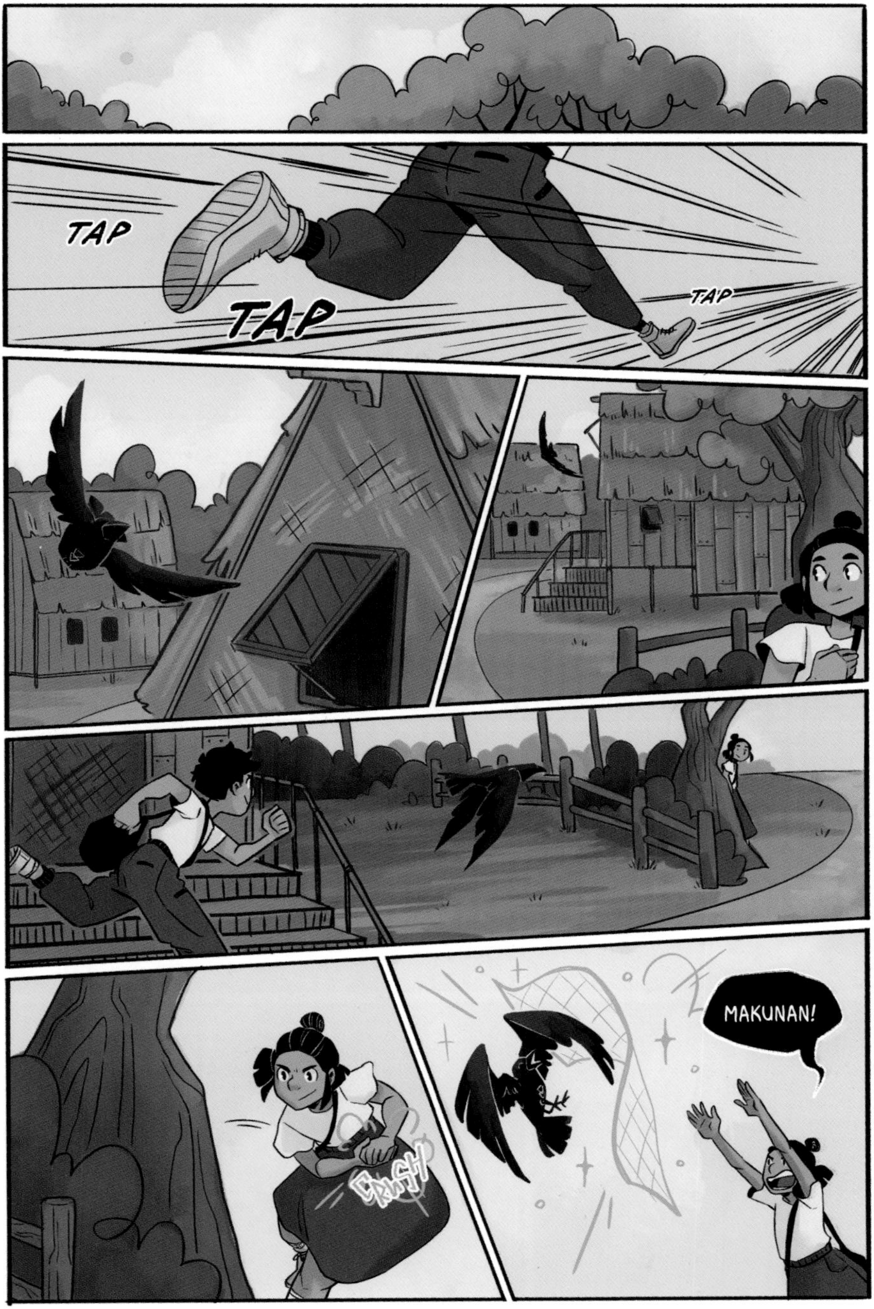
TAP
TAP
TAP
MAKUNAN!

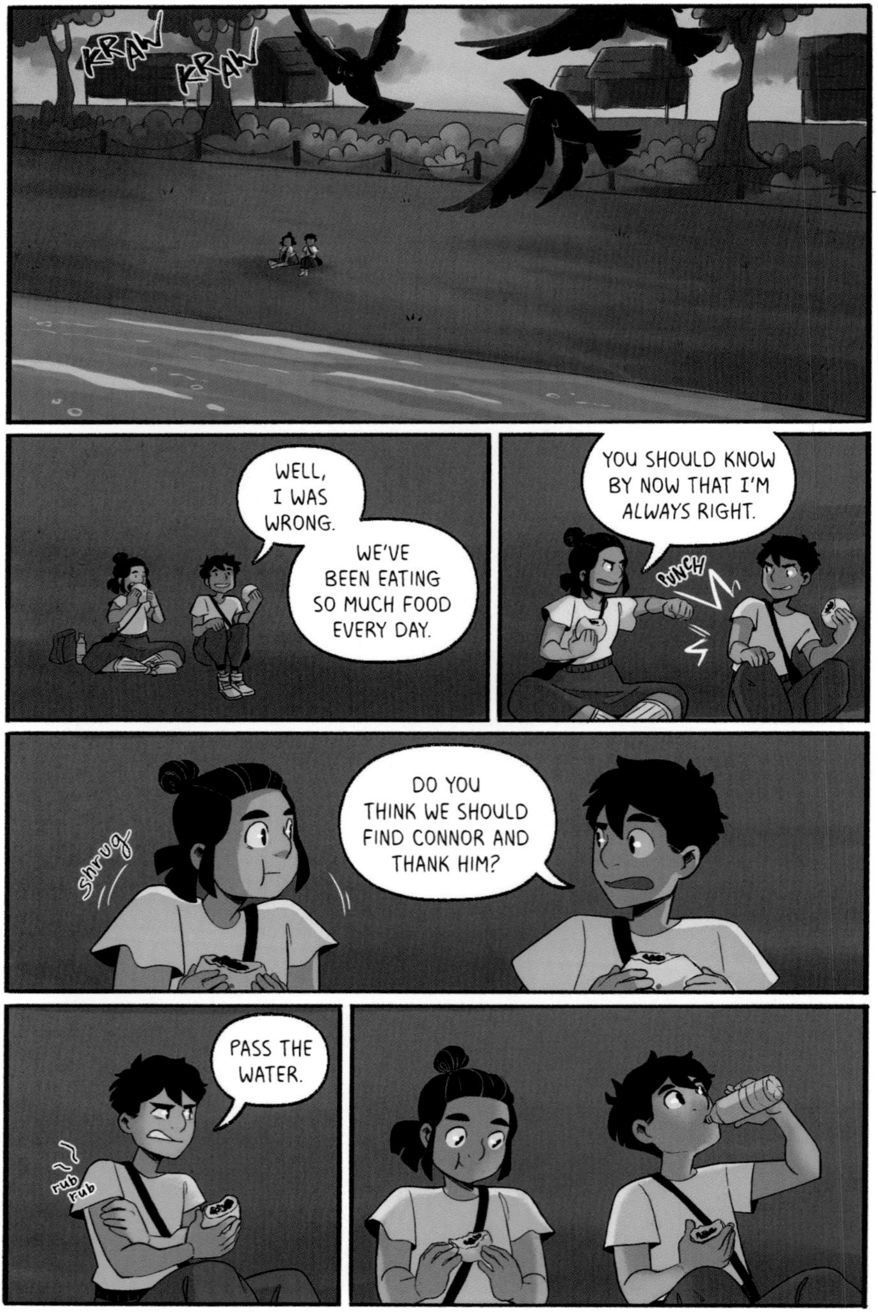
KRAW
KRAW
WELL, I WAS WRONG.
WE'VE BEEN EATING SO MUCH FOOD EVERY DAY.
YOU SHOULD KNOW BY NOW THAT I'M *ALWAYS* RIGHT.
PUNCH
shrug
DO YOU THINK WE SHOULD FIND CONNOR AND THANK HIM?
PASS THE WATER.
rub rub

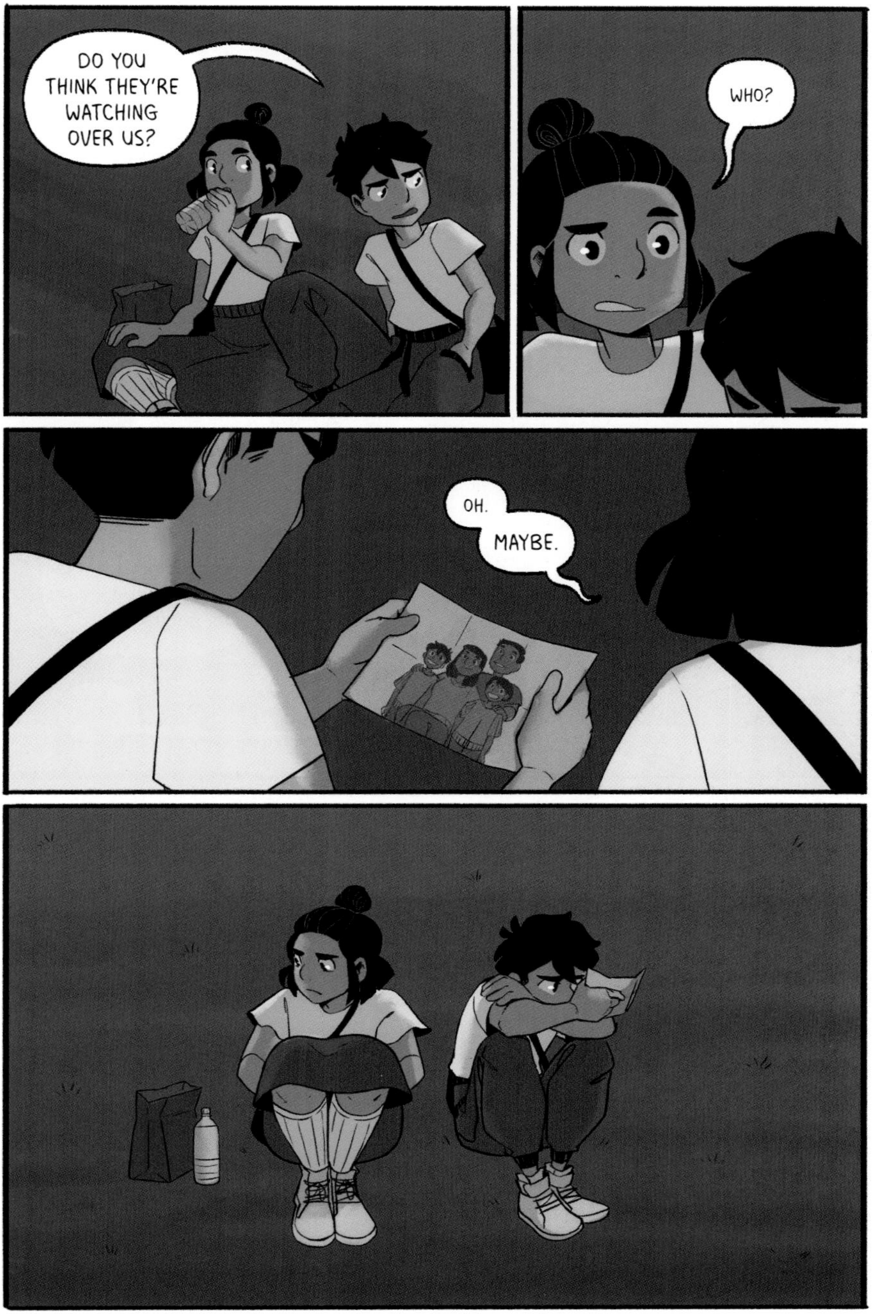
DO YOU THINK THEY'RE WATCHING OVER US?
WHO?
OH.
MAYBE.

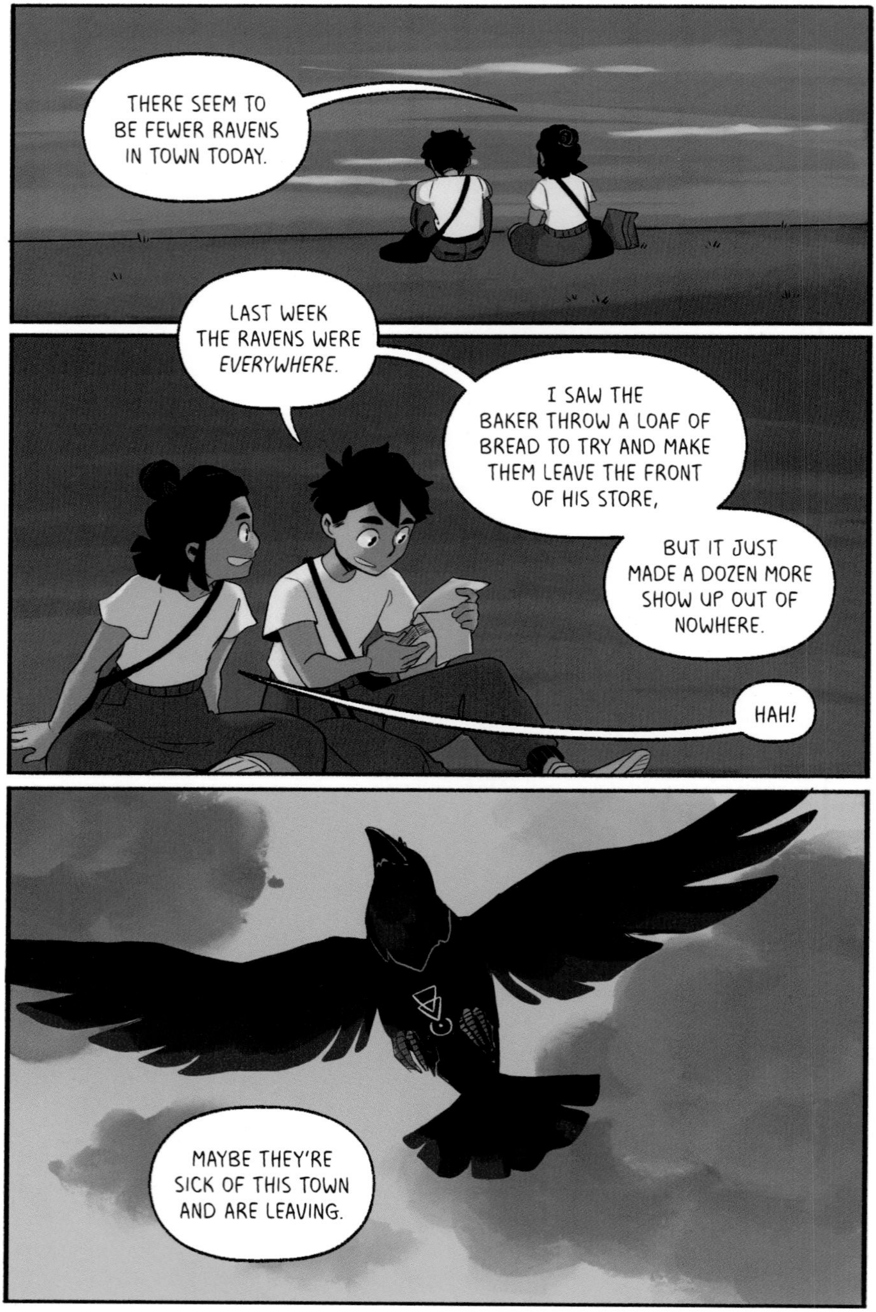
THERE SEEM TO BE FEWER RAVENS IN TOWN TODAY.
LAST WEEK THE RAVENS WERE *EVERYWHERE*.
I SAW THE BAKER THROW A LOAF OF BREAD TO TRY AND MAKE THEM LEAVE THE FRONT OF HIS STORE,
BUT IT JUST MADE A DOZEN MORE SHOW UP OUT OF NOWHERE.
HAH!
MAYBE THEY'RE SICK OF THIS TOWN AND ARE LEAVING.

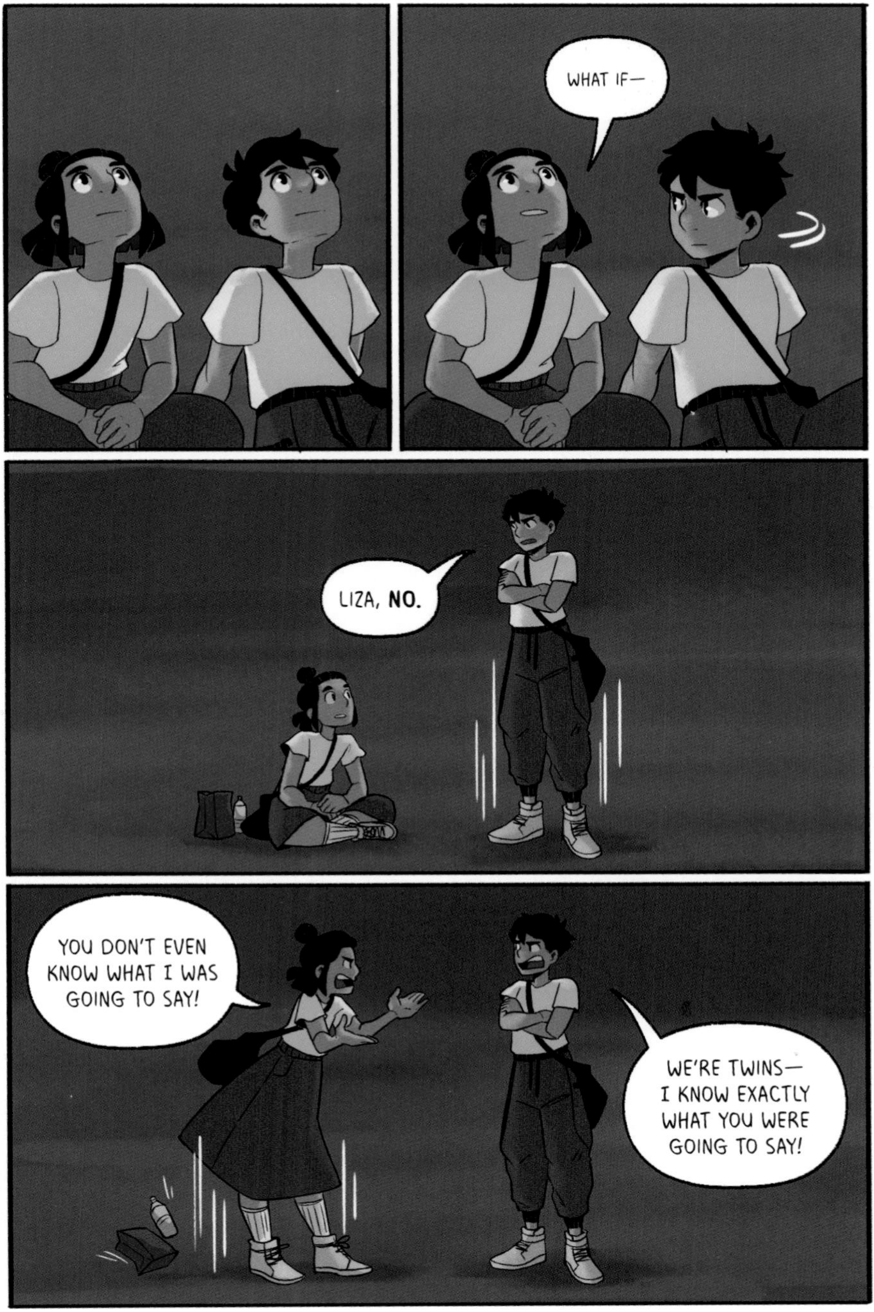
WHAT IF—
LIZA, **NO.**
YOU DON'T EVEN KNOW WHAT I WAS GOING TO SAY!
WE'RE TWINS— I KNOW EXACTLY WHAT YOU WERE GOING TO SAY!

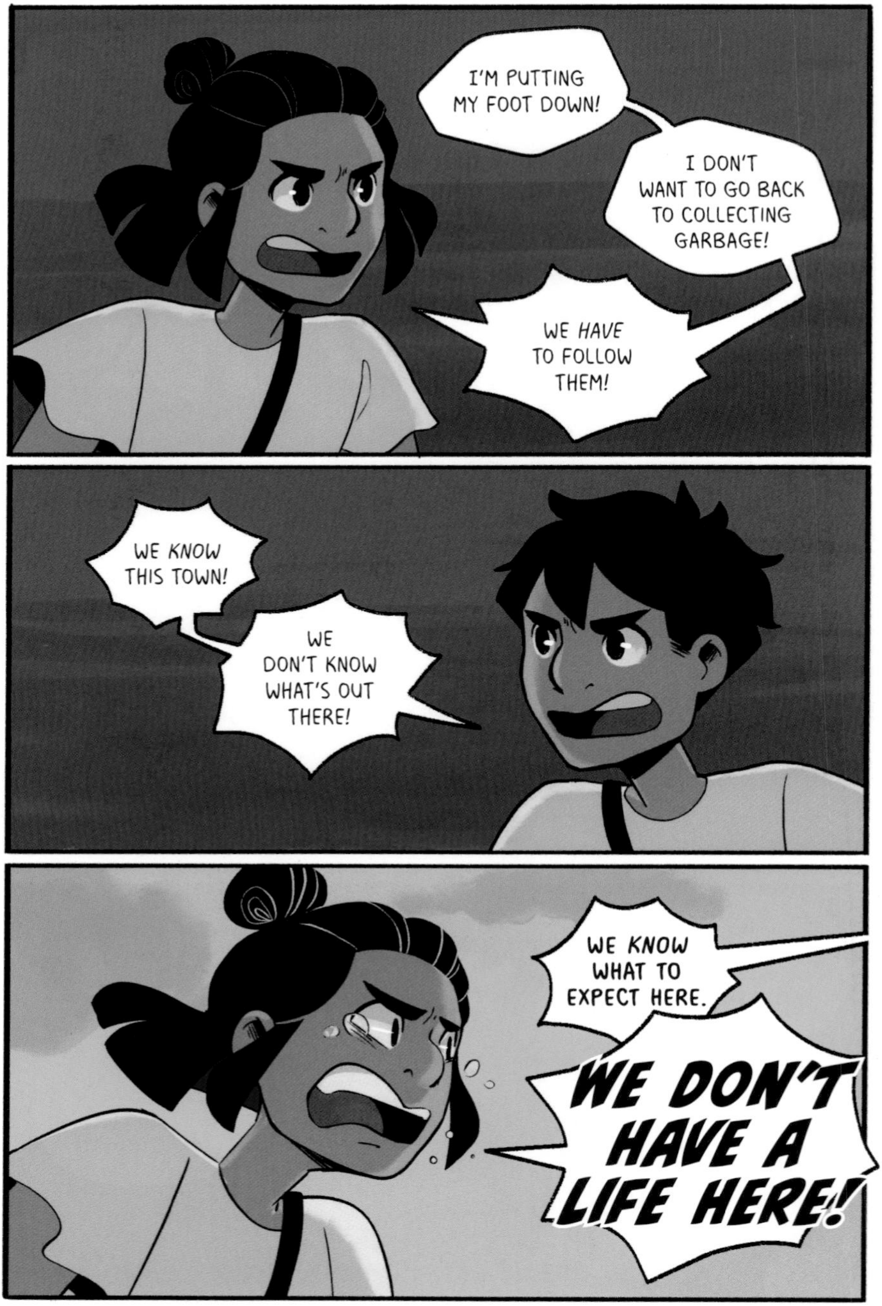
I'M PUTTING MY FOOT DOWN!
I DON'T WANT TO GO BACK TO COLLECTING GARBAGE!
WE *HAVE* TO FOLLOW THEM!
WE *KNOW* THIS TOWN!
WE DON'T KNOW WHAT'S OUT THERE!
WE *KNOW* WHAT TO EXPECT HERE.
WE DON'T HAVE A LIFE HERE!

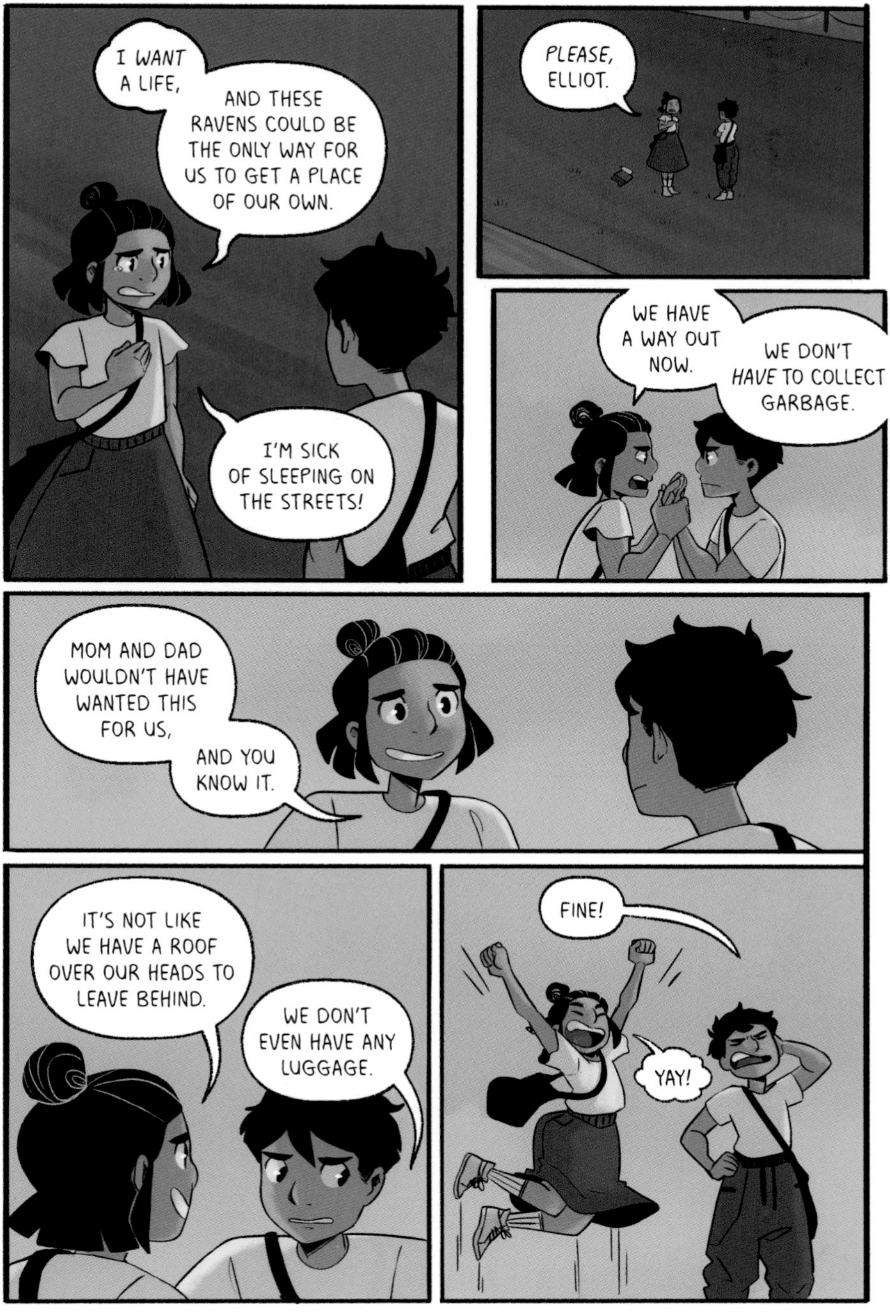
I *WANT* A LIFE,
AND THESE RAVENS COULD BE THE ONLY WAY FOR US TO GET A PLACE OF OUR OWN.
I'M SICK OF SLEEPING ON THE STREETS!
PLEASE, ELLIOT.
WE HAVE A WAY OUT NOW.
WE DON'T *HAVE* TO COLLECT GARBAGE.
MOM AND DAD WOULDN'T HAVE WANTED THIS FOR US,
AND YOU KNOW IT.
IT'S NOT LIKE WE HAVE A ROOF OVER OUR HEADS TO LEAVE BEHIND.
WE DON'T EVEN HAVE ANY LUGGAGE.
FINE!
YAY!

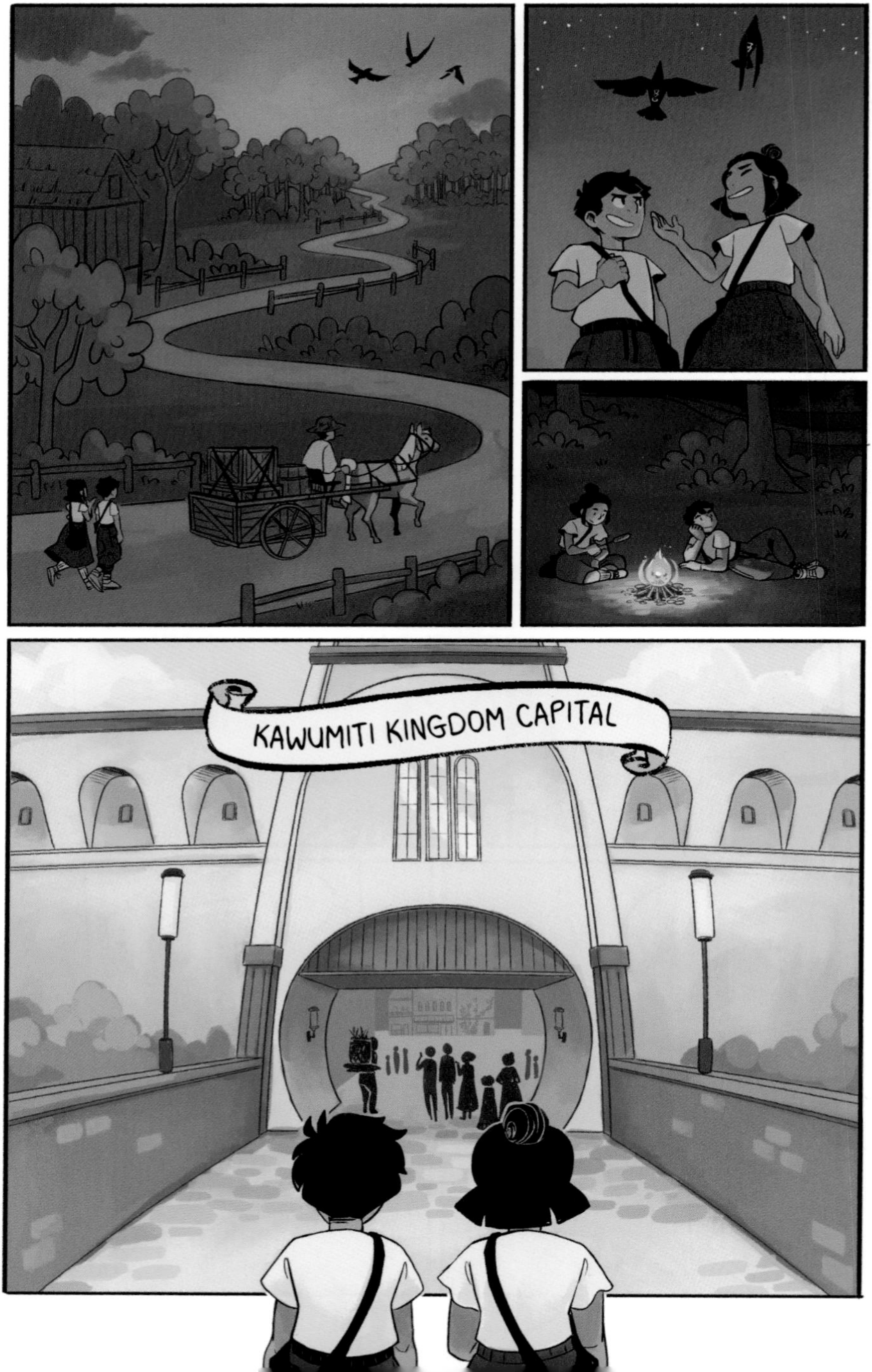
KAWUMITI KINGDOM CAPITAL

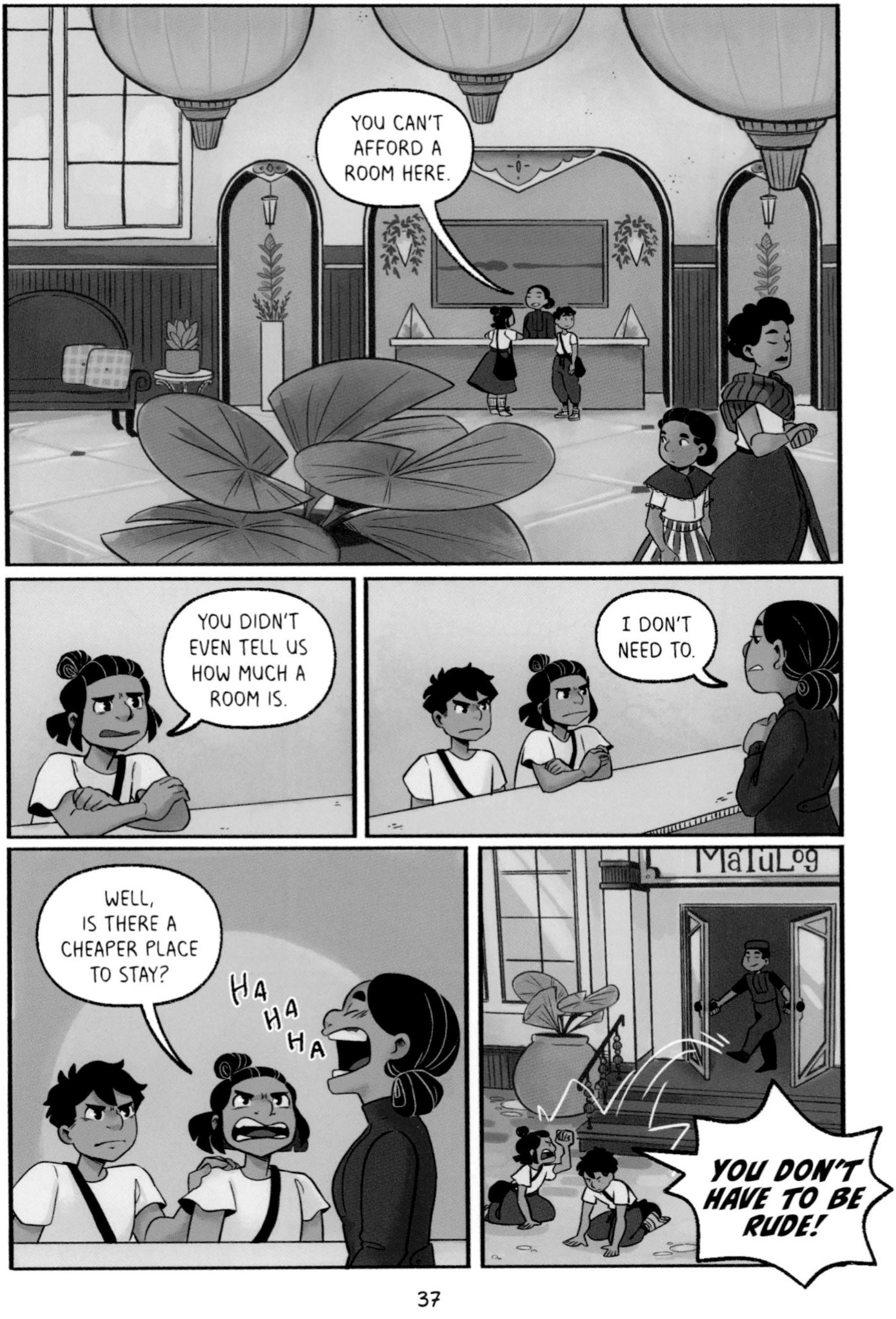
YOU CAN'T AFFORD A ROOM HERE.
YOU DIDN'T EVEN TELL US HOW MUCH A ROOM IS.
I DON'T NEED TO.
WELL, IS THERE A CHEAPER PLACE TO STAY?
HA HA HA
MaTuLog
YOU DON'T HAVE TO BE RUDE!

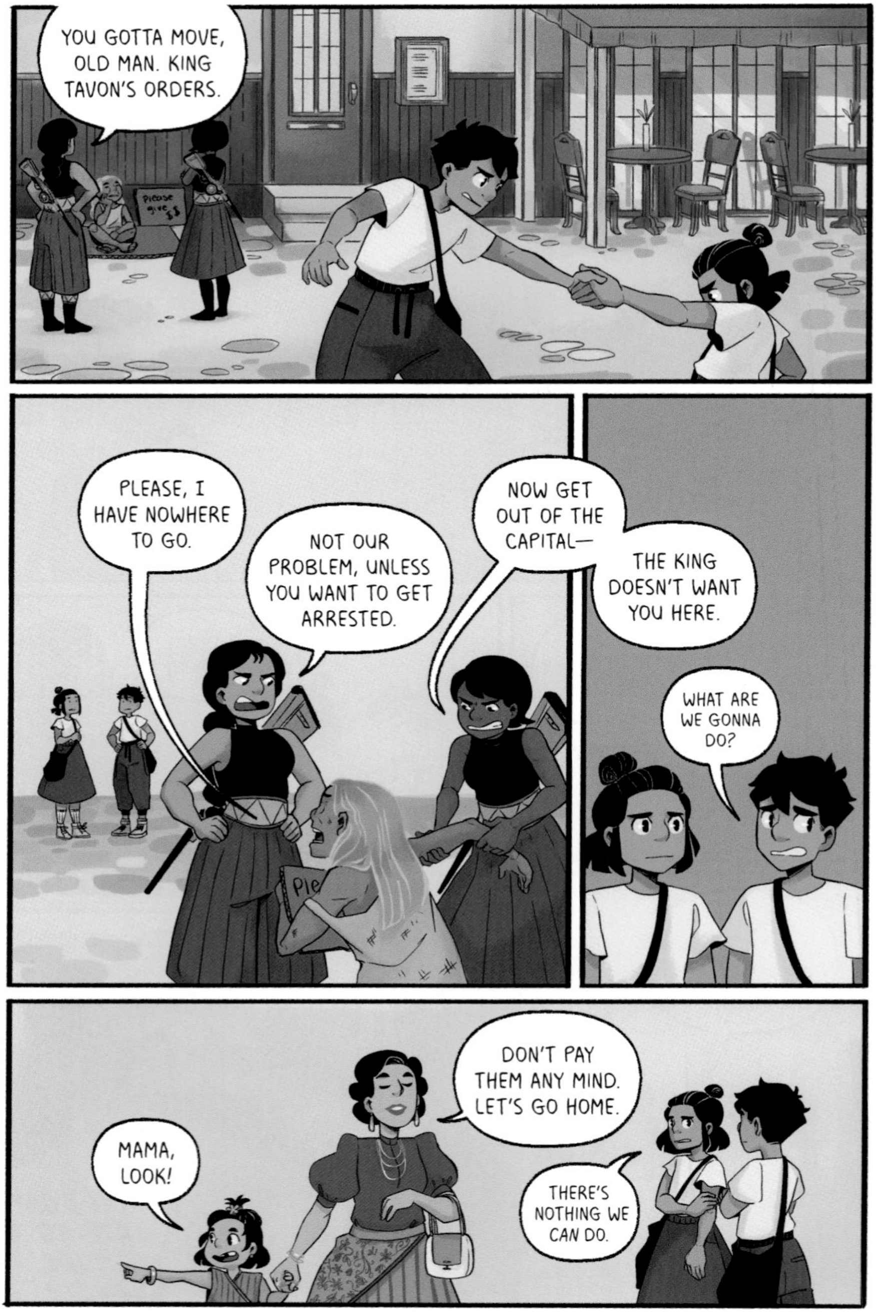

YOU GOTTA MOVE, OLD MAN. KING TAVON'S ORDERS.
Please give $$
PLEASE, I HAVE NOWHERE TO GO.
NOT OUR PROBLEM, UNLESS YOU WANT TO GET ARRESTED.
NOW GET OUT OF THE CAPITAL—
THE KING DOESN'T WANT YOU HERE.
WHAT ARE WE GONNA DO?
MAMA, LOOK!
DON'T PAY THEM ANY MIND. LET'S GO HOME.
THERE'S NOTHING WE CAN DO.

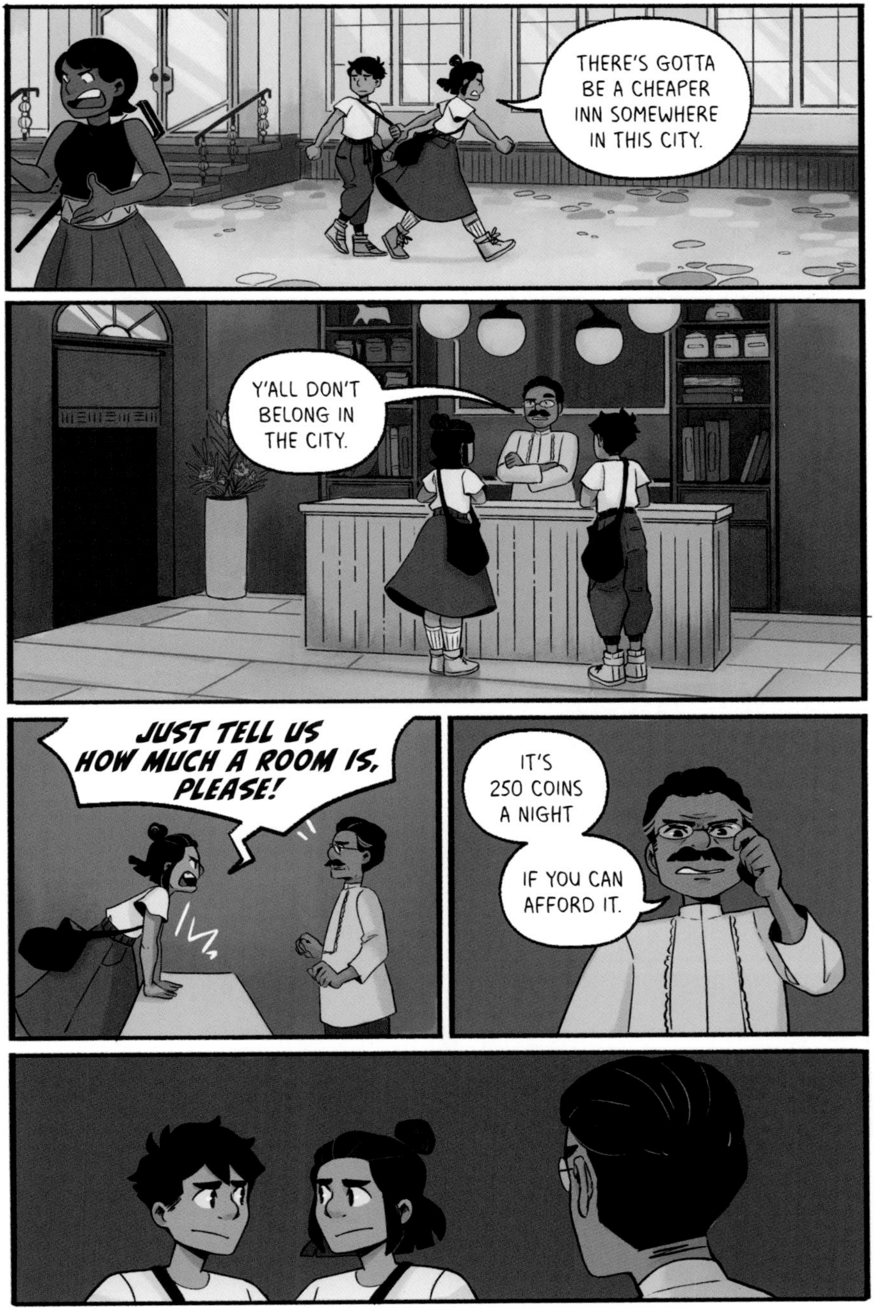
THERE'S GOTTA BE A CHEAPER INN SOMEWHERE IN THIS CITY.
Y'ALL DON'T BELONG IN THE CITY.
JUST TELL US HOW MUCH A ROOM IS, PLEASE!
IT'S 250 COINS A NIGHT
IF YOU CAN AFFORD IT.

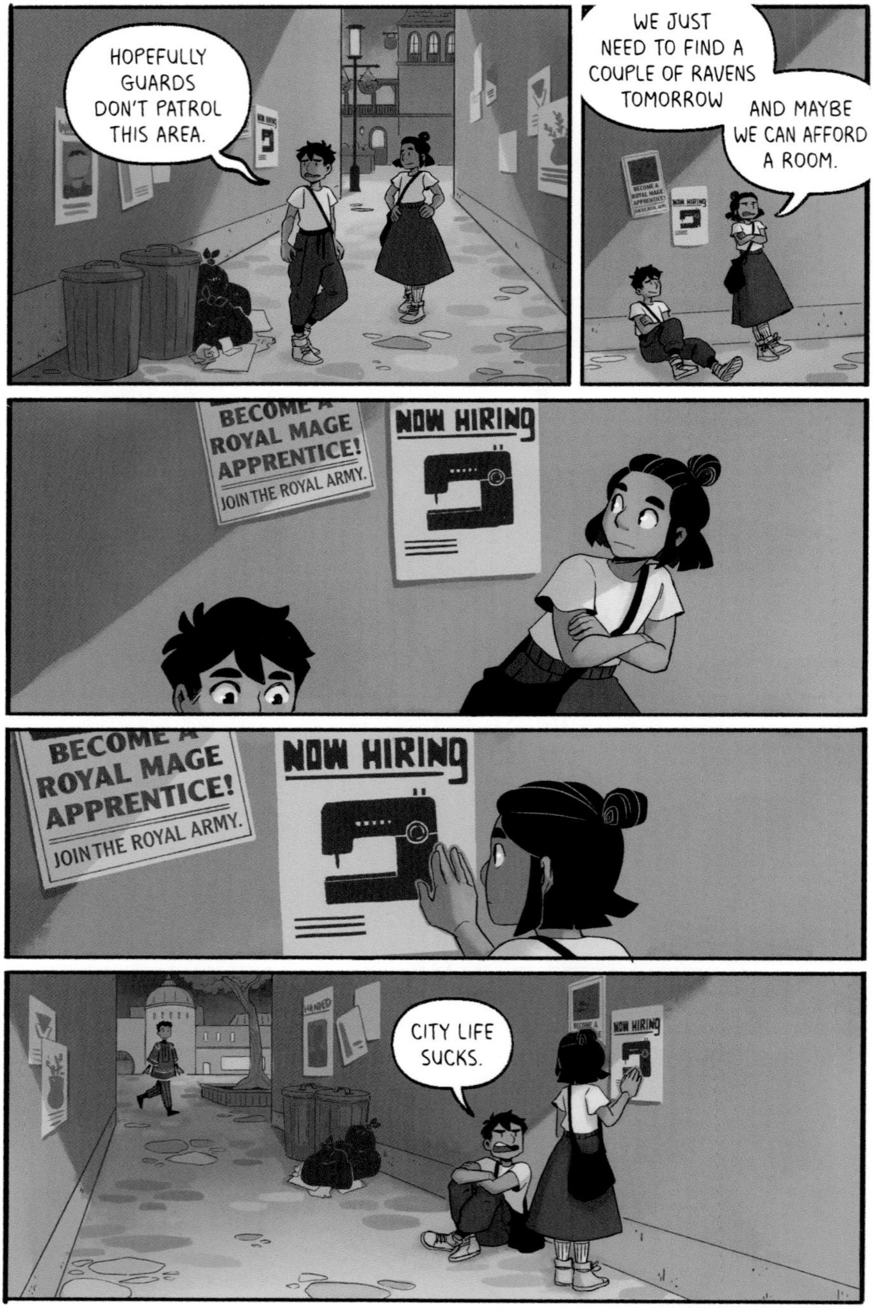
HOPEFULLY GUARDS DON'T PATROL THIS AREA.
NOW HIRING
WE JUST NEED TO FIND A COUPLE OF RAVENS TOMORROW
AND MAYBE WE CAN AFFORD A ROOM.
BECOME A ROYAL MAGE APPRENTICE!
NOW HIRING
BECOME A ROYAL MAGE APPRENTICE!
JOIN THE ROYAL ARMY.
NOW HIRING
BECOME A ROYAL MAGE APPRENTICE!
JOIN THE ROYAL ARMY.
NOW HIRING
CITY LIFE SUCKS.
NOW HIRING

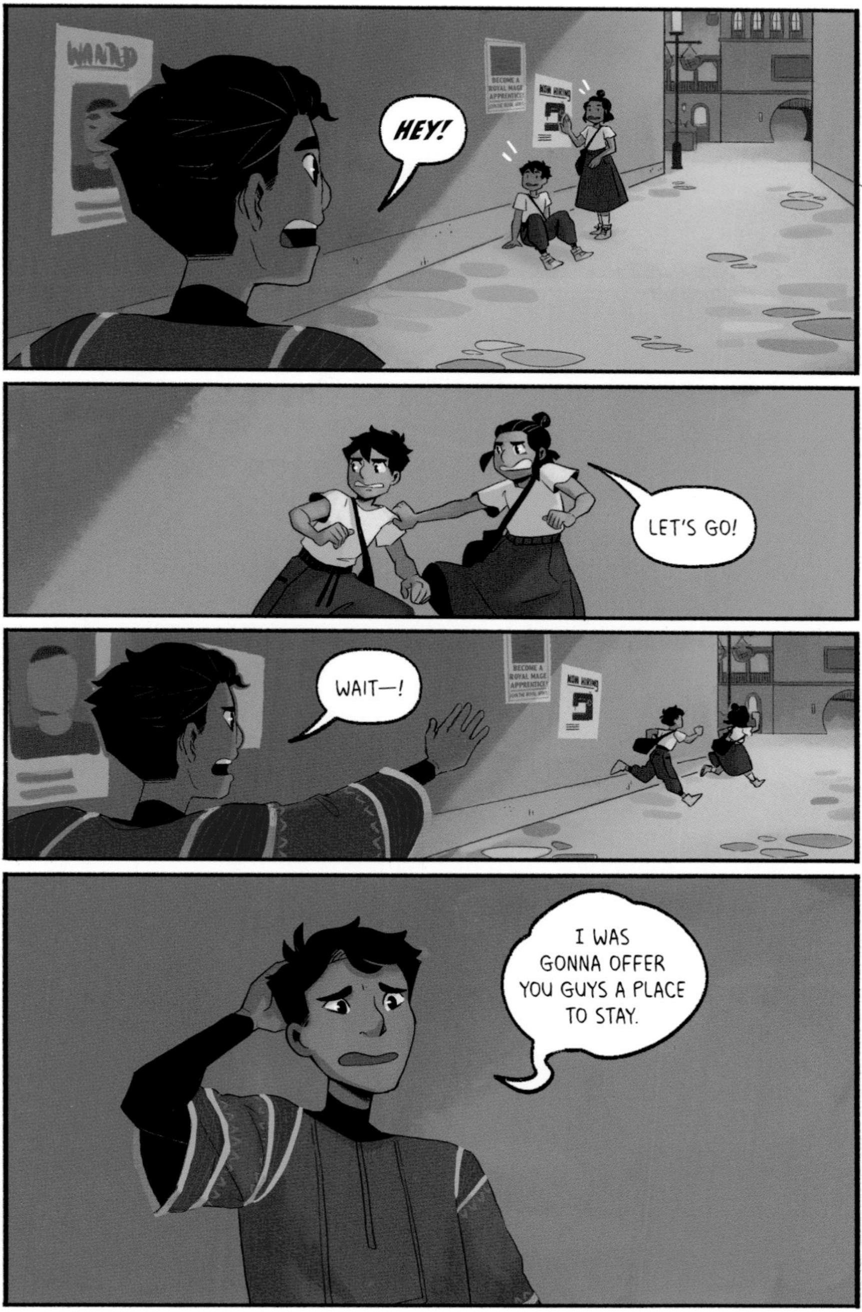
WANTED
BECOME A ROYAL MAGE APPRENTICE!
NOW HIRING
HEY!
LET'S GO!
BECOME A ROYAL MAGE APPRENTICE!
NOW HIRING
WAIT—!
I WAS GONNA OFFER YOU GUYS A PLACE TO STAY.

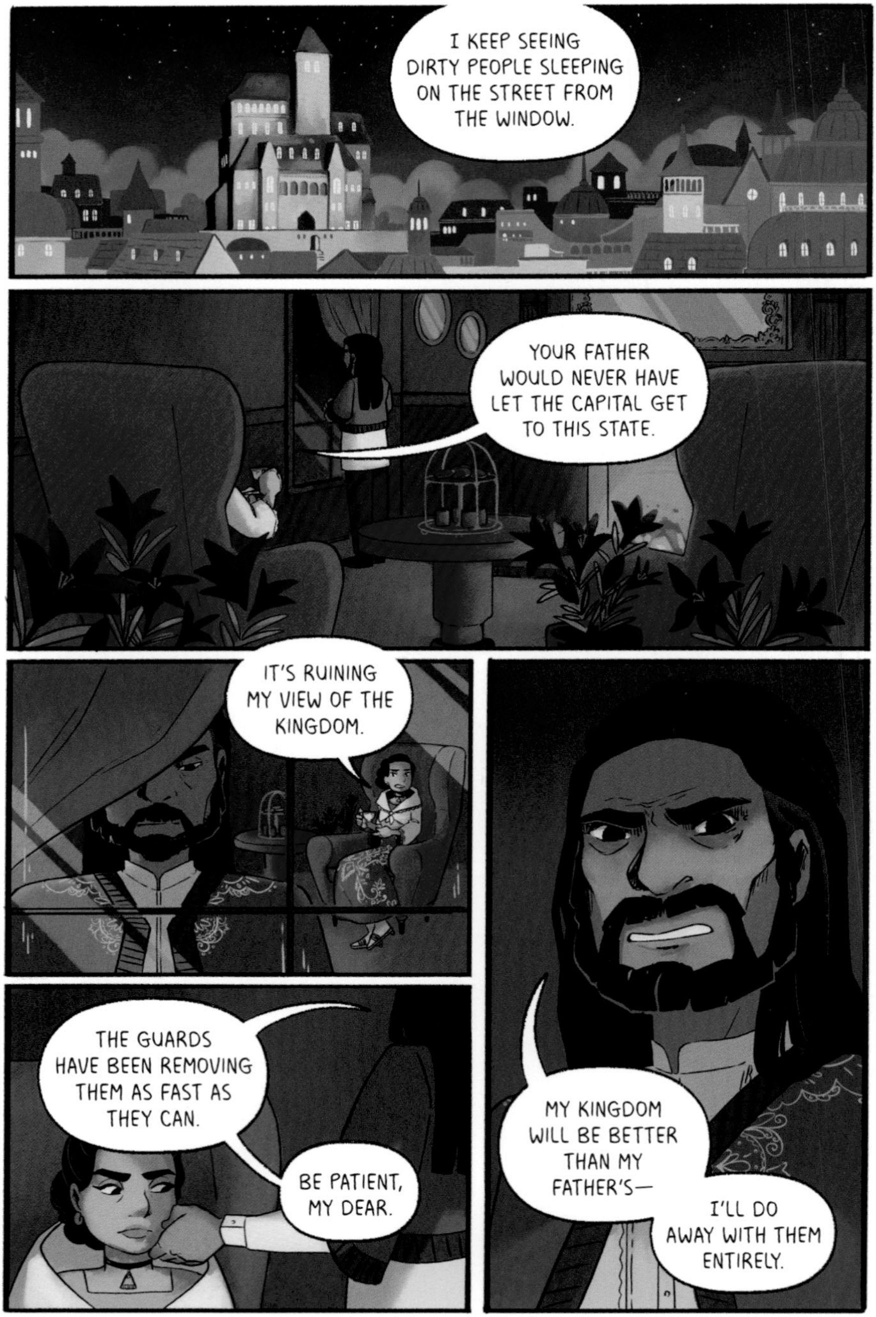
I KEEP SEEING DIRTY PEOPLE SLEEPING ON THE STREET FROM THE WINDOW.
YOUR FATHER WOULD NEVER HAVE LET THE CAPITAL GET TO THIS STATE.
IT'S RUINING MY VIEW OF THE KINGDOM.
THE GUARDS HAVE BEEN REMOVING THEM AS FAST AS THEY CAN.
BE PATIENT, MY DEAR.
MY KINGDOM WILL BE BETTER THAN MY FATHER'S—
I'LL DO AWAY WITH THEM ENTIRELY.

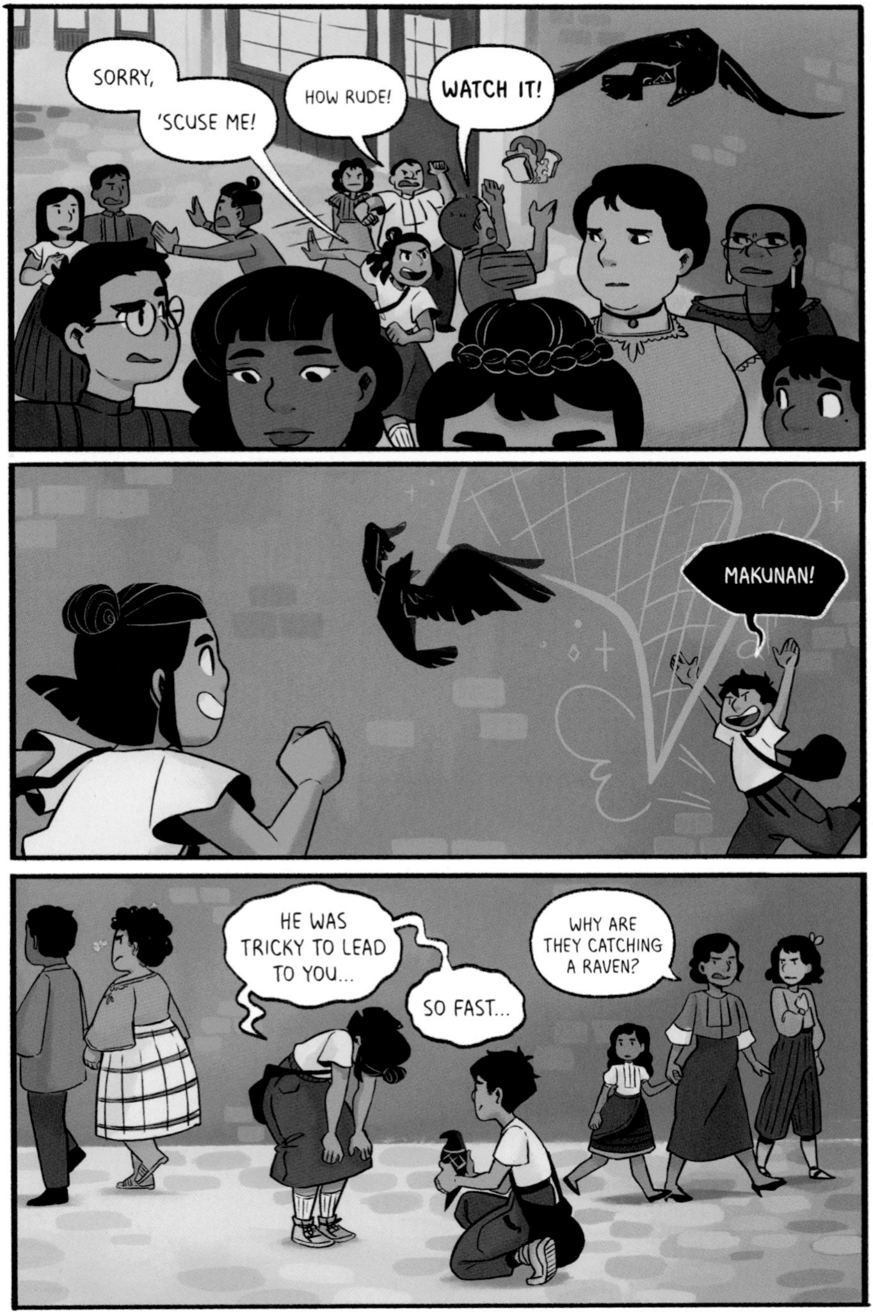
SORRY,
'SCUSE ME!
HOW RUDE!
WATCH IT!
MAKUNAN!
HE WAS TRICKY TO LEAD TO YOU...
SO FAST...
WHY ARE THEY CATCHING A RAVEN?

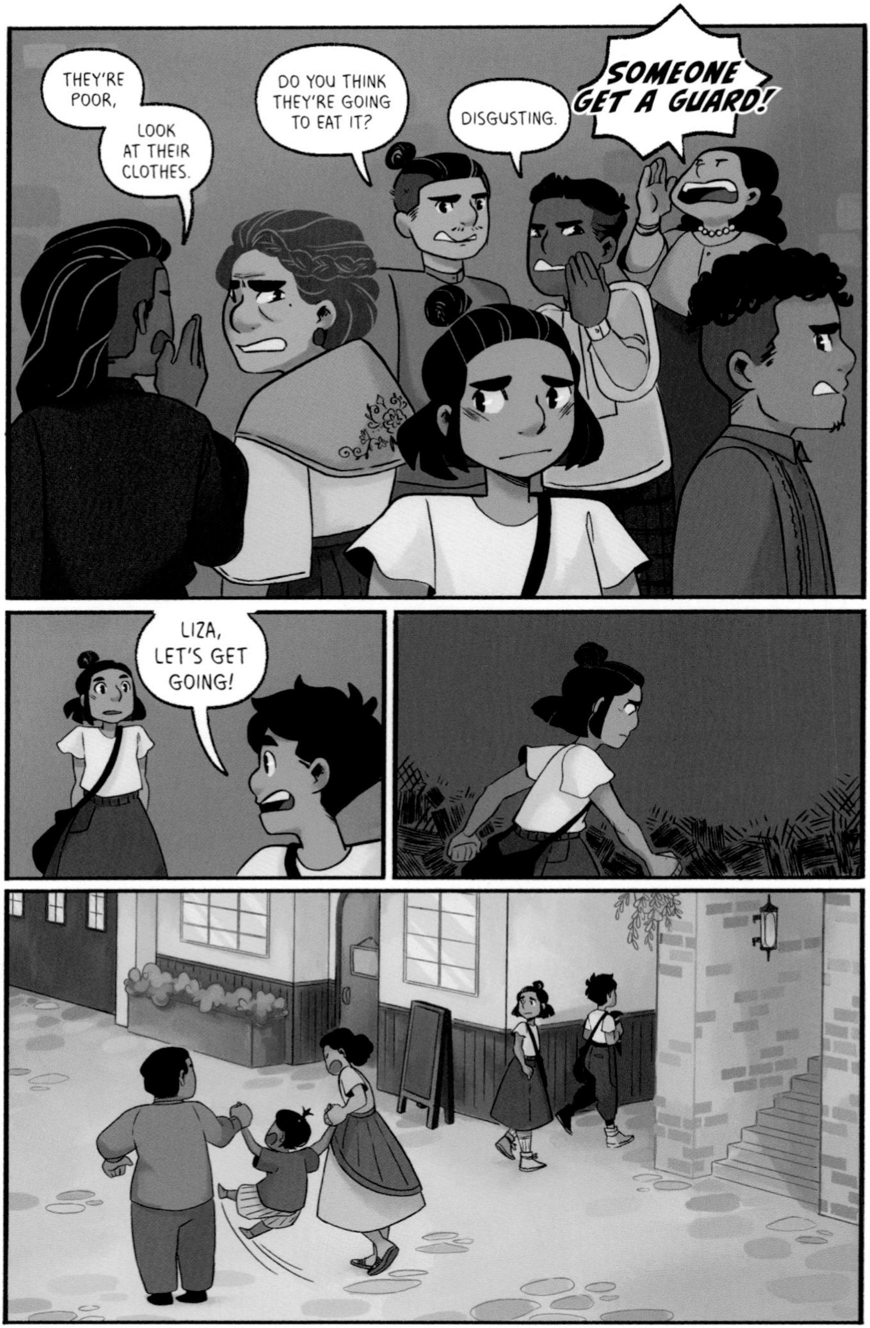
THEY'RE POOR,
LOOK AT THEIR CLOTHES.
DO YOU THINK THEY'RE GOING TO EAT IT?
DISGUSTING.
SOMEONE GET A GUARD!
LIZA, LET'S GET GOING!

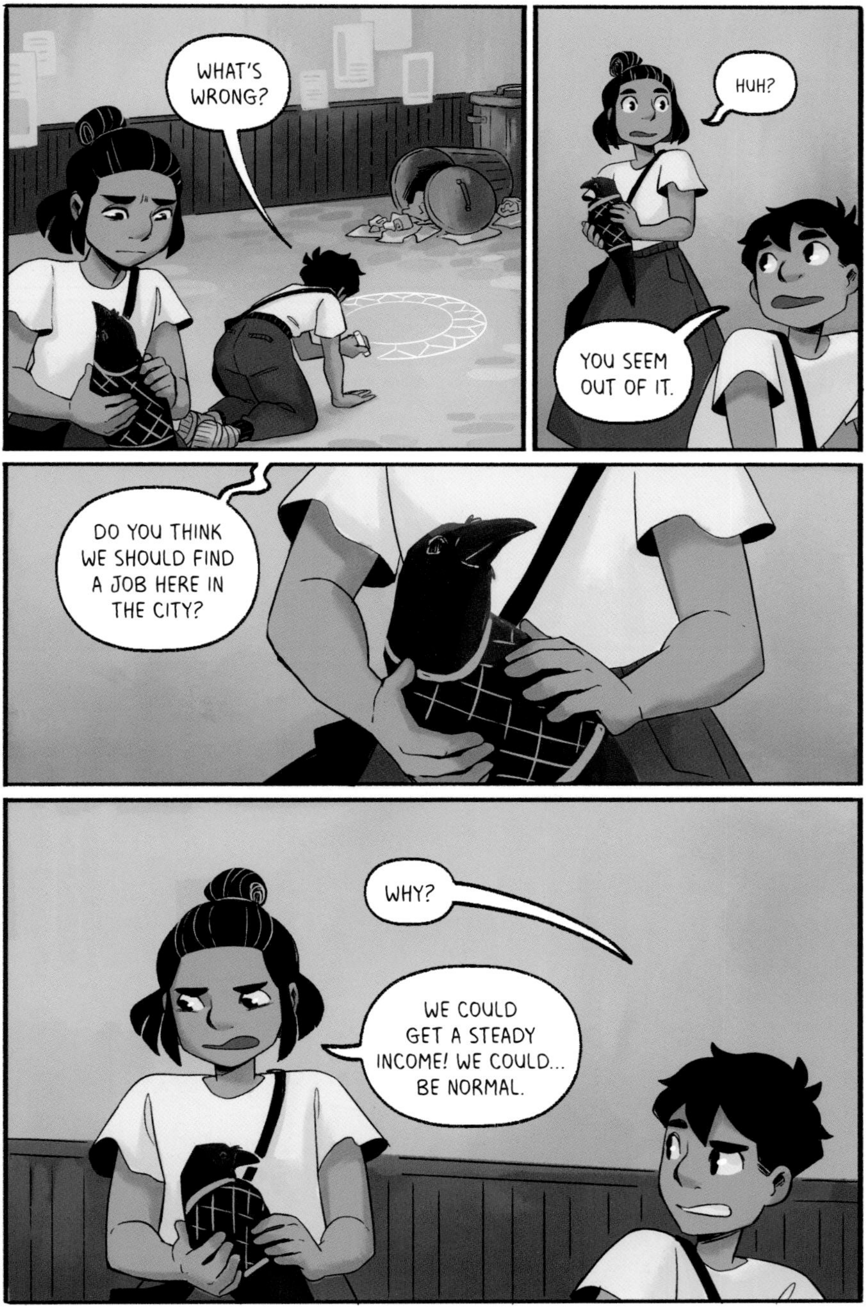
WHAT'S WRONG?
HUH?
YOU SEEM OUT OF IT.
DO YOU THINK WE SHOULD FIND A JOB HERE IN THE CITY?
WHY?
WE COULD GET A STEADY INCOME! WE COULD... BE NORMAL.

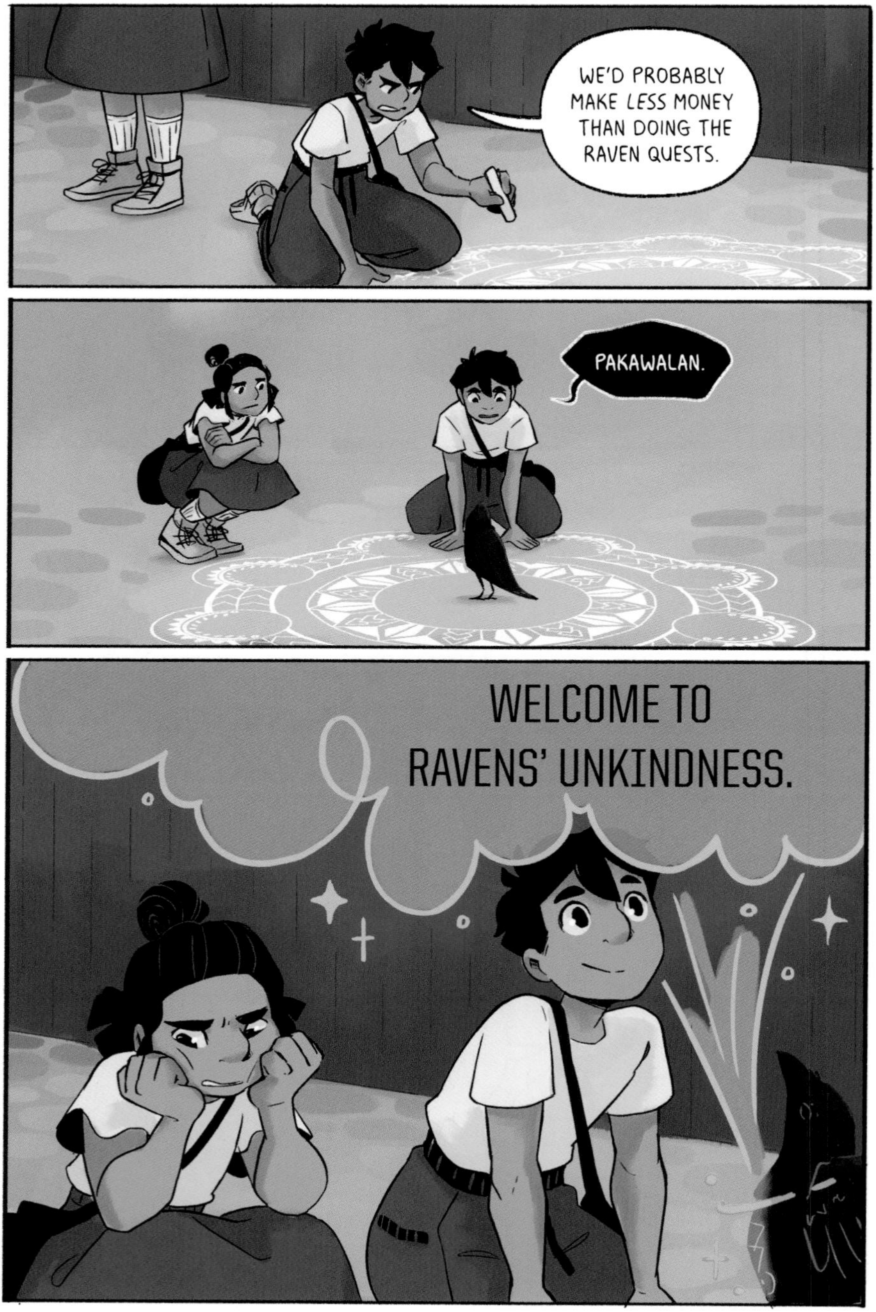
WE'D PROBABLY MAKE LESS MONEY THAN DOING THE RAVEN QUESTS.
PAKAWALAN.
WELCOME TO RAVENS' UNKINDNESS.

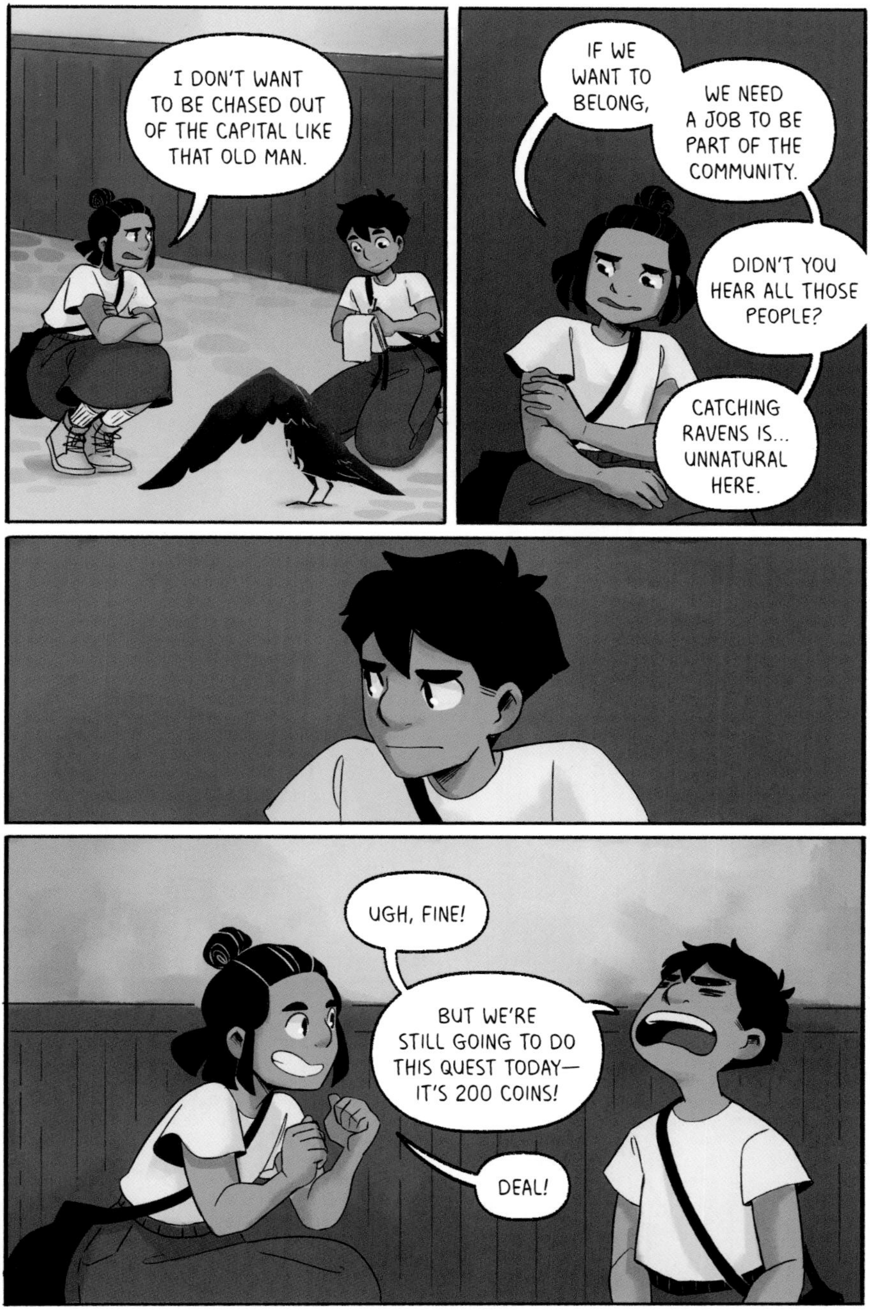
I DON'T WANT TO BE CHASED OUT OF THE CAPITAL LIKE THAT OLD MAN.
IF WE WANT TO BELONG,
WE NEED A JOB TO BE PART OF THE COMMUNITY.
DIDN'T YOU HEAR ALL THOSE PEOPLE?
CATCHING RAVENS IS... UNNATURAL HERE.
UGH, FINE!
BUT WE'RE STILL GOING TO DO THIS QUEST TODAY— IT'S 200 COINS!
DEAL!

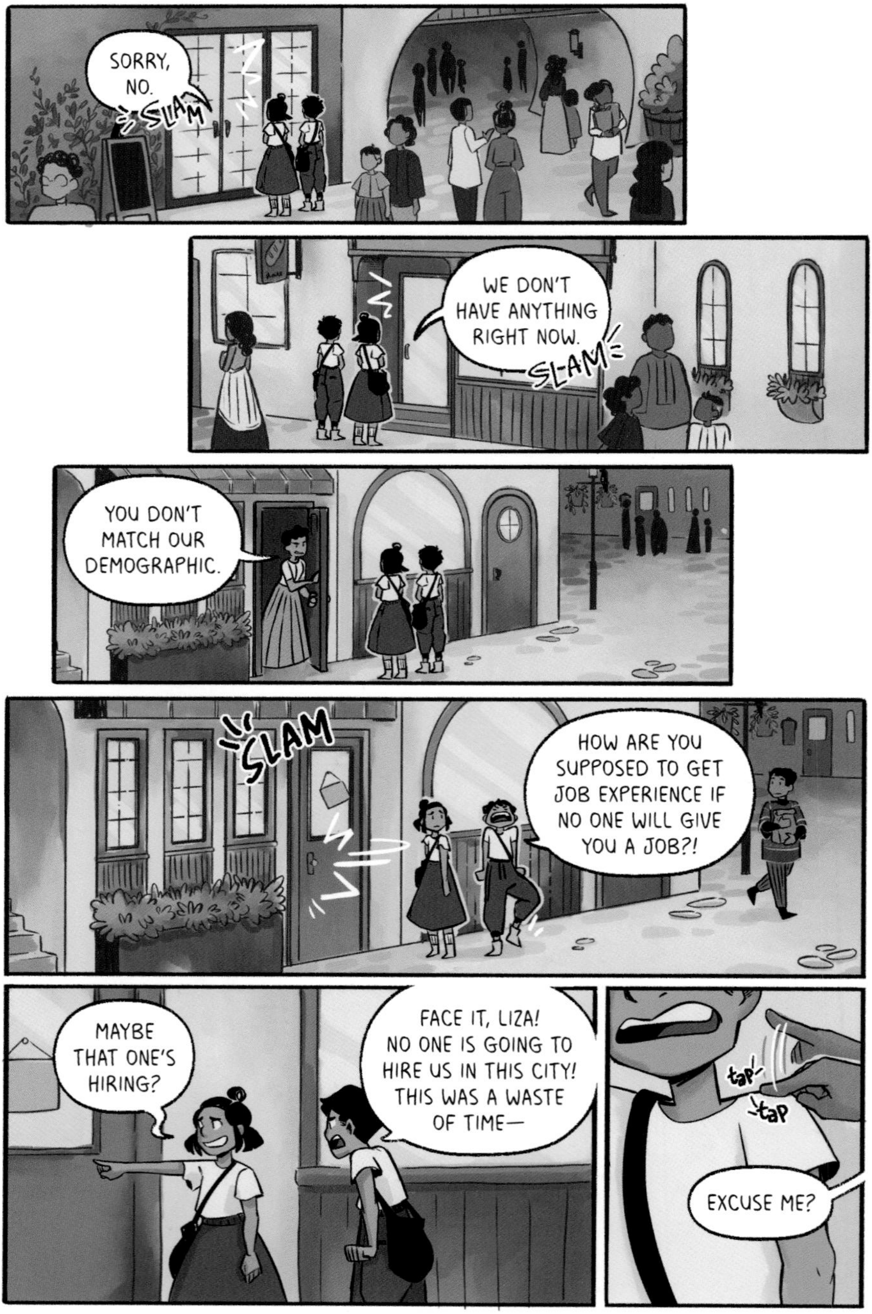
SORRY, NO.
SLAM
WE DON'T HAVE ANYTHING RIGHT NOW.
SLAM
YOU DON'T MATCH OUR DEMOGRAPHIC.
SLAM
HOW ARE YOU SUPPOSED TO GET JOB EXPERIENCE IF NO ONE WILL GIVE YOU A JOB?!
MAYBE THAT ONE'S HIRING?
FACE IT, LIZA! NO ONE IS GOING TO HIRE US IN THIS CITY! THIS WAS A WASTE OF TIME—
tap tap
EXCUSE ME?

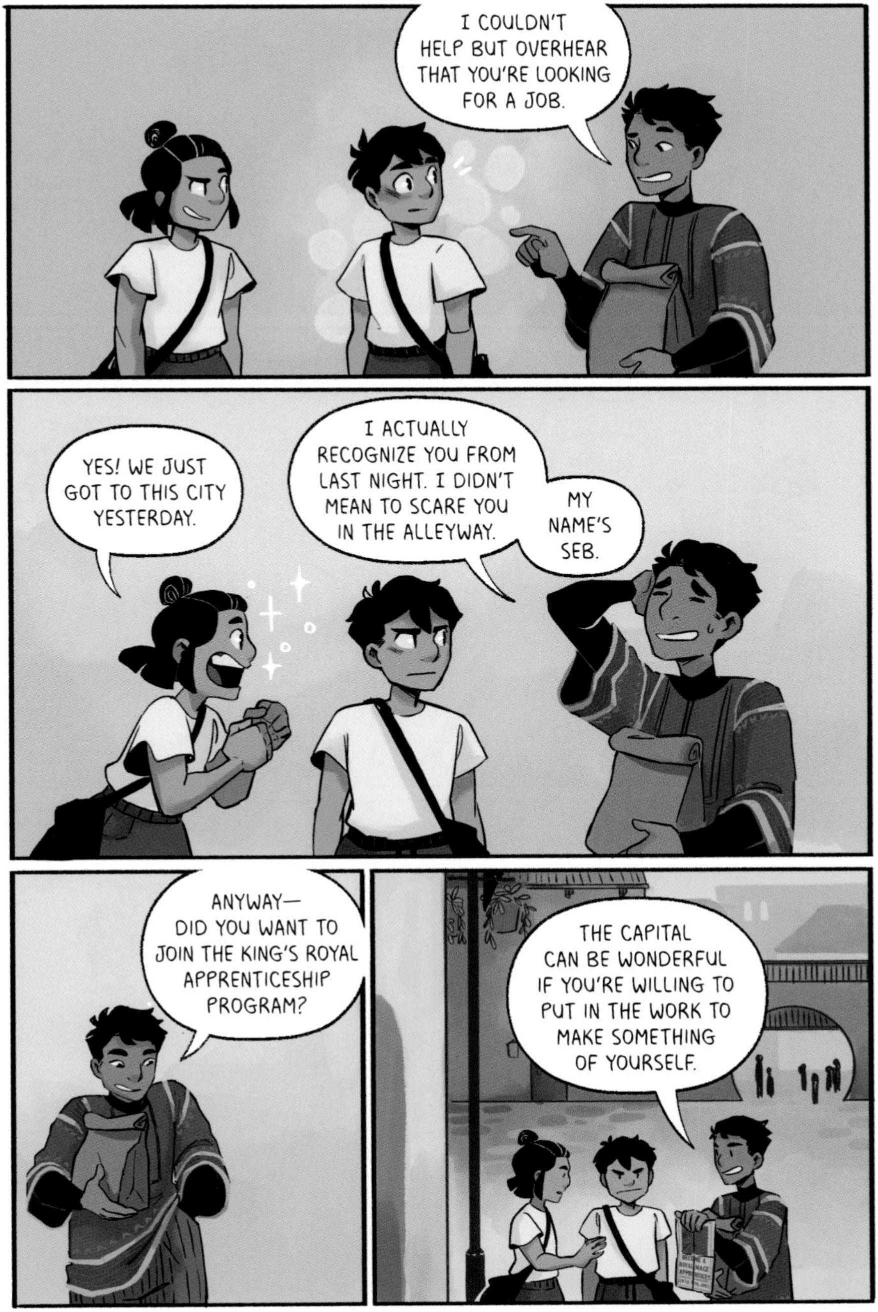
I COULDN'T HELP BUT OVERHEAR THAT YOU'RE LOOKING FOR A JOB.
YES! WE JUST GOT TO THIS CITY YESTERDAY.
I ACTUALLY RECOGNIZE YOU FROM LAST NIGHT. I DIDN'T MEAN TO SCARE YOU IN THE ALLEYWAY.
MY NAME'S SEB.
ANYWAY— DID YOU WANT TO JOIN THE KING'S ROYAL APPRENTICESHIP PROGRAM?
THE CAPITAL CAN BE WONDERFUL IF YOU'RE WILLING TO PUT IN THE WORK TO MAKE SOMETHING OF YOURSELF.

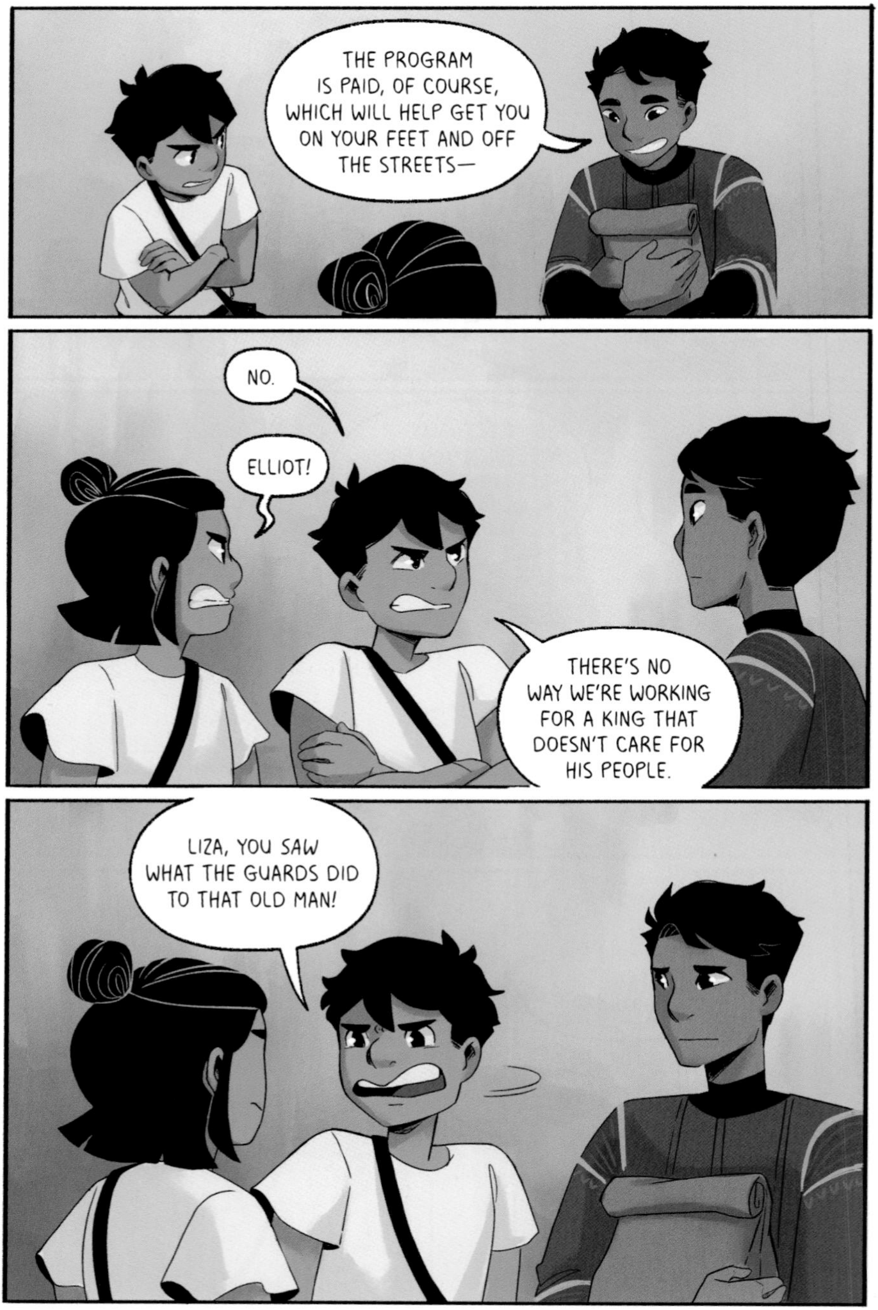
THE PROGRAM IS PAID, OF COURSE, WHICH WILL HELP GET YOU ON YOUR FEET AND OFF THE STREETS—
NO.
ELLIOT!
THERE'S NO WAY WE'RE WORKING FOR A KING THAT DOESN'T CARE FOR HIS PEOPLE.
LIZA, YOU SAW WHAT THE GUARDS DID TO THAT OLD MAN!

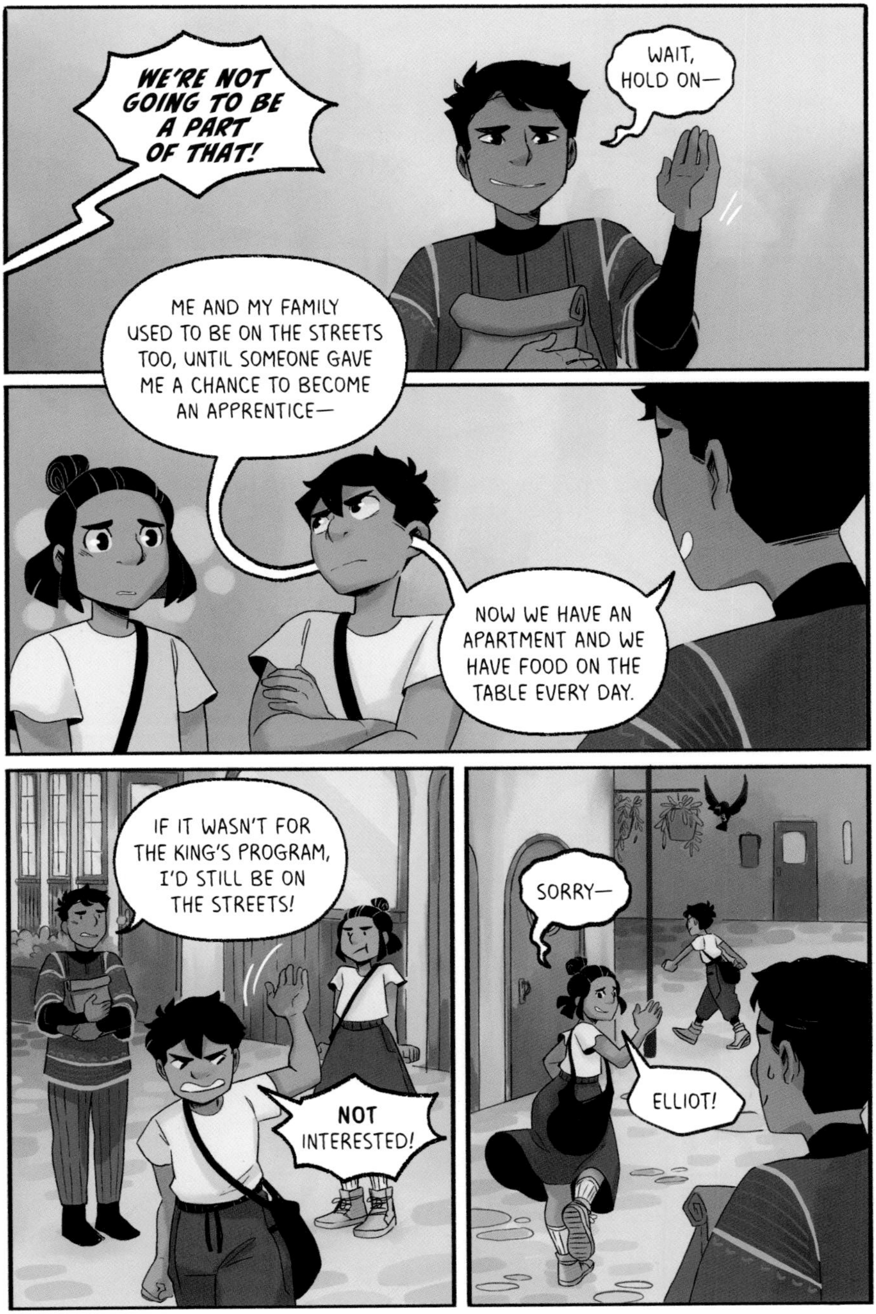
WE'RE NOT GOING TO BE A PART OF THAT!
WAIT, HOLD ON—
ME AND MY FAMILY USED TO BE ON THE STREETS TOO, UNTIL SOMEONE GAVE ME A CHANCE TO BECOME AN APPRENTICE—
NOW WE HAVE AN APARTMENT AND WE HAVE FOOD ON THE TABLE EVERY DAY.
IF IT WASN'T FOR THE KING'S PROGRAM, I'D STILL BE ON THE STREETS!
NOT INTERESTED!
SORRY—
ELLIOT!

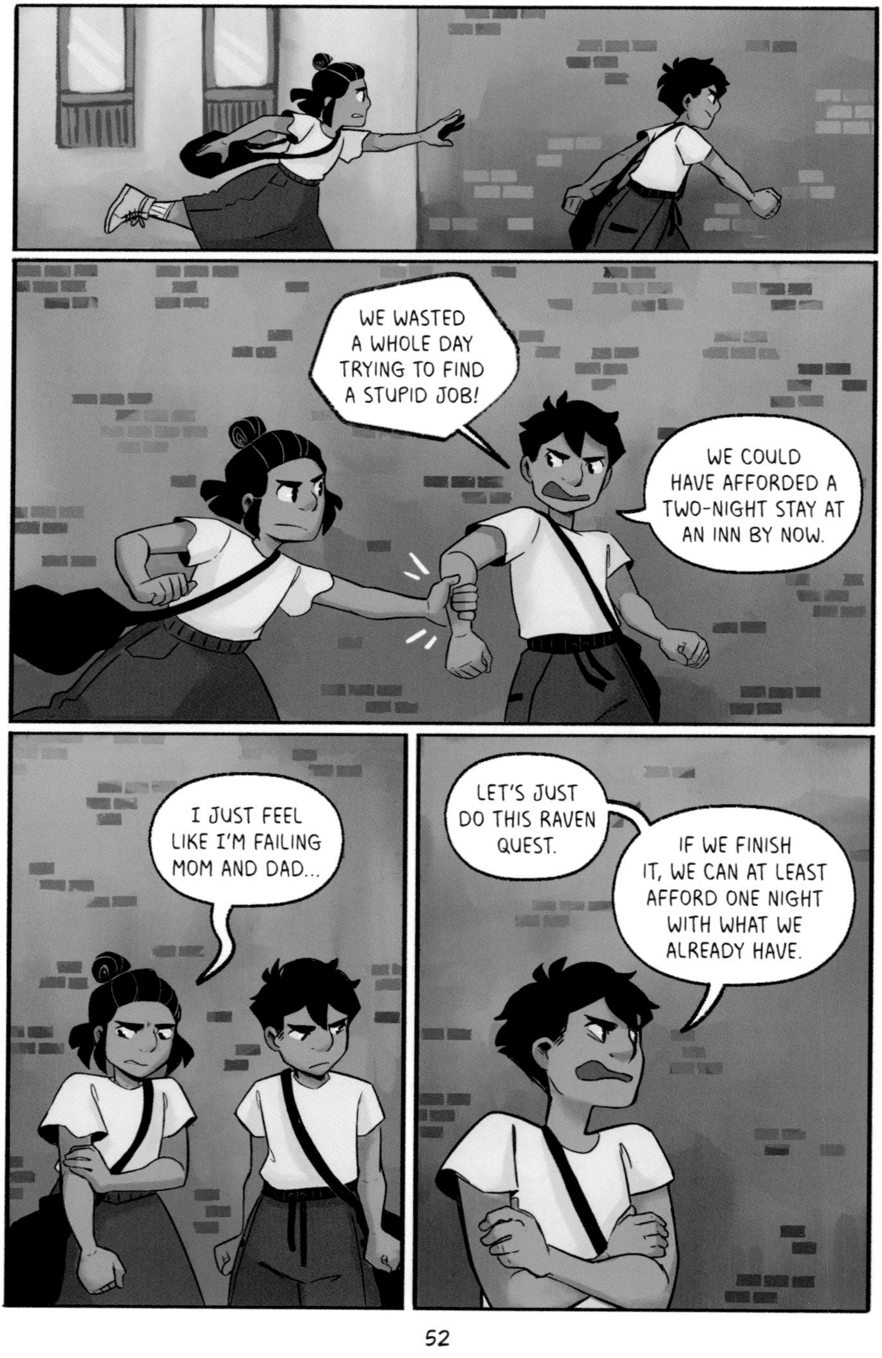
WE WASTED A WHOLE DAY TRYING TO FIND A STUPID JOB!
WE COULD HAVE AFFORDED A TWO-NIGHT STAY AT AN INN BY NOW.
I JUST FEEL LIKE I'M FAILING MOM AND DAD...
LET'S JUST DO THIS RAVEN QUEST.
IF WE FINISH IT, WE CAN AT LEAST AFFORD ONE NIGHT WITH WHAT WE ALREADY HAVE.

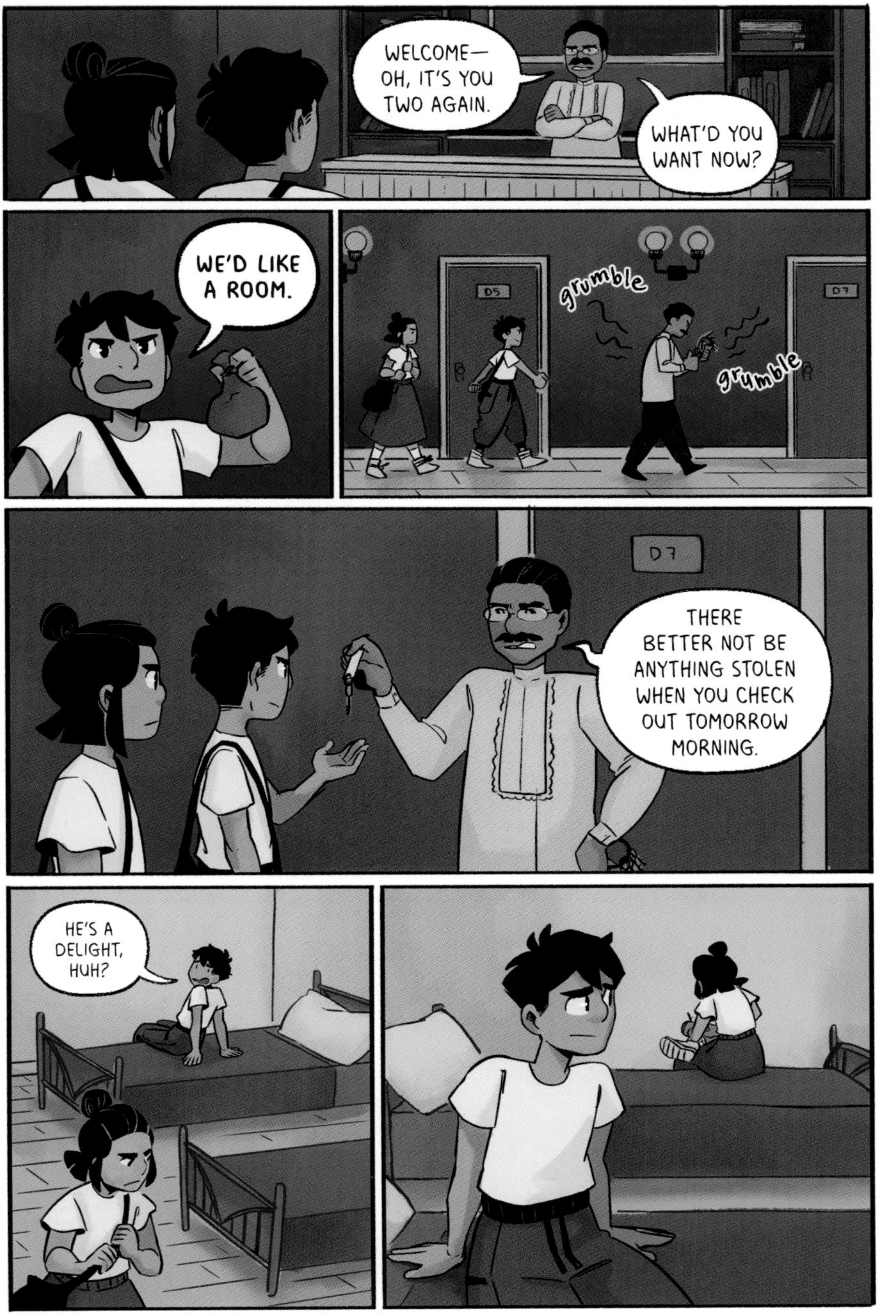
WELCOME—
OH, IT'S YOU
TWO AGAIN.
WHAT'D YOU
WANT NOW?
WE'D LIKE
A ROOM.
grumble
grumble
D5
D7
D7
THERE
BETTER NOT BE
ANYTHING STOLEN
WHEN YOU CHECK
OUT TOMORROW
MORNING.
HE'S A
DELIGHT,
HUH?

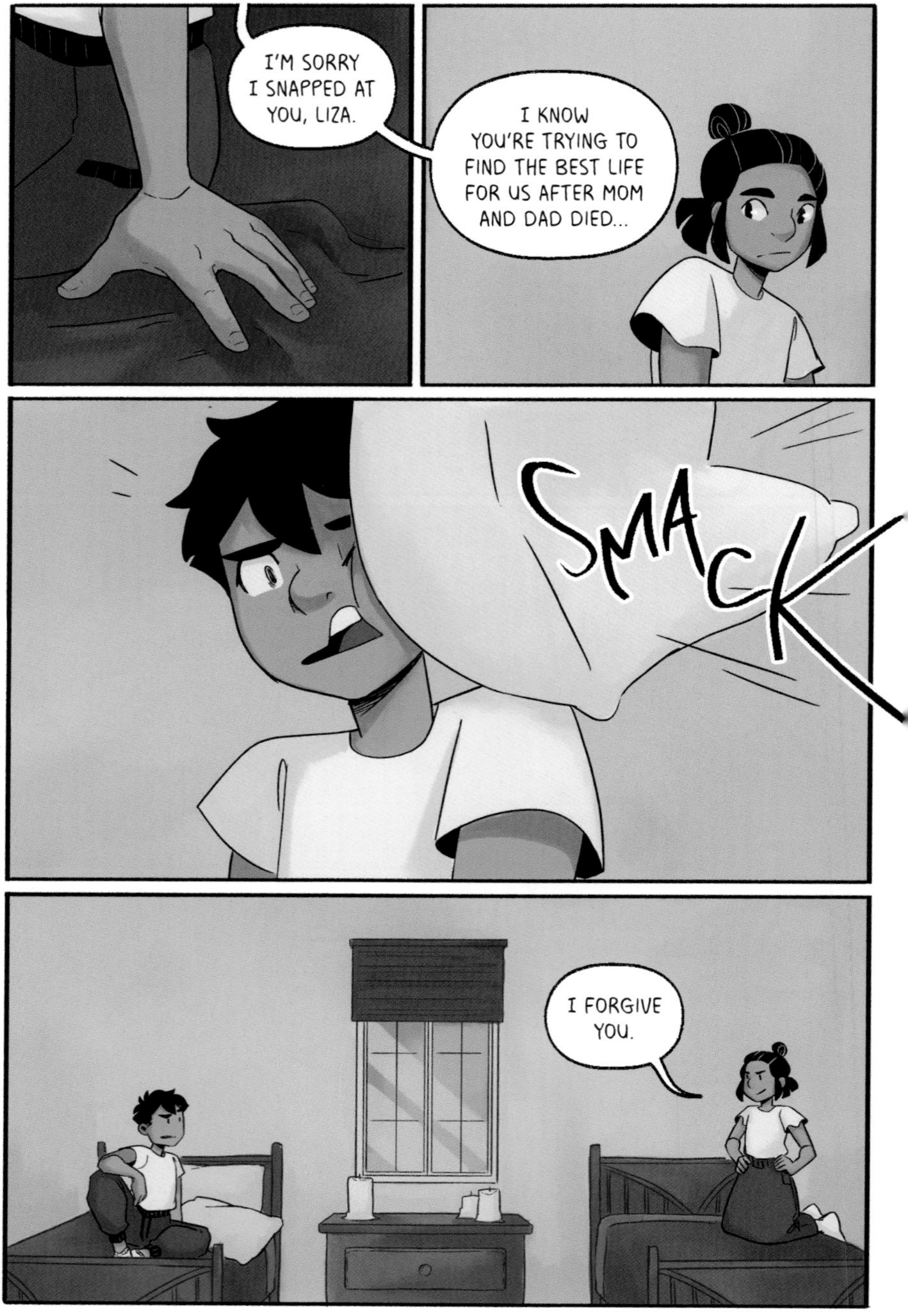
I'M SORRY I SNAPPED AT YOU, LIZA.
I KNOW YOU'RE TRYING TO FIND THE BEST LIFE FOR US AFTER MOM AND DAD DIED...
SMACK
I FORGIVE YOU.

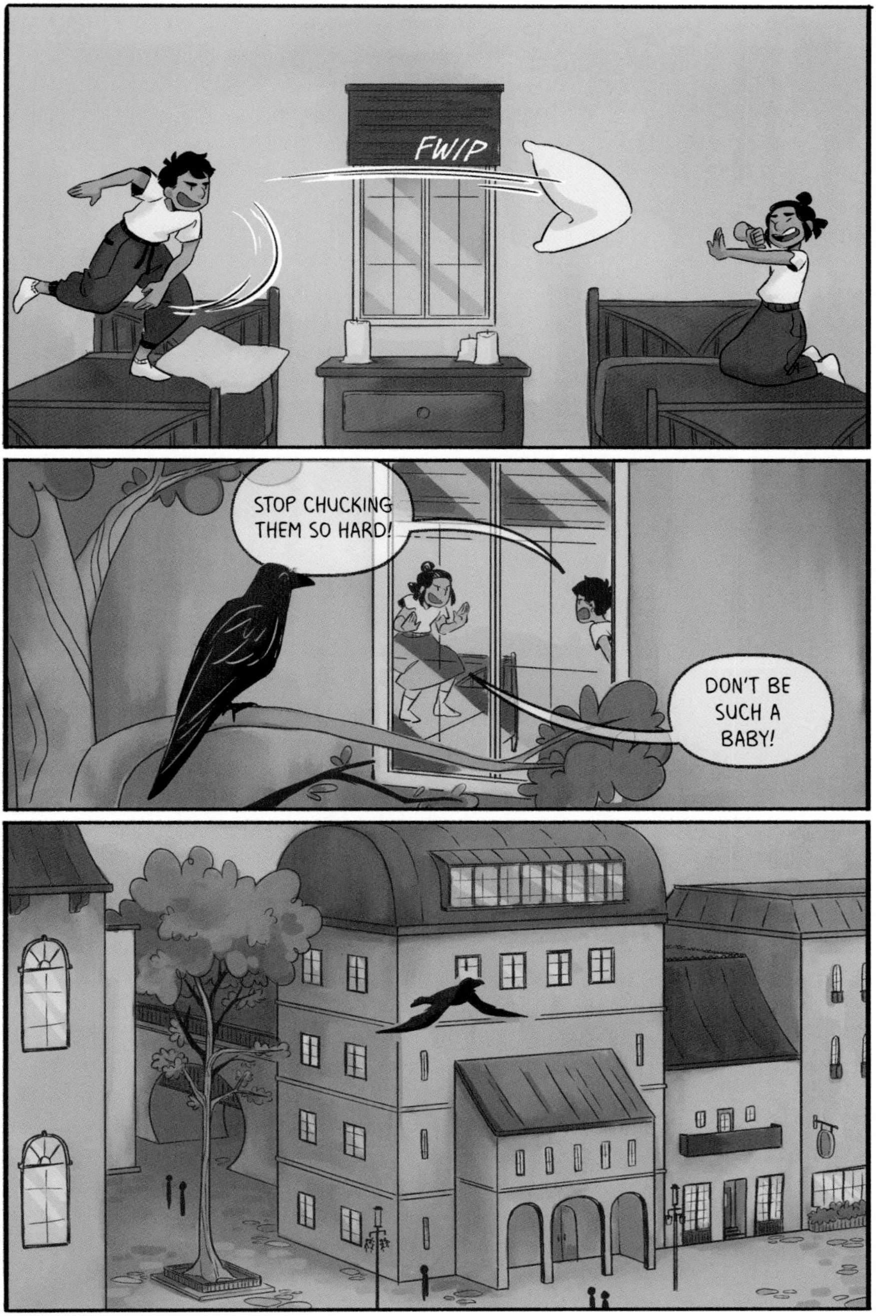
FWIP
STOP CHUCKING THEM SO HARD!
DON'T BE SUCH A BABY!

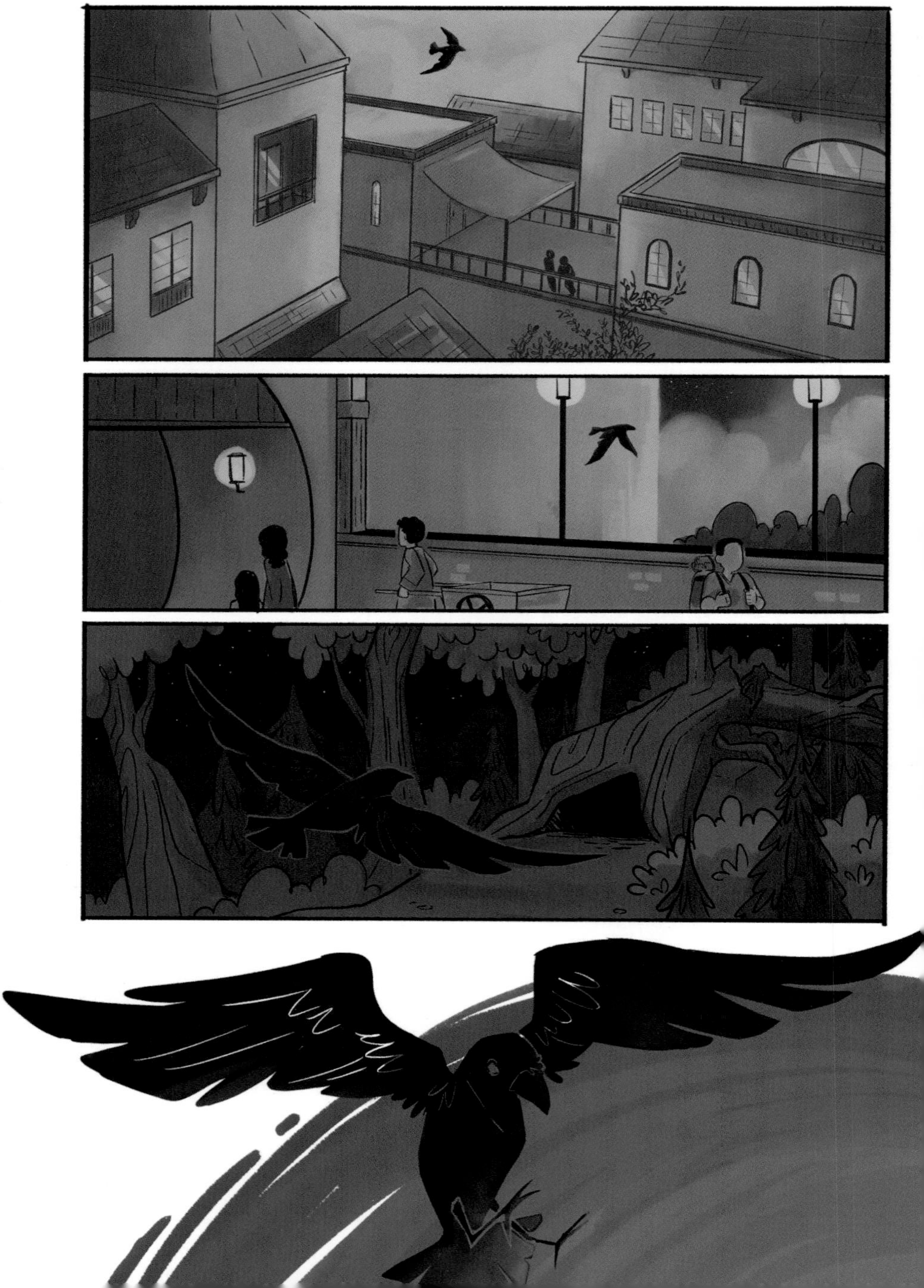

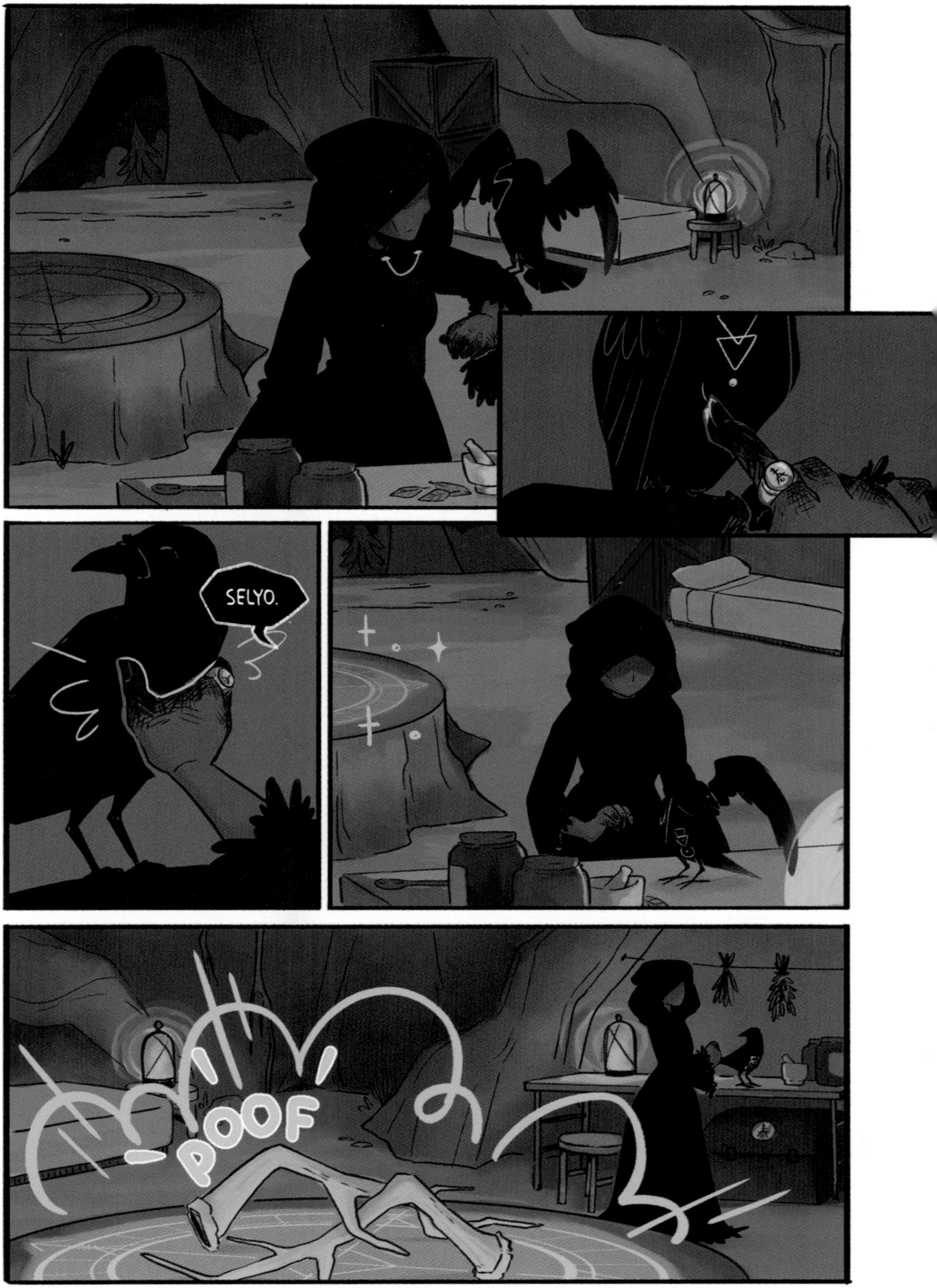
SELYO.
POOF

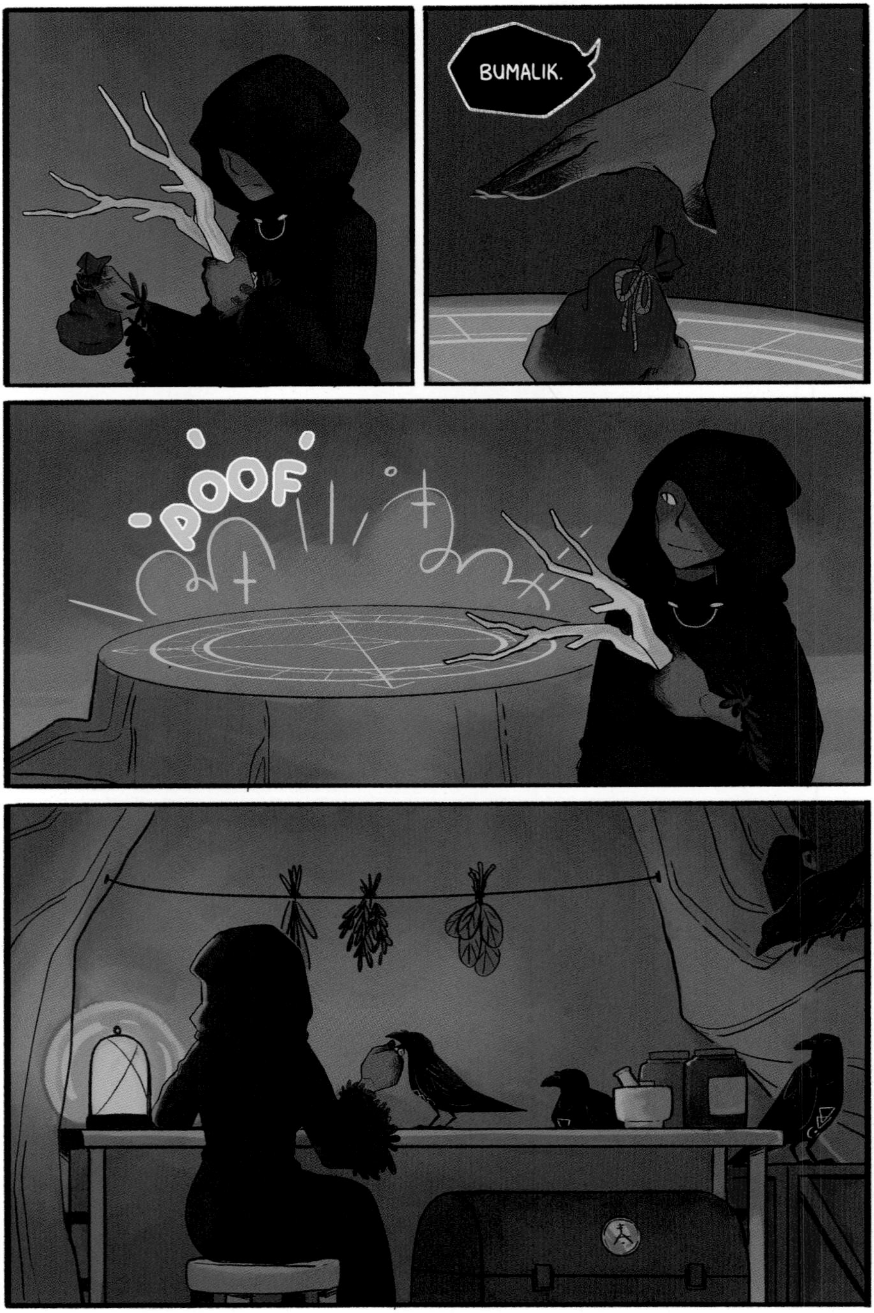
BUMALIK.
POOF

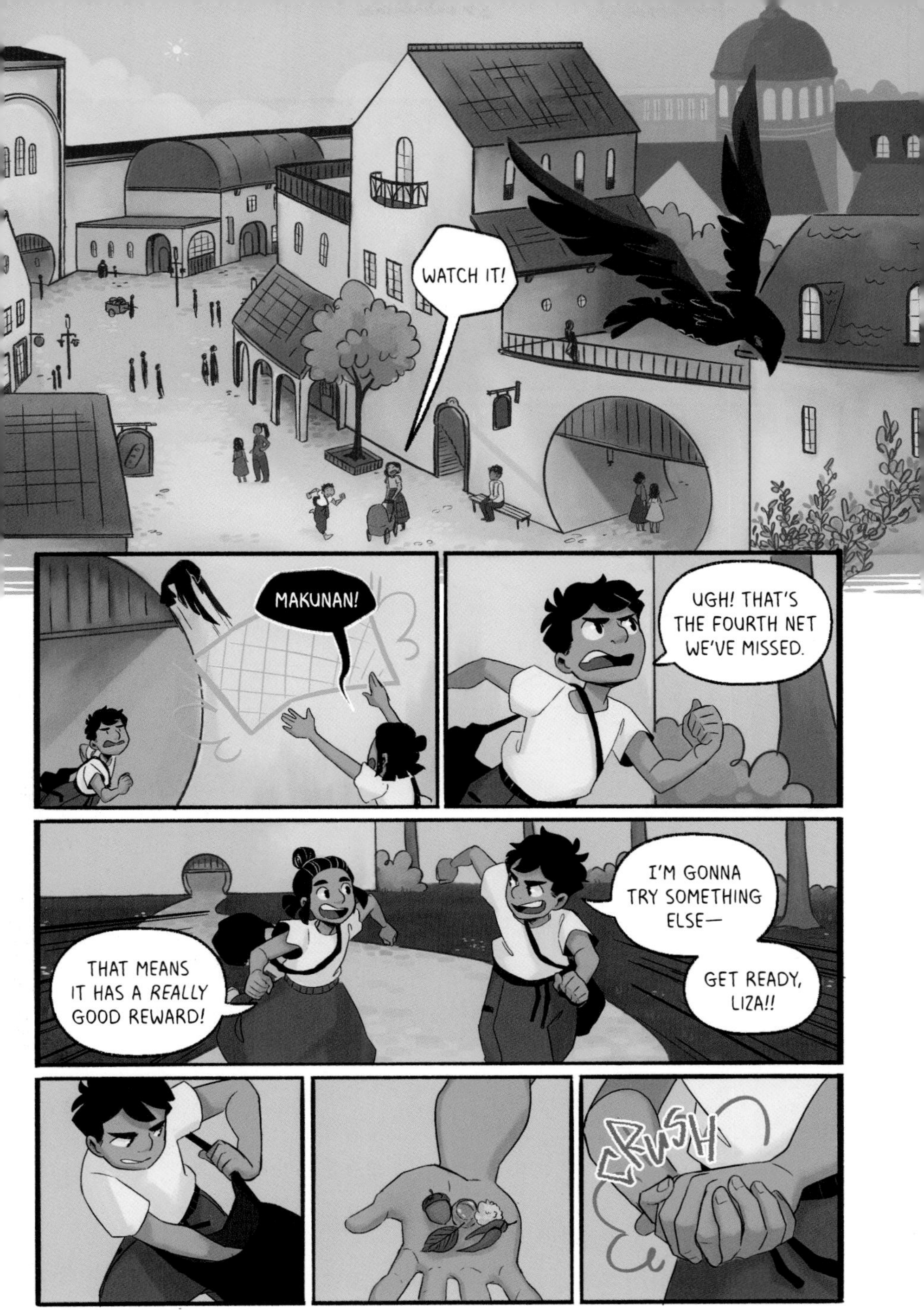
WATCH IT!
MAKUNAN!
UGH! THAT'S THE FOURTH NET WE'VE MISSED.
I'M GONNA TRY SOMETHING ELSE—
GET READY, LIZA!!
THAT MEANS IT HAS A *REALLY* GOOD REWARD!
CRUSH

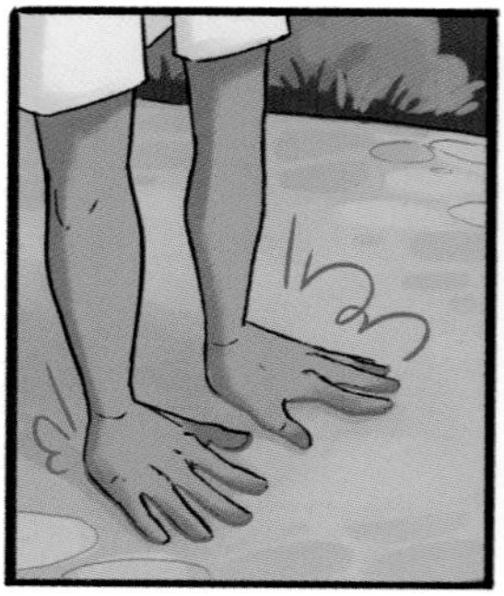

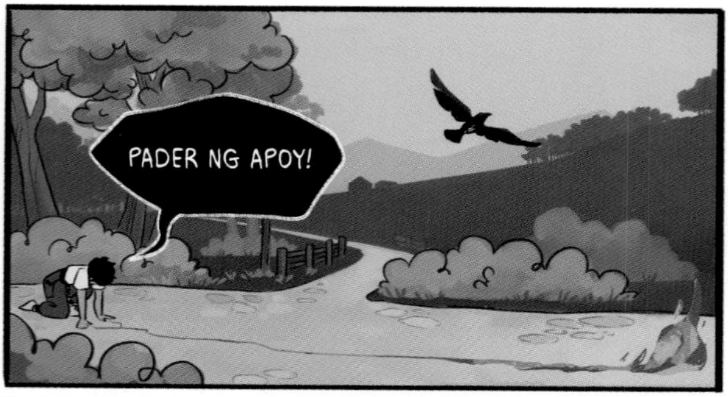

PADER NG APOY!

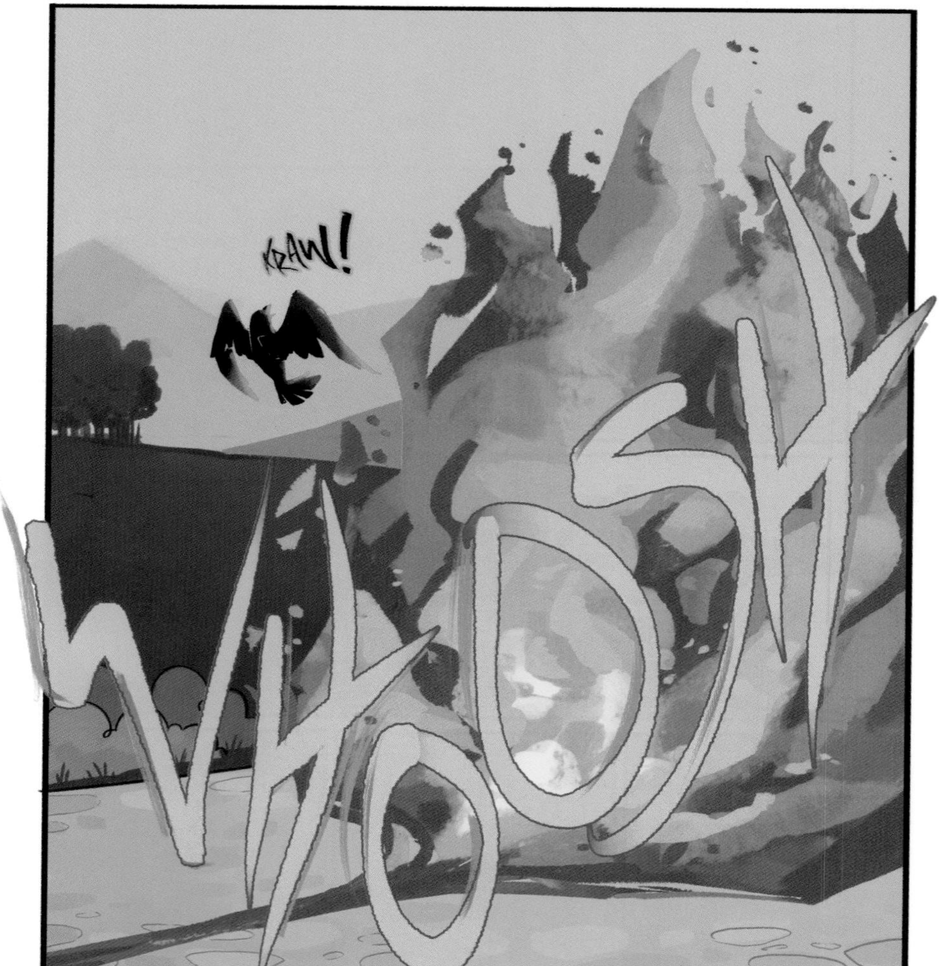

KRAW!
WHOOSH!

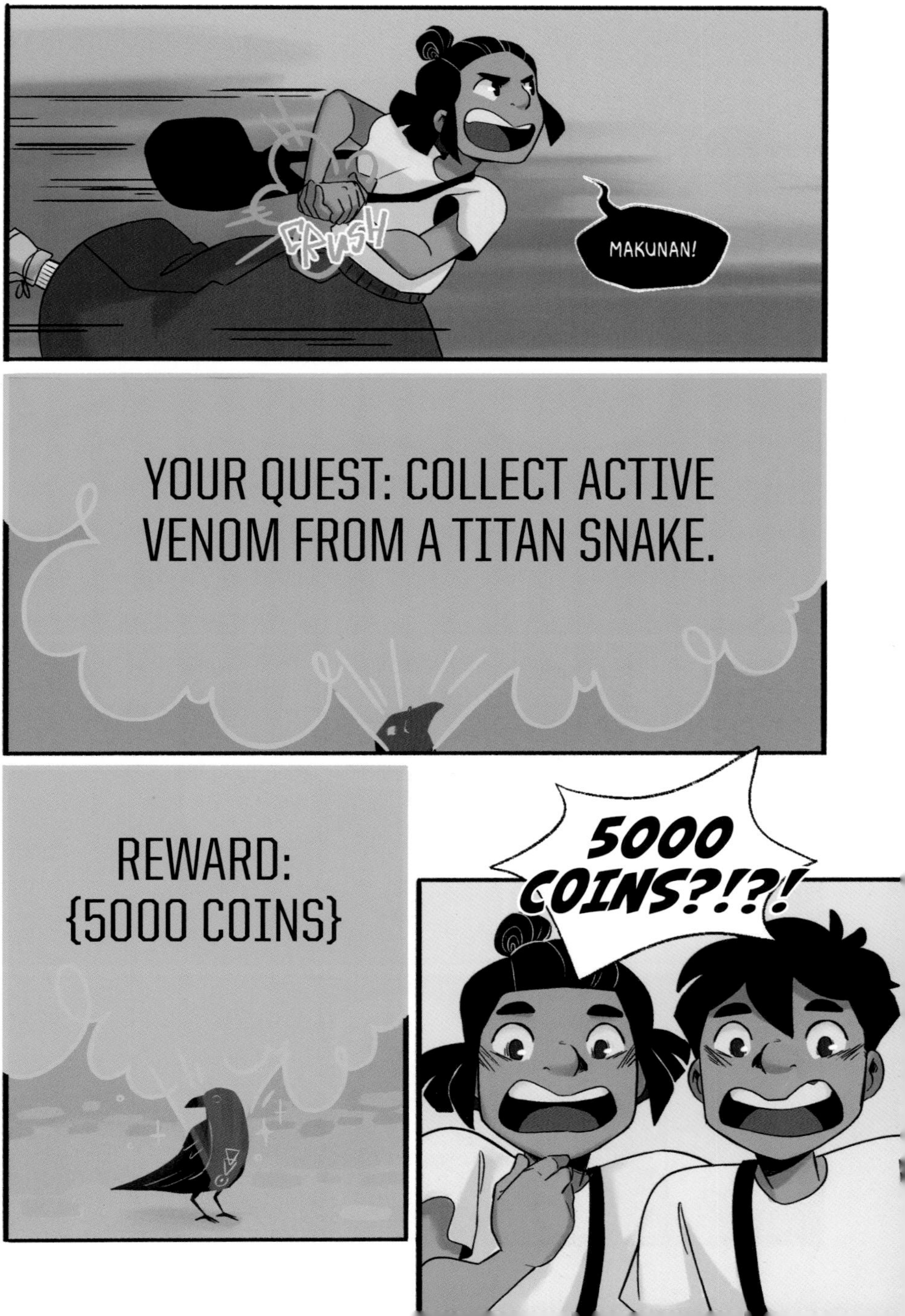
CRUSH
MAKUNAN!
YOUR QUEST: COLLECT ACTIVE VENOM FROM A TITAN SNAKE.
REWARD: {5000 COINS}
5000 COINS?!?!

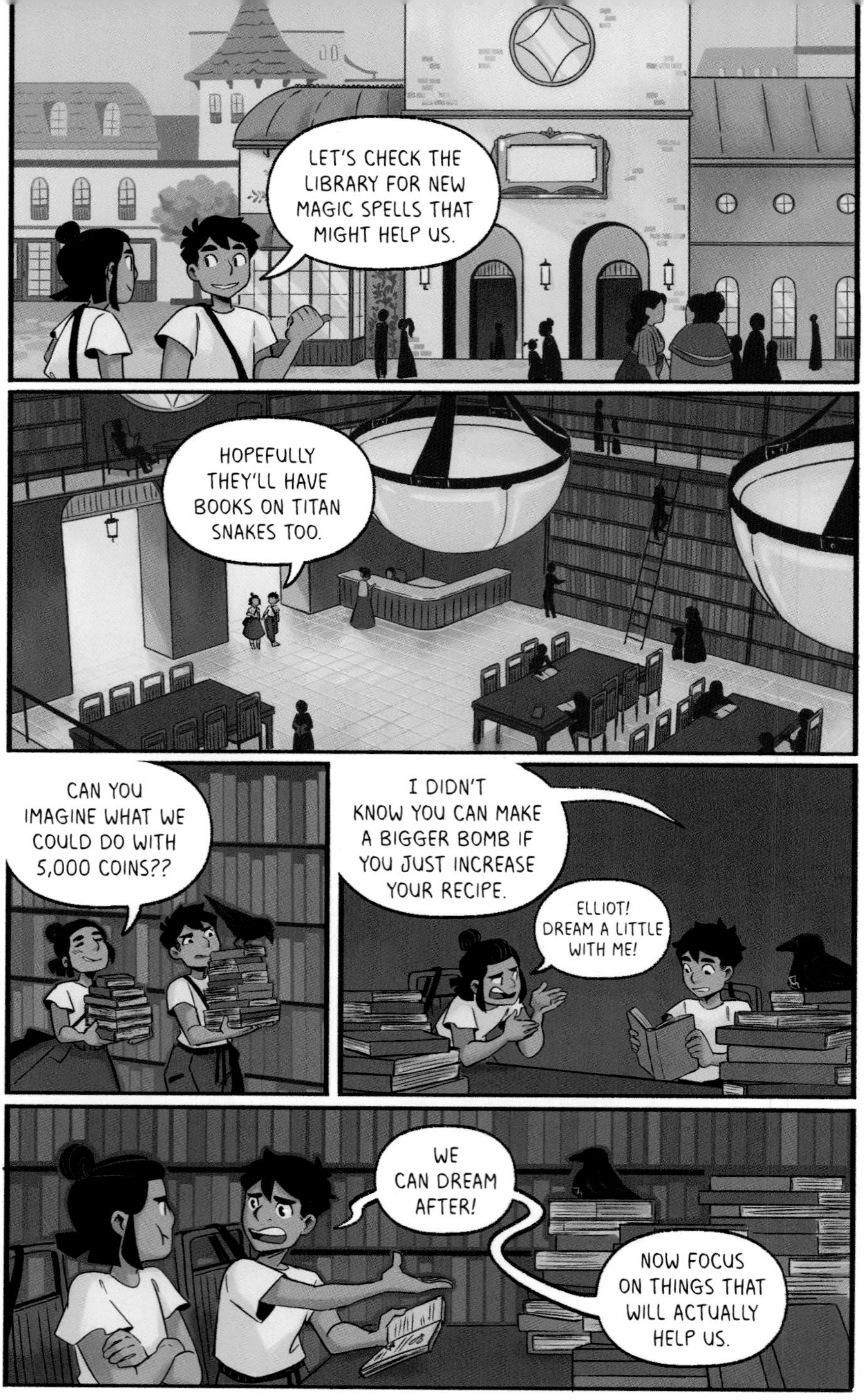
LET'S CHECK THE LIBRARY FOR NEW MAGIC SPELLS THAT MIGHT HELP US.
HOPEFULLY THEY'LL HAVE BOOKS ON TITAN SNAKES TOO.
CAN YOU IMAGINE WHAT WE COULD DO WITH 5,000 COINS??
I DIDN'T KNOW YOU CAN MAKE A BIGGER BOMB IF YOU JUST INCREASE YOUR RECIPE.
ELLIOT! DREAM A LITTLE WITH ME!
WE CAN DREAM AFTER!
NOW FOCUS ON THINGS THAT WILL ACTUALLY HELP US.

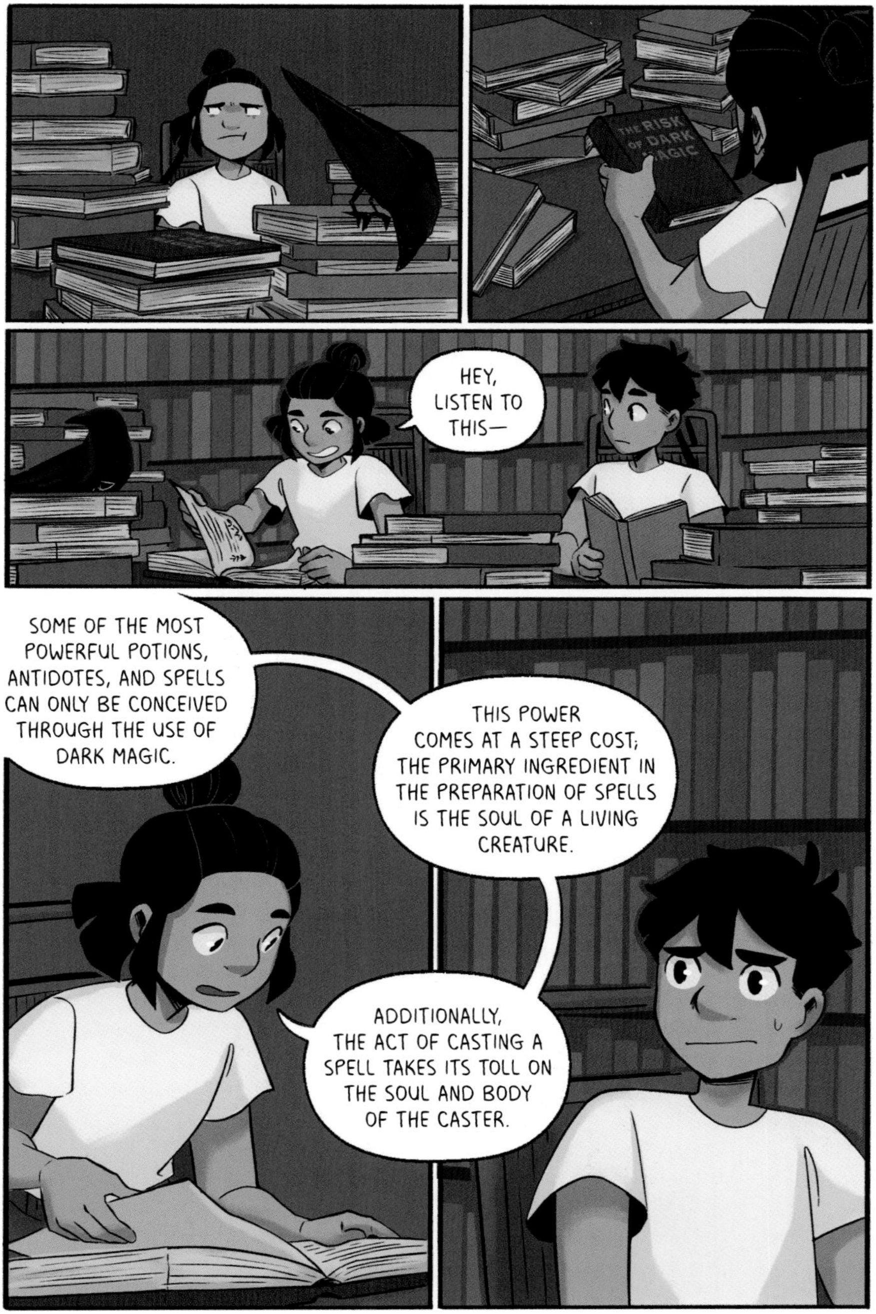
THE RISK OF DARK MAGIC
HEY, LISTEN TO THIS—
SOME OF THE MOST POWERFUL POTIONS, ANTIDOTES, AND SPELLS CAN ONLY BE CONCEIVED THROUGH THE USE OF DARK MAGIC.
THIS POWER COMES AT A STEEP COST; THE PRIMARY INGREDIENT IN THE PREPARATION OF SPELLS IS THE SOUL OF A LIVING CREATURE.
ADDITIONALLY, THE ACT OF CASTING A SPELL TAKES ITS TOLL ON THE SOUL AND BODY OF THE CASTER.

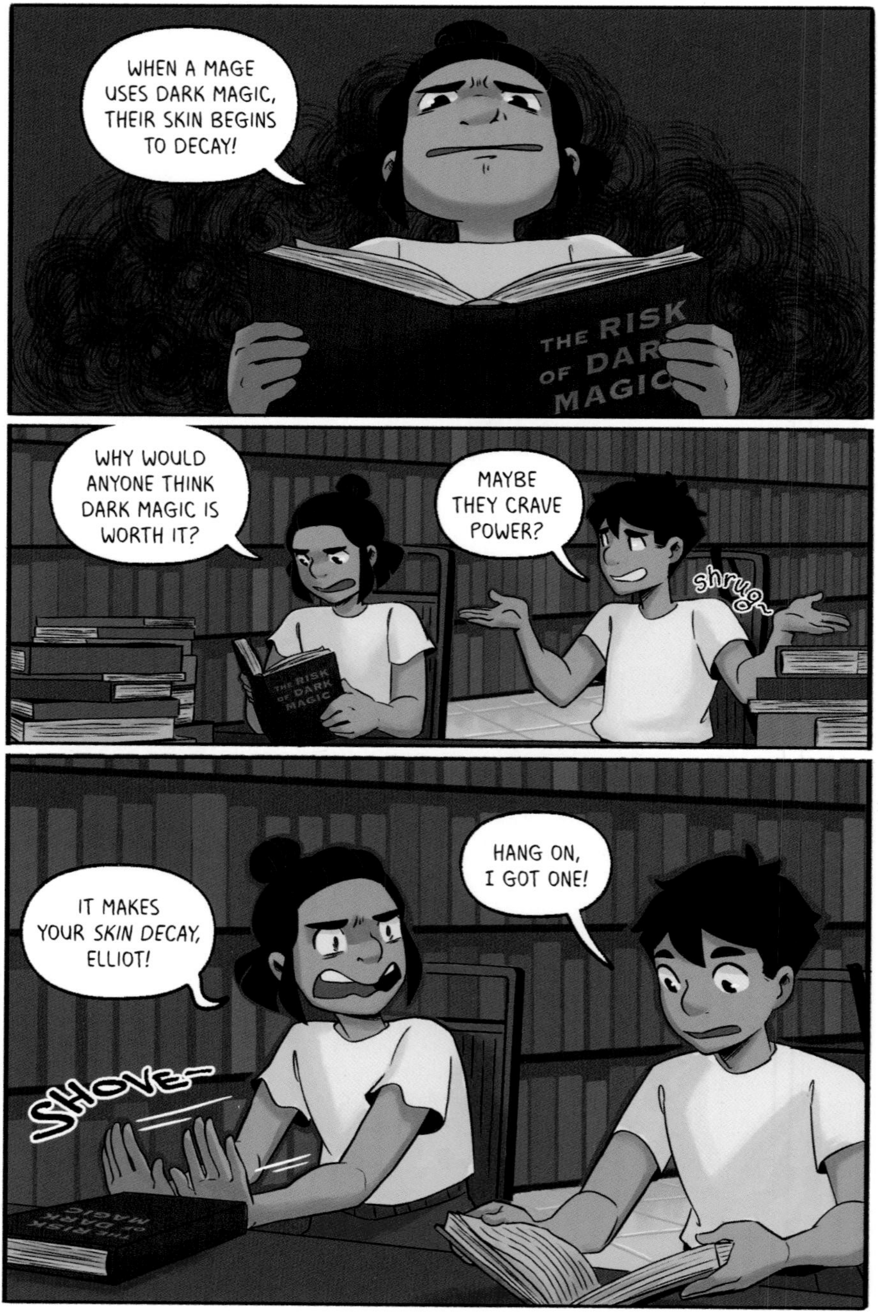
WHEN A MAGE USES DARK MAGIC, THEIR SKIN BEGINS TO DECAY!
THE RISK OF DARK MAGIC
WHY WOULD ANYONE THINK DARK MAGIC IS WORTH IT?
MAYBE THEY CRAVE POWER?
shrug~
THE RISK OF DARK MAGIC
HANG ON, I GOT ONE!
IT MAKES YOUR *SKIN DECAY*, ELLIOT!
SHOVE~

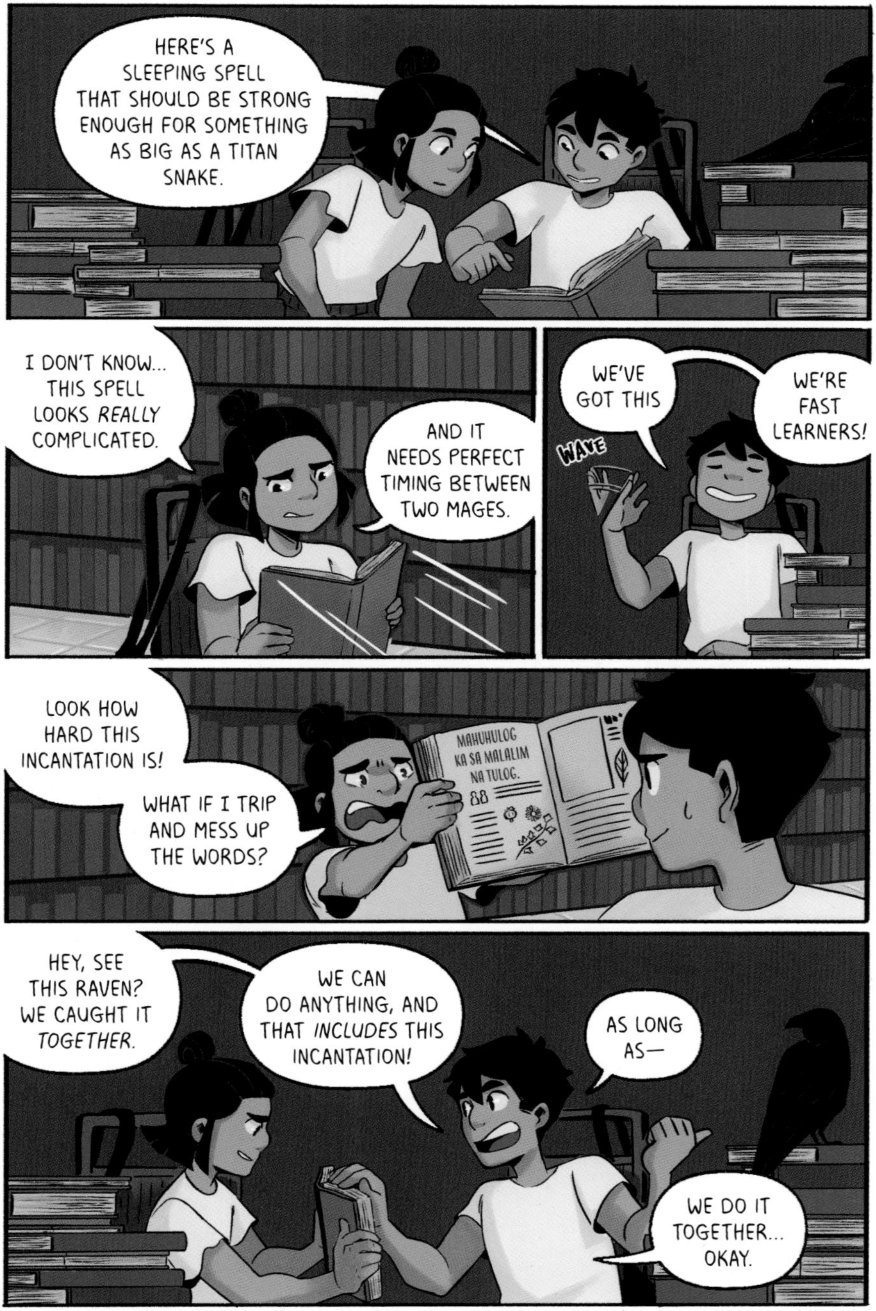
HERE'S A SLEEPING SPELL THAT SHOULD BE STRONG ENOUGH FOR SOMETHING AS BIG AS A TITAN SNAKE.
I DON'T KNOW... THIS SPELL LOOKS *REALLY* COMPLICATED.
AND IT NEEDS PERFECT TIMING BETWEEN TWO MAGES.
WAVE
WE'VE GOT THIS
WE'RE FAST LEARNERS!
LOOK HOW HARD THIS INCANTATION IS!
WHAT IF I TRIP AND MESS UP THE WORDS?
MAHUHULOG KA SA MALALIM NA TULOG.
HEY, SEE THIS RAVEN? WE CAUGHT IT *TOGETHER*.
WE CAN DO ANYTHING, AND THAT *INCLUDES* THIS INCANTATION!
AS LONG AS—
WE DO IT TOGETHER... OKAY.

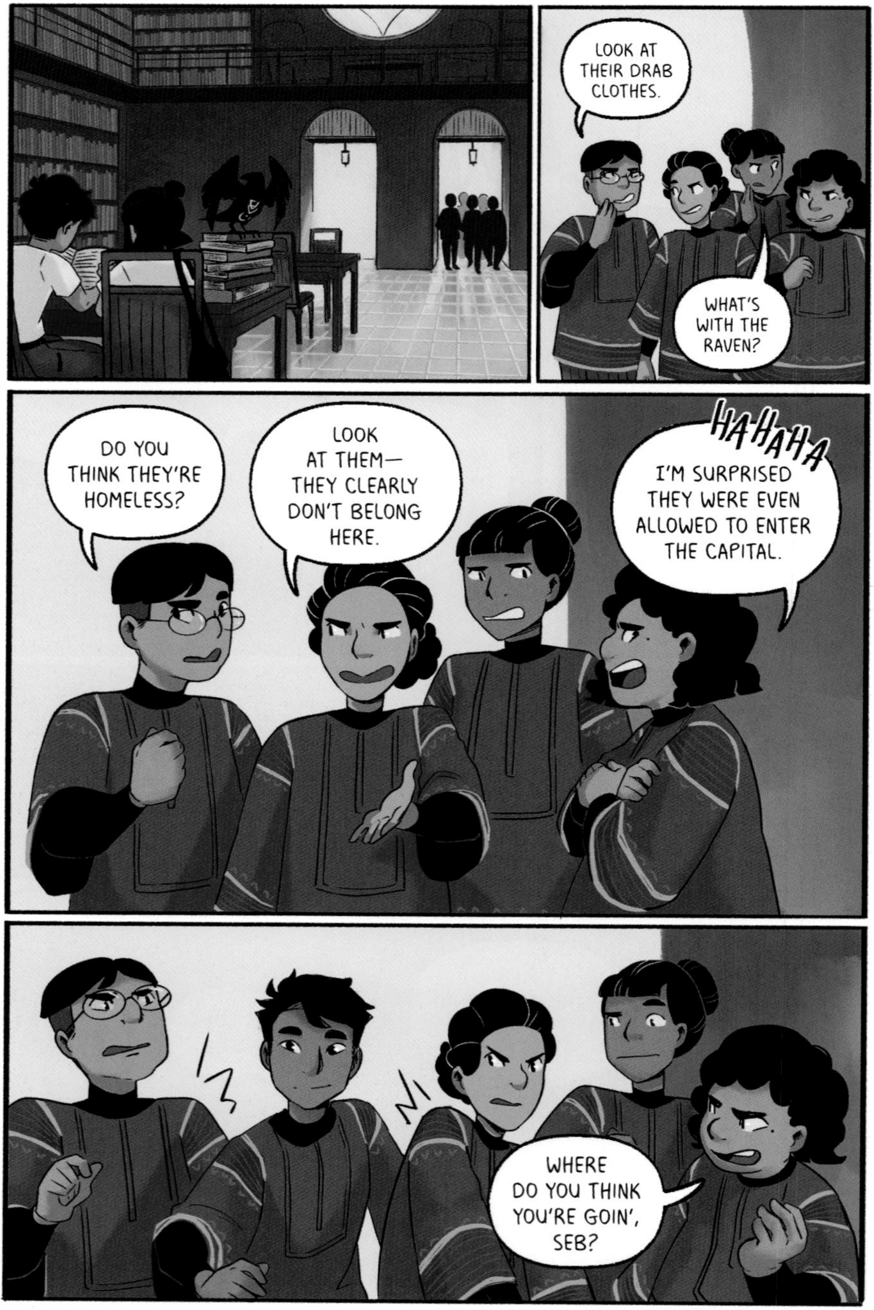
LOOK AT THEIR DRAB CLOTHES.
WHAT'S WITH THE RAVEN?
DO YOU THINK THEY'RE HOMELESS?
LOOK AT THEM— THEY CLEARLY DON'T BELONG HERE.
HAHAHA
I'M SURPRISED THEY WERE EVEN ALLOWED TO ENTER THE CAPITAL.
WHERE DO YOU THINK YOU'RE GOIN', SEB?

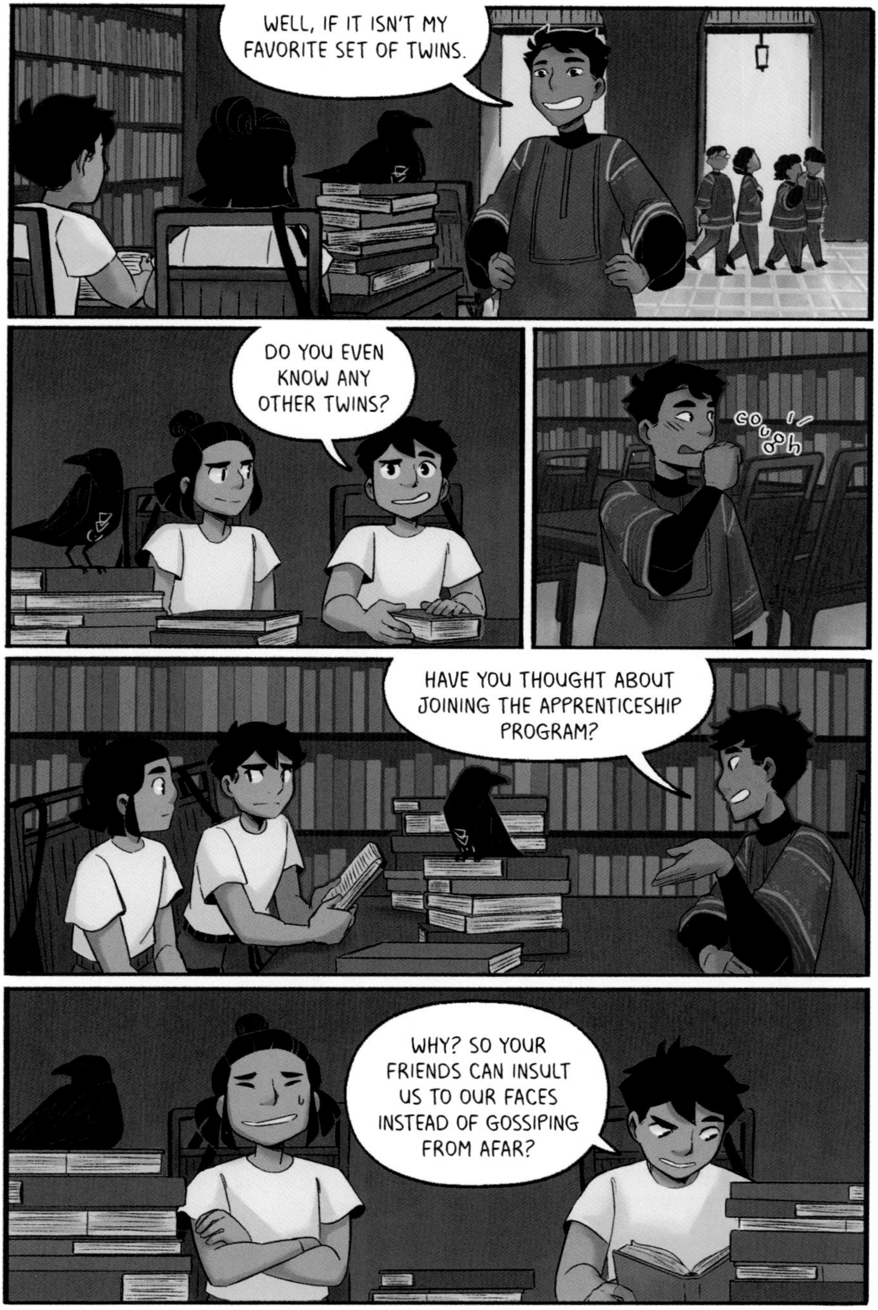
WELL, IF IT ISN'T MY FAVORITE SET OF TWINS.
DO YOU EVEN KNOW ANY OTHER TWINS?
cough
HAVE YOU THOUGHT ABOUT JOINING THE APPRENTICESHIP PROGRAM?
WHY? SO YOUR FRIENDS CAN INSULT US TO OUR FACES INSTEAD OF GOSSIPING FROM AFAR?

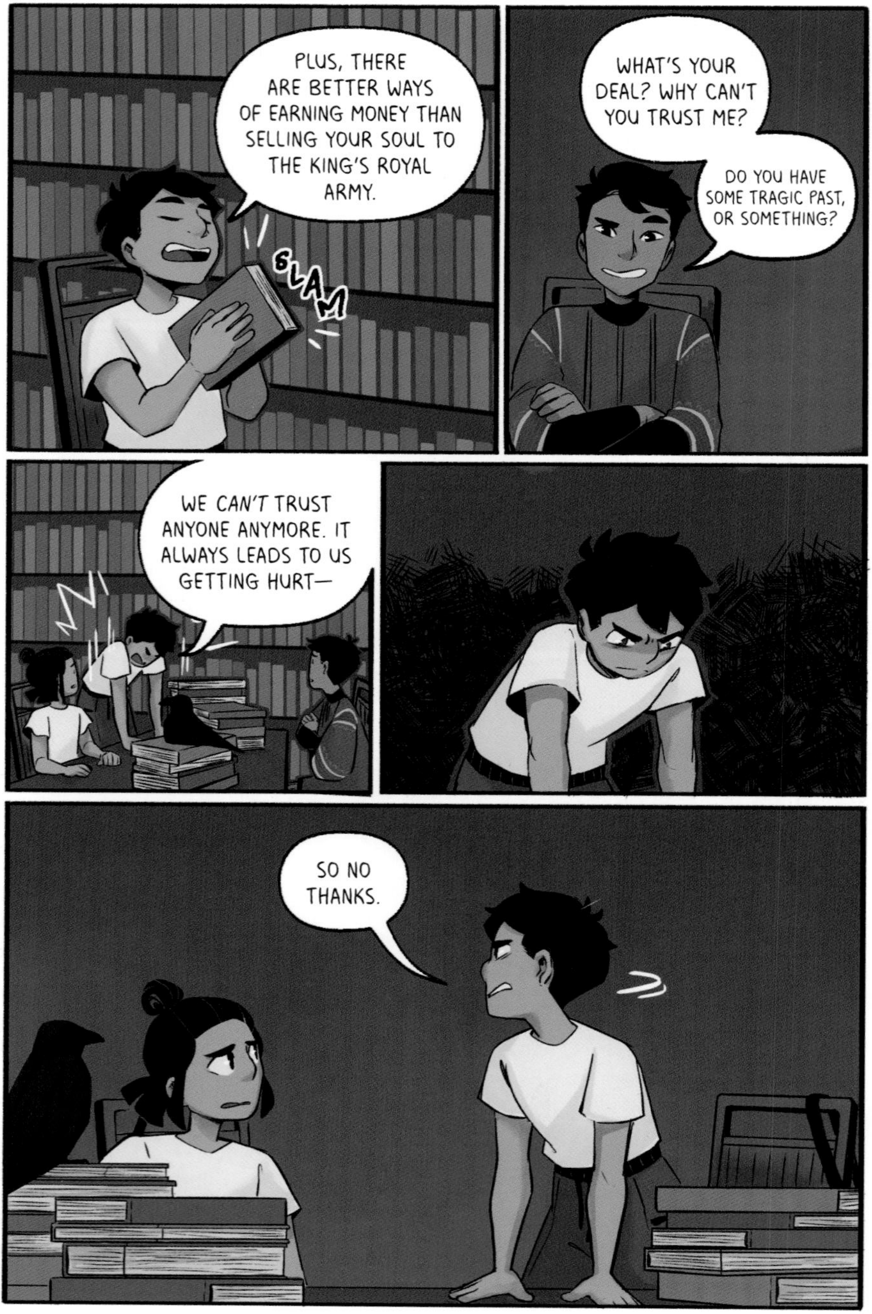
PLUS, THERE ARE BETTER WAYS OF EARNING MONEY THAN SELLING YOUR SOUL TO THE KING'S ROYAL ARMY.
SLAM
WHAT'S YOUR DEAL? WHY CAN'T YOU TRUST ME?
DO YOU HAVE SOME TRAGIC PAST, OR SOMETHING?
WE *CAN'T* TRUST ANYONE ANYMORE. IT ALWAYS LEADS TO US GETTING HURT—
SO NO THANKS.

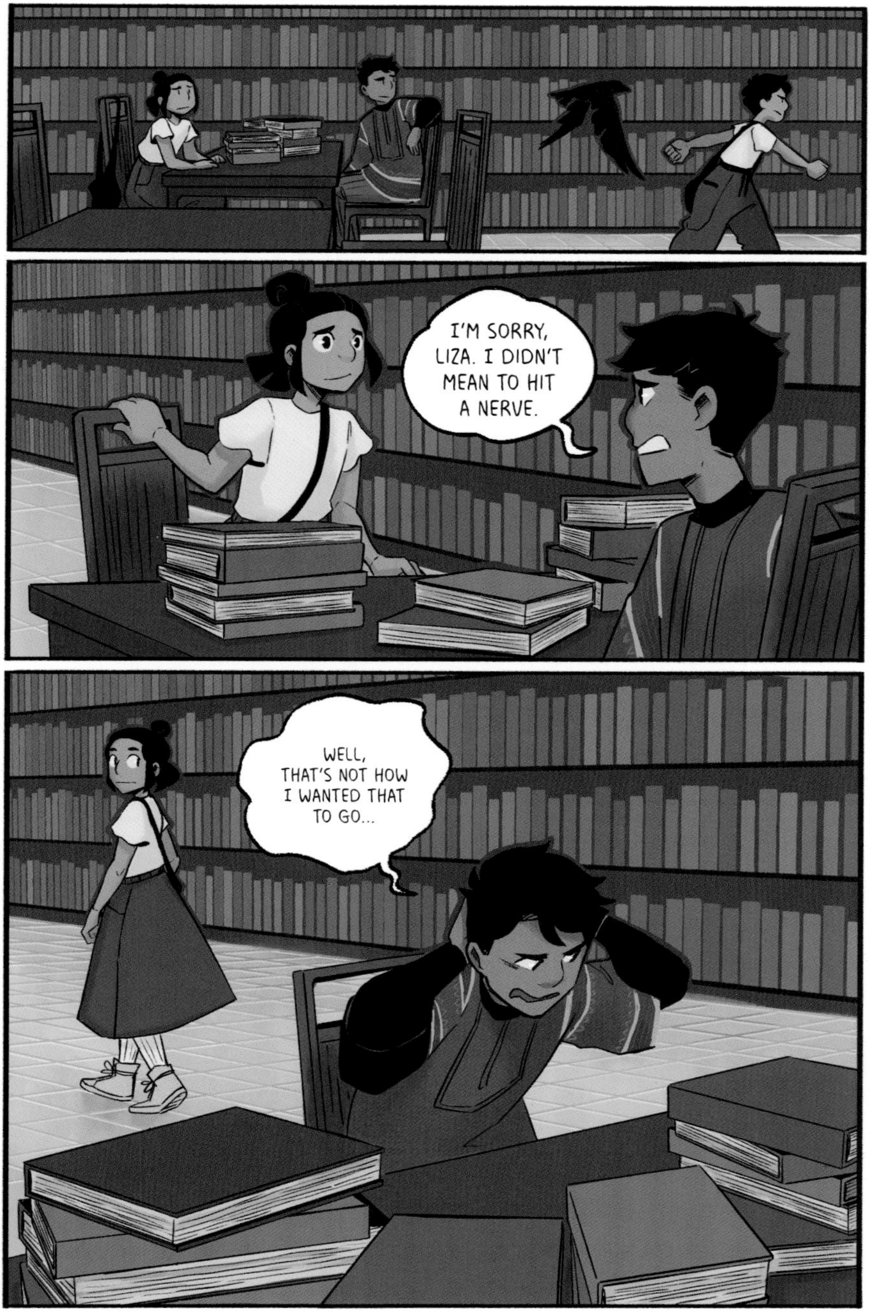
I'M SORRY, LIZA. I DIDN'T MEAN TO HIT A NERVE.
WELL, THAT'S NOT HOW I WANTED THAT TO GO...

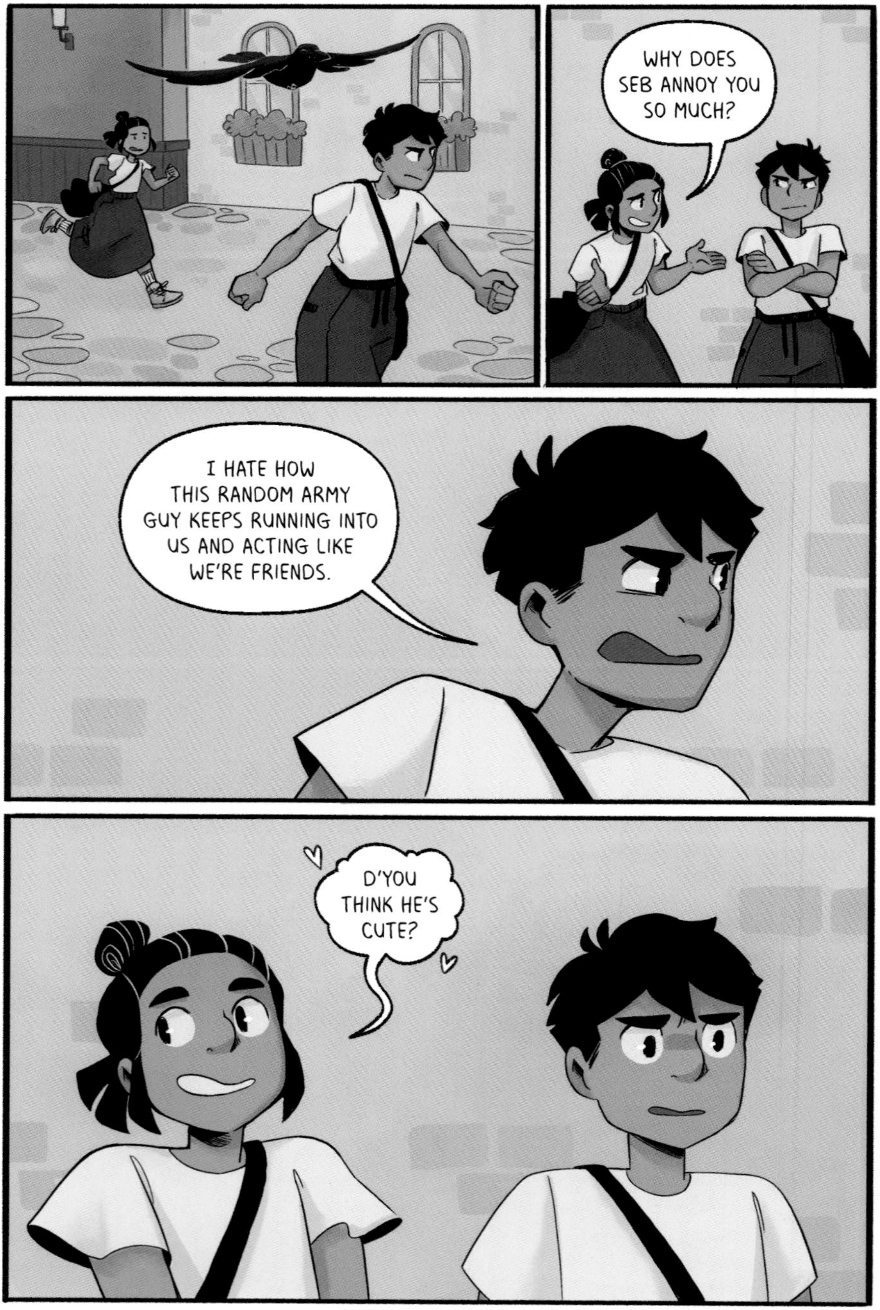
WHY DOES SEB ANNOY YOU SO MUCH?
I HATE HOW THIS RANDOM ARMY GUY KEEPS RUNNING INTO US AND ACTING LIKE WE'RE FRIENDS.
D'YOU THINK HE'S CUTE?

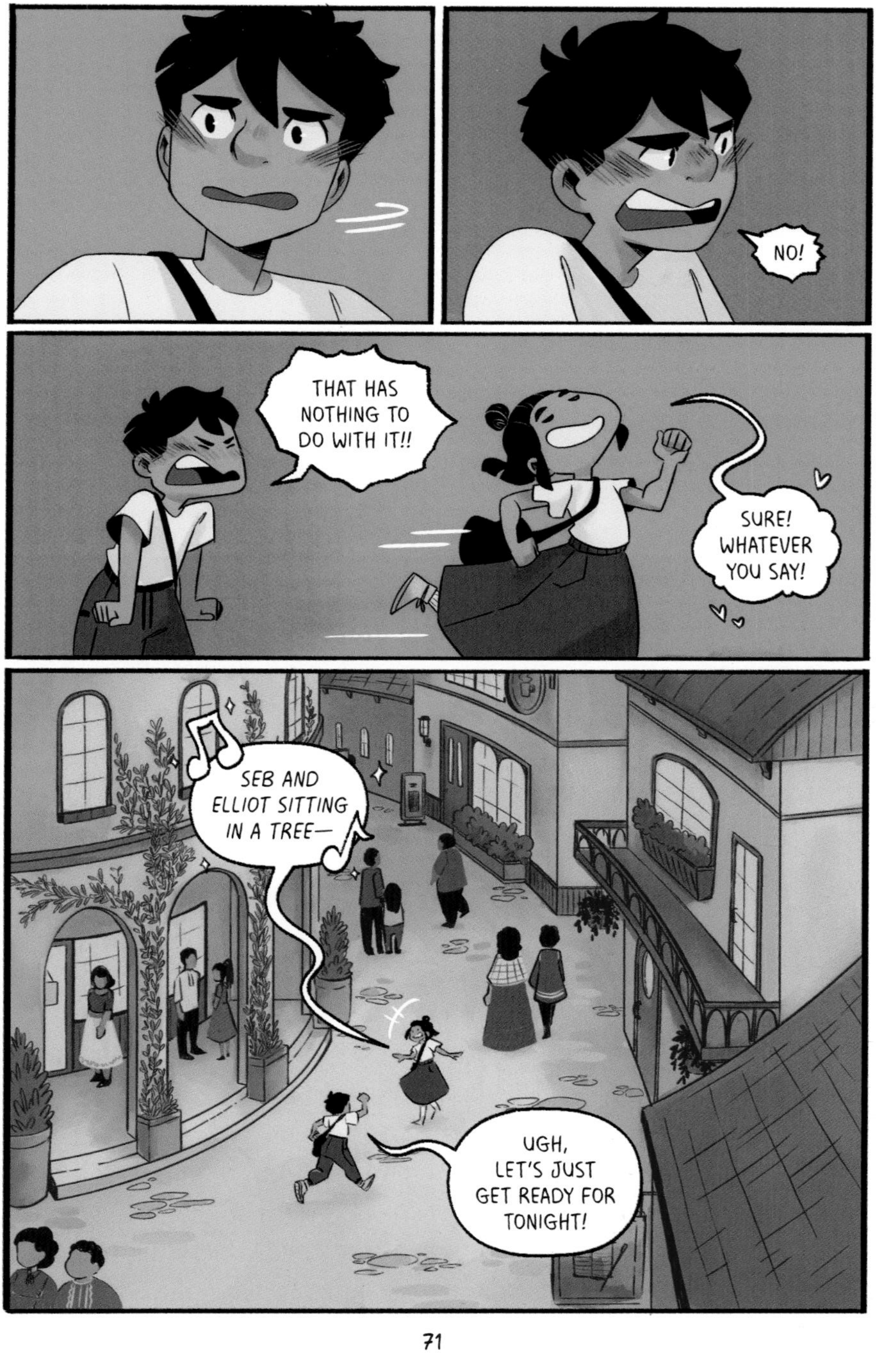
NO!
THAT HAS NOTHING TO DO WITH IT!!
SURE! WHATEVER YOU SAY!
SEB AND ELLIOT SITTING IN A TREE—
UGH, LET'S JUST GET READY FOR TONIGHT!

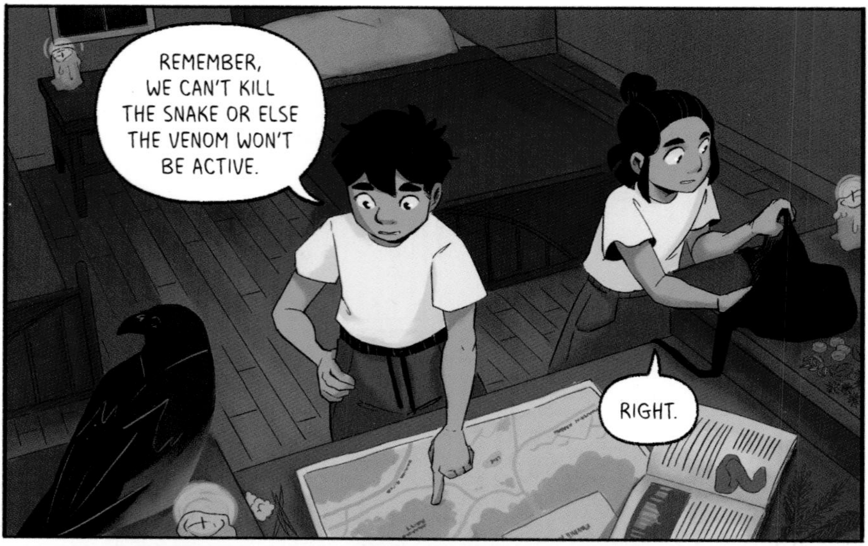
REMEMBER, WE CAN'T KILL THE SNAKE OR ELSE THE VENOM WON'T BE ACTIVE.
RIGHT.

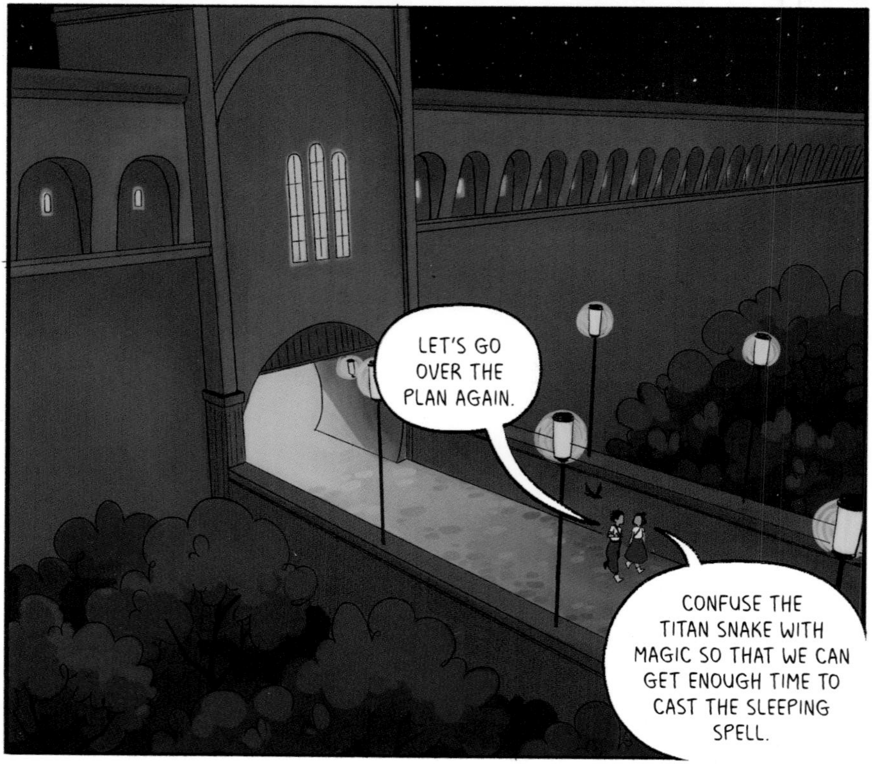
LET'S GO OVER THE PLAN AGAIN.
CONFUSE THE TITAN SNAKE WITH MAGIC SO THAT WE CAN GET ENOUGH TIME TO CAST THE SLEEPING SPELL.

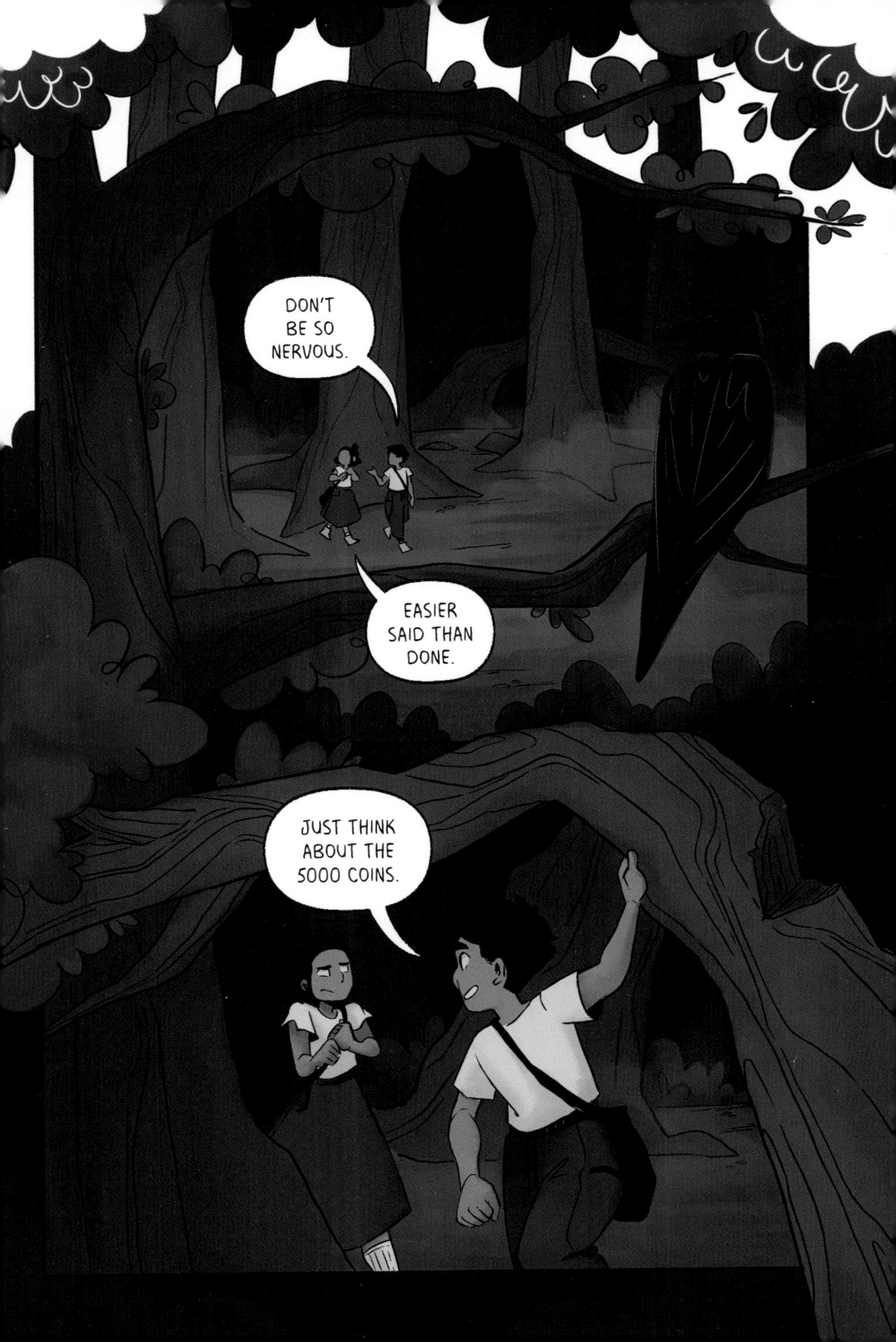
DON'T BE SO NERVOUS.
EASIER SAID THAN DONE.
JUST THINK ABOUT THE 5000 COINS.

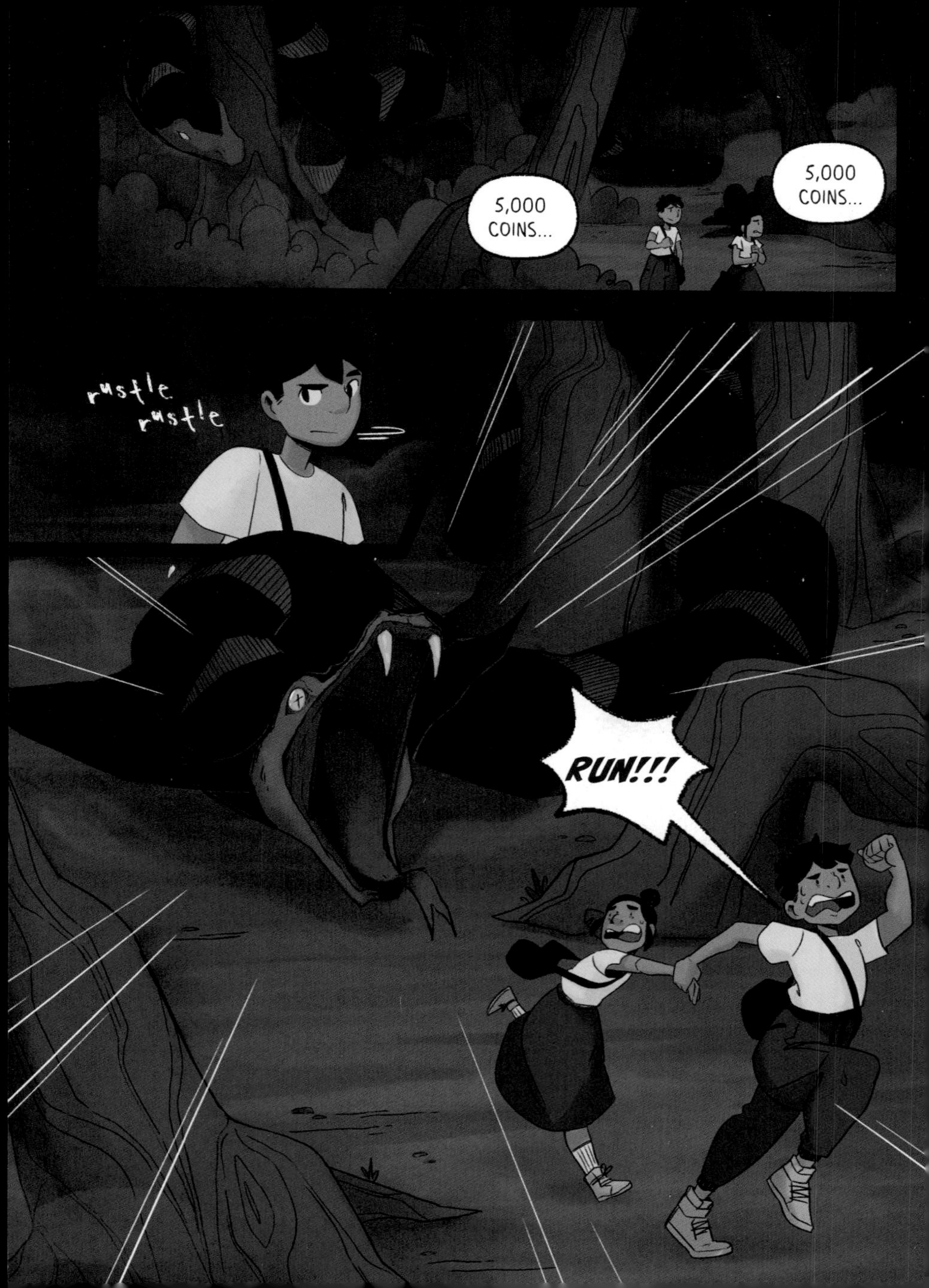
5,000 COINS...
5,000 COINS...
rustle rustle
RUN!!!

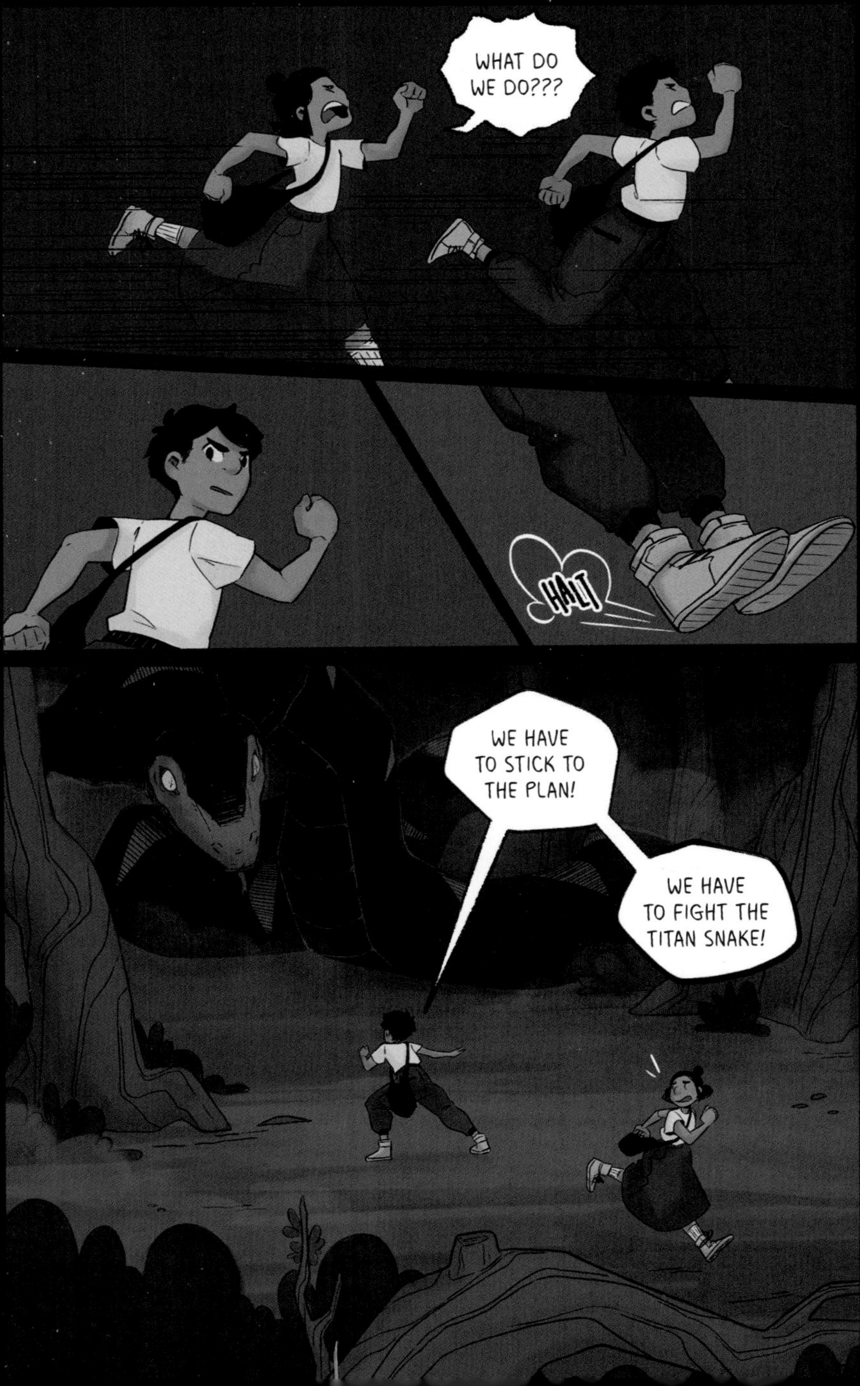
WHAT DO WE DO???
HALT
WE HAVE TO STICK TO THE PLAN!
WE HAVE TO FIGHT THE TITAN SNAKE!

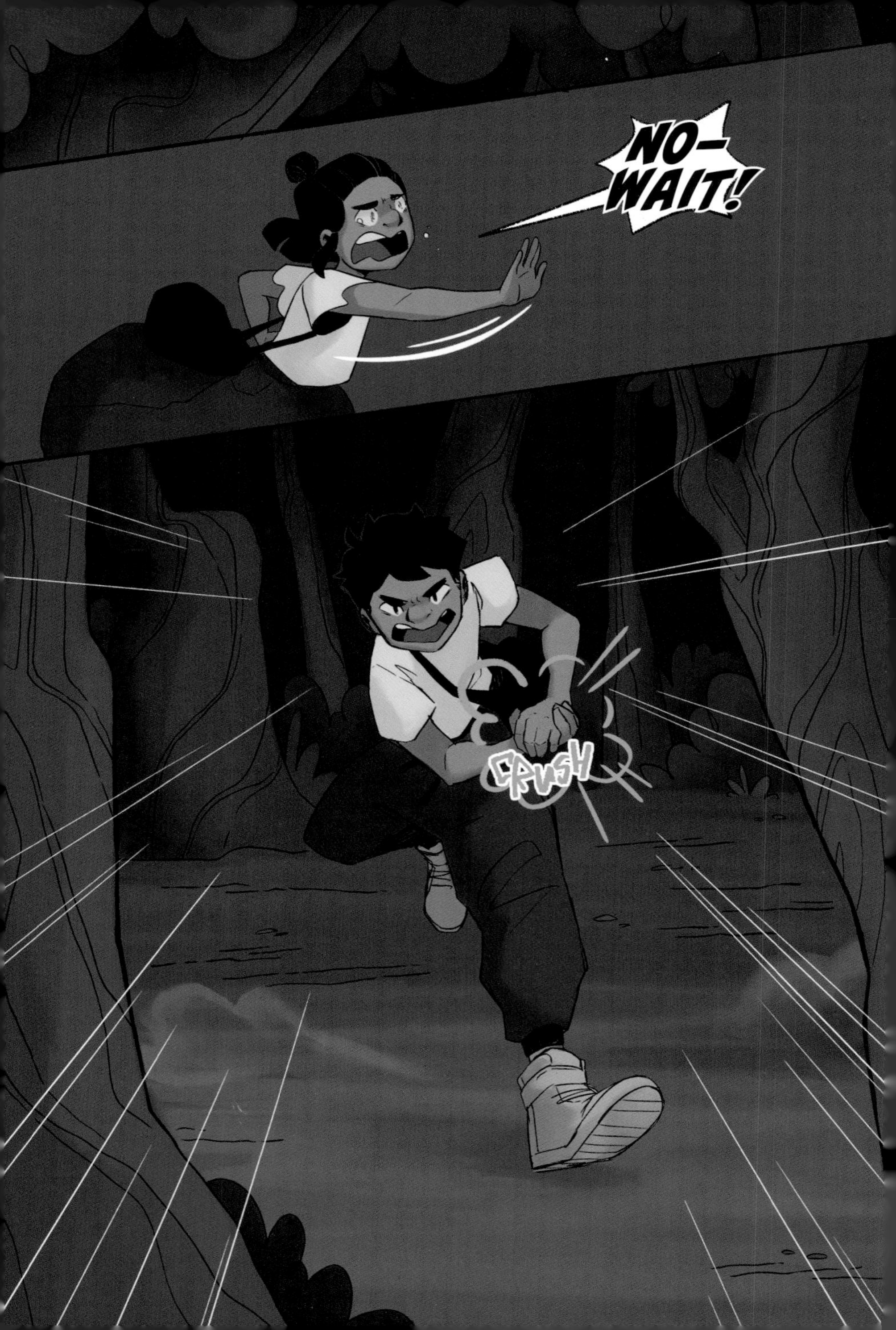
NO–
WAIT!
CRUSH

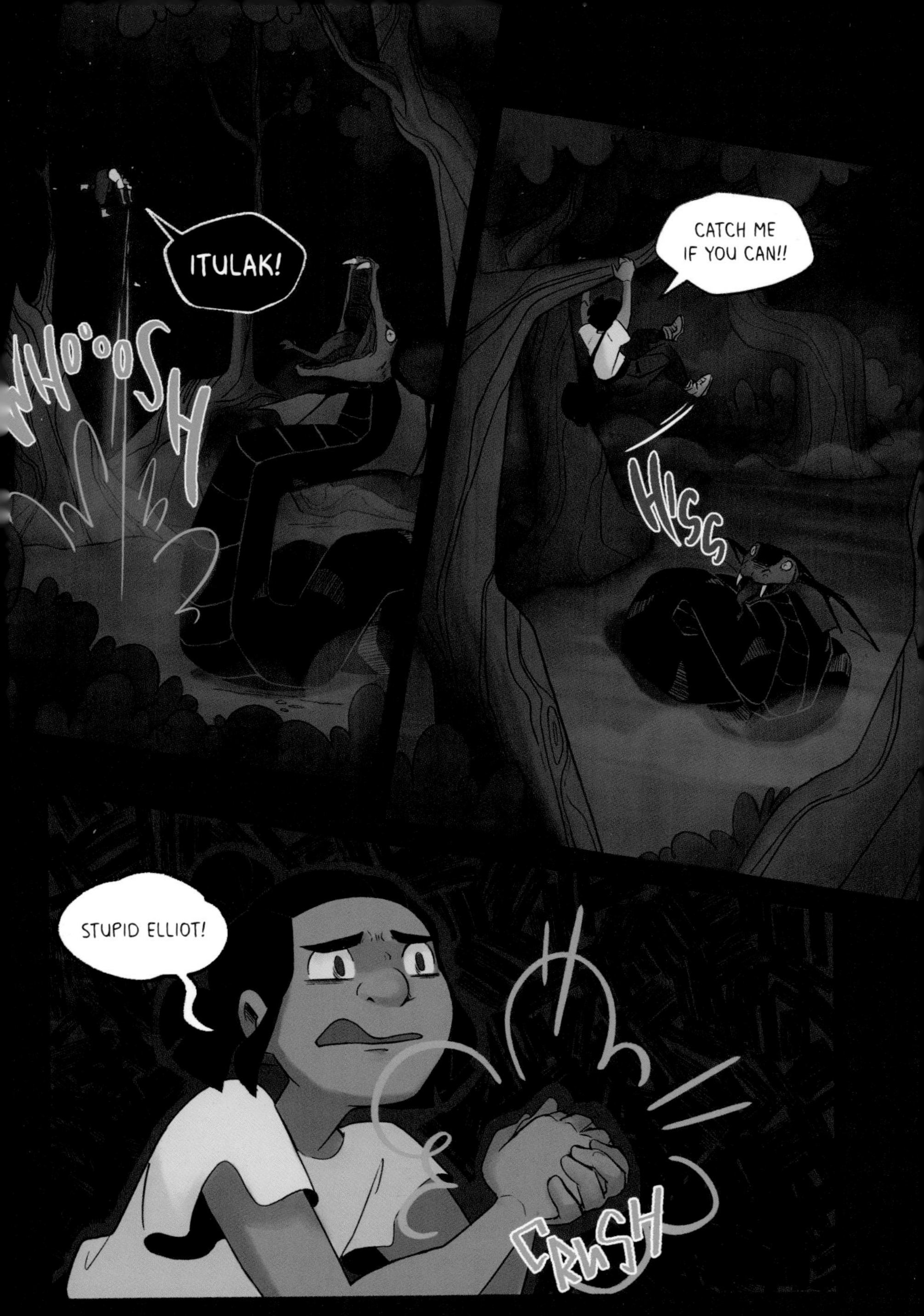
ITULAK!
WHOOOSH
CATCH ME IF YOU CAN!!
HISS
STUPID ELLIOT!
CRUSH

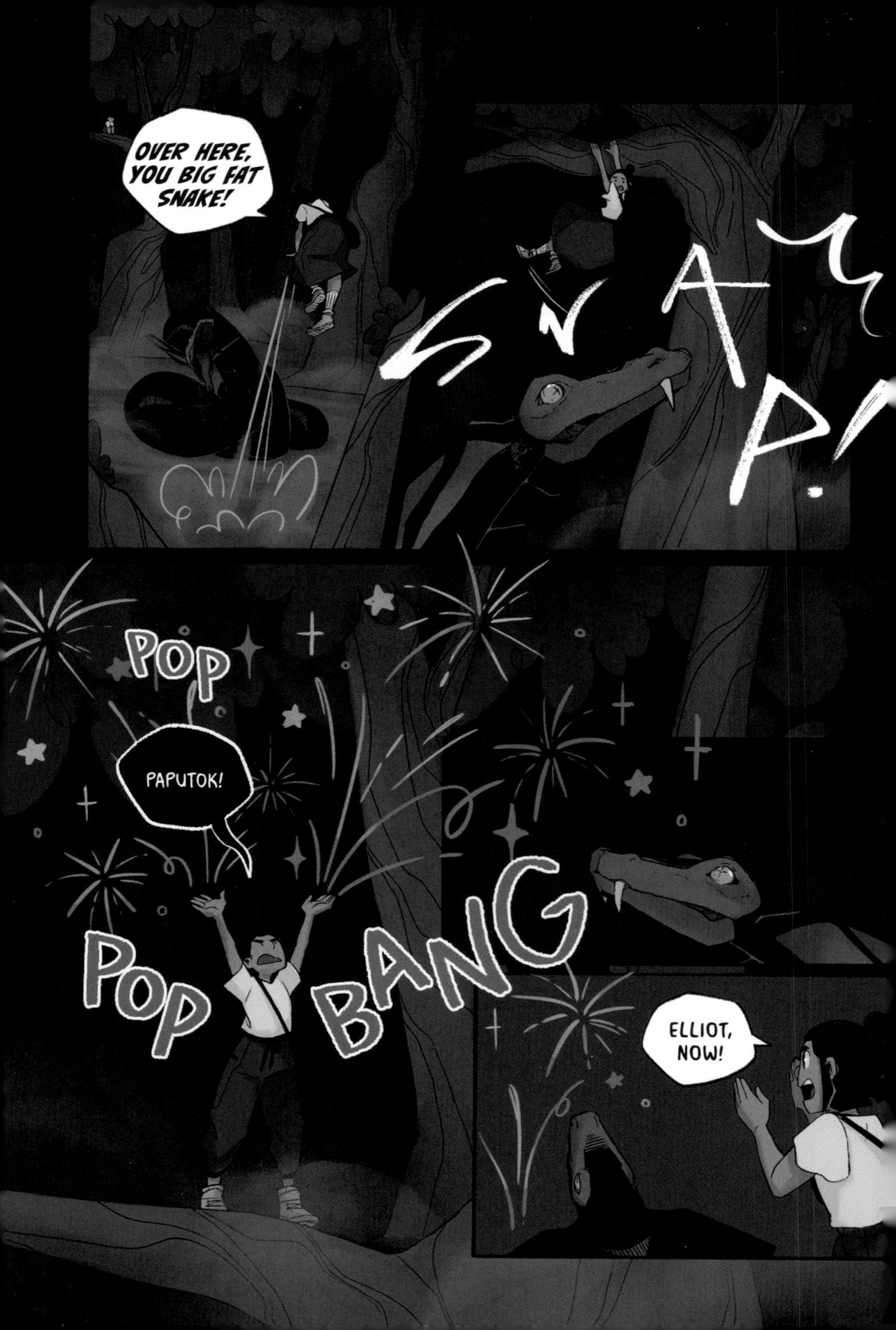
OVER HERE, YOU BIG FAT SNAKE!
SNAP!
POP
PAPUTOK!
POP
BANG
ELLIOT, NOW!

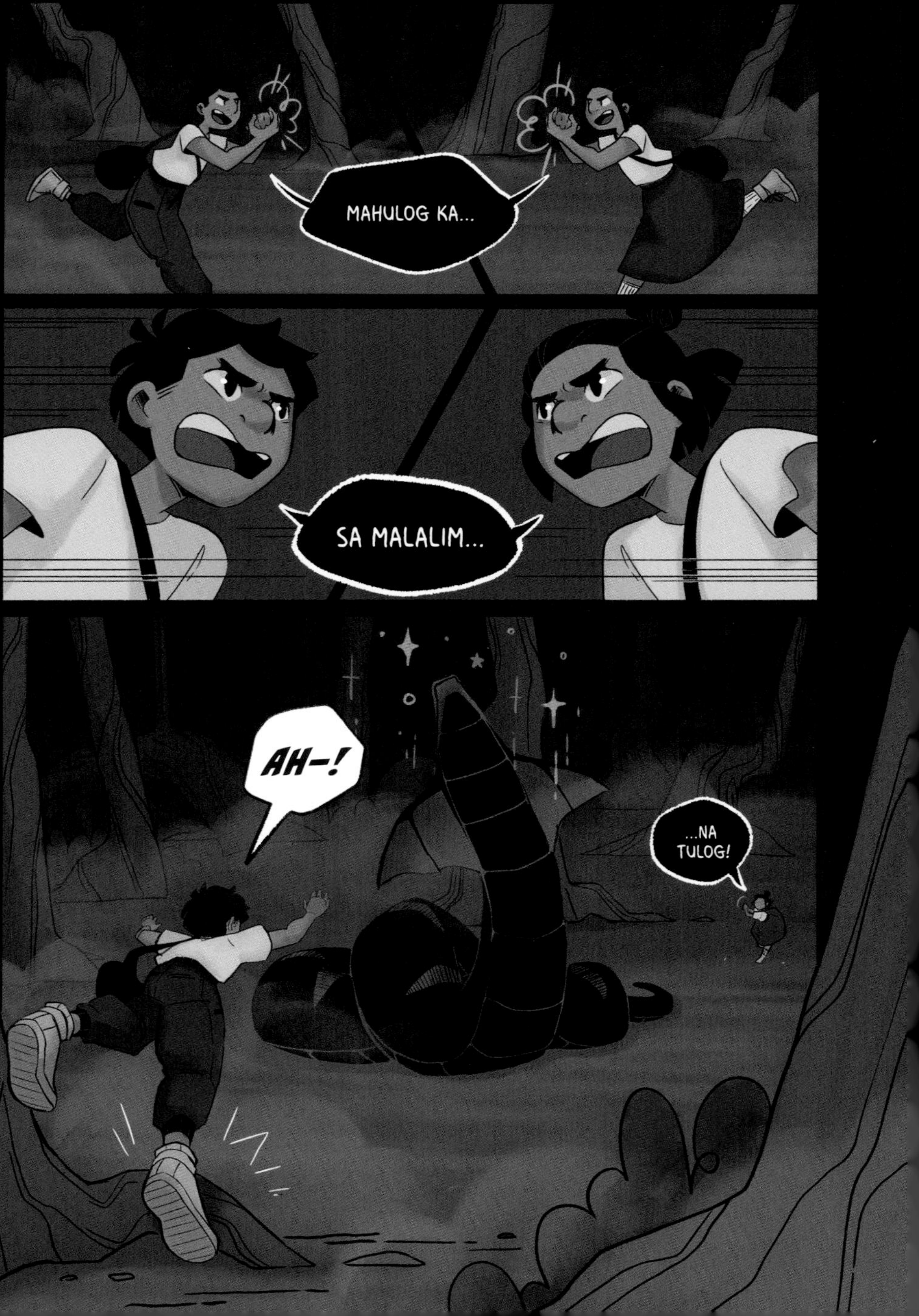
MAHULOG KA...
SA MALALIM...
AH-!
...NA TULOG!

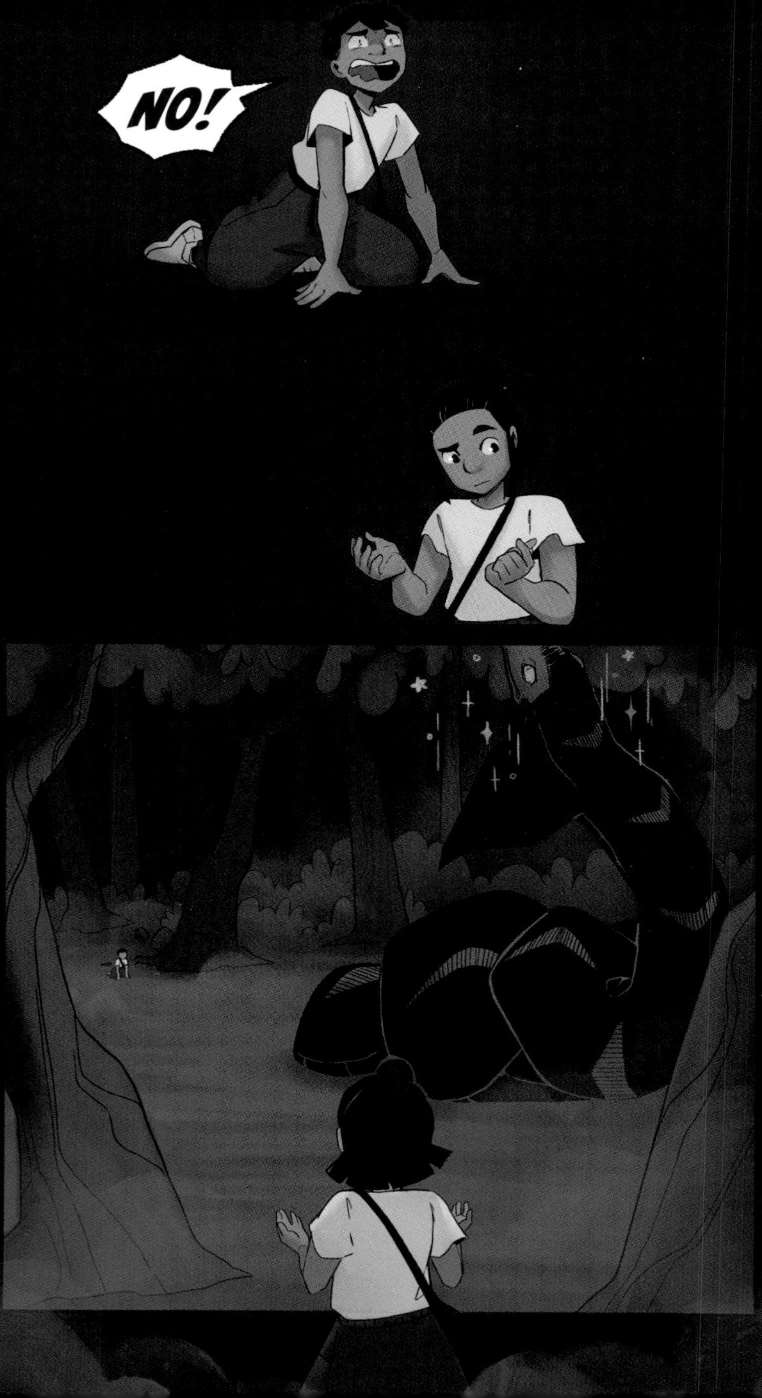
NO!

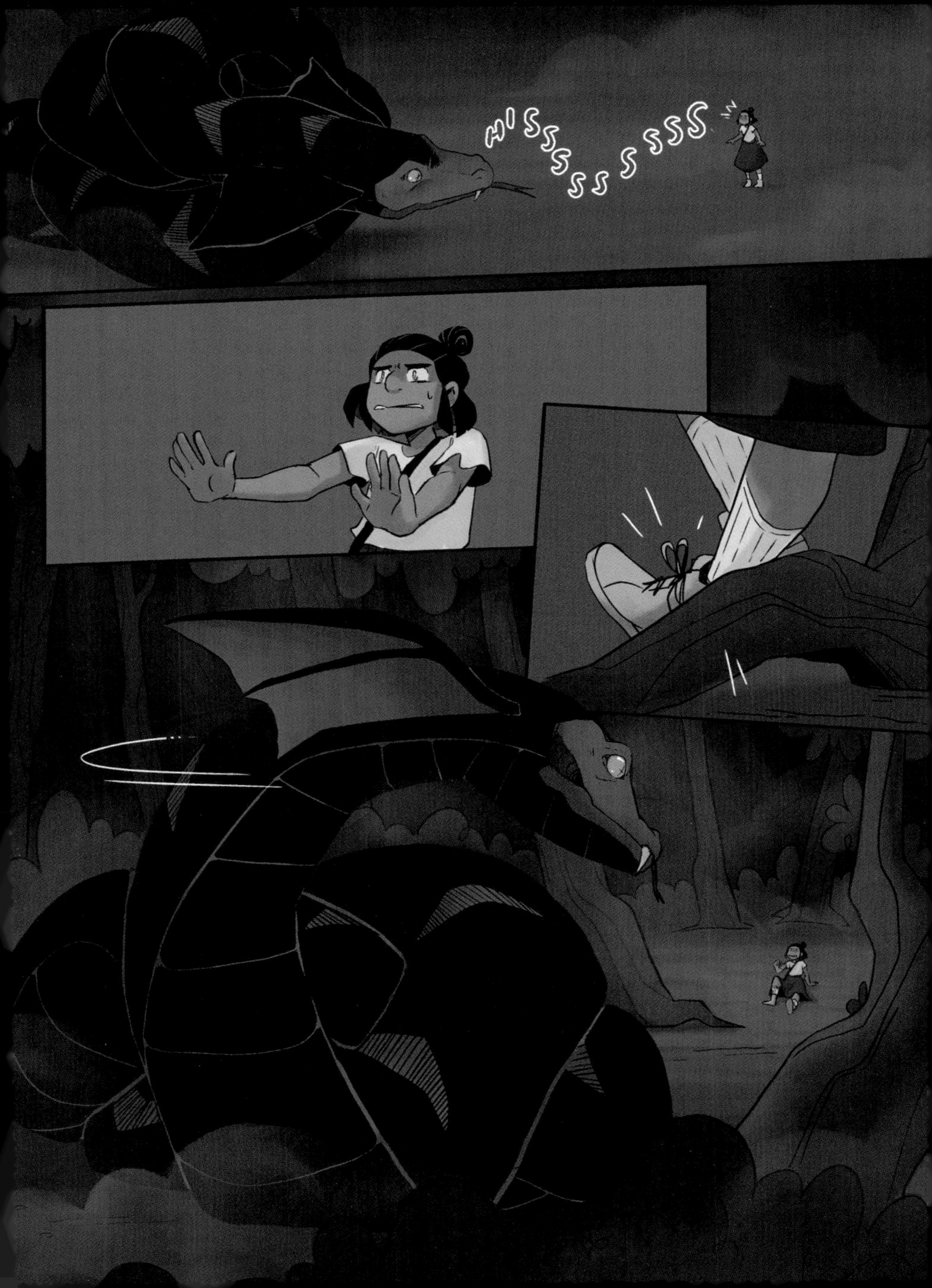
HISSSSSSSSSS

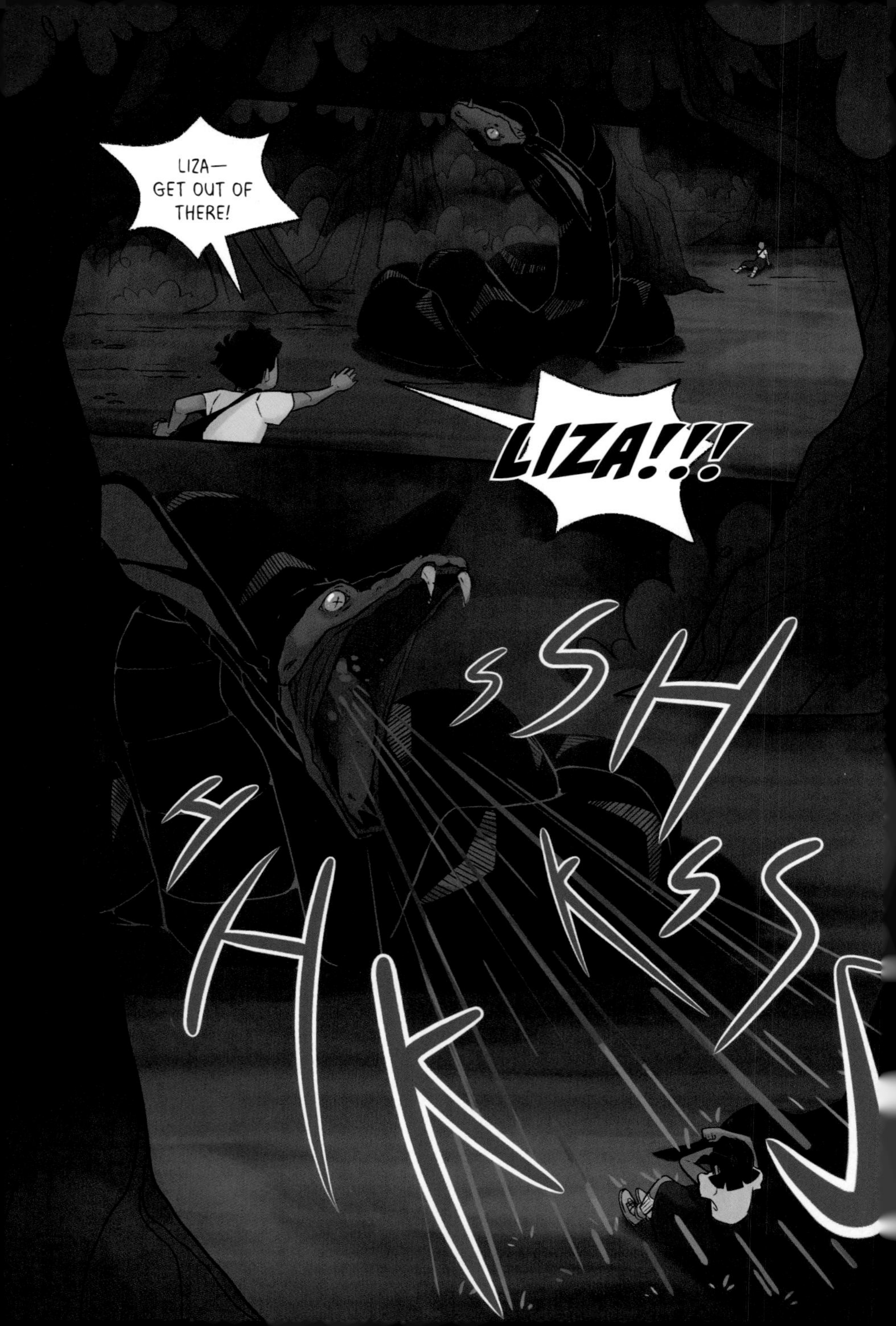
LIZA— GET OUT OF THERE!
LIZA!!!
SSH
HHKKSSS

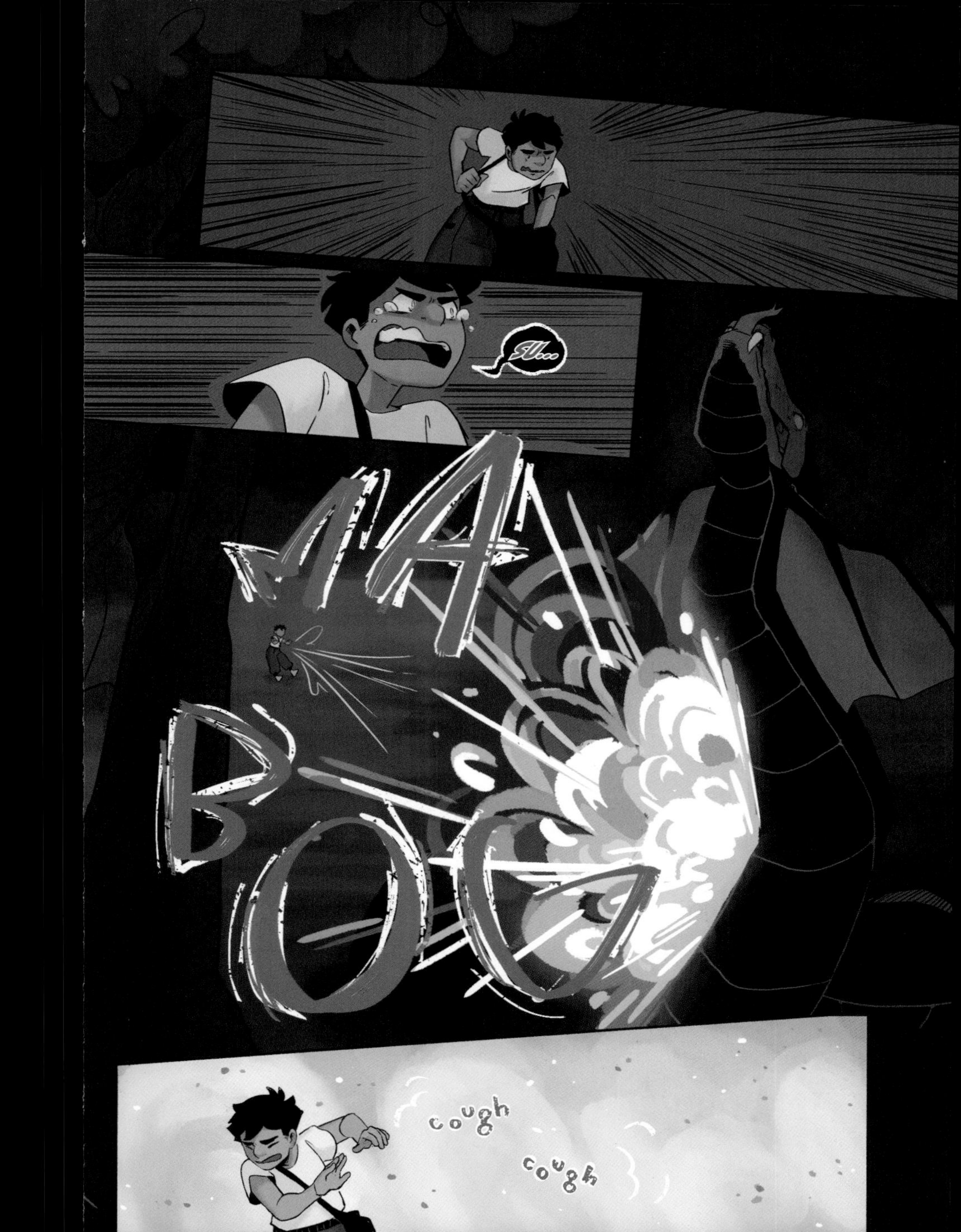
SU...
MAA
BOOM
cough
cough

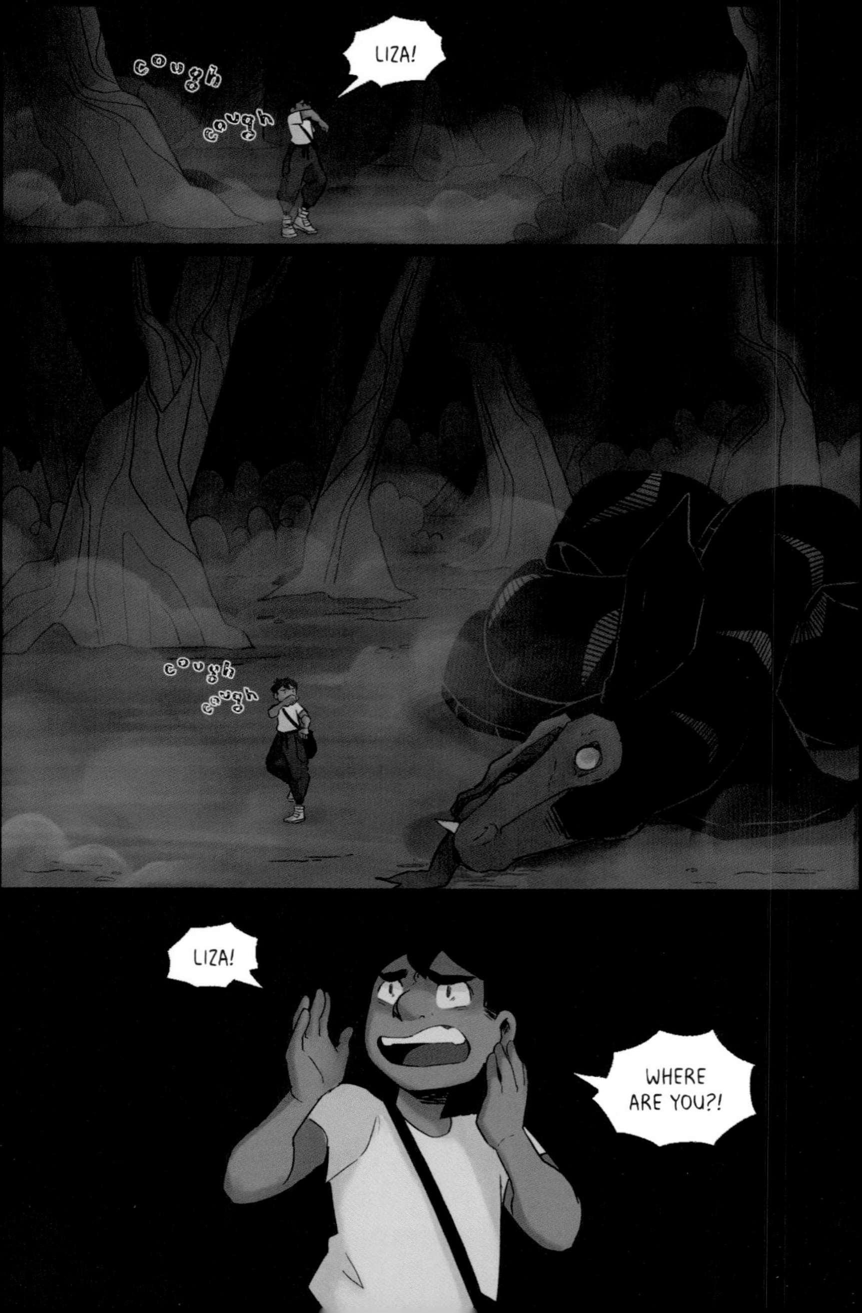
LIZA!
cough
cough
cough
cough
LIZA!
WHERE ARE YOU?!

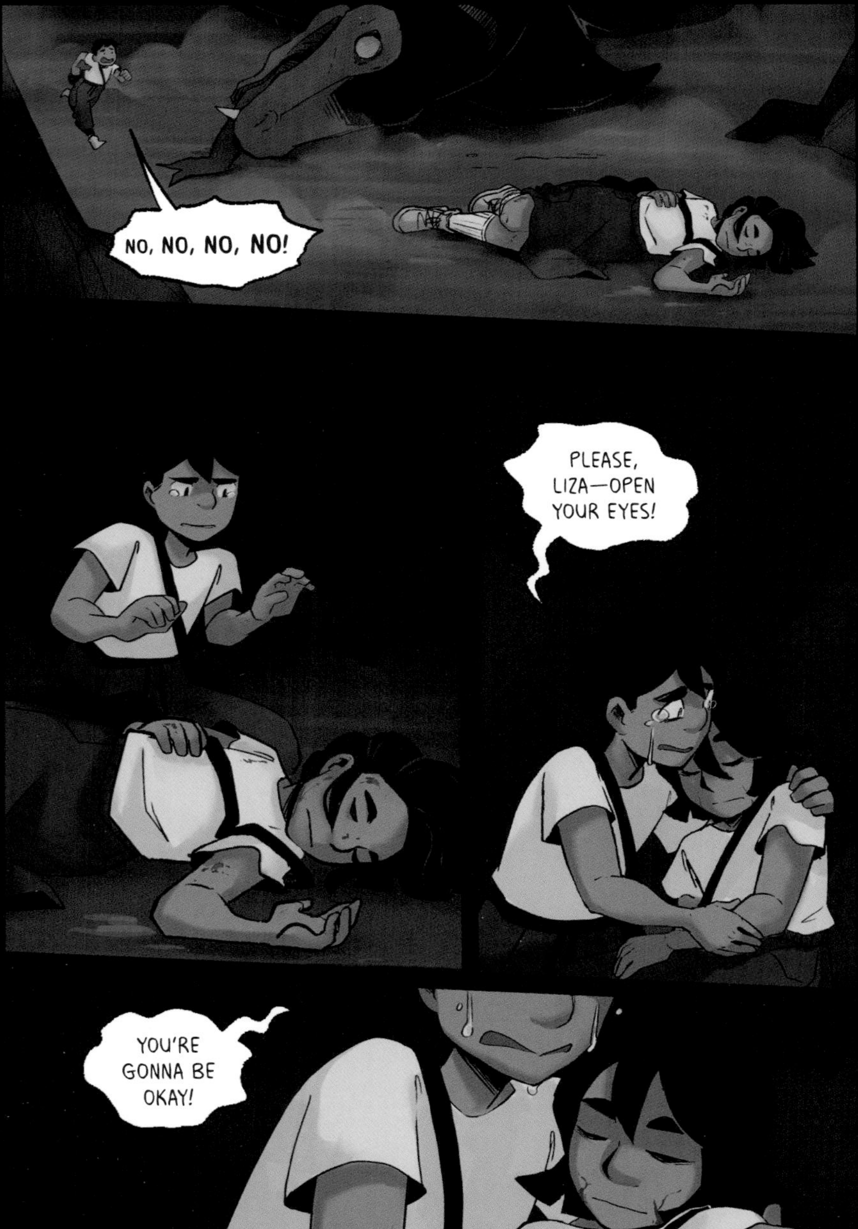
NO, NO, NO, NO!
PLEASE, LIZA—OPEN YOUR EYES!
YOU'RE GONNA BE OKAY!

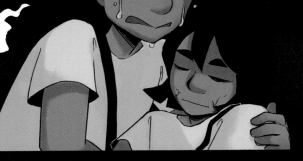

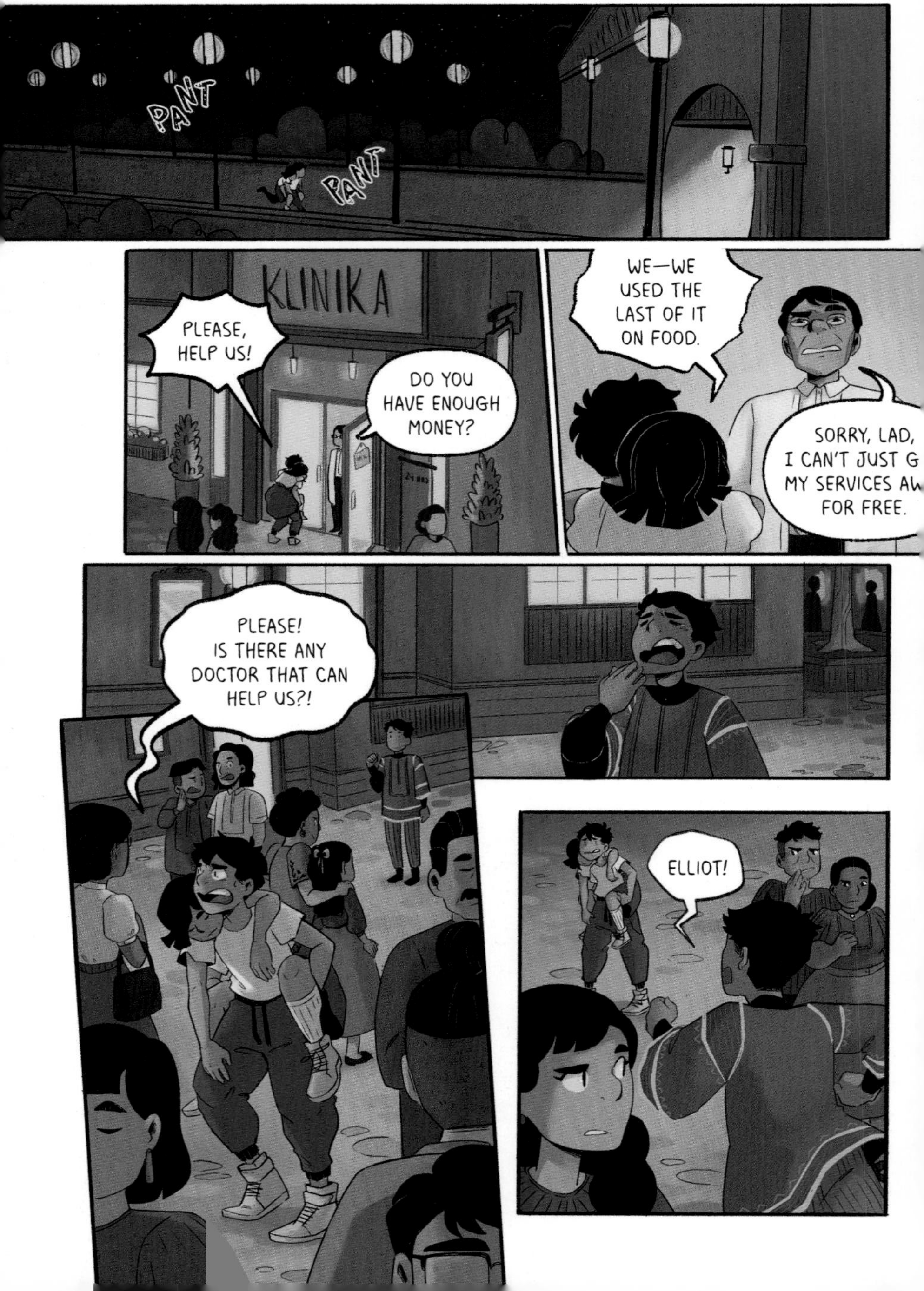
PANT
PANT
KLINIKA
PLEASE, HELP US!
DO YOU HAVE ENOUGH MONEY?
WE—WE USED THE LAST OF IT ON FOOD.
SORRY, LAD, I CAN'T JUST G MY SERVICES AW FOR FREE.
PLEASE! IS THERE ANY DOCTOR THAT CAN HELP US?!
ELLIOT!

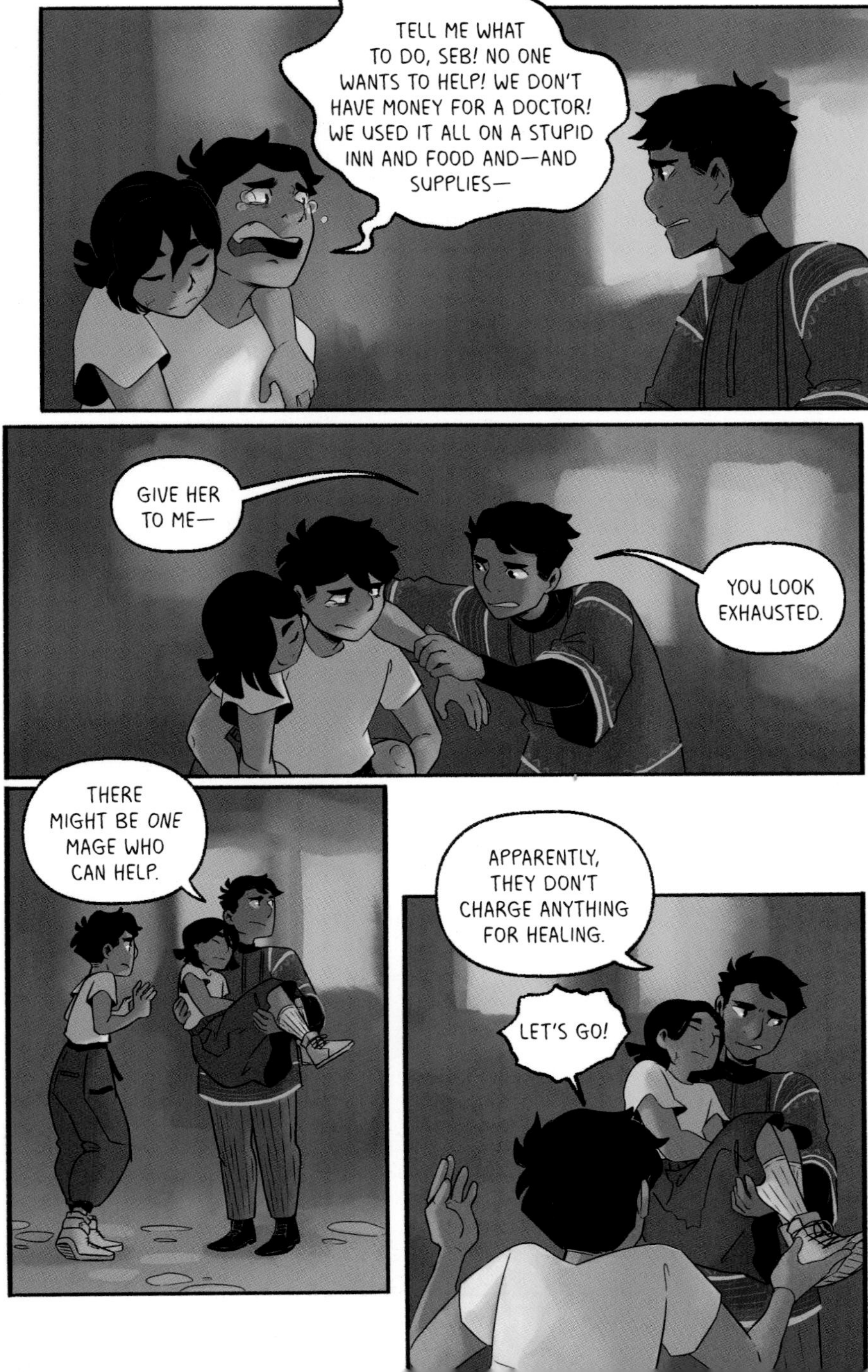
TELL ME WHAT TO DO, SEB! NO ONE WANTS TO HELP! WE DON'T HAVE MONEY FOR A DOCTOR! WE USED IT ALL ON A STUPID INN AND FOOD AND—AND SUPPLIES—
GIVE HER TO ME—
YOU LOOK EXHAUSTED.
THERE MIGHT BE *ONE* MAGE WHO CAN HELP.
APPARENTLY, THEY DON'T CHARGE ANYTHING FOR HEALING.
LET'S GO!

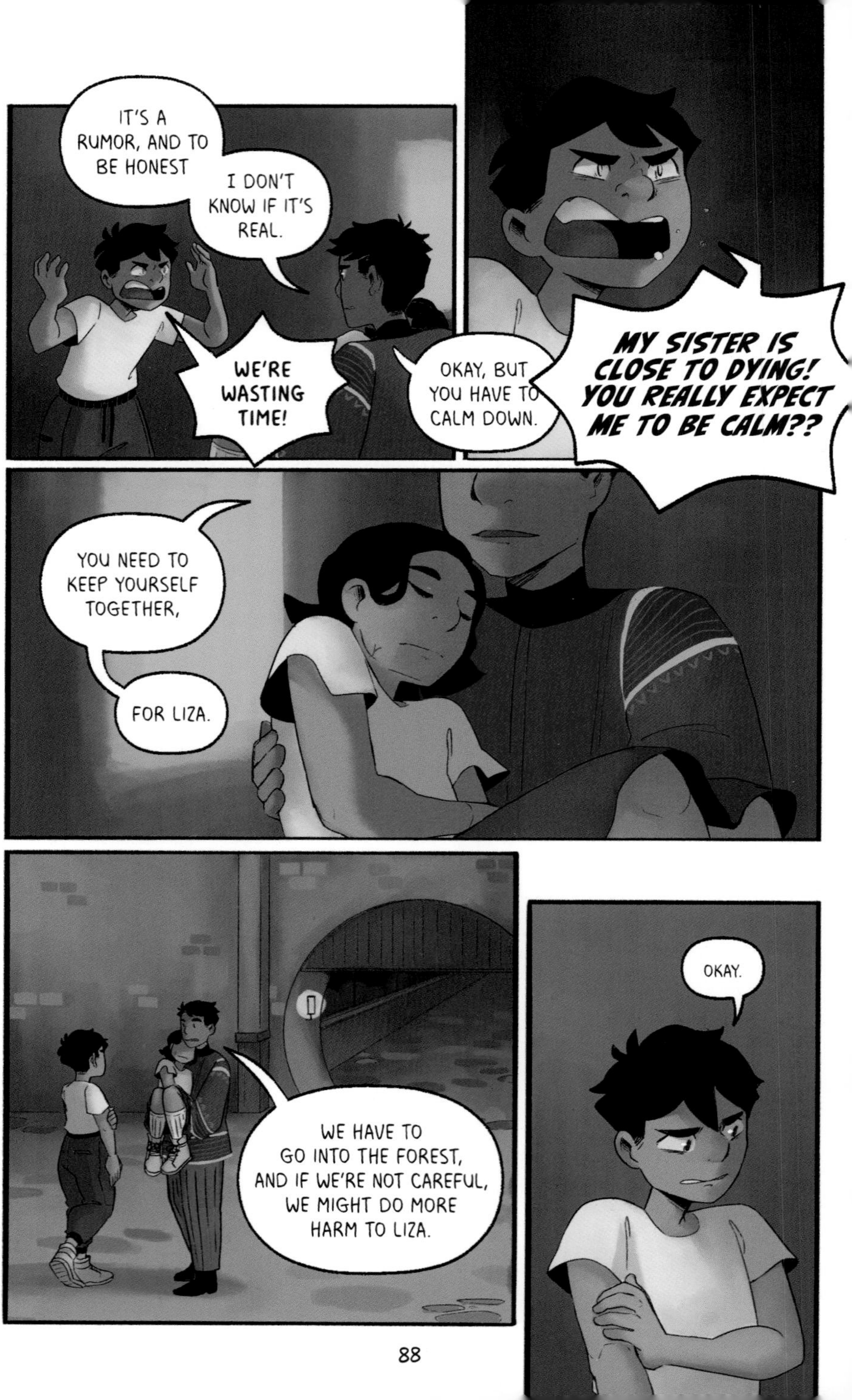
IT'S A RUMOR, AND TO BE HONEST
I DON'T KNOW IF IT'S REAL.
WE'RE WASTING TIME!
OKAY, BUT YOU HAVE TO CALM DOWN.
MY SISTER IS CLOSE TO DYING! YOU REALLY EXPECT ME TO BE CALM??
YOU NEED TO KEEP YOURSELF TOGETHER,
FOR LIZA.
WE HAVE TO GO INTO THE FOREST, AND IF WE'RE NOT CAREFUL, WE MIGHT DO MORE HARM TO LIZA.
OKAY.

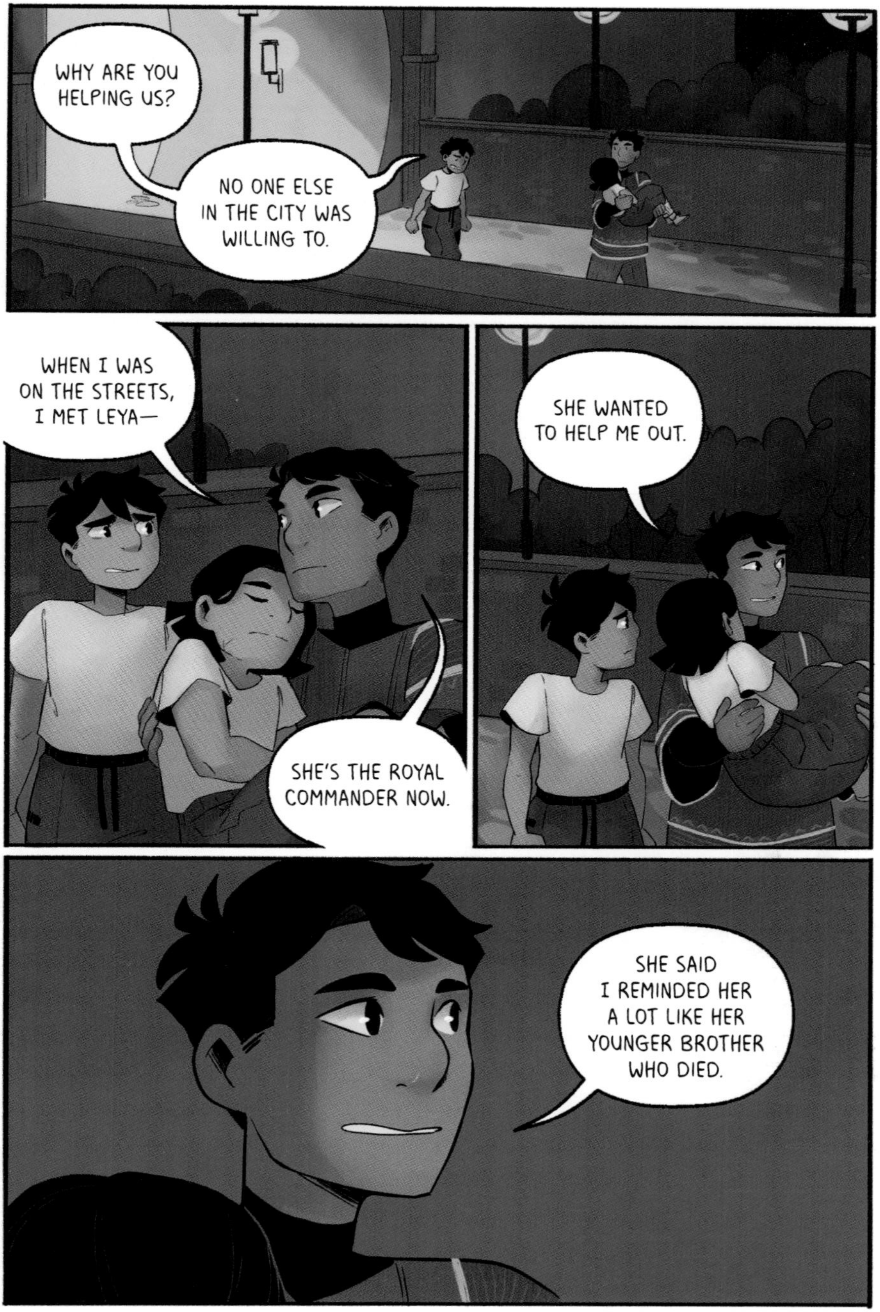
WHY ARE YOU HELPING US?
NO ONE ELSE IN THE CITY WAS WILLING TO.
WHEN I WAS ON THE STREETS, I MET LEYA—
SHE'S THE ROYAL COMMANDER NOW.
SHE WANTED TO HELP ME OUT.
SHE SAID I REMINDED HER A LOT LIKE HER YOUNGER BROTHER WHO DIED.

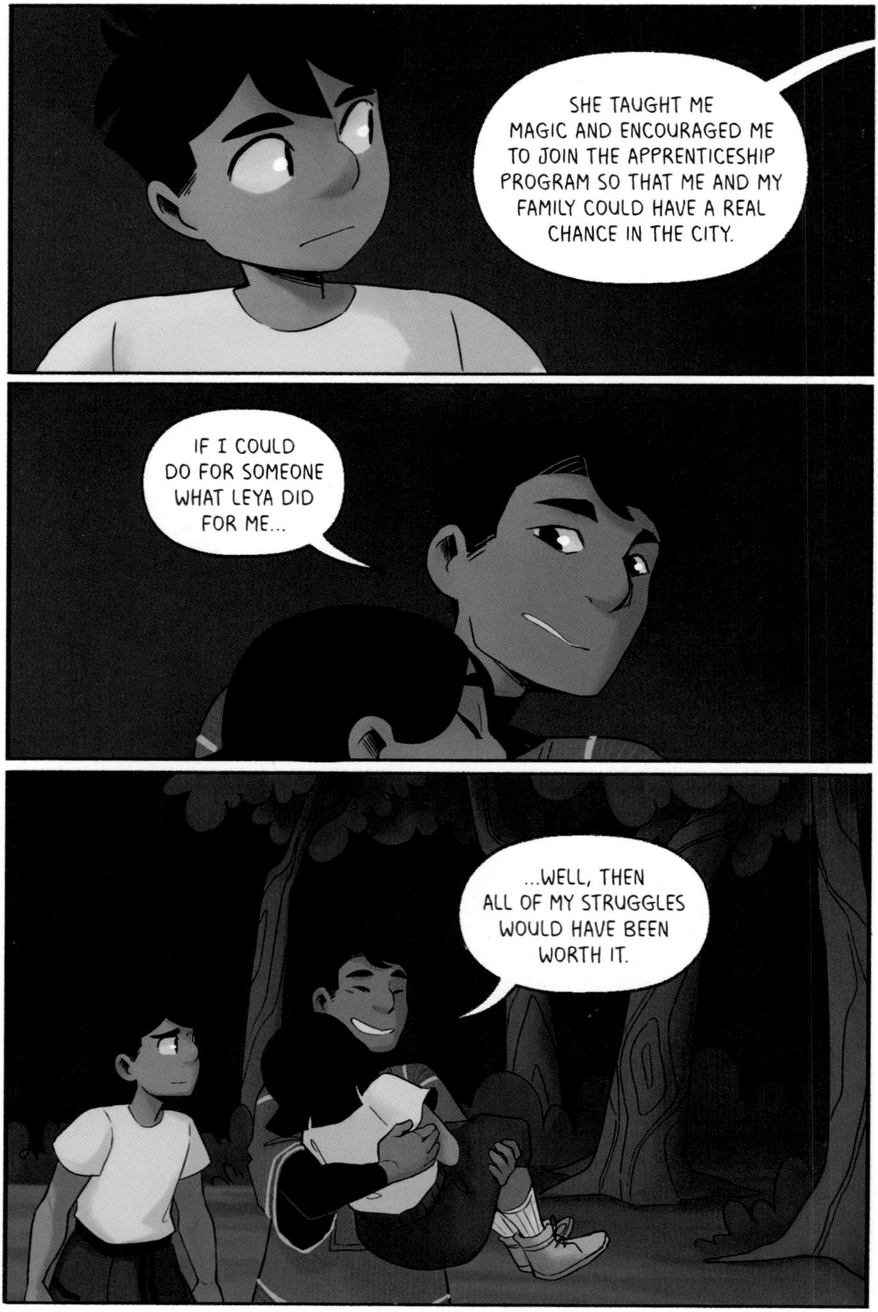
SHE TAUGHT ME MAGIC AND ENCOURAGED ME TO JOIN THE APPRENTICESHIP PROGRAM SO THAT ME AND MY FAMILY COULD HAVE A REAL CHANCE IN THE CITY.
IF I COULD DO FOR SOMEONE WHAT LEYA DID FOR ME...
...WELL, THEN ALL OF MY STRUGGLES WOULD HAVE BEEN WORTH IT.

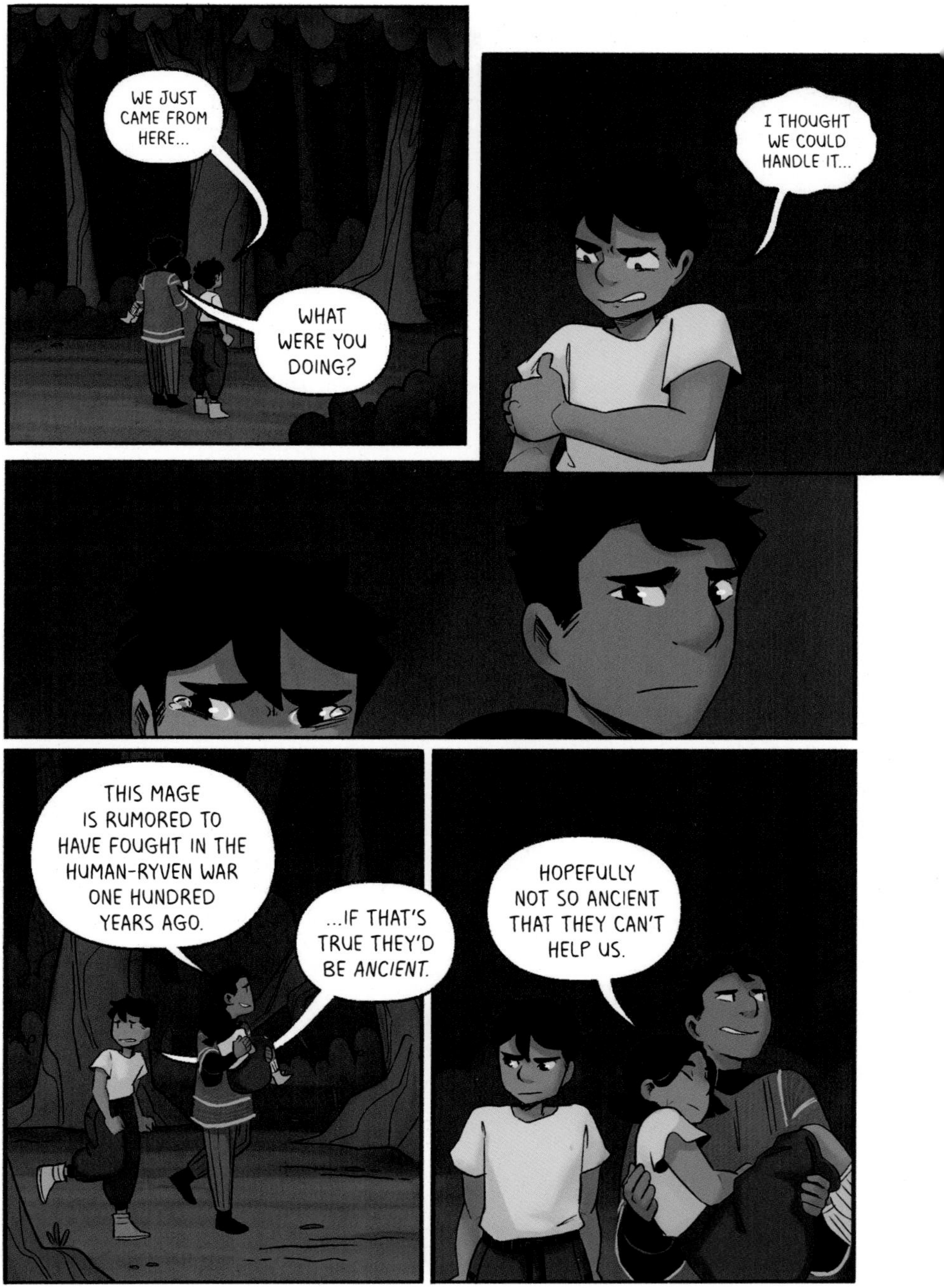
WE JUST CAME FROM HERE...
WHAT WERE YOU DOING?
I THOUGHT WE COULD HANDLE IT...
THIS MAGE IS RUMORED TO HAVE FOUGHT IN THE HUMAN-RYVEN WAR ONE HUNDRED YEARS AGO.
...IF THAT'S TRUE THEY'D BE *ANCIENT*.
HOPEFULLY NOT SO ANCIENT THAT THEY CAN'T HELP US.

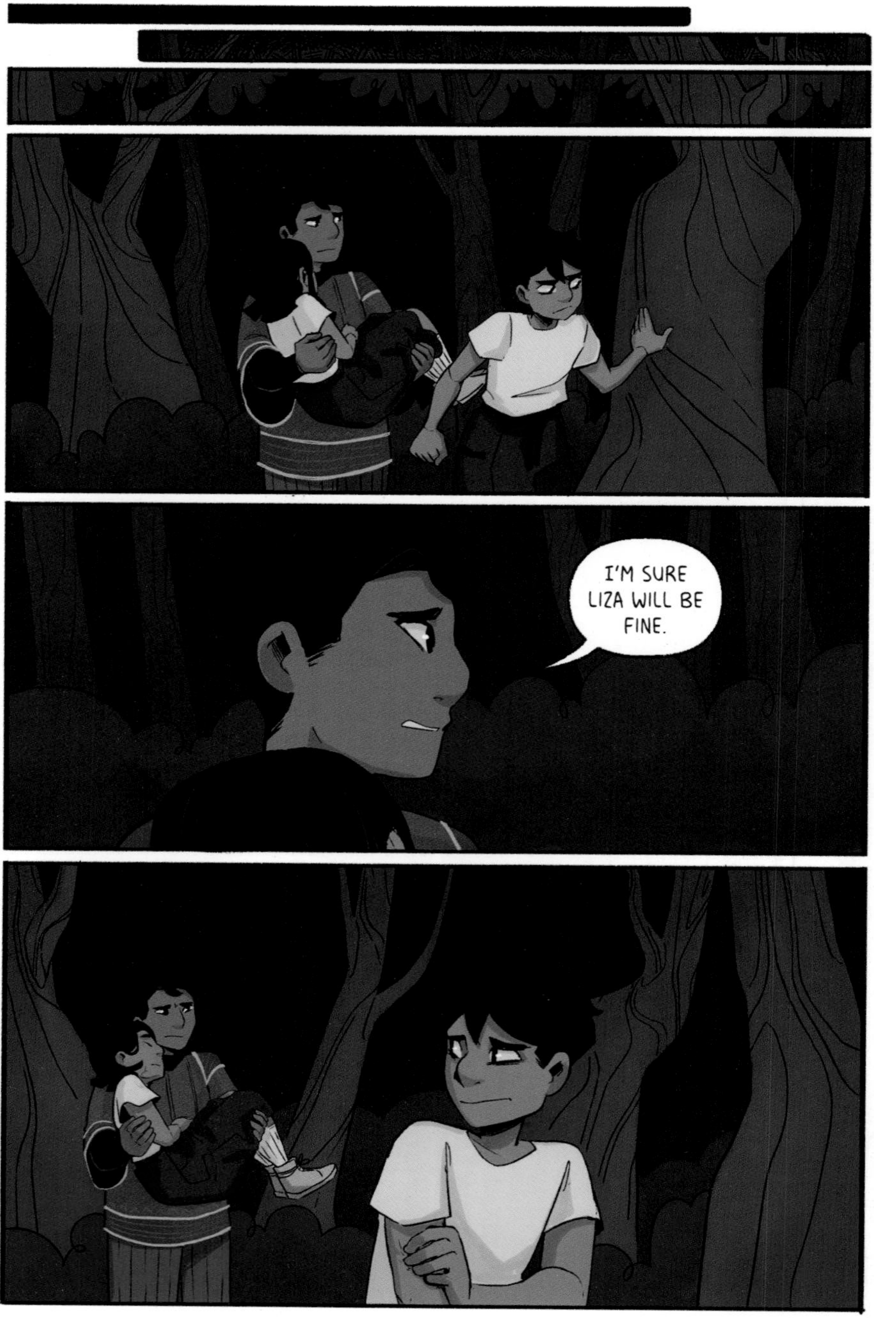
I'M SURE LIZA WILL BE FINE.

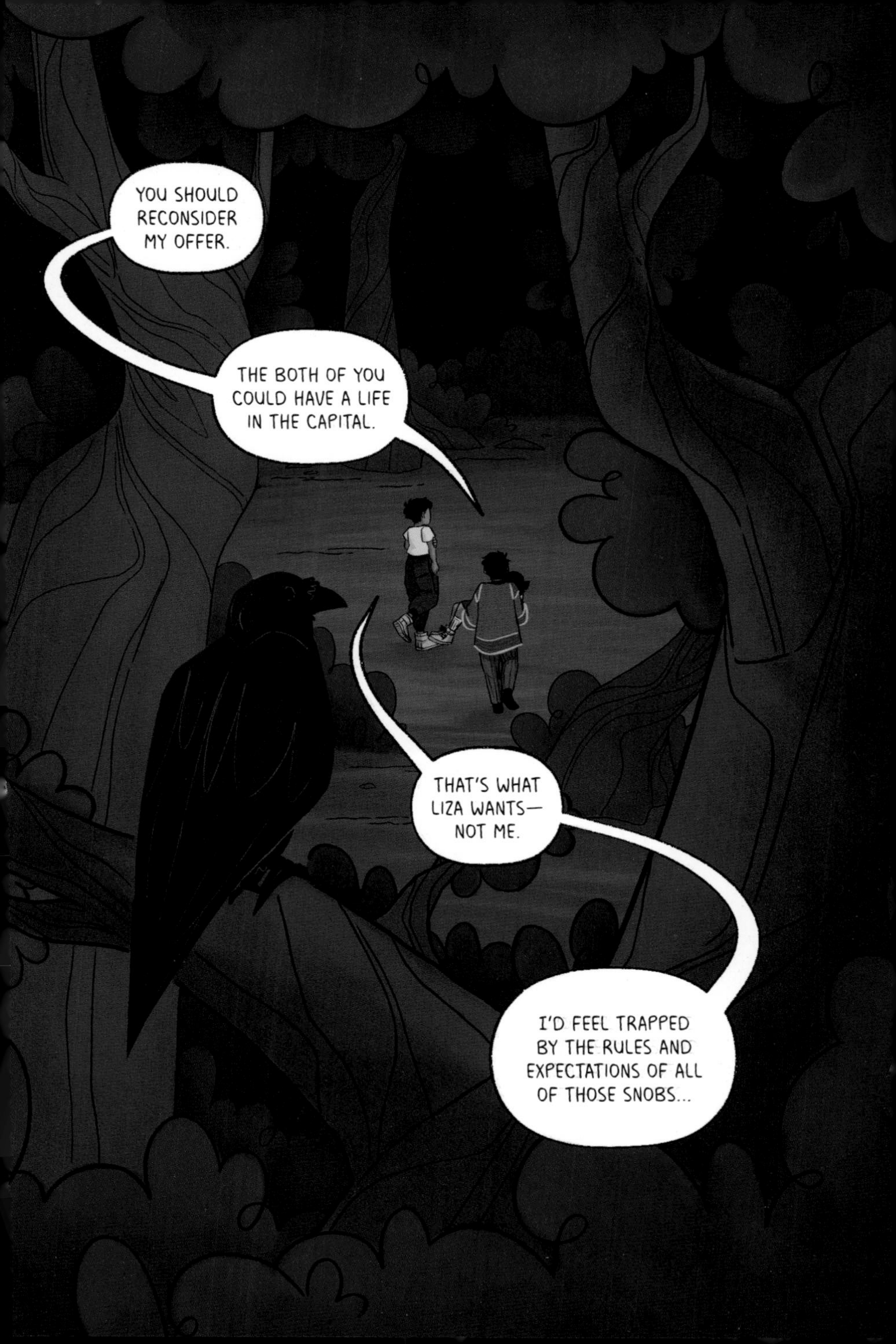
YOU SHOULD RECONSIDER MY OFFER.
THE BOTH OF YOU COULD HAVE A LIFE IN THE CAPITAL.
THAT'S WHAT LIZA WANTS— NOT ME.
I'D FEEL TRAPPED BY THE RULES AND EXPECTATIONS OF ALL OF THOSE SNOBS...

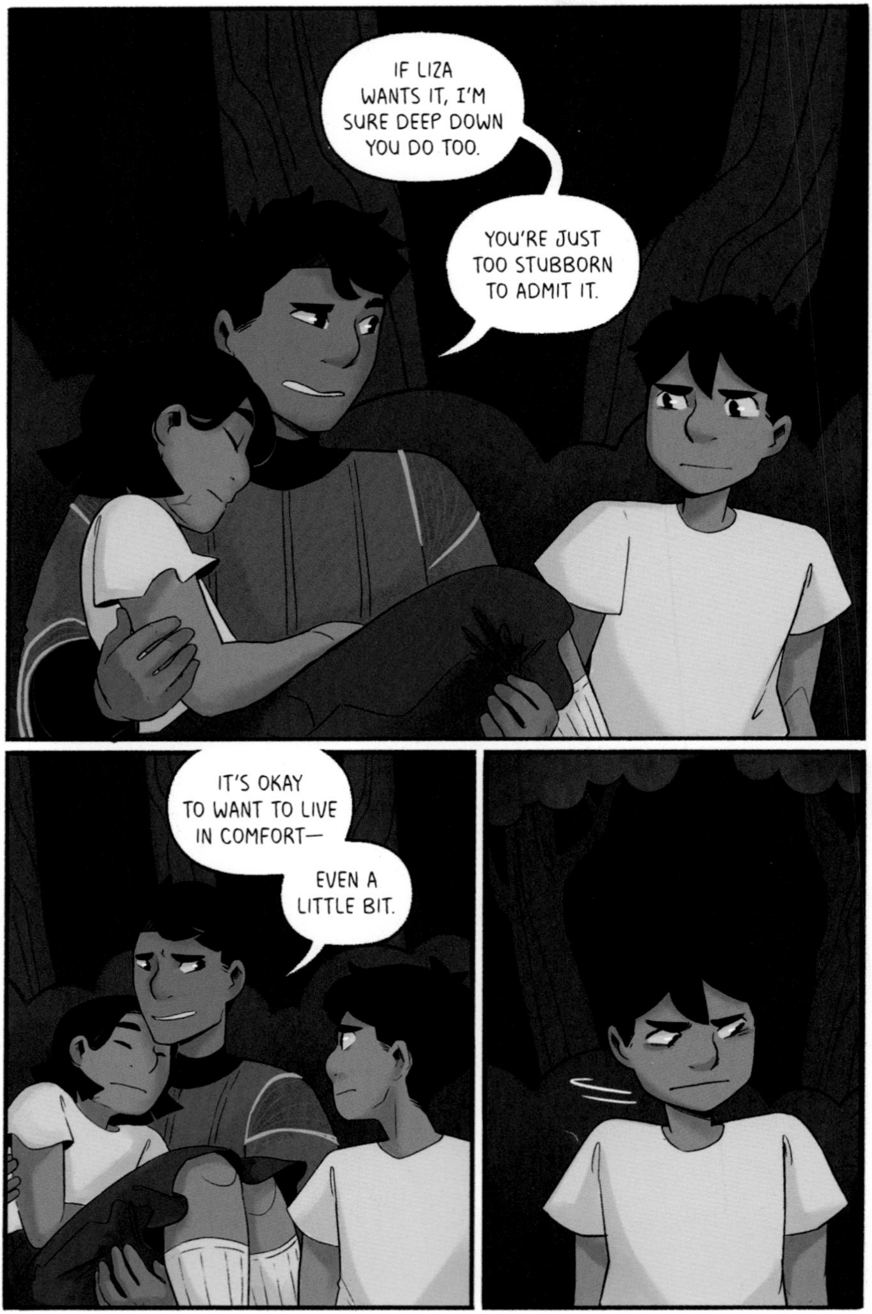
IF LIZA WANTS IT, I'M SURE DEEP DOWN YOU DO TOO.
YOU'RE JUST TOO STUBBORN TO ADMIT IT.
IT'S OKAY TO WANT TO LIVE IN COMFORT—
EVEN A LITTLE BIT.

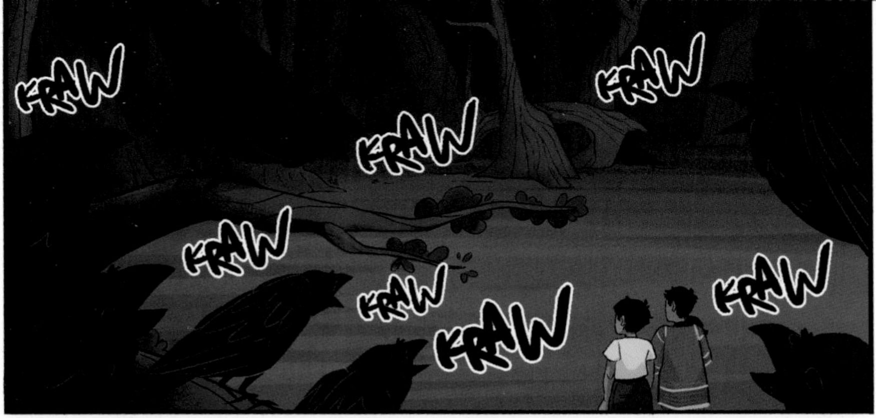
KRAW
KRAW
KRAW
KRAW
KRAW
KRAW
KRAW

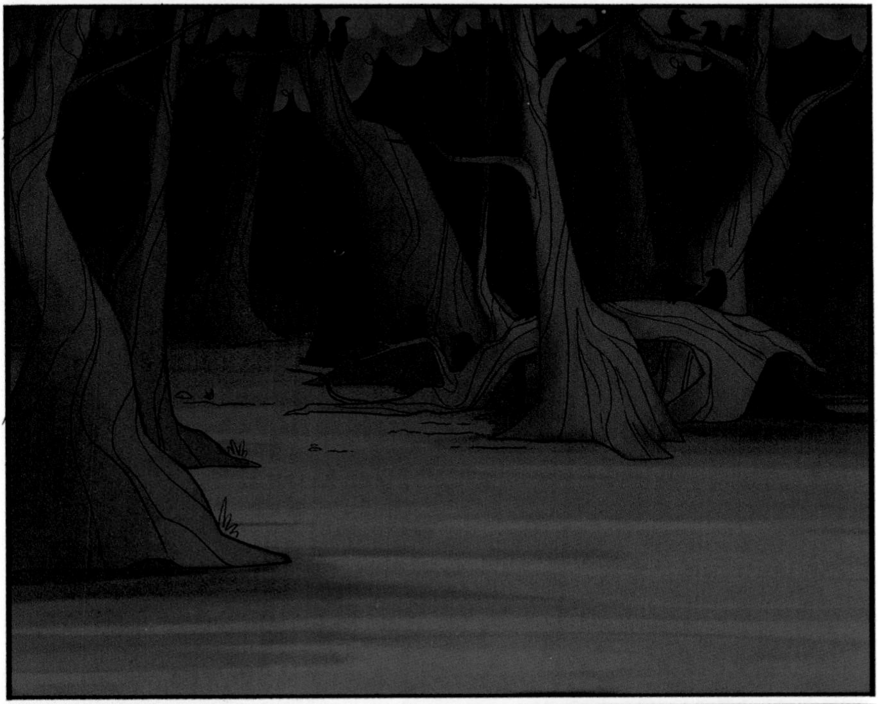

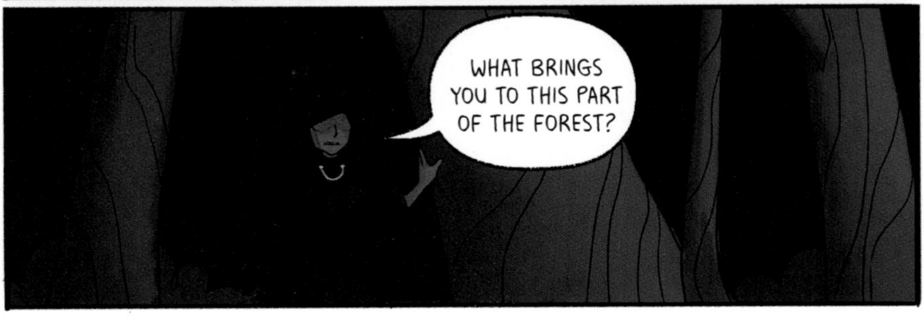
WHAT BRINGS YOU TO THIS PART OF THE FOREST?

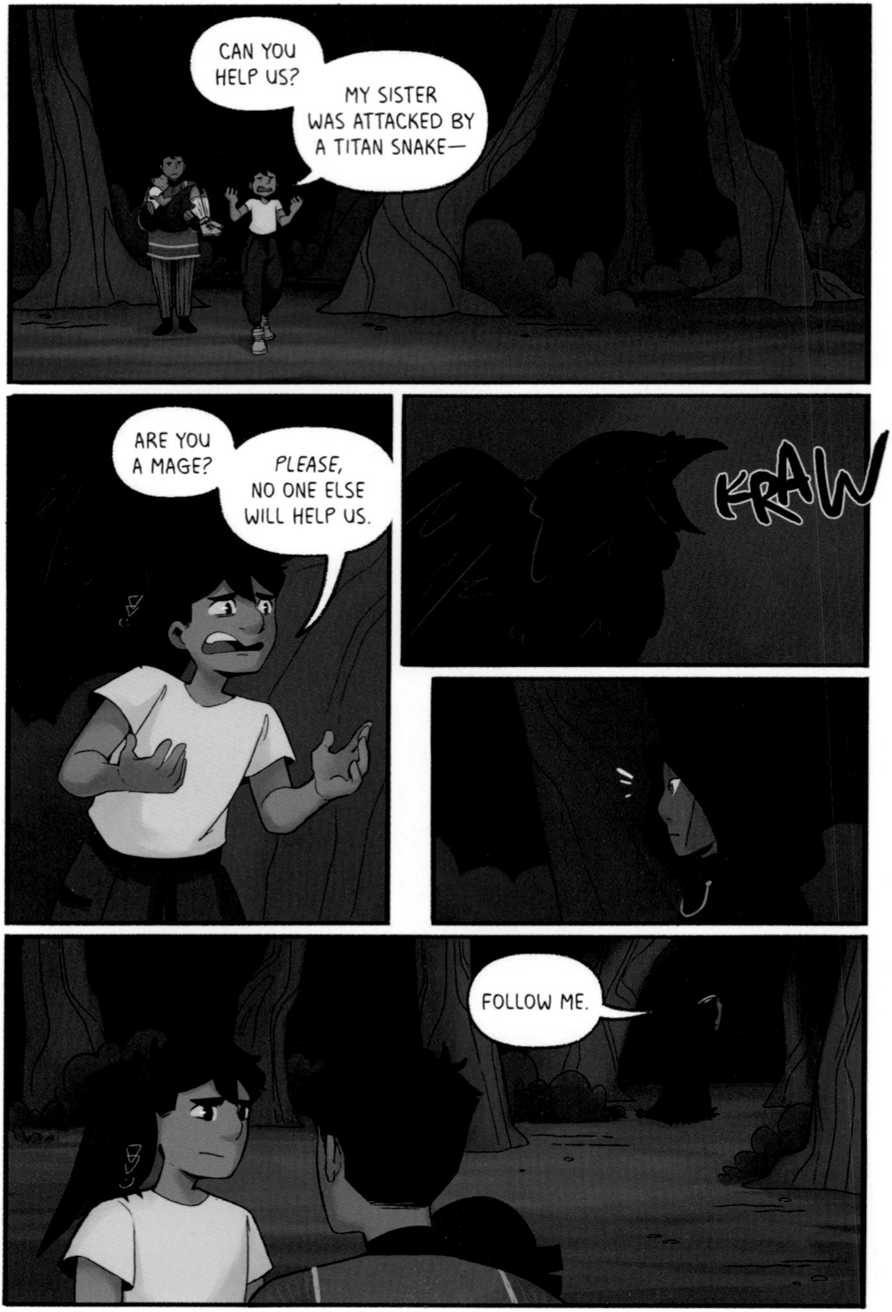
CAN YOU HELP US?
MY SISTER WAS ATTACKED BY A TITAN SNAKE—
ARE YOU A MAGE?
PLEASE, NO ONE ELSE WILL HELP US.
KRAW
FOLLOW ME.

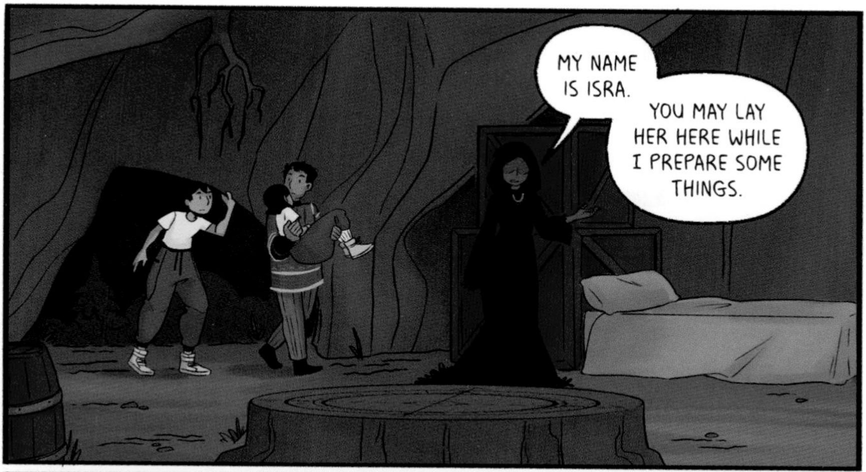
MY NAME IS ISRA.
YOU MAY LAY HER HERE WHILE I PREPARE SOME THINGS.

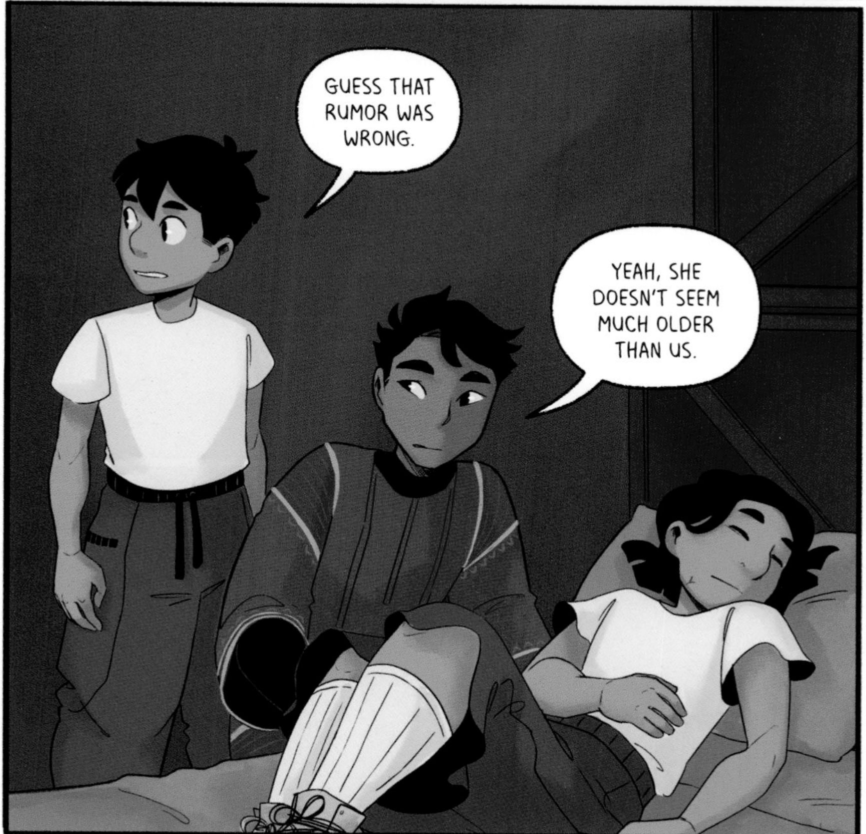
GUESS THAT RUMOR WAS WRONG.
YEAH, SHE DOESN'T SEEM MUCH OLDER THAN US.

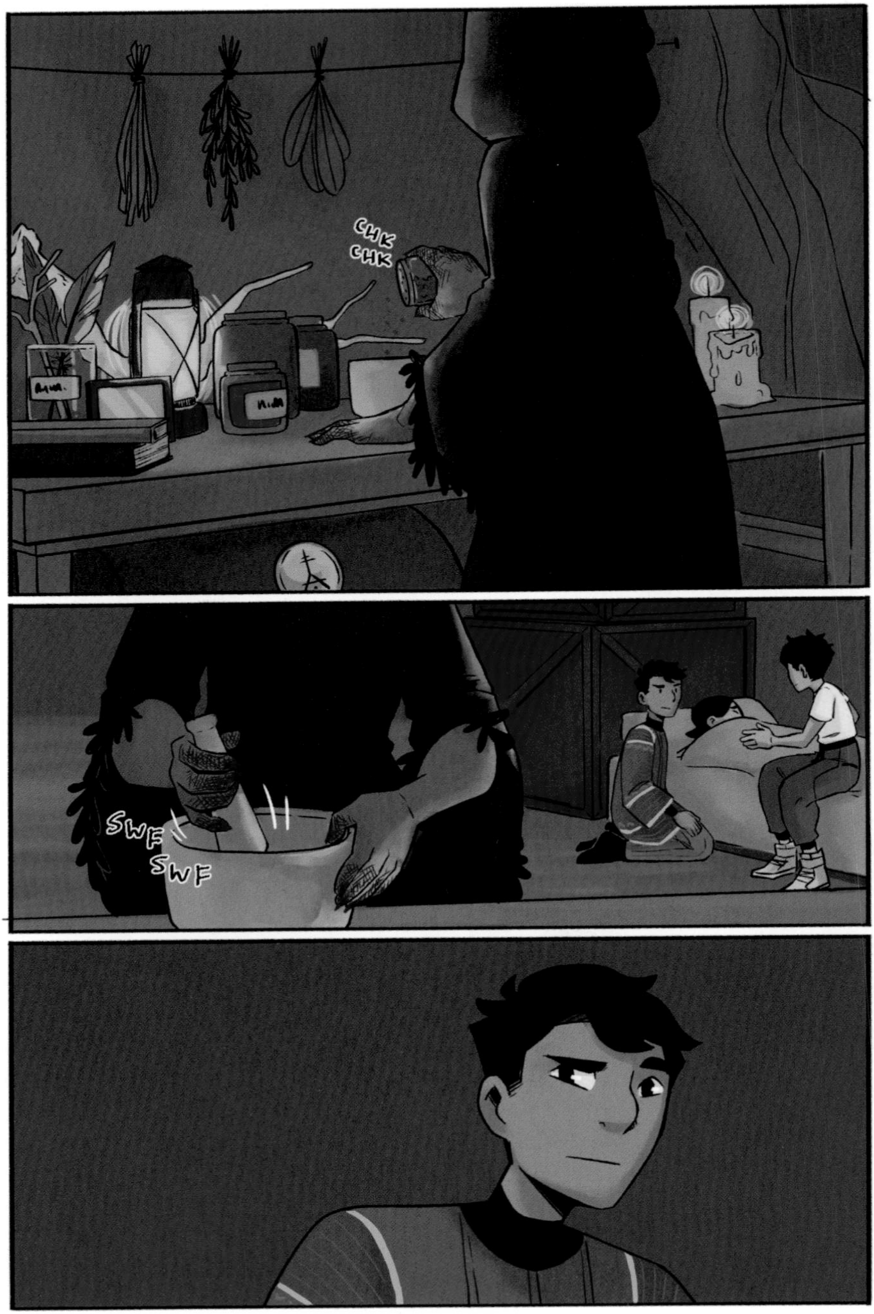
CHK
CHK
SWF
SWF

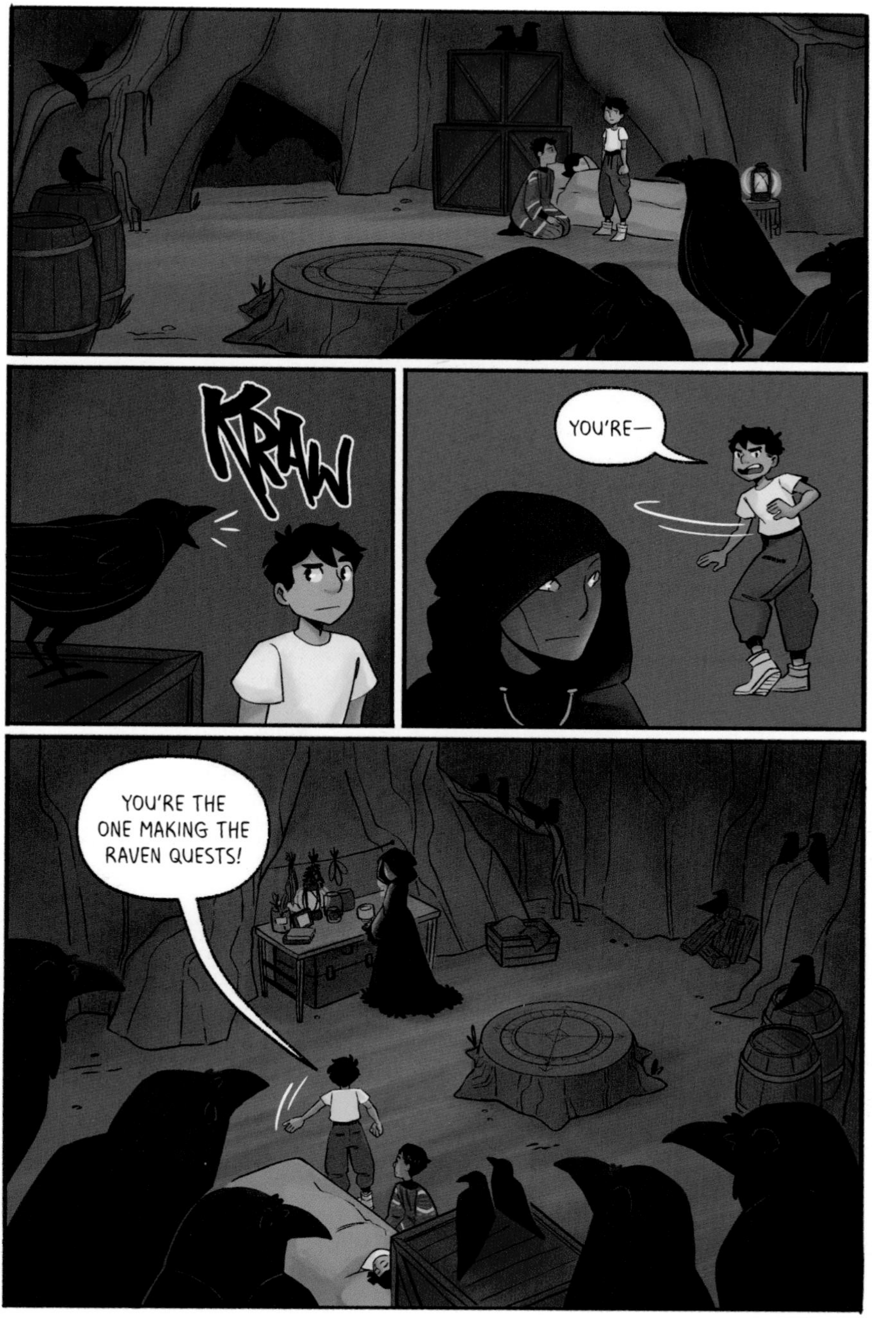
KRAW
YOU'RE—
YOU'RE THE ONE MAKING THE RAVEN QUESTS!

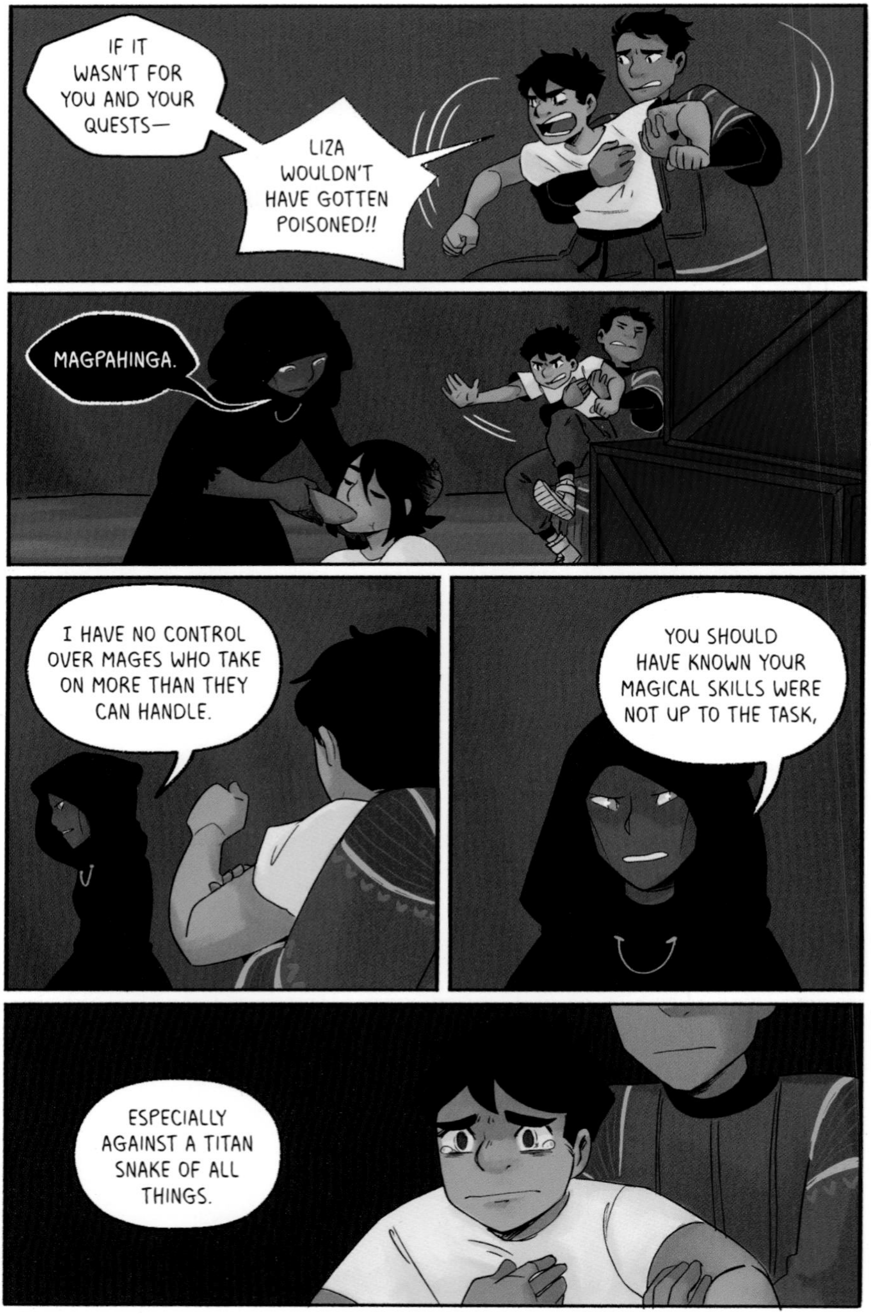

IF IT WASN'T FOR YOU AND YOUR QUESTS—
LIZA WOULDN'T HAVE GOTTEN POISONED!!
MAGPAHINGA.
I HAVE NO CONTROL OVER MAGES WHO TAKE ON MORE THAN THEY CAN HANDLE.
YOU SHOULD HAVE KNOWN YOUR MAGICAL SKILLS WERE NOT UP TO THE TASK,
ESPECIALLY AGAINST A TITAN SNAKE OF ALL THINGS.

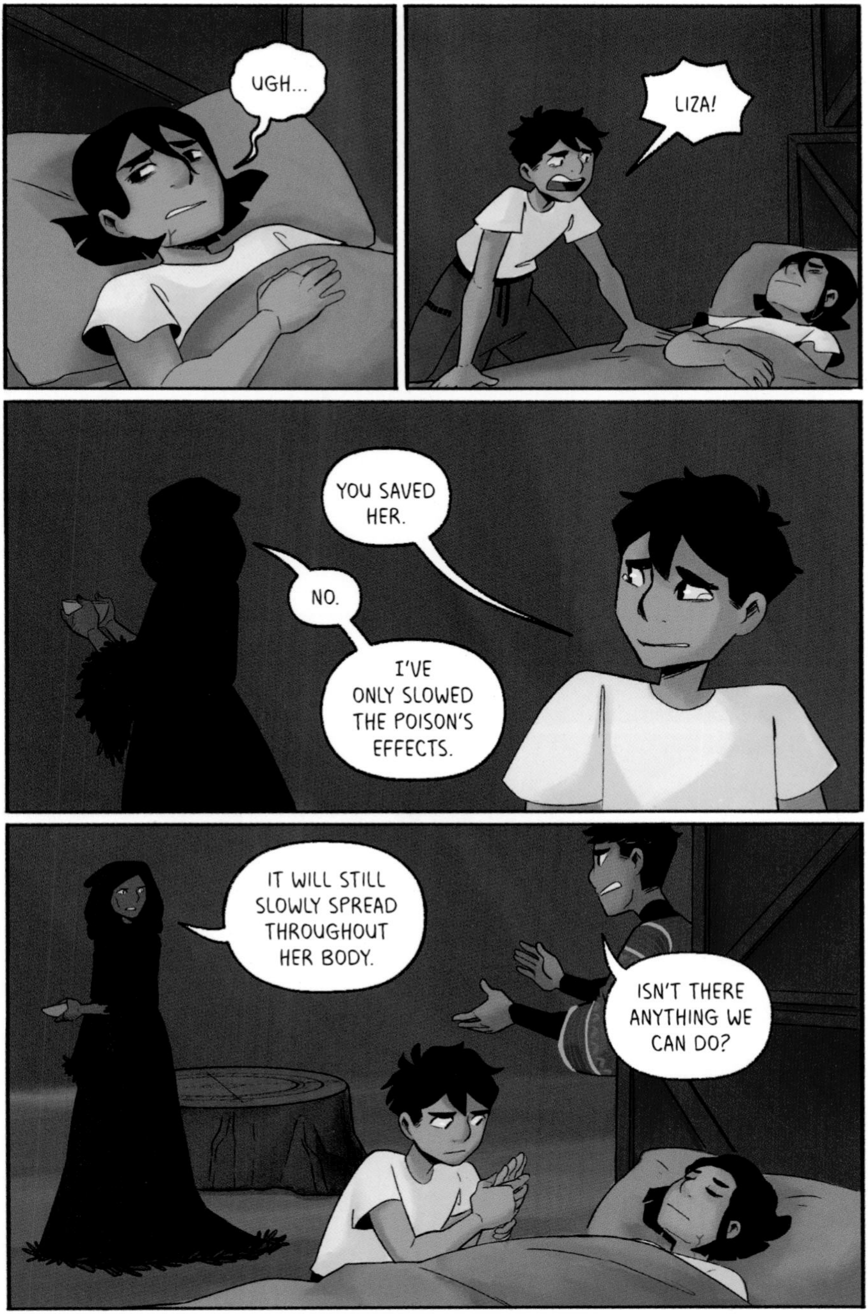
UGH...
LIZA!
YOU SAVED HER.
NO.
I'VE ONLY SLOWED THE POISON'S EFFECTS.
IT WILL STILL SLOWLY SPREAD THROUGHOUT HER BODY.
ISN'T THERE ANYTHING WE CAN DO?

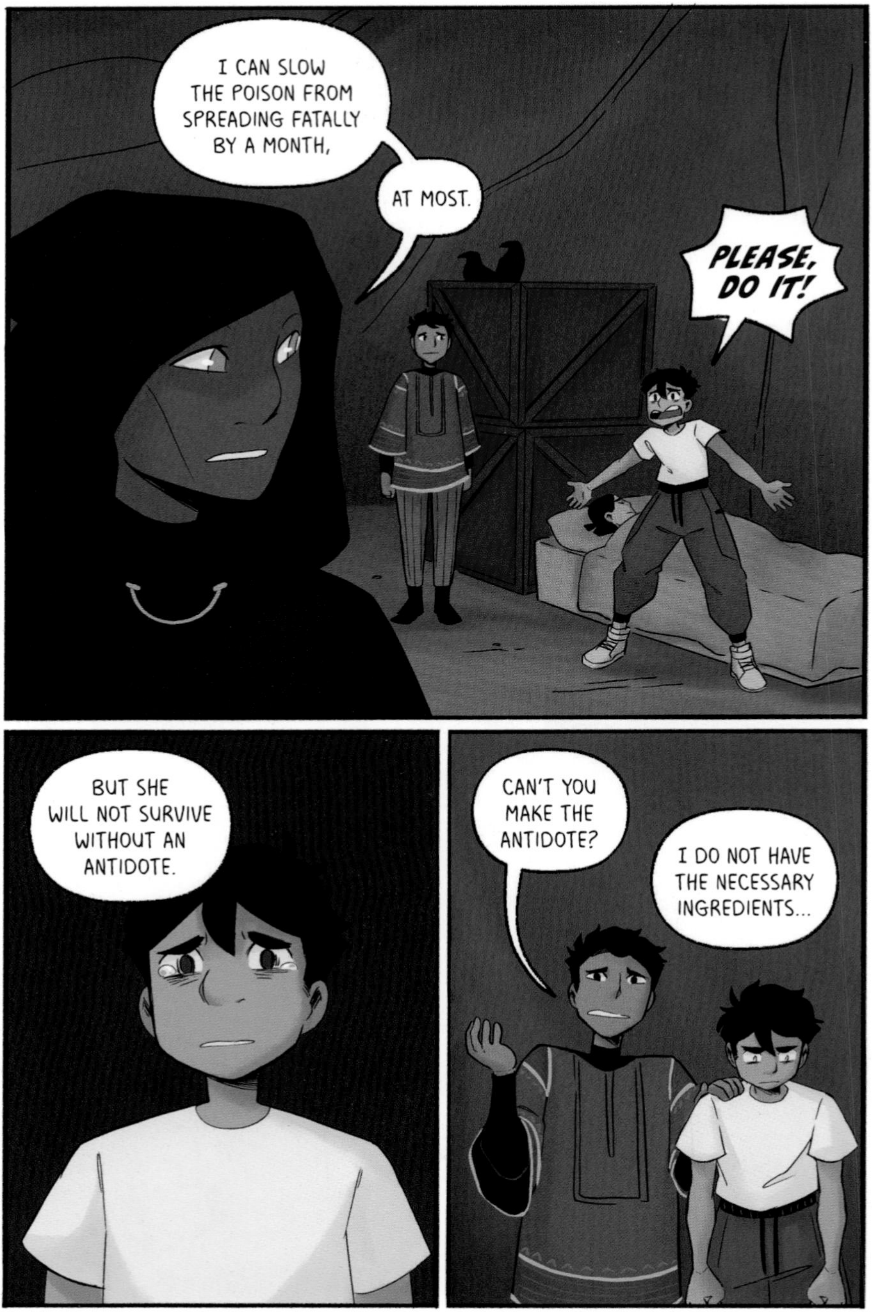
I CAN SLOW THE POISON FROM SPREADING FATALLY BY A MONTH,
AT MOST.
PLEASE, DO IT!
BUT SHE WILL NOT SURVIVE WITHOUT AN ANTIDOTE.
CAN'T YOU MAKE THE ANTIDOTE?
I DO NOT HAVE THE NECESSARY INGREDIENTS...

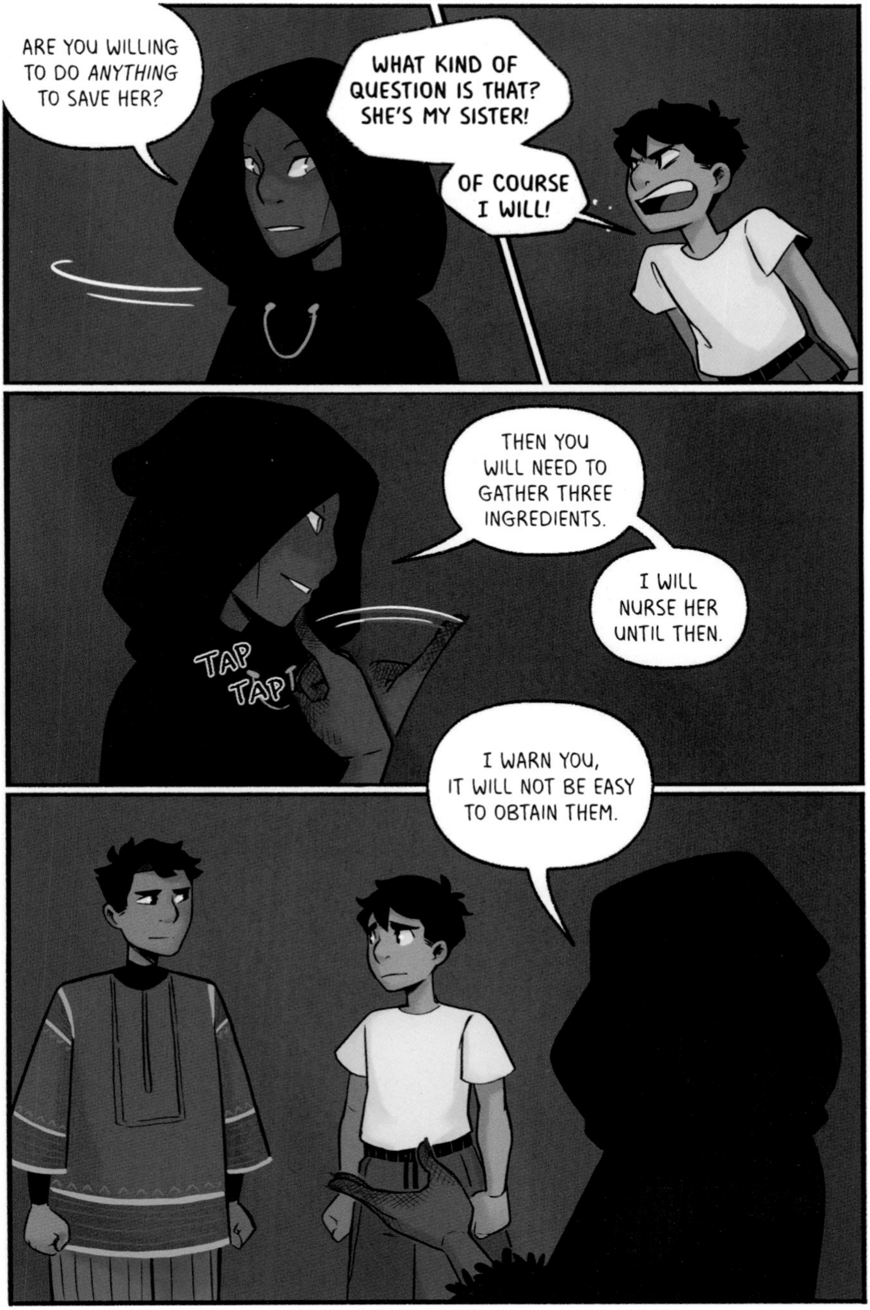
ARE YOU WILLING TO DO *ANYTHING* TO SAVE HER?
WHAT KIND OF QUESTION IS THAT? SHE'S MY SISTER!
OF COURSE I WILL!
THEN YOU WILL NEED TO GATHER THREE INGREDIENTS.
I WILL NURSE HER UNTIL THEN.
TAP TAP
I WARN YOU, IT WILL NOT BE EASY TO OBTAIN THEM.

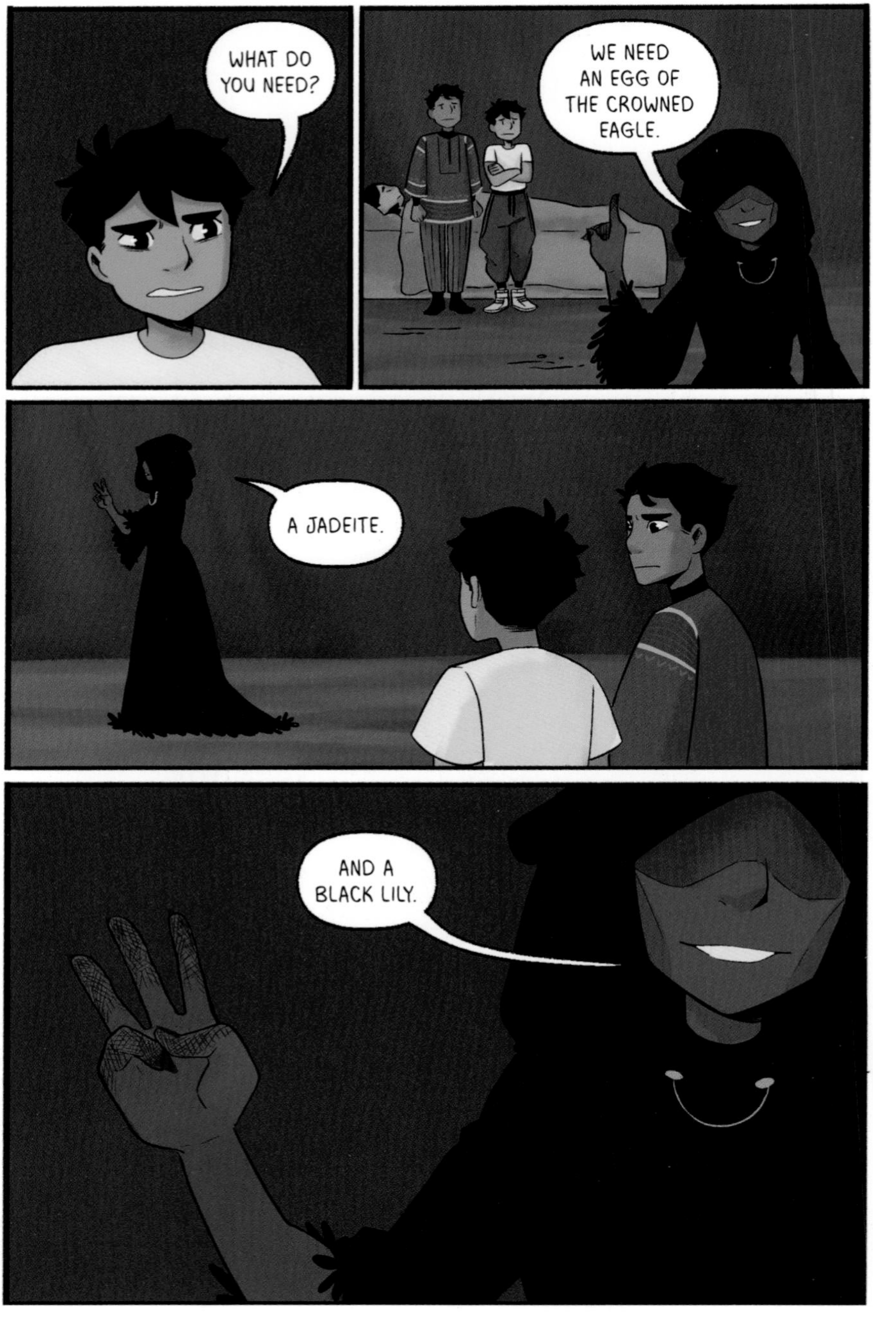
WHAT DO YOU NEED?
WE NEED AN EGG OF THE CROWNED EAGLE.
A JADEITE.
AND A BLACK LILY.

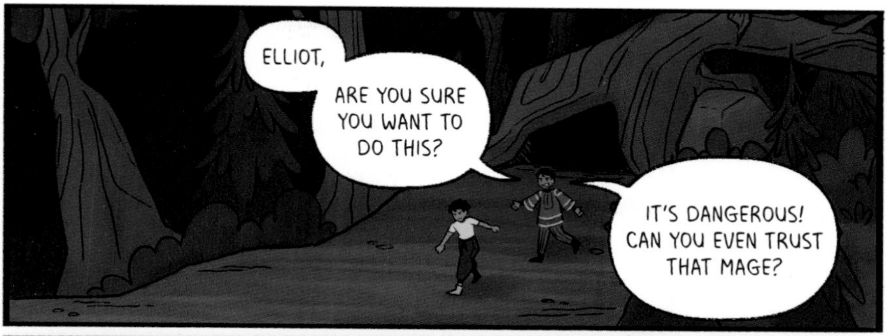
ELLIOT,
ARE YOU SURE YOU WANT TO DO THIS?
IT'S DANGEROUS! CAN YOU EVEN TRUST THAT MAGE?

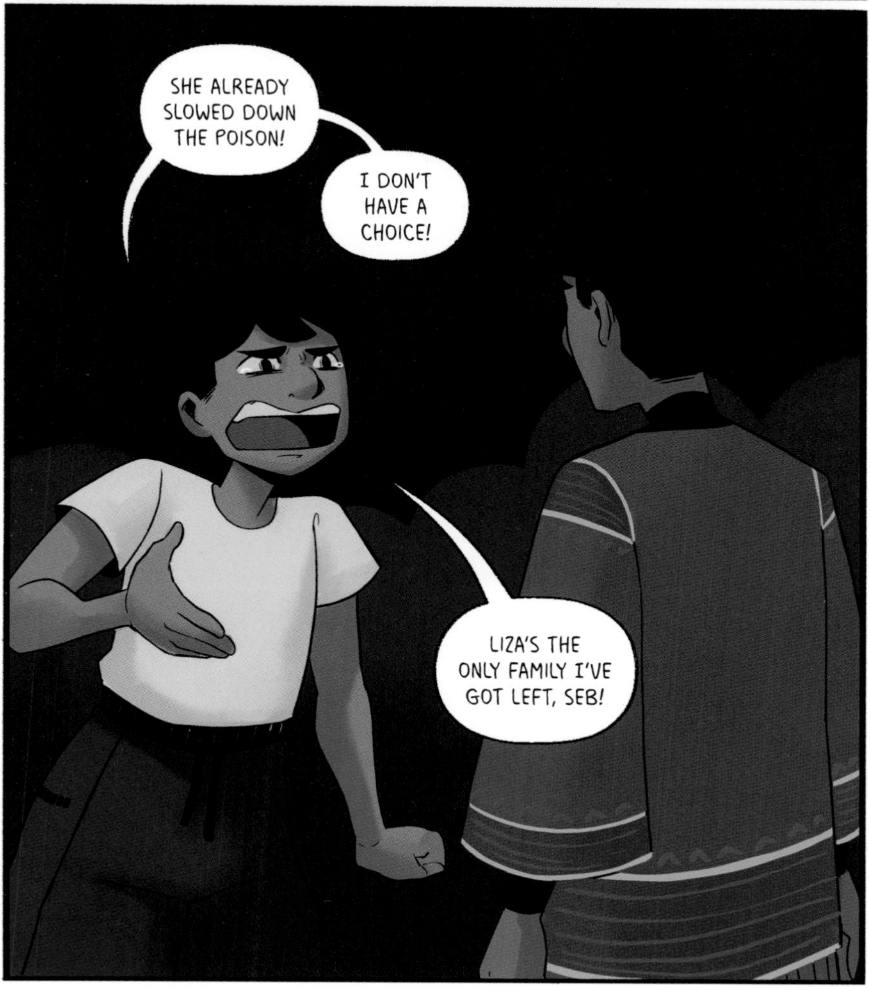
SHE ALREADY SLOWED DOWN THE POISON!
I DON'T HAVE A CHOICE!
LIZA'S THE ONLY FAMILY I'VE GOT LEFT, SEB!

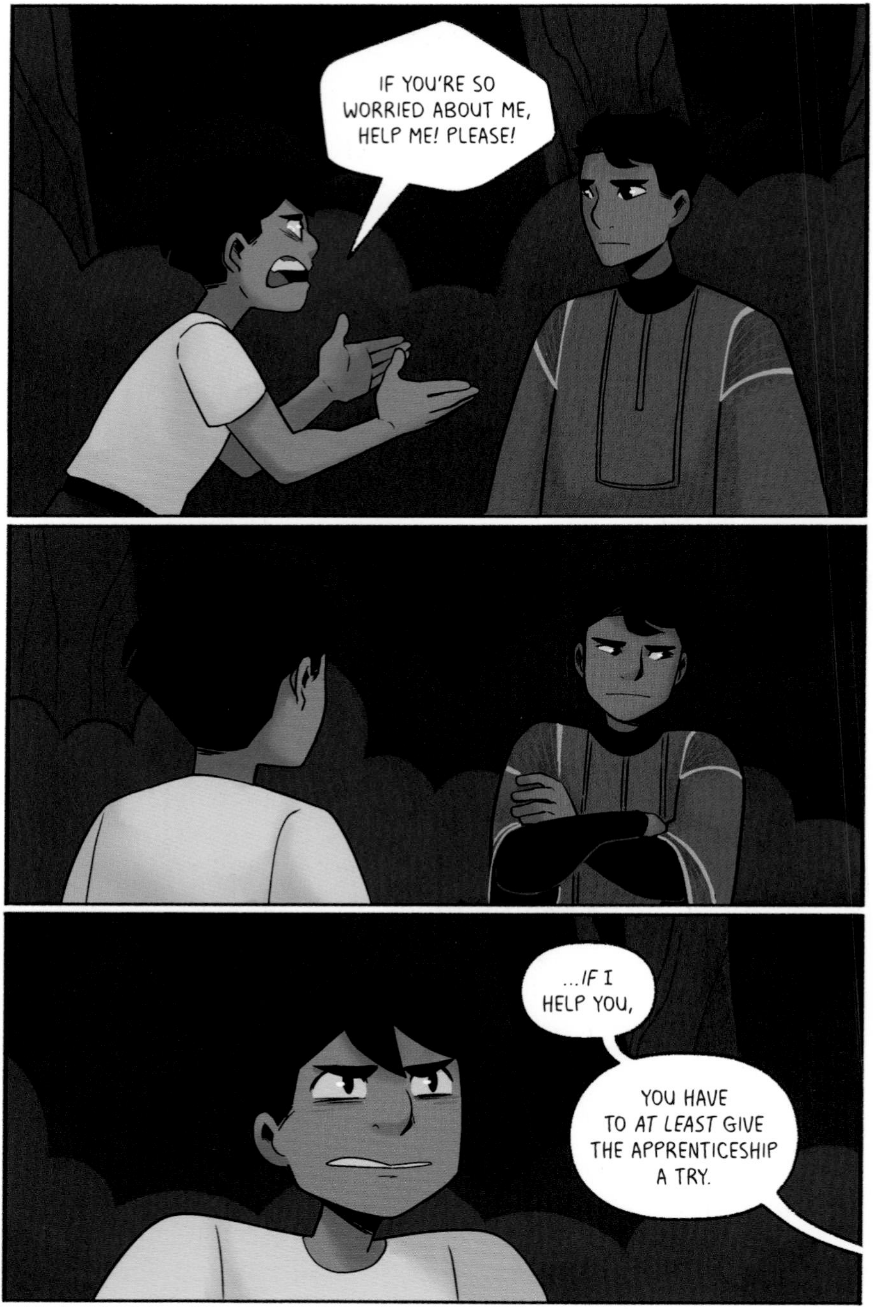
IF YOU'RE SO WORRIED ABOUT ME, HELP ME! PLEASE!
...IF I HELP YOU,
YOU HAVE TO AT LEAST GIVE THE APPRENTICESHIP A TRY.

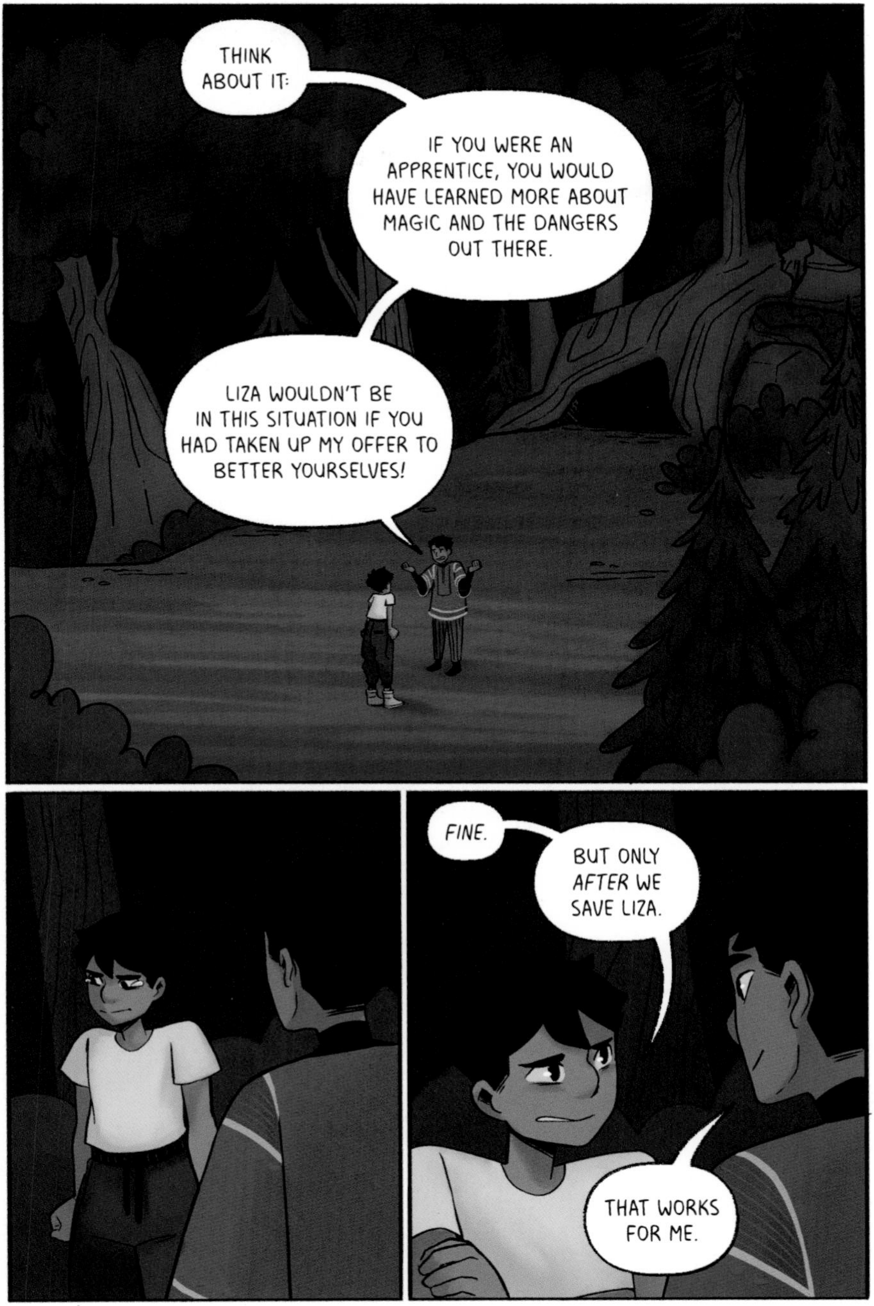
THINK ABOUT IT:
IF YOU WERE AN APPRENTICE, YOU WOULD HAVE LEARNED MORE ABOUT MAGIC AND THE DANGERS OUT THERE.
LIZA WOULDN'T BE IN THIS SITUATION IF YOU HAD TAKEN UP MY OFFER TO BETTER YOURSELVES!
FINE.
BUT ONLY *AFTER* WE SAVE LIZA.
THAT WORKS FOR ME.

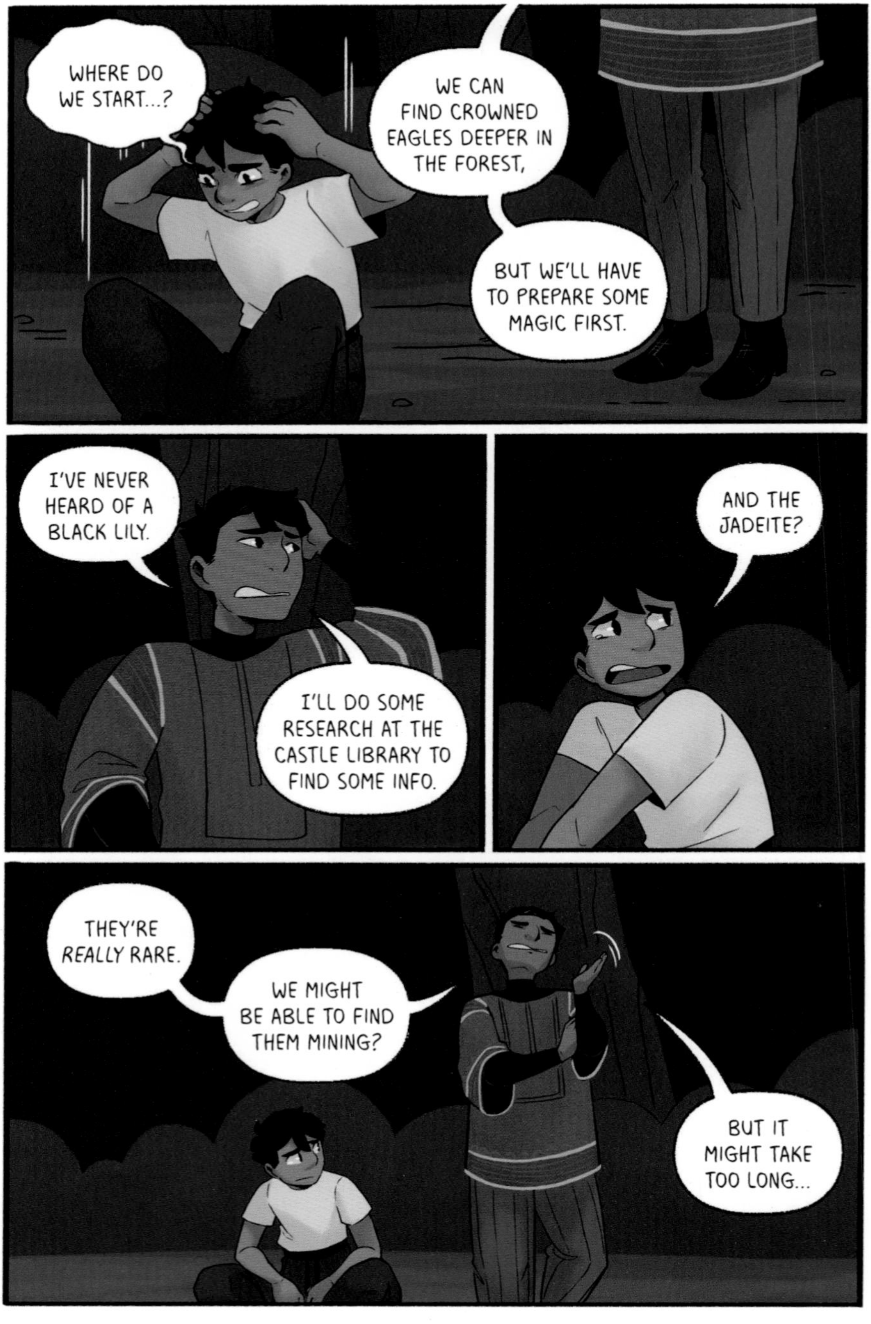
WHERE DO WE START...?
WE CAN FIND CROWNED EAGLES DEEPER IN THE FOREST,
BUT WE'LL HAVE TO PREPARE SOME MAGIC FIRST.
I'VE NEVER HEARD OF A BLACK LILY.
I'LL DO SOME RESEARCH AT THE CASTLE LIBRARY TO FIND SOME INFO.
AND THE JADEITE?
THEY'RE *REALLY* RARE.
WE MIGHT BE ABLE TO FIND THEM MINING?
BUT IT MIGHT TAKE TOO LONG...

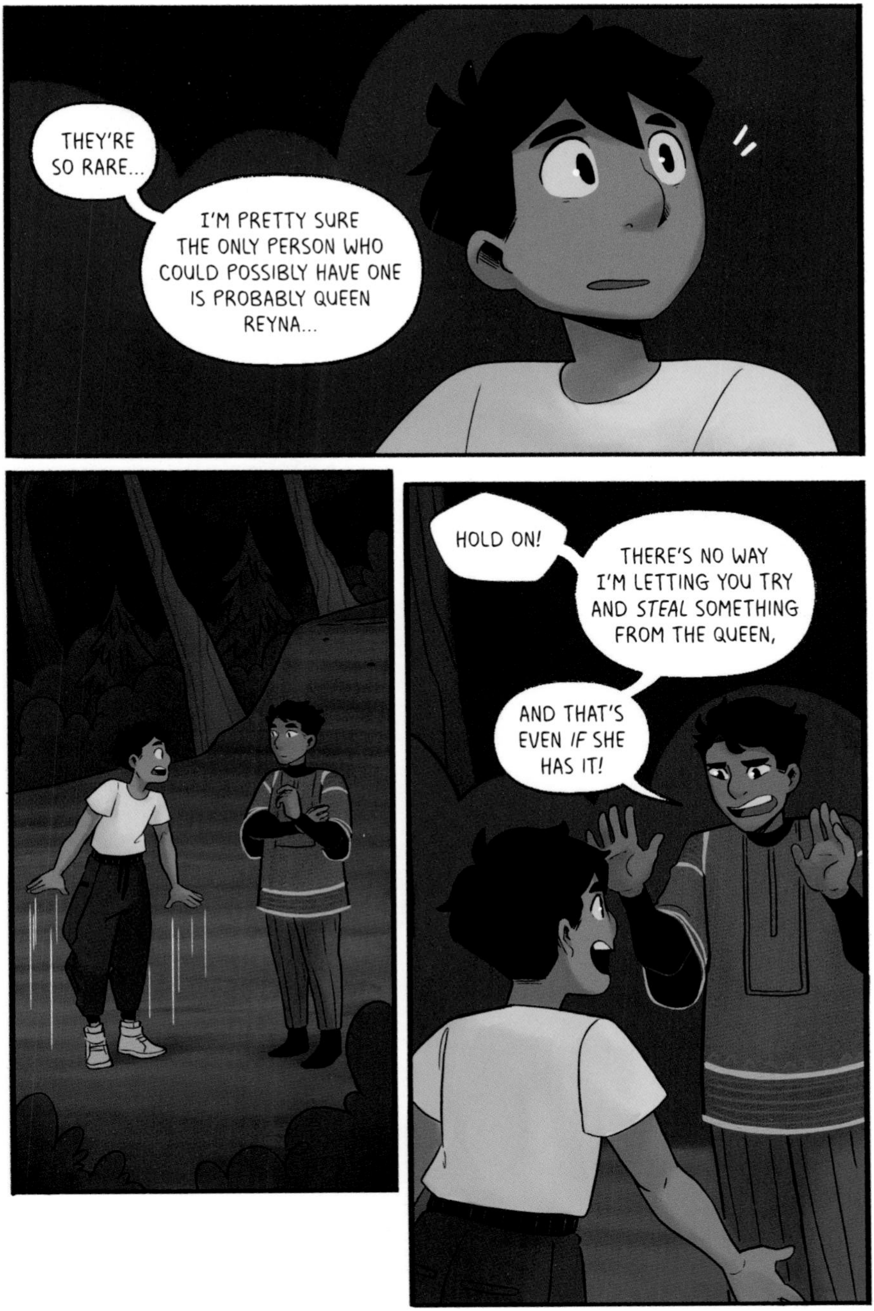
THEY'RE SO RARE...
I'M PRETTY SURE THE ONLY PERSON WHO COULD POSSIBLY HAVE ONE IS PROBABLY QUEEN REYNA...
HOLD ON!
THERE'S NO WAY I'M LETTING YOU TRY AND *STEAL* SOMETHING FROM THE QUEEN,
AND THAT'S EVEN *IF* SHE HAS IT!

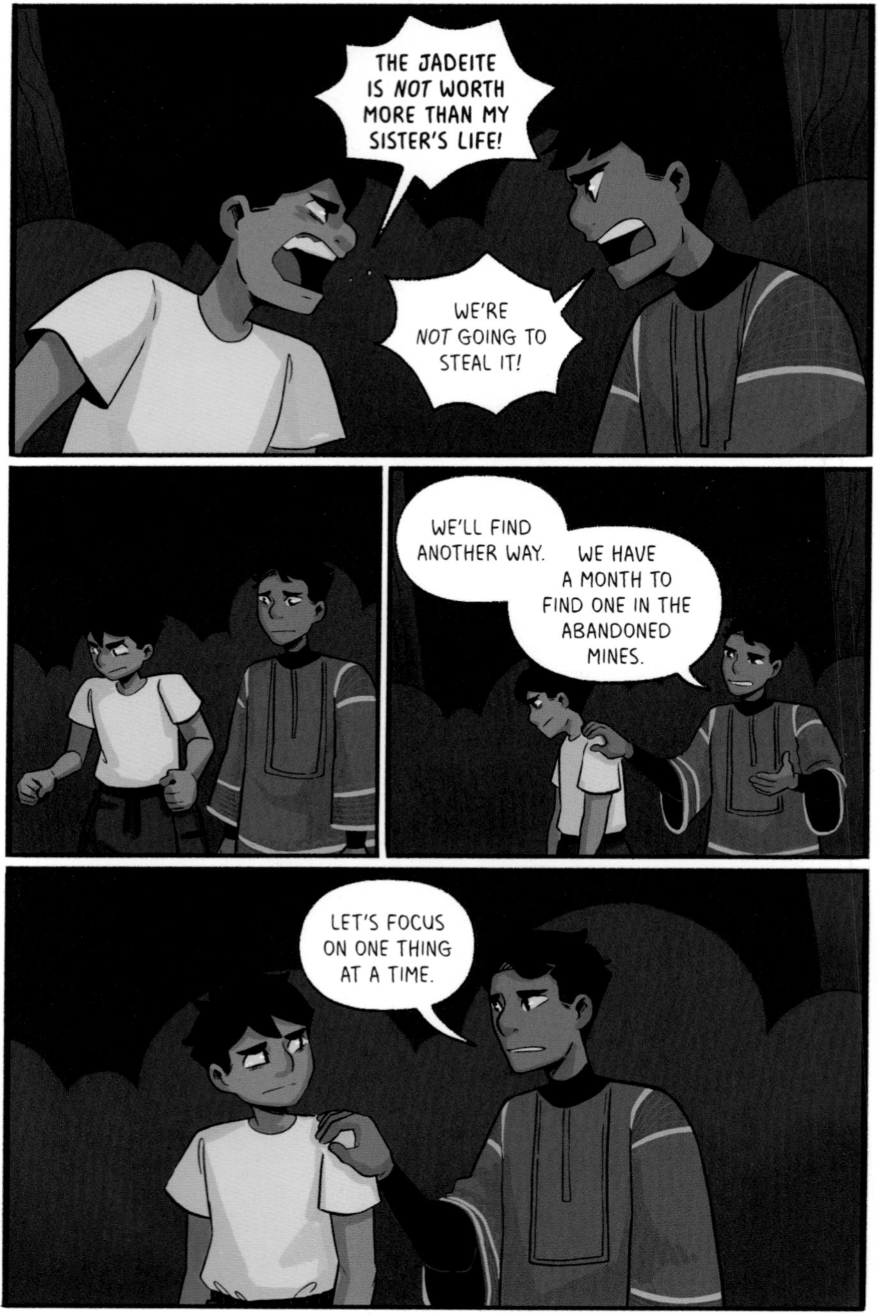
THE JADEITE IS *NOT* WORTH MORE THAN MY SISTER'S LIFE!
WE'RE *NOT* GOING TO STEAL IT!
WE'LL FIND ANOTHER WAY.
WE HAVE A MONTH TO FIND ONE IN THE ABANDONED MINES.
LET'S FOCUS ON ONE THING AT A TIME.

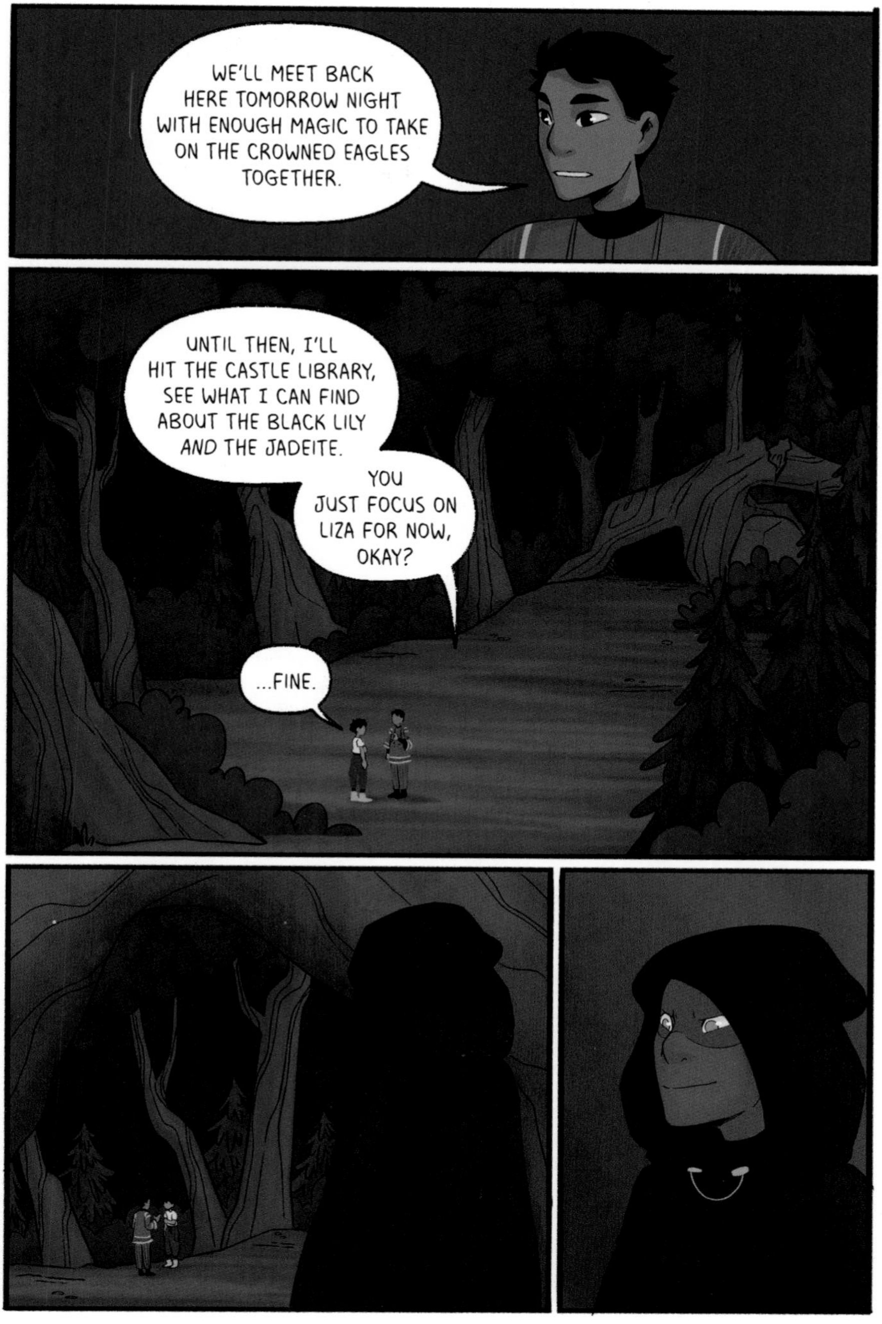
WE'LL MEET BACK HERE TOMORROW NIGHT WITH ENOUGH MAGIC TO TAKE ON THE CROWNED EAGLES TOGETHER.
UNTIL THEN, I'LL HIT THE CASTLE LIBRARY, SEE WHAT I CAN FIND ABOUT THE BLACK LILY *AND* THE JADEITE.
YOU JUST FOCUS ON LIZA FOR NOW, OKAY?
...FINE.

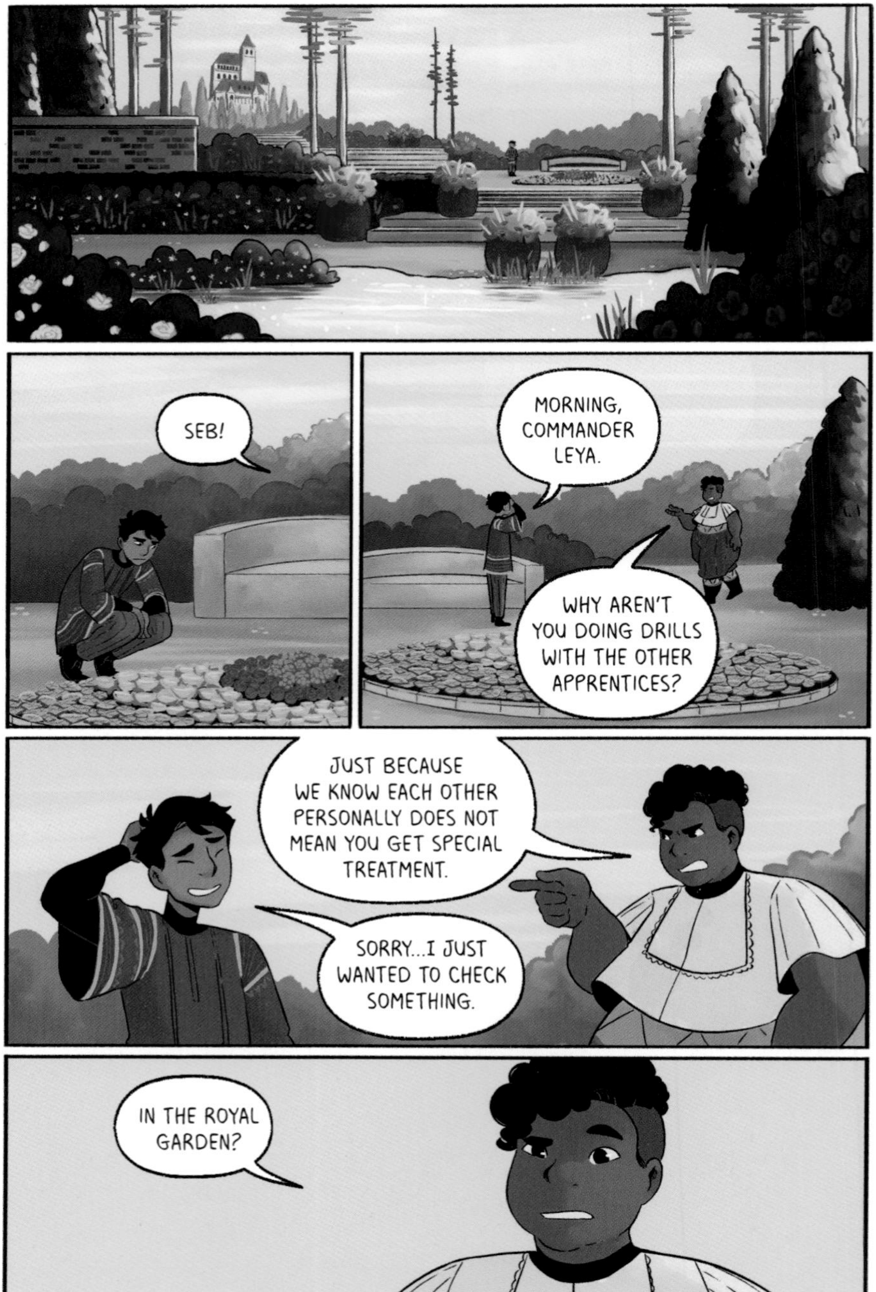
SEB!
MORNING, COMMANDER LEYA.
WHY AREN'T YOU DOING DRILLS WITH THE OTHER APPRENTICES?
JUST BECAUSE WE KNOW EACH OTHER PERSONALLY DOES NOT MEAN YOU GET SPECIAL TREATMENT.
SORRY...I JUST WANTED TO CHECK SOMETHING.
IN THE ROYAL GARDEN?

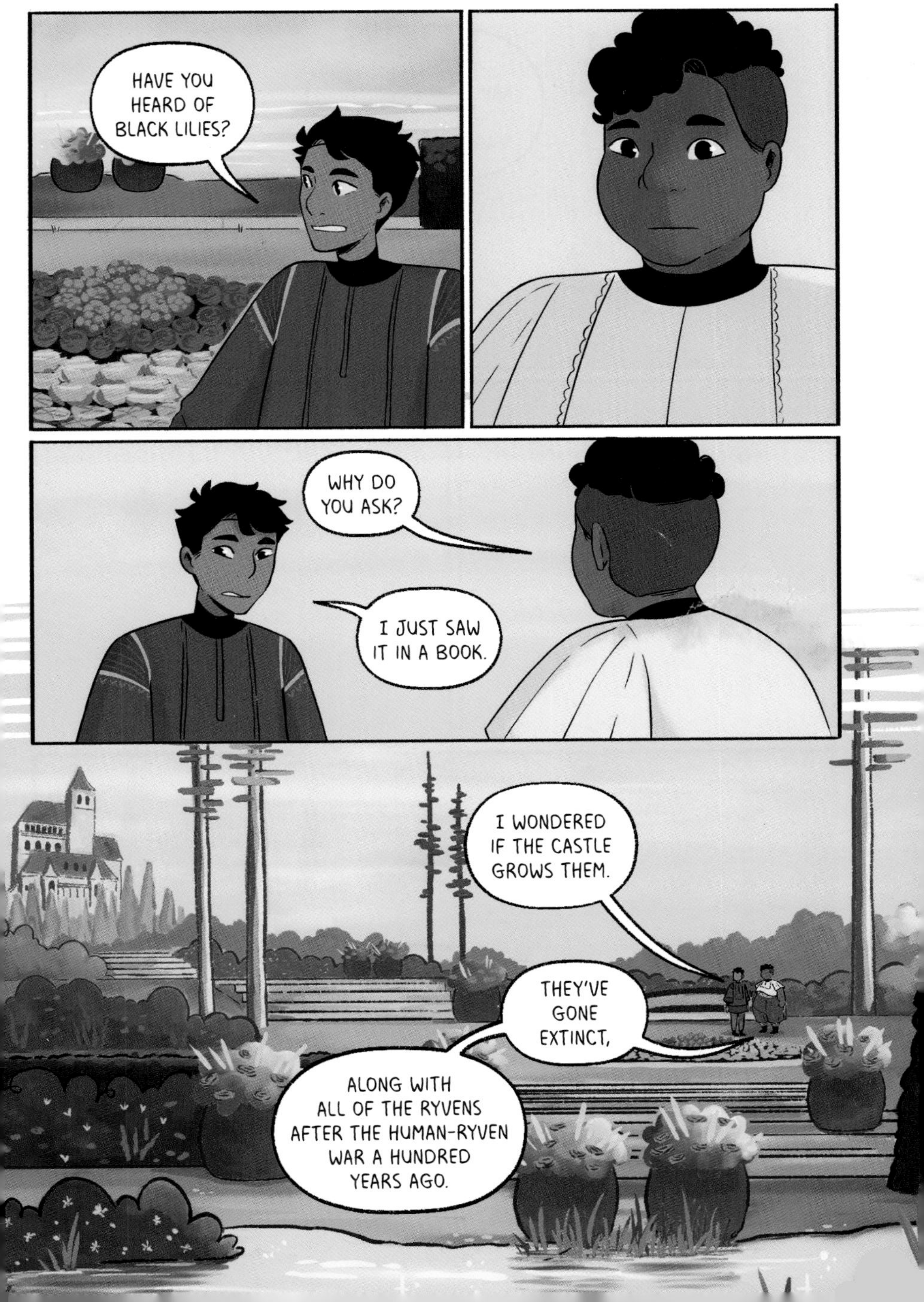
HAVE YOU HEARD OF BLACK LILIES?
WHY DO YOU ASK?
I JUST SAW IT IN A BOOK.
I WONDERED IF THE CASTLE GROWS THEM.
THEY'VE GONE EXTINCT,
ALONG WITH ALL OF THE RYVENS AFTER THE HUMAN-RYVEN WAR A HUNDRED YEARS AGO.

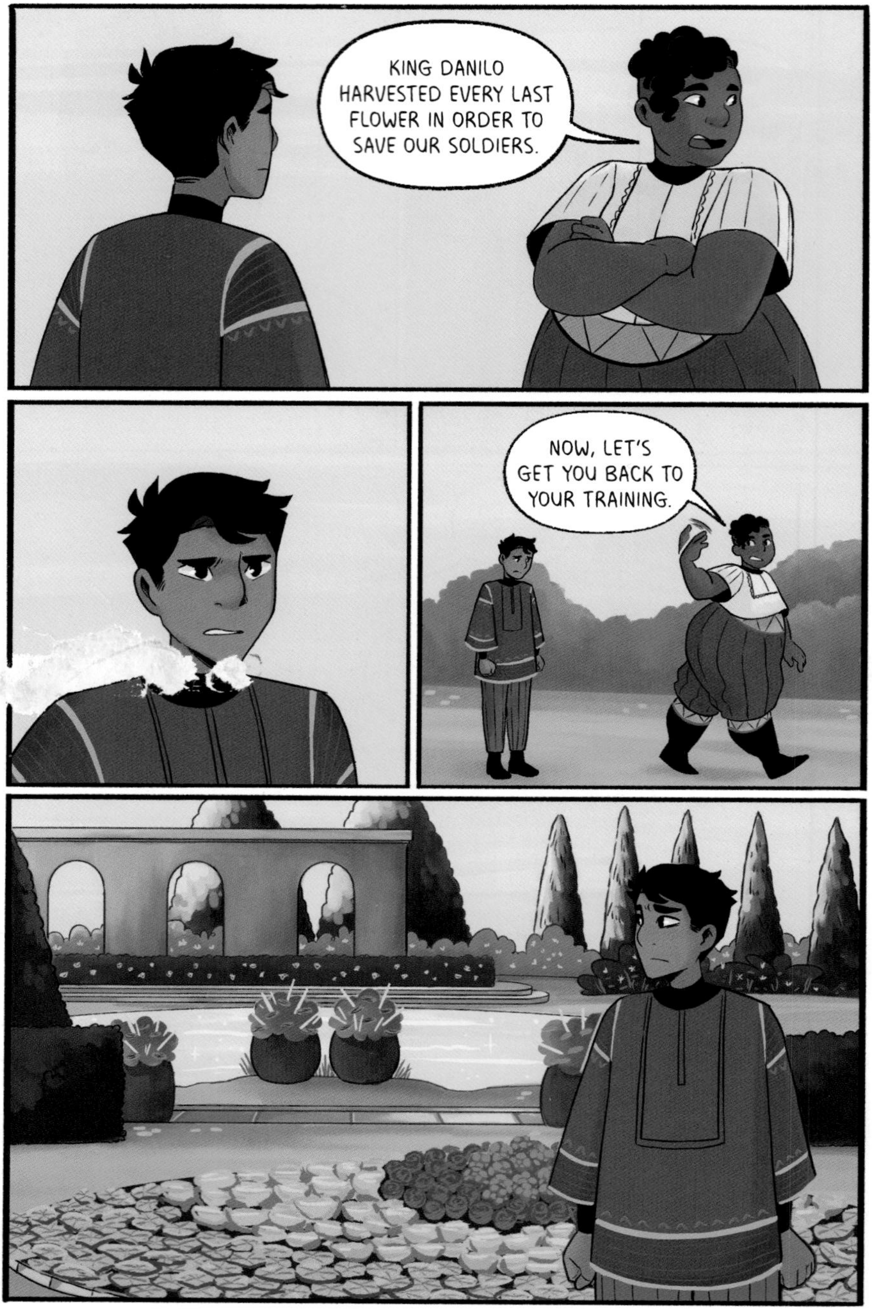
KING DANILO HARVESTED EVERY LAST FLOWER IN ORDER TO SAVE OUR SOLDIERS.
NOW, LET'S GET YOU BACK TO YOUR TRAINING.

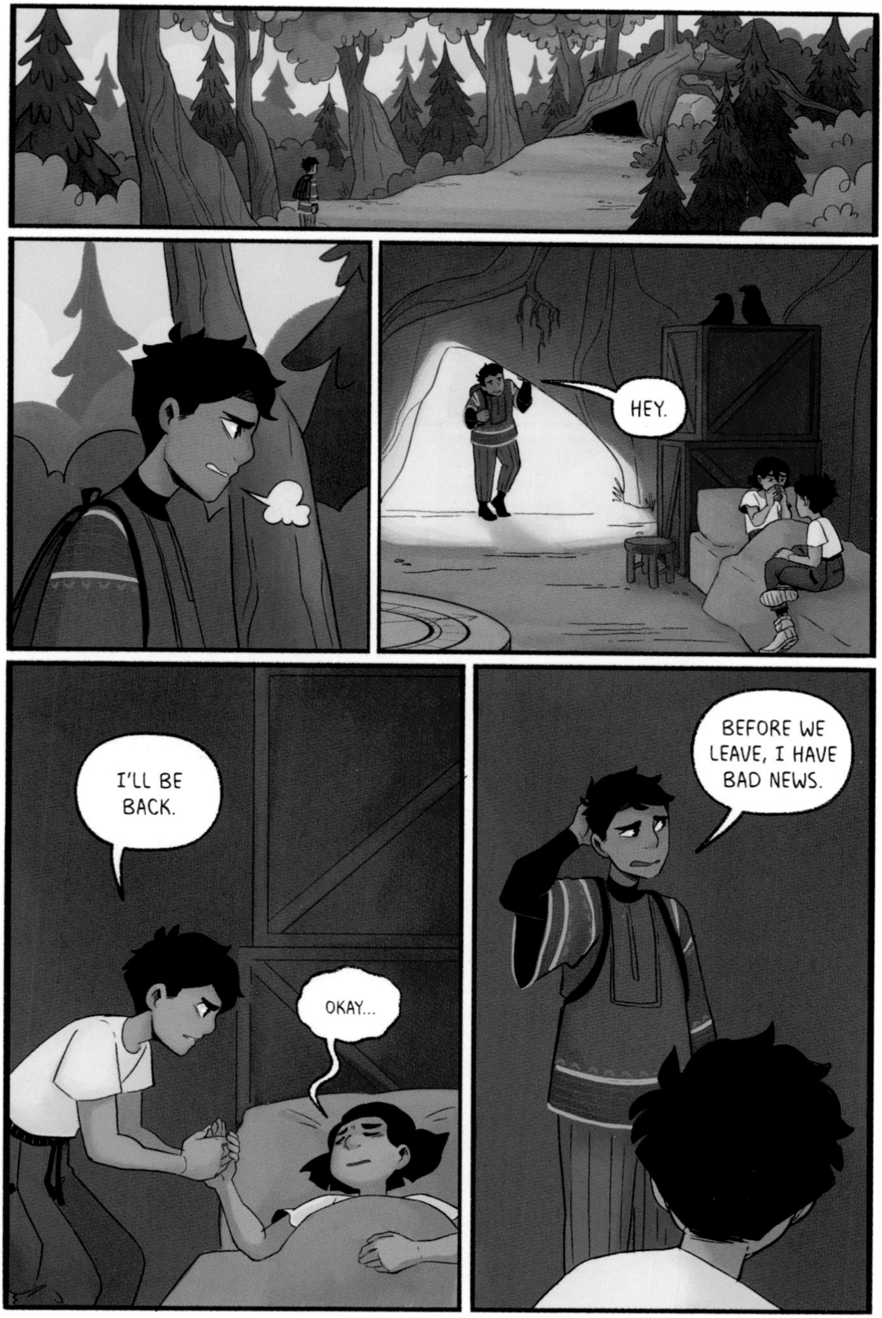
HEY.
I'LL BE BACK.
OKAY...
BEFORE WE LEAVE, I HAVE BAD NEWS.

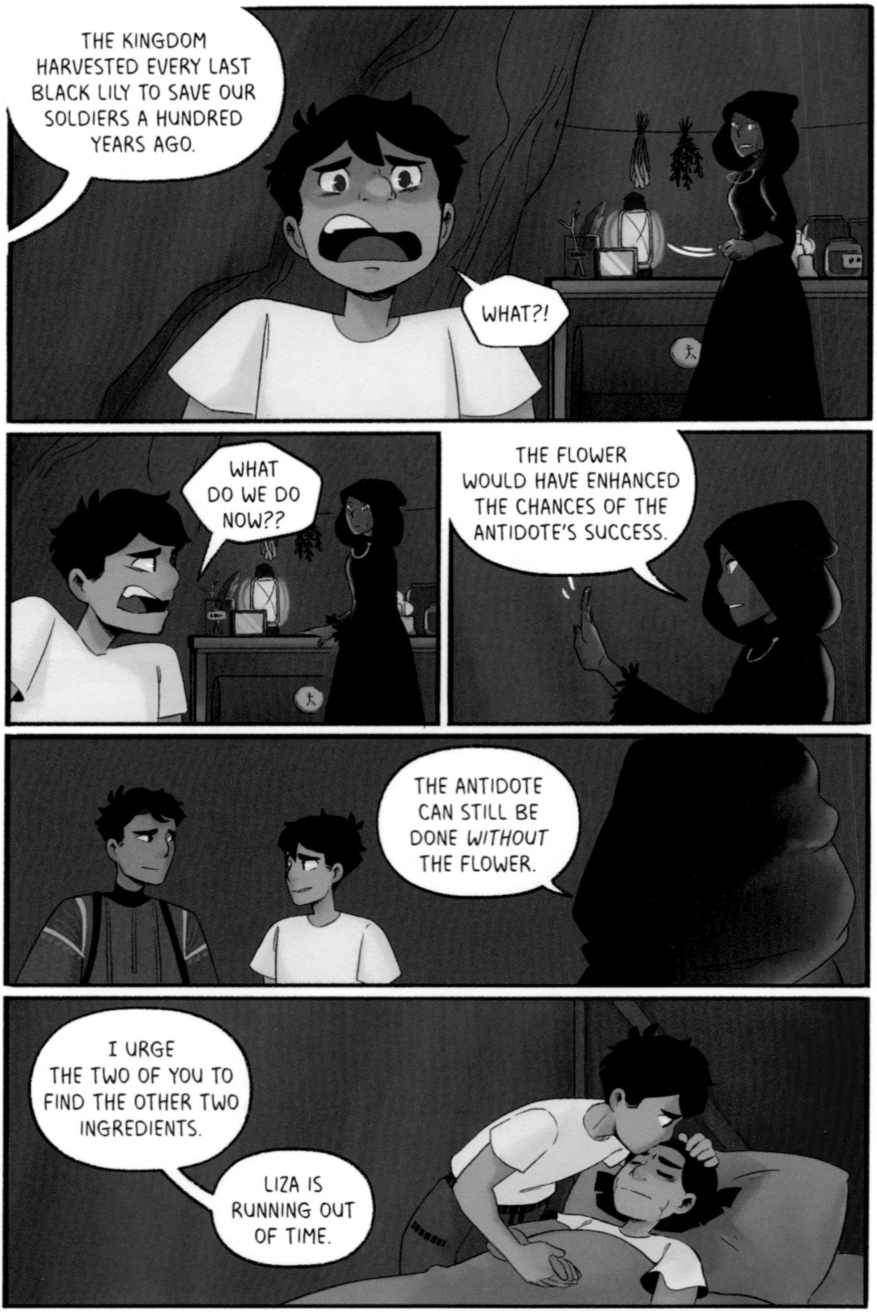
THE KINGDOM HARVESTED EVERY LAST BLACK LILY TO SAVE OUR SOLDIERS A HUNDRED YEARS AGO.
WHAT?!
WHAT DO WE DO NOW??
THE FLOWER WOULD HAVE ENHANCED THE CHANCES OF THE ANTIDOTE'S SUCCESS.
THE ANTIDOTE CAN STILL BE DONE *WITHOUT* THE FLOWER.
I URGE THE TWO OF YOU TO FIND THE OTHER TWO INGREDIENTS.
LIZA IS RUNNING OUT OF TIME.

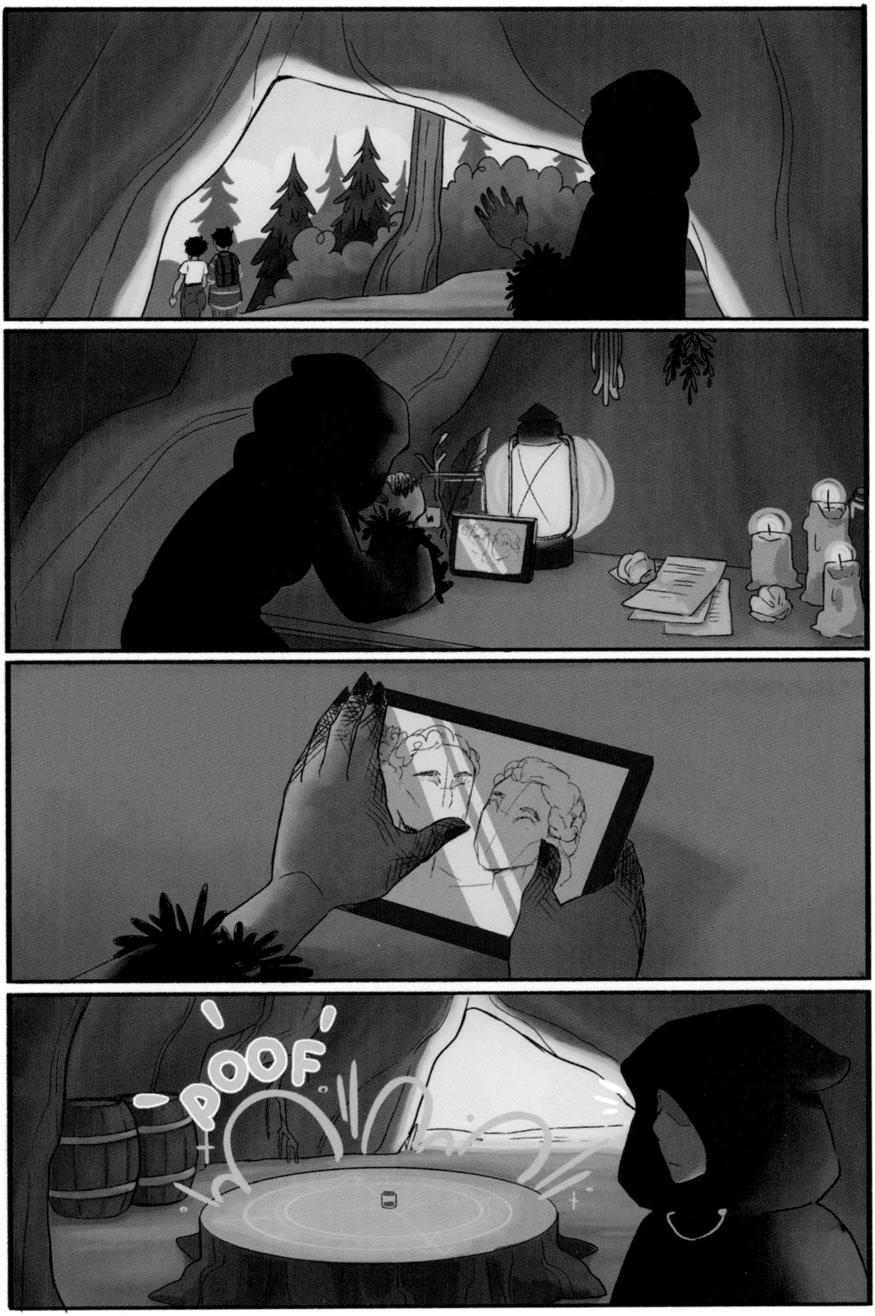
POOF

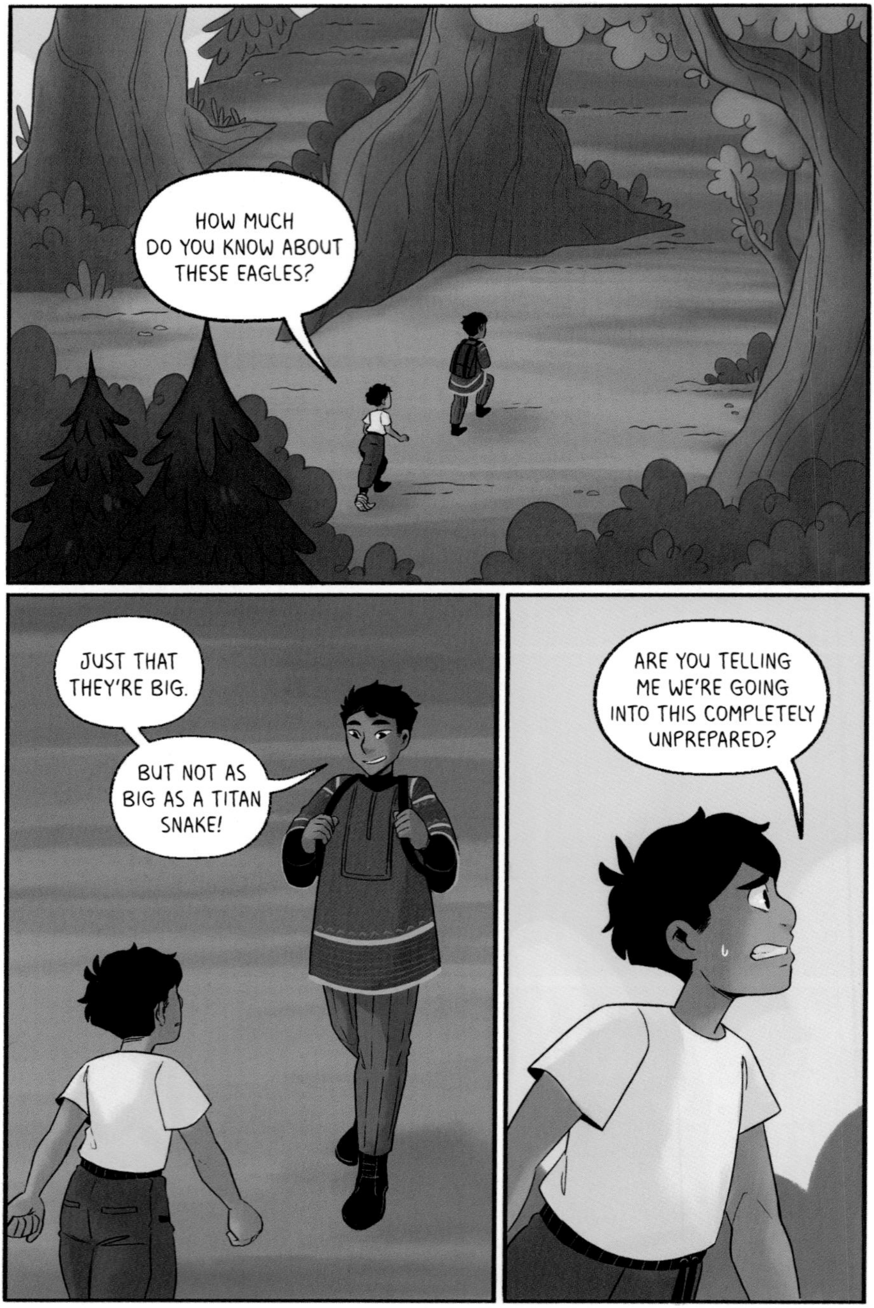

HOW MUCH DO YOU KNOW ABOUT THESE EAGLES?
JUST THAT THEY'RE BIG.
BUT NOT AS BIG AS A TITAN SNAKE!
ARE YOU TELLING ME WE'RE GOING INTO THIS COMPLETELY UNPREPARED?

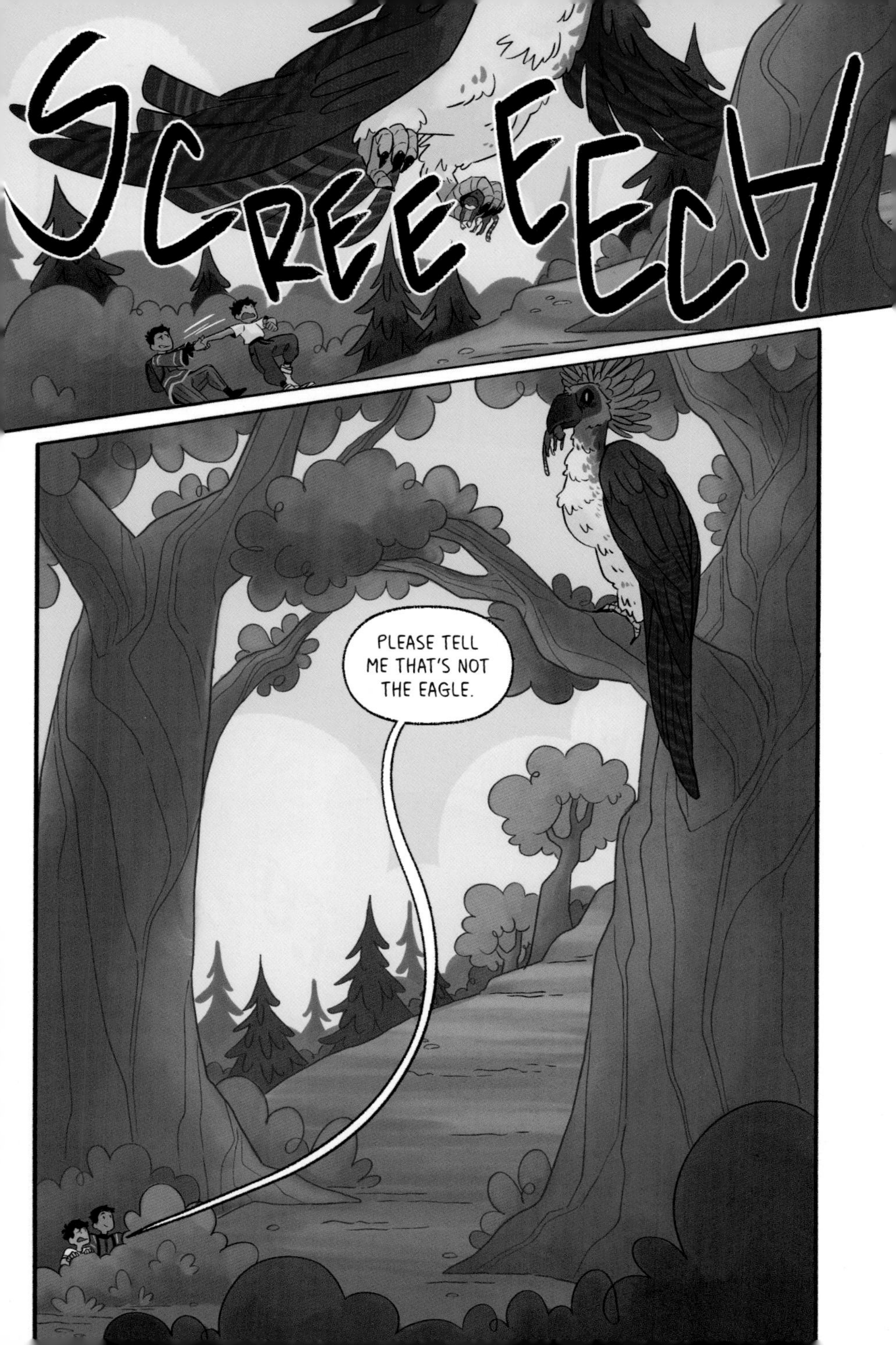
SCREEEECH
PLEASE TELL ME THAT'S NOT THE EAGLE.

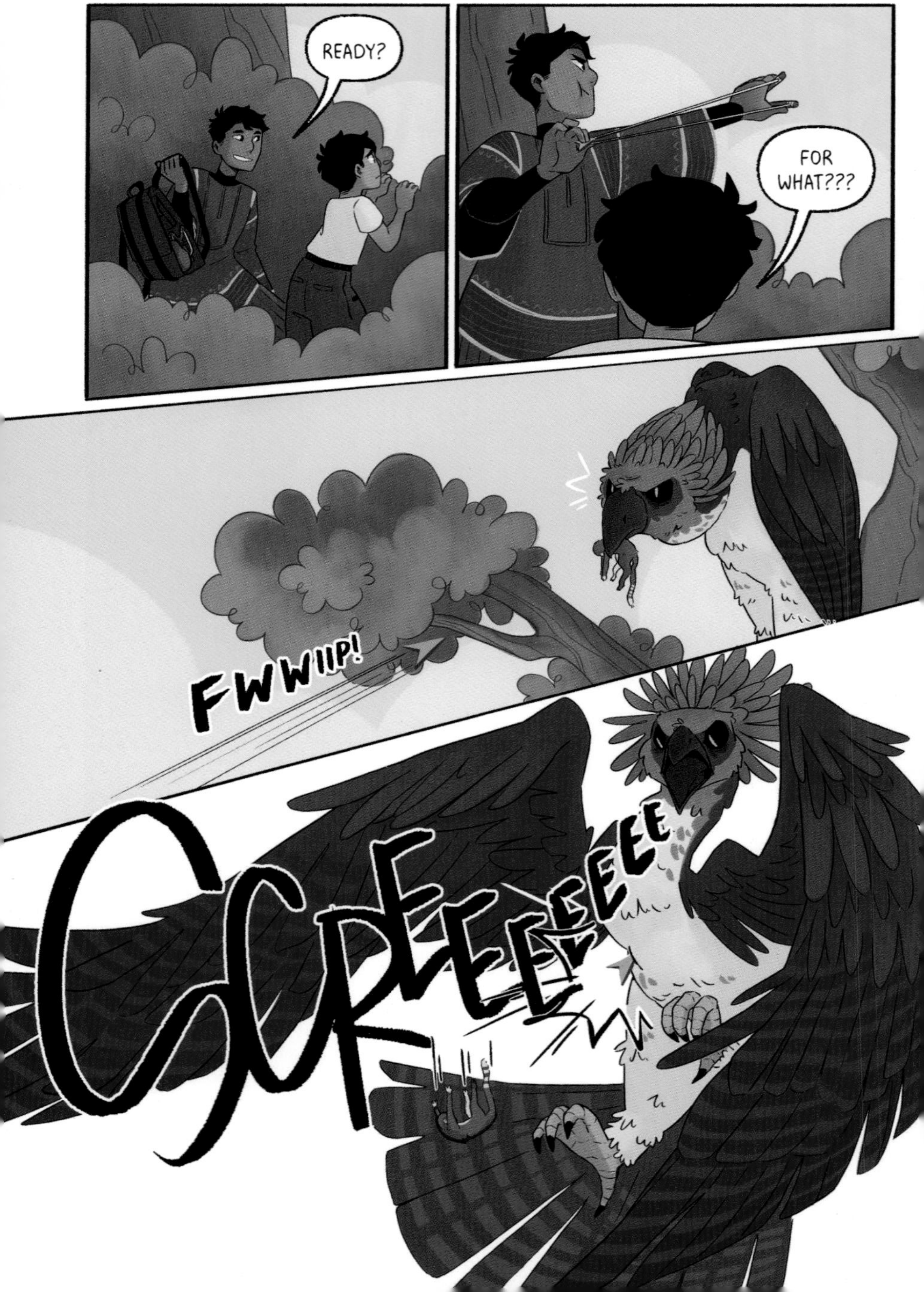
READY?
FOR WHAT???
FWWIIP!
SCREEEEEEEE

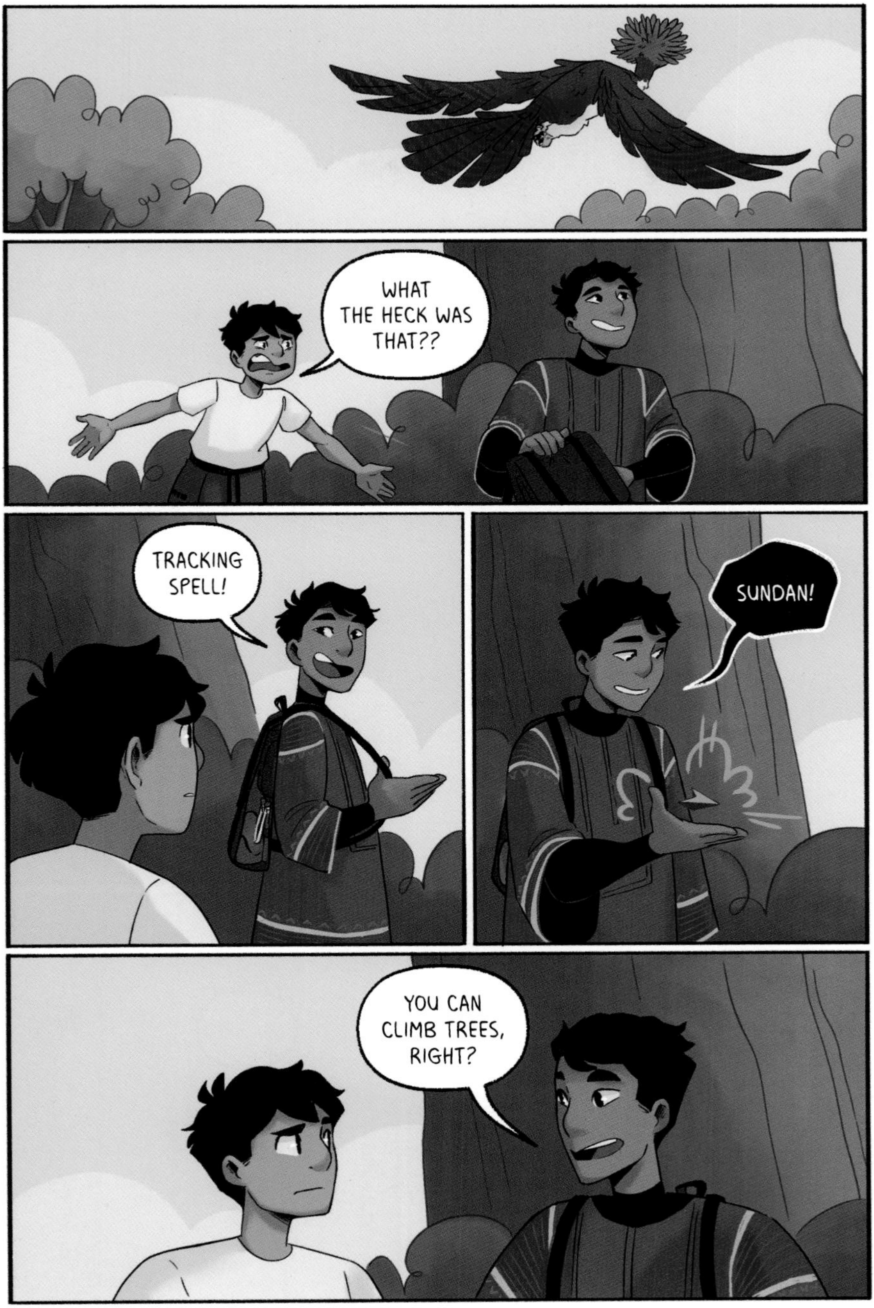
WHAT THE HECK WAS THAT??
TRACKING SPELL!
SUNDAN!
YOU CAN CLIMB TREES, RIGHT?

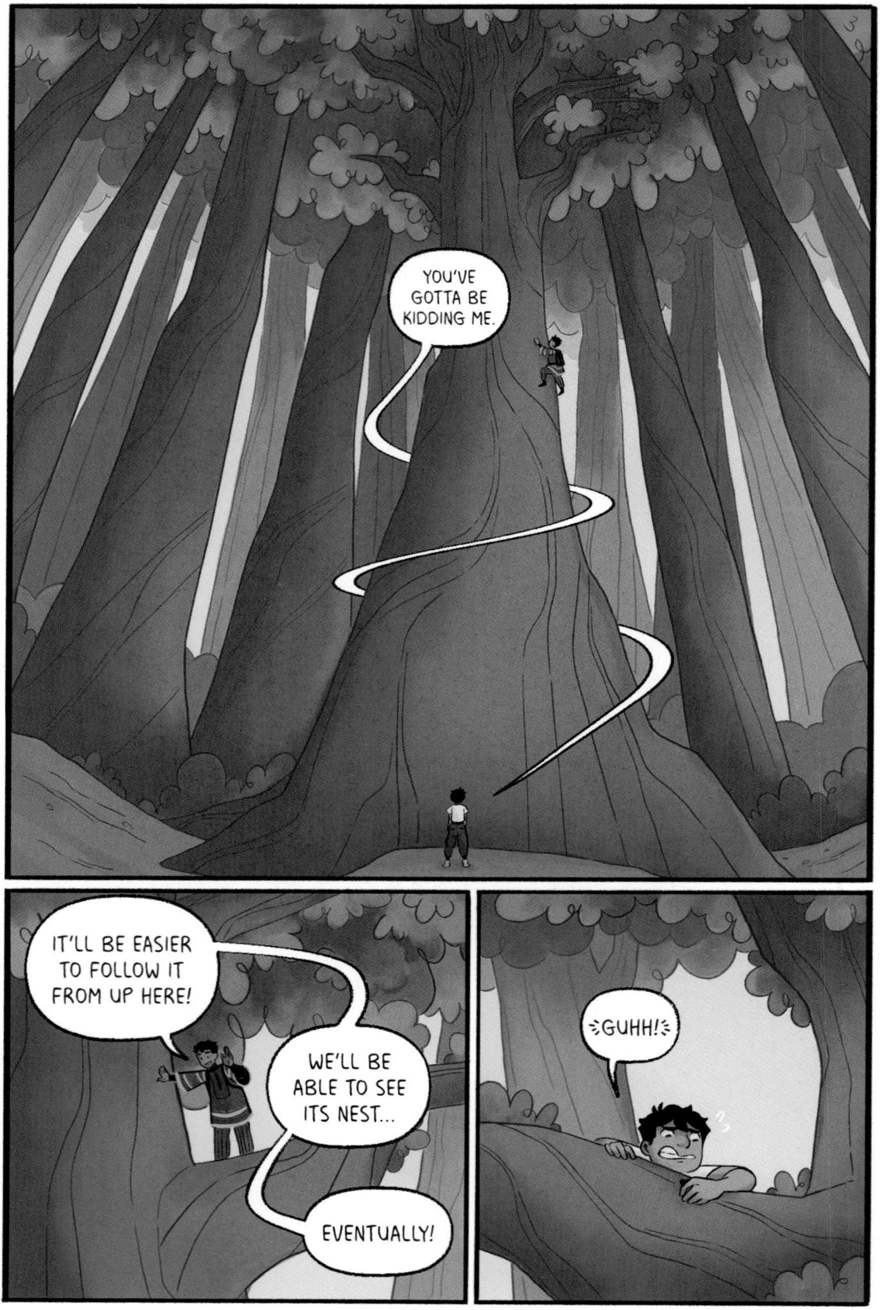
YOU'VE GOTTA BE KIDDING ME.
IT'LL BE EASIER TO FOLLOW IT FROM UP HERE!
WE'LL BE ABLE TO SEE ITS NEST...
EVENTUALLY!
GUHH!

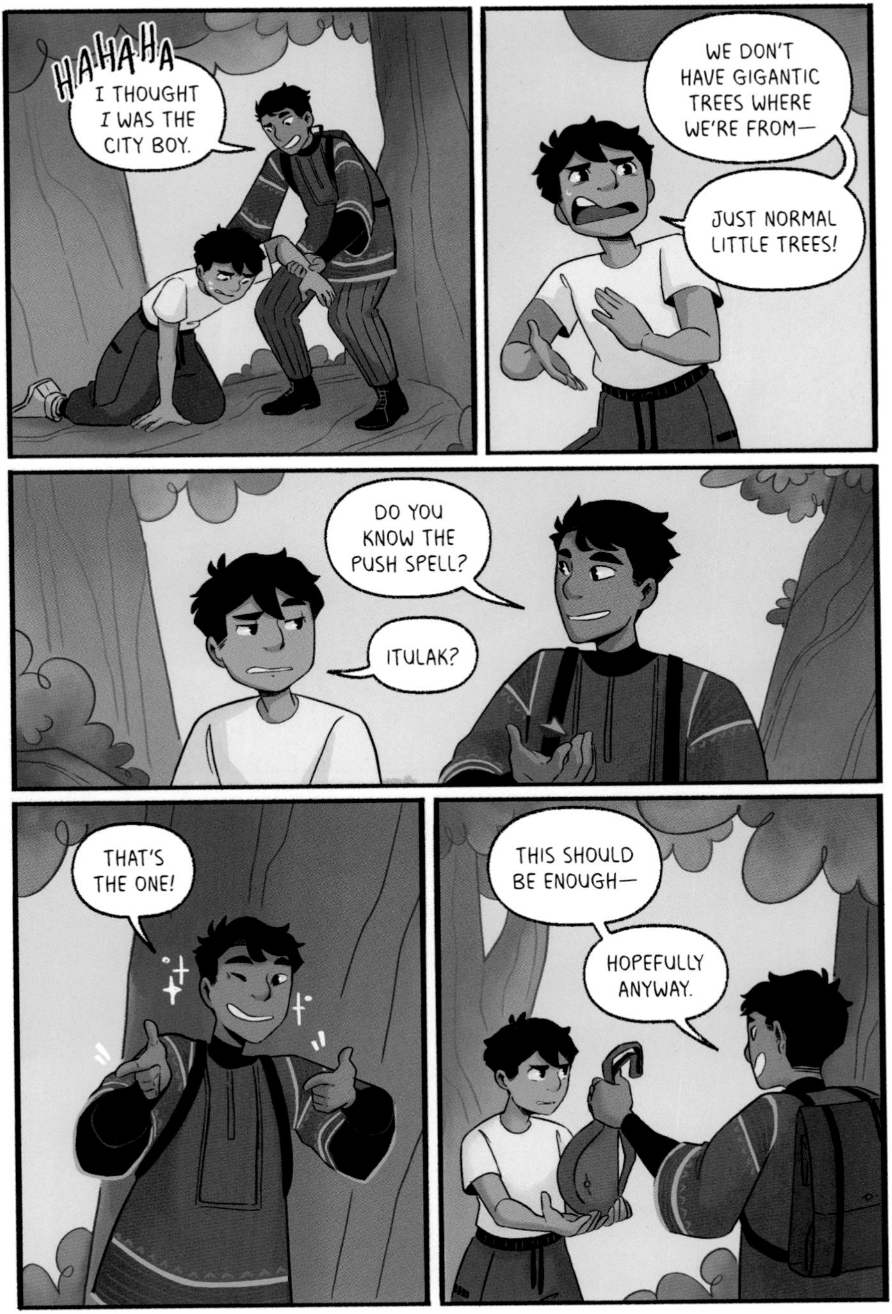
HAHAHA
I THOUGHT I WAS THE CITY BOY.
WE DON'T HAVE GIGANTIC TREES WHERE WE'RE FROM—
JUST NORMAL LITTLE TREES!
DO YOU KNOW THE PUSH SPELL?
ITULAK?
THAT'S THE ONE!
THIS SHOULD BE ENOUGH—
HOPEFULLY ANYWAY.

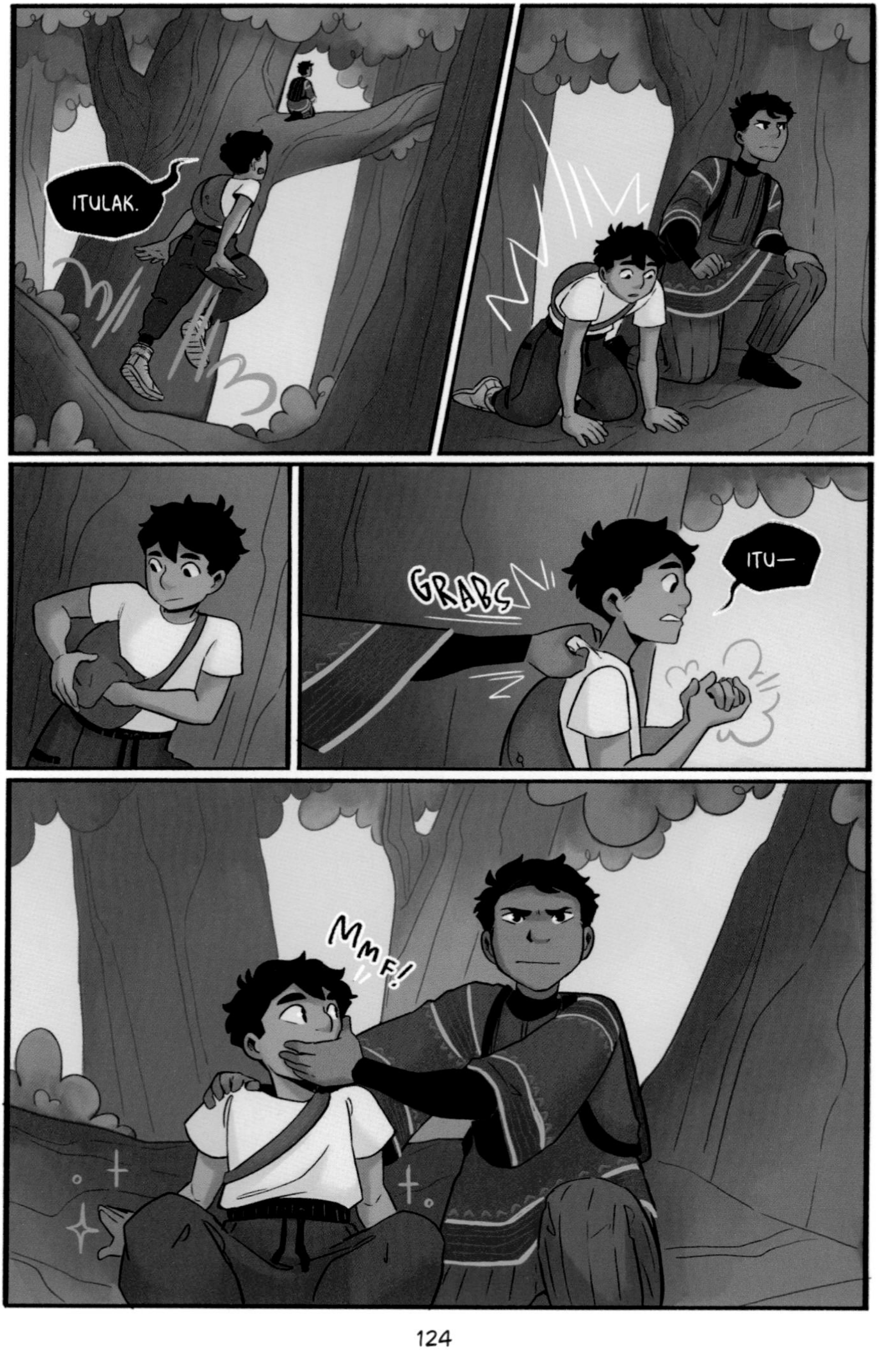
ITULAK.
GRABS
ITU—
MMF!

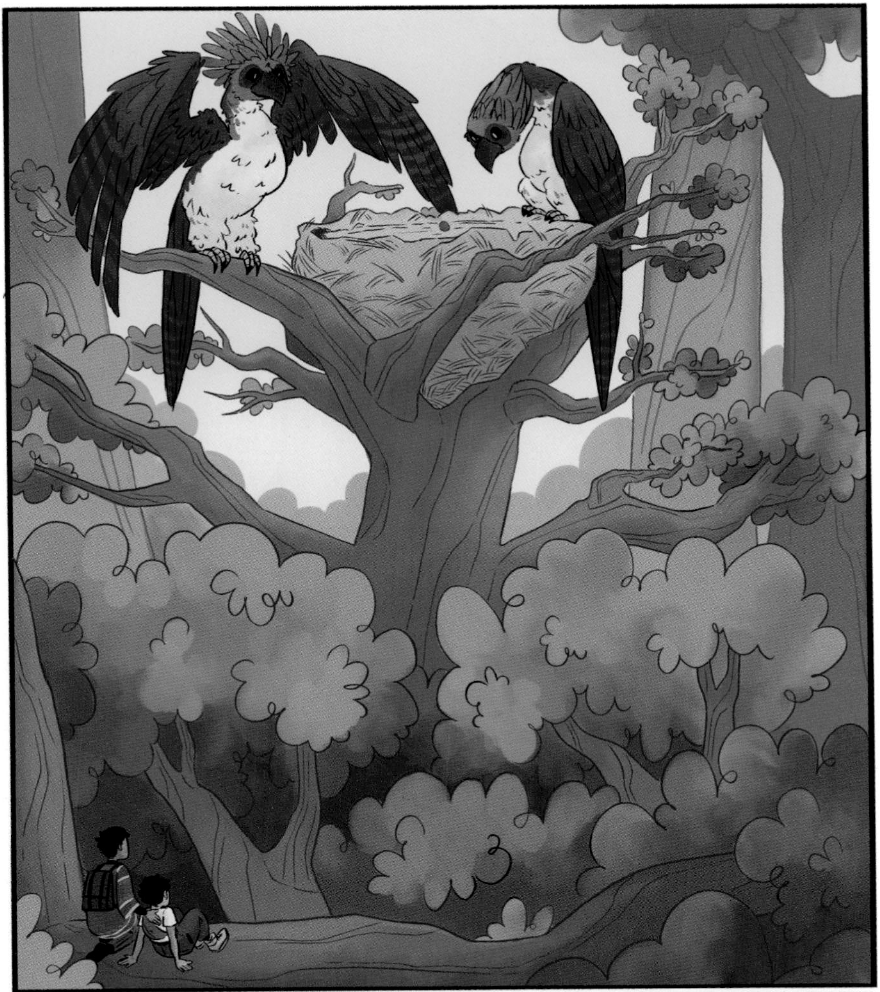

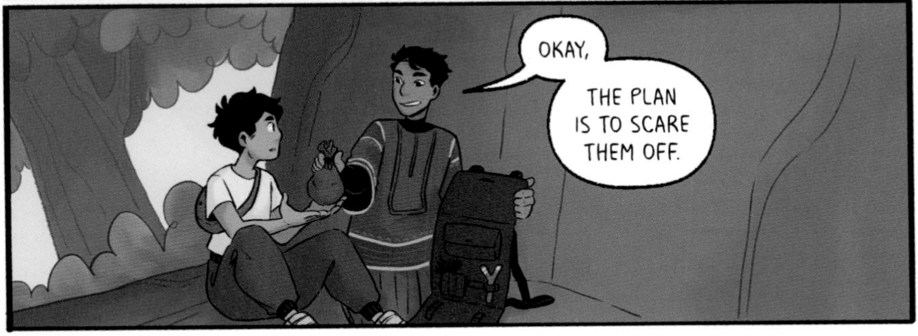
OKAY,
THE PLAN IS TO SCARE THEM OFF.

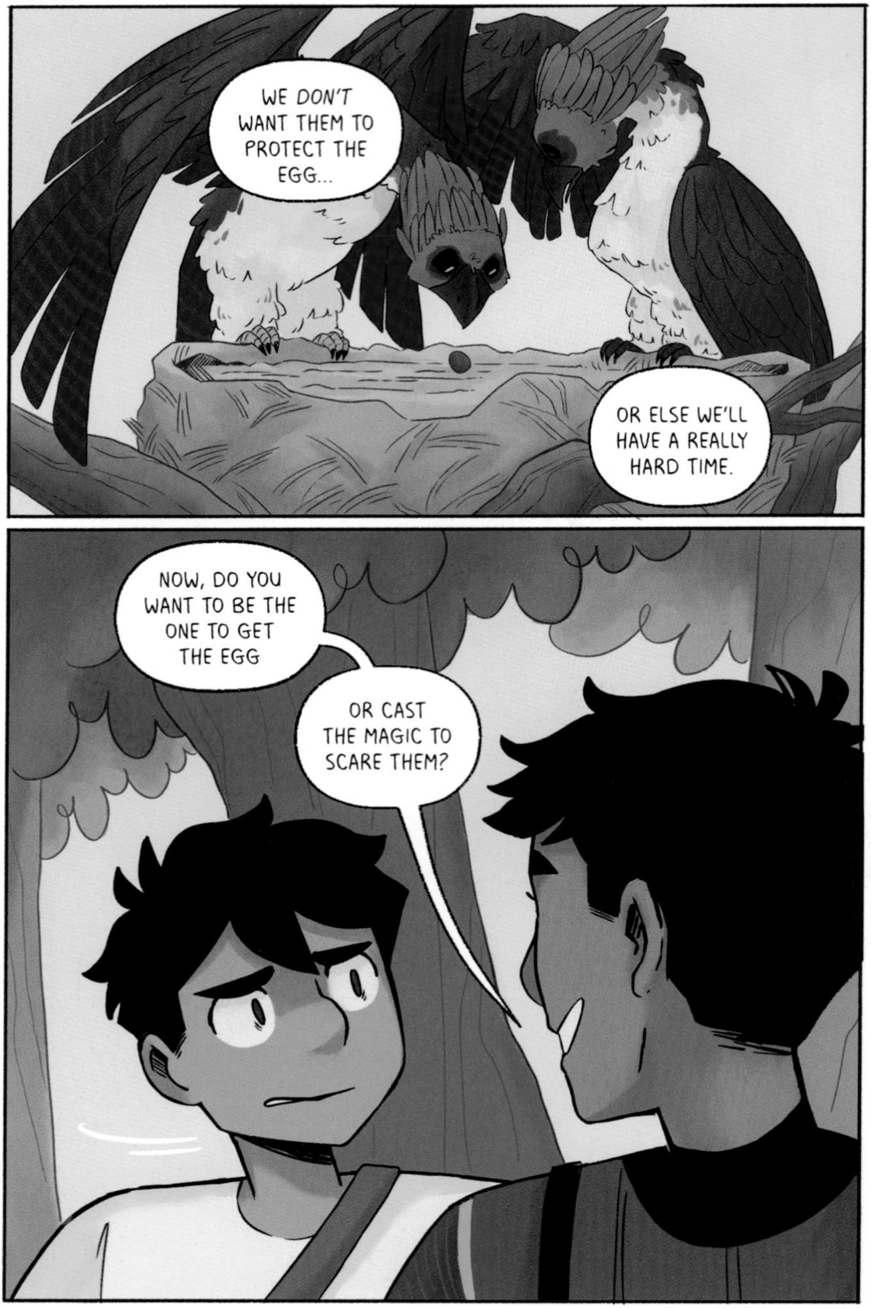
WE *DON'T* WANT THEM TO PROTECT THE EGG...
OR ELSE WE'LL HAVE A REALLY HARD TIME.
NOW, DO YOU WANT TO BE THE ONE TO GET THE EGG
OR CAST THE MAGIC TO SCARE THEM?

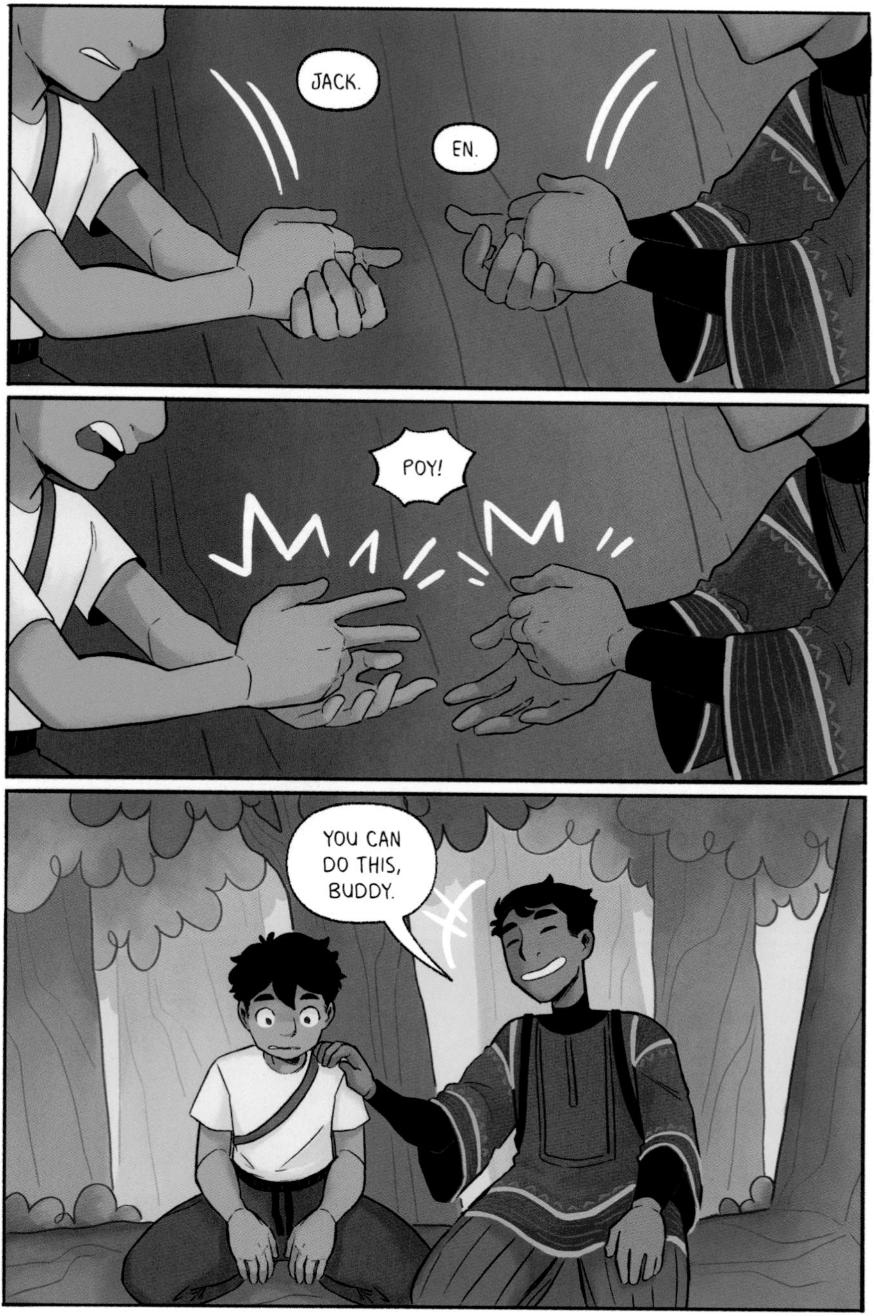
JACK.
EN.
POY!
YOU CAN DO THIS, BUDDY.

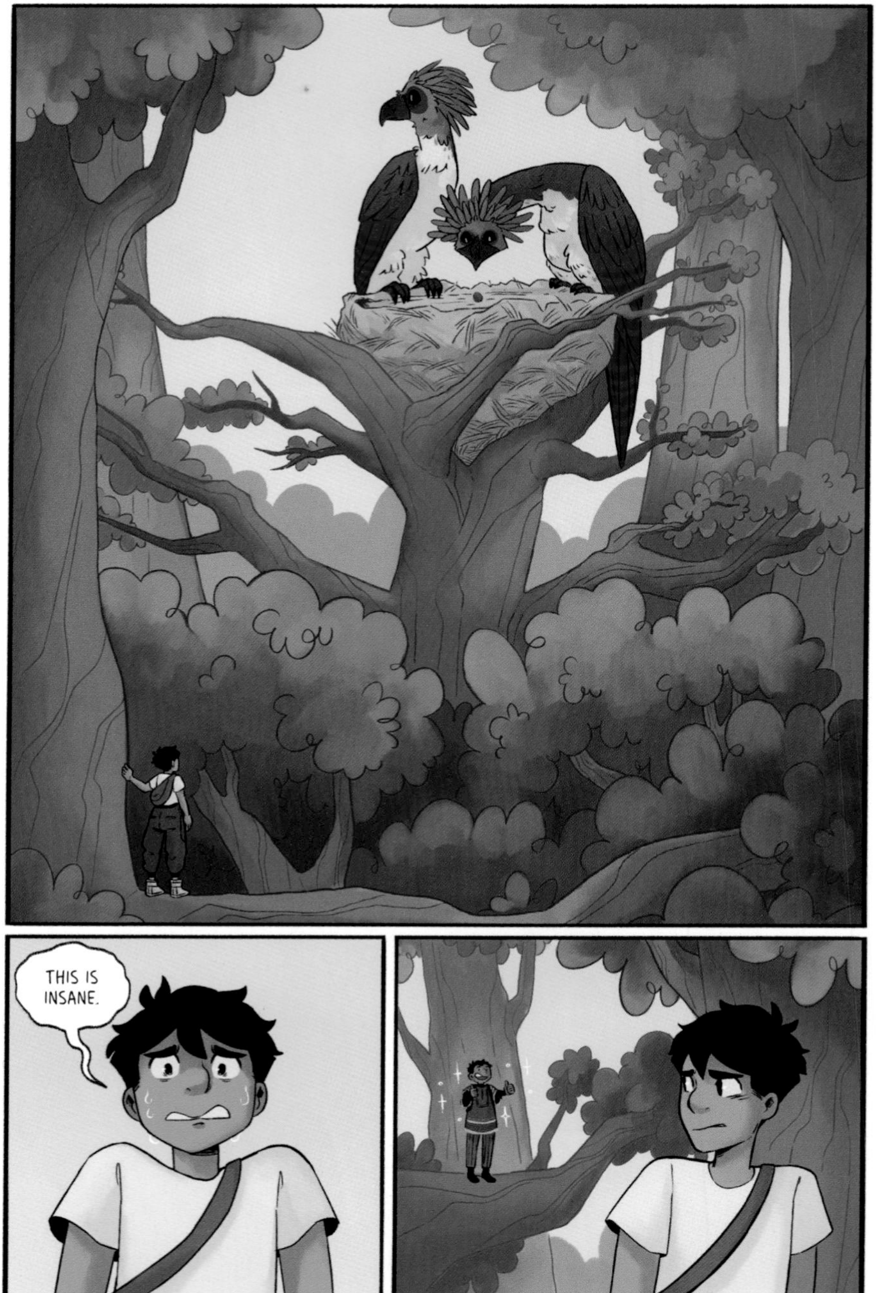
THIS IS INSANE.

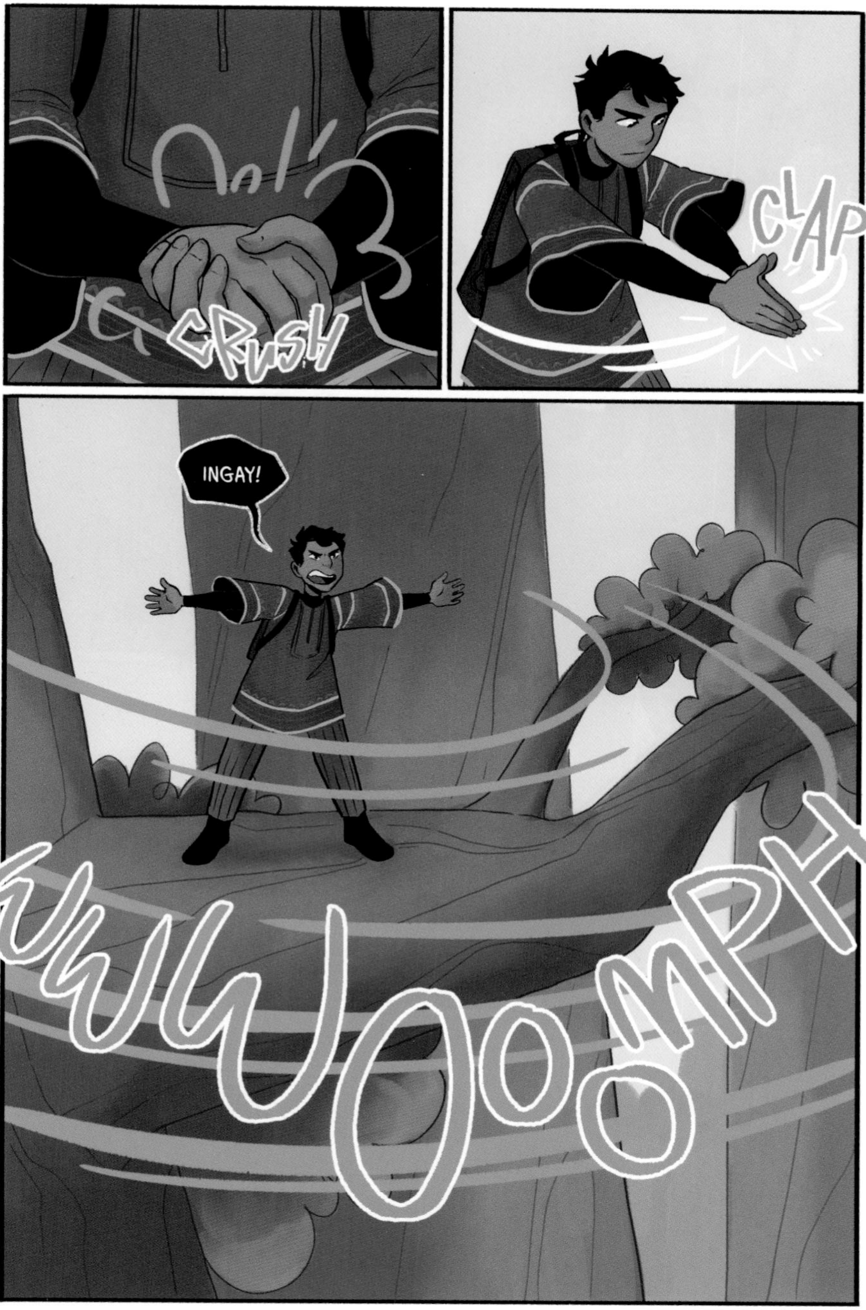
CRUSH
CLAP
INGAY!
WWWOOOMPH

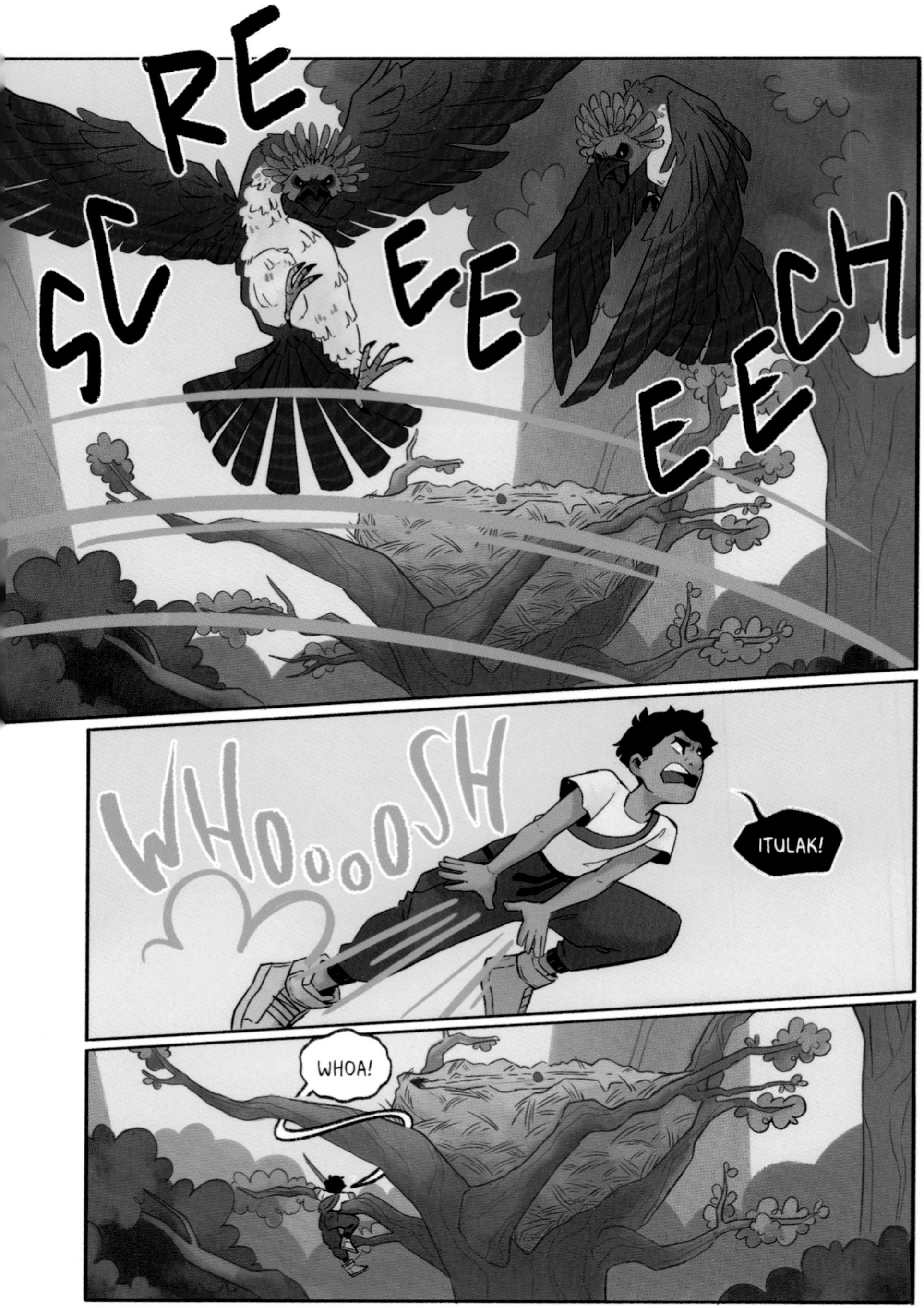
SCREEEEECH
WHOOOOSH
ITULAK!
WHOA!

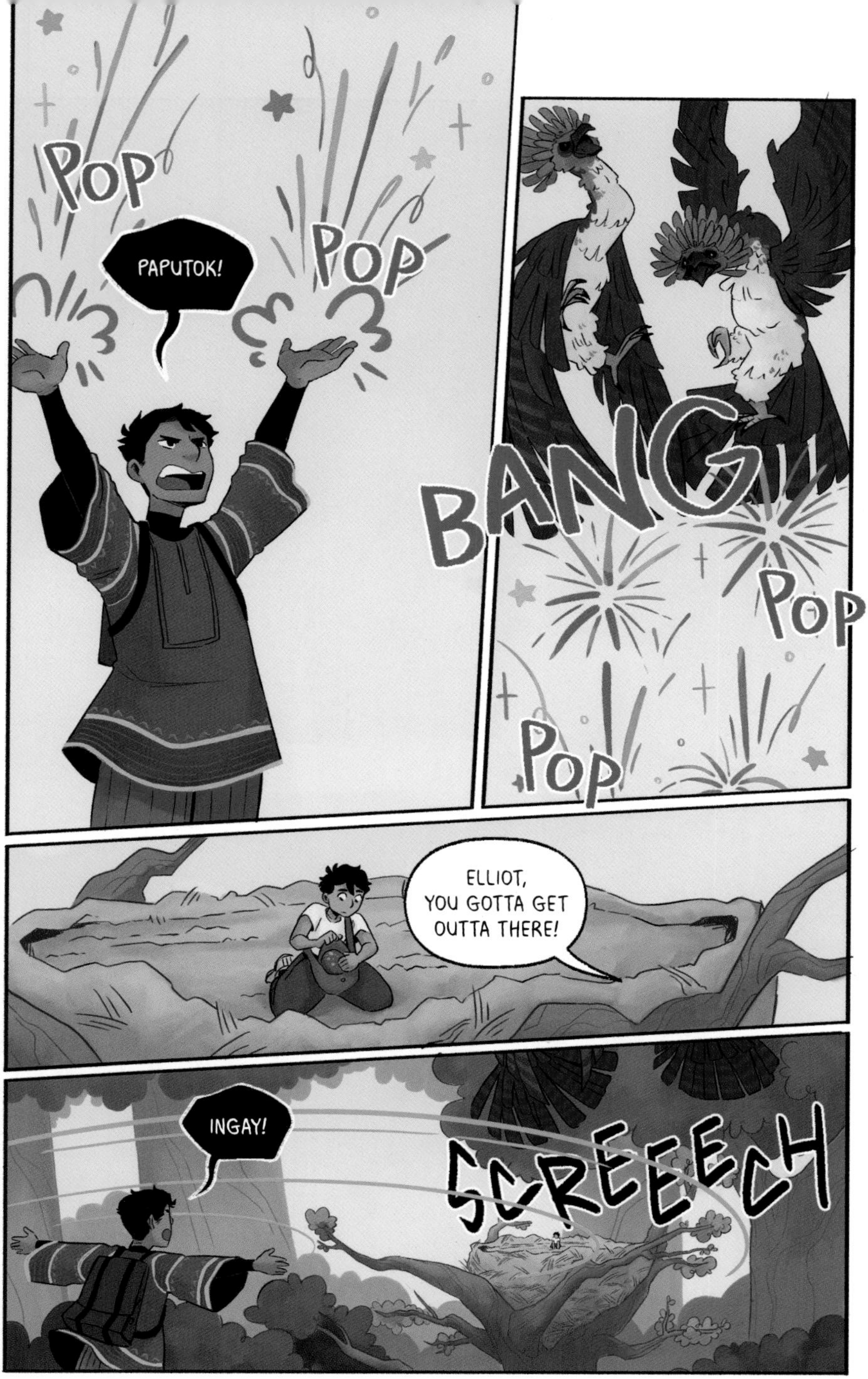
POP
PAPUTOK!
POP
BANG
POP
POP
ELLIOT, YOU GOTTA GET OUTTA THERE!
INGAY!
SCREEECH

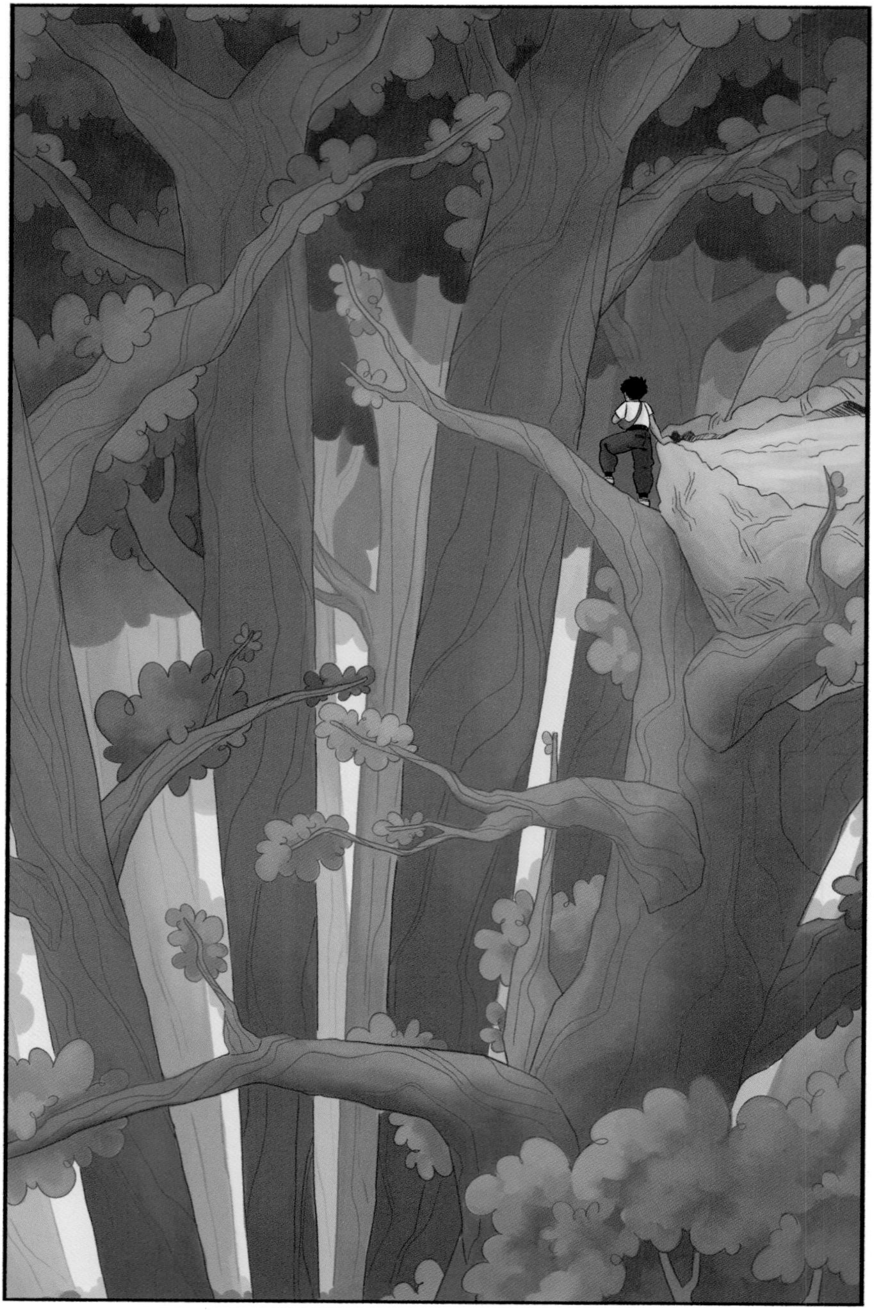

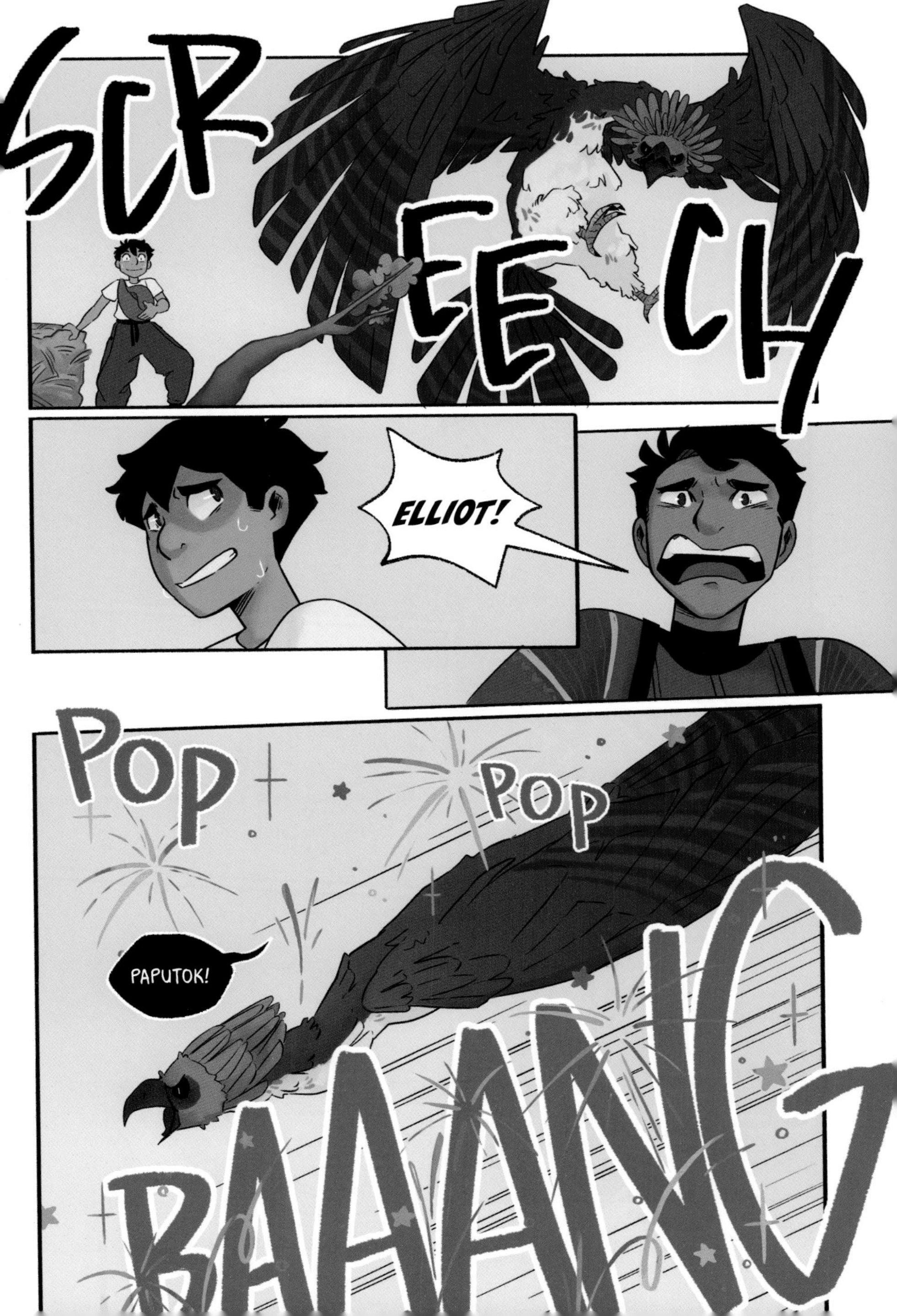
SCREECH
ELLIOT!
POP
POP
PAPUTOK!
BAAANG

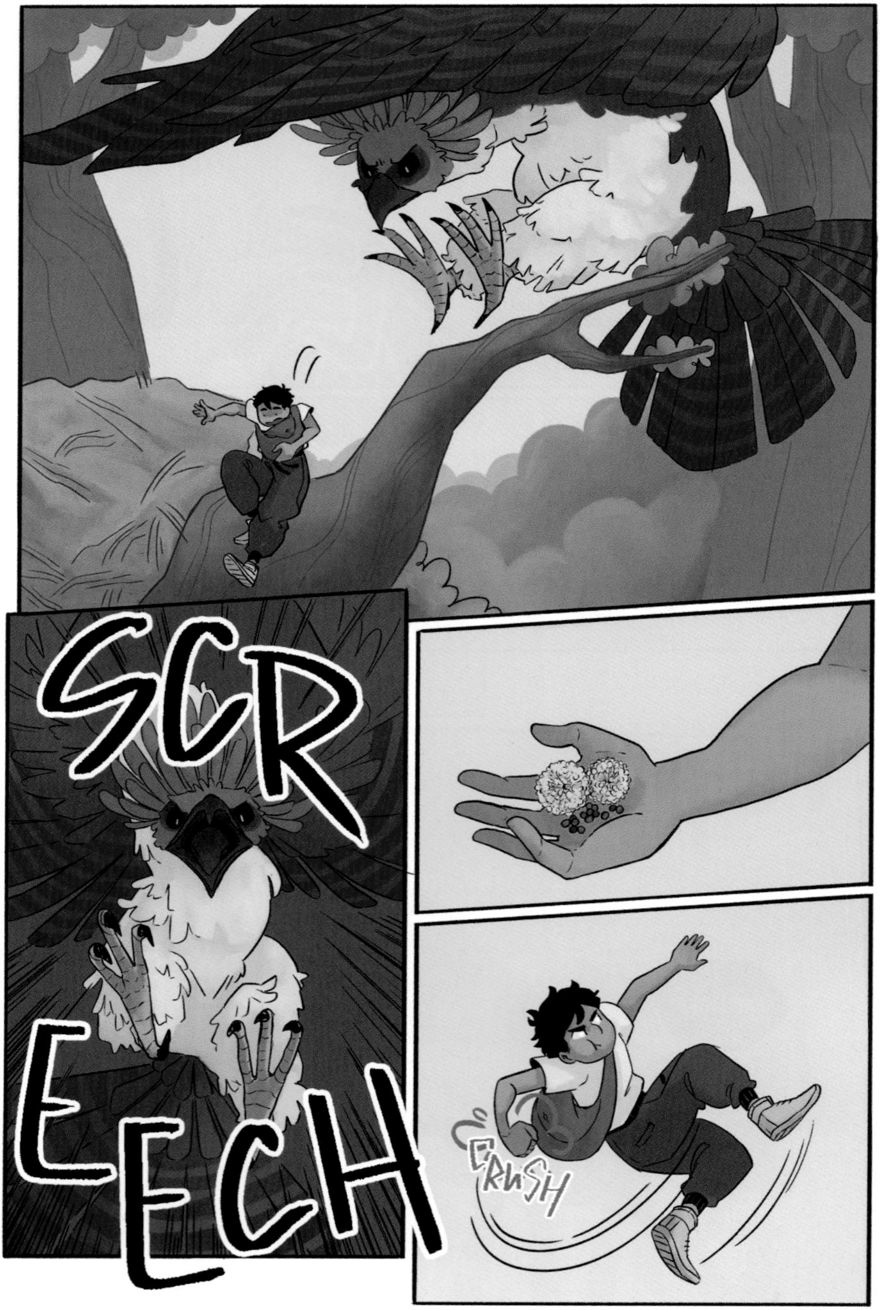
SCR
EECH
CRUSH

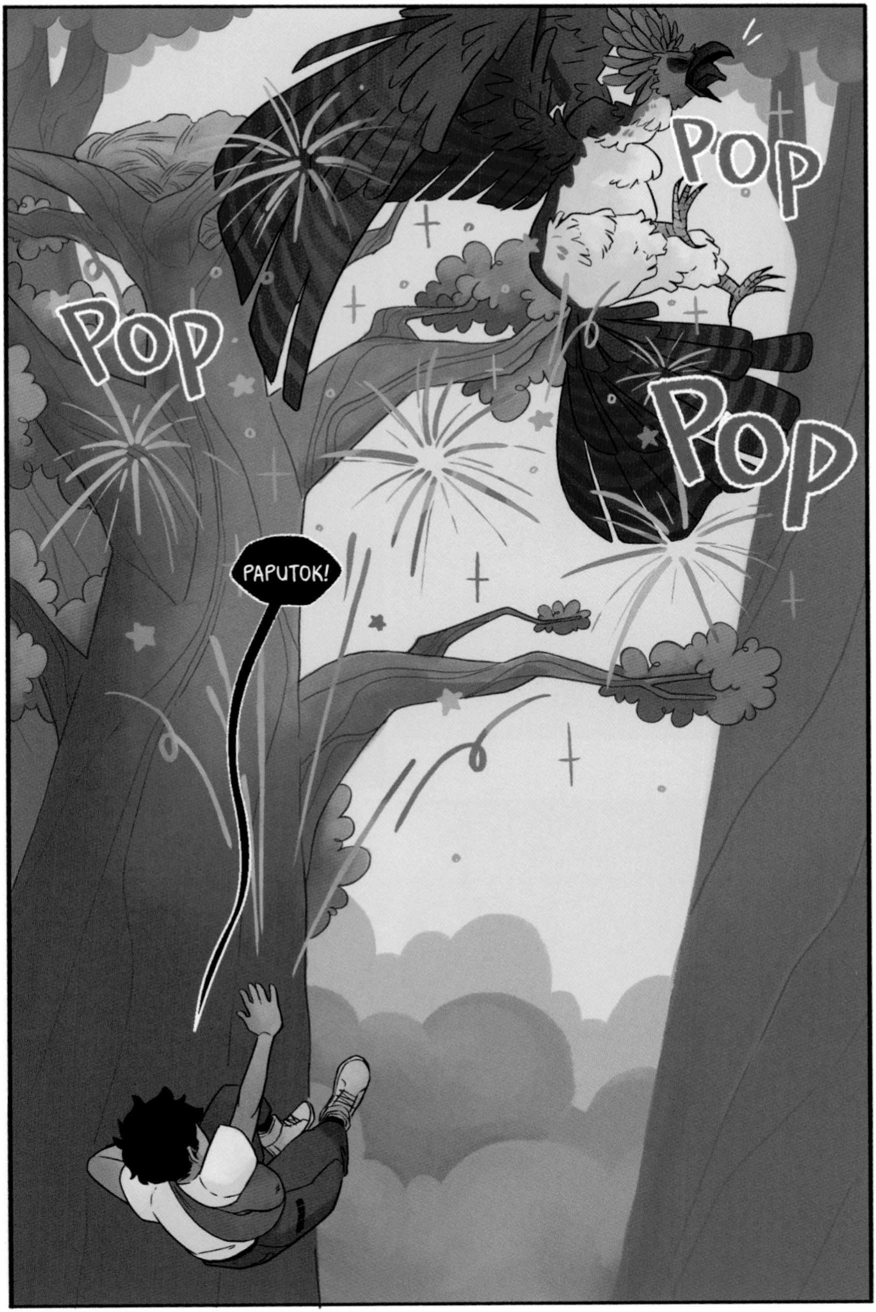
POP
POP
POP
PAPUTOK!

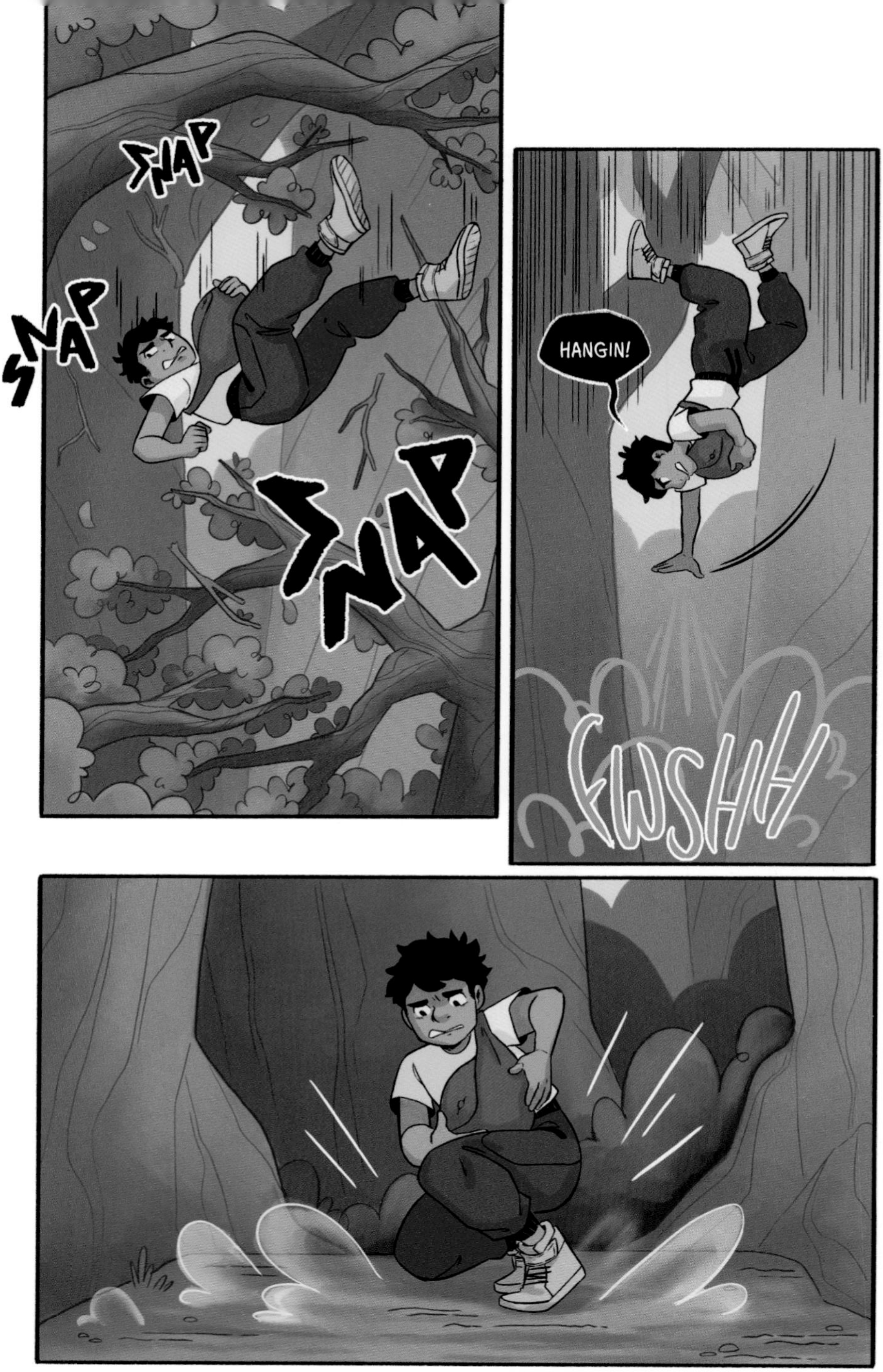
SNAP
SNAP
SNAP
HANGIN!
FWSHH

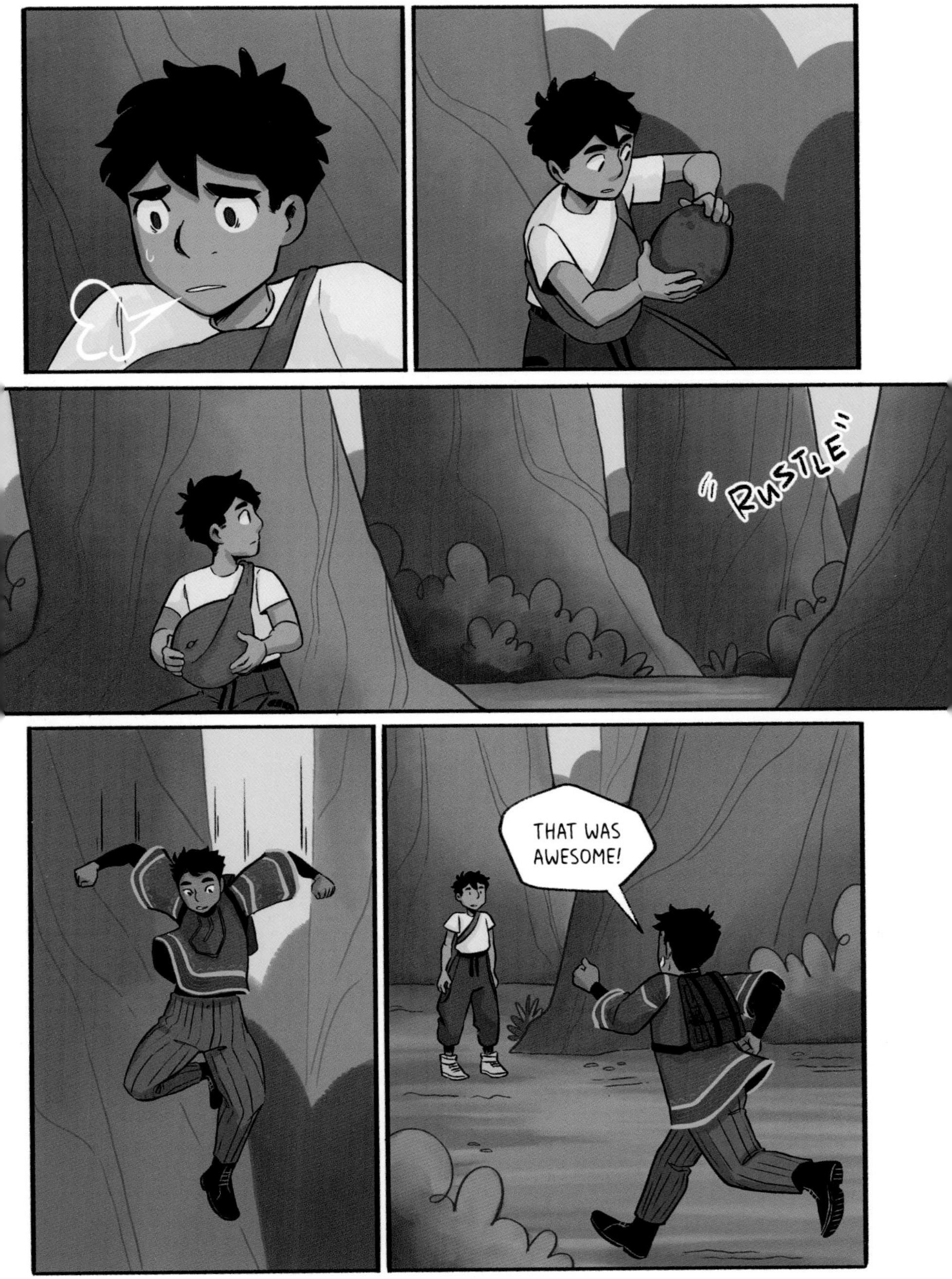
RUSTLE
THAT WAS AWESOME!

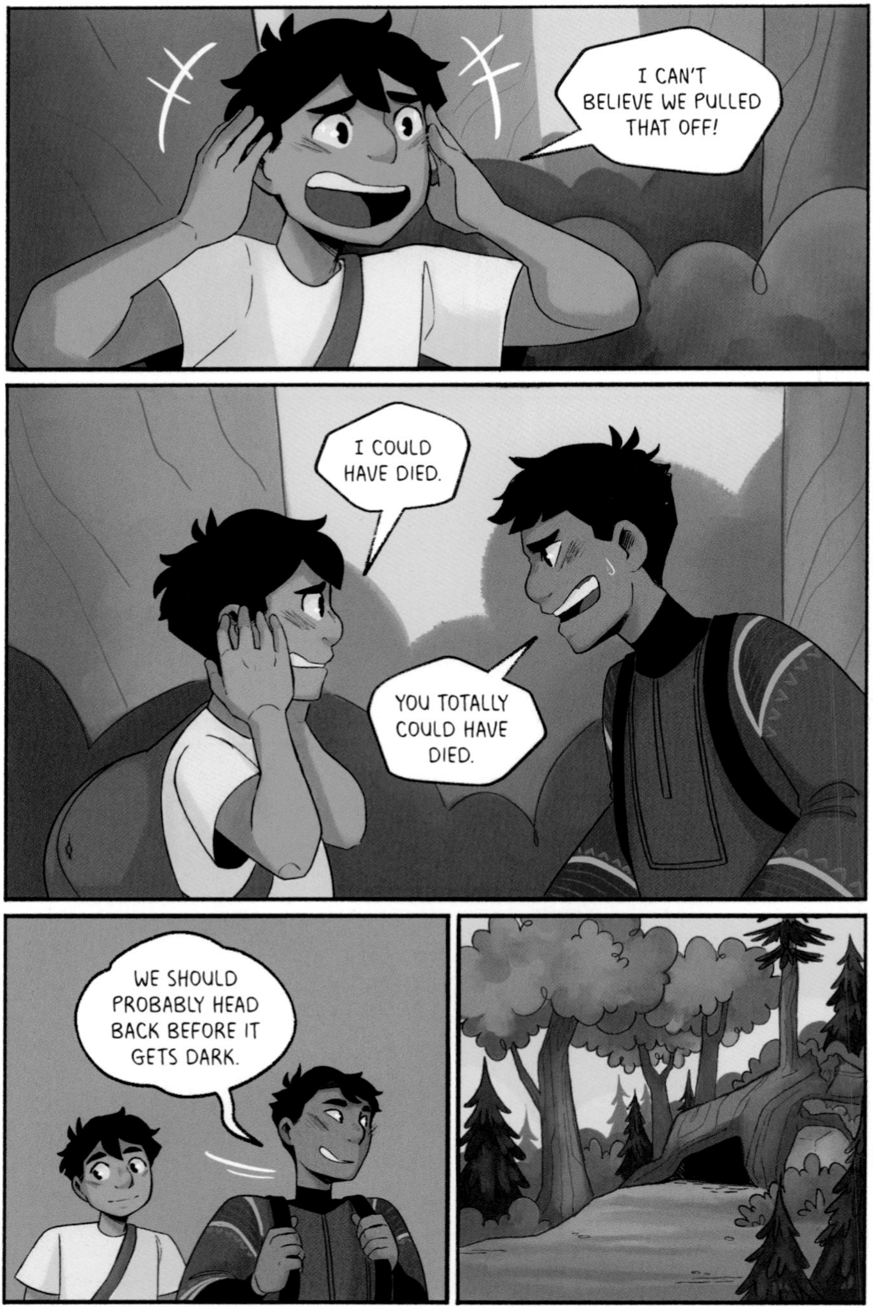
I CAN'T BELIEVE WE PULLED THAT OFF!
I COULD HAVE DIED.
YOU TOTALLY COULD HAVE DIED.
WE SHOULD PROBABLY HEAD BACK BEFORE IT GETS DARK.

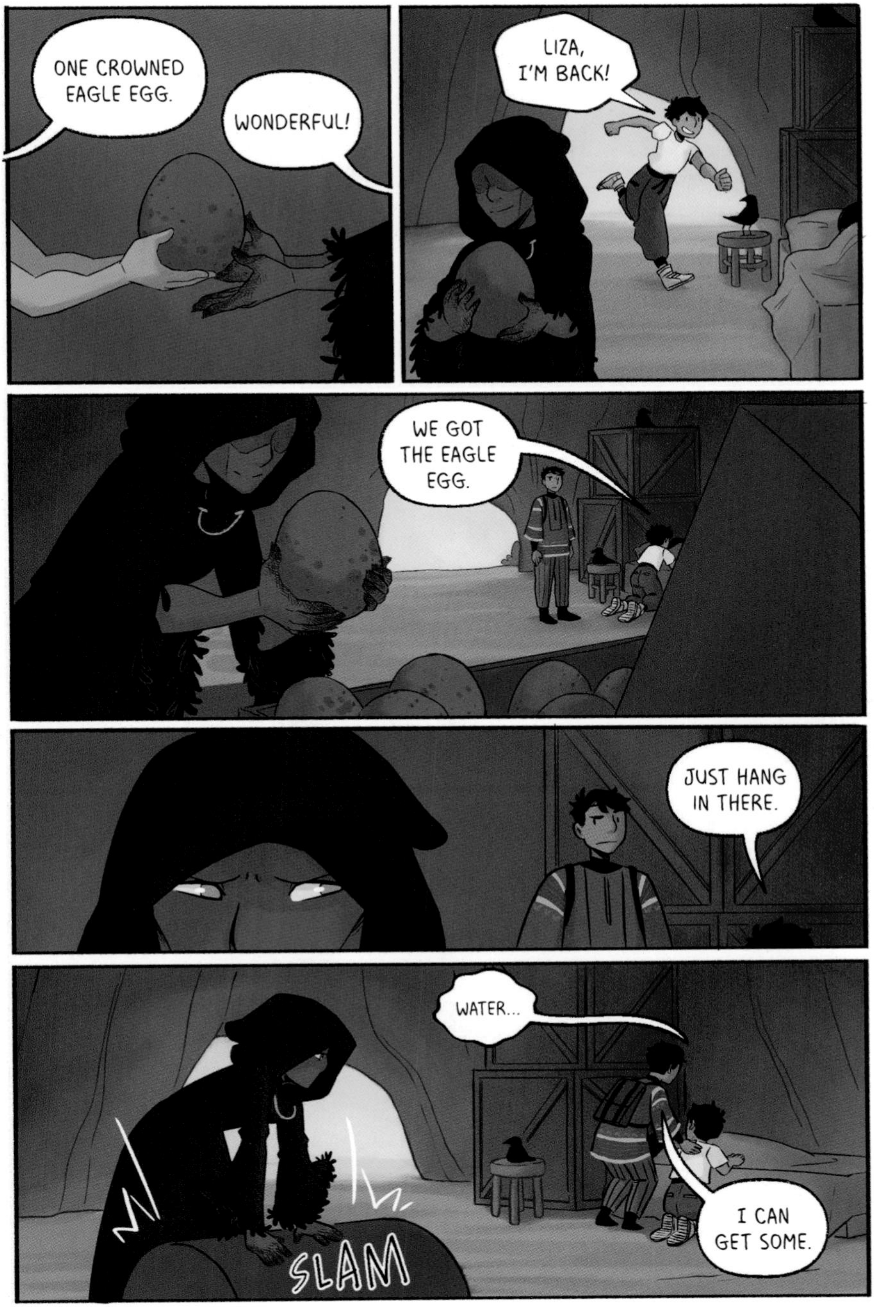
ONE CROWNED EAGLE EGG.
WONDERFUL!
LIZA, I'M BACK!
WE GOT THE EAGLE EGG.
JUST HANG IN THERE.
WATER...
I CAN GET SOME.
SLAM

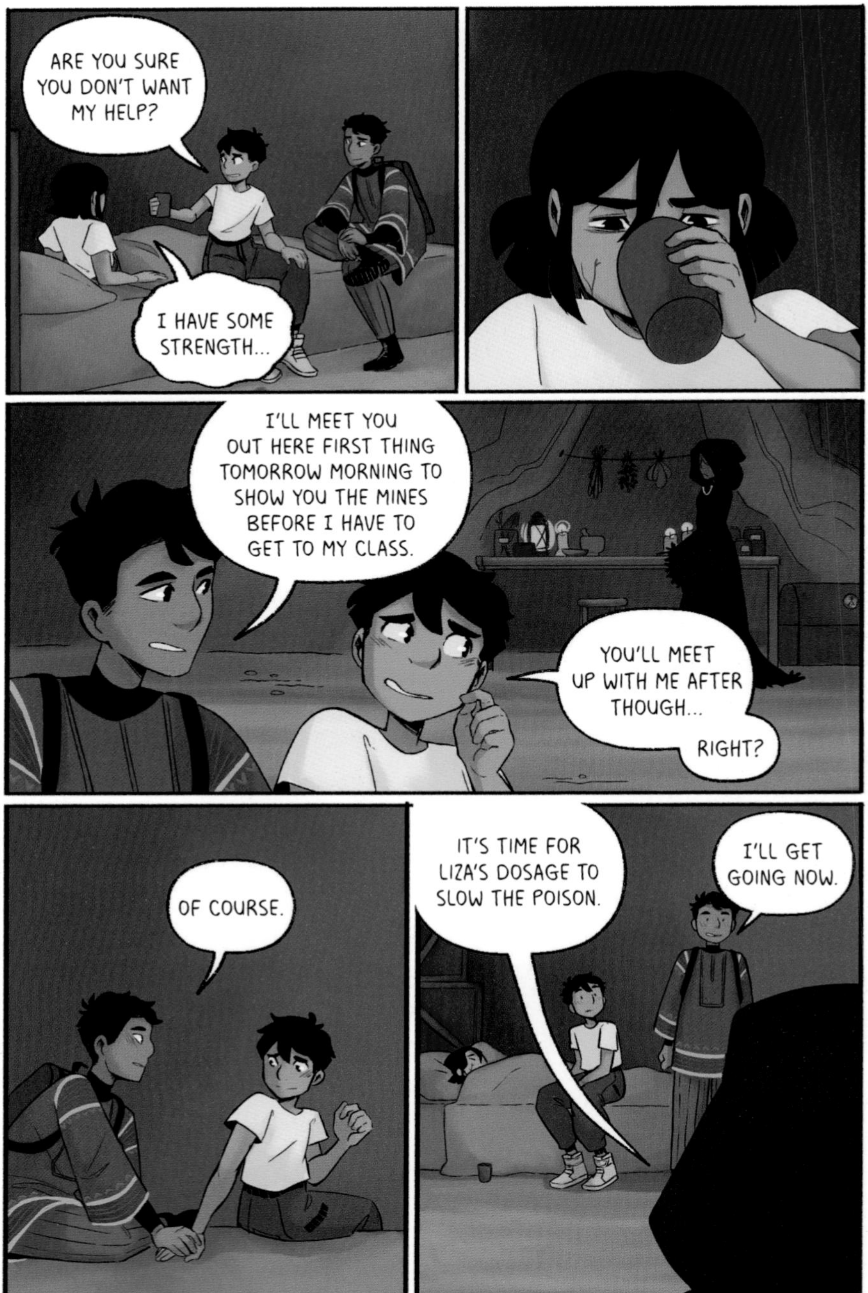
ARE YOU SURE YOU DON'T WANT MY HELP?
I HAVE SOME STRENGTH...
I'LL MEET YOU OUT HERE FIRST THING TOMORROW MORNING TO SHOW YOU THE MINES BEFORE I HAVE TO GET TO MY CLASS.
YOU'LL MEET UP WITH ME AFTER THOUGH...
RIGHT?
OF COURSE.
IT'S TIME FOR LIZA'S DOSAGE TO SLOW THE POISON.
I'LL GET GOING NOW.

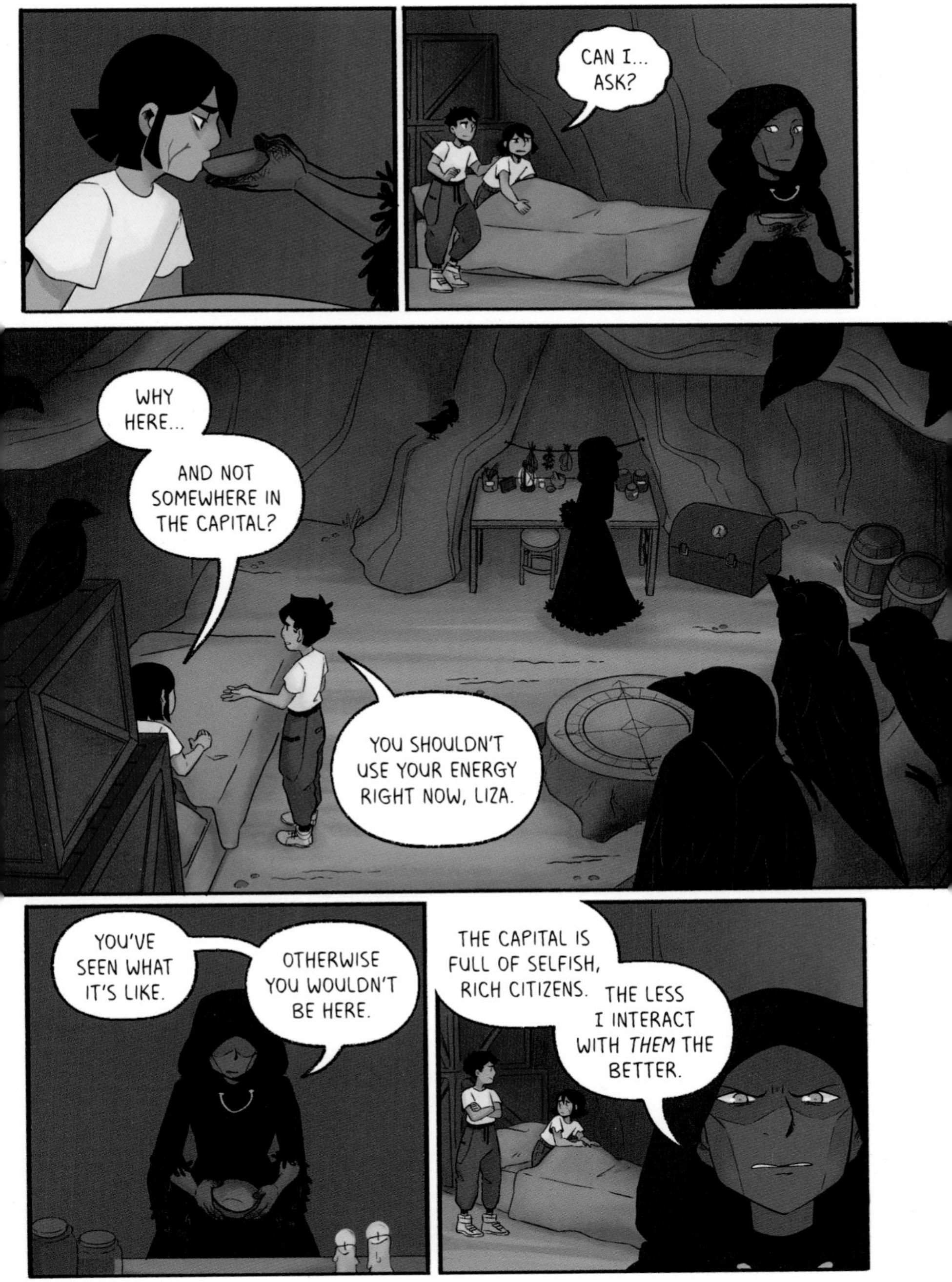
CAN I... ASK?
WHY HERE...
AND NOT SOMEWHERE IN THE CAPITAL?
YOU SHOULDN'T USE YOUR ENERGY RIGHT NOW, LIZA.
YOU'VE SEEN WHAT IT'S LIKE.
OTHERWISE YOU WOULDN'T BE HERE.
THE CAPITAL IS FULL OF SELFISH, RICH CITIZENS.
THE LESS I INTERACT WITH *THEM* THE BETTER.

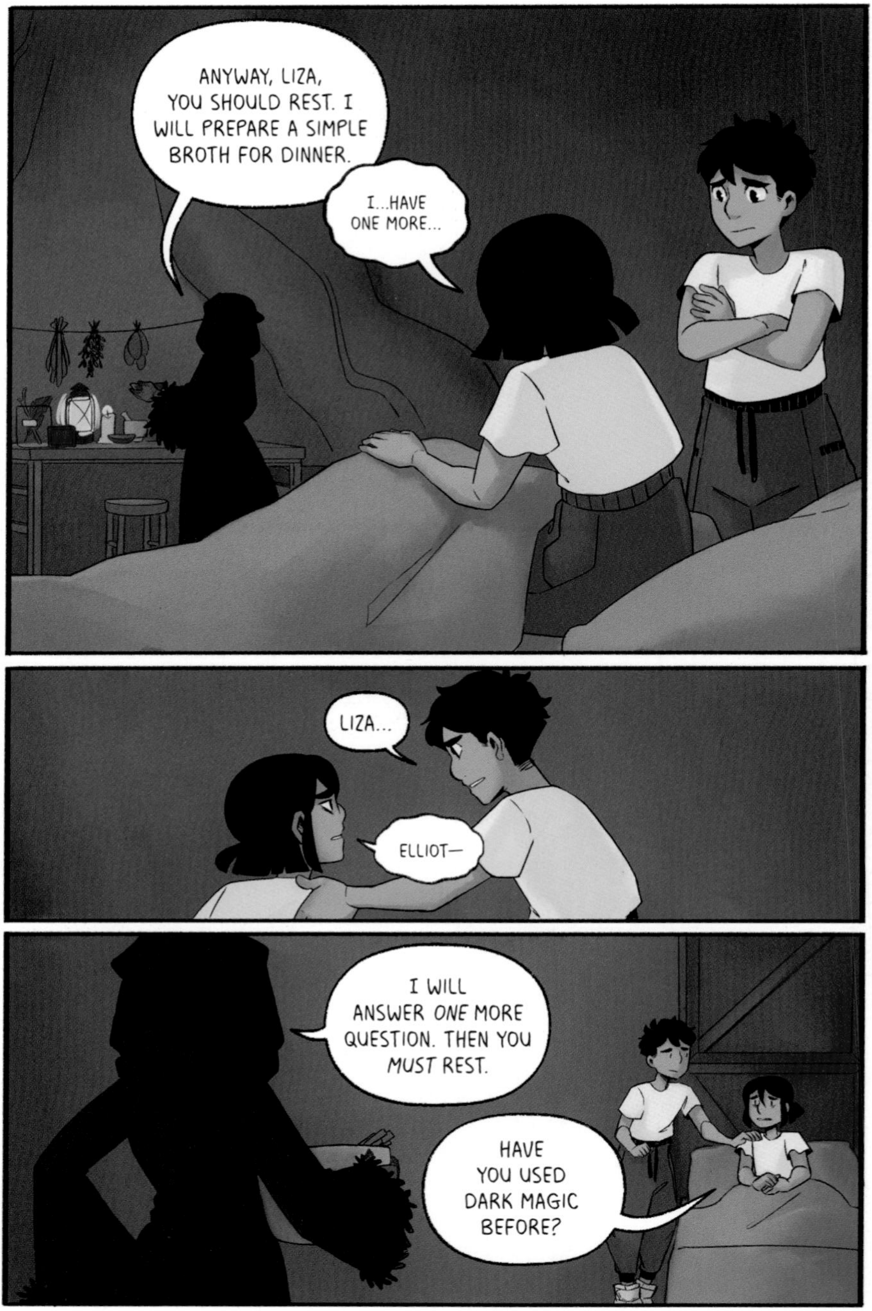
ANYWAY, LIZA, YOU SHOULD REST. I WILL PREPARE A SIMPLE BROTH FOR DINNER.
I...HAVE ONE MORE...
LIZA...
ELLIOT—
I WILL ANSWER *ONE* MORE QUESTION. THEN YOU *MUST* REST.
HAVE YOU USED DARK MAGIC BEFORE?

IS...IS THAT WHY YOUR HANDS LOOK LIKE THAT?

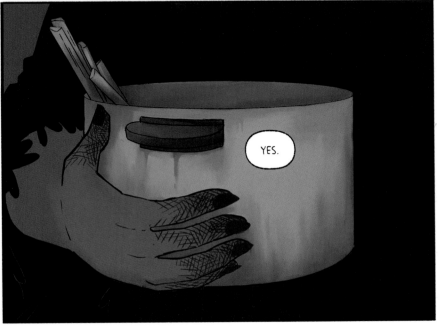

YES.

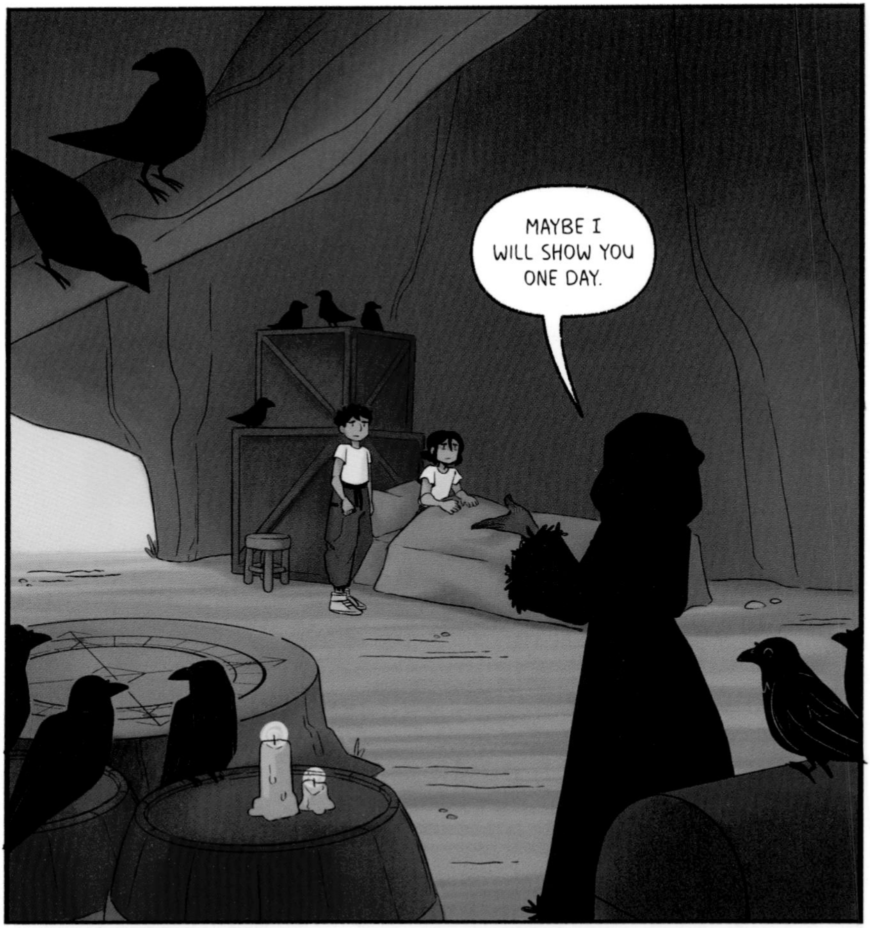
MAYBE I WILL SHOW YOU ONE DAY.

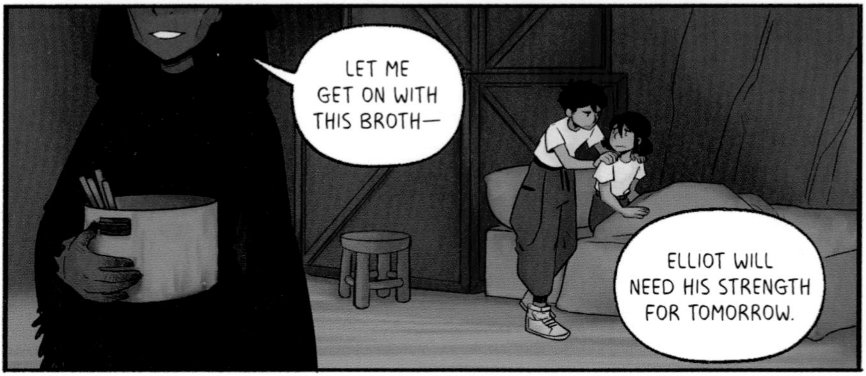
LET ME GET ON WITH THIS BROTH—
ELLIOT WILL NEED HIS STRENGTH FOR TOMORROW.

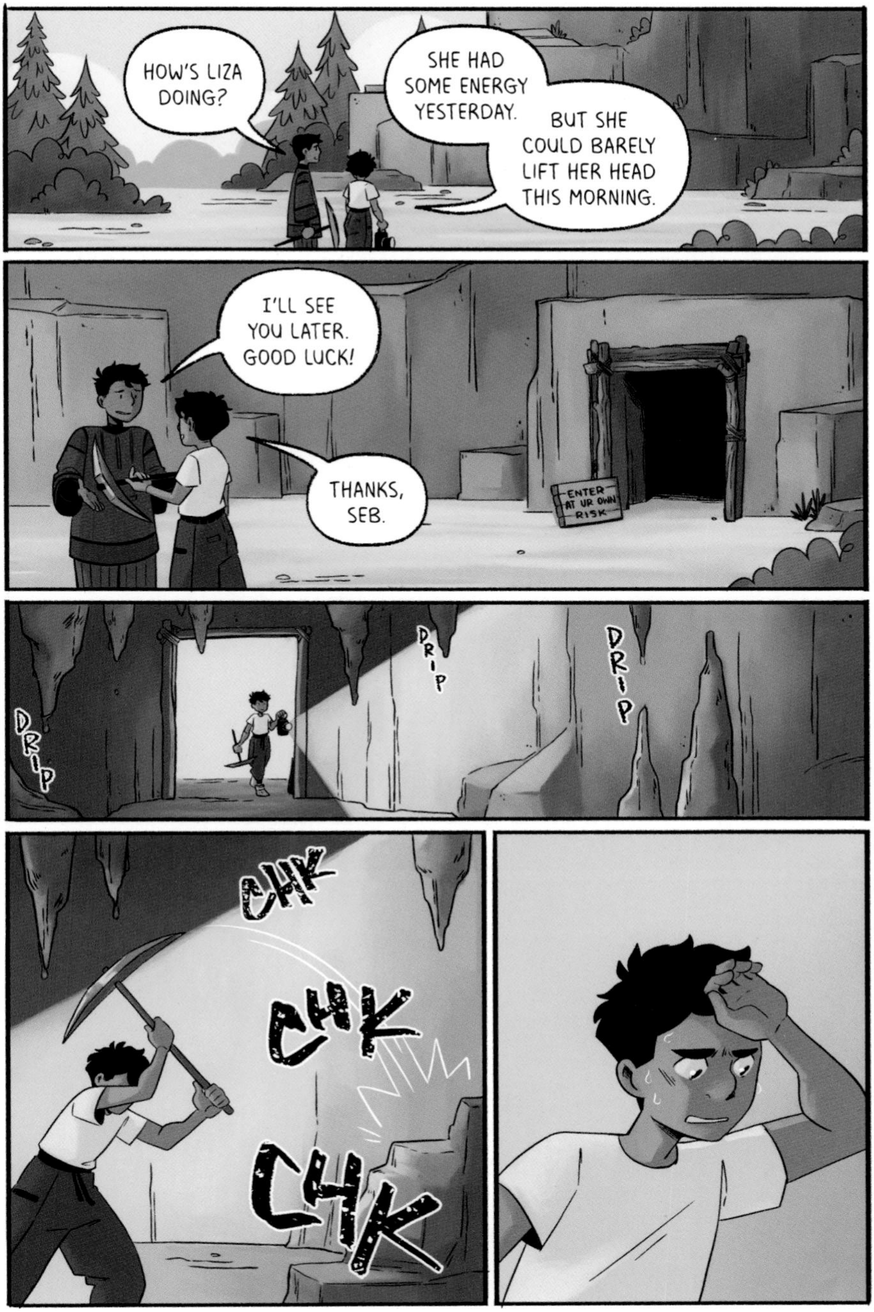
HOW'S LIZA DOING?
SHE HAD SOME ENERGY YESTERDAY.
BUT SHE COULD BARELY LIFT HER HEAD THIS MORNING.
I'LL SEE YOU LATER. GOOD LUCK!
THANKS, SEB.
ENTER AT UR OWN RISK
DRIP
DRIP
DRIP
CHK
CHK
CHK

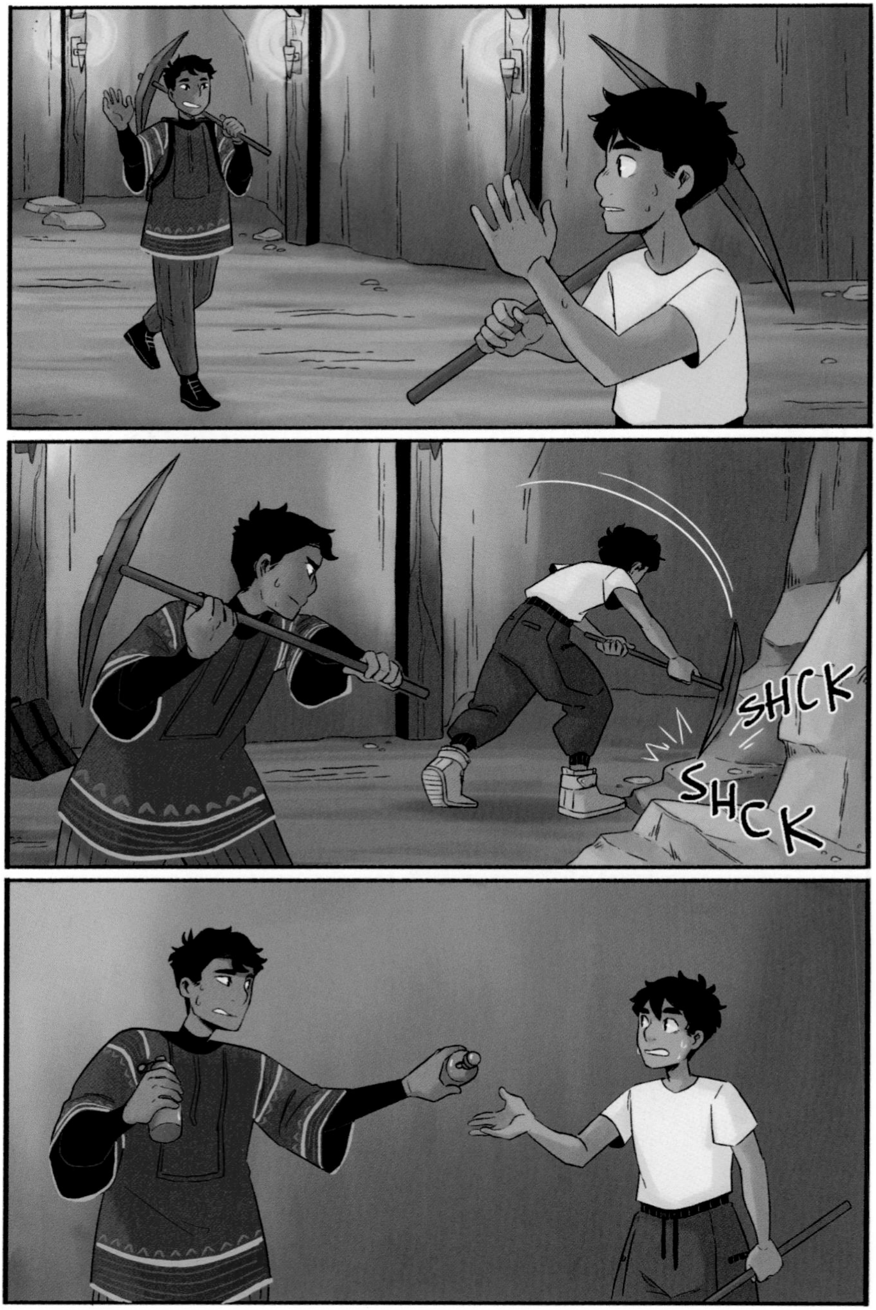
SHCK
SHCK

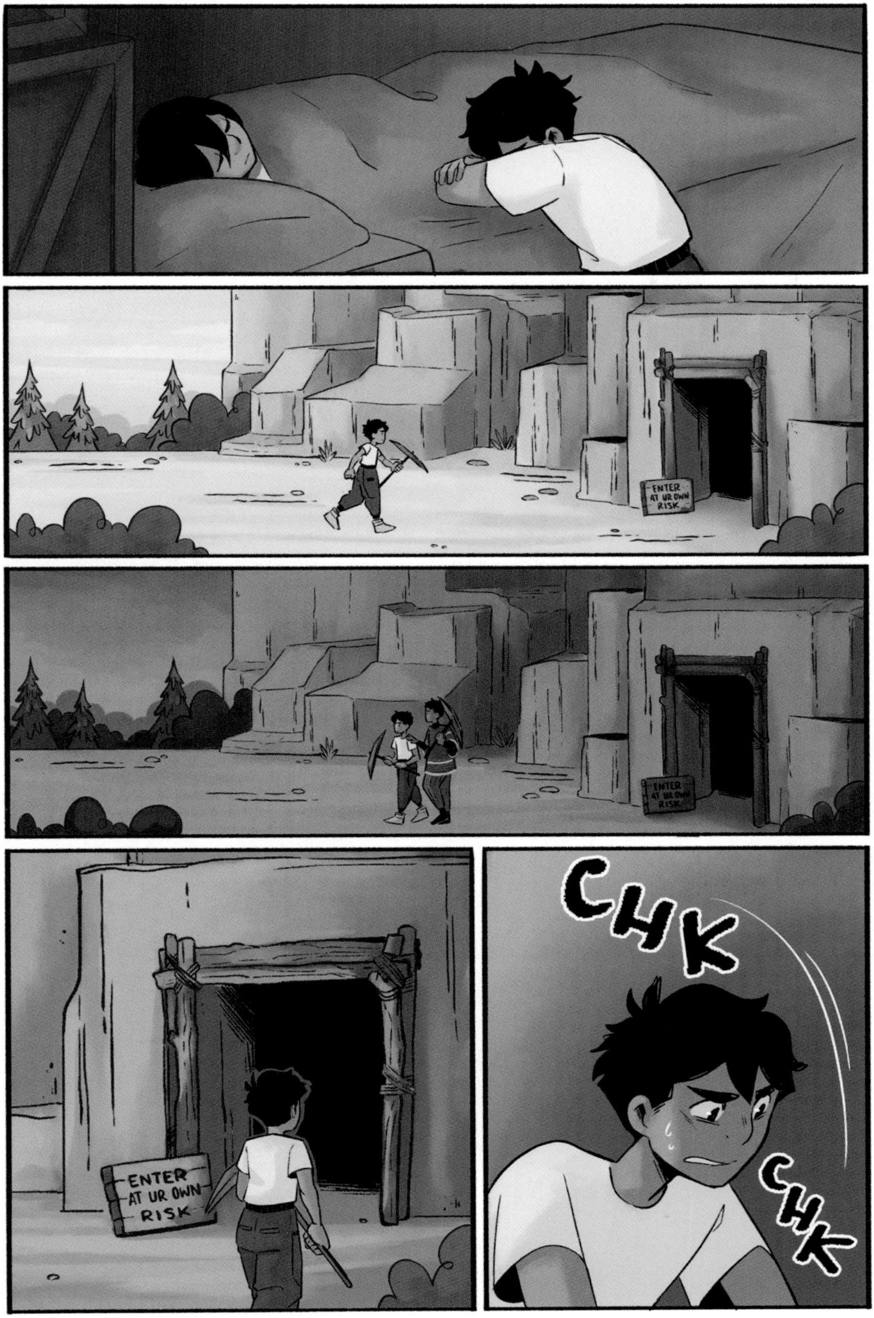
ENTER AT UR OWN RISK
ENTER AT UR OWN RISK
ENTER AT UR OWN RISK
CHK
CHK

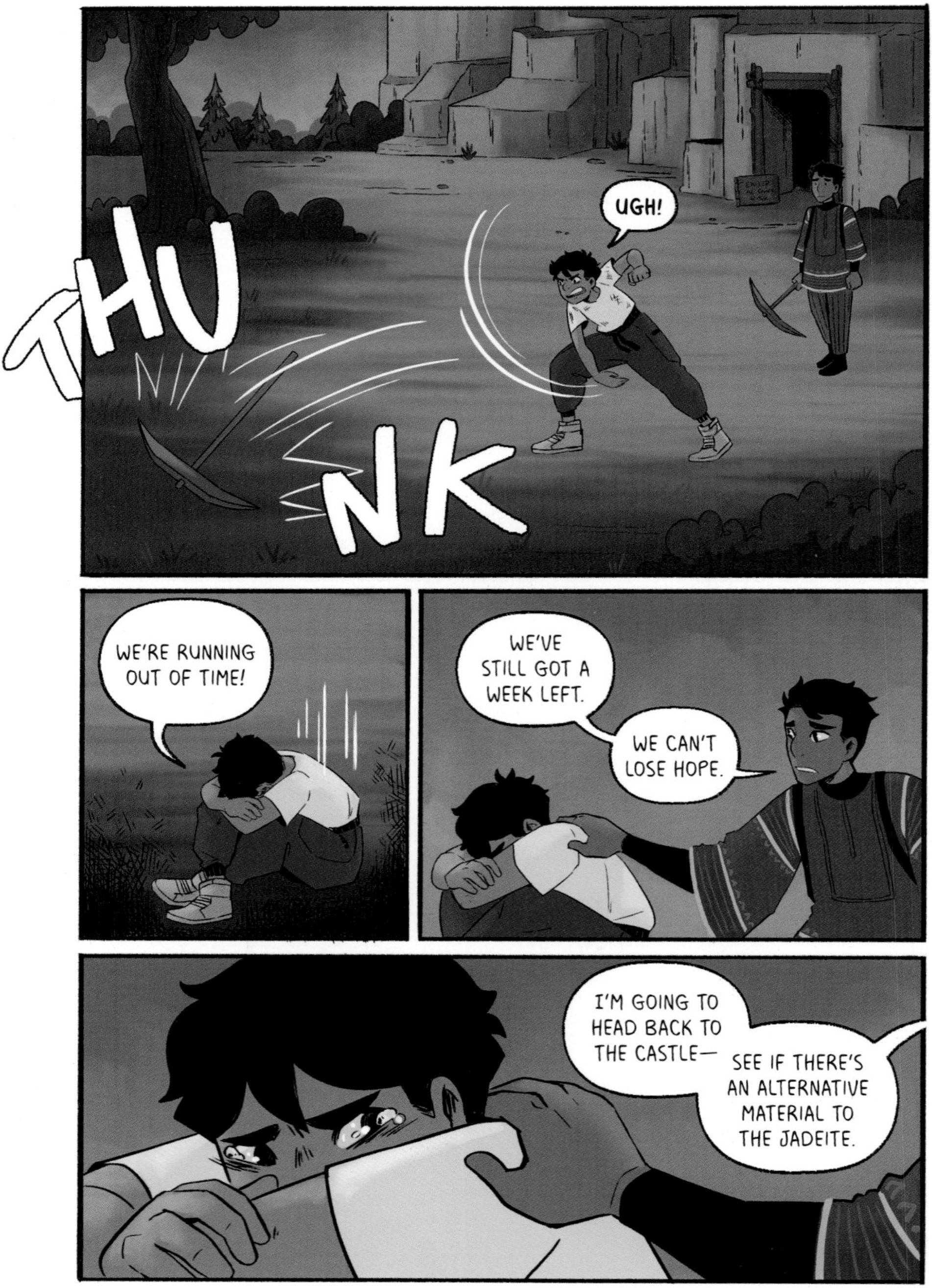
UGH!
THU
NK
WE'RE RUNNING OUT OF TIME!
WE'VE STILL GOT A WEEK LEFT.
WE CAN'T LOSE HOPE.
I'M GOING TO HEAD BACK TO THE CASTLE—
SEE IF THERE'S AN ALTERNATIVE MATERIAL TO THE JADEITE.

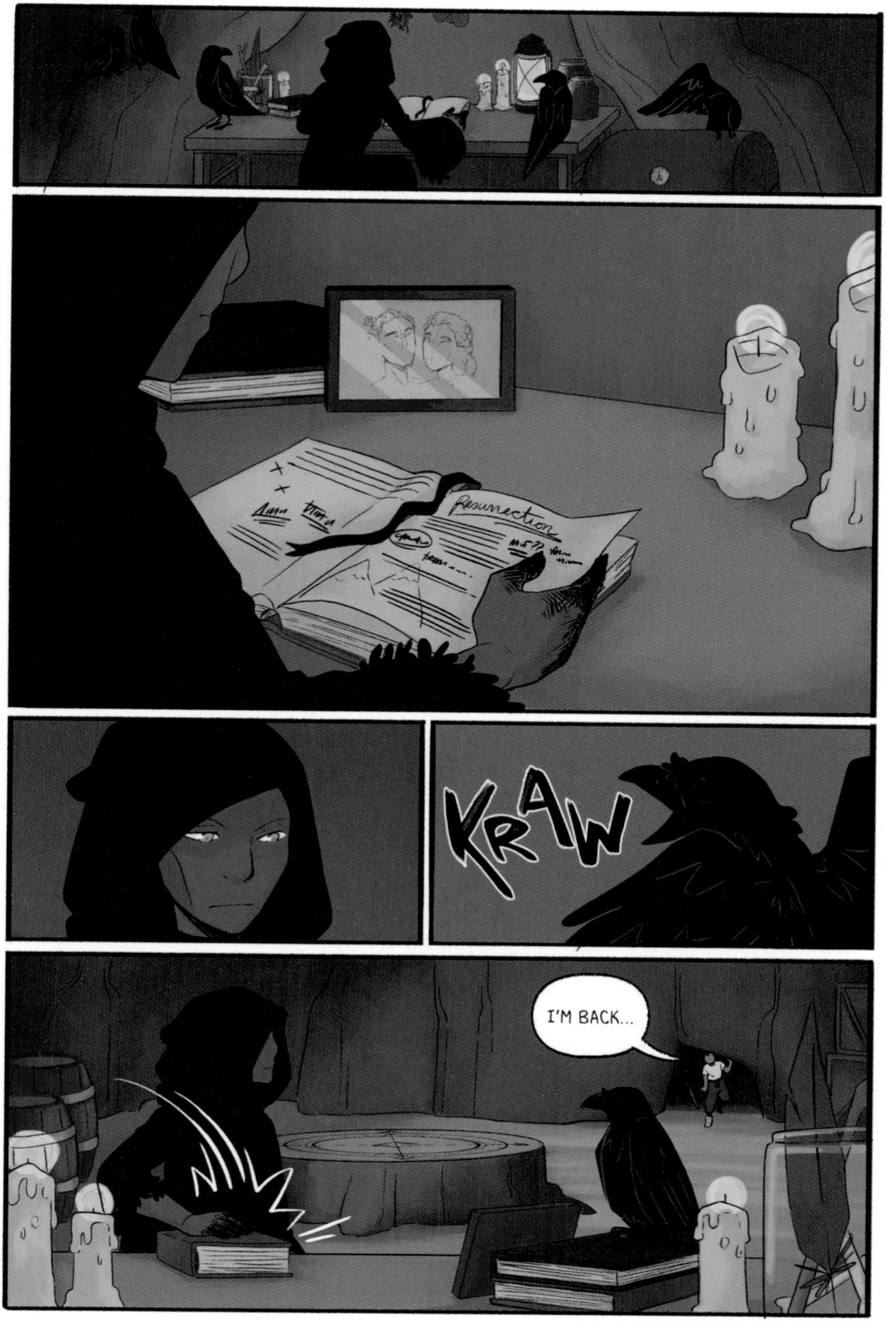
Resurrection
KRAW
I'M BACK...

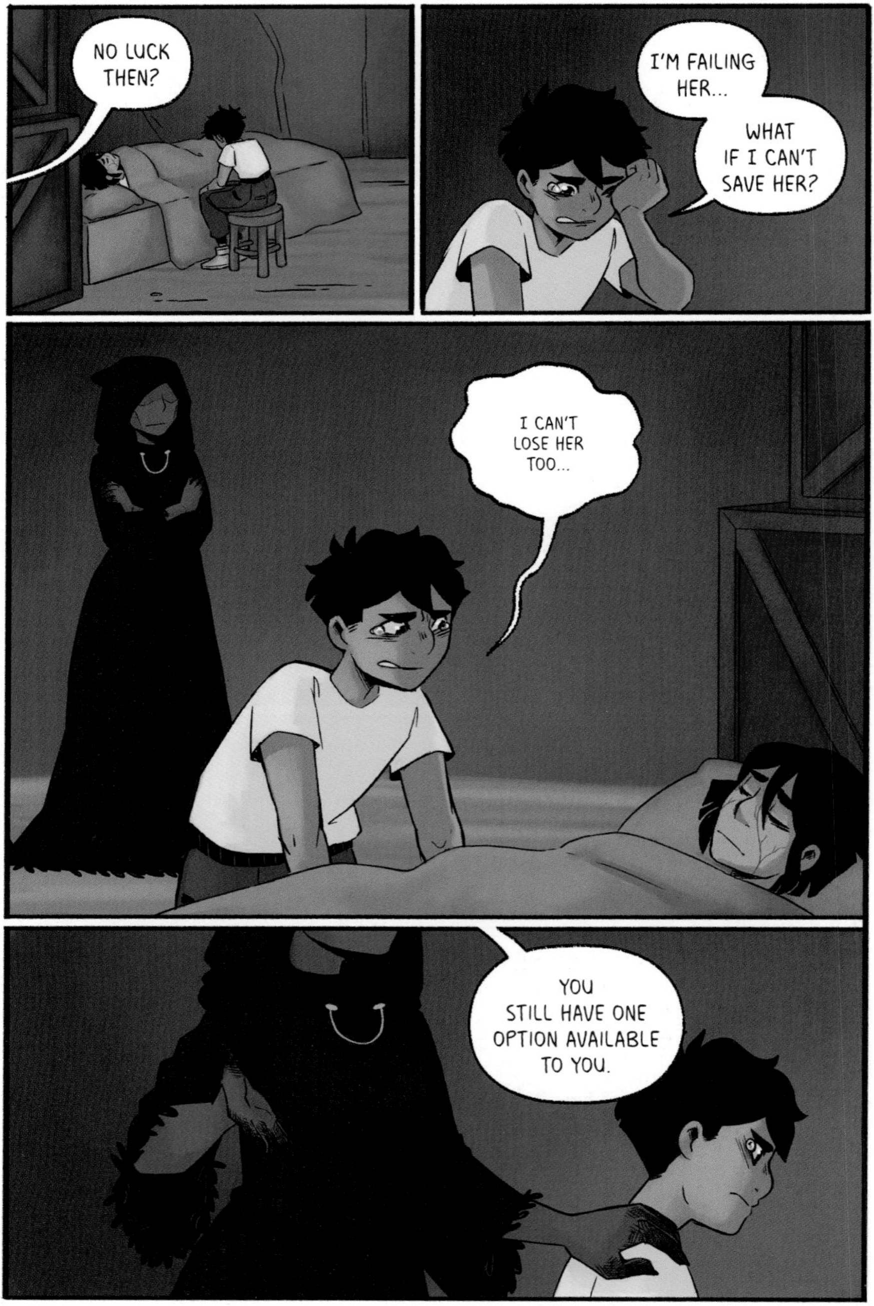
NO LUCK THEN?
I'M FAILING HER...
WHAT IF I CAN'T SAVE HER?
I CAN'T LOSE HER TOO...
YOU STILL HAVE ONE OPTION AVAILABLE TO YOU.

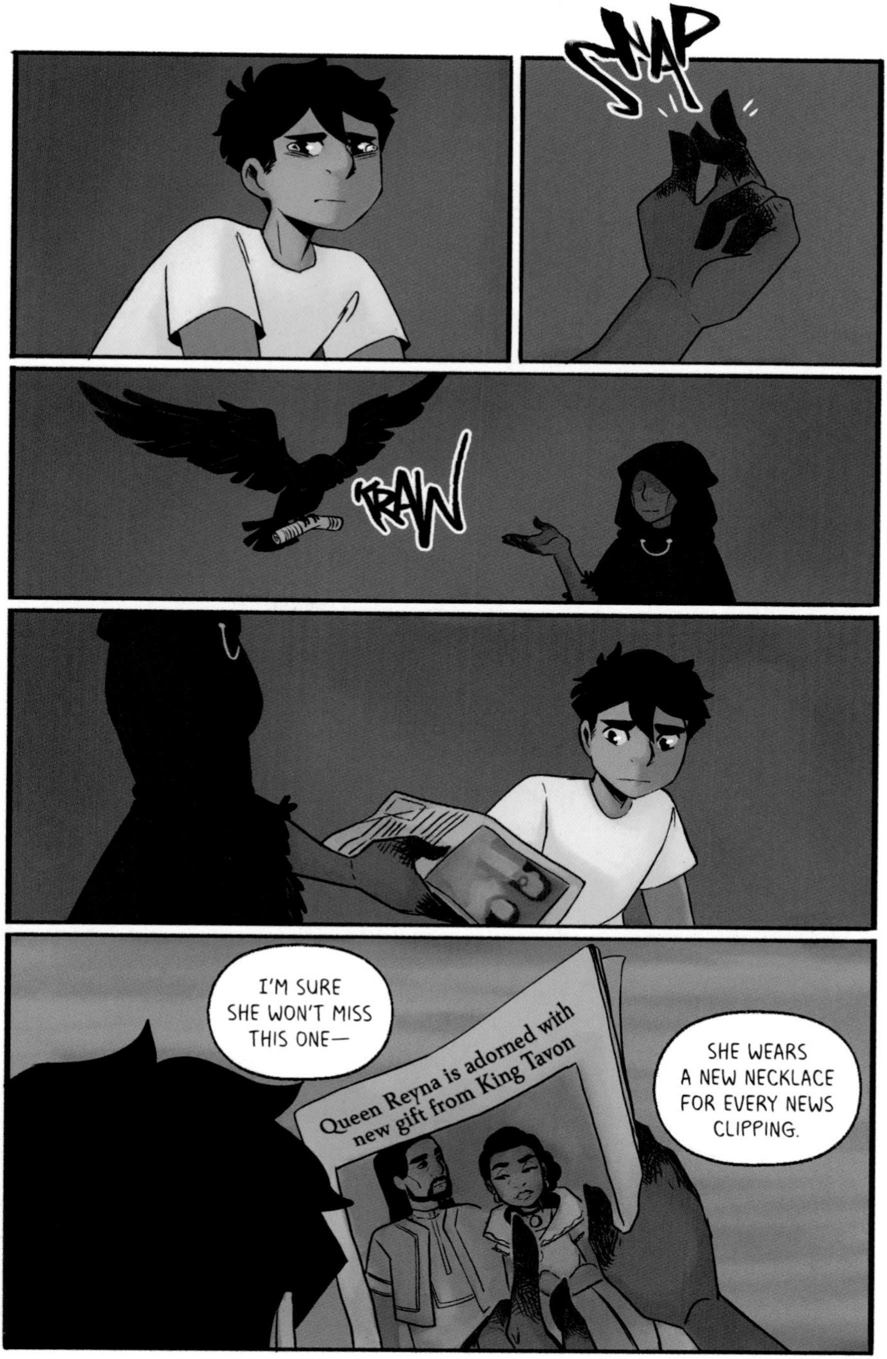
SNAP
KRAW
I'M SURE SHE WON'T MISS THIS ONE—
Queen Reyna is adorned with new gift from King Tavon
SHE WEARS A NEW NECKLACE FOR EVERY NEWS CLIPPING.

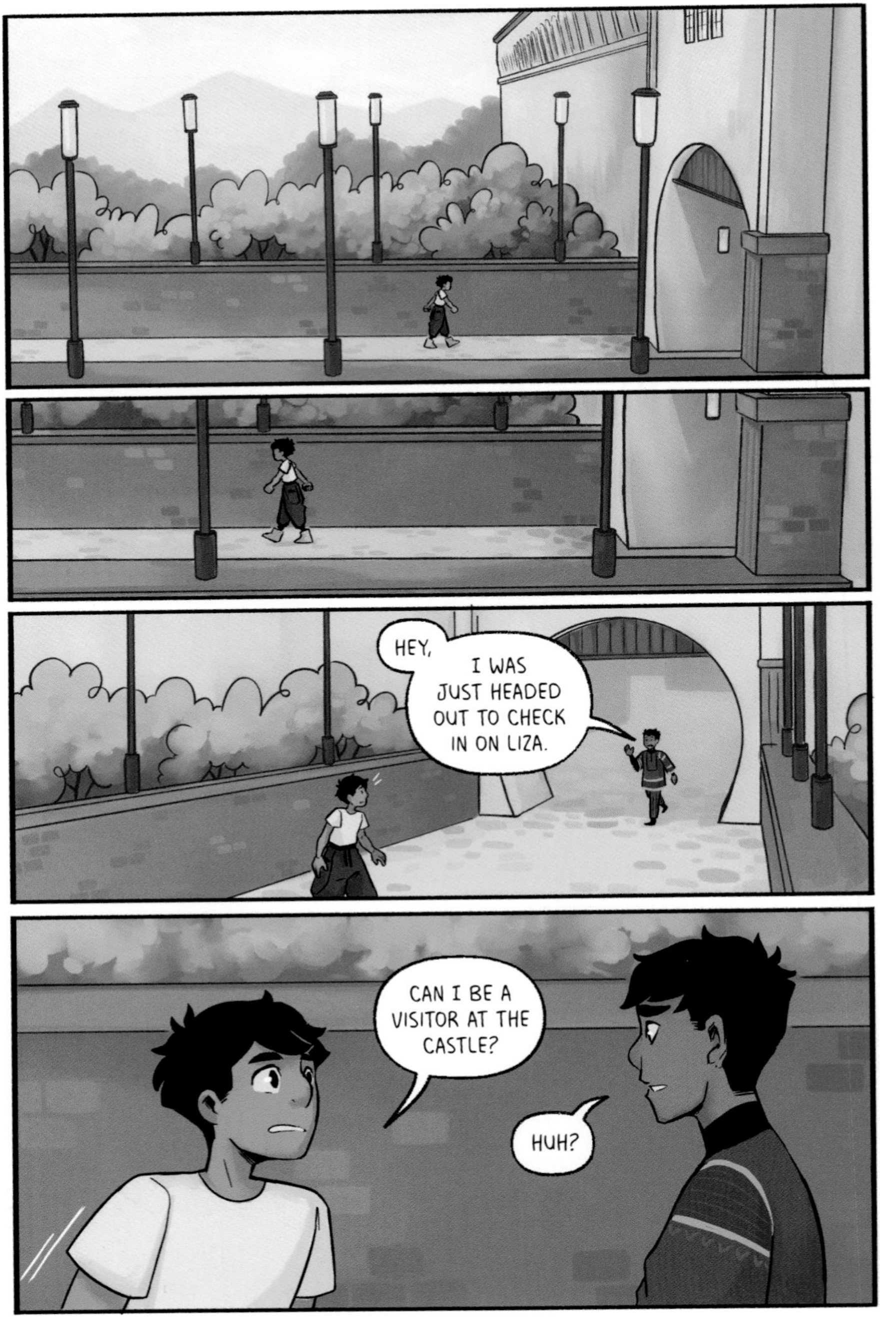
HEY,
I WAS JUST HEADED OUT TO CHECK IN ON LIZA.
CAN I BE A VISITOR AT THE CASTLE?
HUH?

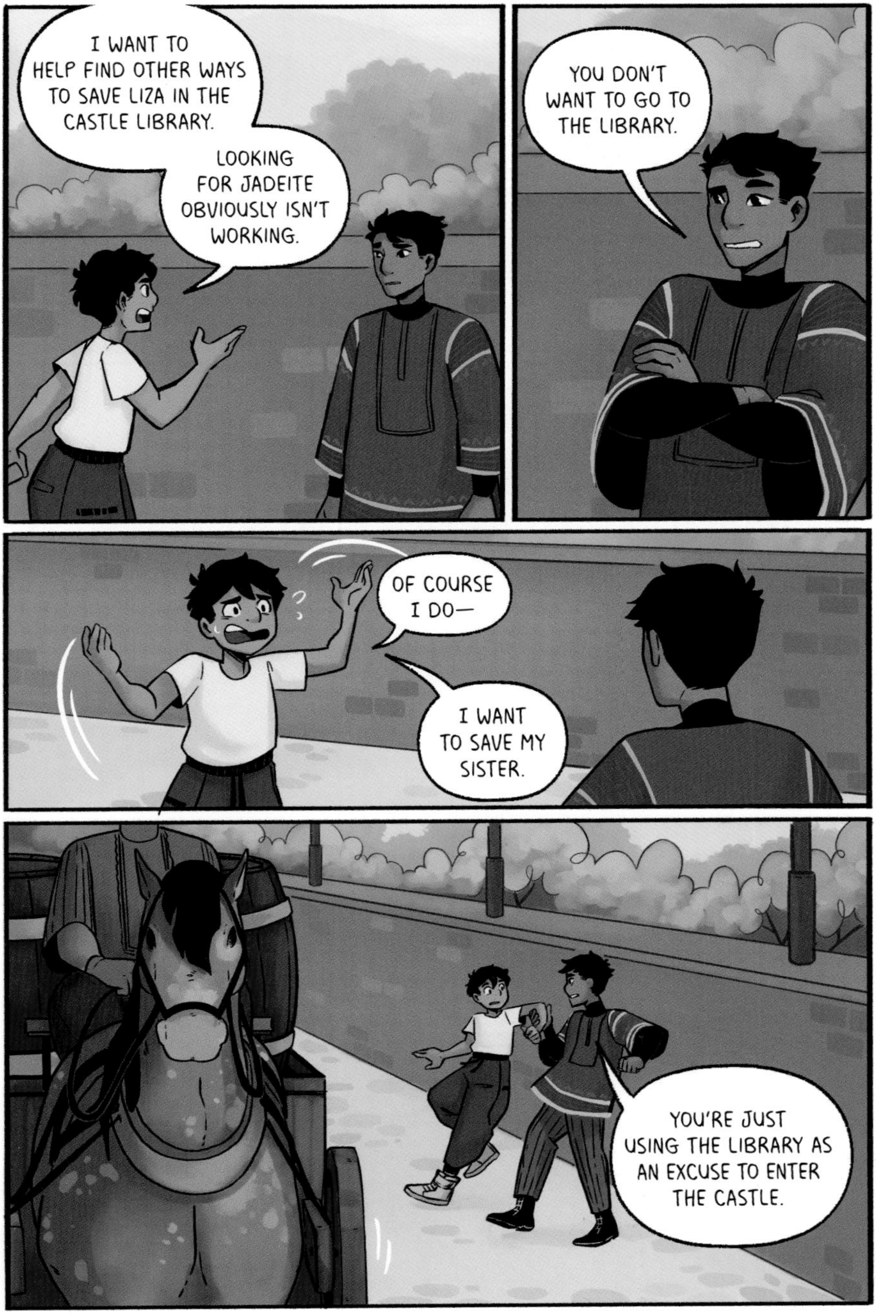
I WANT TO HELP FIND OTHER WAYS TO SAVE LIZA IN THE CASTLE LIBRARY.
LOOKING FOR JADEITE OBVIOUSLY ISN'T WORKING.
YOU DON'T WANT TO GO TO THE LIBRARY.
OF COURSE I DO—
I WANT TO SAVE MY SISTER.
YOU'RE JUST USING THE LIBRARY AS AN EXCUSE TO ENTER THE CASTLE.

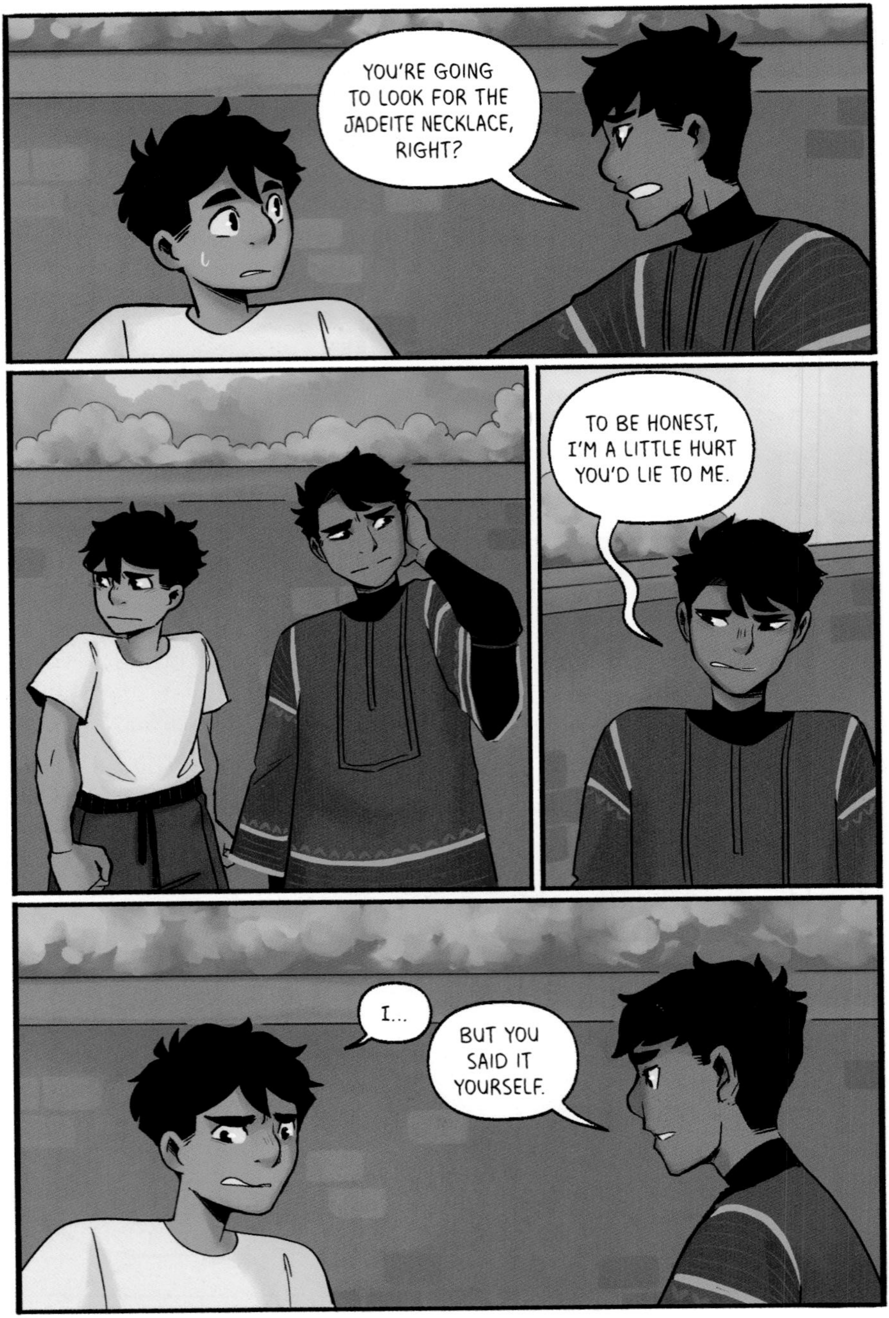
YOU'RE GOING TO LOOK FOR THE JADEITE NECKLACE, RIGHT?
TO BE HONEST, I'M A LITTLE HURT YOU'D LIE TO ME.
I...
BUT YOU SAID IT YOURSELF.

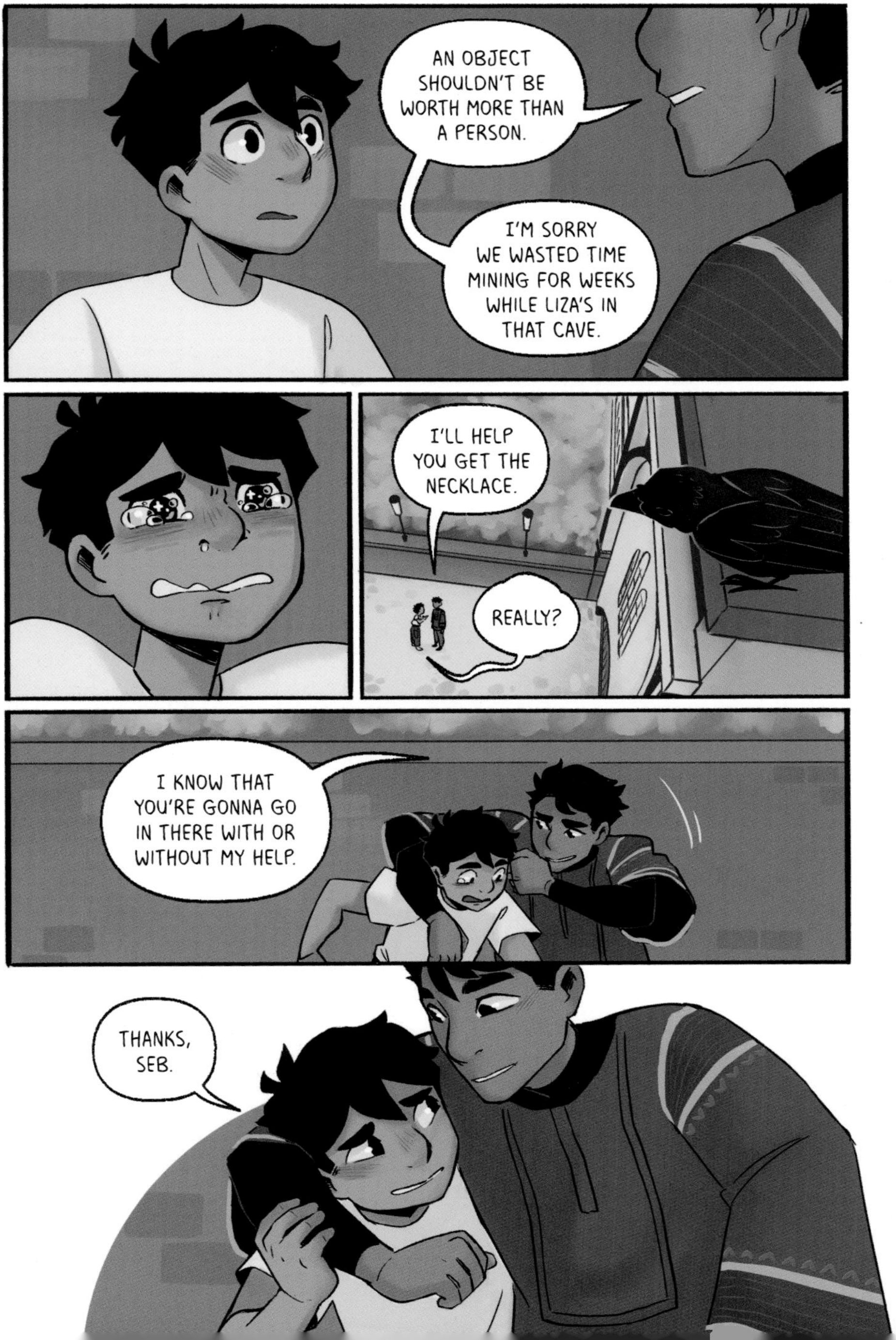
AN OBJECT SHOULDN'T BE WORTH MORE THAN A PERSON.
I'M SORRY WE WASTED TIME MINING FOR WEEKS WHILE LIZA'S IN THAT CAVE.
I'LL HELP YOU GET THE NECKLACE.
REALLY?
I KNOW THAT YOU'RE GONNA GO IN THERE WITH OR WITHOUT MY HELP.
THANKS, SEB.

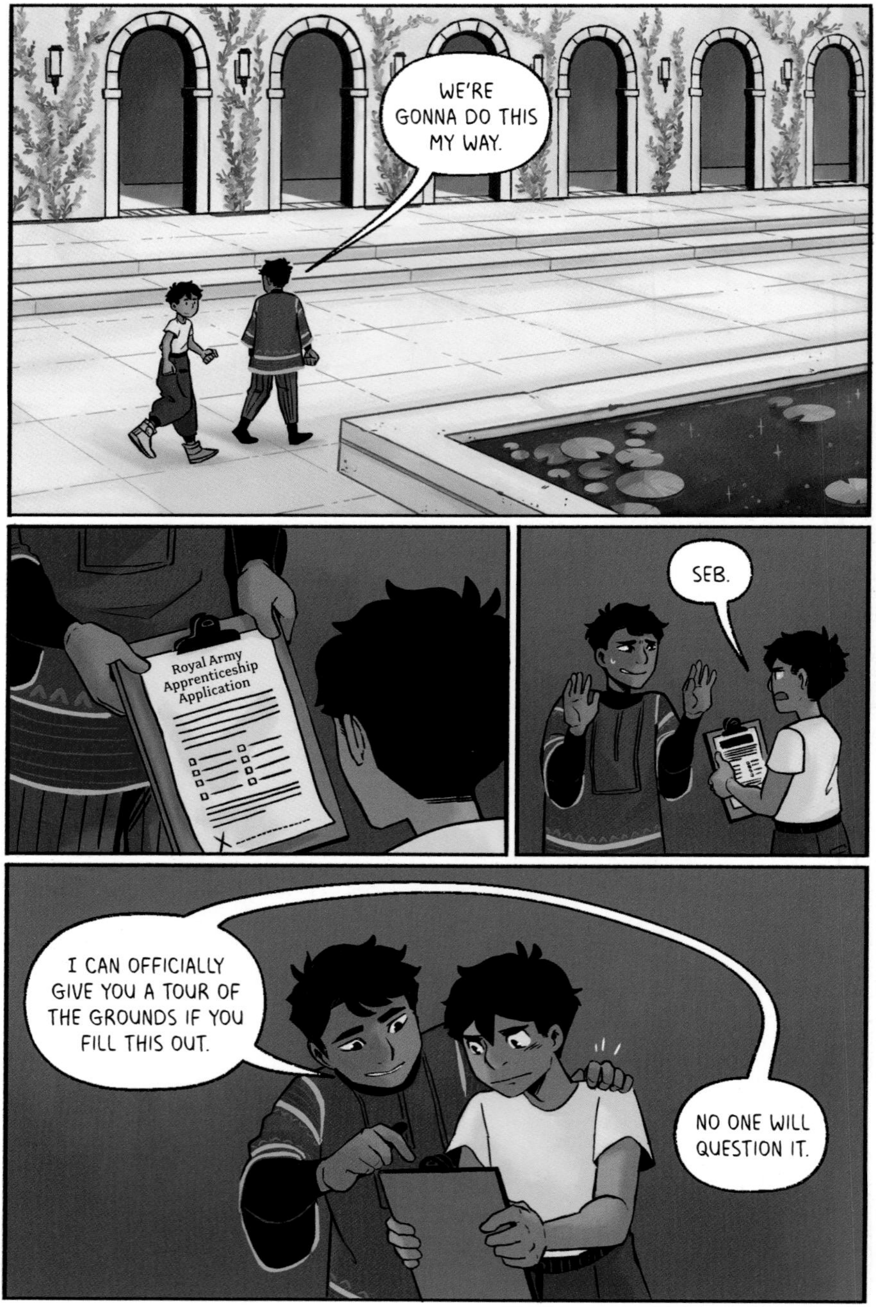
WE'RE GONNA DO THIS MY WAY.
Royal Army Apprenticeship Application
SEB.
I CAN OFFICIALLY GIVE YOU A TOUR OF THE GROUNDS IF YOU FILL THIS OUT.
NO ONE WILL QUESTION IT.

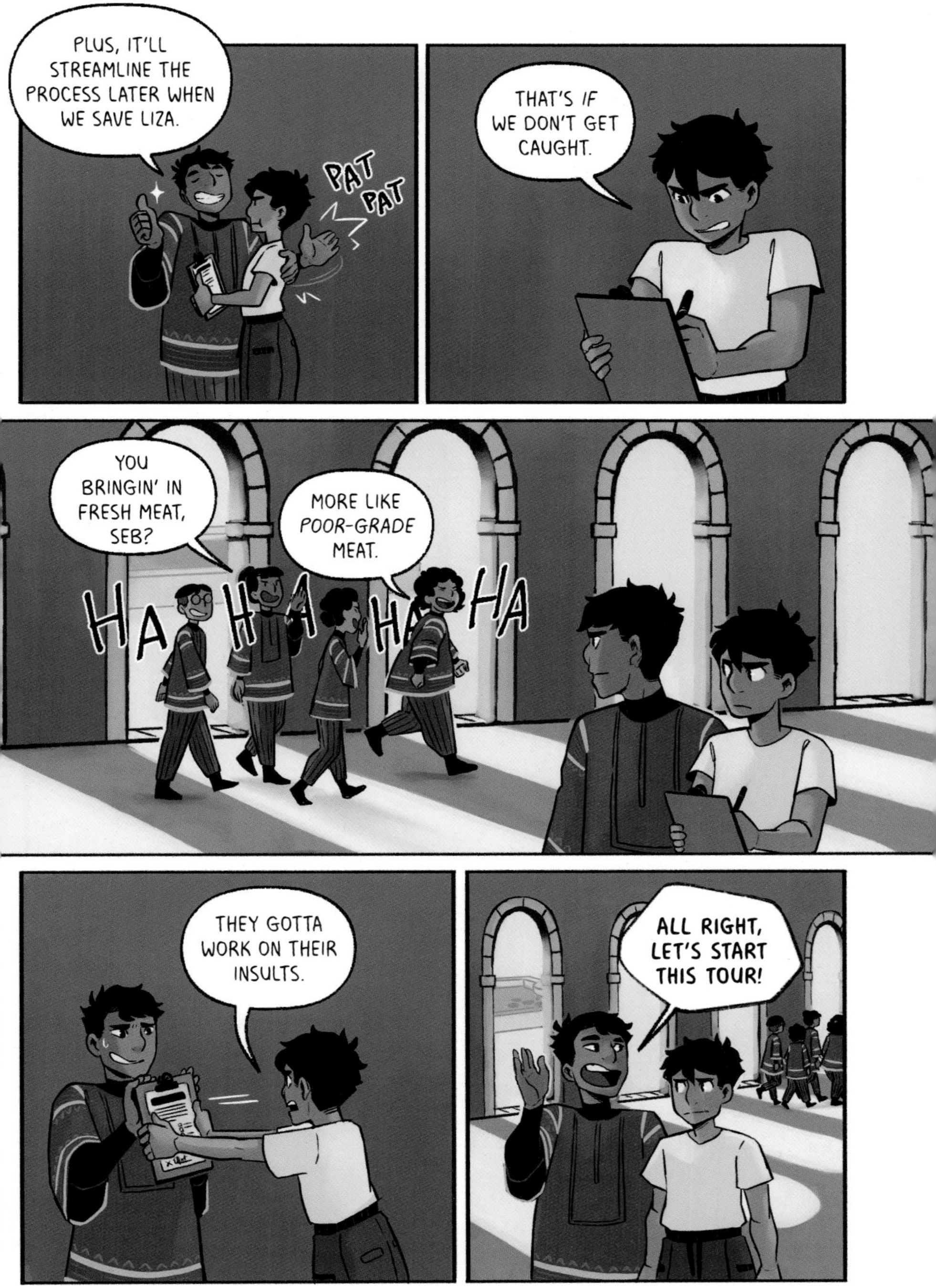
PLUS, IT'LL STREAMLINE THE PROCESS LATER WHEN WE SAVE LIZA.
PAT PAT
THAT'S *IF* WE DON'T GET CAUGHT.
YOU BRINGIN' IN FRESH MEAT, SEB?
MORE LIKE *POOR-GRADE* MEAT.
HA HA HA HA
THEY GOTTA WORK ON THEIR INSULTS.
ALL RIGHT, LET'S START THIS TOUR!

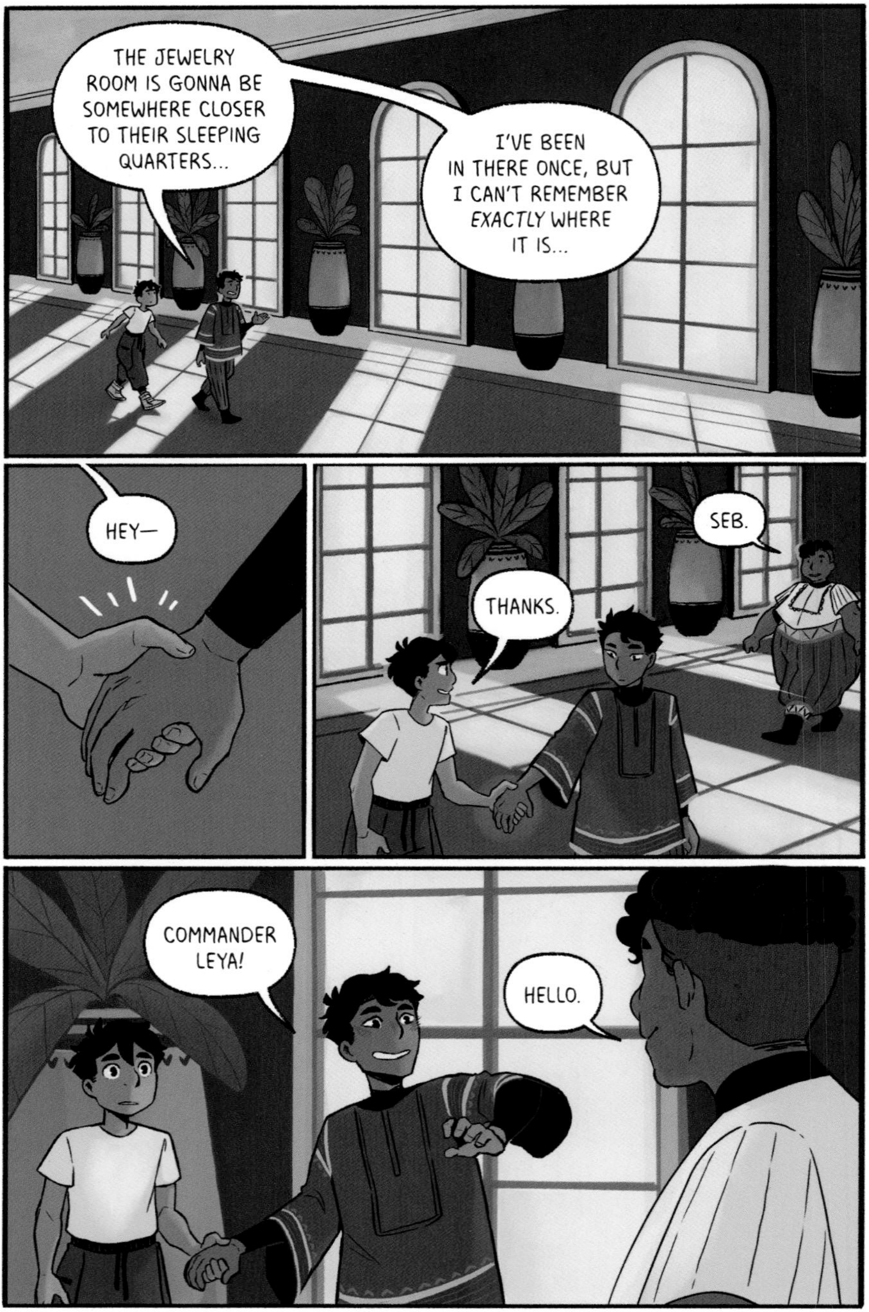
THE JEWELRY ROOM IS GONNA BE SOMEWHERE CLOSER TO THEIR SLEEPING QUARTERS...
I'VE BEEN IN THERE ONCE, BUT I CAN'T REMEMBER *EXACTLY* WHERE IT IS...
HEY—
THANKS.
SEB.
COMMANDER LEYA!
HELLO.

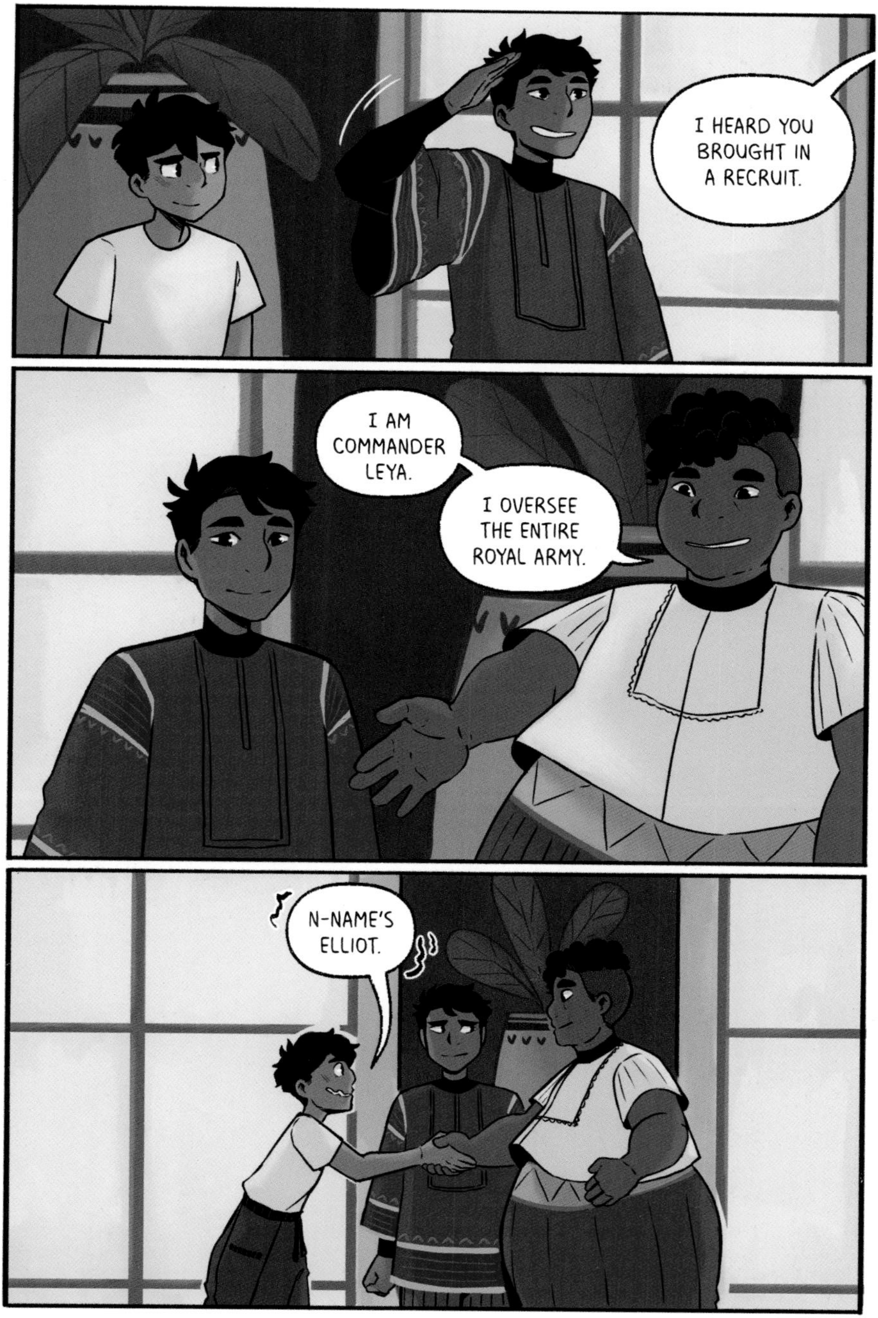
I HEARD YOU BROUGHT IN A RECRUIT.
I AM COMMANDER LEYA.
I OVERSEE THE ENTIRE ROYAL ARMY.
N-NAME'S ELLIOT.

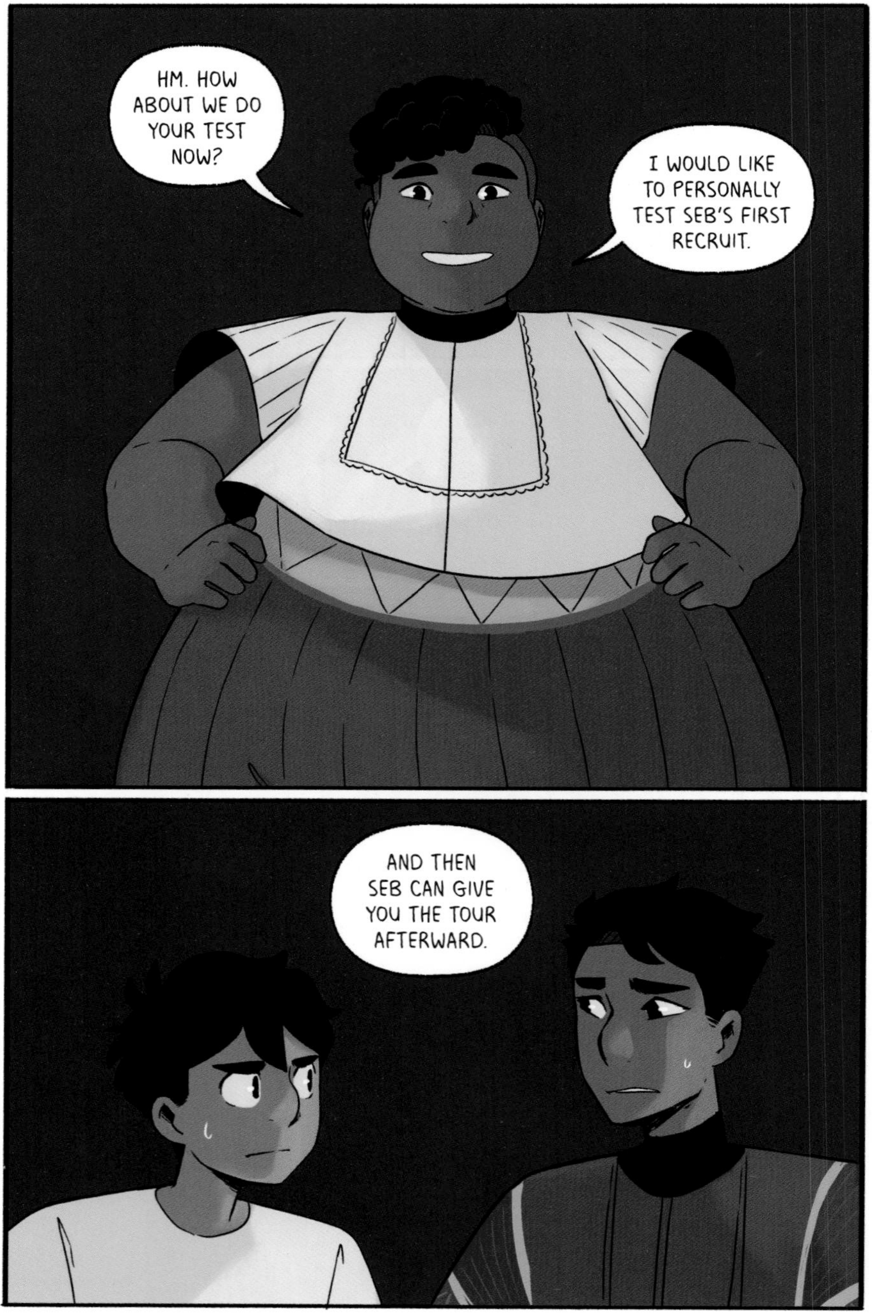
HM. HOW ABOUT WE DO YOUR TEST NOW?
I WOULD LIKE TO PERSONALLY TEST SEB'S FIRST RECRUIT.
AND THEN SEB CAN GIVE YOU THE TOUR AFTERWARD.

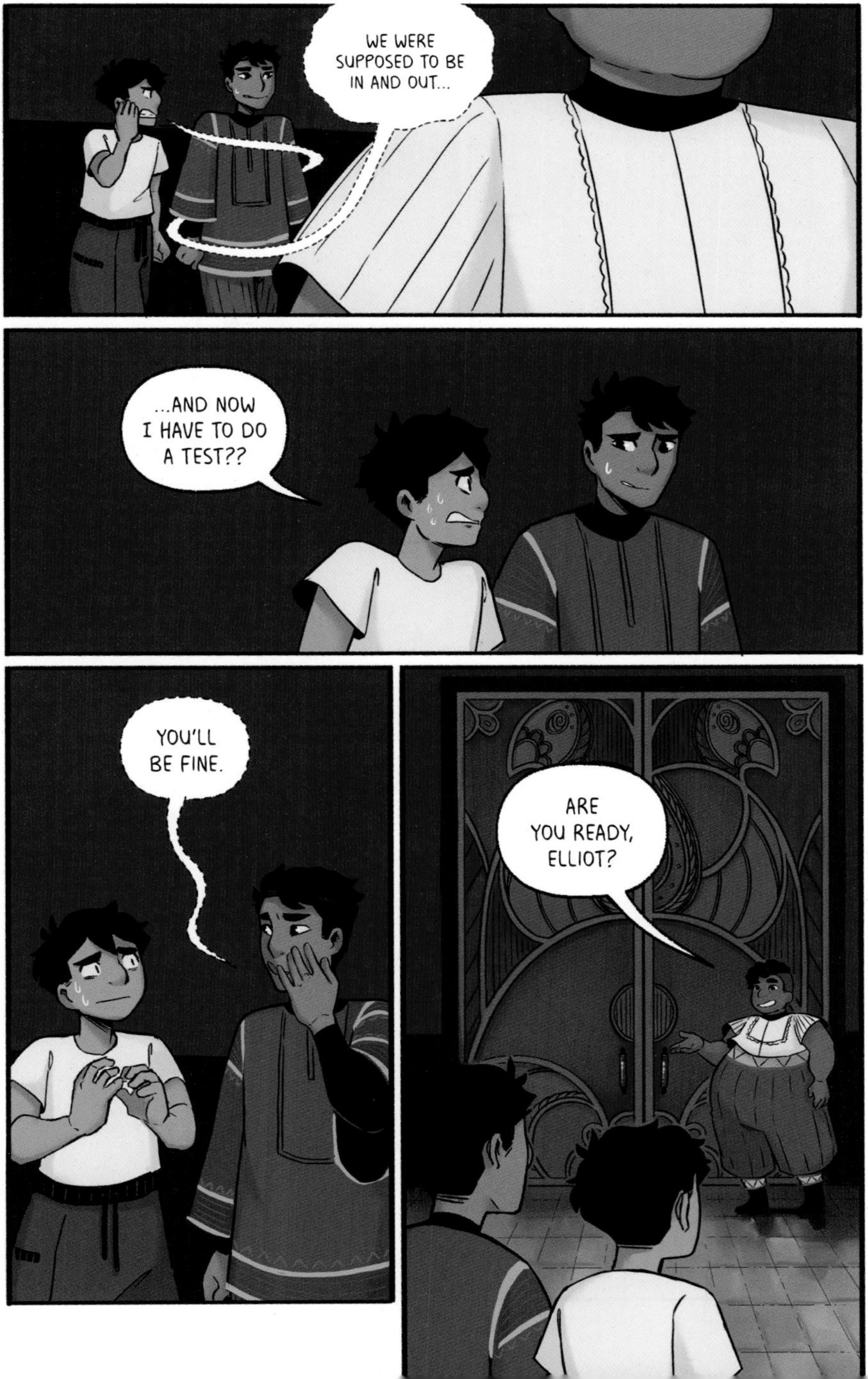
WE WERE SUPPOSED TO BE IN AND OUT...
...AND NOW I HAVE TO DO A TEST??
YOU'LL BE FINE.
ARE YOU READY, ELLIOT?

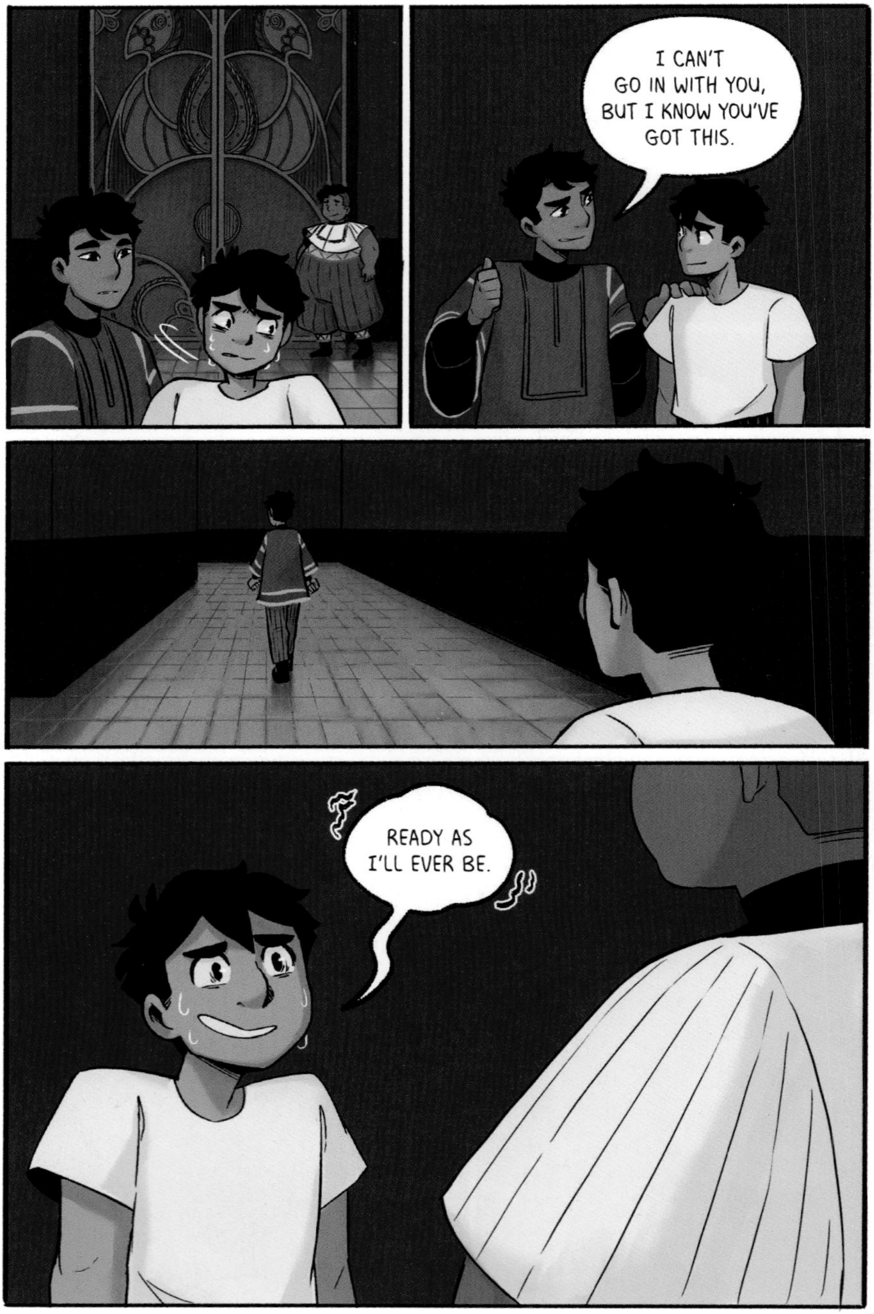
I CAN'T GO IN WITH YOU, BUT I KNOW YOU'VE GOT THIS.
READY AS I'LL EVER BE.

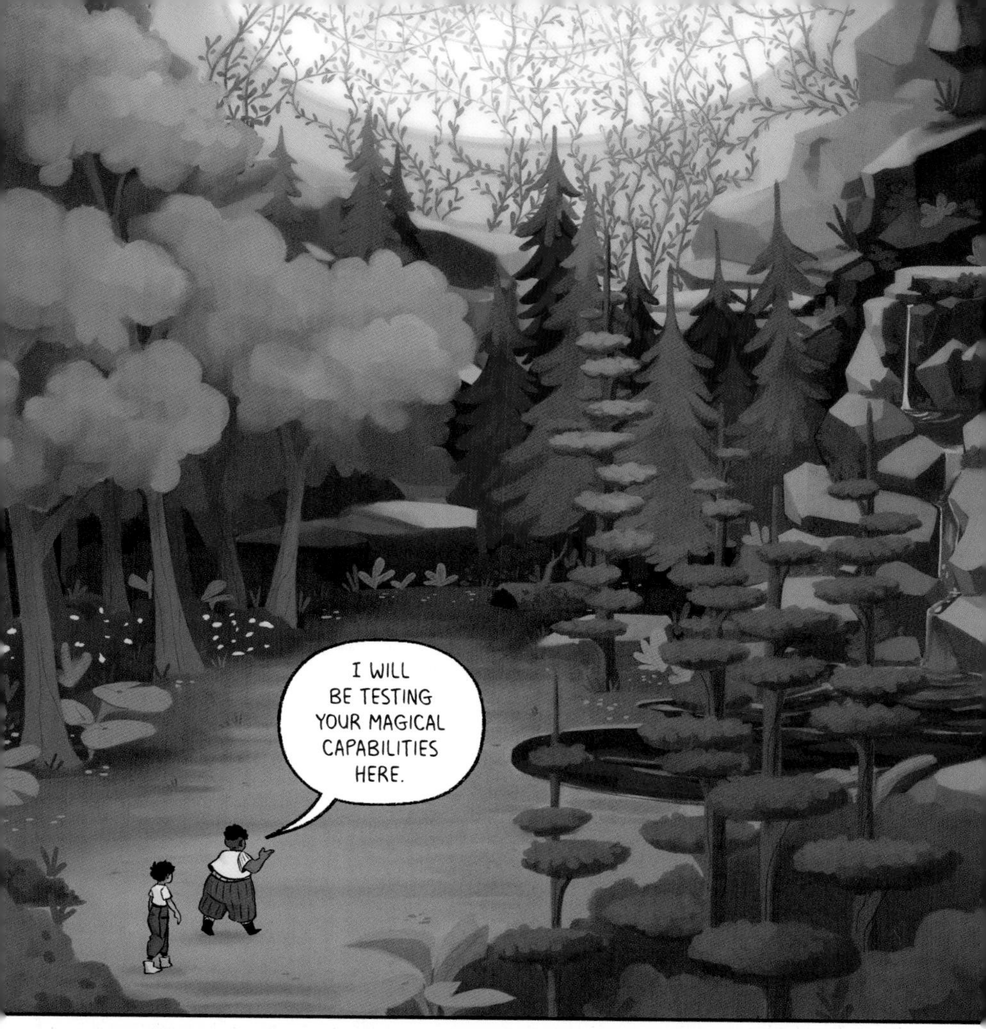
I WILL BE TESTING YOUR MAGICAL CAPABILITIES HERE.

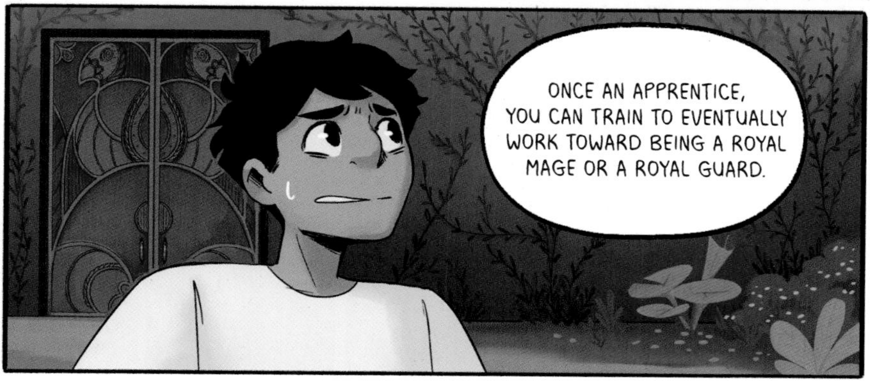
ONCE AN APPRENTICE, YOU CAN TRAIN TO EVENTUALLY WORK TOWARD BEING A ROYAL MAGE OR A ROYAL GUARD.

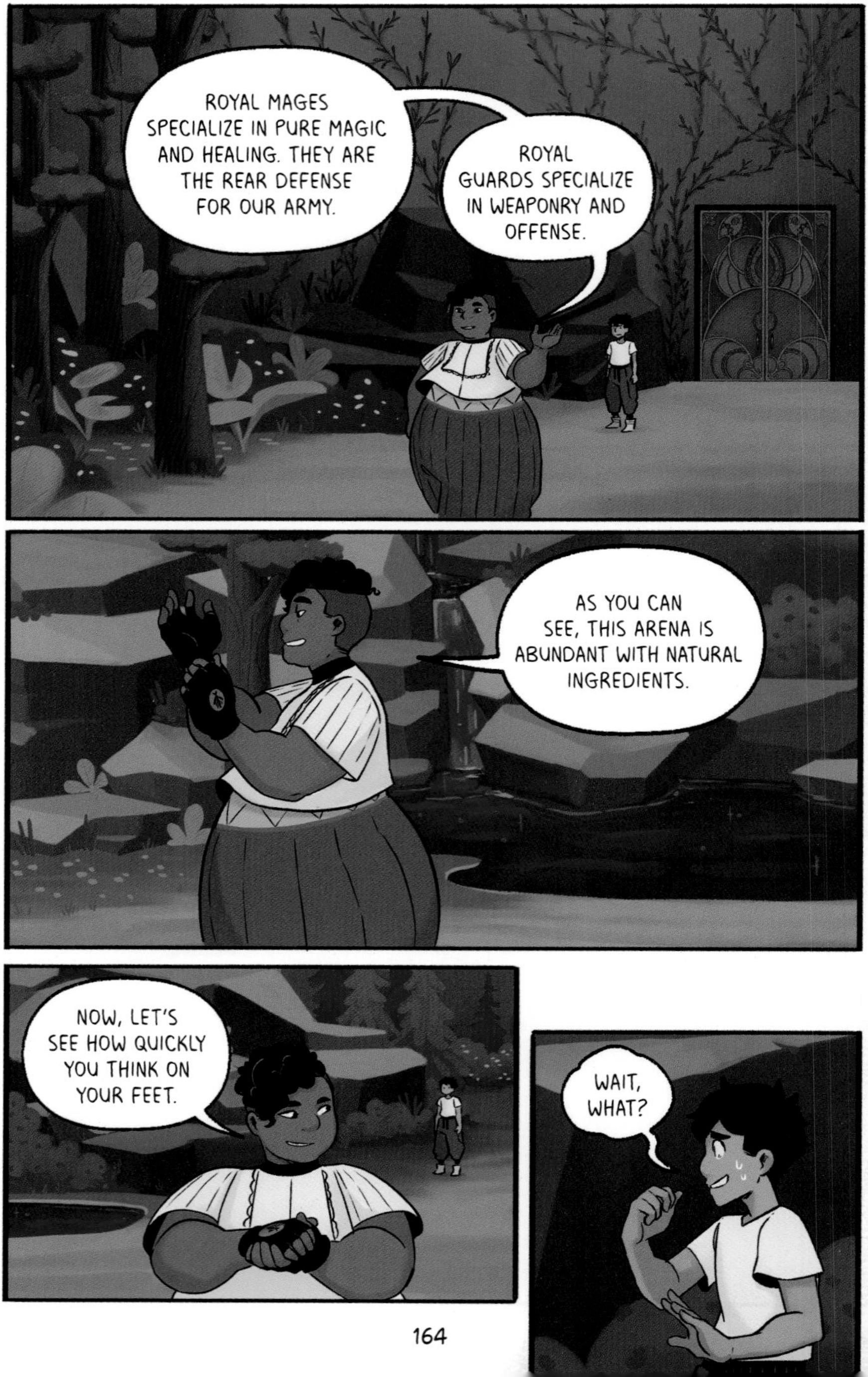
ROYAL MAGES SPECIALIZE IN PURE MAGIC AND HEALING. THEY ARE THE REAR DEFENSE FOR OUR ARMY.
ROYAL GUARDS SPECIALIZE IN WEAPONRY AND OFFENSE.
AS YOU CAN SEE, THIS ARENA IS ABUNDANT WITH NATURAL INGREDIENTS.
NOW, LET'S SEE HOW QUICKLY YOU THINK ON YOUR FEET.
WAIT, WHAT?

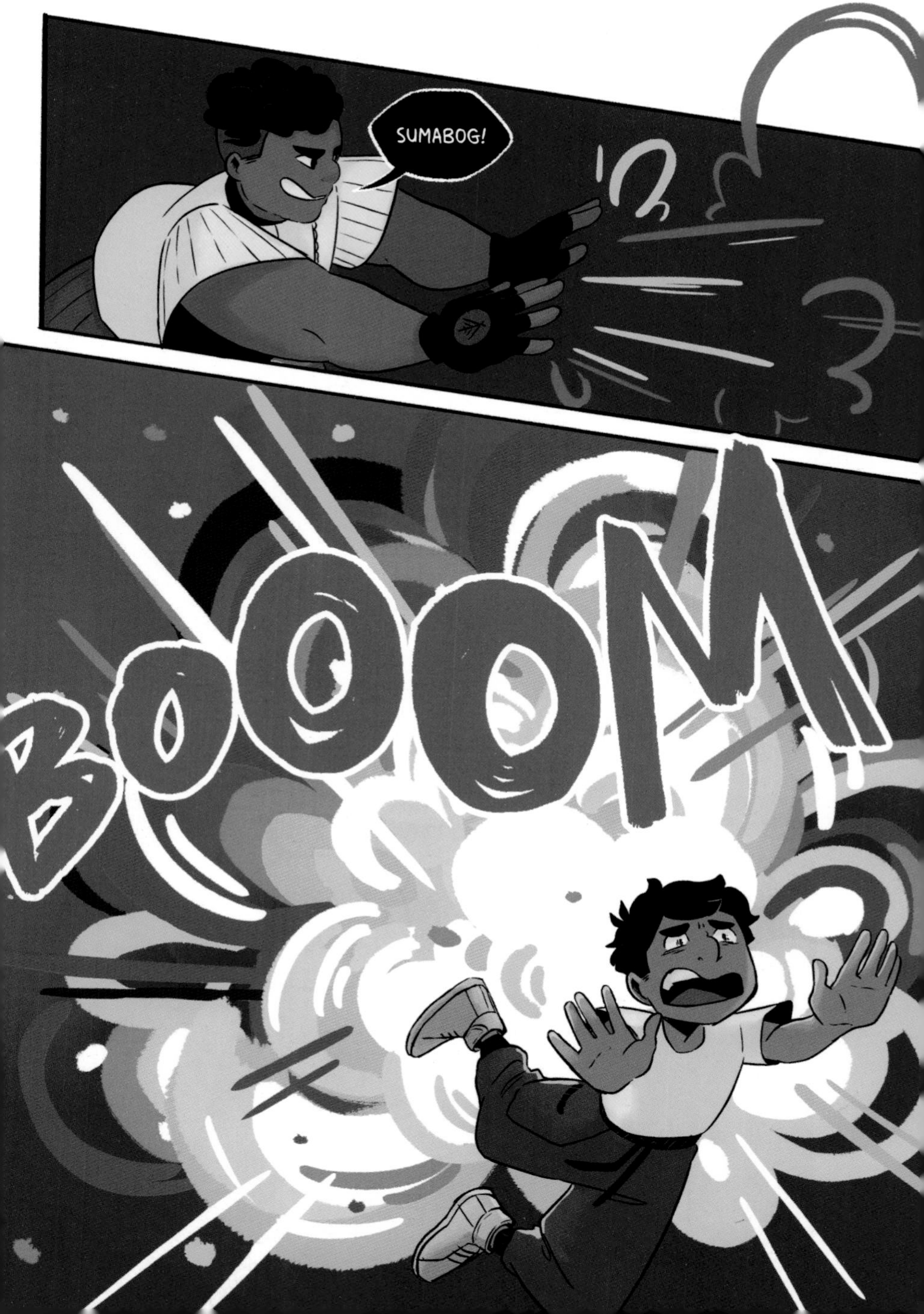
SUMABOG!
BOOOM

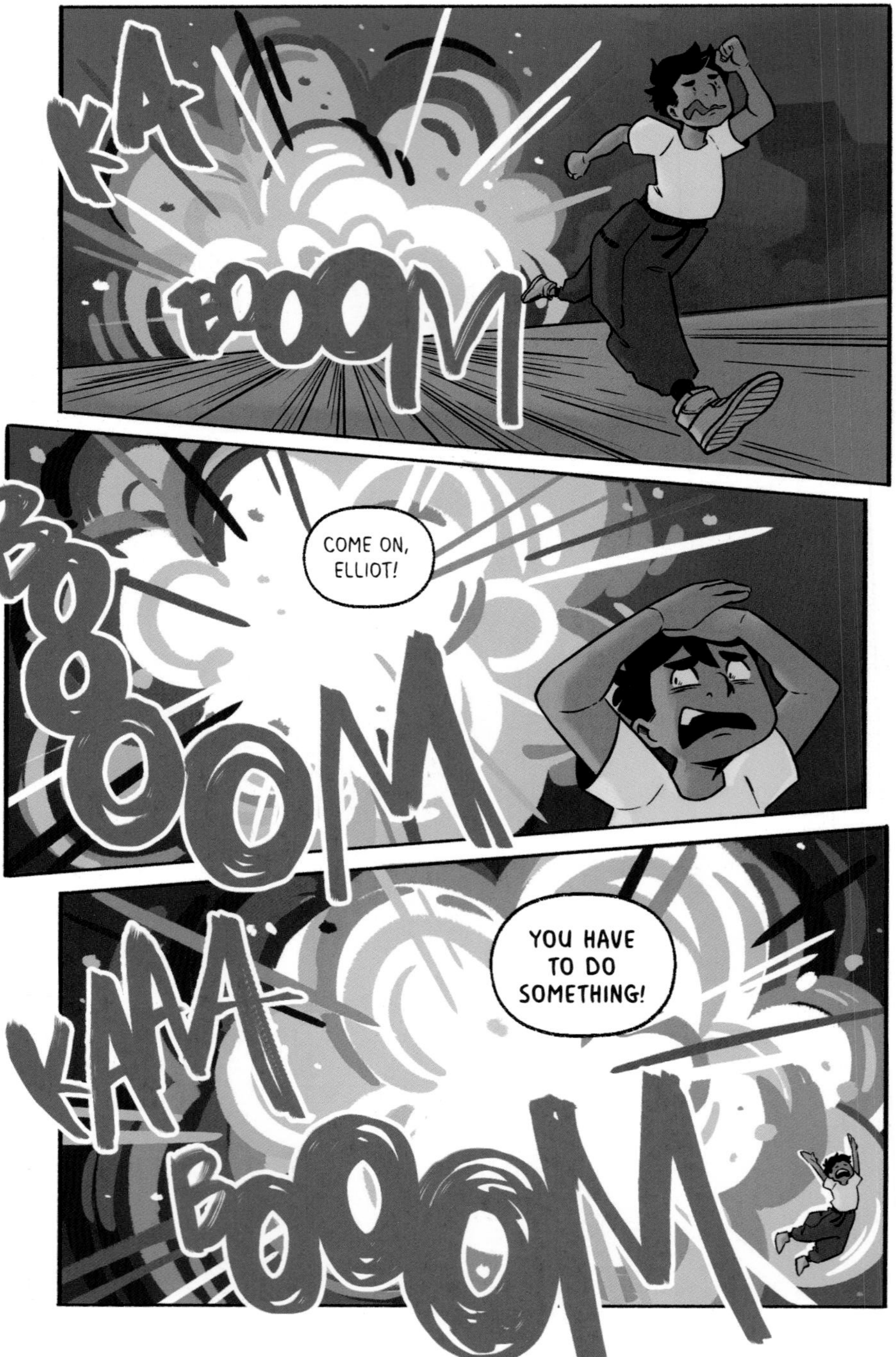
COME ON, ELLIOT!
YOU HAVE TO DO SOMETHING!

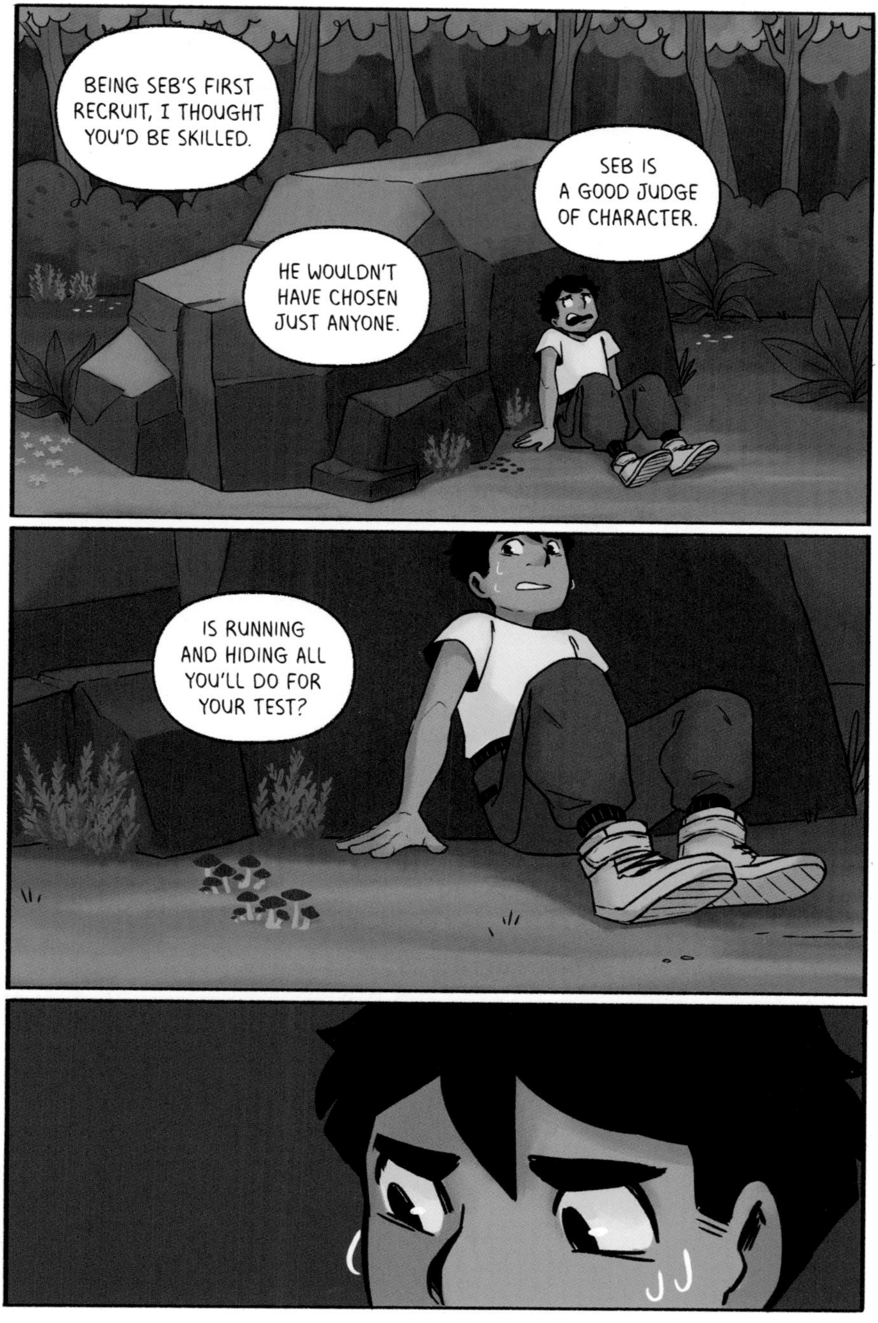
BEING SEB'S FIRST RECRUIT, I THOUGHT YOU'D BE SKILLED.
SEB IS A GOOD JUDGE OF CHARACTER.
HE WOULDN'T HAVE CHOSEN JUST ANYONE.
IS RUNNING AND HIDING ALL YOU'LL DO FOR YOUR TEST?

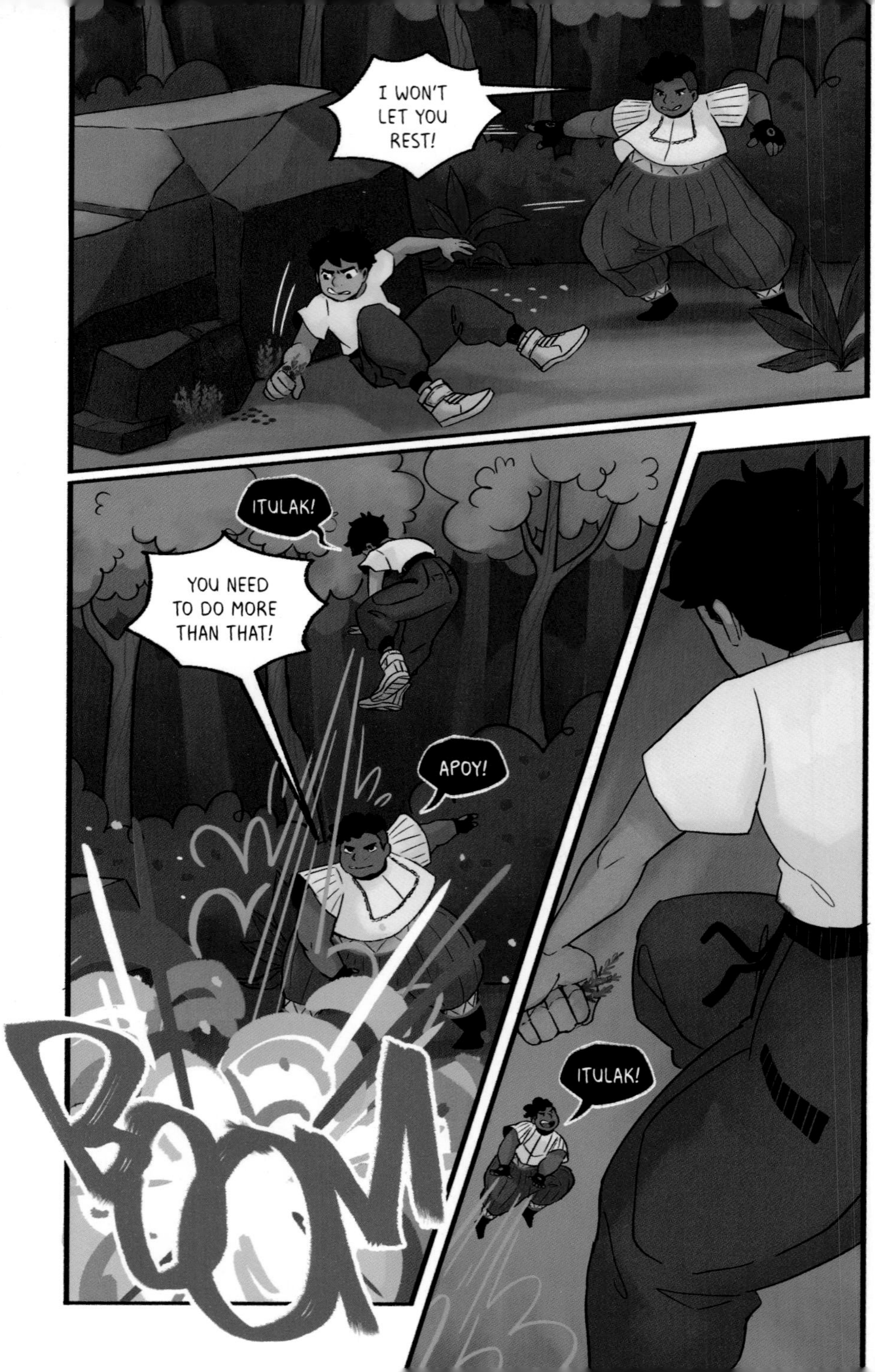
I WON'T LET YOU REST!
ITULAK!
YOU NEED TO DO MORE THAN THAT!
APOY!
BOOM
ITULAK!

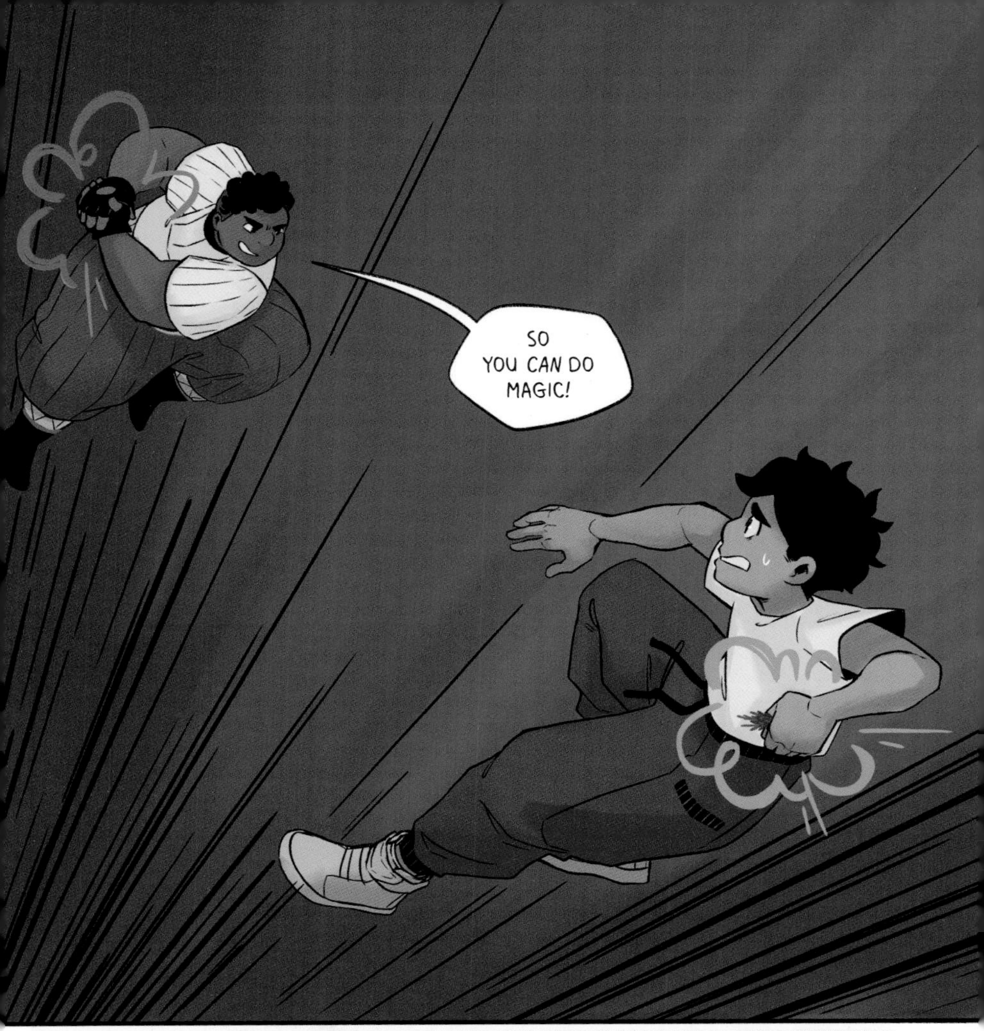
SO
YOU CAN DO
MAGIC!

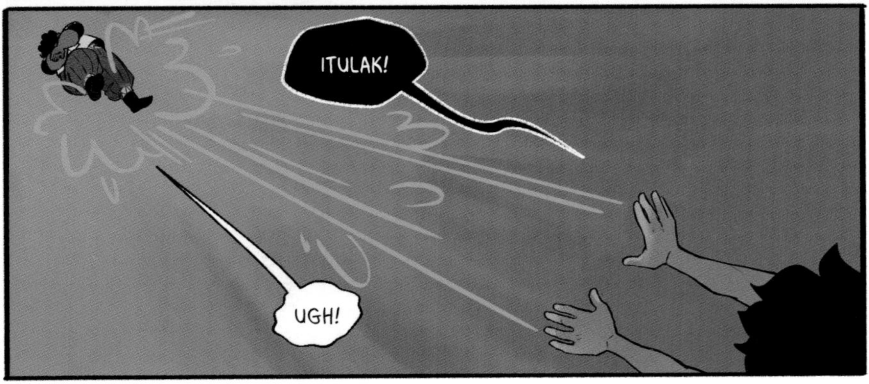
ITULAK!
UGH!

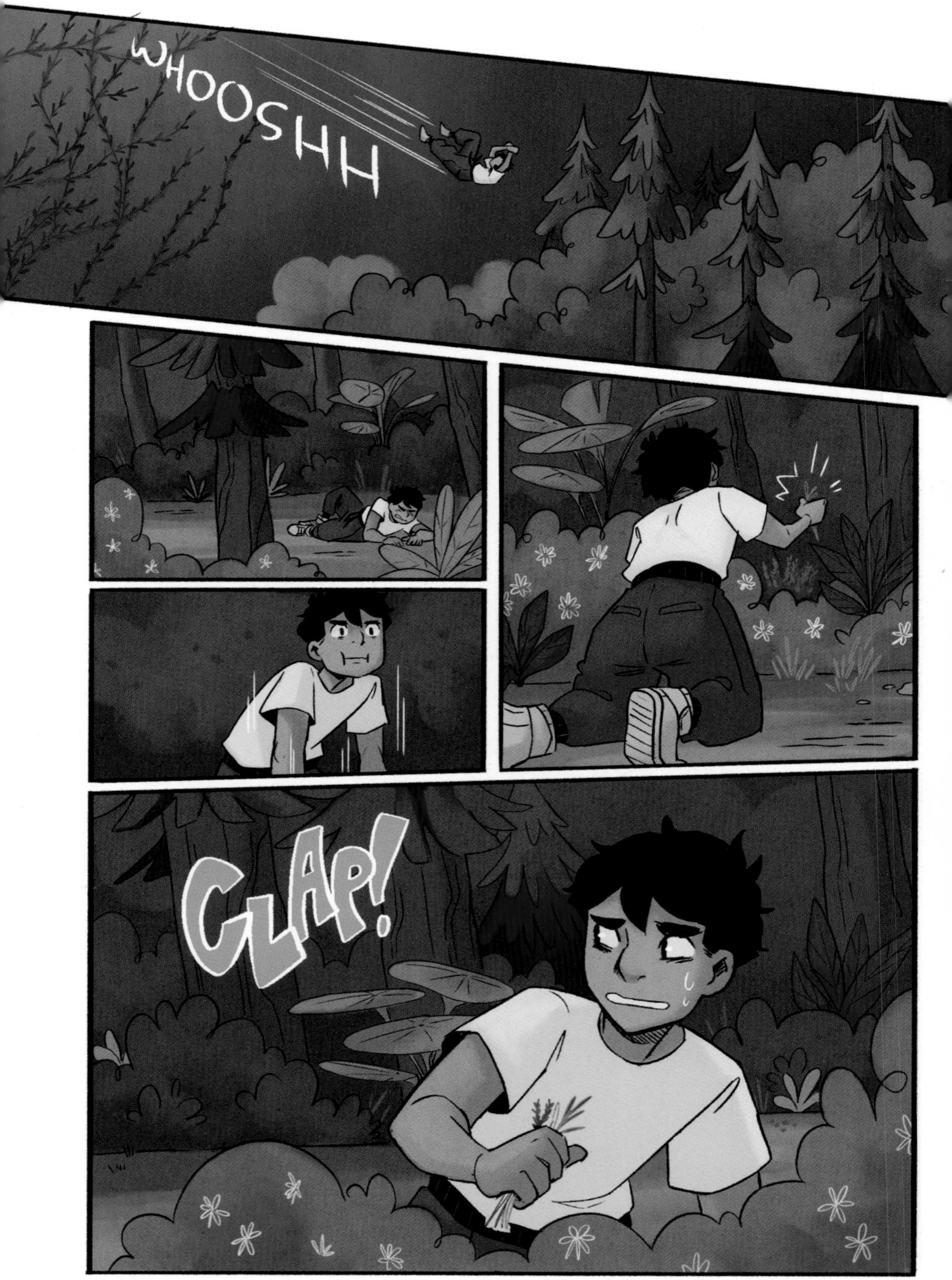
WHOOSHH
CLAP!

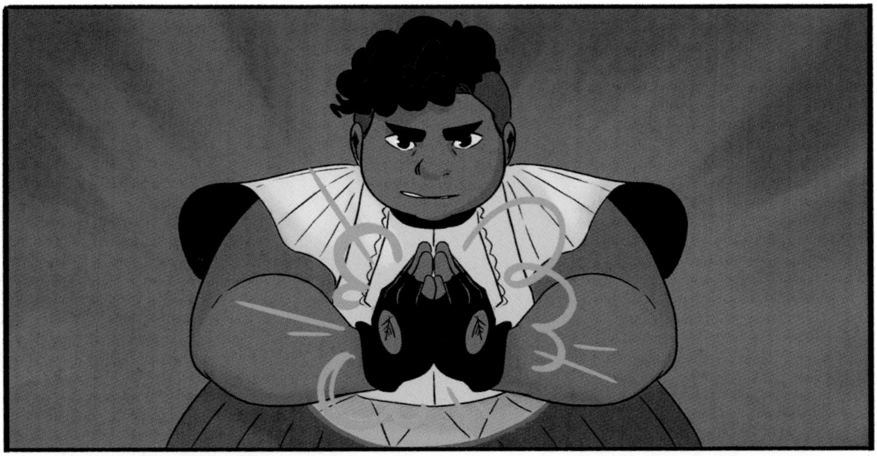

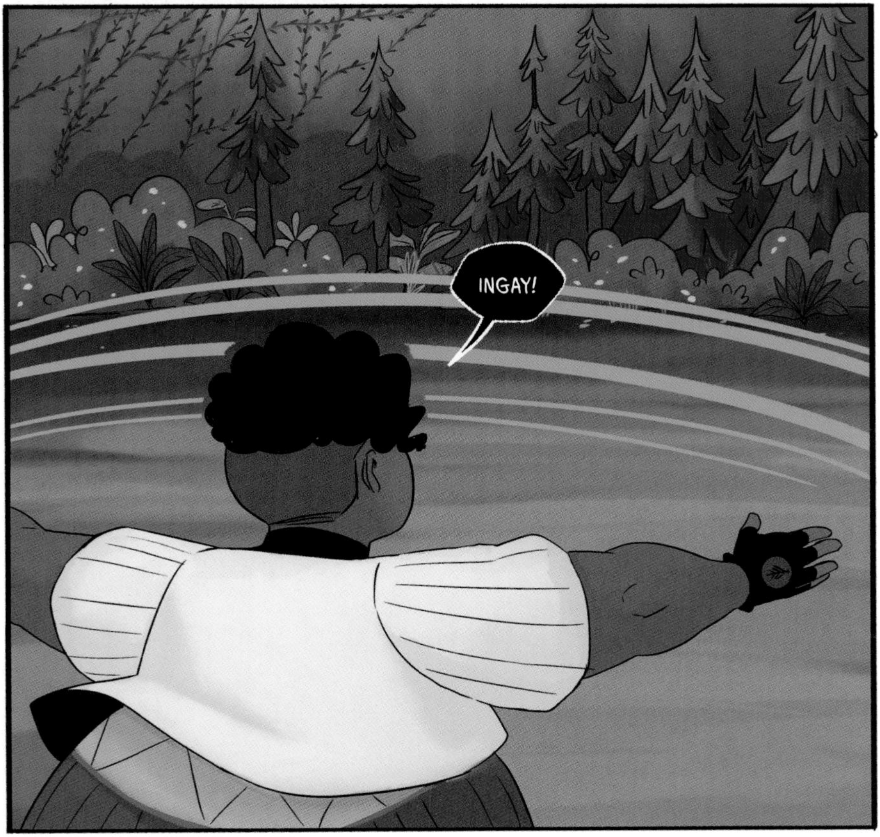
INGAY!

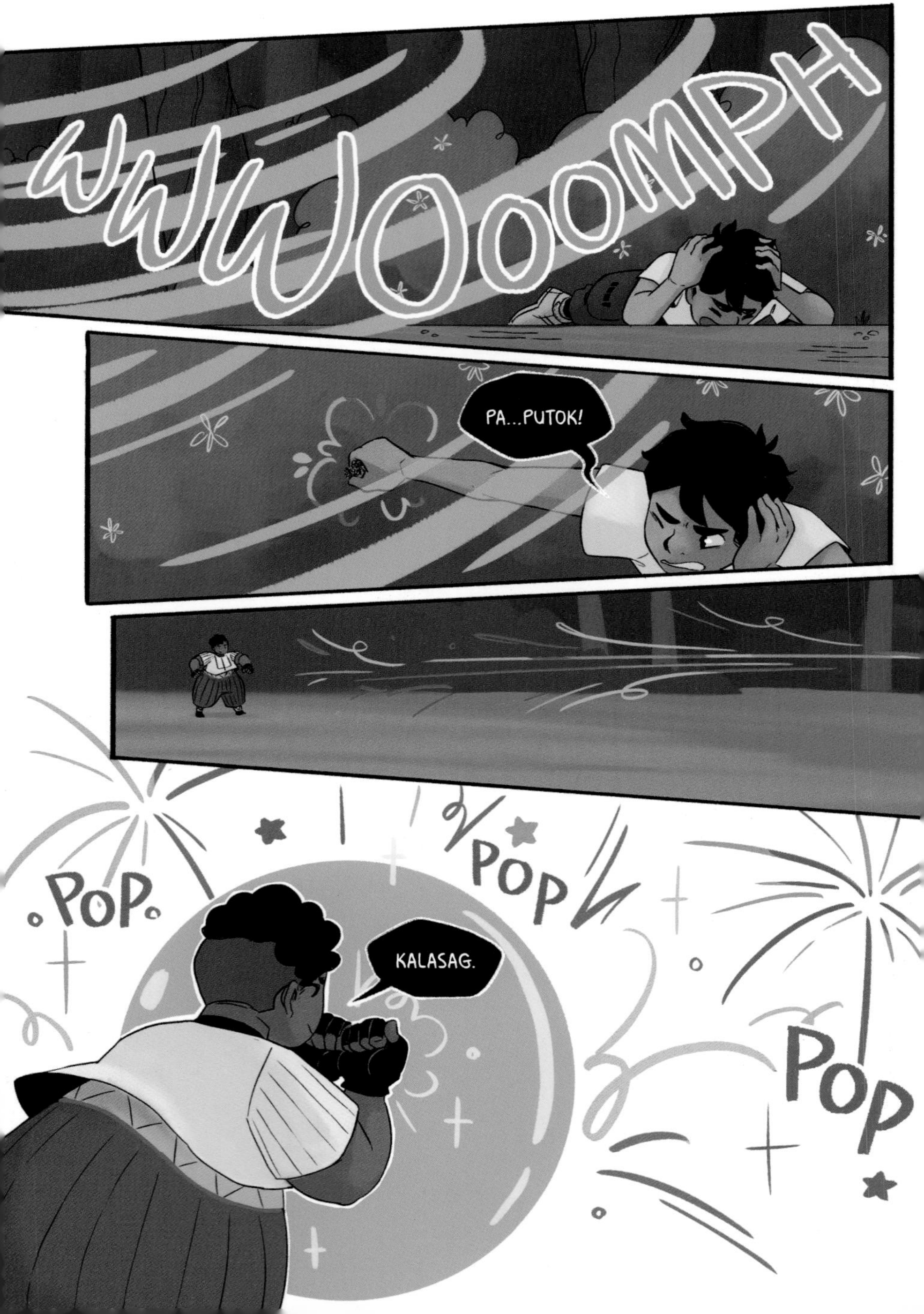
WWWOOOMPH
PA...PUTOK!
POP
POP
KALASAG.
POP

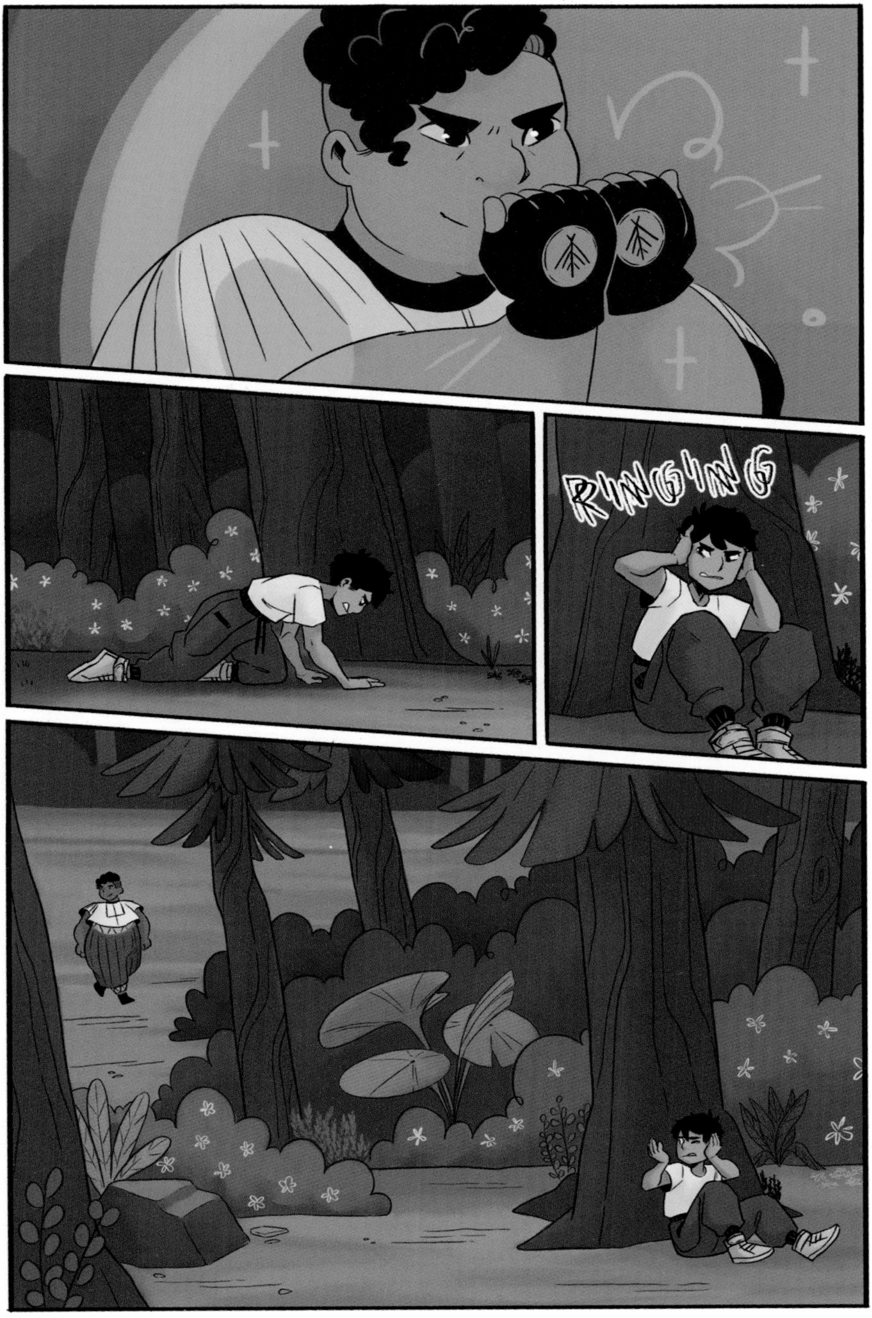
RINGING

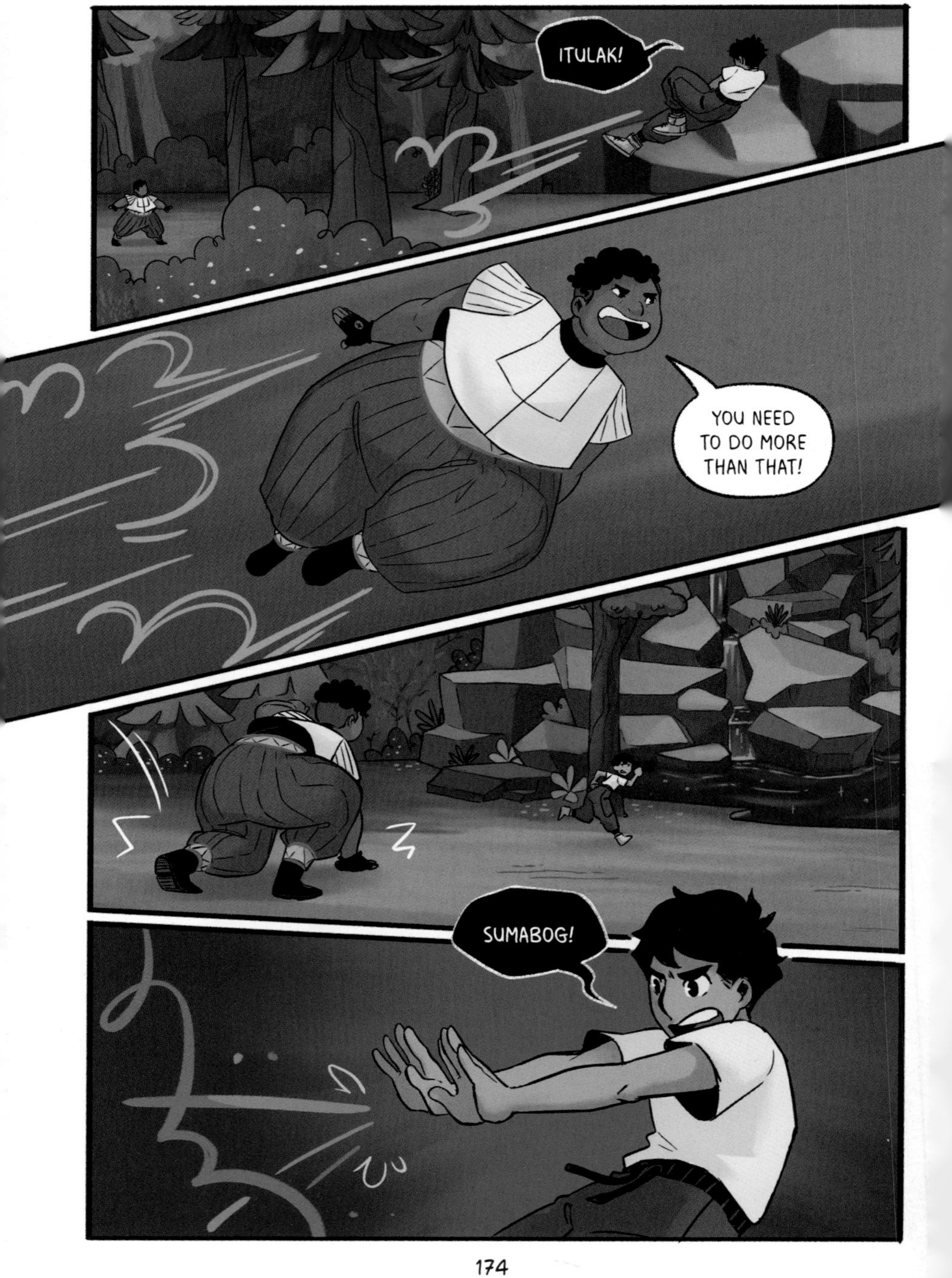
ITULAK!
YOU NEED TO DO MORE THAN THAT!
SUMABOG!

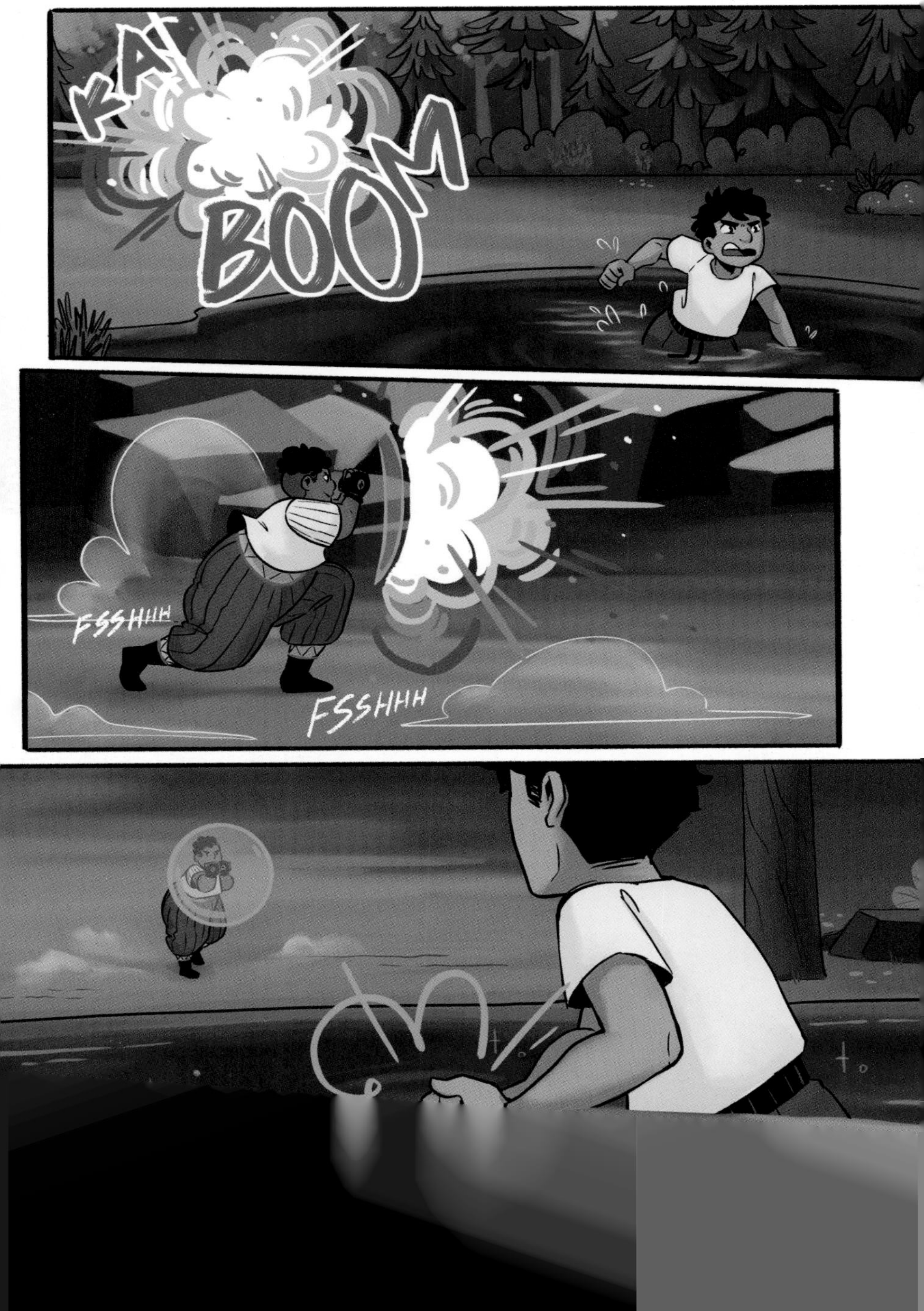
KA-BOOM
FSSHHH
FSSHHH

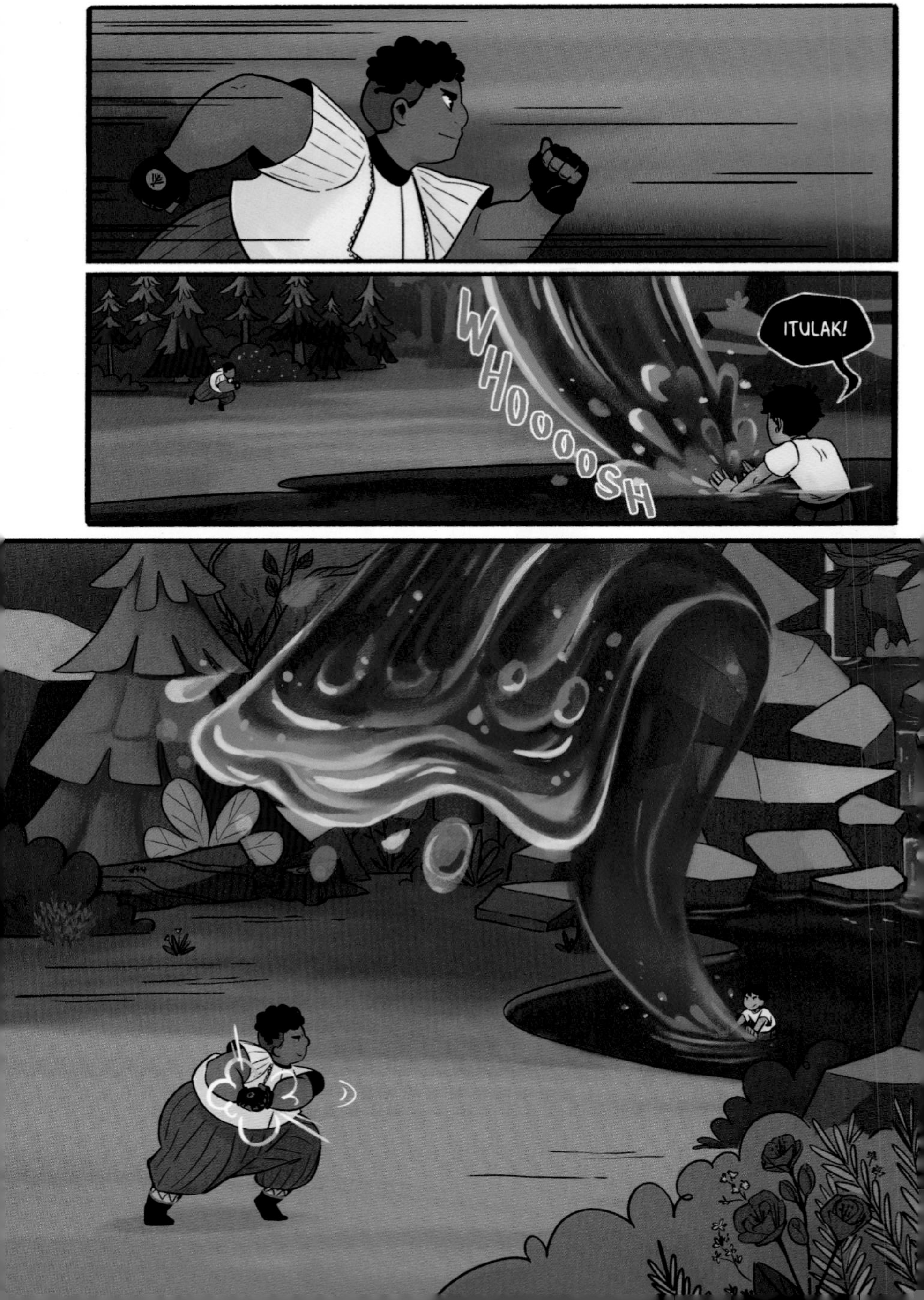
WHOOOOOSH
ITULAK!

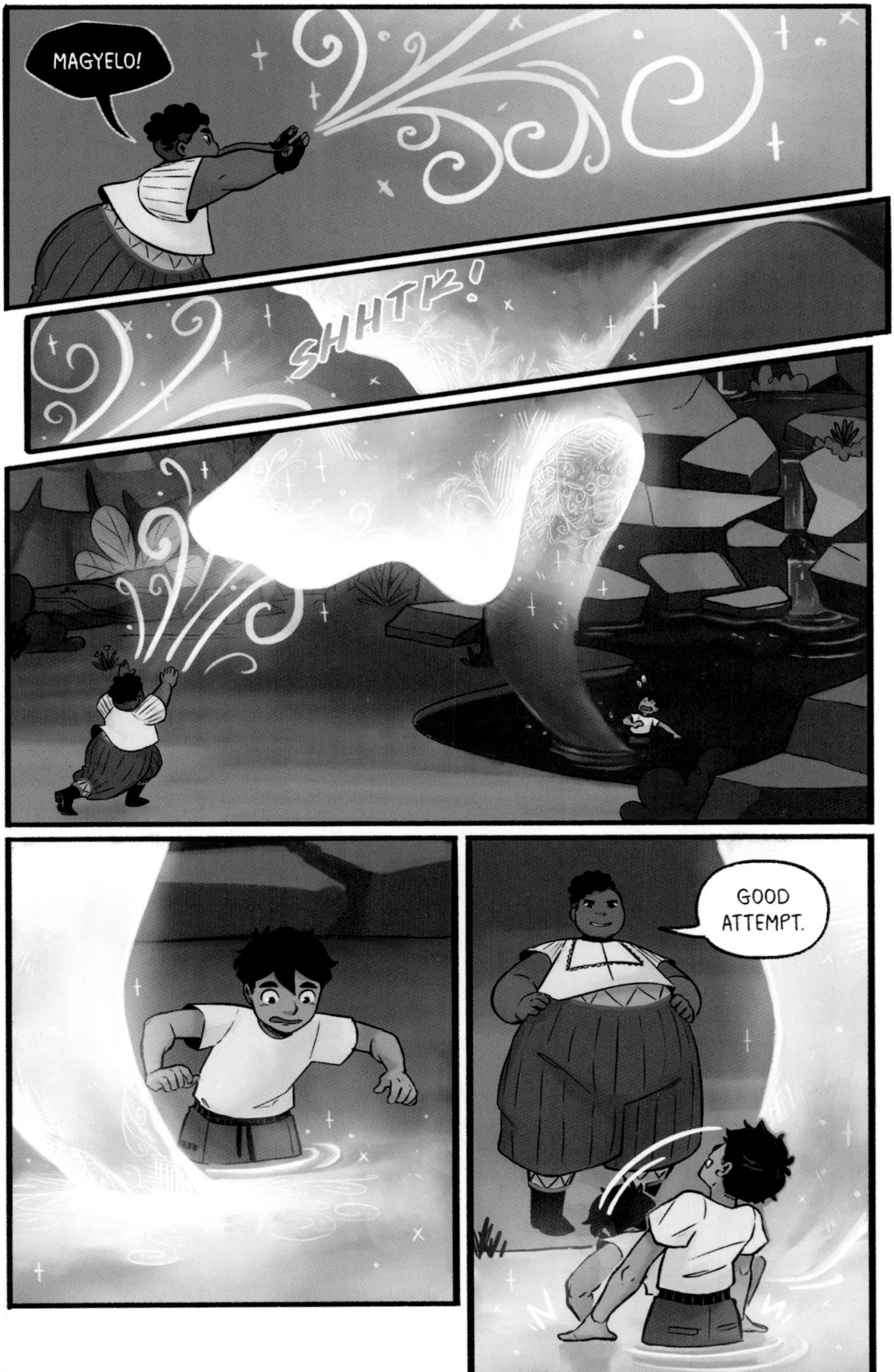
MAGYELO!
SHHTK!
GOOD ATTEMPT.

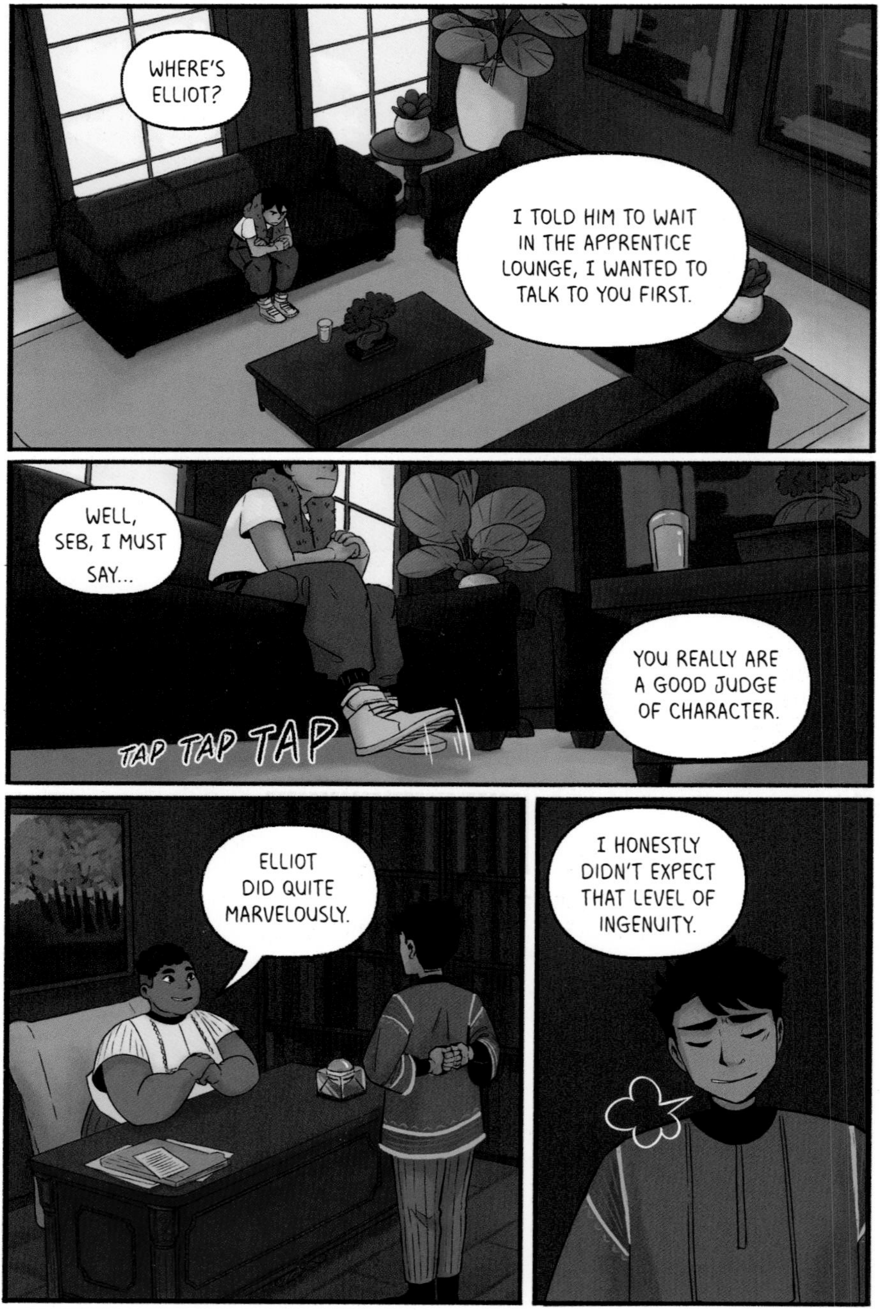
WHERE'S ELLIOT?
I TOLD HIM TO WAIT IN THE APPRENTICE LOUNGE, I WANTED TO TALK TO YOU FIRST.
WELL, SEB, I MUST SAY...
YOU REALLY ARE A GOOD JUDGE OF CHARACTER.
TAP TAP TAP
ELLIOT DID QUITE MARVELOUSLY.
I HONESTLY DIDN'T EXPECT THAT LEVEL OF INGENUITY.

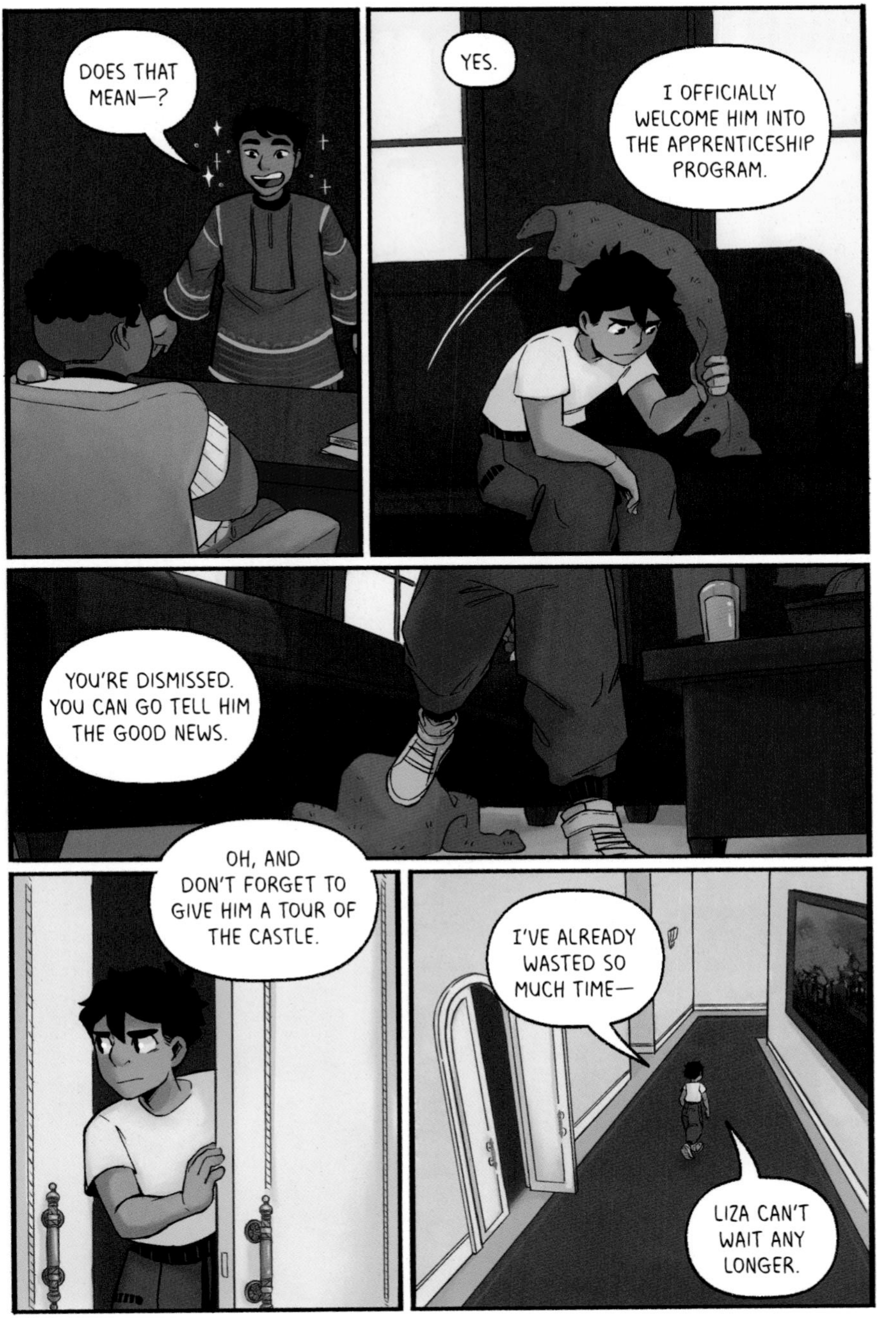
DOES THAT MEAN—?
YES.
I OFFICIALLY WELCOME HIM INTO THE APPRENTICESHIP PROGRAM.
YOU'RE DISMISSED. YOU CAN GO TELL HIM THE GOOD NEWS.
OH, AND DON'T FORGET TO GIVE HIM A TOUR OF THE CASTLE.
I'VE ALREADY WASTED SO MUCH TIME—
LIZA CAN'T WAIT ANY LONGER.

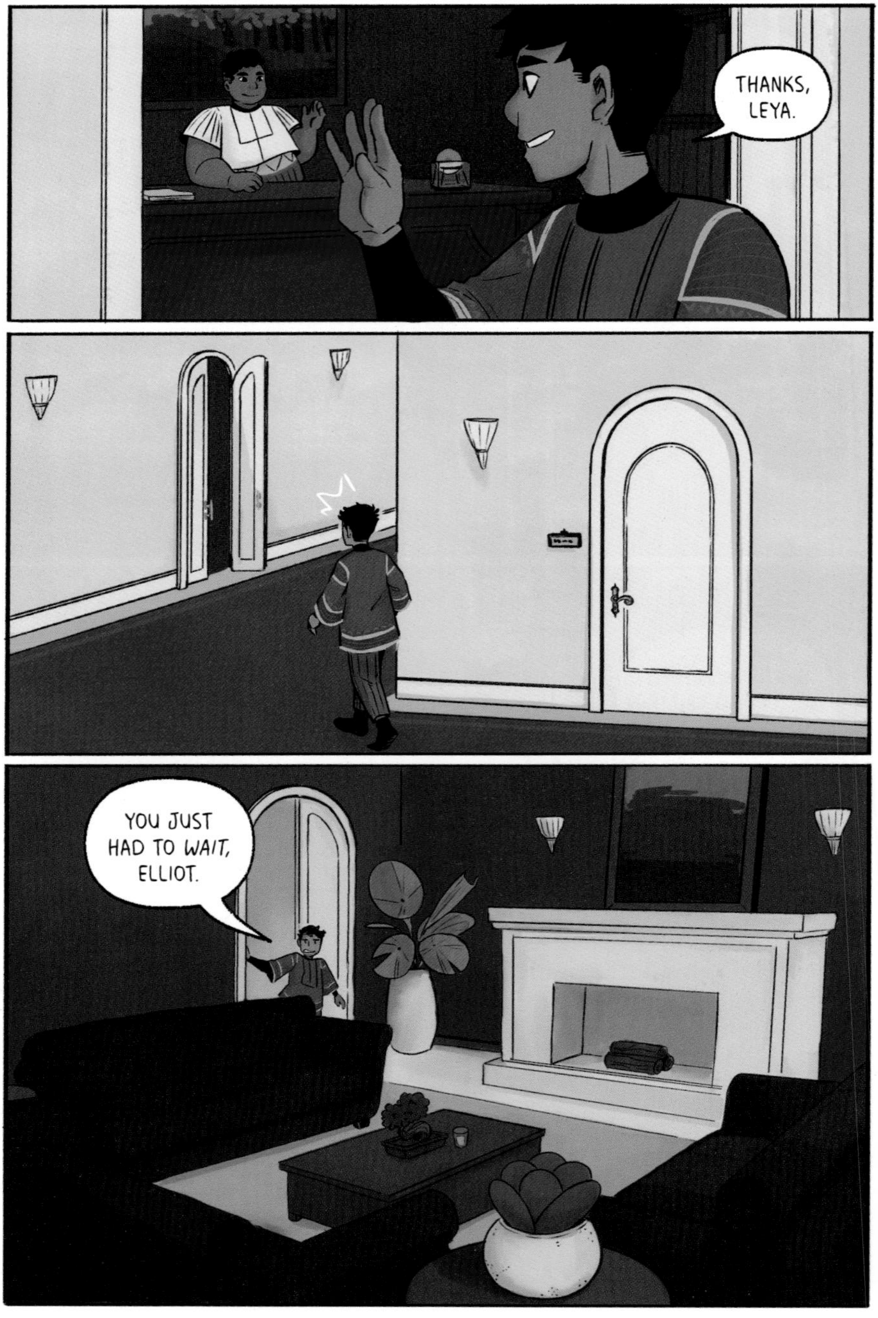
THANKS, LEYA.
YOU JUST HAD TO WAIT, ELLIOT.

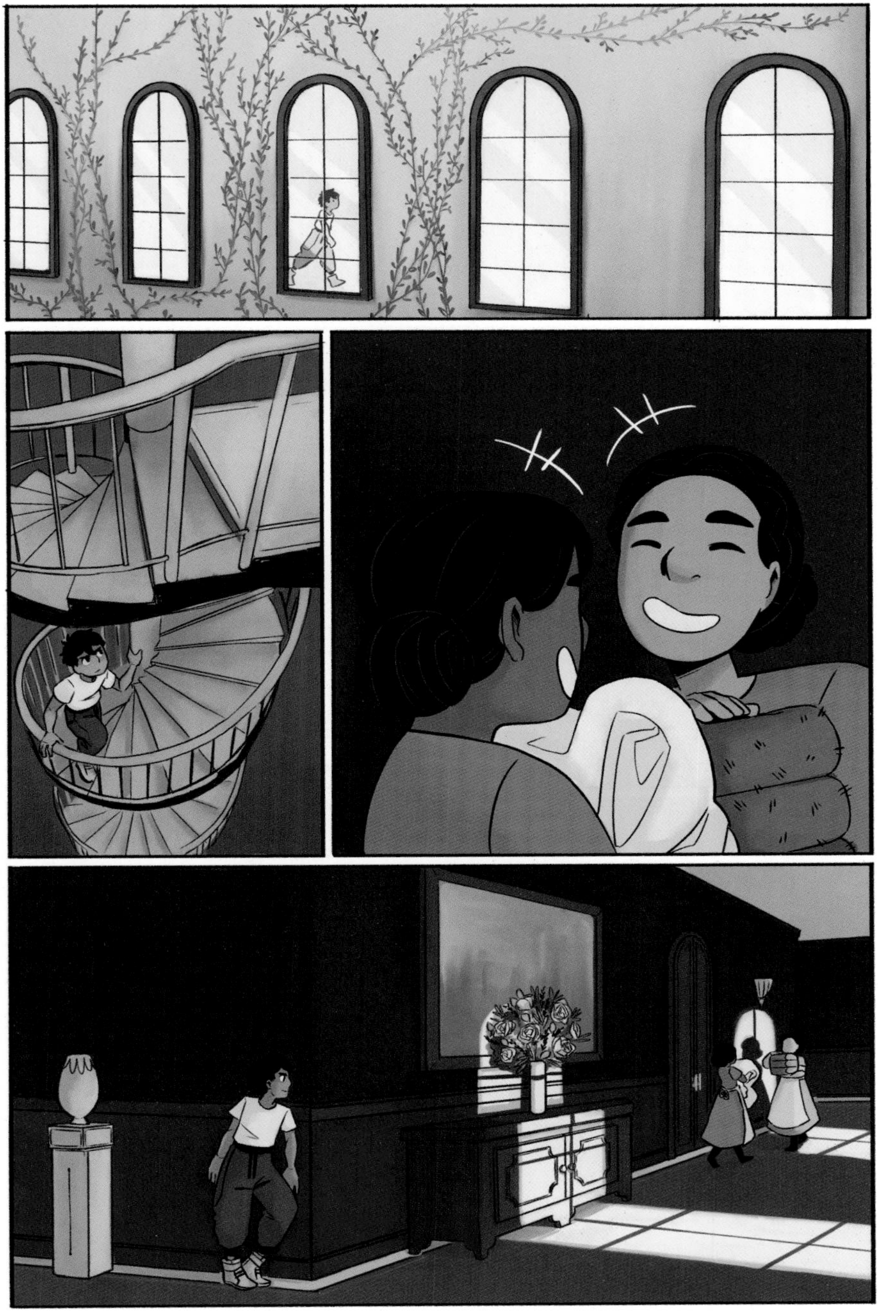

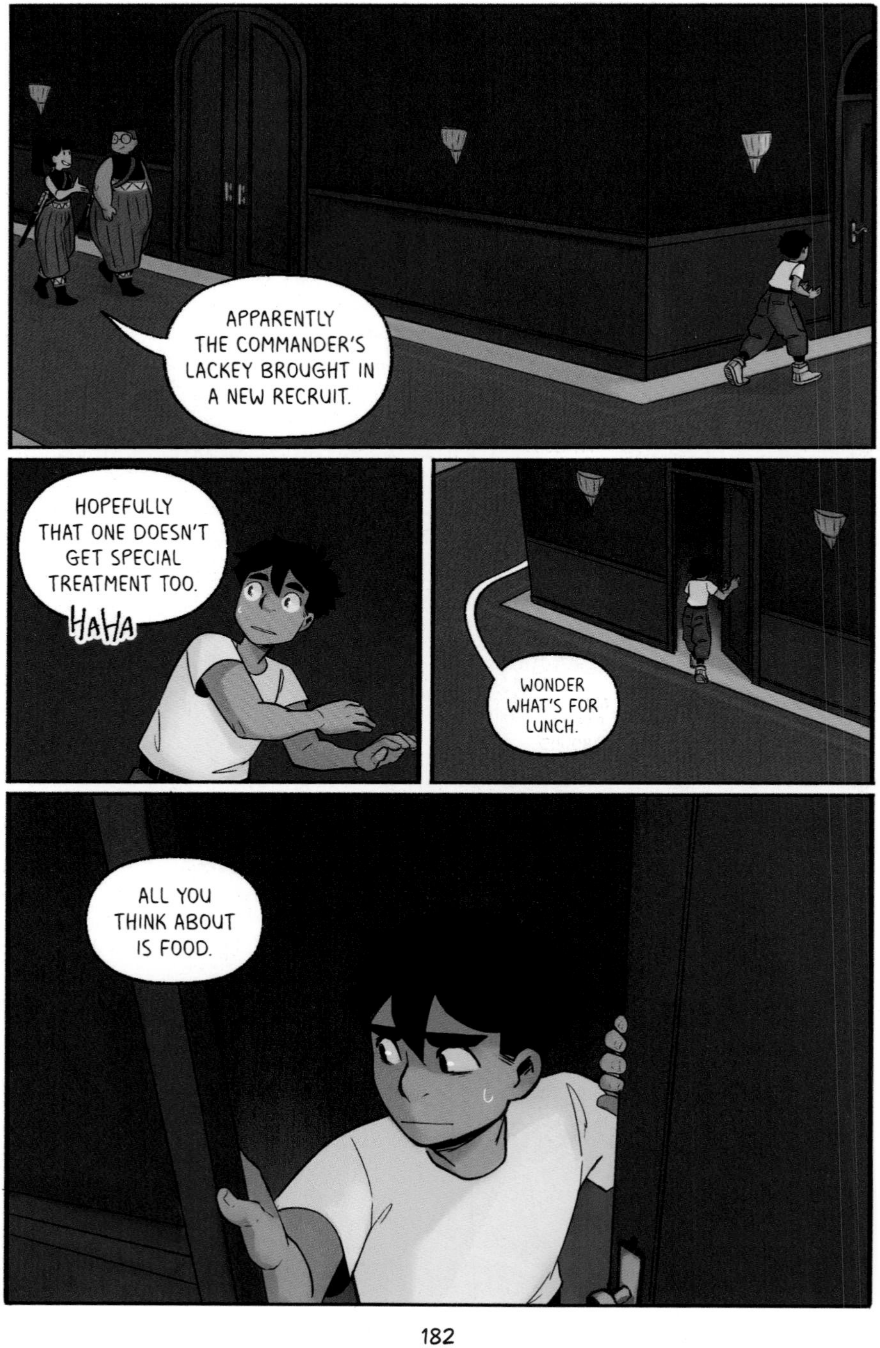
APPARENTLY THE COMMANDER'S LACKEY BROUGHT IN A NEW RECRUIT.
HOPEFULLY THAT ONE DOESN'T GET SPECIAL TREATMENT TOO.
HAHA
WONDER WHAT'S FOR LUNCH.
ALL YOU THINK ABOUT IS FOOD.

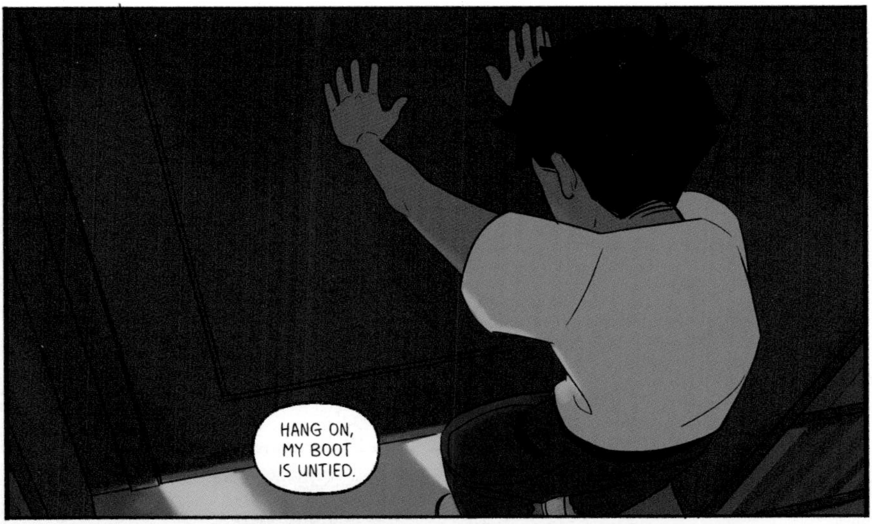
HANG ON, MY BOOT IS UNTIED.

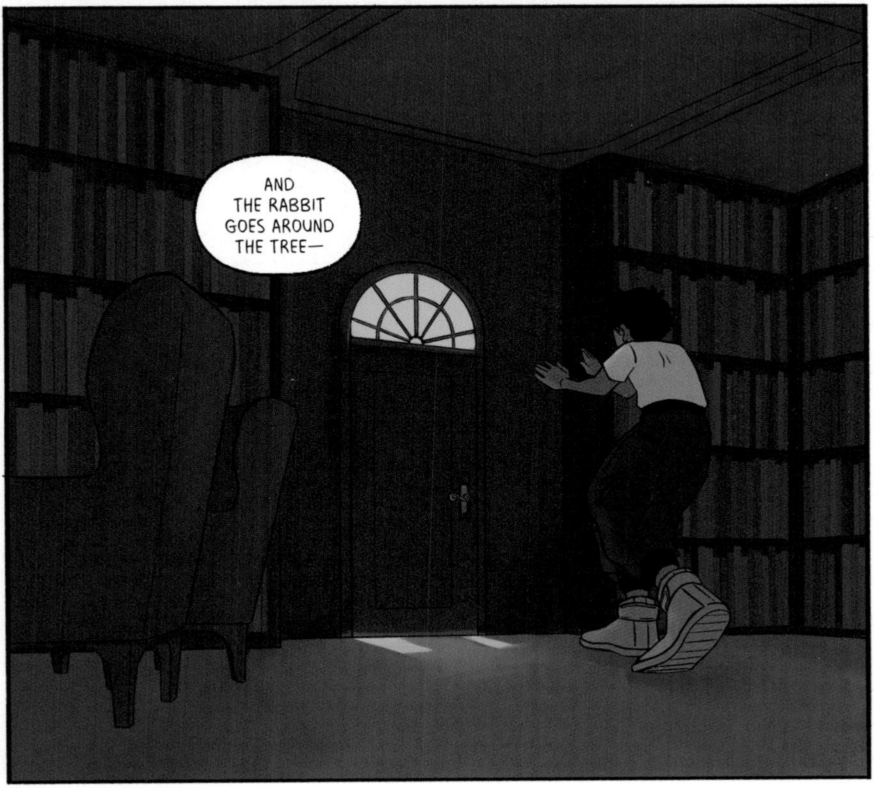
AND THE RABBIT GOES AROUND THE TREE—

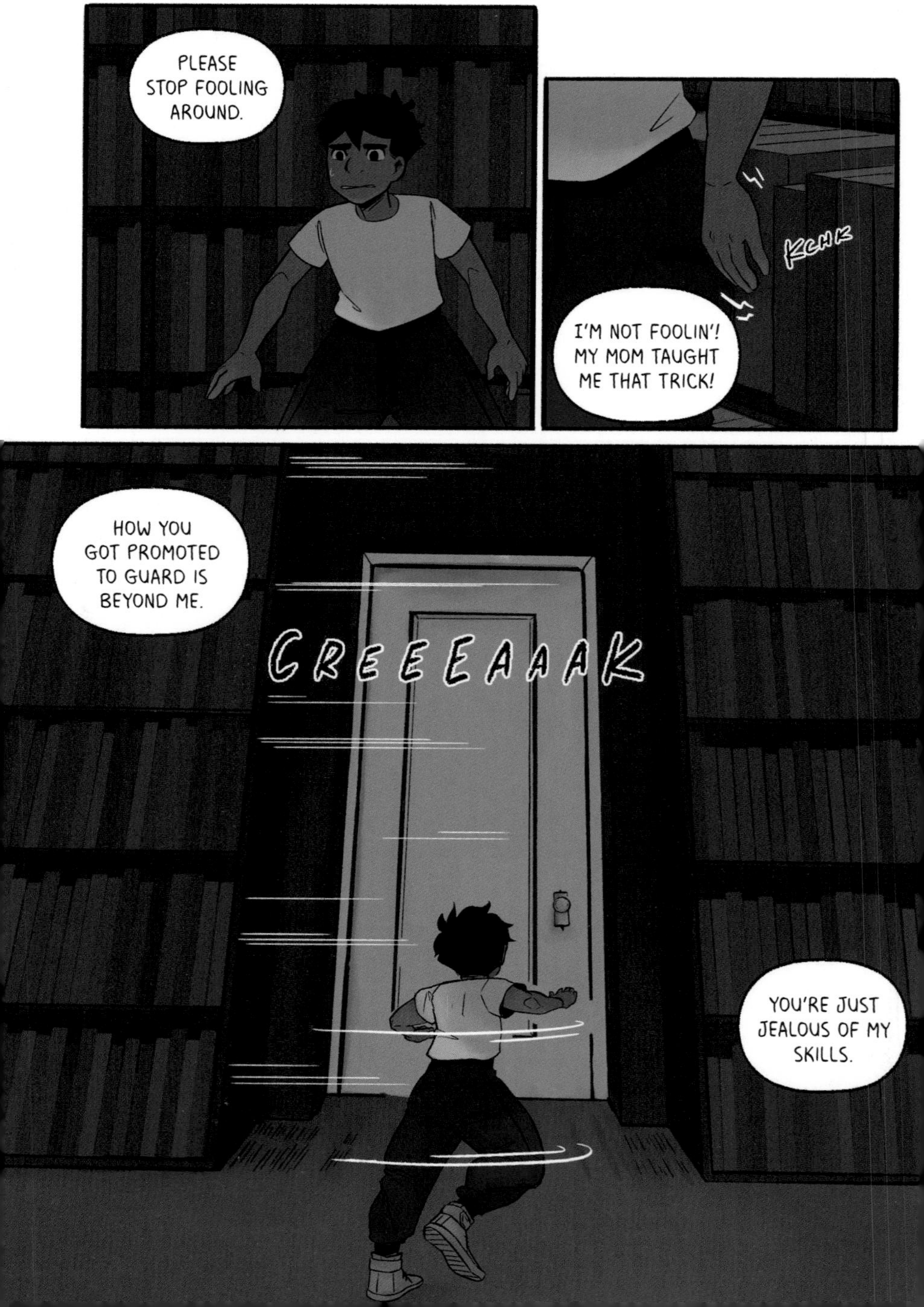
PLEASE STOP FOOLING AROUND.
KCHK
I'M NOT FOOLIN'! MY MOM TAUGHT ME THAT TRICK!
HOW YOU GOT PROMOTED TO GUARD IS BEYOND ME.
CREEEAAAK
YOU'RE JUST JEALOUS OF MY SKILLS.

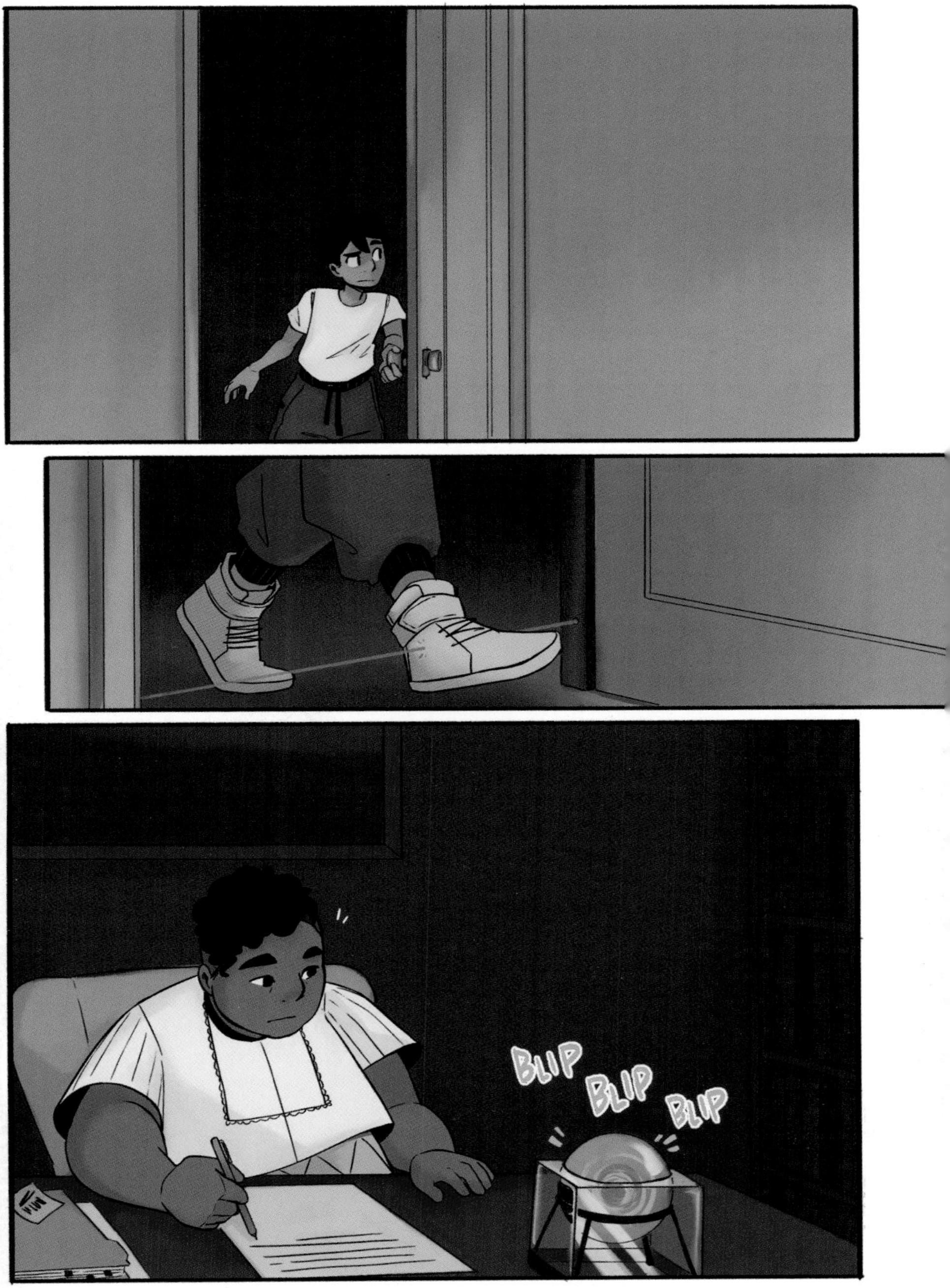
BLIP
BLIP
BLIP

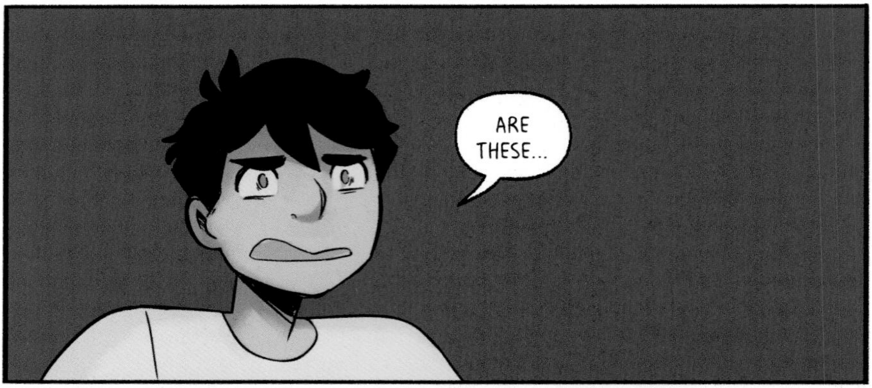
ARE THESE...

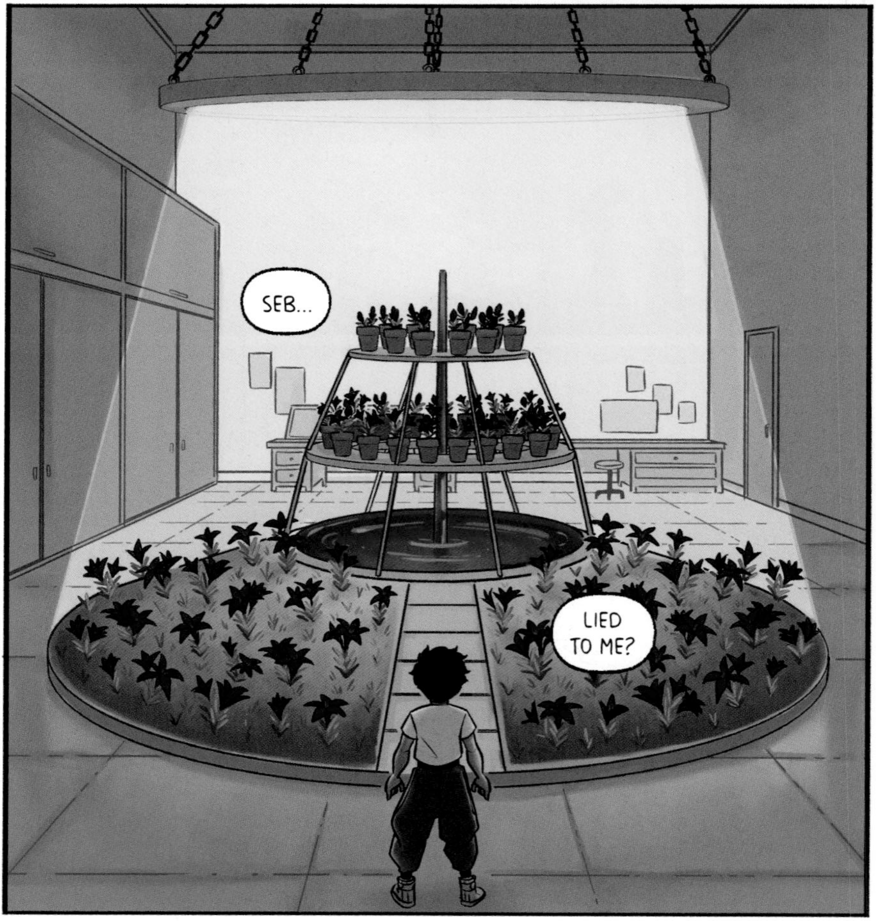
SEB...
LIED TO ME?

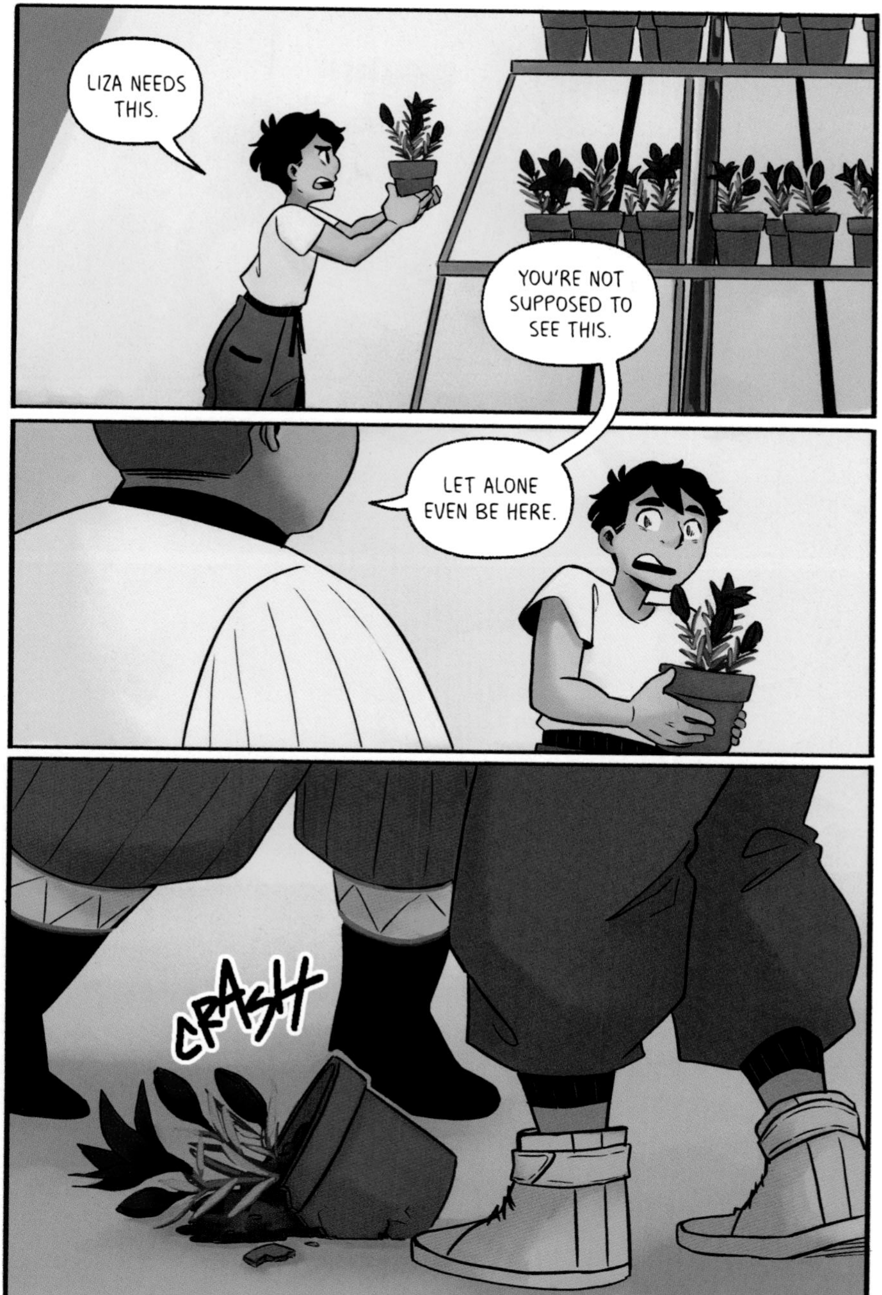
LIZA NEEDS THIS.
YOU'RE NOT SUPPOSED TO SEE THIS.
LET ALONE EVEN BE HERE.
CRASH

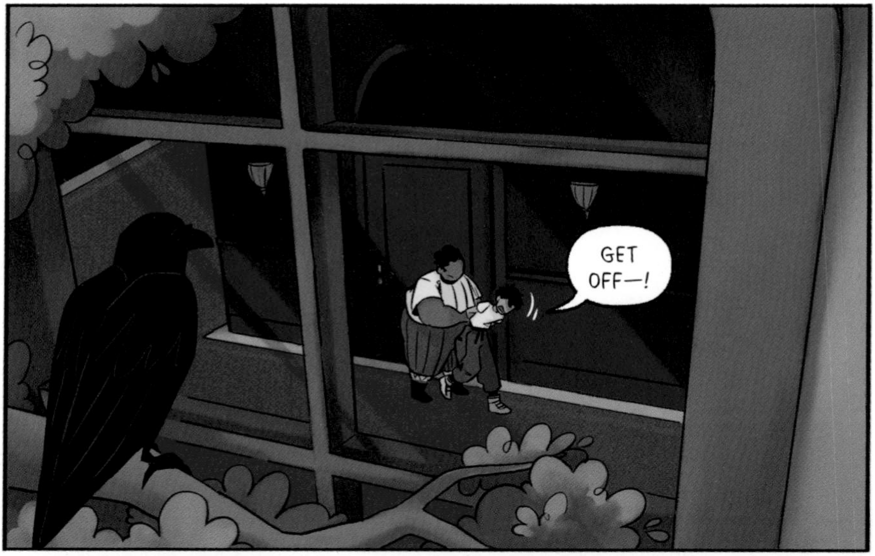
GET OFF—!

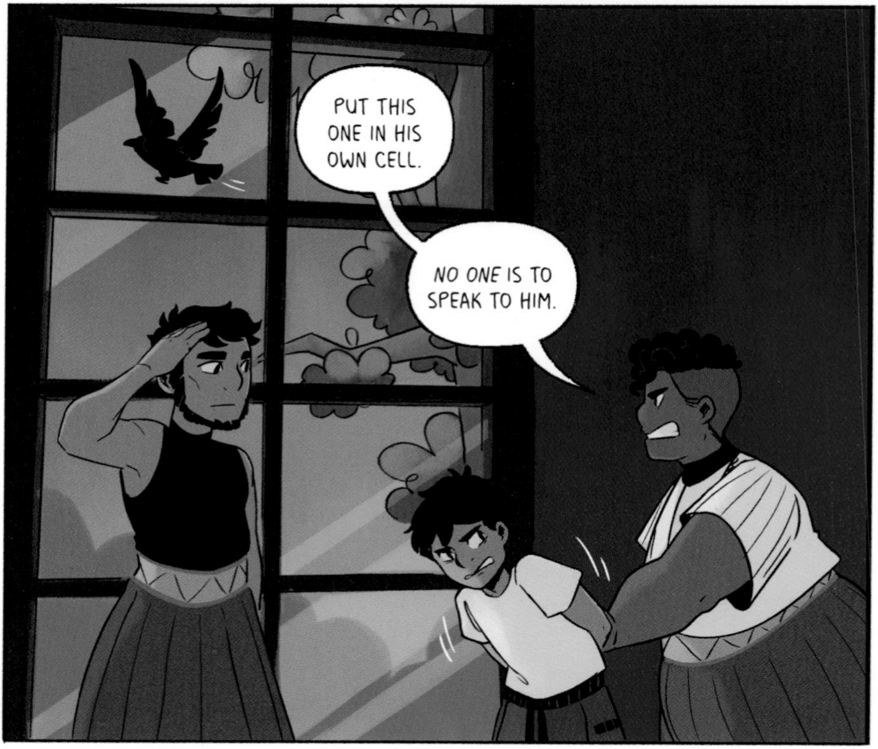
PUT THIS ONE IN HIS OWN CELL.
NO ONE IS TO SPEAK TO HIM.

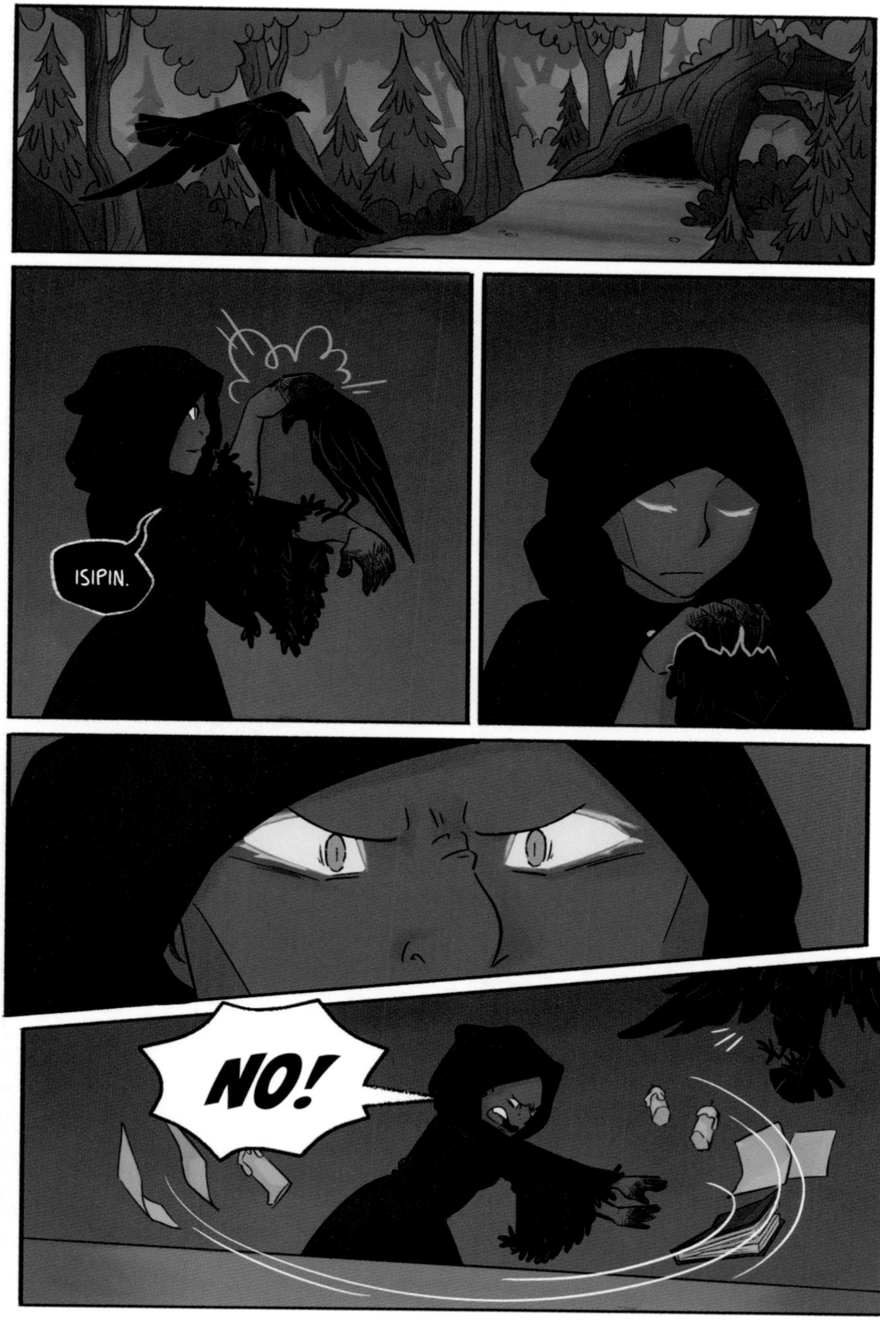
ISIPIN.
NO!

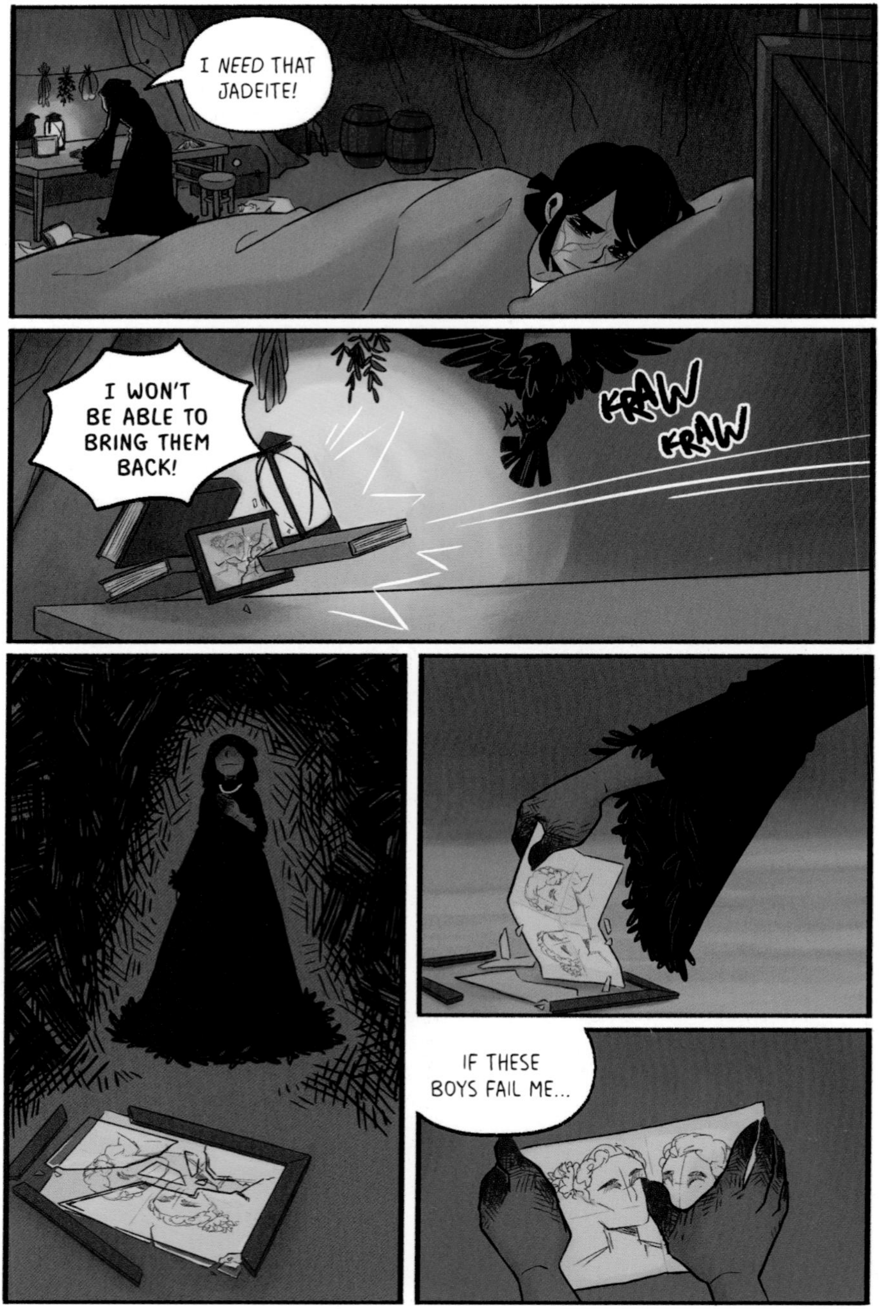
I NEED THAT JADEITE!
I WON'T BE ABLE TO BRING THEM BACK!
KRAW KRAW
IF THESE BOYS FAIL ME...

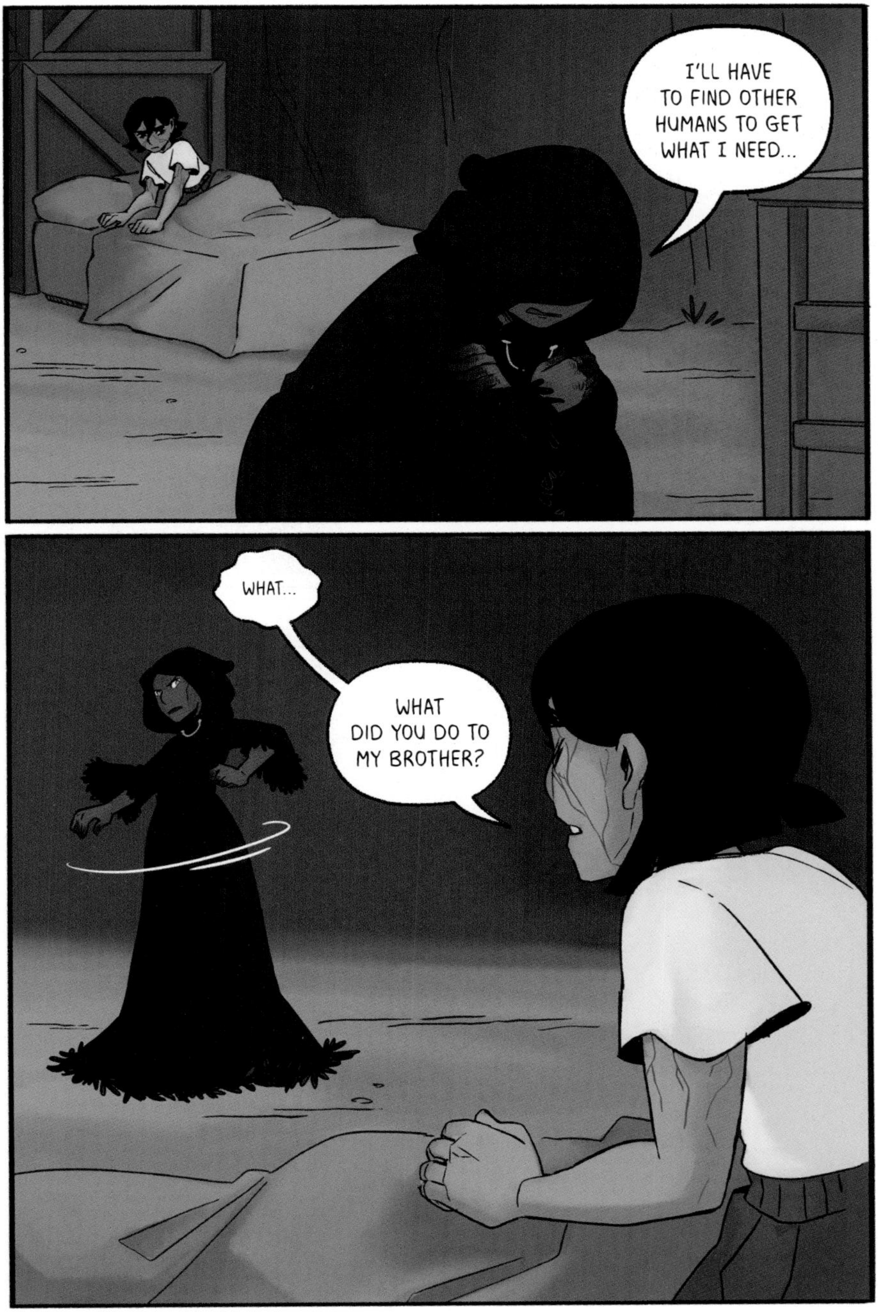
I'LL HAVE TO FIND OTHER HUMANS TO GET WHAT I NEED...
WHAT...
WHAT DID YOU DO TO MY BROTHER?

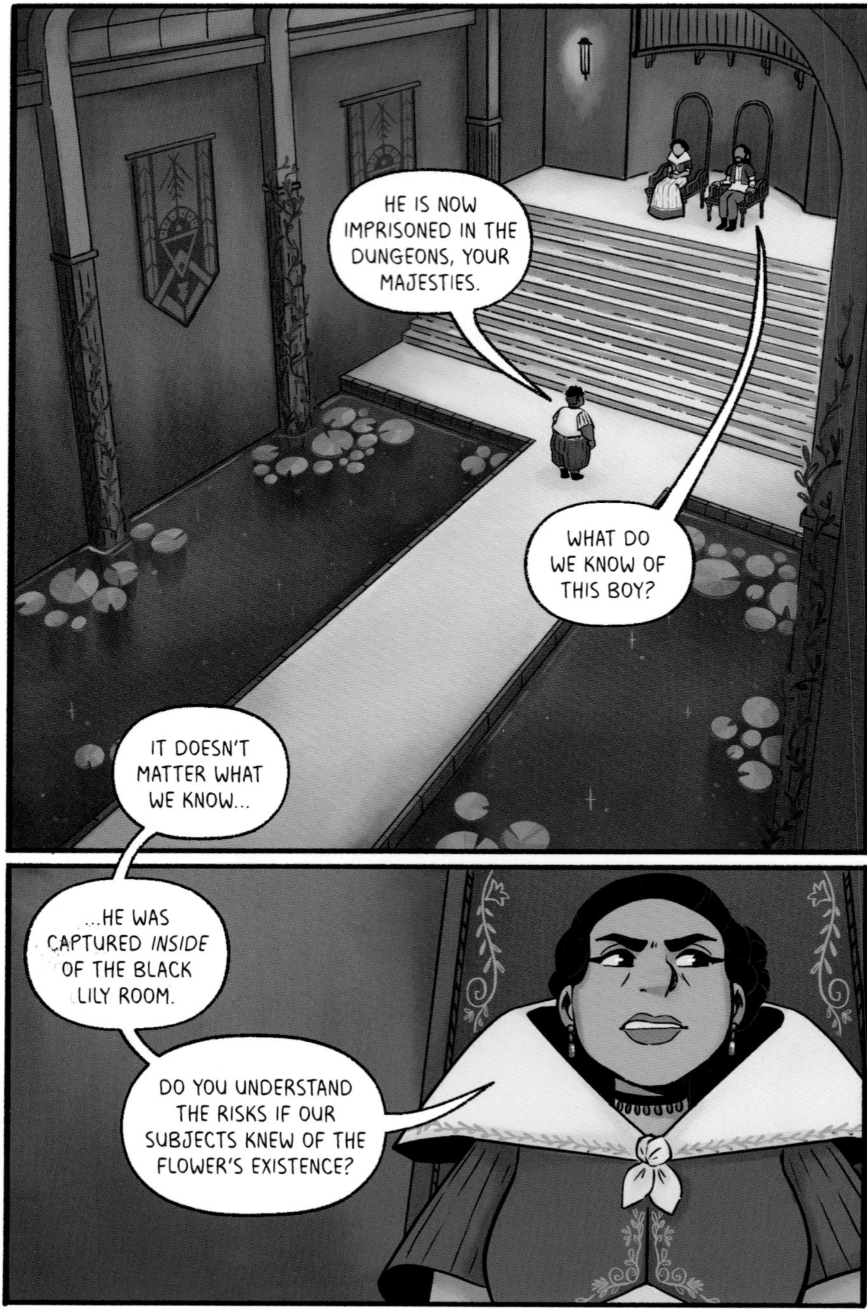
HE IS NOW IMPRISONED IN THE DUNGEONS, YOUR MAJESTIES.
WHAT DO WE KNOW OF THIS BOY?
IT DOESN'T MATTER WHAT WE KNOW...
...HE WAS CAPTURED *INSIDE* OF THE BLACK LILY ROOM.
DO YOU UNDERSTAND THE RISKS IF OUR SUBJECTS KNEW OF THE FLOWER'S EXISTENCE?

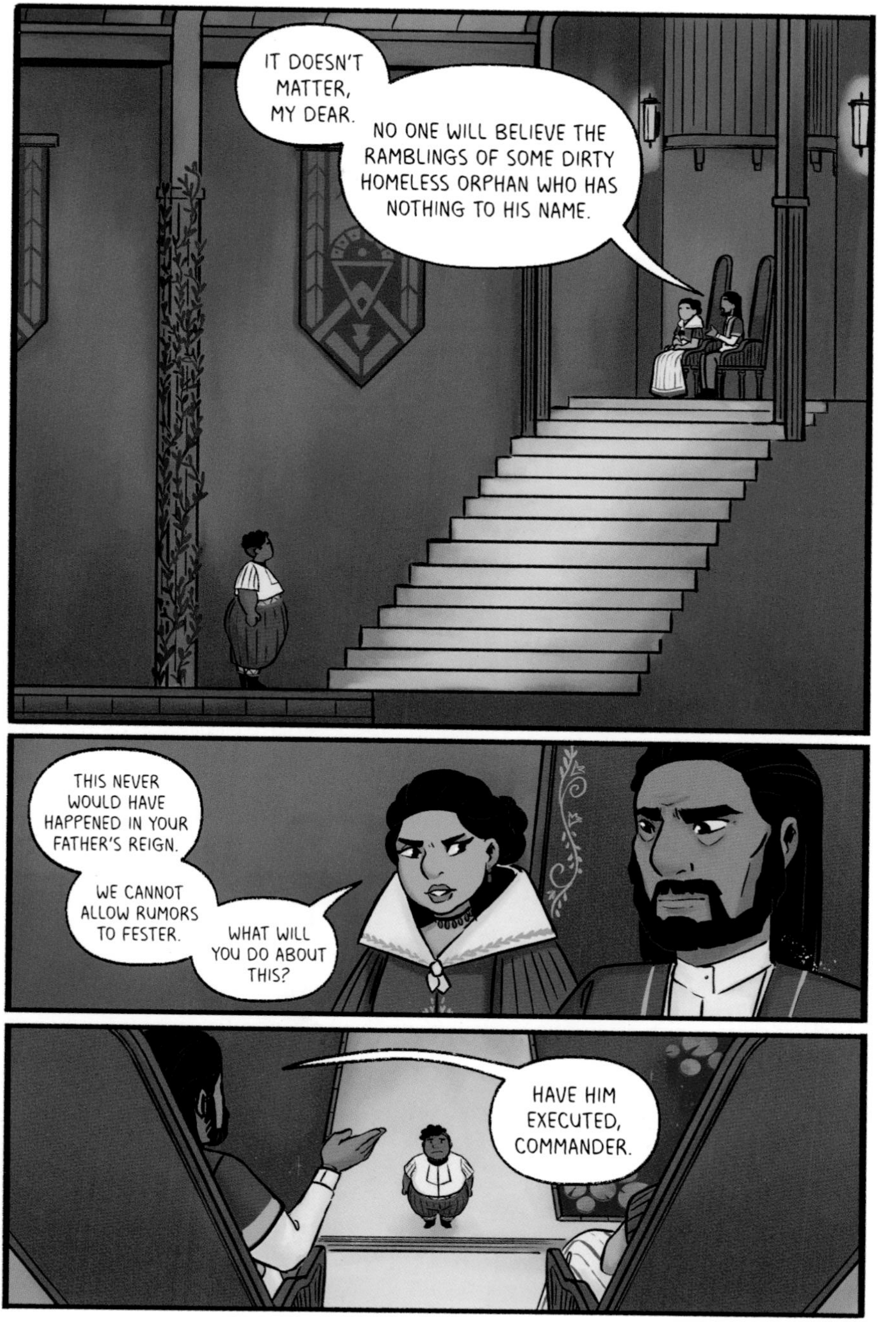
IT DOESN'T MATTER, MY DEAR.
NO ONE WILL BELIEVE THE RAMBLINGS OF SOME DIRTY HOMELESS ORPHAN WHO HAS NOTHING TO HIS NAME.
THIS NEVER WOULD HAVE HAPPENED IN YOUR FATHER'S REIGN.
WE CANNOT ALLOW RUMORS TO FESTER.
WHAT WILL YOU DO ABOUT THIS?
HAVE HIM EXECUTED, COMMANDER.

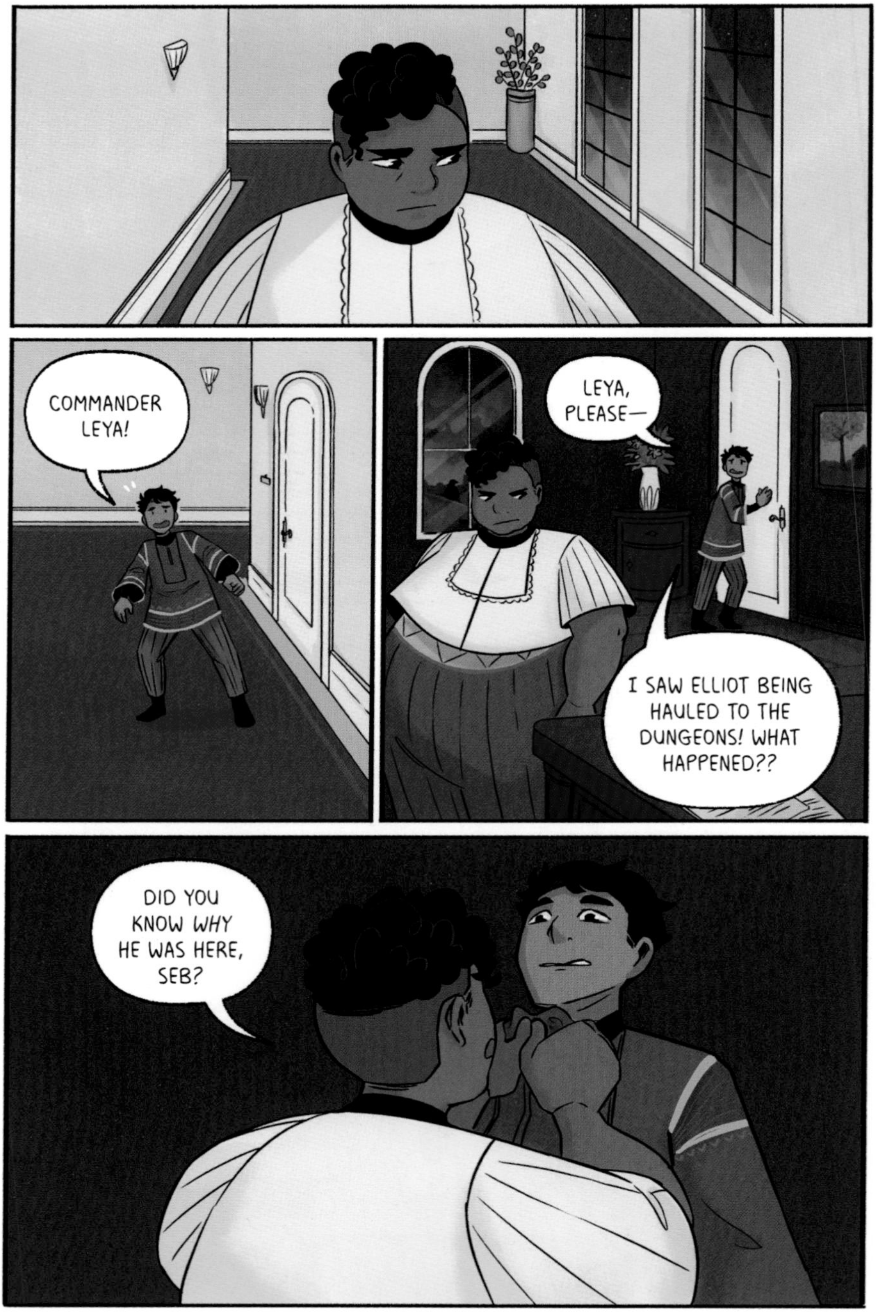
COMMANDER LEYA!
LEYA, PLEASE—
I SAW ELLIOT BEING HAULED TO THE DUNGEONS! WHAT HAPPENED??
DID YOU KNOW *WHY* HE WAS HERE, SEB?

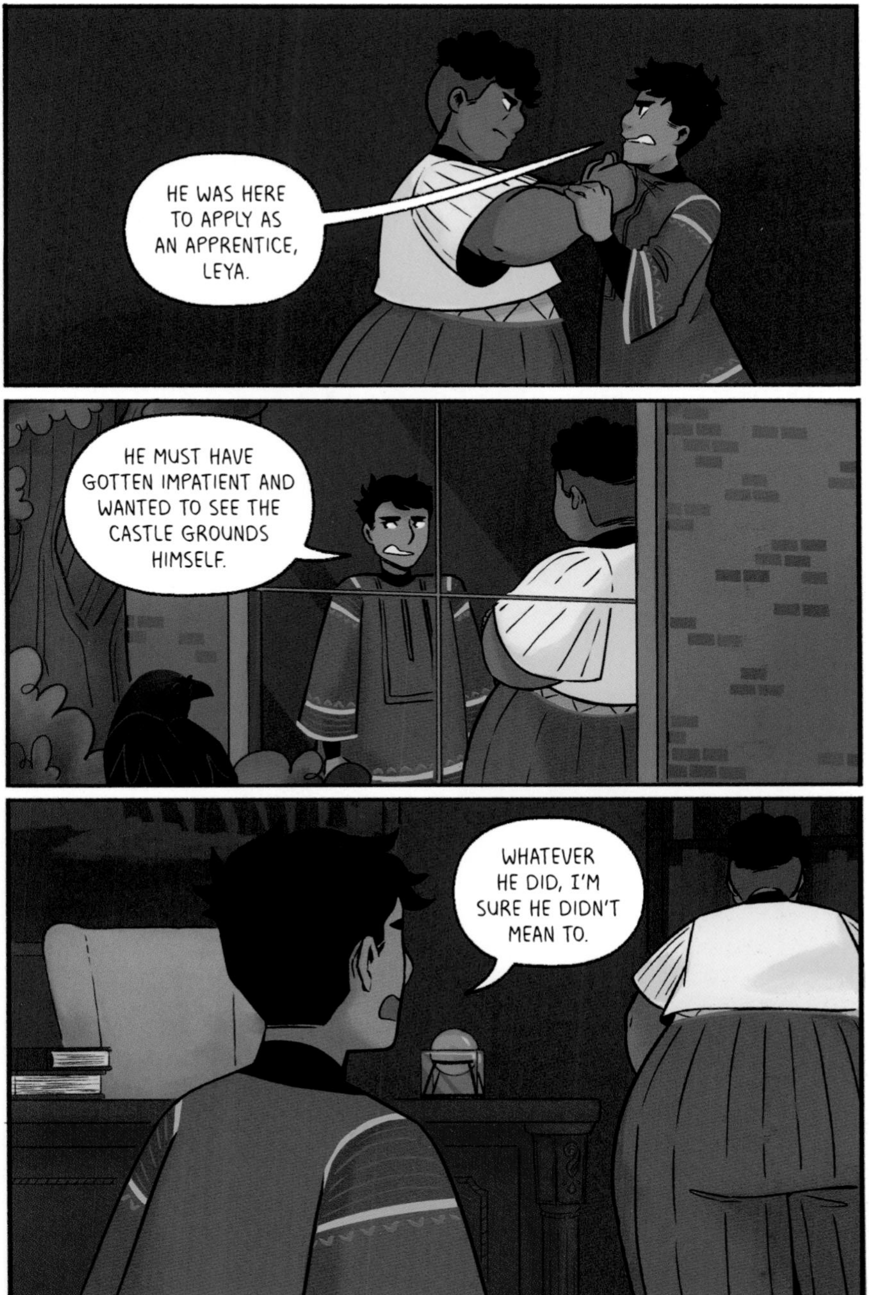
HE WAS HERE TO APPLY AS AN APPRENTICE, LEYA.
HE MUST HAVE GOTTEN IMPATIENT AND WANTED TO SEE THE CASTLE GROUNDS HIMSELF.
WHATEVER HE DID, I'M SURE HE DIDN'T MEAN TO.

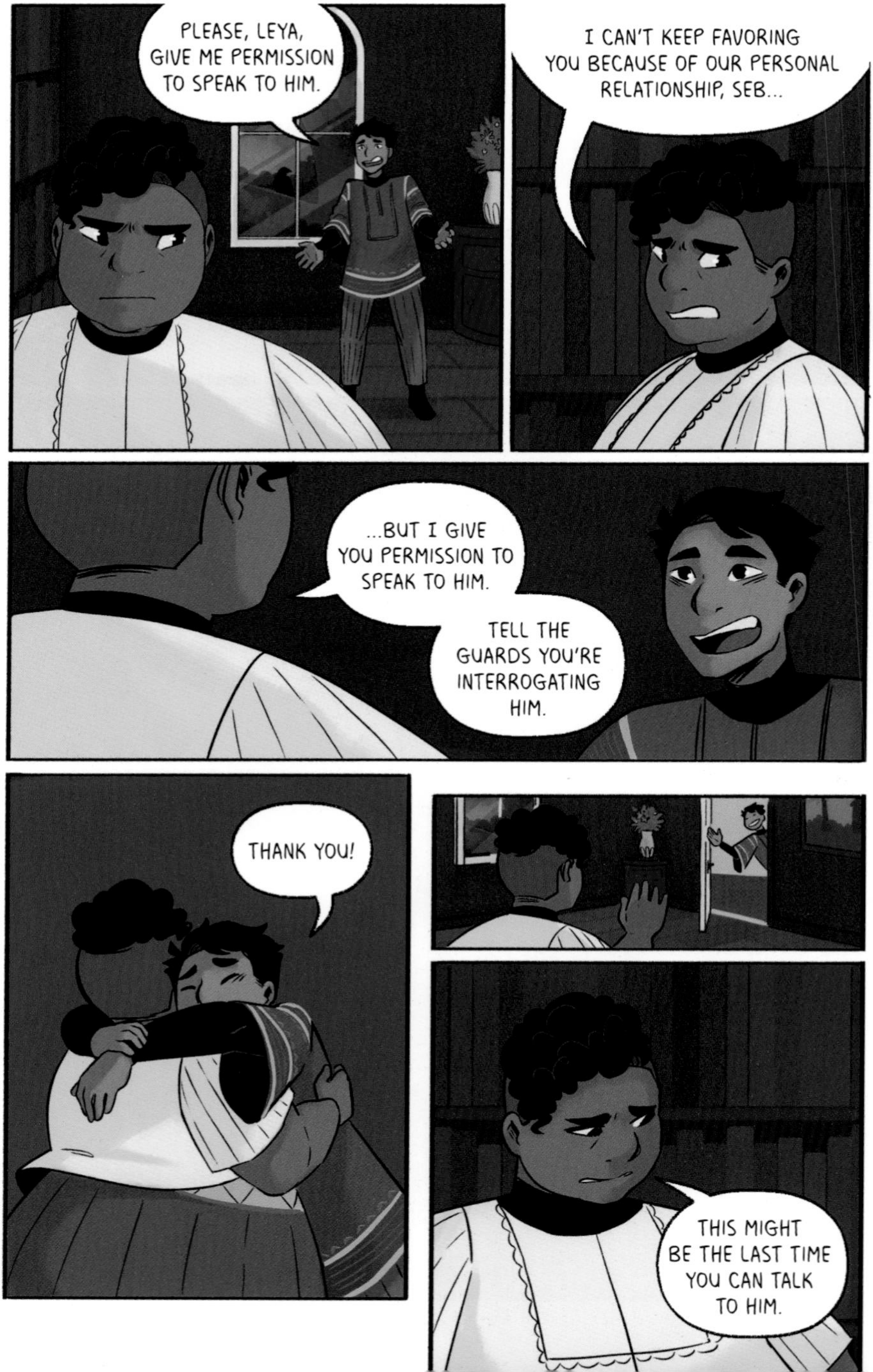
PLEASE, LEYA, GIVE ME PERMISSION TO SPEAK TO HIM.
I CAN'T KEEP FAVORING YOU BECAUSE OF OUR PERSONAL RELATIONSHIP, SEB...
...BUT I GIVE YOU PERMISSION TO SPEAK TO HIM.
TELL THE GUARDS YOU'RE INTERROGATING HIM.
THANK YOU!
THIS MIGHT BE THE LAST TIME YOU CAN TALK TO HIM.

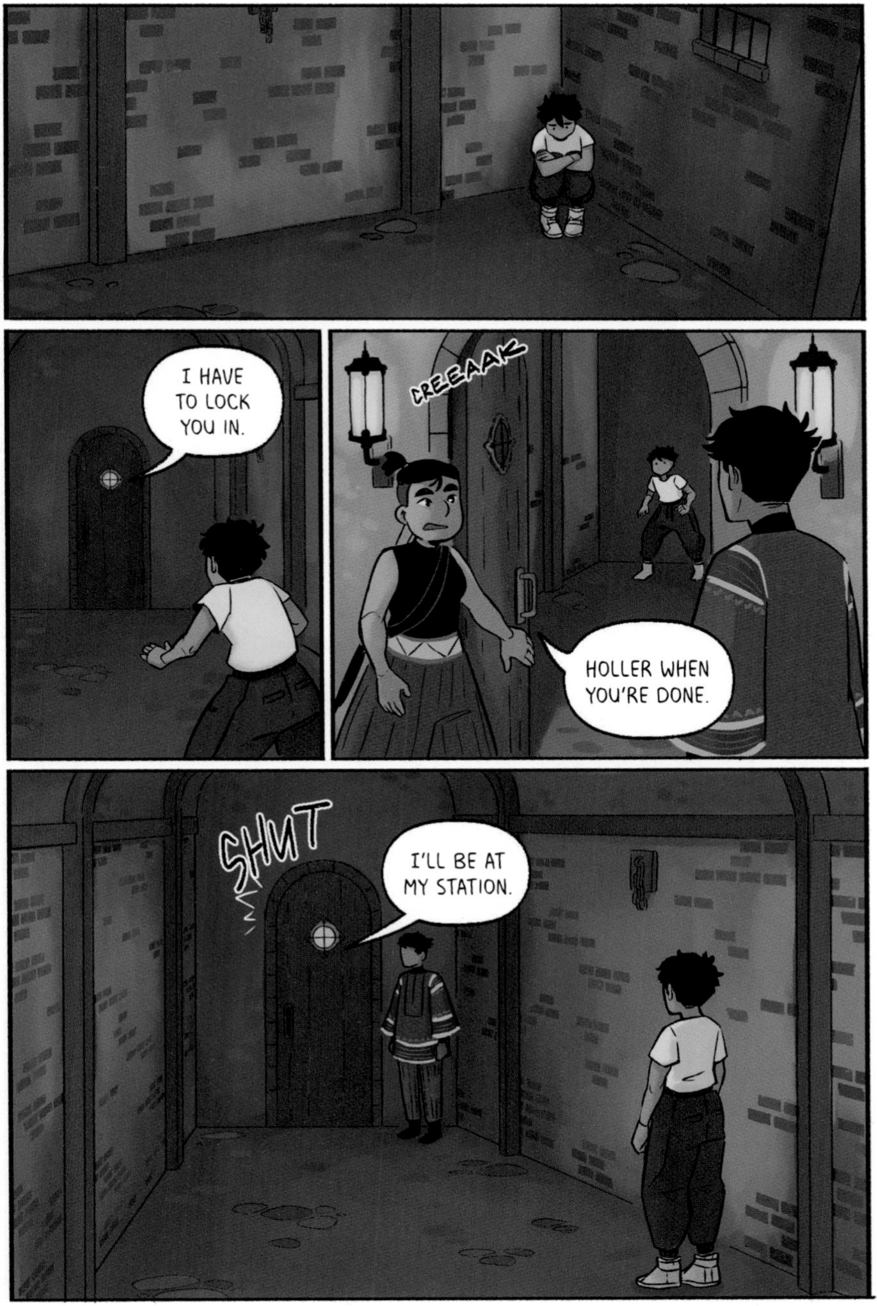
I HAVE TO LOCK YOU IN.
CREEAAK
HOLLER WHEN YOU'RE DONE.
SHUT
I'LL BE AT MY STATION.

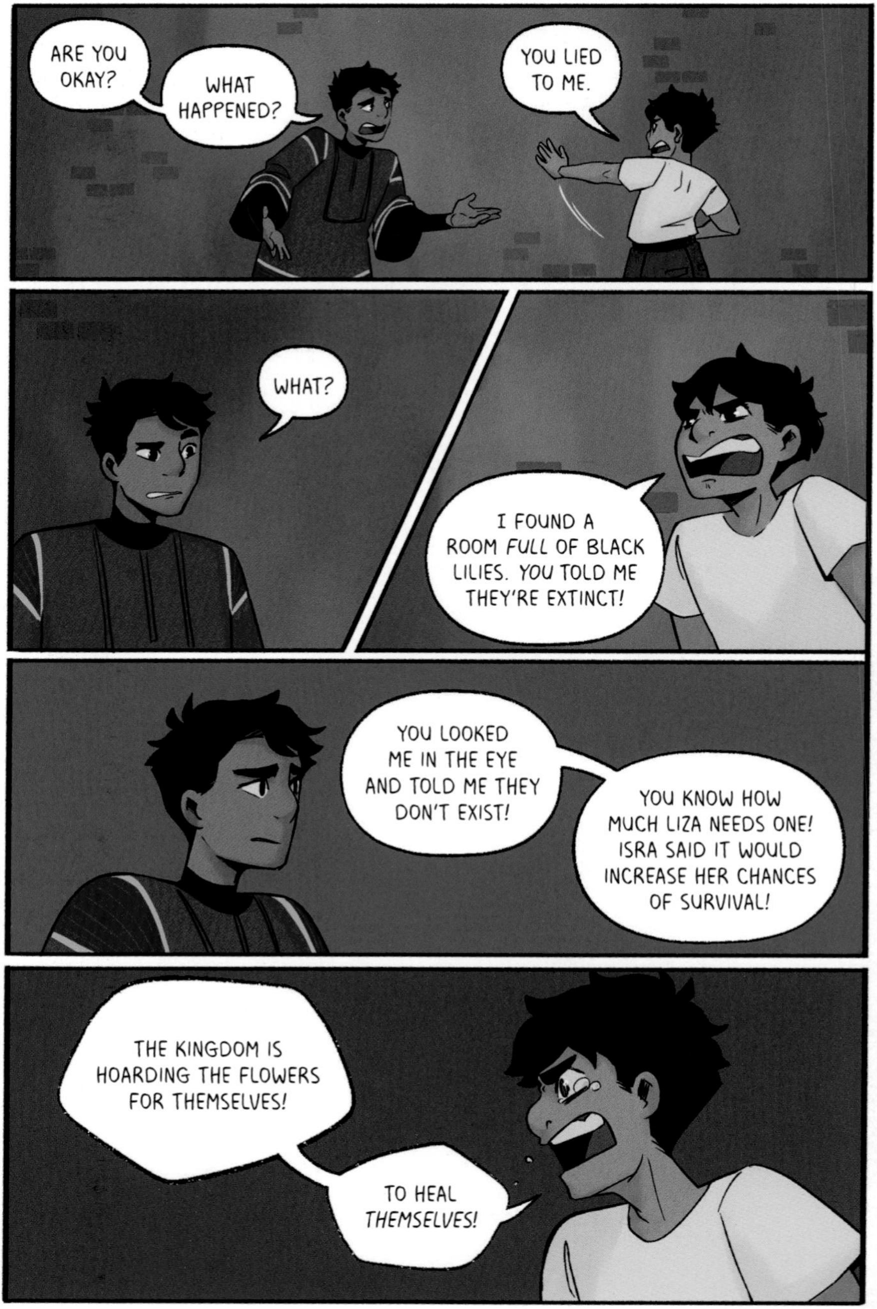
ARE YOU OKAY?
WHAT HAPPENED?
YOU LIED TO ME.
WHAT?
I FOUND A ROOM *FULL* OF BLACK LILIES. *YOU* TOLD ME THEY'RE EXTINCT!
YOU LOOKED ME IN THE EYE AND TOLD ME THEY DON'T EXIST!
YOU KNOW HOW MUCH LIZA NEEDS ONE! ISRA SAID IT WOULD INCREASE HER CHANCES OF SURVIVAL!
THE KINGDOM IS HOARDING THE FLOWERS FOR THEMSELVES!
TO HEAL *THEMSELVES!*

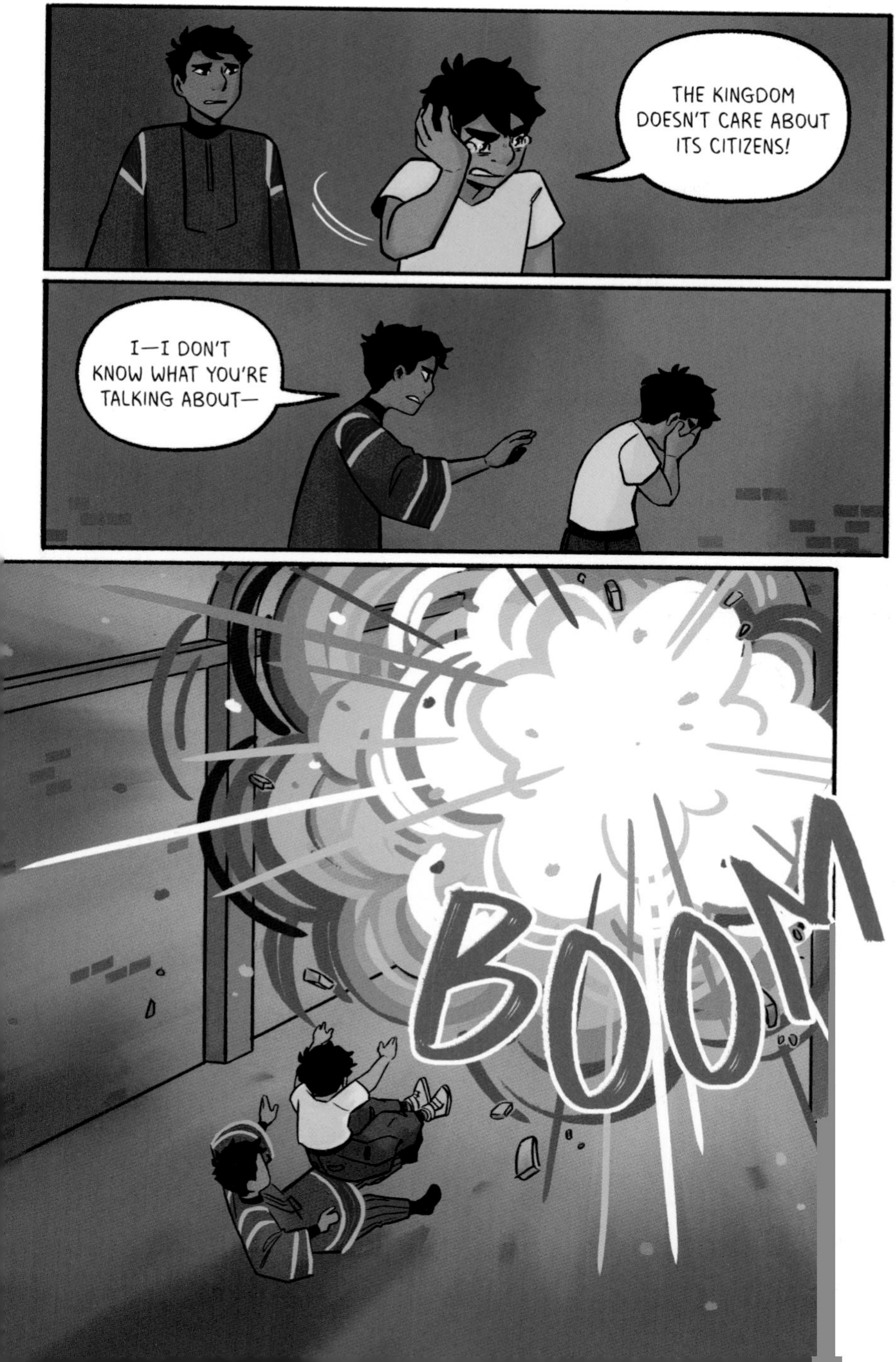
THE KINGDOM DOESN'T CARE ABOUT ITS CITIZENS!
I—I DON'T KNOW WHAT YOU'RE TALKING ABOUT—
BOOM

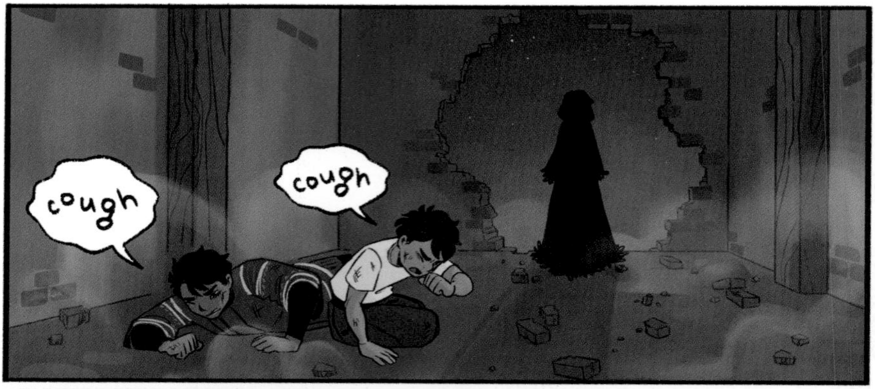
cough
cough

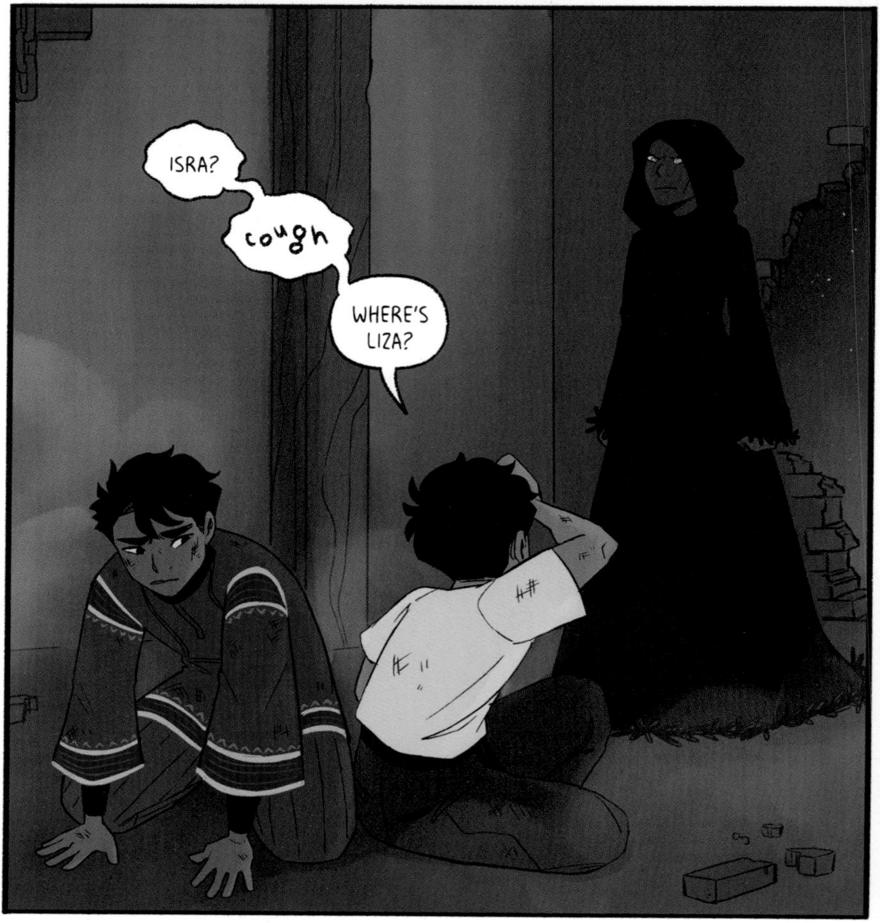
ISRA?
cough
WHERE'S LIZA?

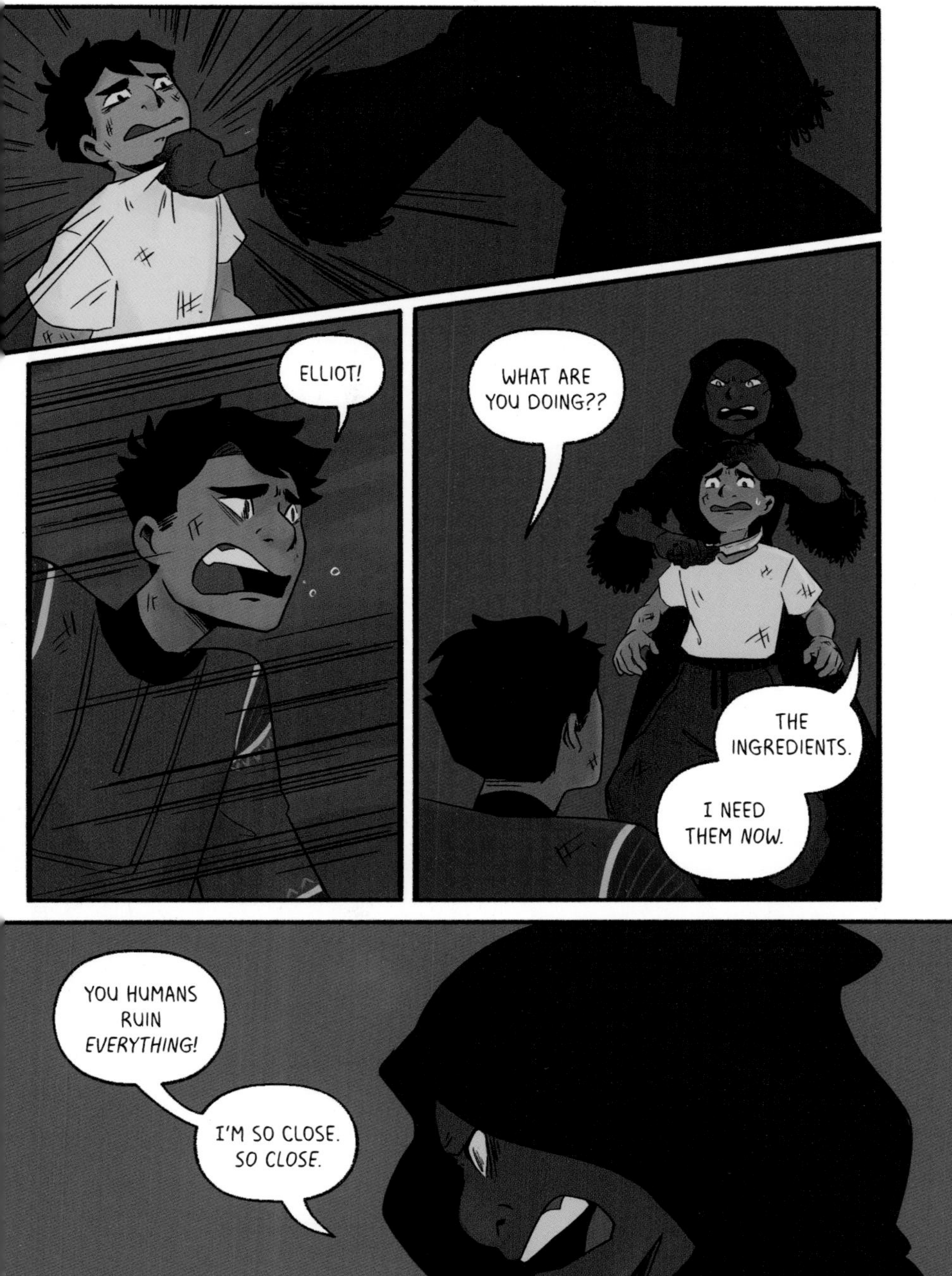
ELLIOT!
WHAT ARE YOU DOING??
THE INGREDIENTS.
I NEED THEM NOW.
YOU HUMANS RUIN EVERYTHING!
I'M SO CLOSE. SO CLOSE.

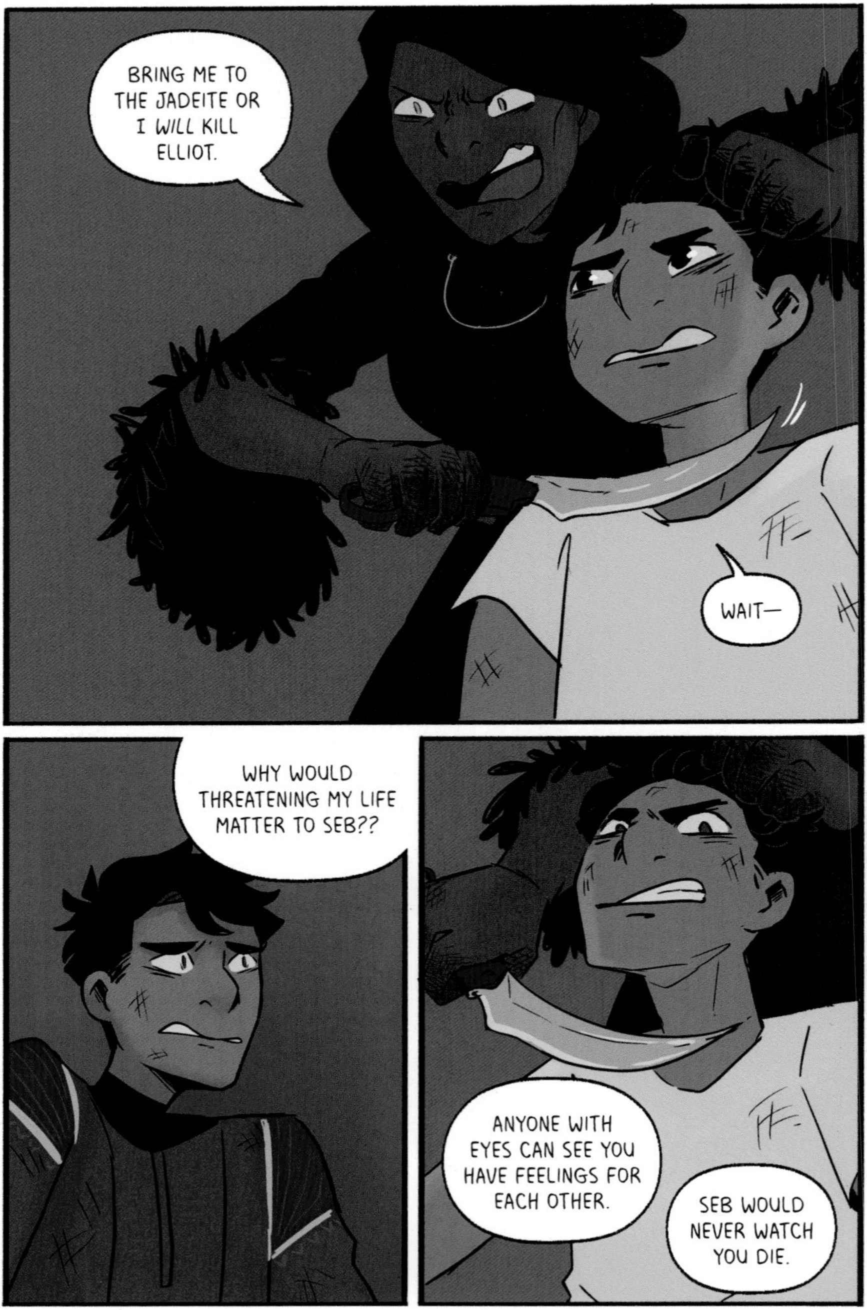
BRING ME TO THE JADEITE OR I *WILL* KILL ELLIOT.
WAIT—
WHY WOULD THREATENING MY LIFE MATTER TO SEB??
ANYONE WITH EYES CAN SEE YOU HAVE FEELINGS FOR EACH OTHER.
SEB WOULD NEVER WATCH YOU DIE.

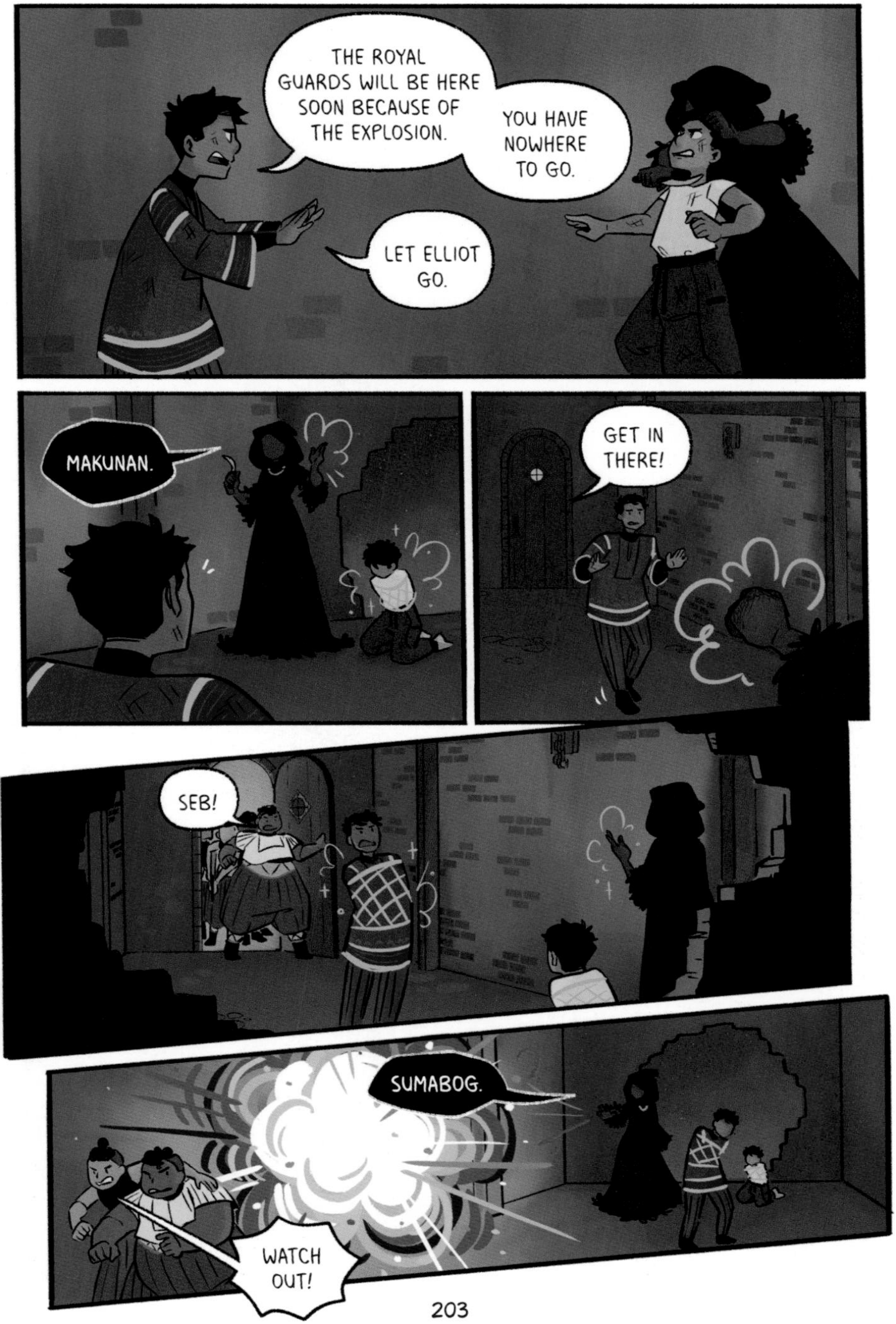
THE ROYAL GUARDS WILL BE HERE SOON BECAUSE OF THE EXPLOSION.
YOU HAVE NOWHERE TO GO.
LET ELLIOT GO.
MAKUNAN.
GET IN THERE!
SEB!
SUMABOG.
WATCH OUT!

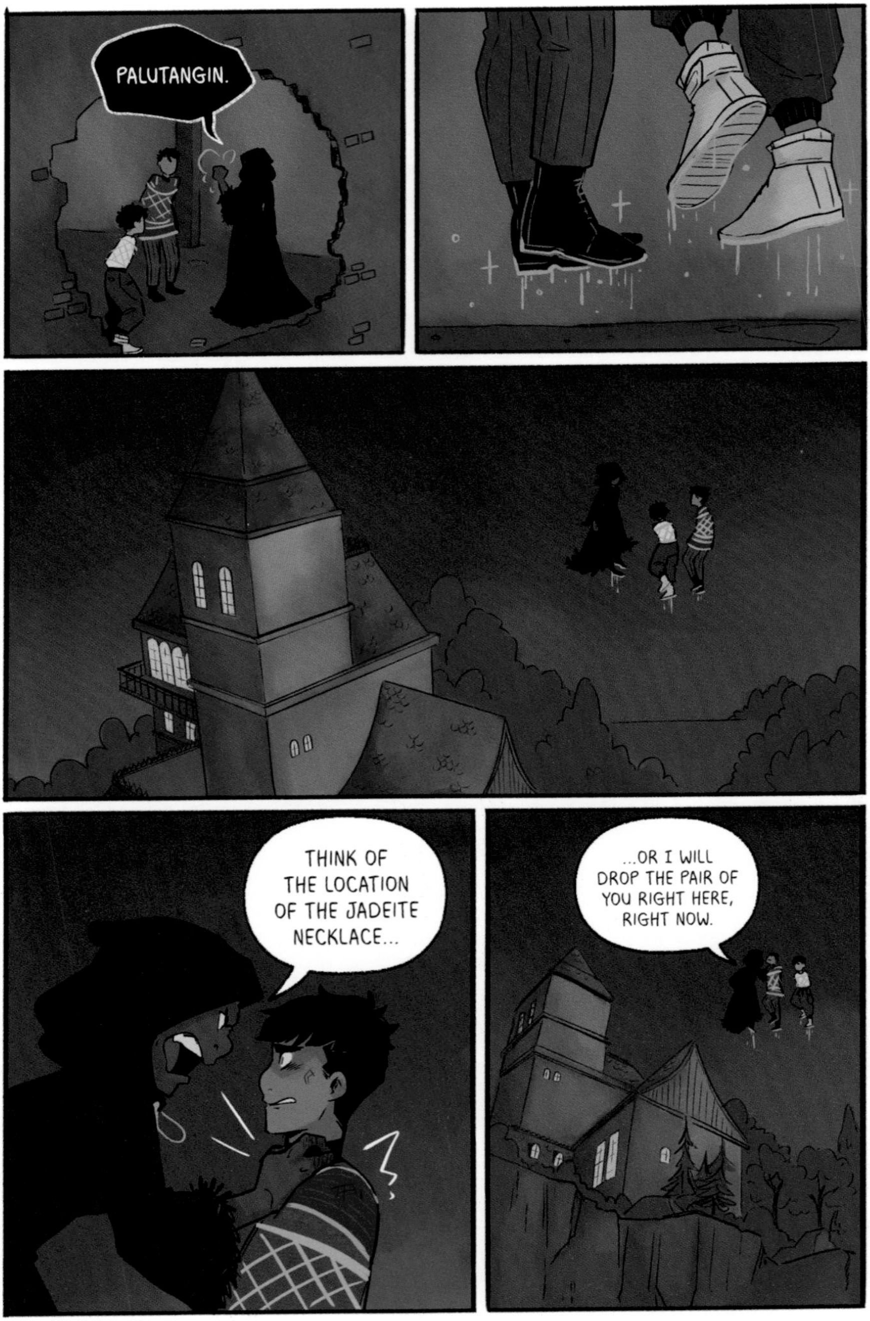
PALUTANGIN.
THINK OF THE LOCATION OF THE JADEITE NECKLACE...
...OR I WILL DROP THE PAIR OF YOU RIGHT HERE, RIGHT NOW.

TAKE IT!

ISIPIN ANG LUGAR.

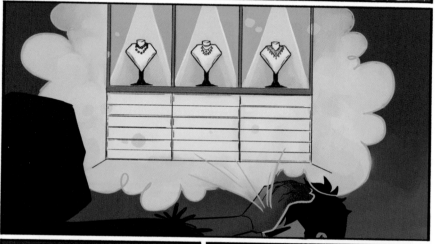

POOF

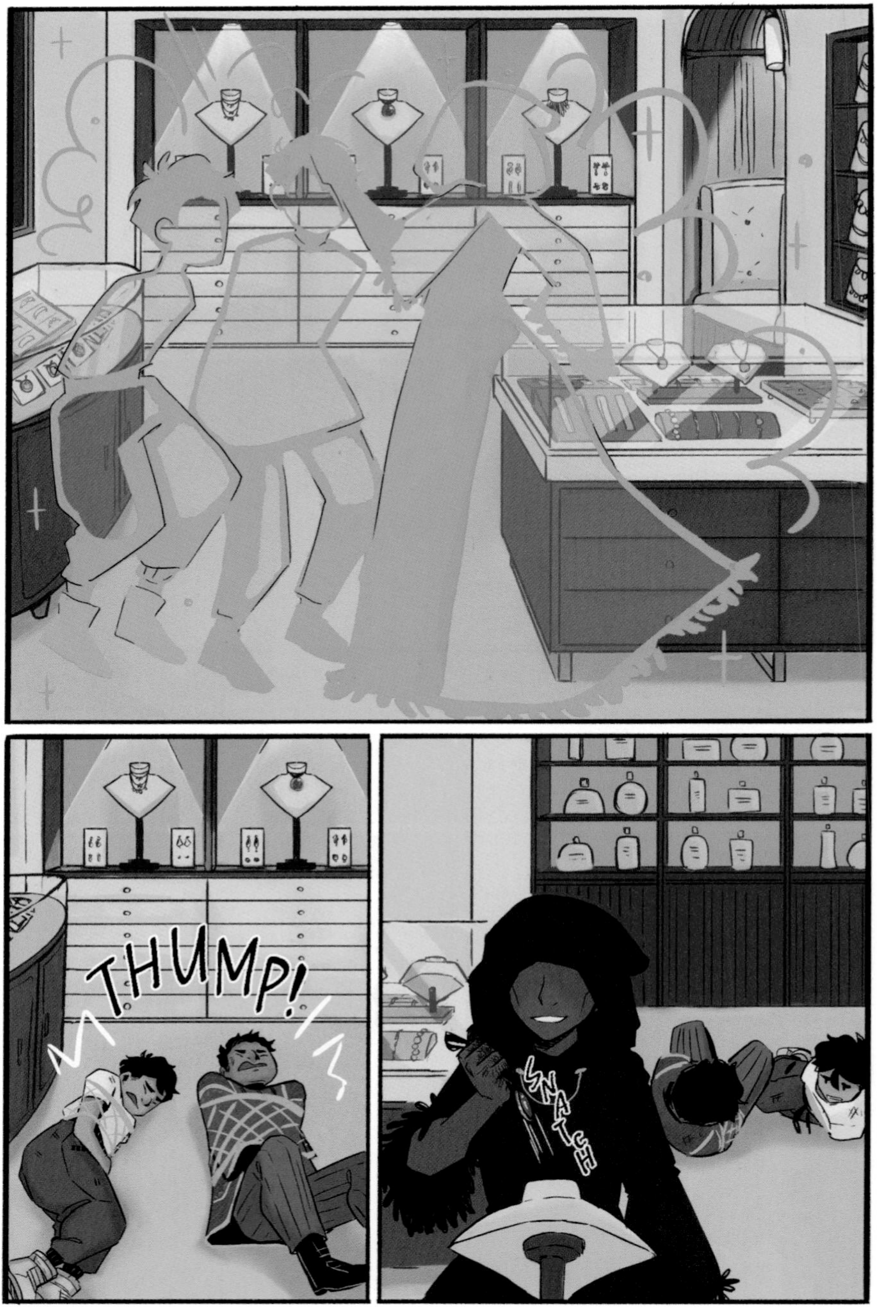
THUMP!
SNATCH

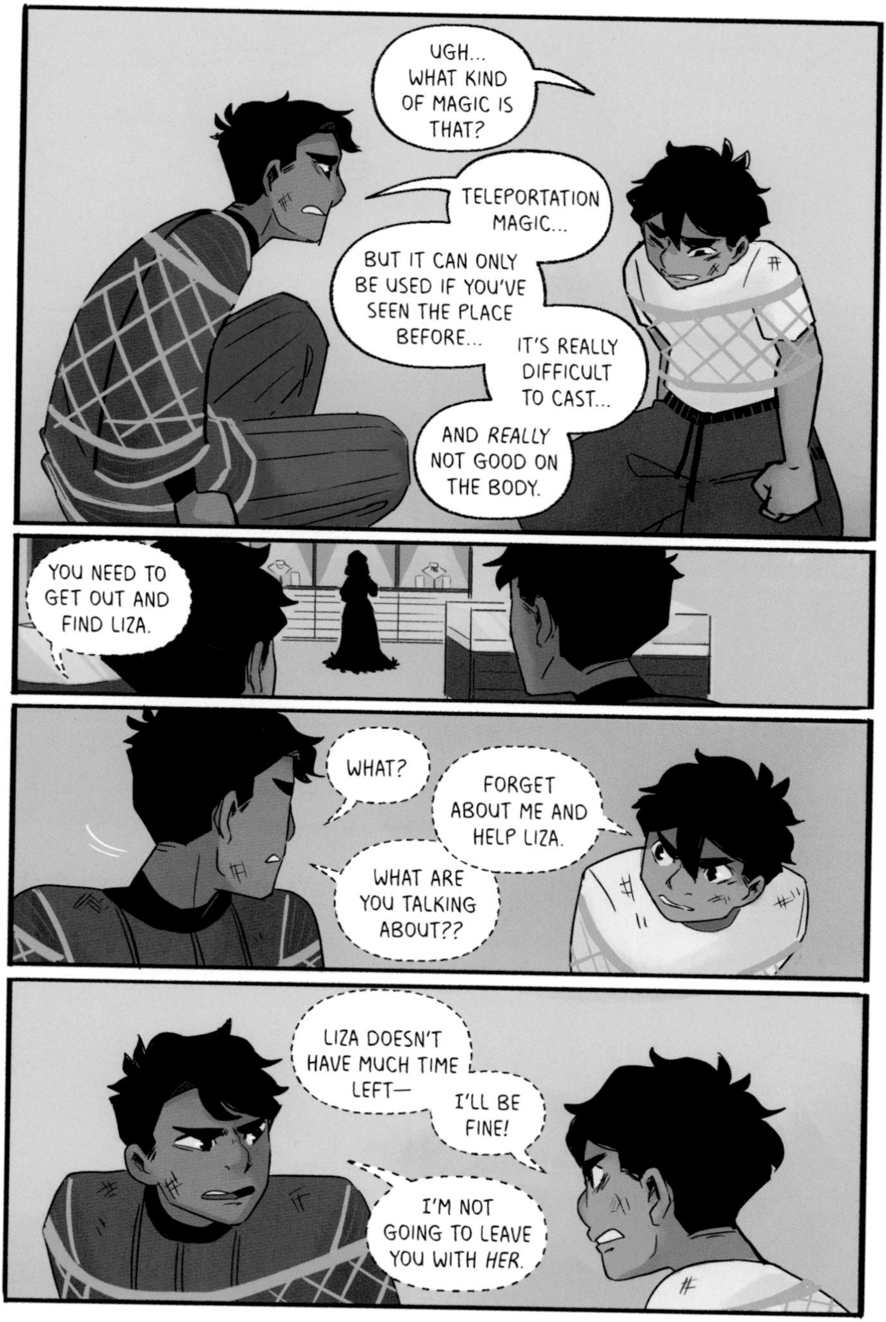
UGH... WHAT KIND OF MAGIC IS THAT?
TELEPORTATION MAGIC...
BUT IT CAN ONLY BE USED IF YOU'VE SEEN THE PLACE BEFORE...
IT'S REALLY DIFFICULT TO CAST...
AND *REALLY* NOT GOOD ON THE BODY.
YOU NEED TO GET OUT AND FIND LIZA.
WHAT?
FORGET ABOUT ME AND HELP LIZA.
WHAT ARE YOU TALKING ABOUT??
LIZA DOESN'T HAVE MUCH TIME LEFT—
I'LL BE FINE!
I'M NOT GOING TO LEAVE YOU WITH *HER*.

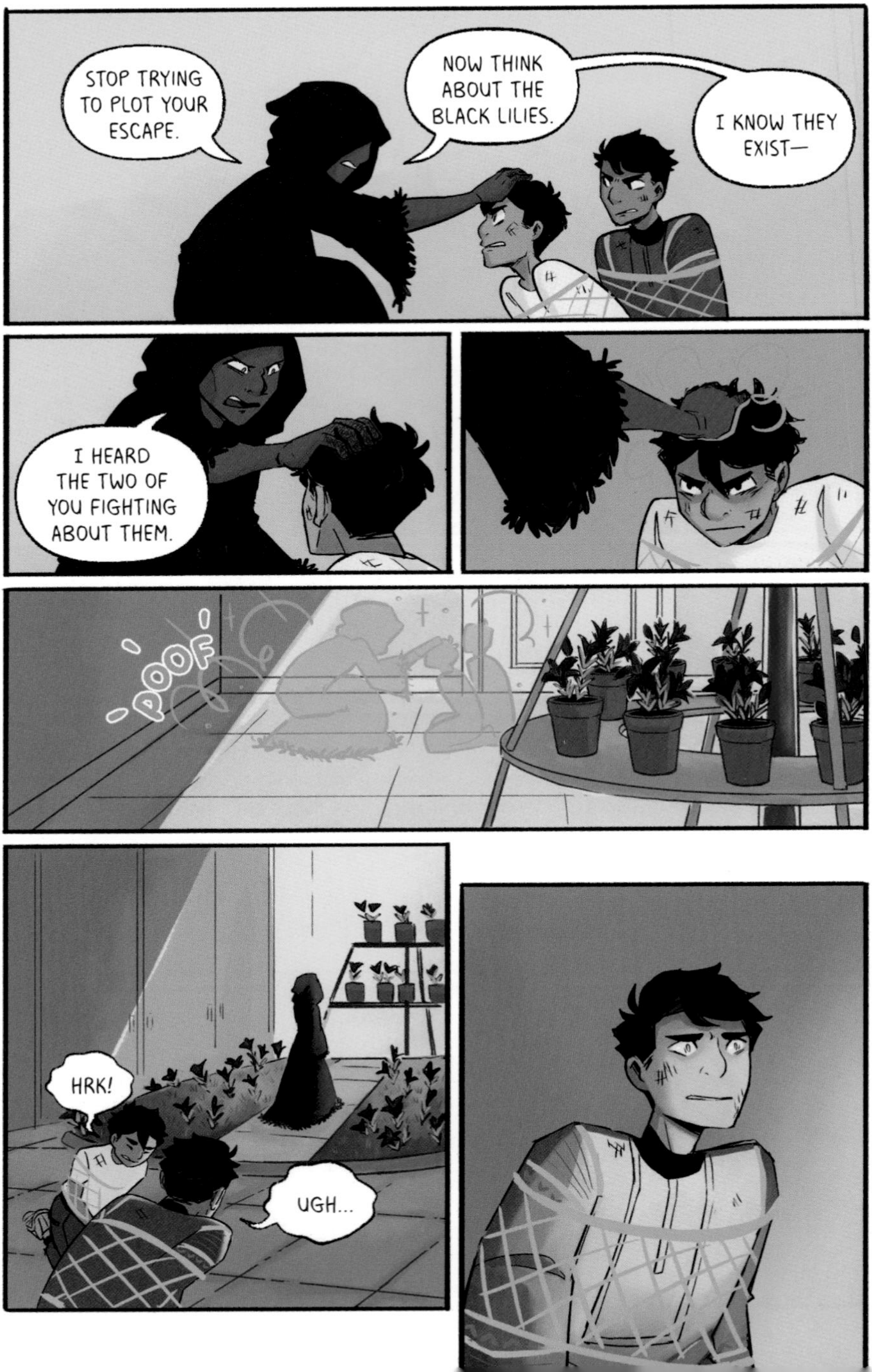
STOP TRYING TO PLOT YOUR ESCAPE.
NOW THINK ABOUT THE BLACK LILIES.
I KNOW THEY EXIST—
I HEARD THE TWO OF YOU FIGHTING ABOUT THEM.
POOF
HRK!
UGH...

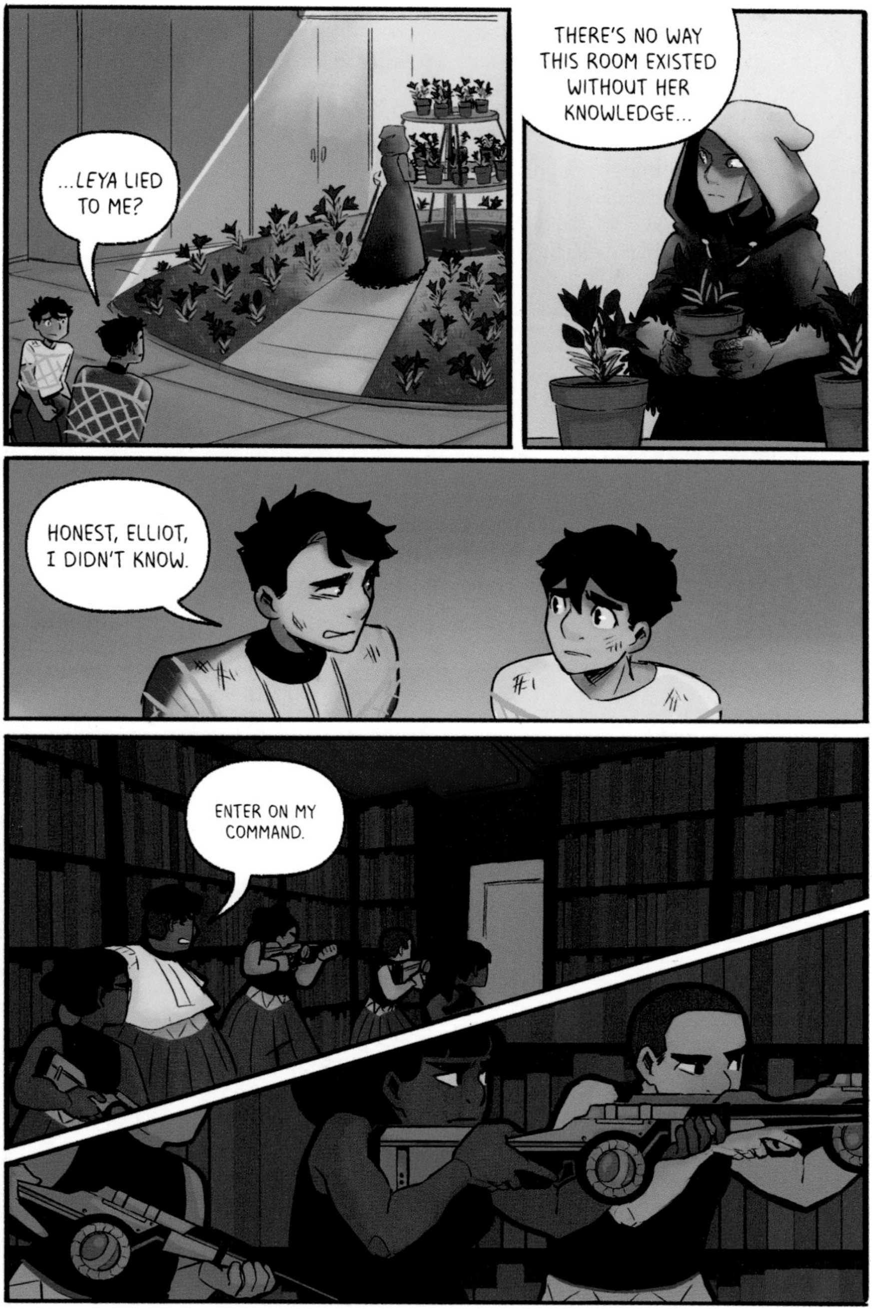
...LEYA LIED TO ME?
THERE'S NO WAY THIS ROOM EXISTED WITHOUT HER KNOWLEDGE...
HONEST, ELLIOT, I DIDN'T KNOW.
ENTER ON MY COMMAND.

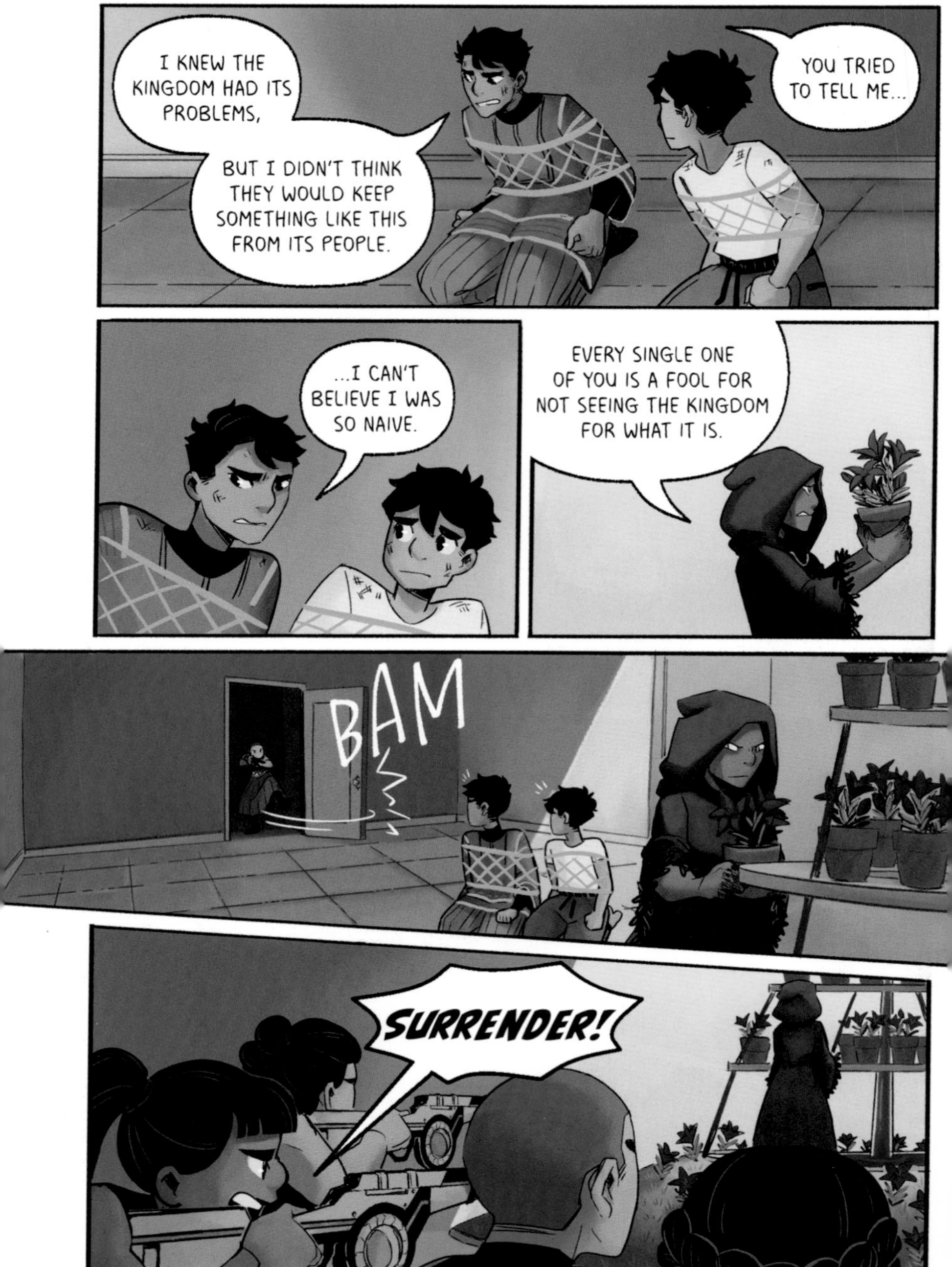
I KNEW THE KINGDOM HAD ITS PROBLEMS,
BUT I DIDN'T THINK THEY WOULD KEEP SOMETHING LIKE THIS FROM ITS PEOPLE.
YOU TRIED TO TELL ME...
...I CAN'T BELIEVE I WAS SO NAIVE.
EVERY SINGLE ONE OF YOU IS A FOOL FOR NOT SEEING THE KINGDOM FOR WHAT IT IS.
BAM
SURRENDER!

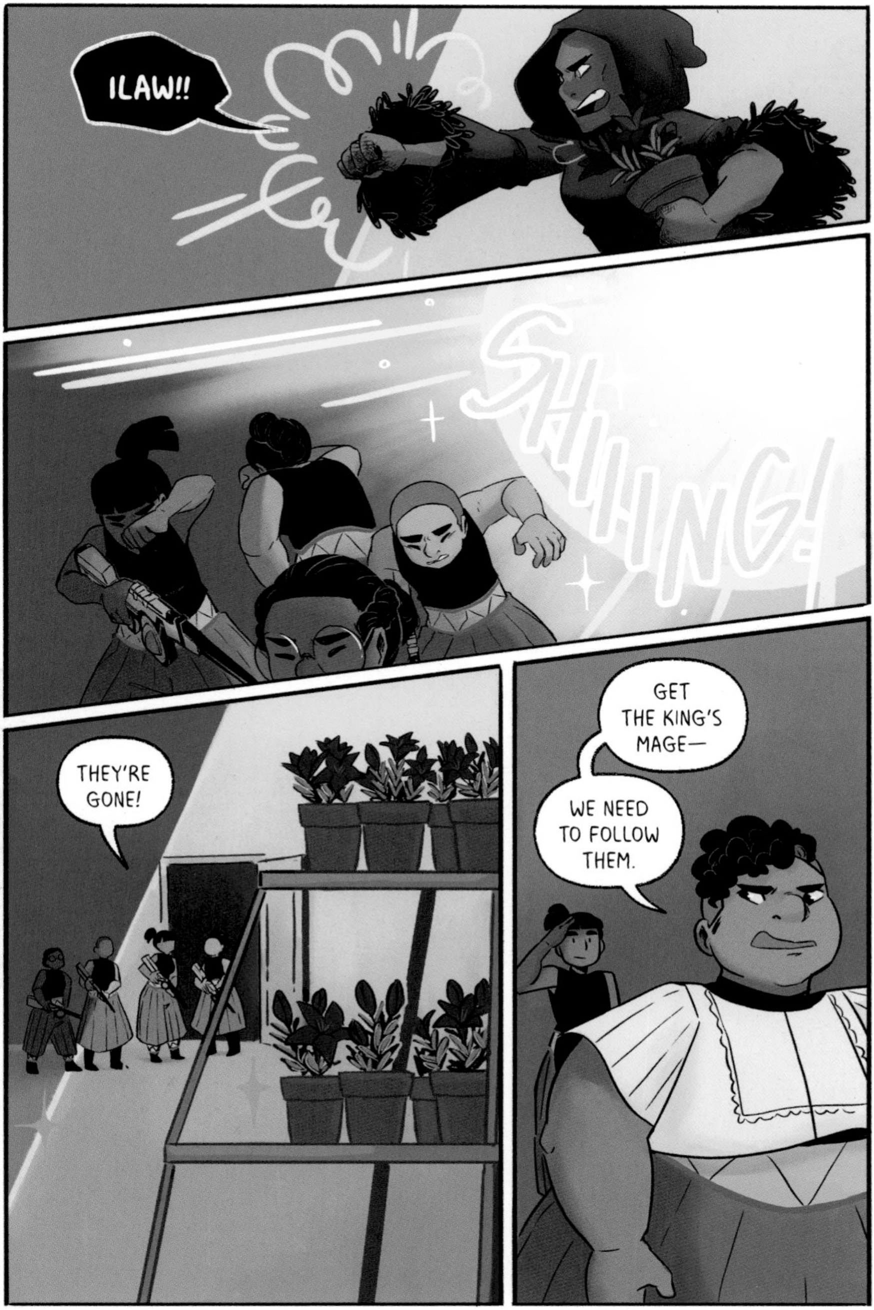
ILAW!!
SHIIING!
THEY'RE GONE!
GET THE KING'S MAGE—
WE NEED TO FOLLOW THEM.

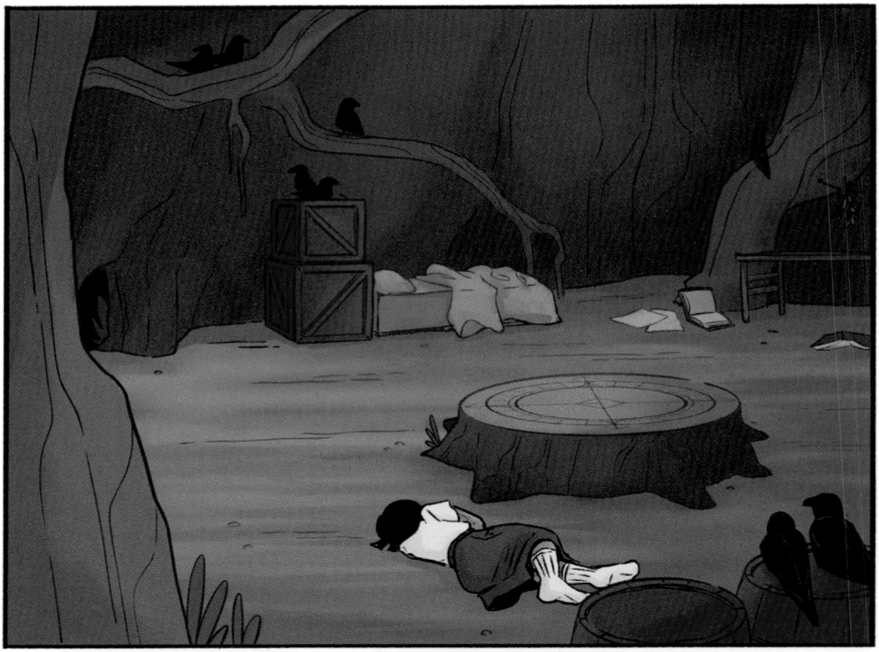

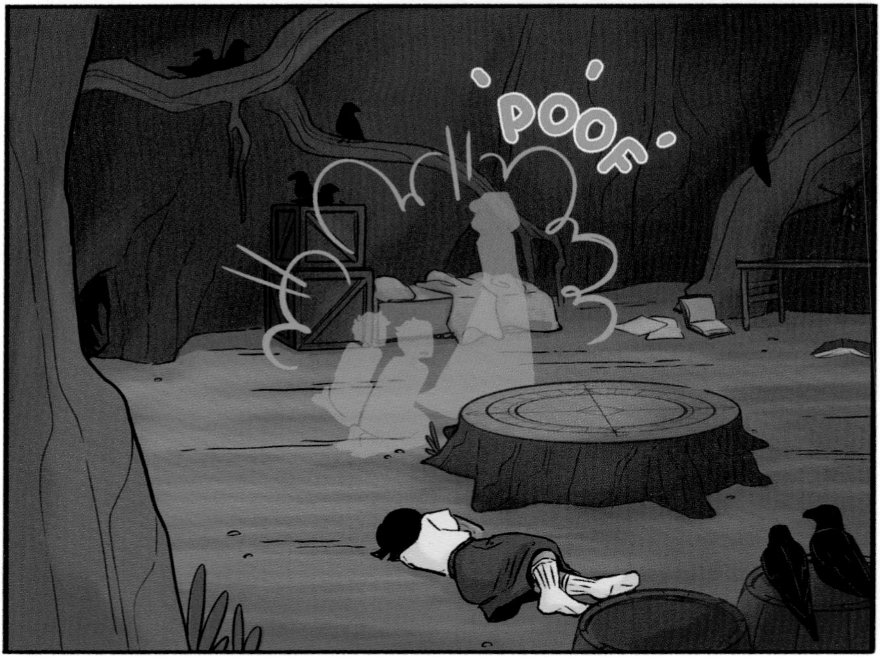
POOF

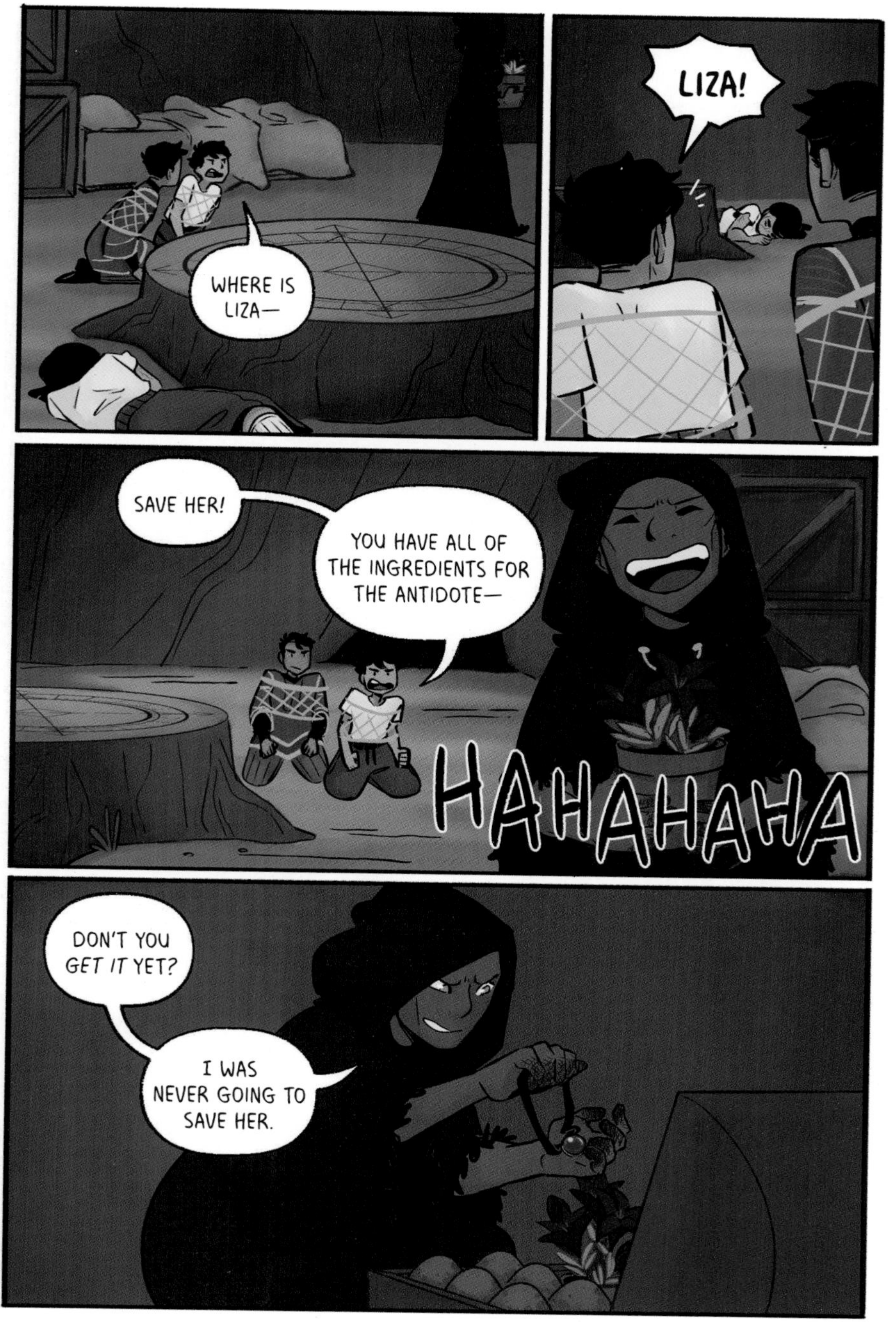
WHERE IS LIZA—
LIZA!
SAVE HER!
YOU HAVE ALL OF THE INGREDIENTS FOR THE ANTIDOTE—
HAHAHAHA
DON'T YOU GET *IT* YET?
I WAS NEVER GOING TO SAVE HER.

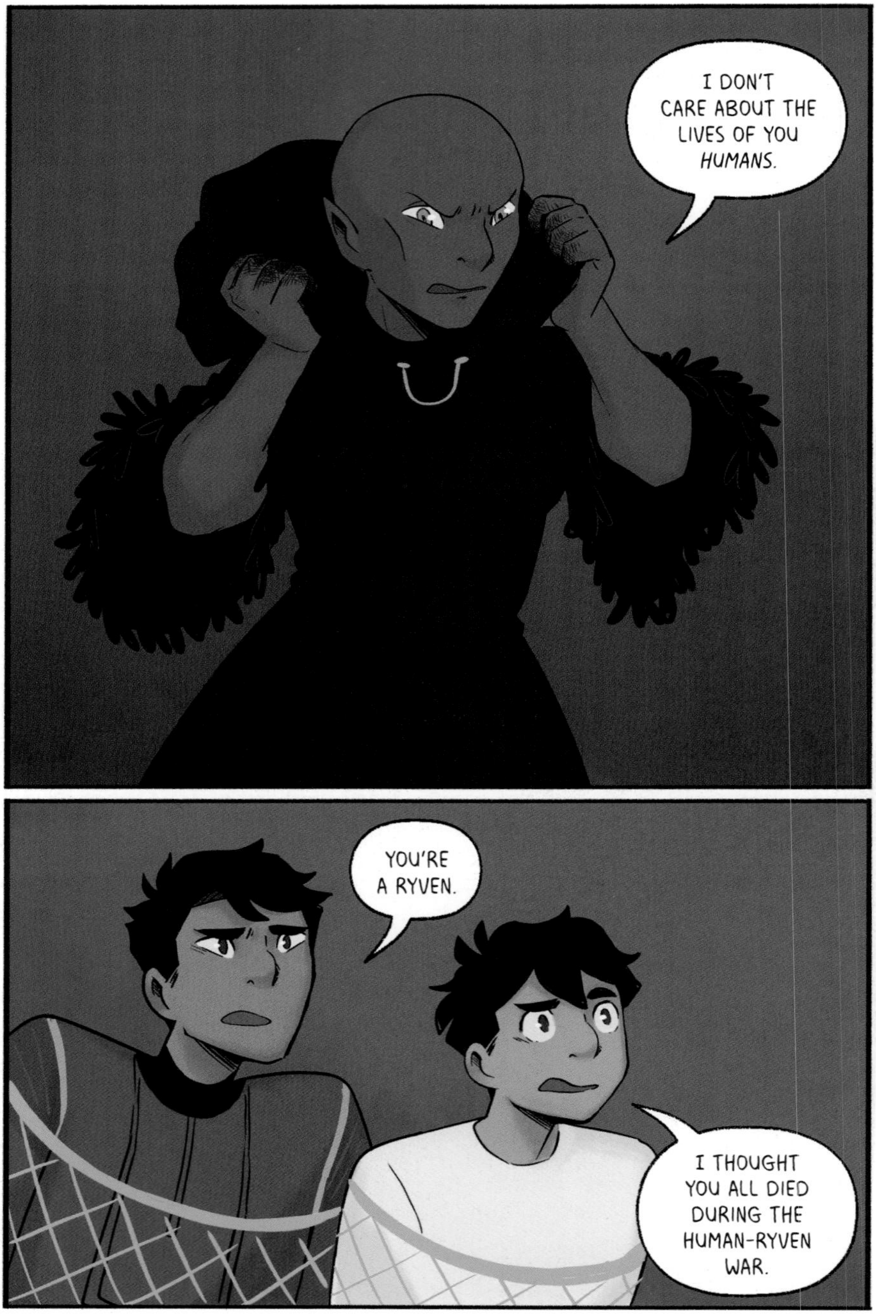
I DON'T CARE ABOUT THE LIVES OF YOU *HUMANS*.
YOU'RE A RYVEN.
I THOUGHT YOU ALL DIED DURING THE HUMAN-RYVEN WAR.

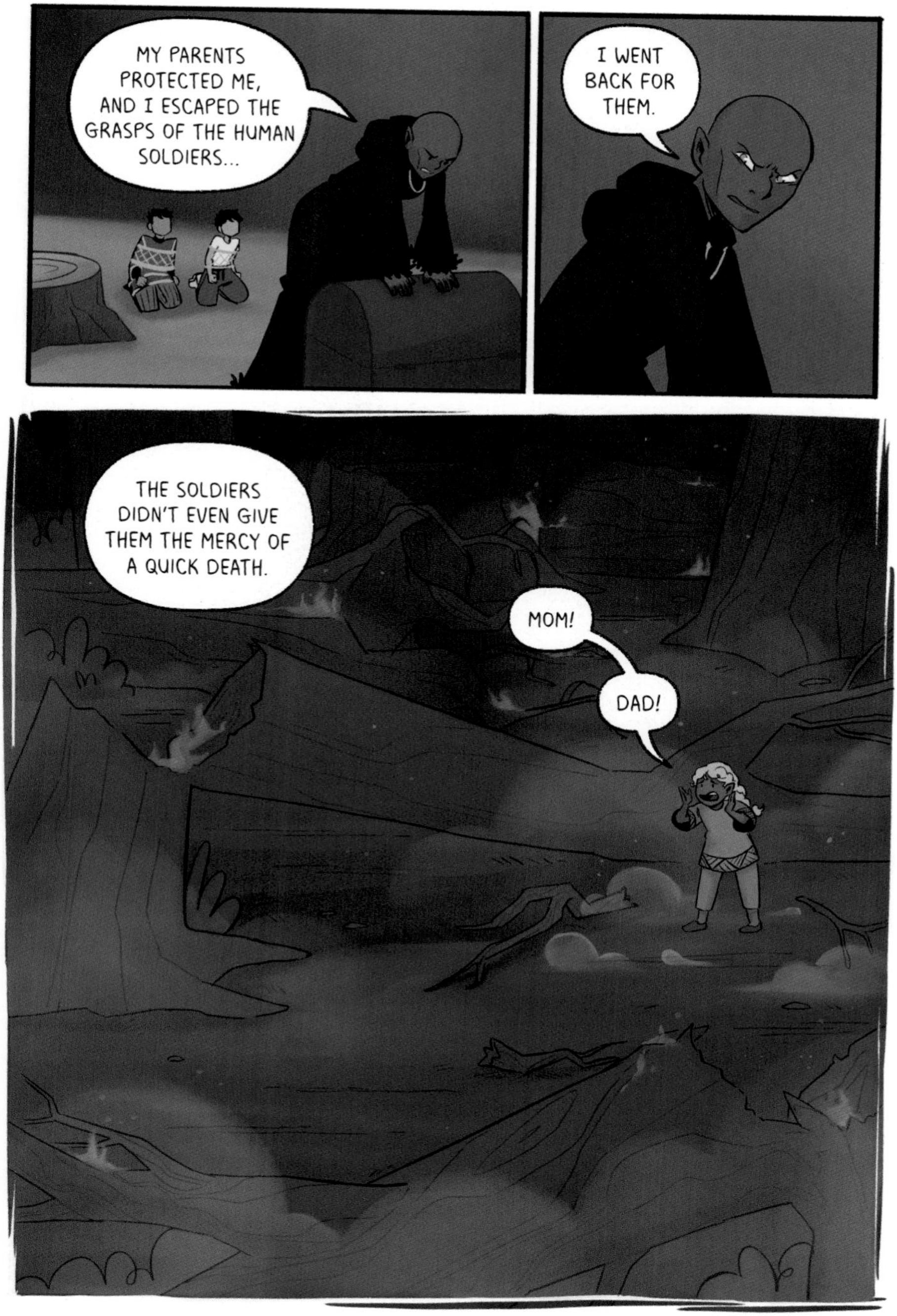
MY PARENTS PROTECTED ME, AND I ESCAPED THE GRASPS OF THE HUMAN SOLDIERS...
I WENT BACK FOR THEM.
THE SOLDIERS DIDN'T EVEN GIVE THEM THE MERCY OF A QUICK DEATH.
MOM!
DAD!

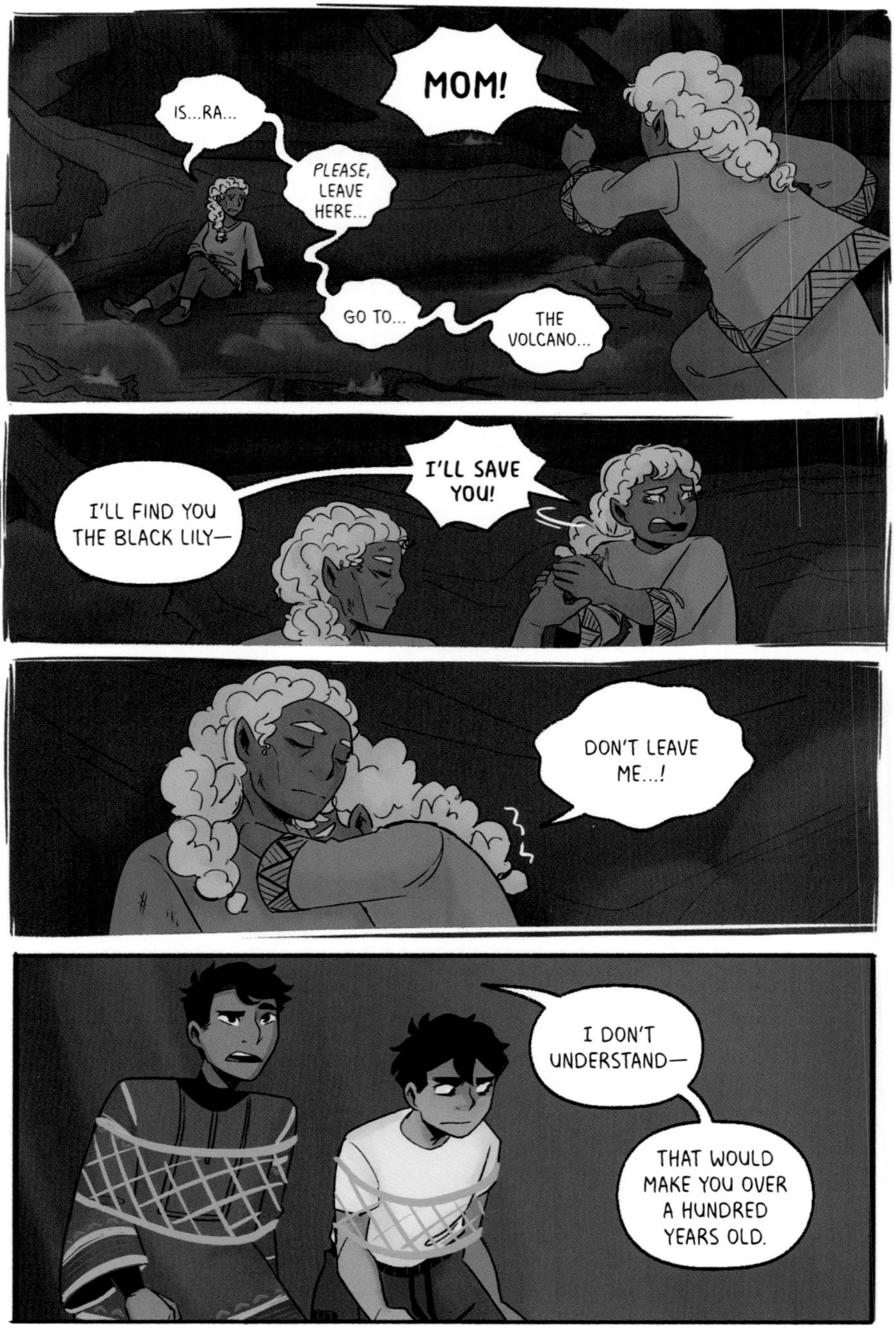
MOM!
IS...RA...
PLEASE, LEAVE HERE...
GO TO...
THE VOLCANO...
I'LL FIND YOU THE BLACK LILY—
I'LL SAVE YOU!
DON'T LEAVE ME...!
I DON'T UNDERSTAND—
THAT WOULD MAKE YOU OVER A HUNDRED YEARS OLD.

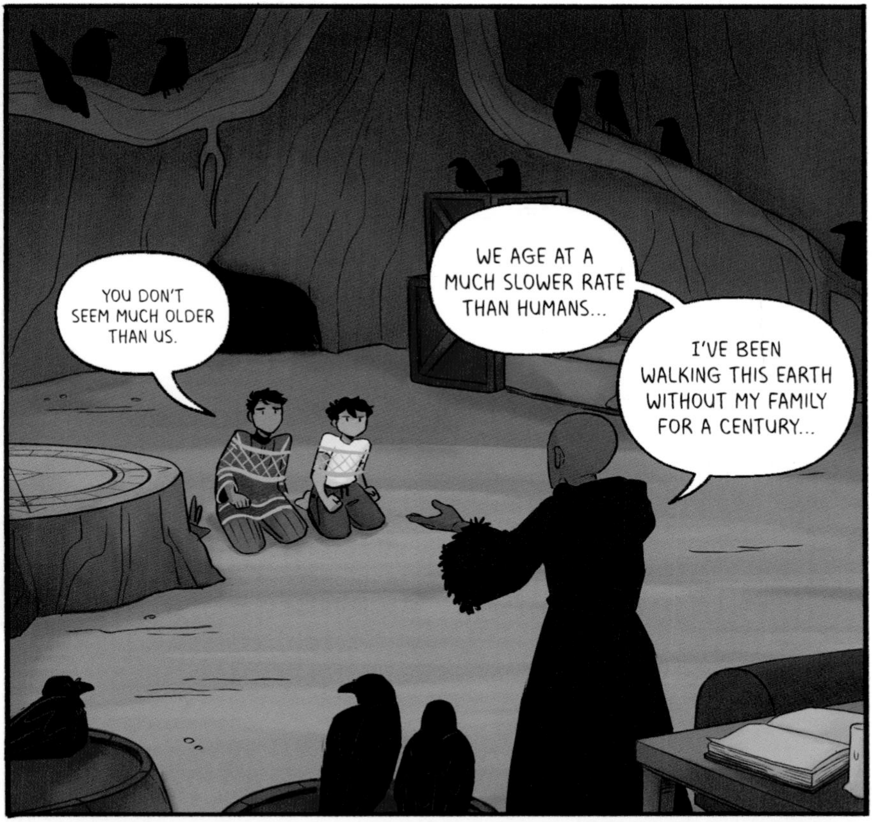
YOU DON'T SEEM MUCH OLDER THAN US.
WE AGE AT A MUCH SLOWER RATE THAN HUMANS...
I'VE BEEN WALKING THIS EARTH WITHOUT MY FAMILY FOR A CENTURY...

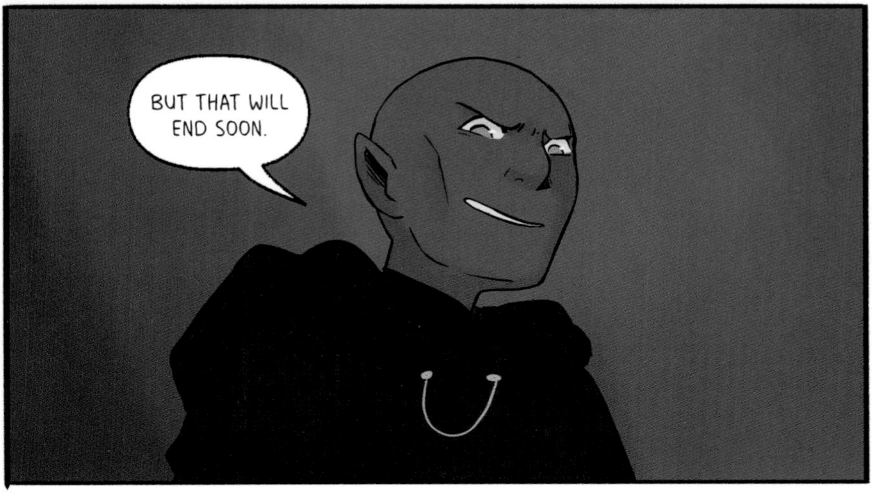
BUT THAT WILL END SOON.

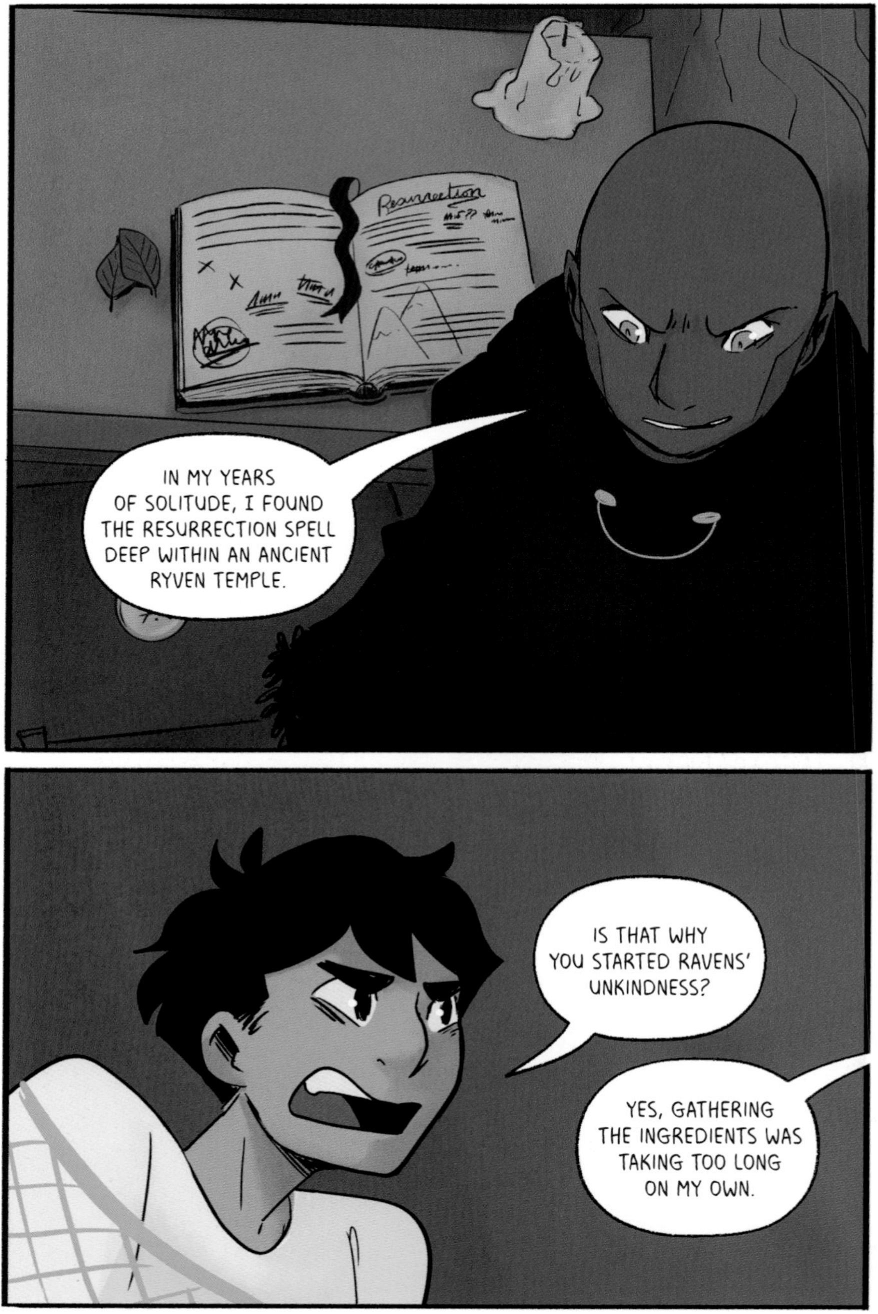
Resurrection
IN MY YEARS OF SOLITUDE, I FOUND THE RESURRECTION SPELL DEEP WITHIN AN ANCIENT RYVEN TEMPLE.
IS THAT WHY YOU STARTED RAVENS' UNKINDNESS?
YES, GATHERING THE INGREDIENTS WAS TAKING TOO LONG ON MY OWN.

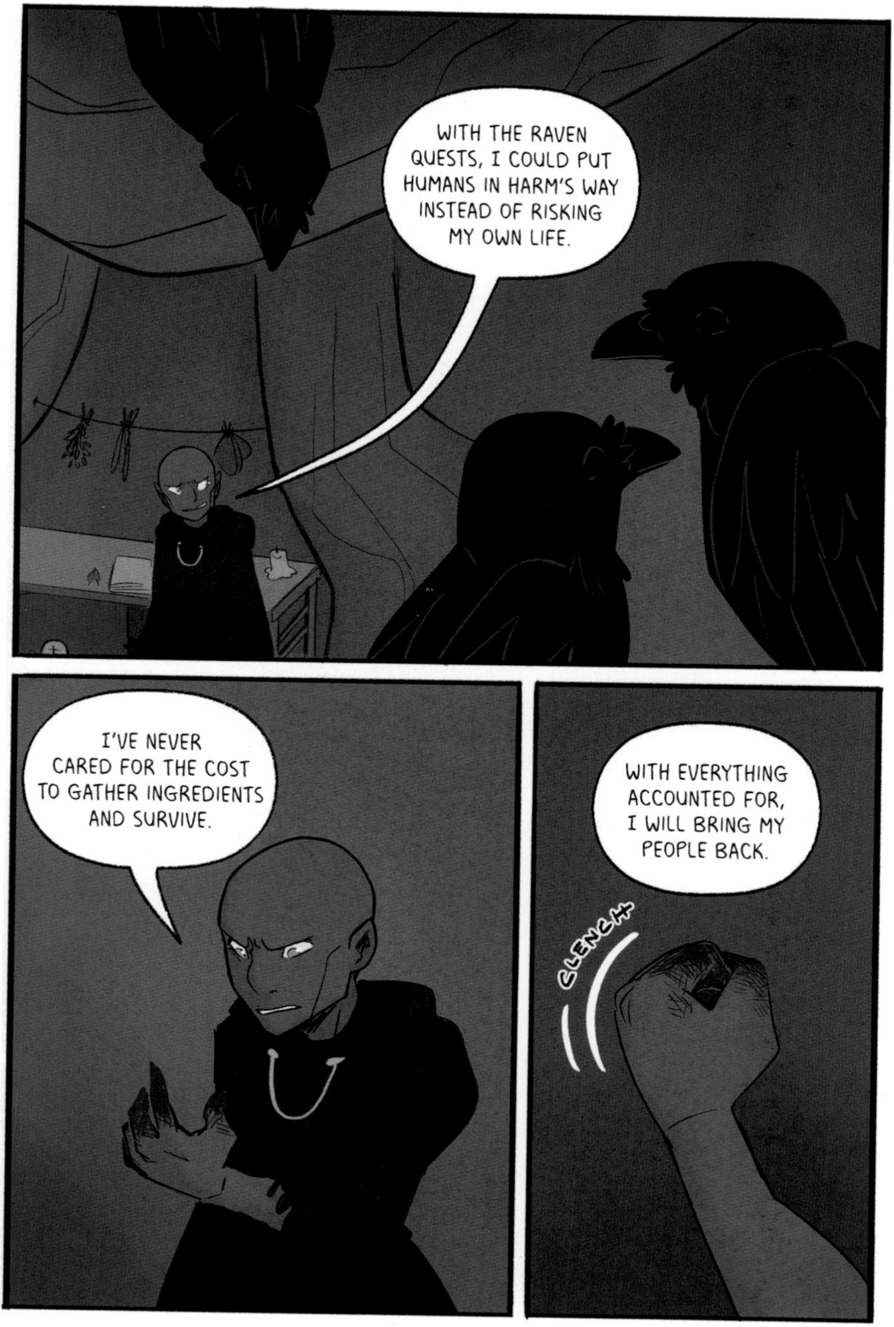
WITH THE RAVEN QUESTS, I COULD PUT HUMANS IN HARM'S WAY INSTEAD OF RISKING MY OWN LIFE.
I'VE NEVER CARED FOR THE COST TO GATHER INGREDIENTS AND SURVIVE.
WITH EVERYTHING ACCOUNTED FOR, I WILL BRING MY PEOPLE BACK.
CLENCH

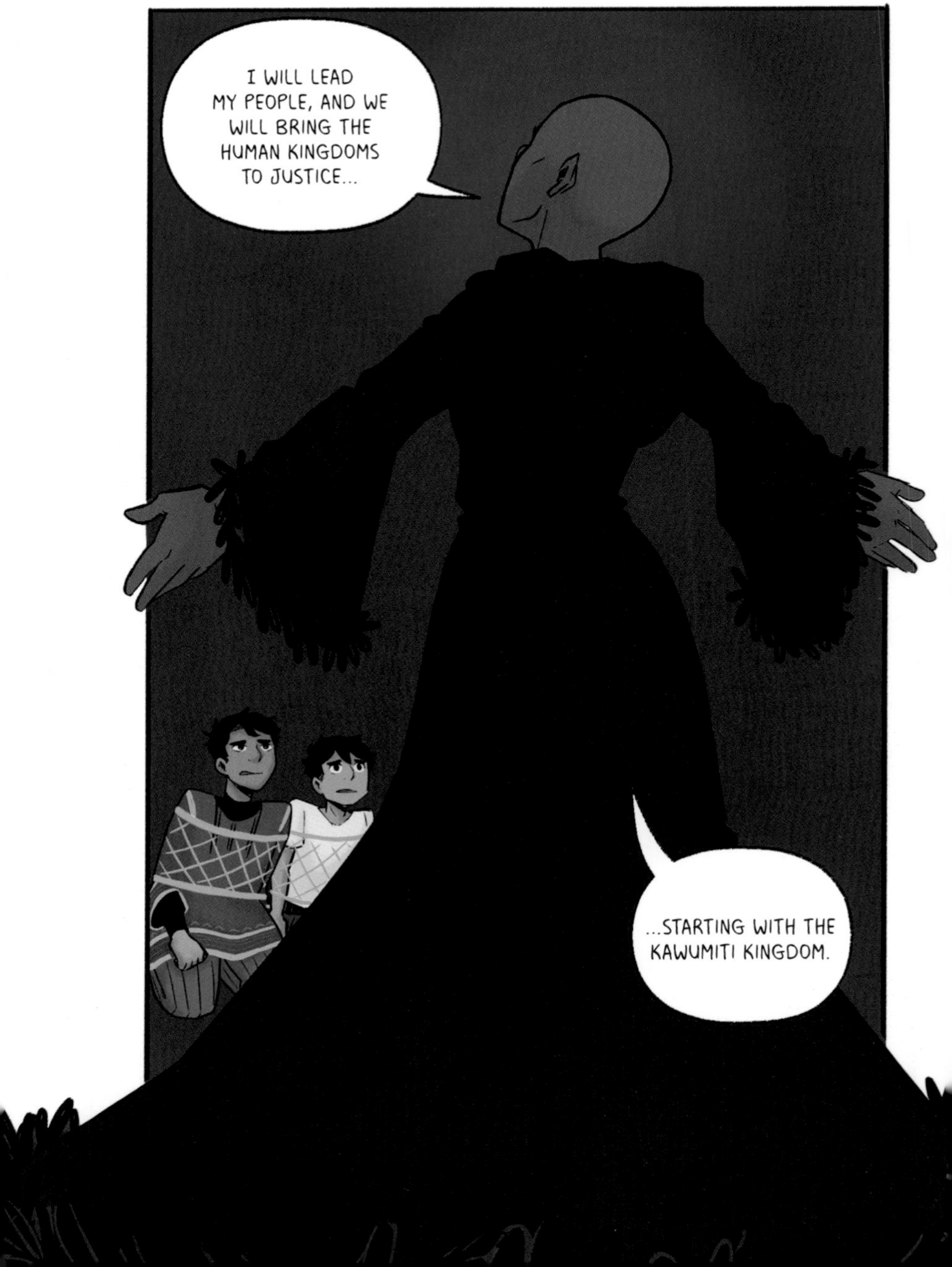
I WILL LEAD MY PEOPLE, AND WE WILL BRING THE HUMAN KINGDOMS TO JUSTICE...
...STARTING WITH THE KAWUMITI KINGDOM.

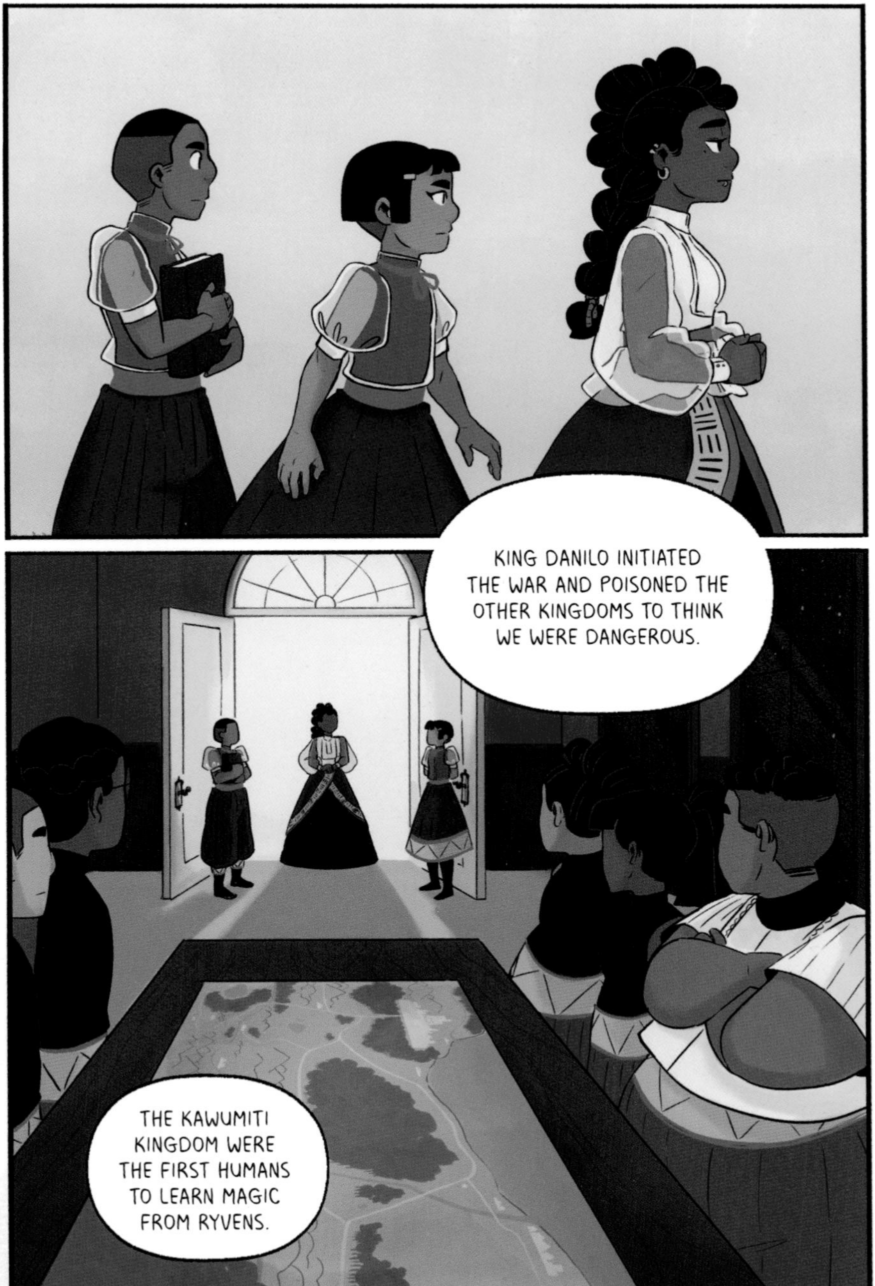
KING DANILO INITIATED THE WAR AND POISONED THE OTHER KINGDOMS TO THINK WE WERE DANGEROUS.
THE KAWUMITI KINGDOM WERE THE FIRST HUMANS TO LEARN MAGIC FROM RYVENS.

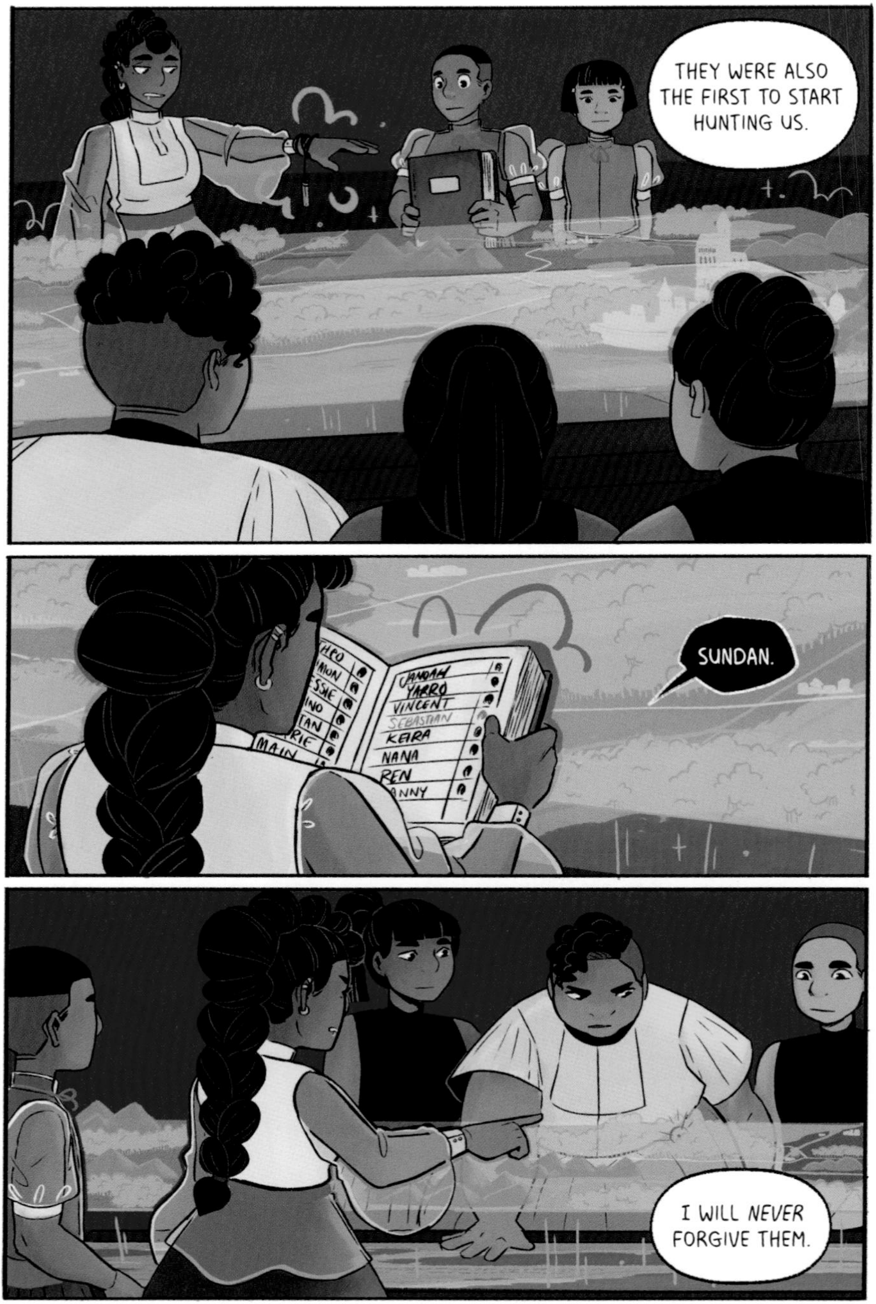
THEY WERE ALSO THE FIRST TO START HUNTING US.
YARRO
VINCENT
SEBASTIAN
KEIRA
NANA
REN
SUNDAN.
I WILL *NEVER* FORGIVE THEM.

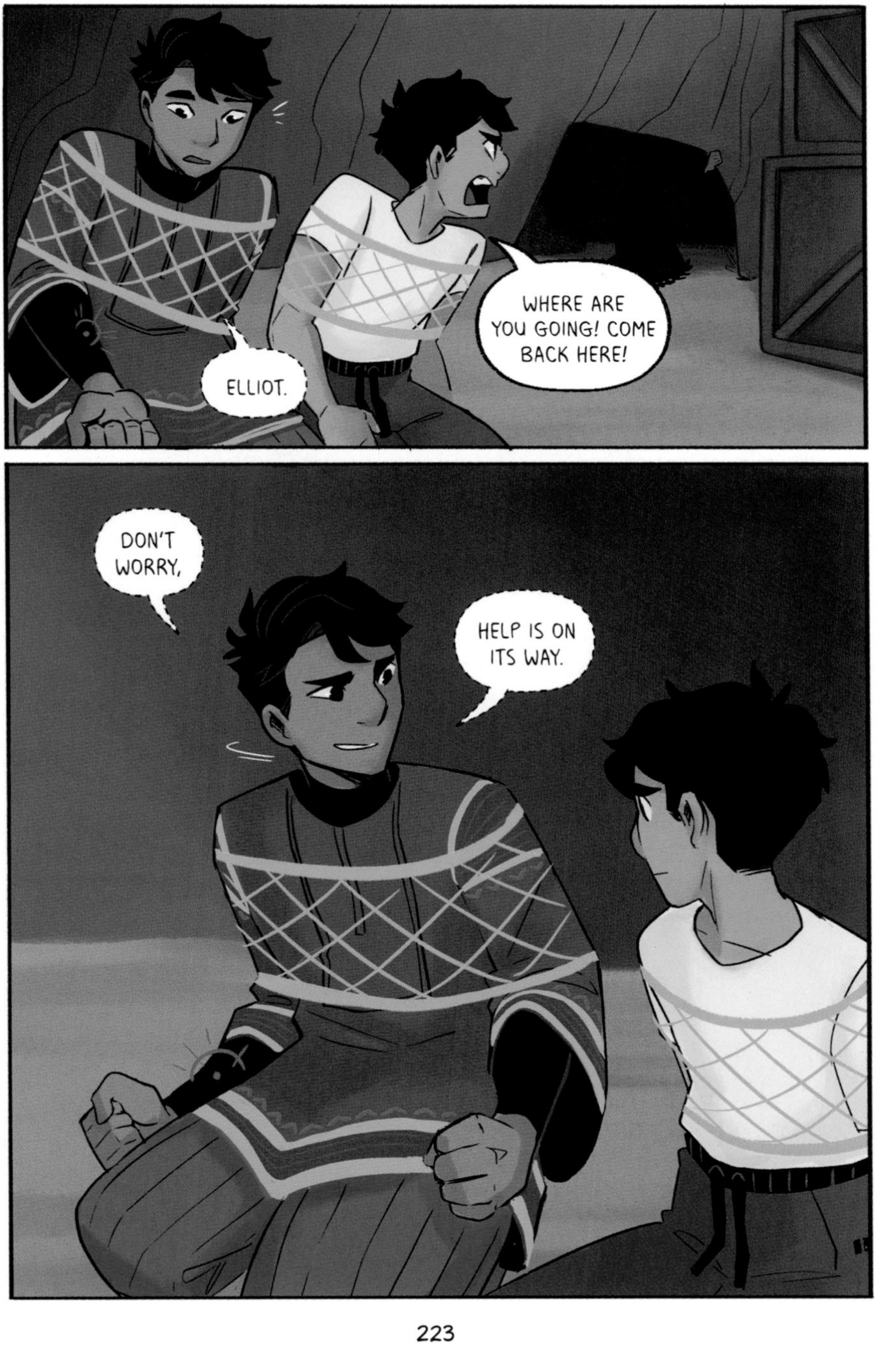
ELLIOT.
WHERE ARE YOU GOING! COME BACK HERE!
DON'T WORRY,
HELP IS ON ITS WAY.

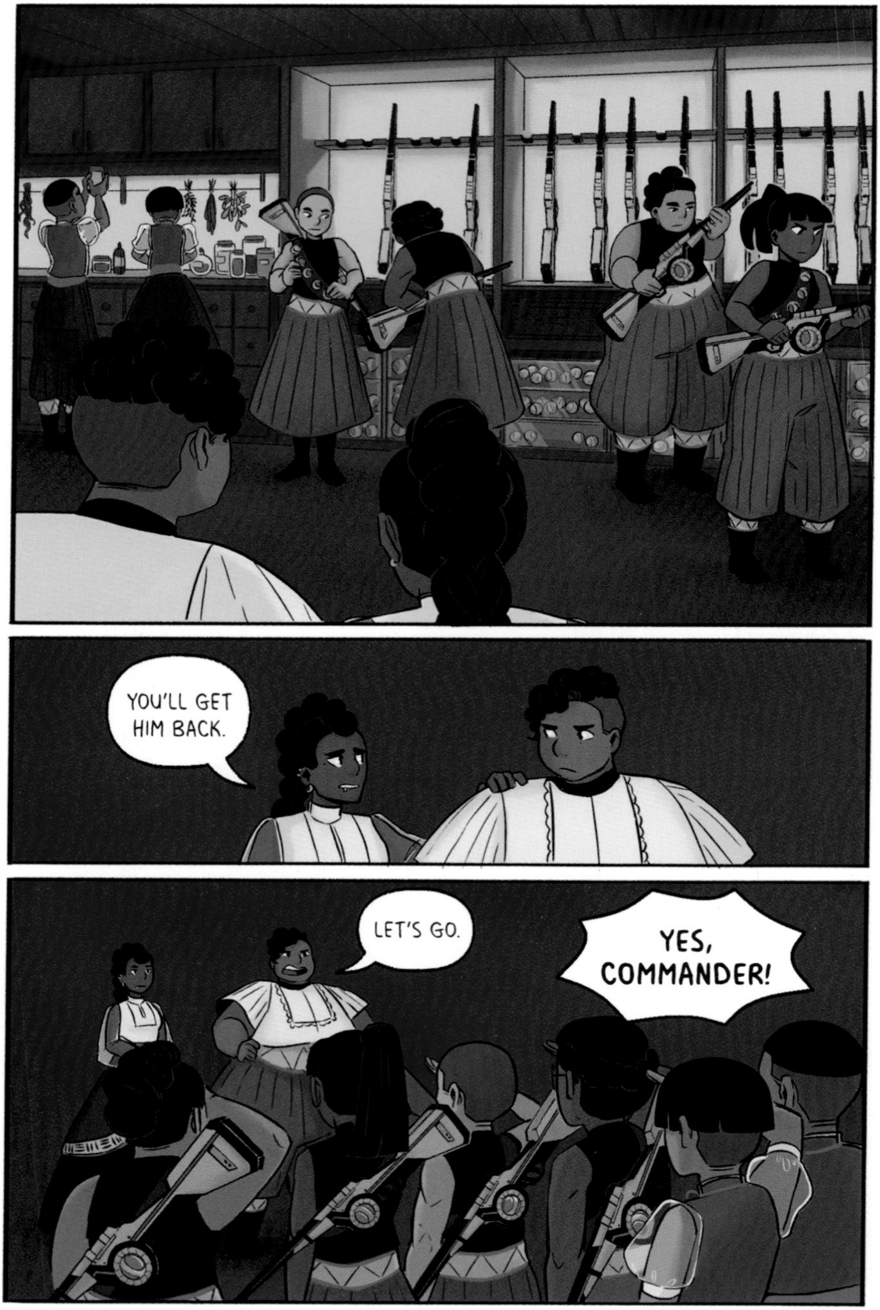
YOU'LL GET HIM BACK.
LET'S GO.
YES, COMMANDER!

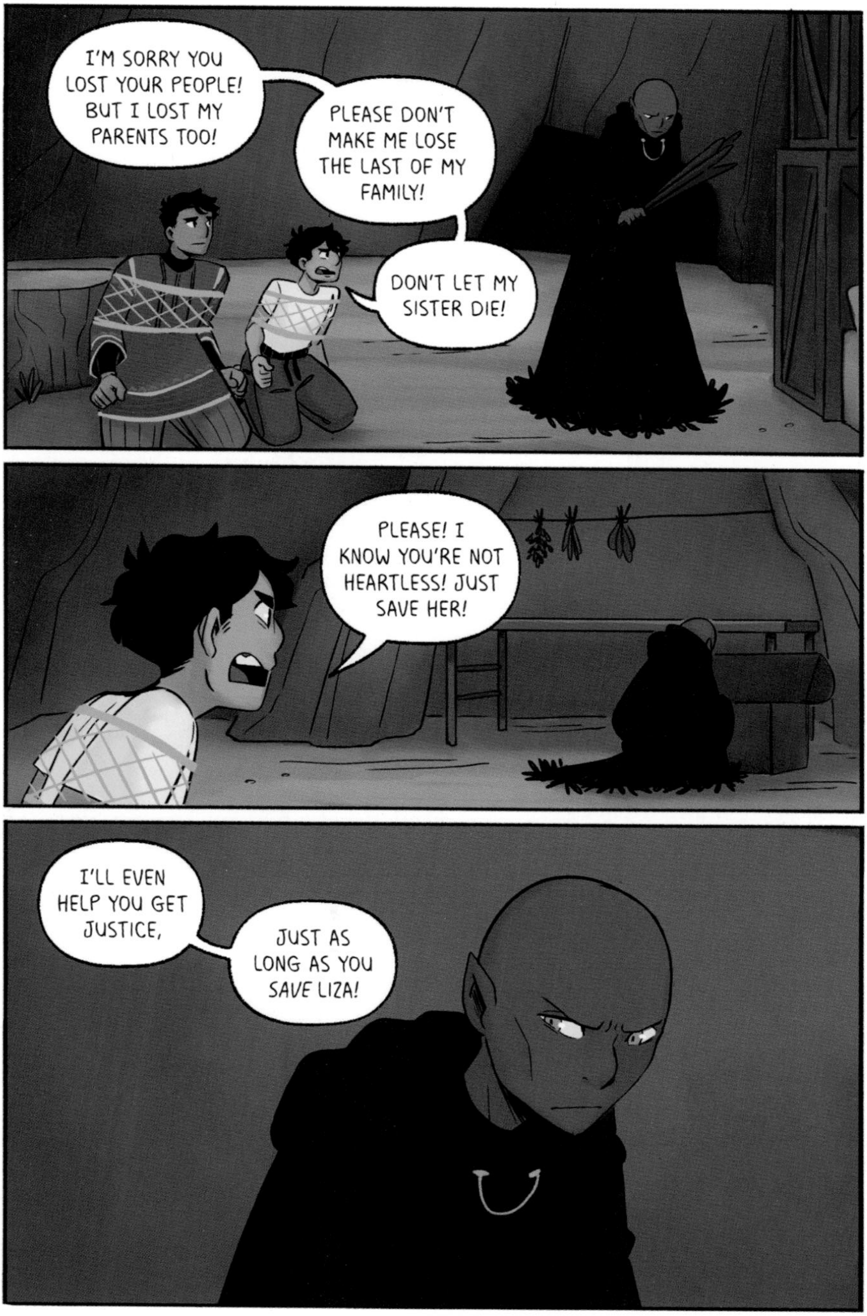
I'M SORRY YOU LOST YOUR PEOPLE! BUT I LOST MY PARENTS TOO!
PLEASE DON'T MAKE ME LOSE THE LAST OF MY FAMILY!
DON'T LET MY SISTER DIE!
PLEASE! I KNOW YOU'RE NOT HEARTLESS! JUST SAVE HER!
I'LL EVEN HELP YOU GET JUSTICE,
JUST AS LONG AS YOU *SAVE* LIZA!

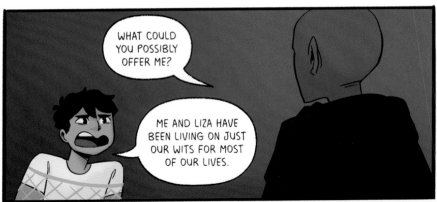

WHAT COULD YOU POSSIBLY OFFER ME?

ME AND LIZA HAVE BEEN LIVING ON JUST OUR WITS FOR MOST OF OUR LIVES.

I CAN HELP YOU SURVIVE IN THE WILD. I'LL BE YOUR SERVANT, ANYTHING!

I CAN EVEN GO PLACES THAT YOU CAN'T *BECAUSE* I'M HUMAN—

I GOT INTO THE CASTLE, DIDN'T I??

ELLIOT.

WHATEVER IT TAKES TO SAVE MY SISTER.

PLEASE, ISRA.

YOU MUST TAKE THE DEATH OATH.

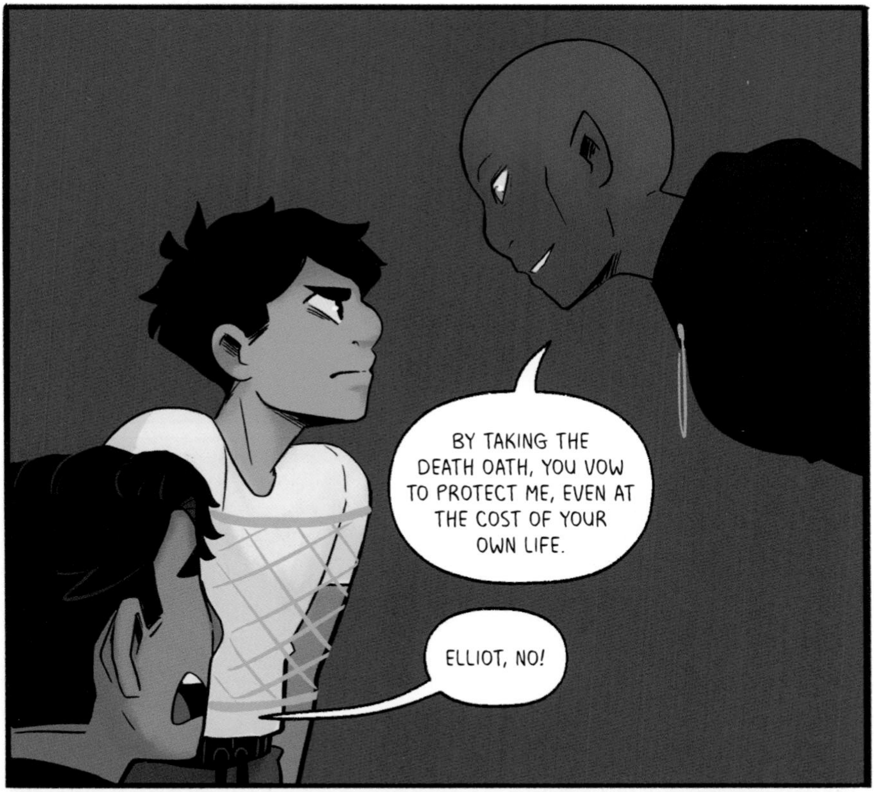
BY TAKING THE DEATH OATH, YOU VOW TO PROTECT ME, EVEN AT THE COST OF YOUR OWN LIFE.
ELLIOT, NO!

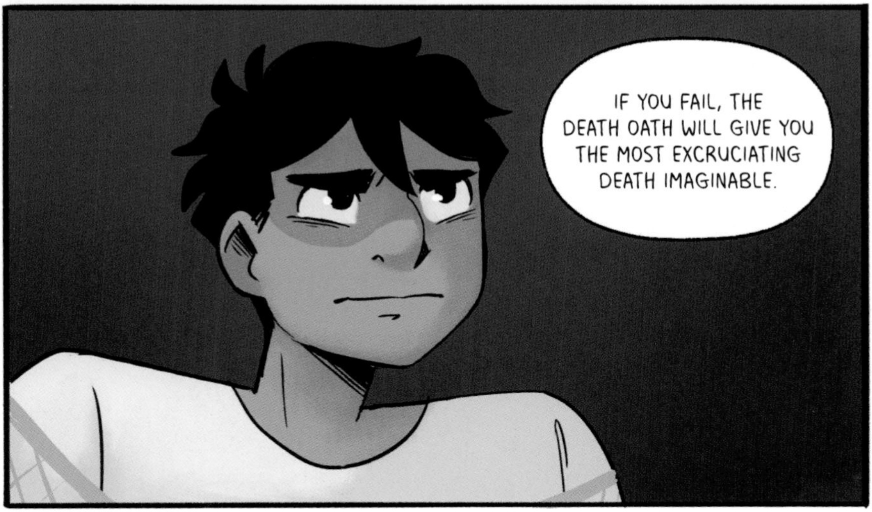
IF YOU FAIL, THE DEATH OATH WILL GIVE YOU THE MOST EXCRUCIATING DEATH IMAGINABLE.

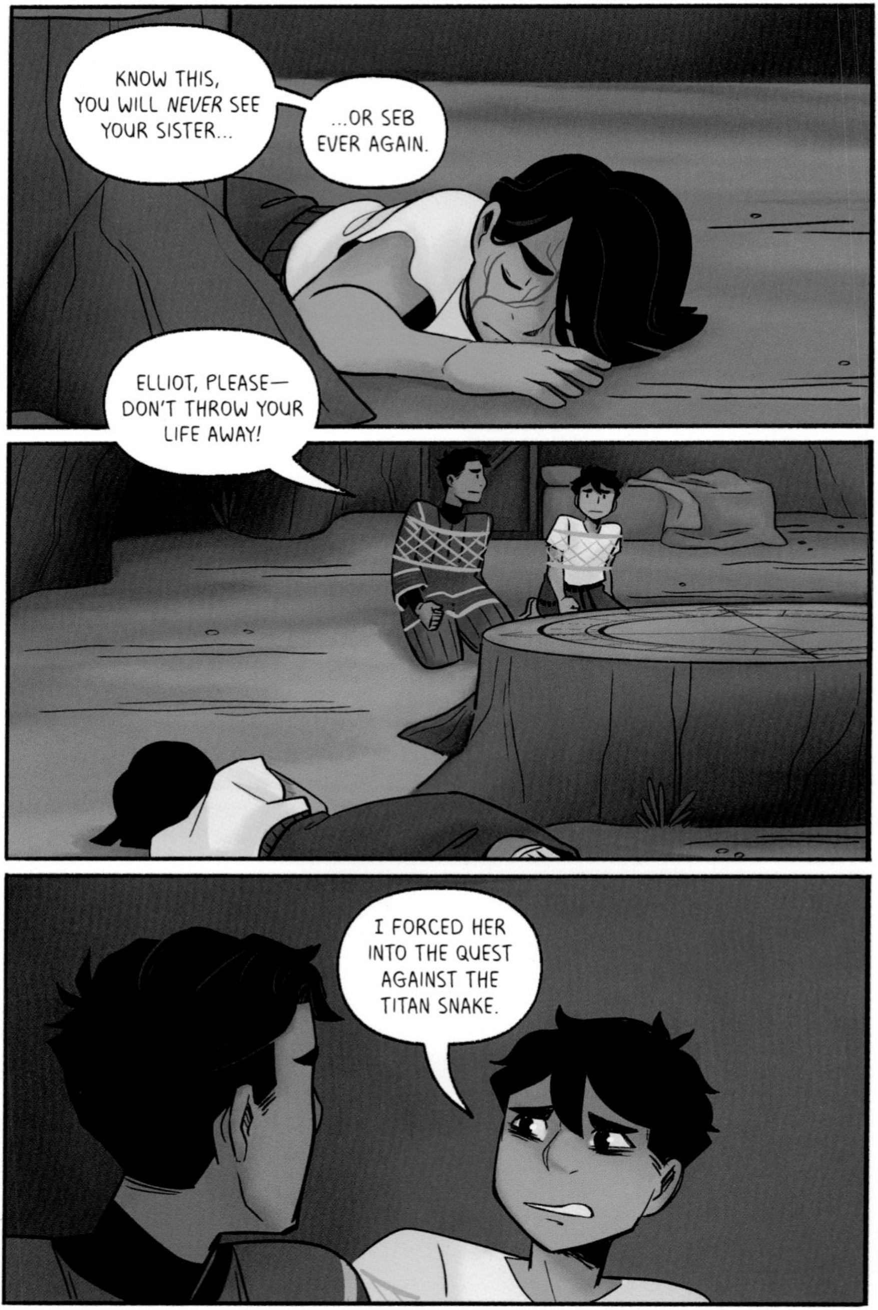
KNOW THIS, YOU WILL *NEVER* SEE YOUR SISTER...
...OR SEB EVER AGAIN.
ELLIOT, PLEASE— DON'T THROW YOUR LIFE AWAY!
I FORCED HER INTO THE QUEST AGAINST THE TITAN SNAKE.

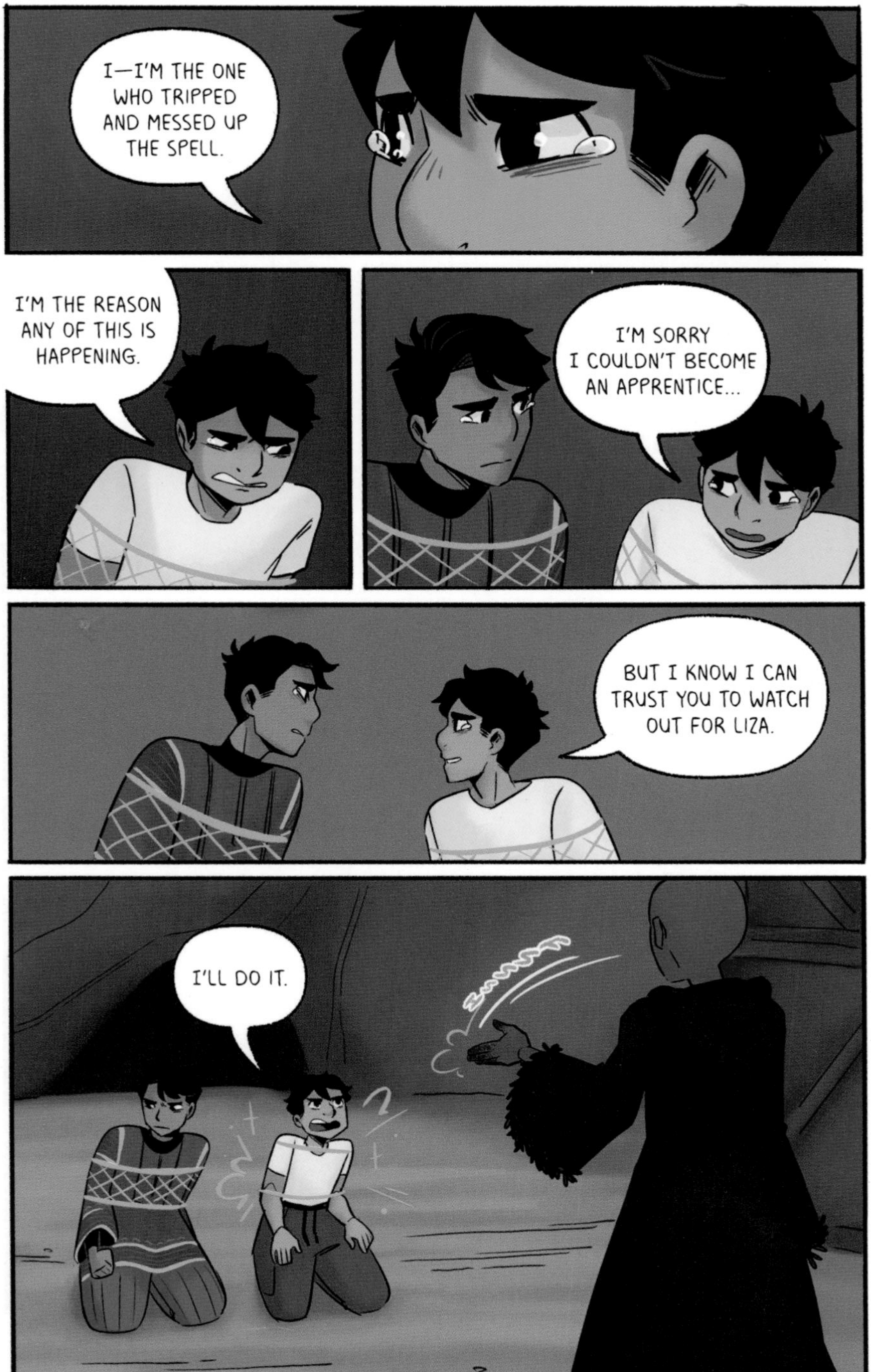
I—I'M THE ONE WHO TRIPPED AND MESSED UP THE SPELL.
I'M THE REASON ANY OF THIS IS HAPPENING.
I'M SORRY I COULDN'T BECOME AN APPRENTICE...
BUT I KNOW I CAN TRUST YOU TO WATCH OUT FOR LIZA.
I'LL DO IT.

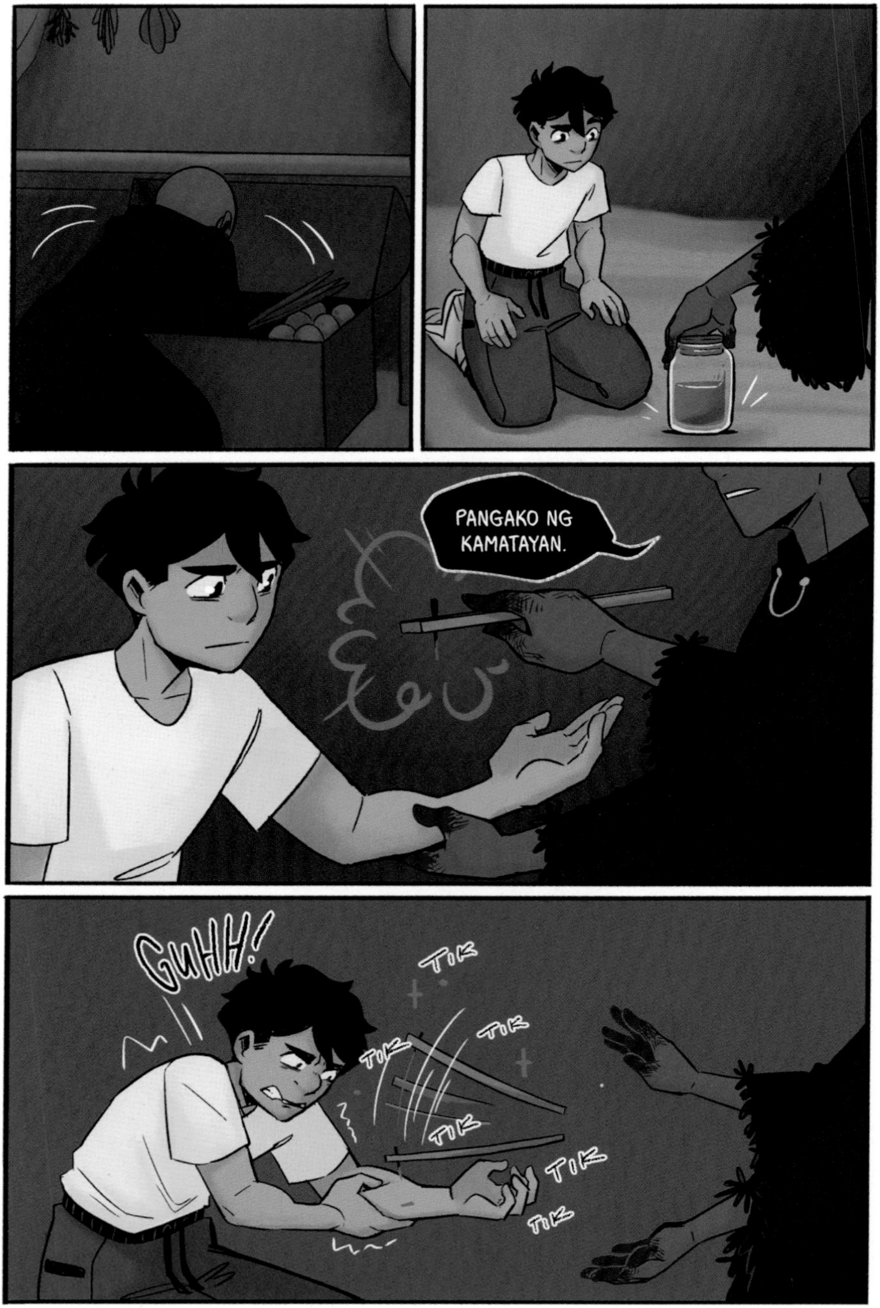
PANGAKO NG KAMATAYAN.
GUHH!
TIK
TIK
TIK
TIK
TIK
TIK

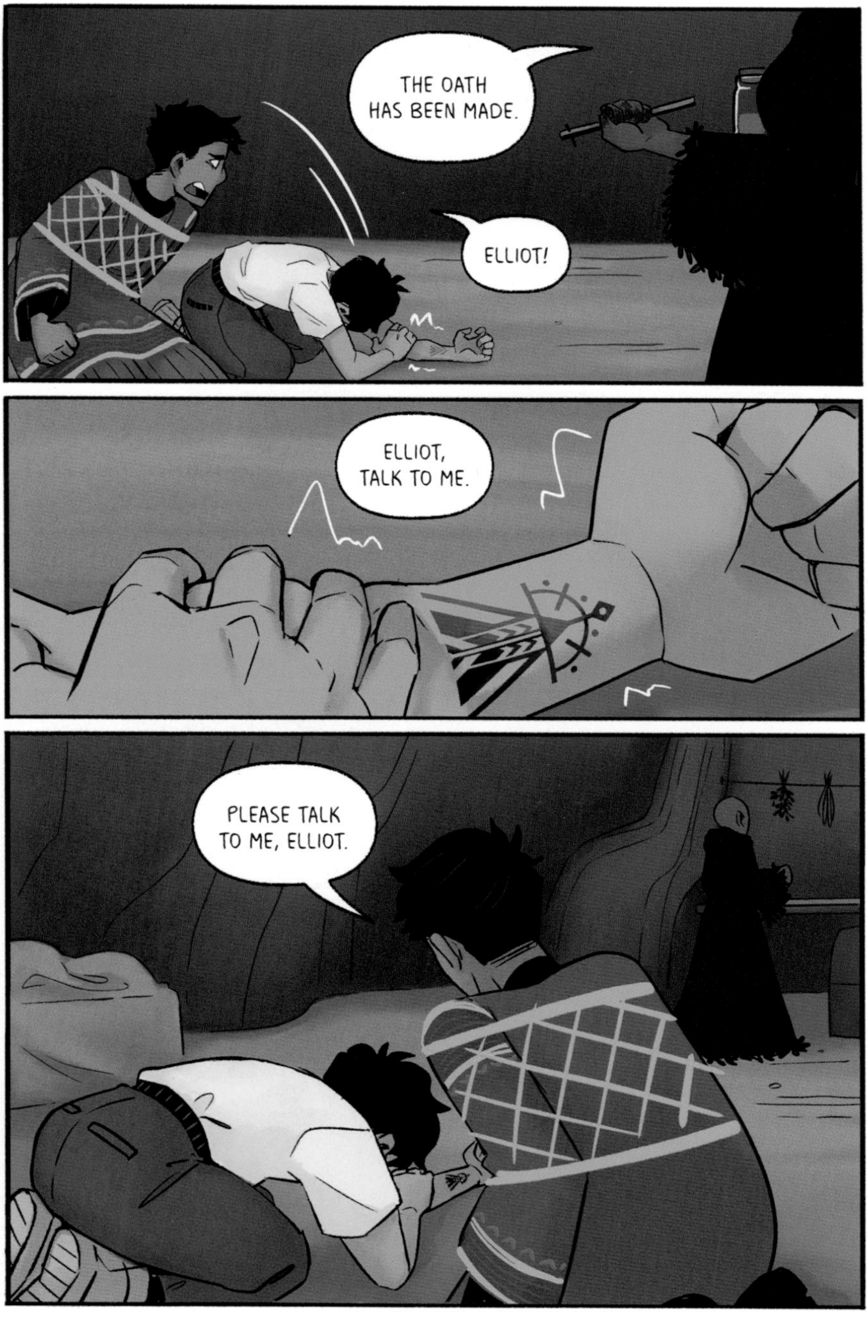
THE OATH HAS BEEN MADE.
ELLIOT!
ELLIOT, TALK TO ME.
PLEASE TALK TO ME, ELLIOT.

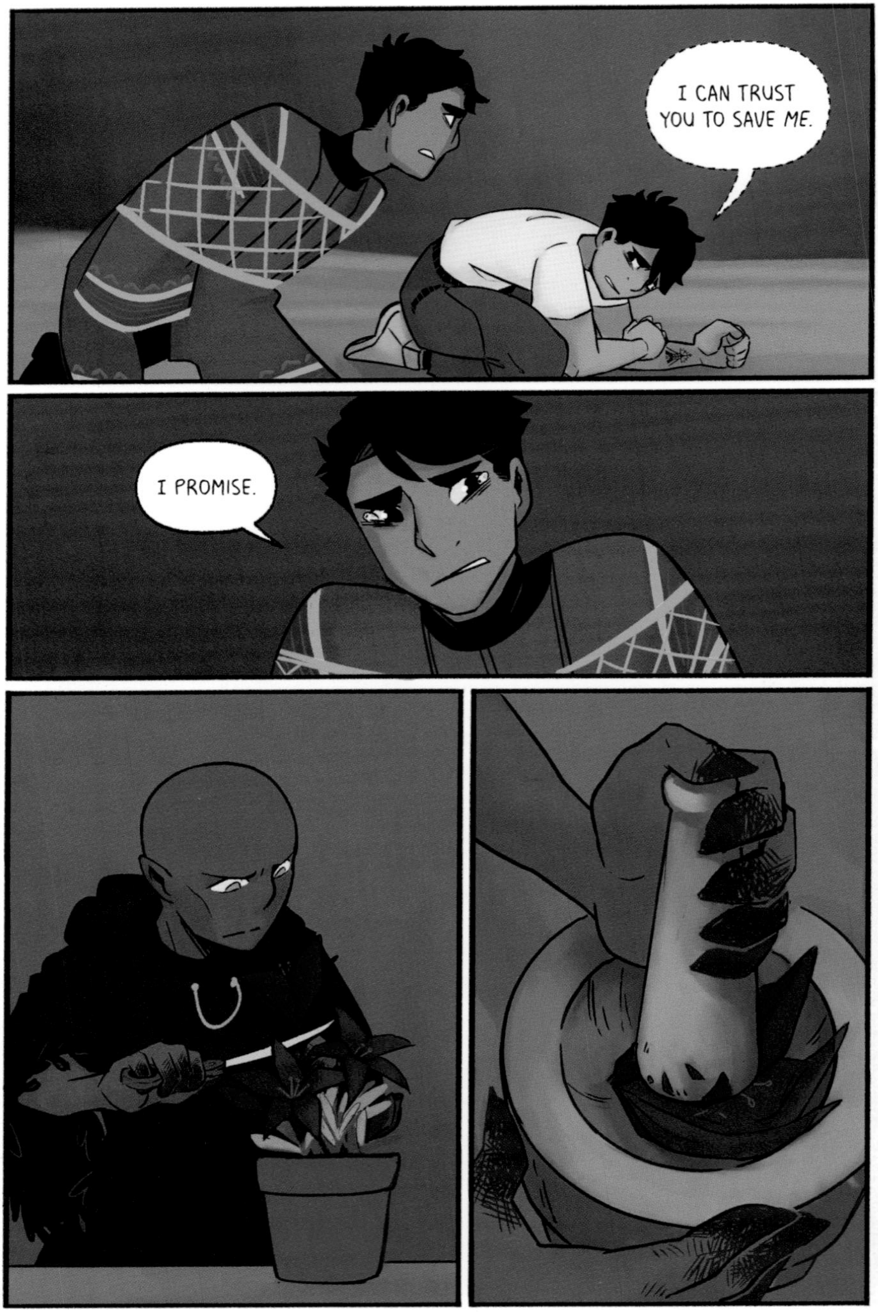
I CAN TRUST YOU TO SAVE *ME*.
I PROMISE.

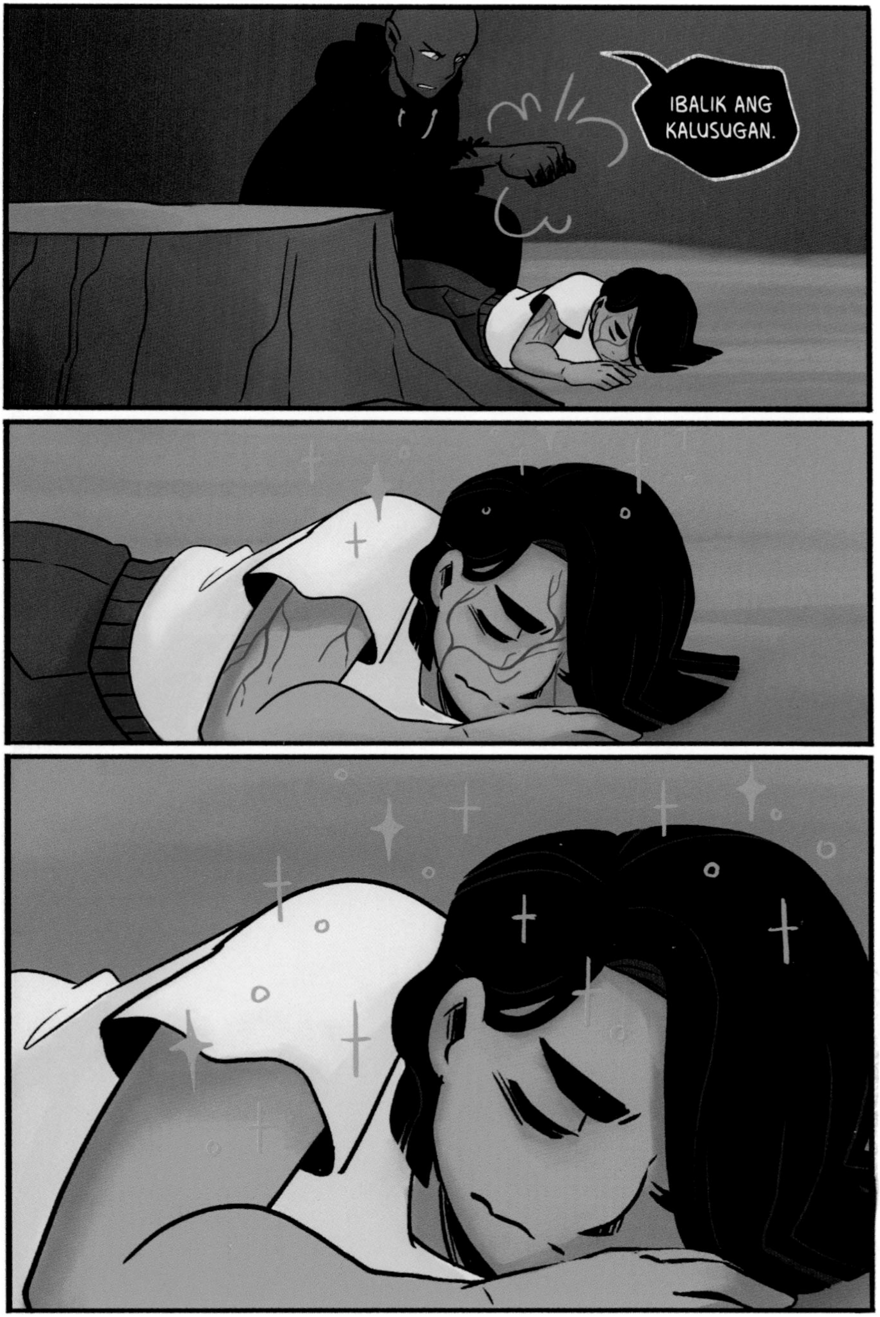
IBALIK ANG KALUSUGAN.

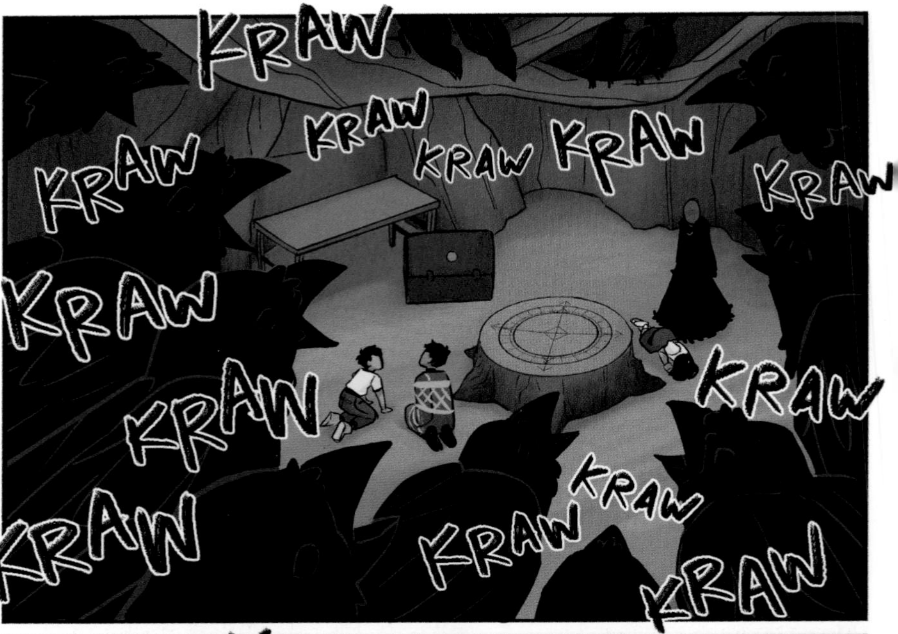
KRAW
KRAW
KRAW
KRAW
KRAW
KRAW
KRAW
KRAW
KRAW
KRAW
KRAW
KRAW
KRAW

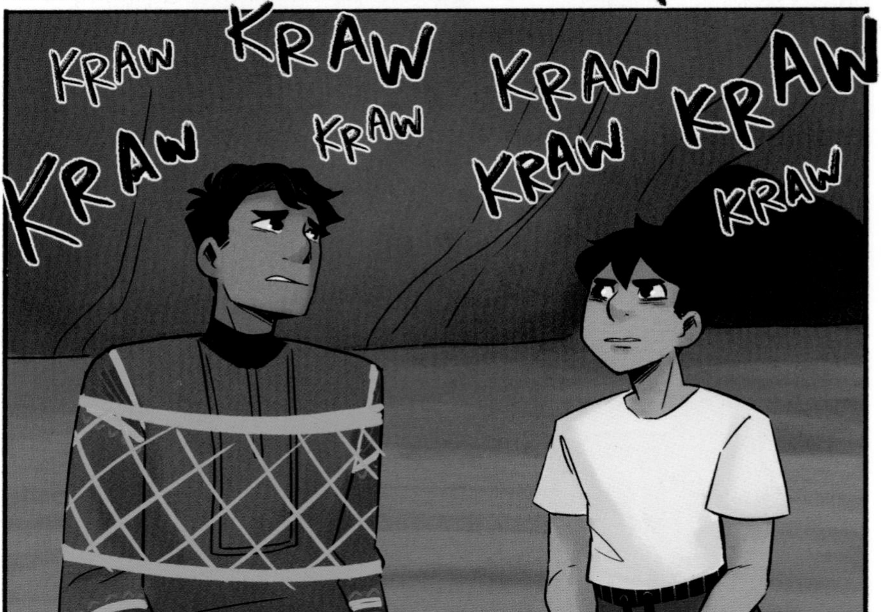
KRAW
KRAW
KRAW
KRAW
KRAW
KRAW
KRAW
KRAW

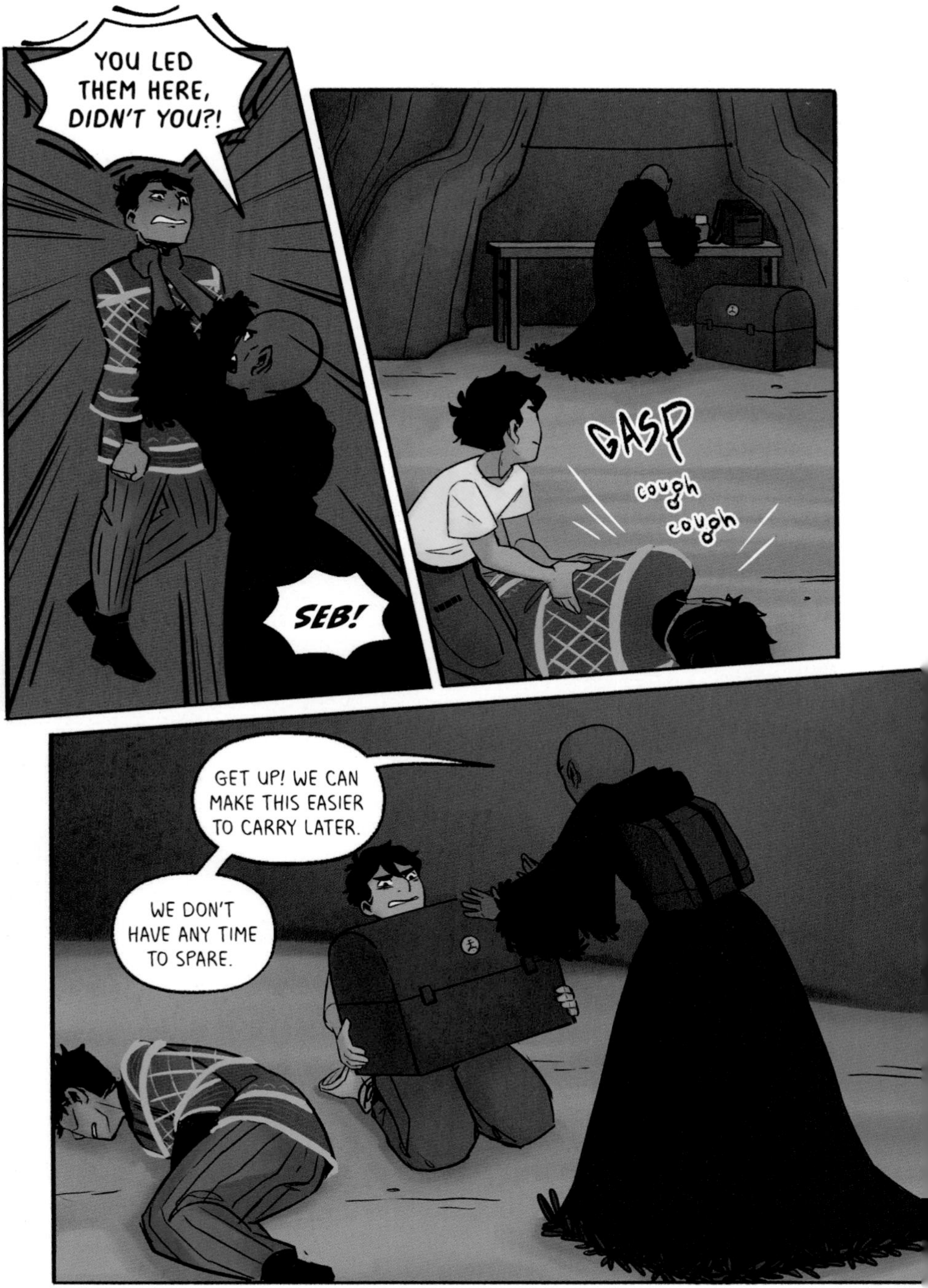
YOU LED THEM HERE, DIDN'T YOU?!
SEB!
GASP
cough cough
GET UP! WE CAN MAKE THIS EASIER TO CARRY LATER.
WE DON'T HAVE ANY TIME TO SPARE.

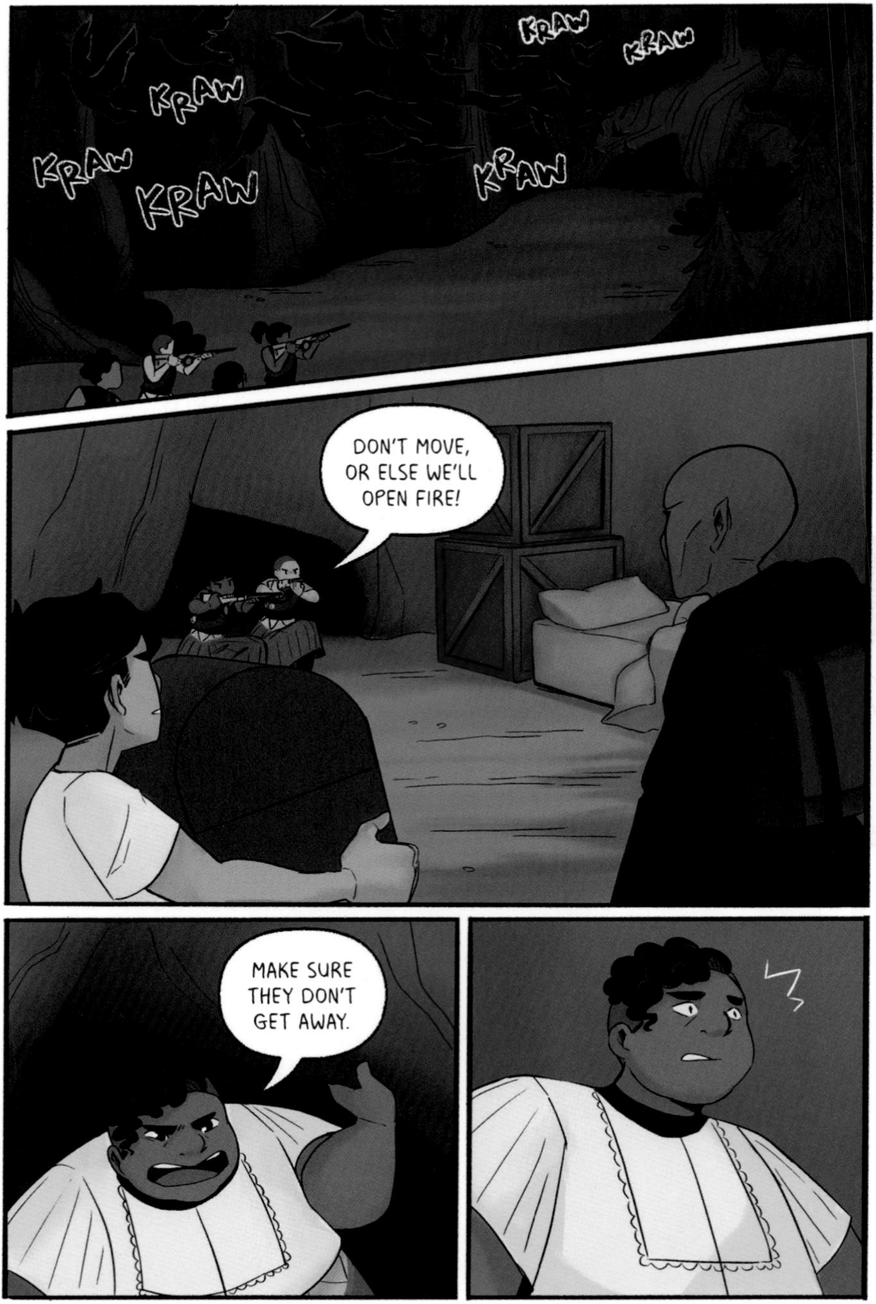
KRAW
KRAW
KRAW
KRAW
KRAW
KRAW
DON'T MOVE, OR ELSE WE'LL OPEN FIRE!
MAKE SURE THEY DON'T GET AWAY.

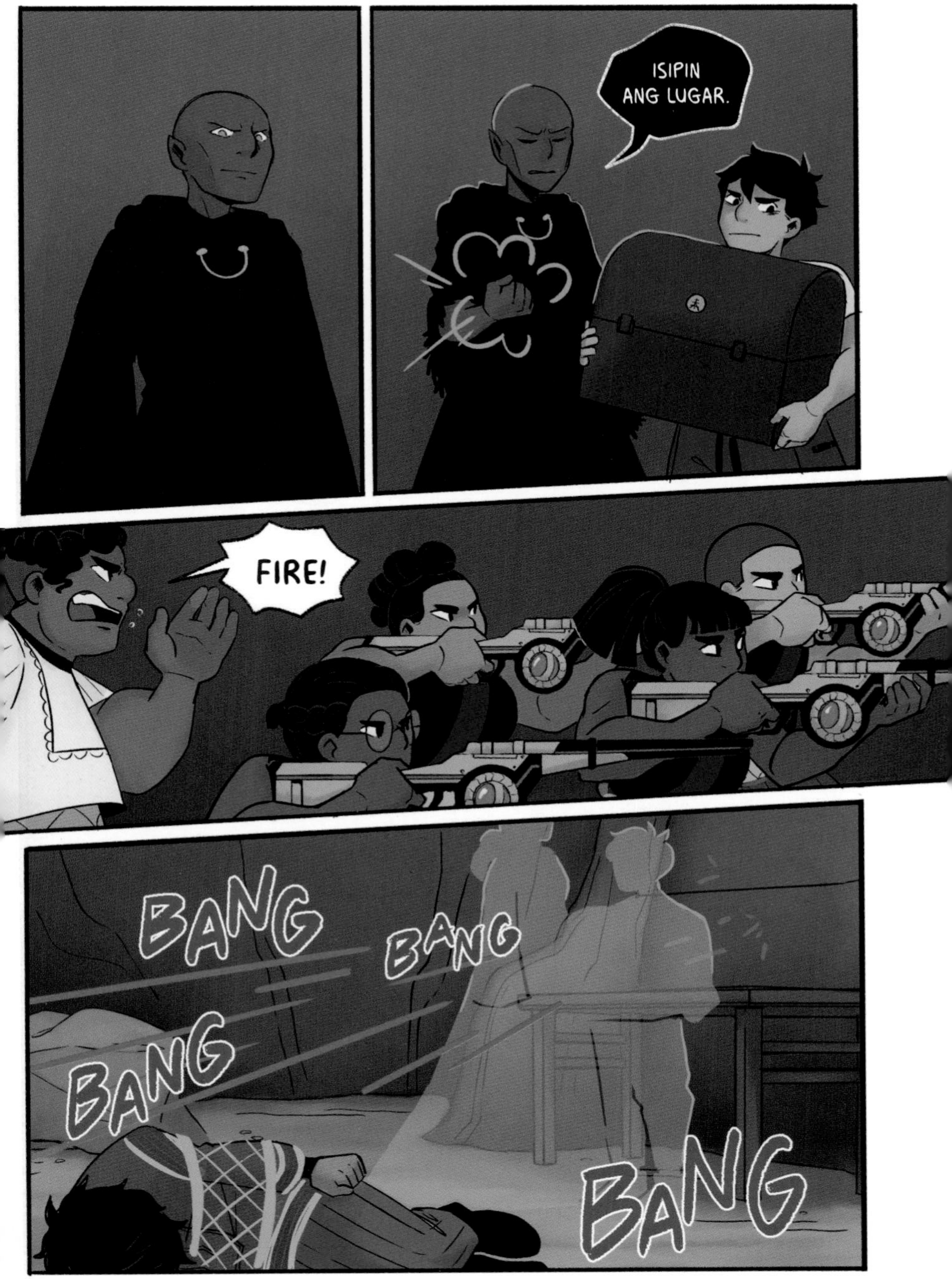
ISIPIN ANG LUGAR.
FIRE!
BANG
BANG
BANG
BANG

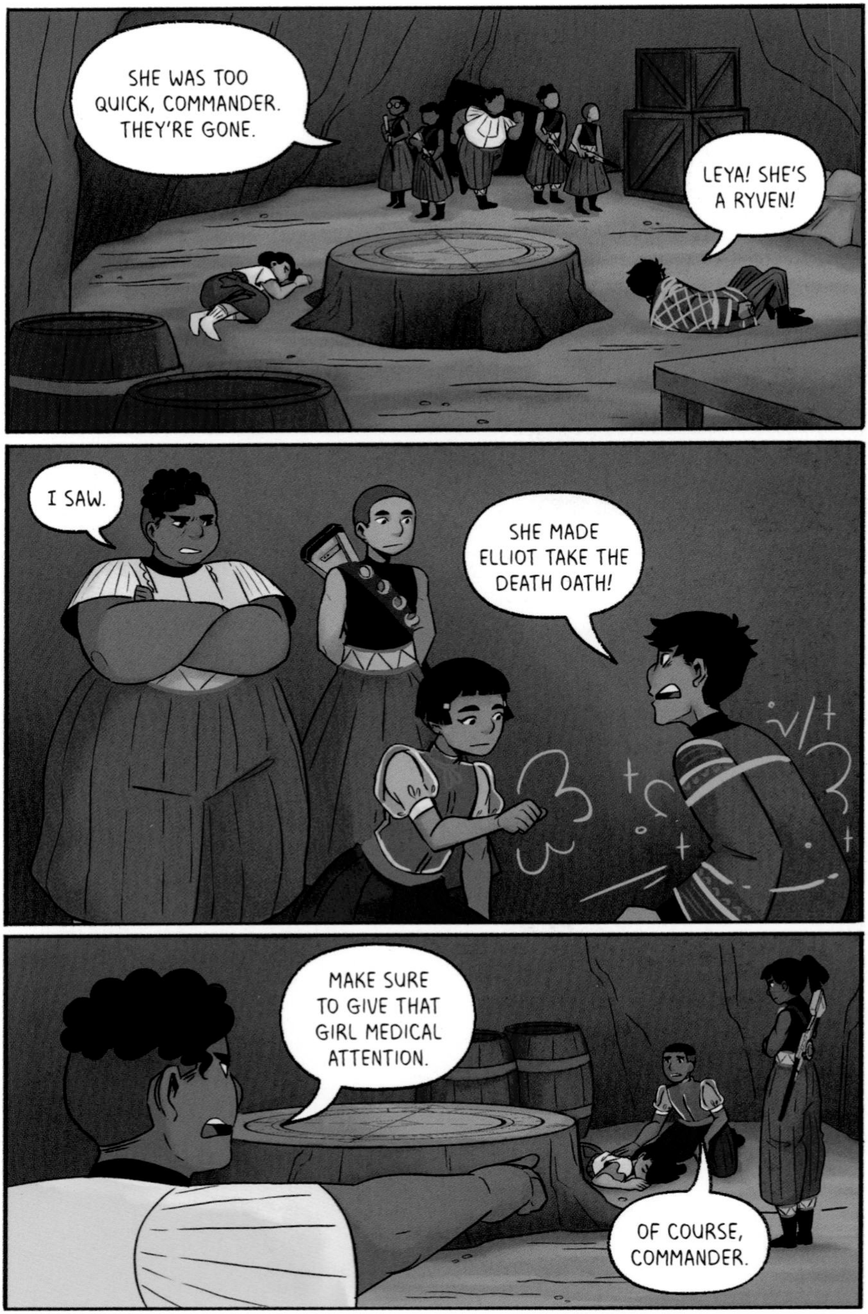
SHE WAS TOO QUICK, COMMANDER. THEY'RE GONE.
LEYA! SHE'S A RYVEN!
I SAW.
SHE MADE ELLIOT TAKE THE DEATH OATH!
MAKE SURE TO GIVE THAT GIRL MEDICAL ATTENTION.
OF COURSE, COMMANDER.

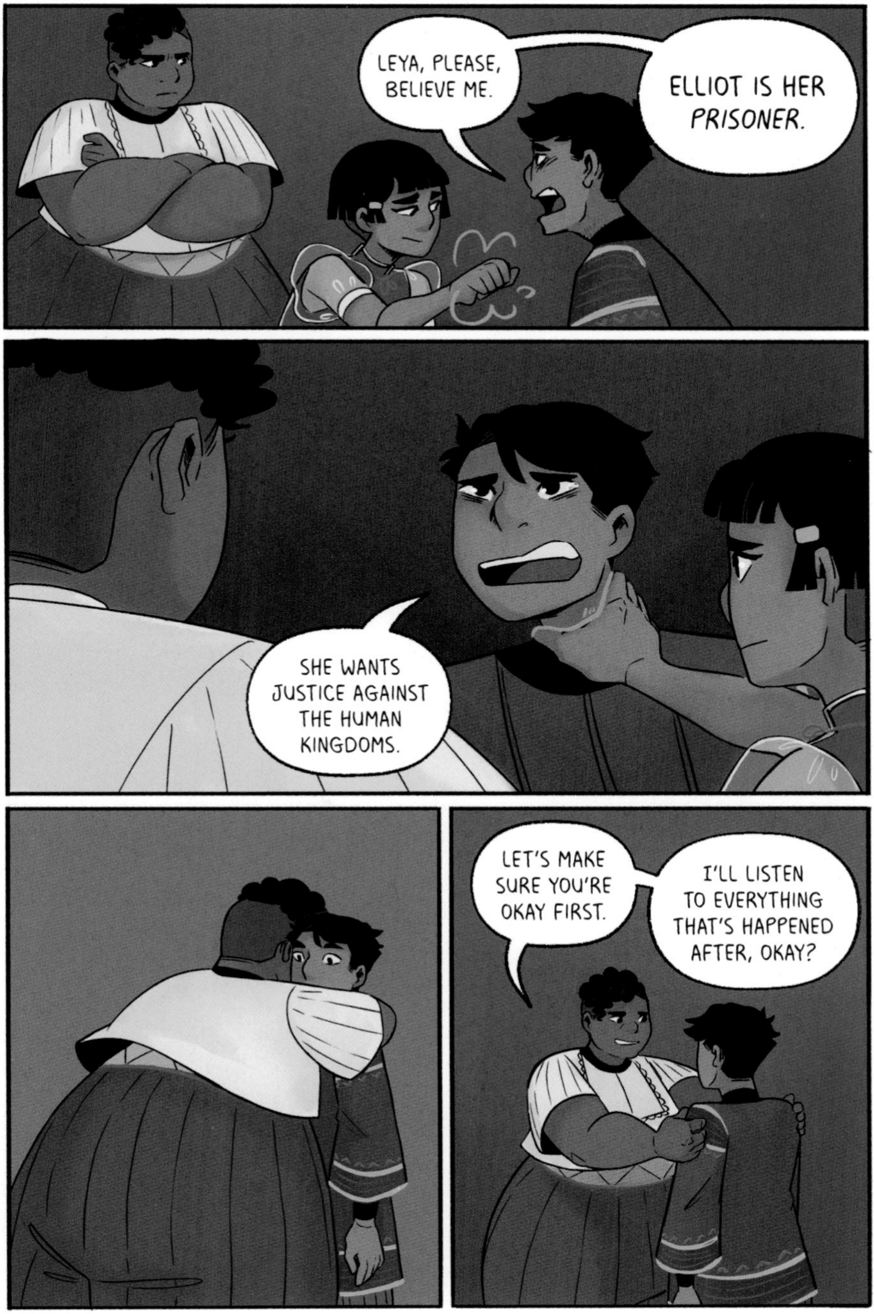
LEYA, PLEASE, BELIEVE ME.
ELLIOT IS HER *PRISONER*.
SHE WANTS JUSTICE AGAINST THE HUMAN KINGDOMS.
LET'S MAKE SURE YOU'RE OKAY FIRST.
I'LL LISTEN TO EVERYTHING THAT'S HAPPENED AFTER, OKAY?

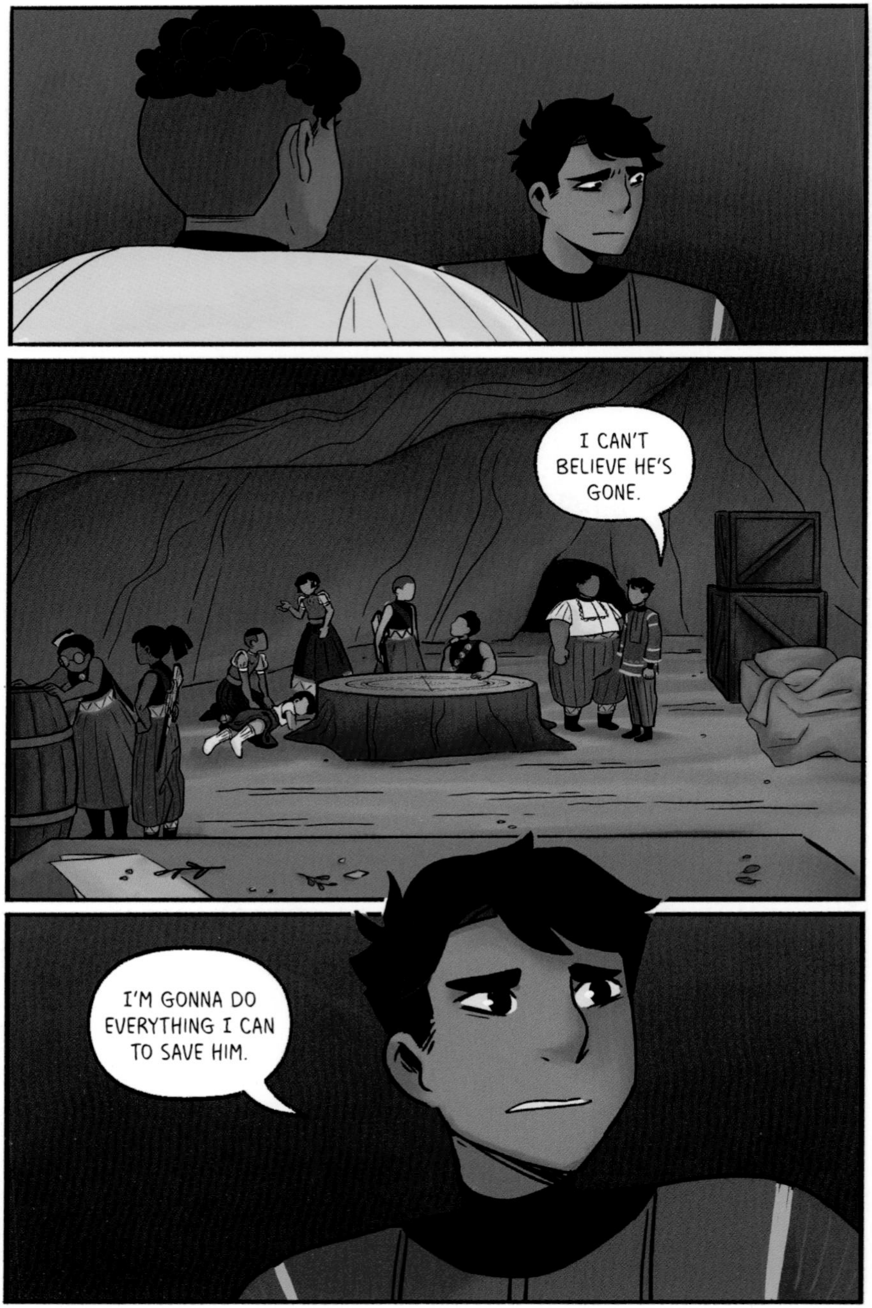
I CAN'T BELIEVE HE'S GONE.
I'M GONNA DO EVERYTHING I CAN TO SAVE HIM.

ONE WEEK LATER

LIZA!

HOW ARE YOU FEELING?

BETTER.

WE BROUGHT YOU SOME MANGOS.

THOSE ARE ACTUALLY ELLIOT'S FAVORITE...

DO YOU REMEMBER ANYTHING ABOUT YOUR TIME WITH THE RYVEN?

DID SHE SAY ANYTHING THAT STANDS OUT?

HMM...

I REMEMBER HER TALKING ABOUT BRINGING HER PARENTS BACK.

I DON'T REALLY KNOW WHAT THAT MEANS.

I'M SORRY I CAN'T REMEMBER MUCH...

DON'T BE SO HARD ON YOURSELF.

YOU WERE UNCONSCIOUS MOST OF THE TIME BECAUSE OF THE POISON.

PLEASE LET SEB OR MYSELF KNOW IF YOU REMEMBER ANYTHING ELSE.

THE ROYAL MAGES HAVE ASSURED ME THAT YOU NO LONGER HAVE *ANY* POISON IN YOUR SYSTEM.
YOU'LL STILL NEED REST TO RECOVER FROM THE TOLL IT HAD ON YOUR BODY.
SO SHE KEPT HER END OF THE BARGAIN TO ELLIOT, THEN?
IT APPEARS SO.
ON THAT TOPIC, THE TWO OF YOU *MUST* PROMISE TO KEEP THE BLACK LILIES A SECRET.

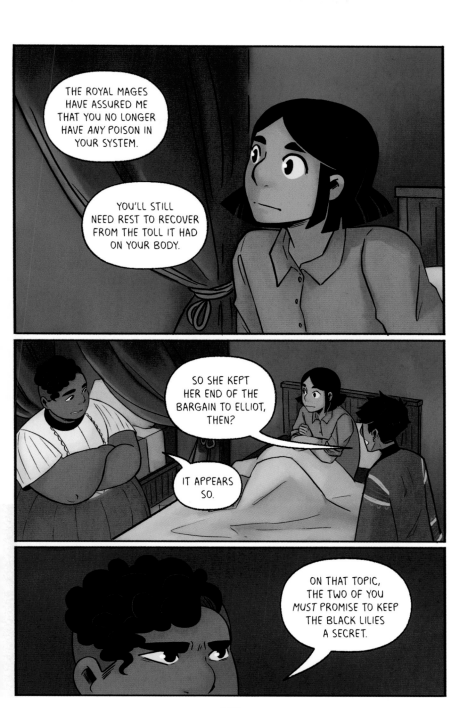

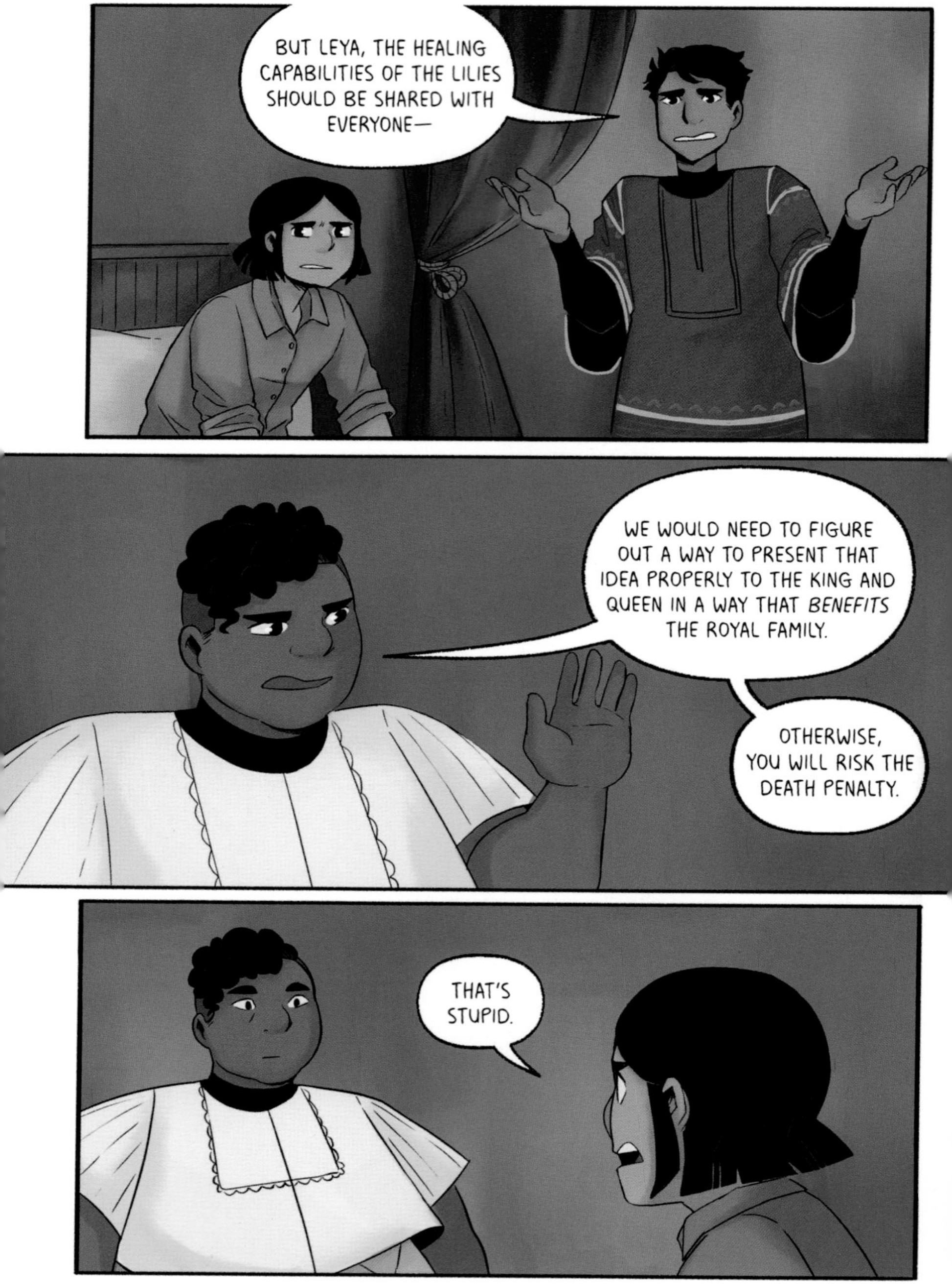
BUT LEYA, THE HEALING CAPABILITIES OF THE LILIES SHOULD BE SHARED WITH EVERYONE—
WE WOULD NEED TO FIGURE OUT A WAY TO PRESENT THAT IDEA PROPERLY TO THE KING AND QUEEN IN A WAY THAT *BENEFITS* THE ROYAL FAMILY.
OTHERWISE, YOU WILL RISK THE DEATH PENALTY.
THAT'S STUPID.

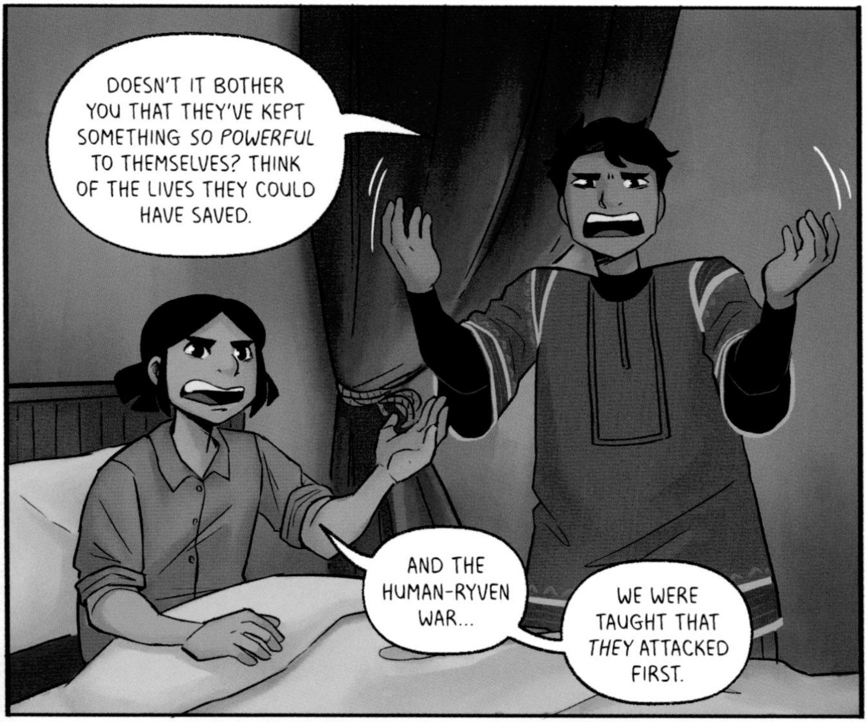
DOESN'T IT BOTHER YOU THAT THEY'VE KEPT SOMETHING *SO POWERFUL* TO THEMSELVES? THINK OF THE LIVES THEY COULD HAVE SAVED.
AND THE HUMAN-RYVEN WAR...
WE WERE TAUGHT THAT *THEY* ATTACKED FIRST.

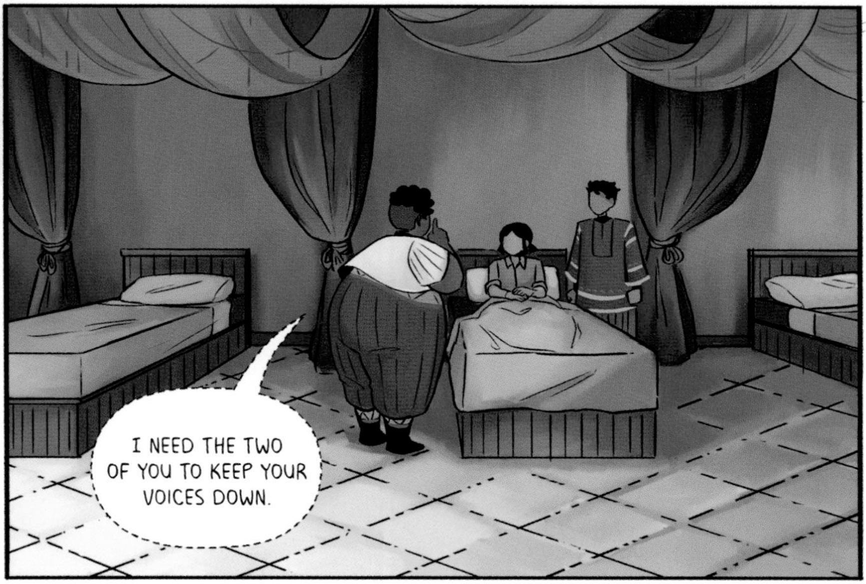
I NEED THE TWO OF YOU TO KEEP YOUR VOICES DOWN.

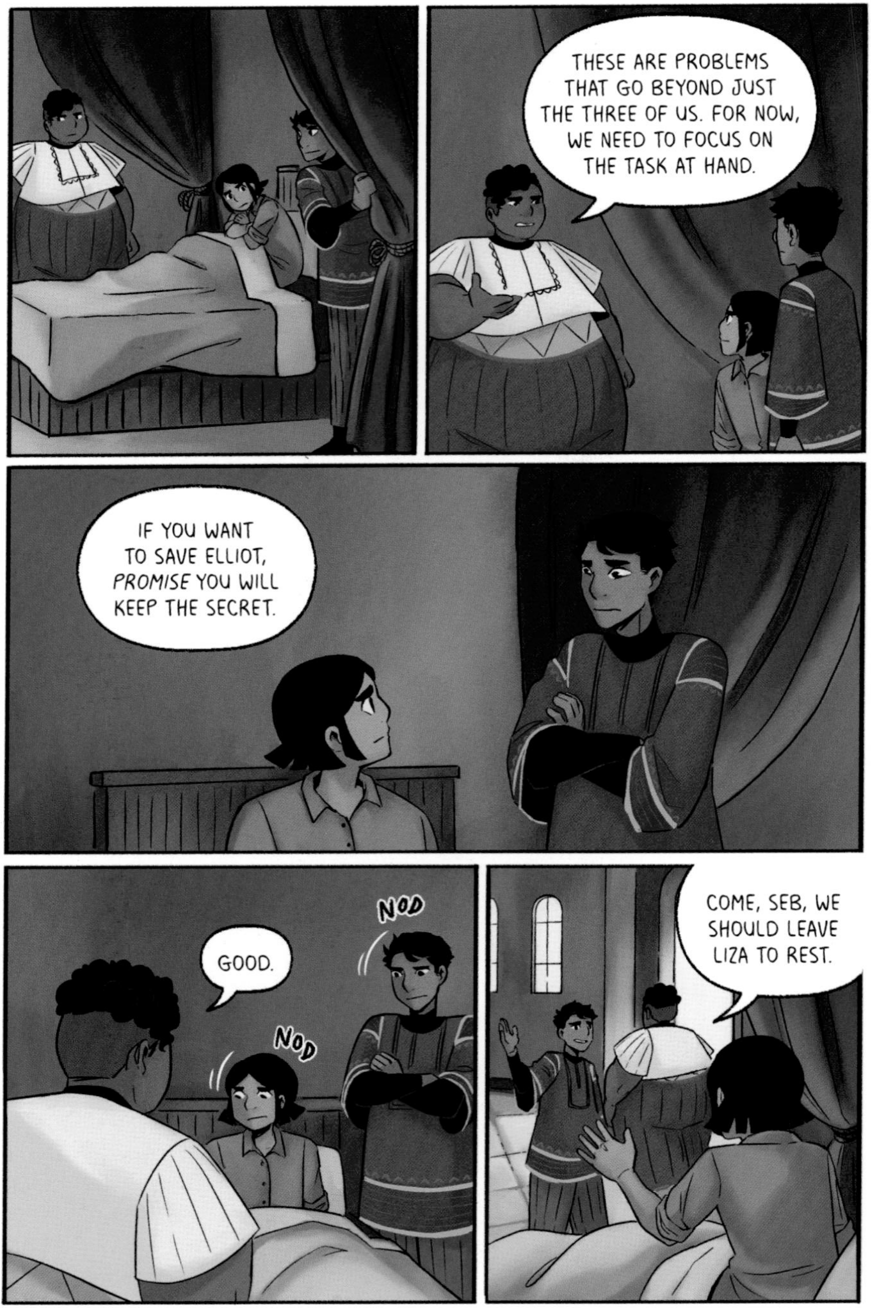
THESE ARE PROBLEMS THAT GO BEYOND JUST THE THREE OF US. FOR NOW, WE NEED TO FOCUS ON THE TASK AT HAND.
IF YOU WANT TO SAVE ELLIOT, *PROMISE* YOU WILL KEEP THE SECRET.
GOOD.
NOD
NOD
COME, SEB, WE SHOULD LEAVE LIZA TO REST.

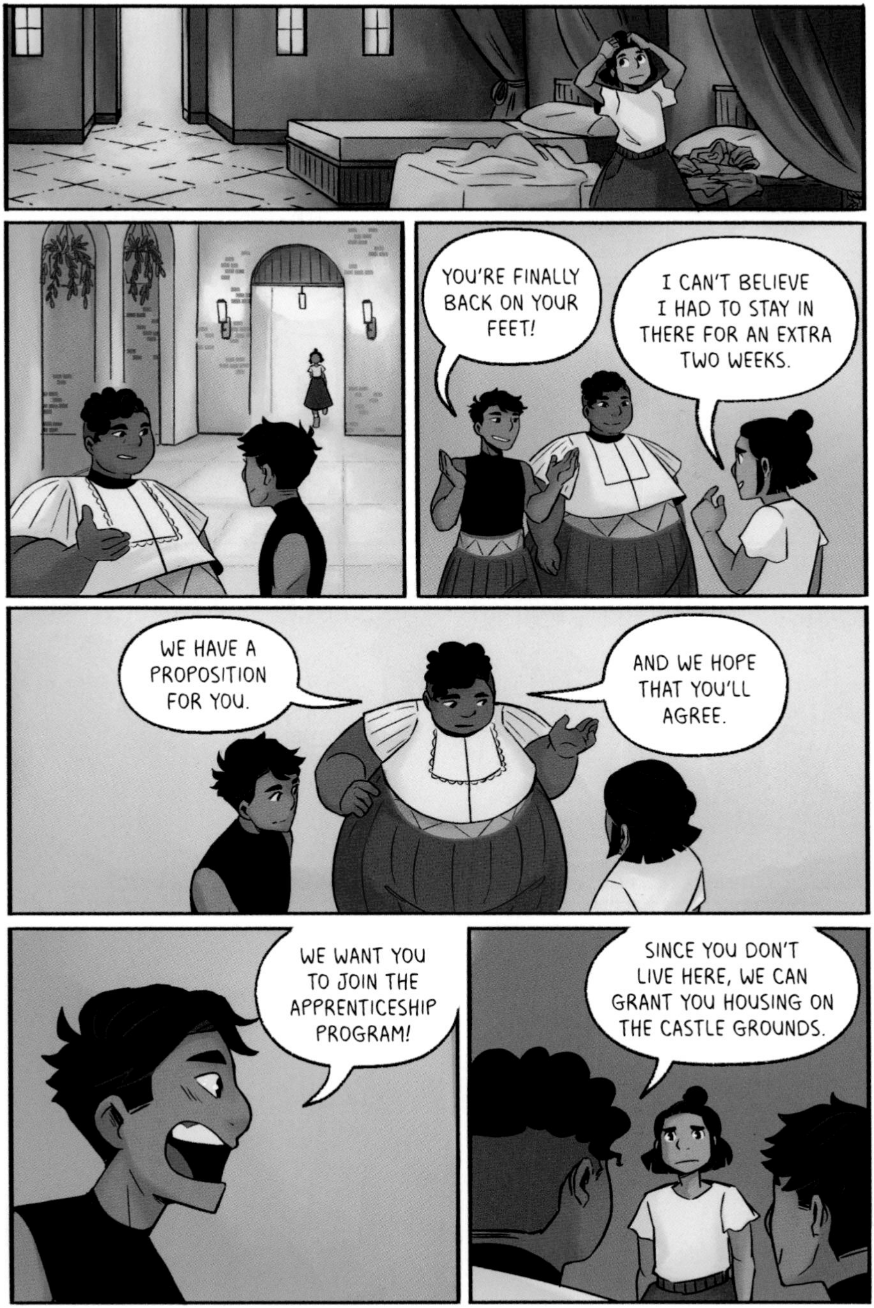
YOU'RE FINALLY BACK ON YOUR FEET!
I CAN'T BELIEVE I HAD TO STAY IN THERE FOR AN EXTRA TWO WEEKS.
WE HAVE A PROPOSITION FOR YOU.
AND WE HOPE THAT YOU'LL AGREE.
WE WANT YOU TO JOIN THE APPRENTICESHIP PROGRAM!
SINCE YOU DON'T LIVE HERE, WE CAN GRANT YOU HOUSING ON THE CASTLE GROUNDS.

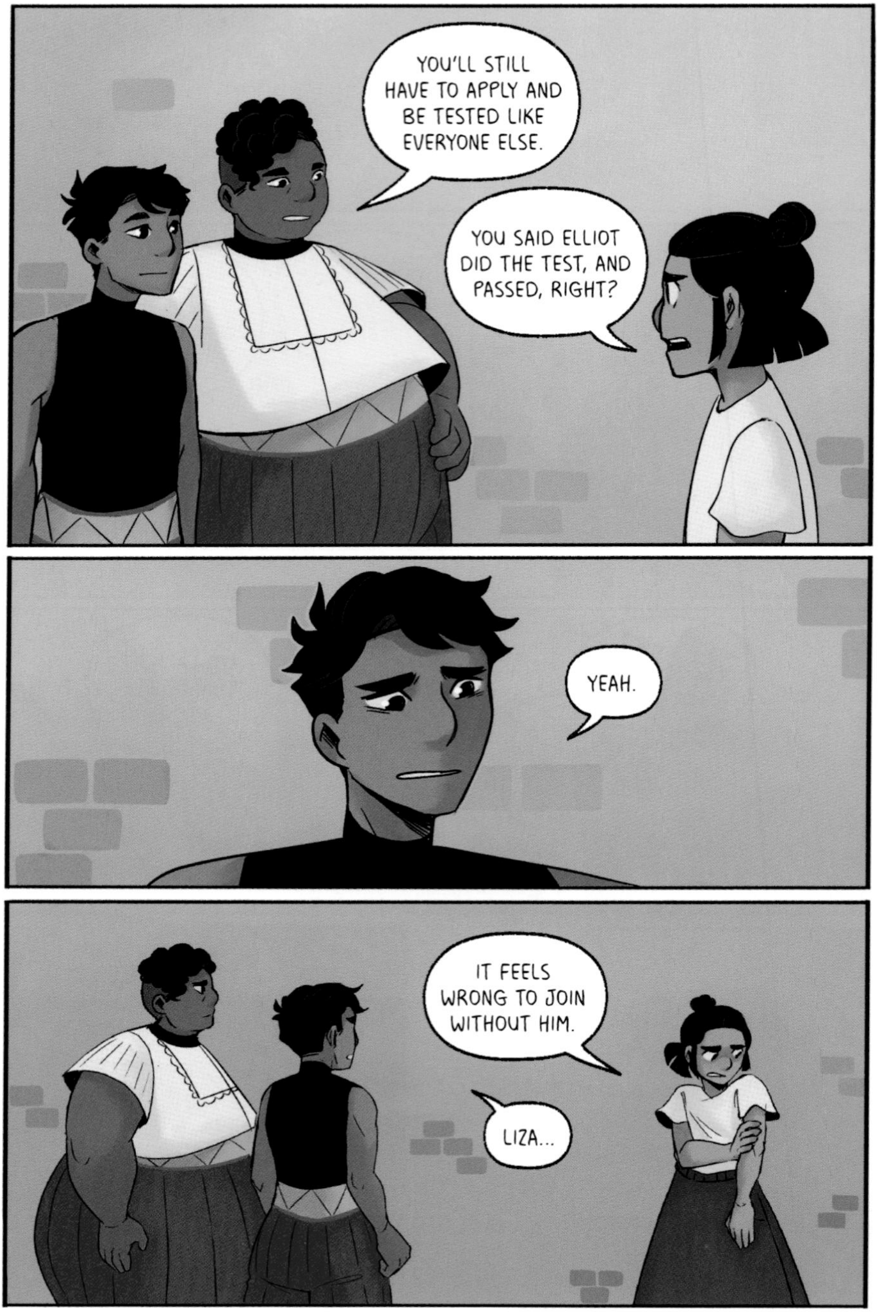
YOU'LL STILL HAVE TO APPLY AND BE TESTED LIKE EVERYONE ELSE.
YOU SAID ELLIOT DID THE TEST, AND PASSED, RIGHT?
YEAH.
IT FEELS WRONG TO JOIN WITHOUT HIM.
LIZA...

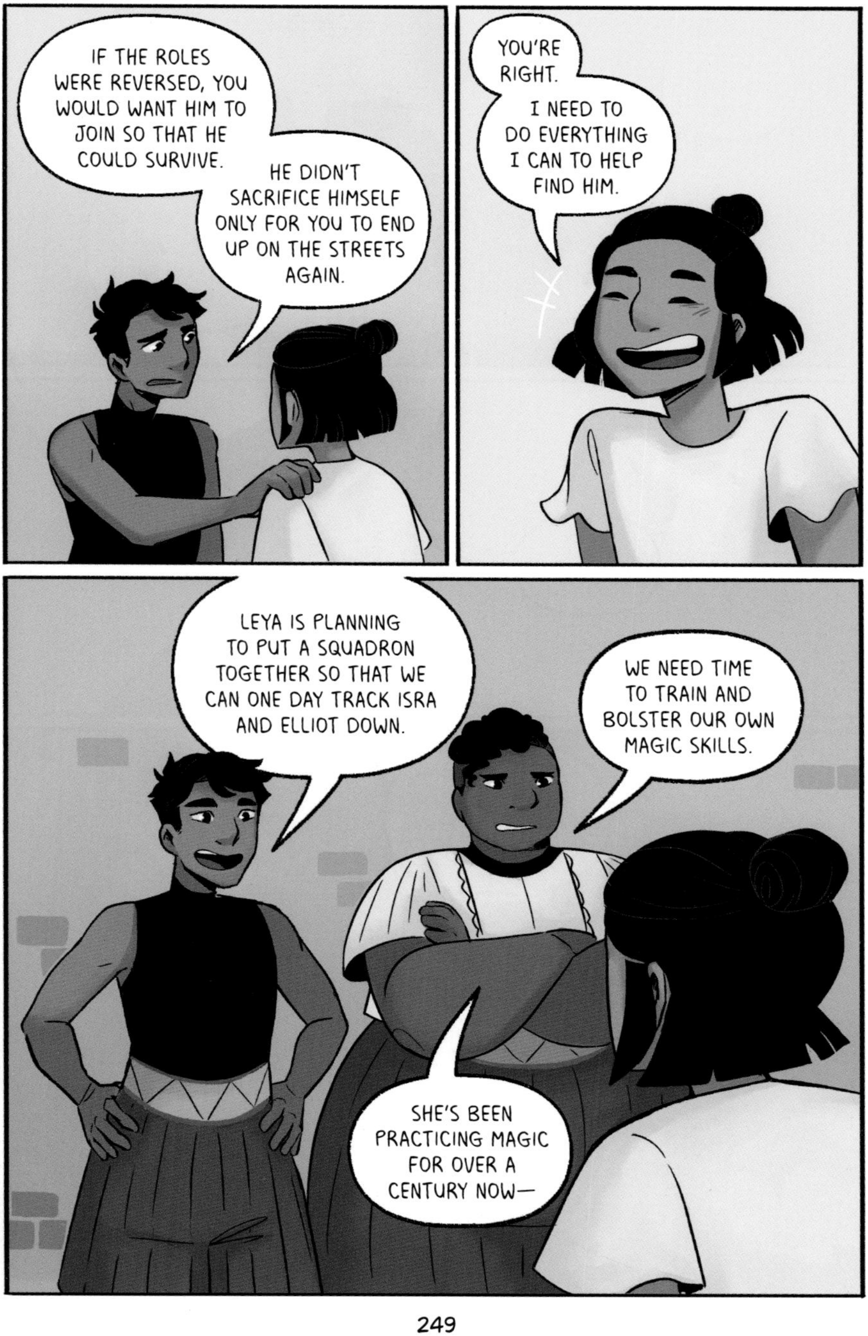
IF THE ROLES WERE REVERSED, YOU WOULD WANT HIM TO JOIN SO THAT HE COULD SURVIVE.
HE DIDN'T SACRIFICE HIMSELF ONLY FOR YOU TO END UP ON THE STREETS AGAIN.
YOU'RE RIGHT.
I NEED TO DO EVERYTHING I CAN TO HELP FIND HIM.
LEYA IS PLANNING TO PUT A SQUADRON TOGETHER SO THAT WE CAN ONE DAY TRACK ISRA AND ELLIOT DOWN.
WE NEED TIME TO TRAIN AND BOLSTER OUR OWN MAGIC SKILLS.
SHE'S BEEN PRACTICING MAGIC FOR OVER A CENTURY NOW—

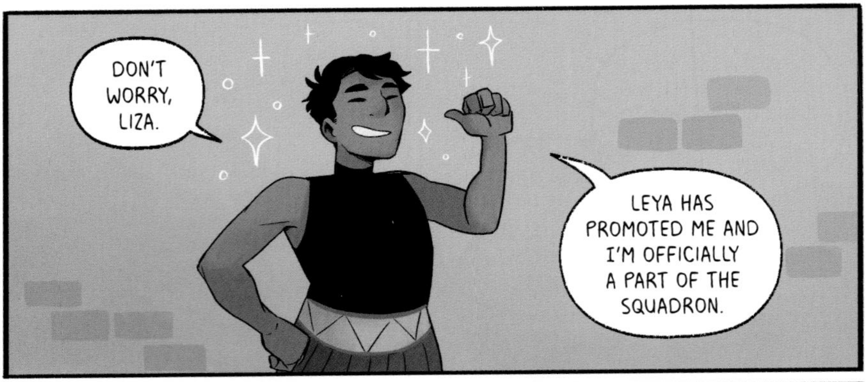
DON'T WORRY, LIZA.
LEYA HAS PROMOTED ME AND I'M OFFICIALLY A PART OF THE SQUADRON.
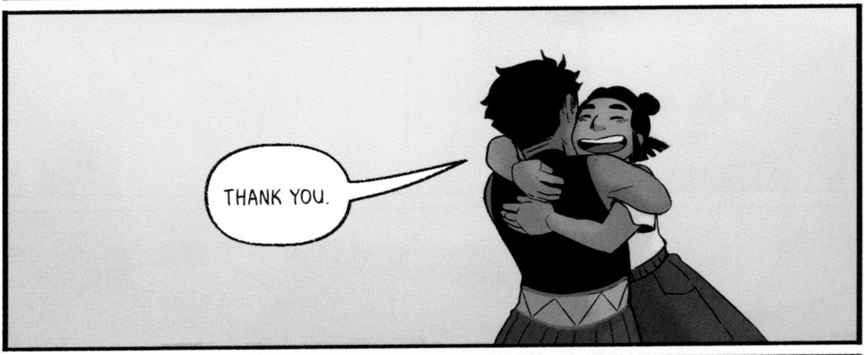
THANK YOU.
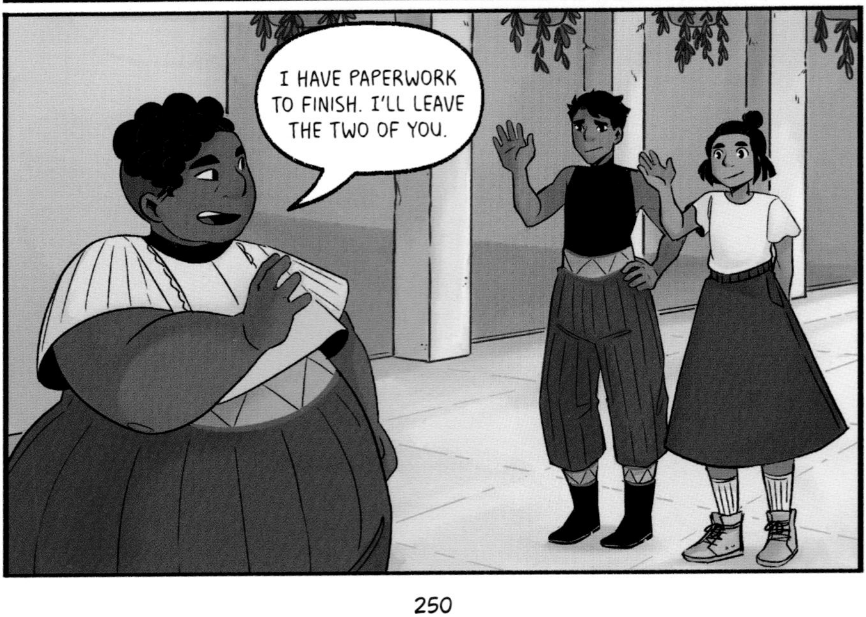
I HAVE PAPERWORK TO FINISH. I'LL LEAVE THE TWO OF YOU.

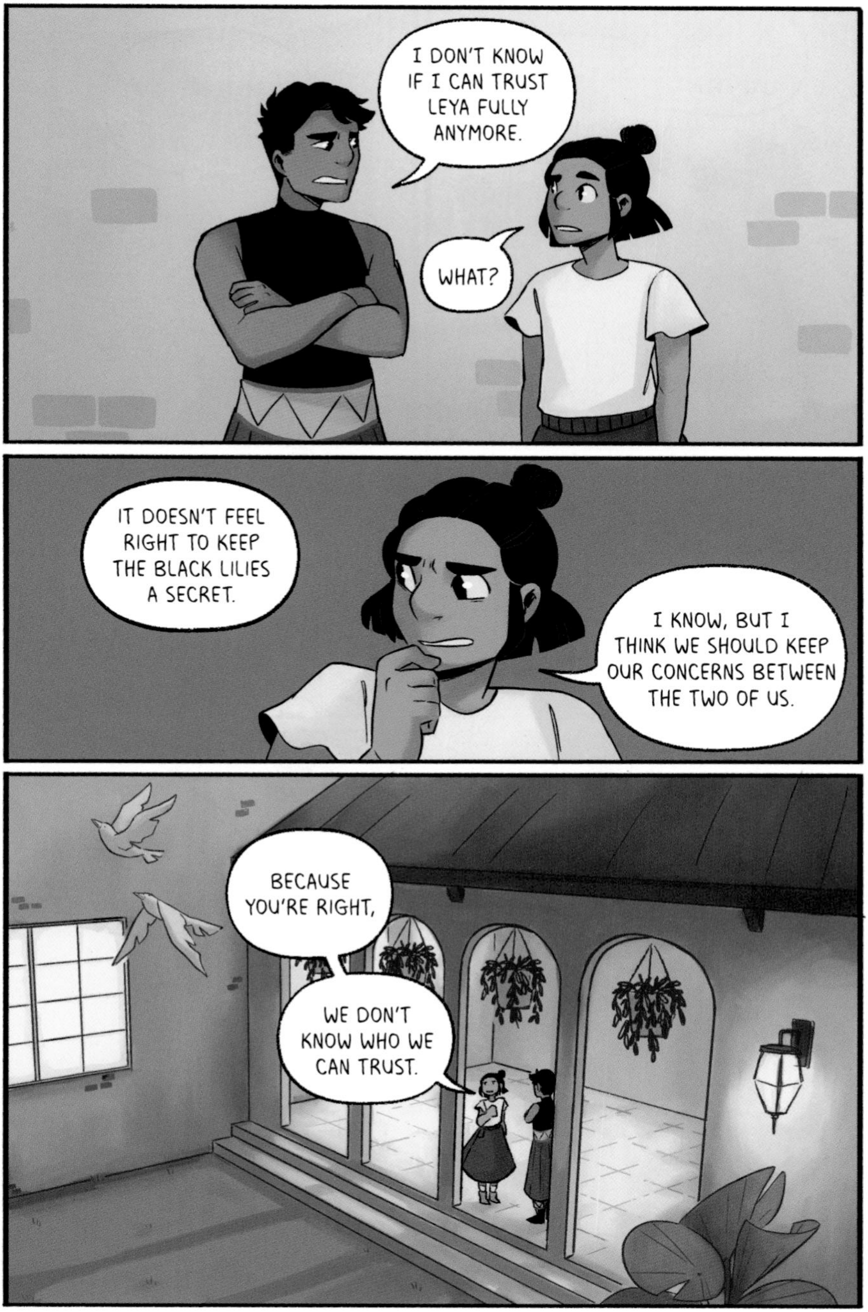
I DON'T KNOW IF I CAN TRUST LEYA FULLY ANYMORE.
WHAT?
IT DOESN'T FEEL RIGHT TO KEEP THE BLACK LILIES A SECRET.
I KNOW, BUT I THINK WE SHOULD KEEP OUR CONCERNS BETWEEN THE TWO OF US.
BECAUSE YOU'RE RIGHT,
WE DON'T KNOW WHO WE CAN TRUST.

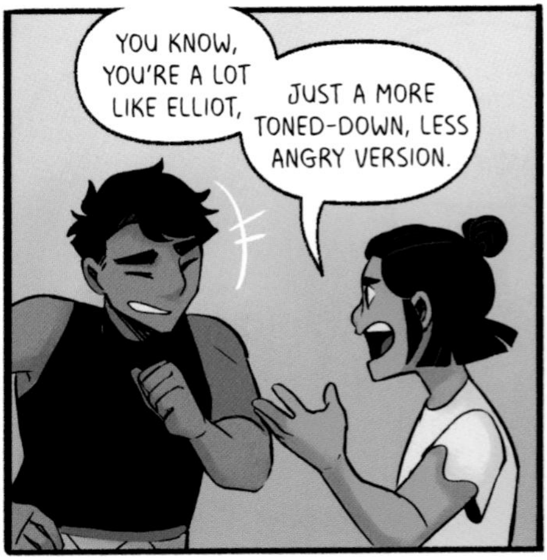
YOU KNOW, YOU'RE A LOT LIKE ELLIOT,
JUST A MORE TONED-DOWN, LESS ANGRY VERSION.

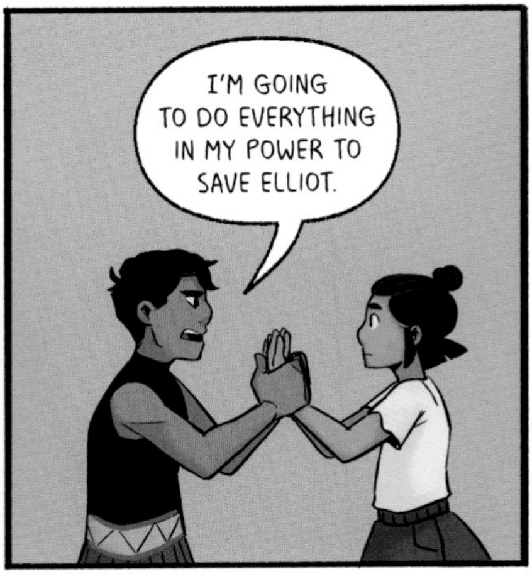
I'M GOING TO DO EVERYTHING IN MY POWER TO SAVE ELLIOT.

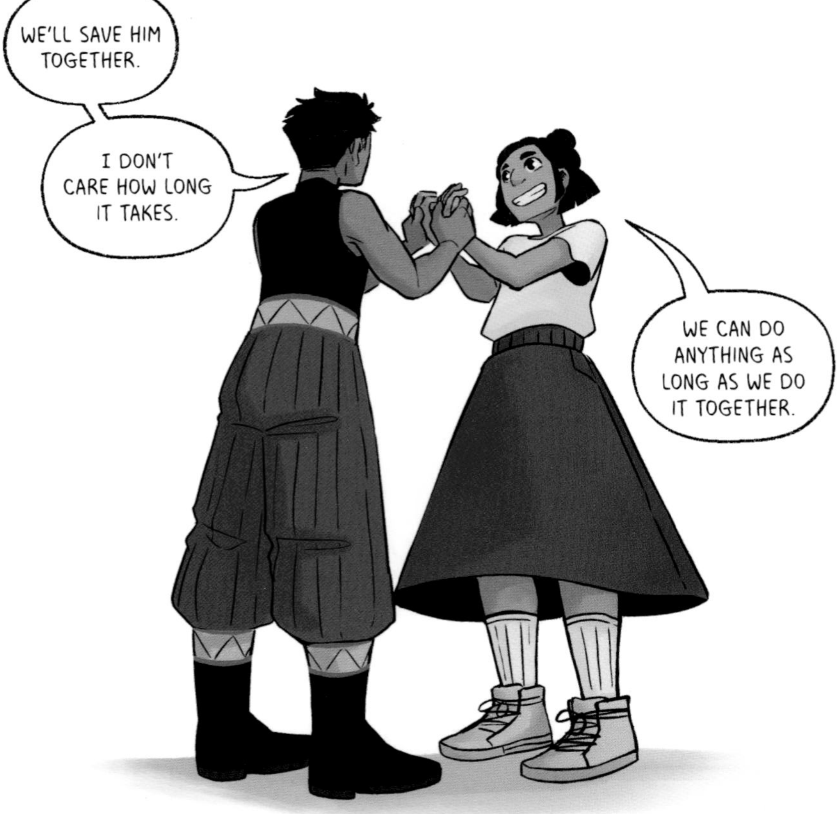
WE'LL SAVE HIM TOGETHER.
I DON'T CARE HOW LONG IT TAKES.
WE CAN DO ANYTHING AS LONG AS WE DO IT TOGETHER.

EPILOGUE

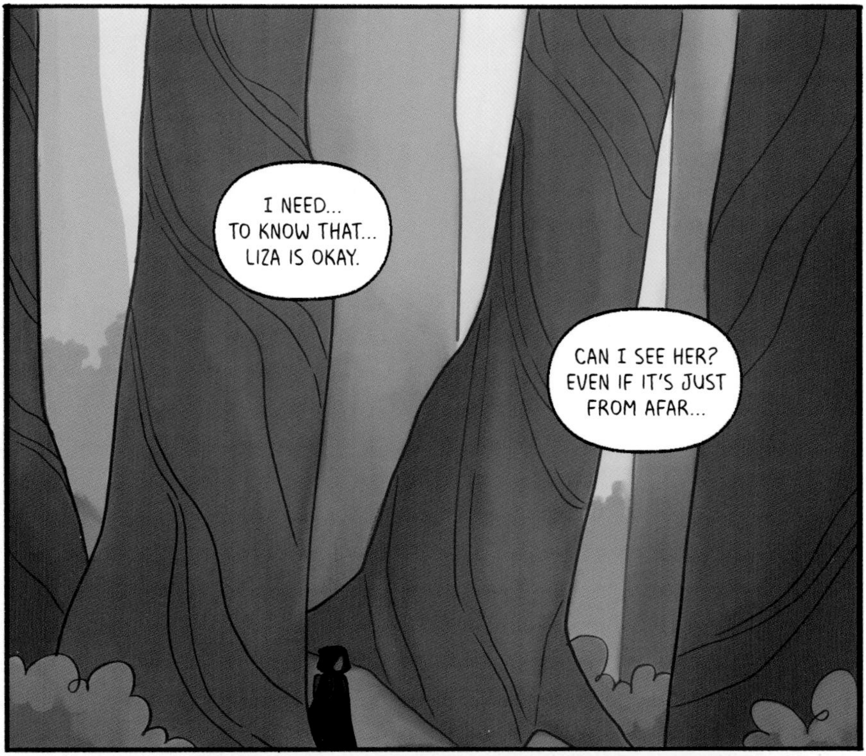

I NEED... TO KNOW THAT... LIZA IS OKAY.
CAN I SEE HER? EVEN IF IT'S JUST FROM AFAR...

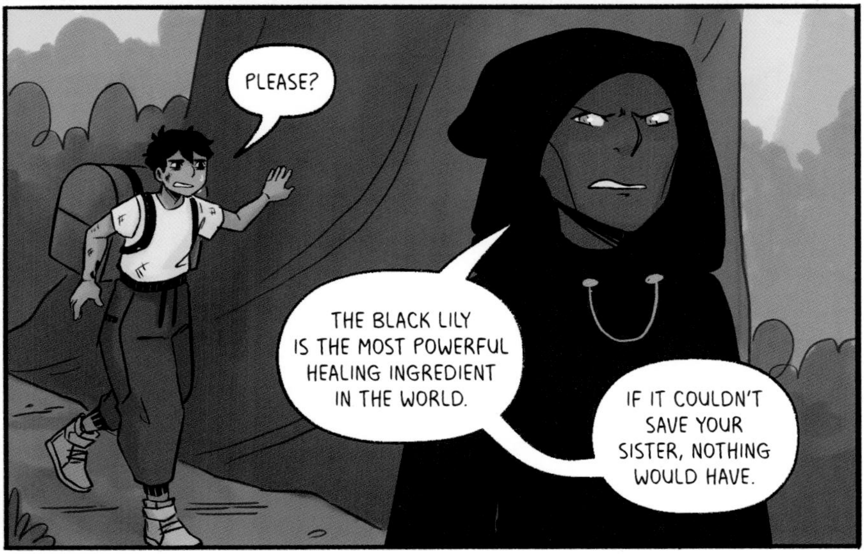

PLEASE?
THE BLACK LILY IS THE MOST POWERFUL HEALING INGREDIENT IN THE WORLD.
IF IT COULDN'T SAVE YOUR SISTER, NOTHING WOULD HAVE.

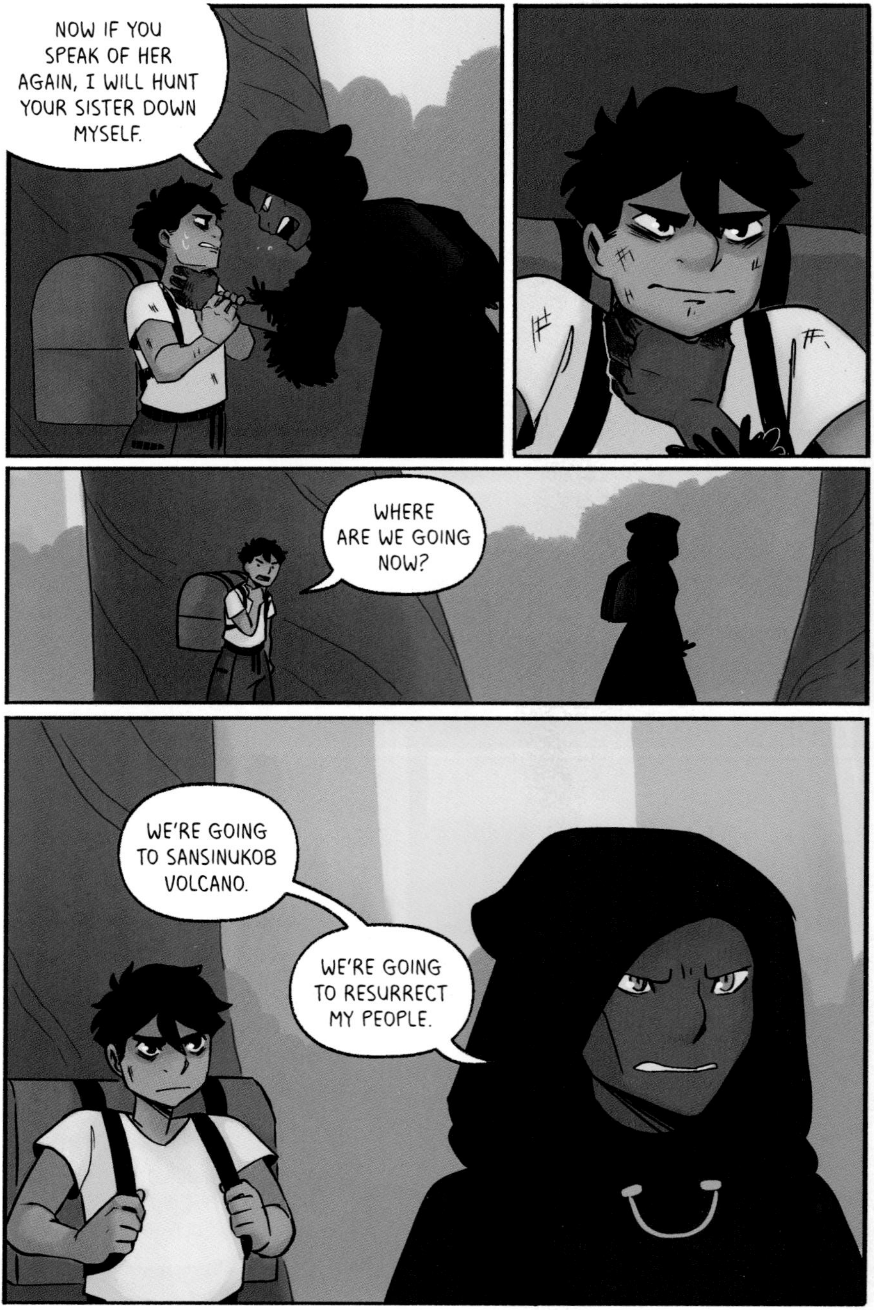
NOW IF YOU SPEAK OF HER AGAIN, I WILL HUNT YOUR SISTER DOWN MYSELF.
WHERE ARE WE GOING NOW?
WE'RE GOING TO SANSINUKOB VOLCANO.
WE'RE GOING TO RESURRECT MY PEOPLE.

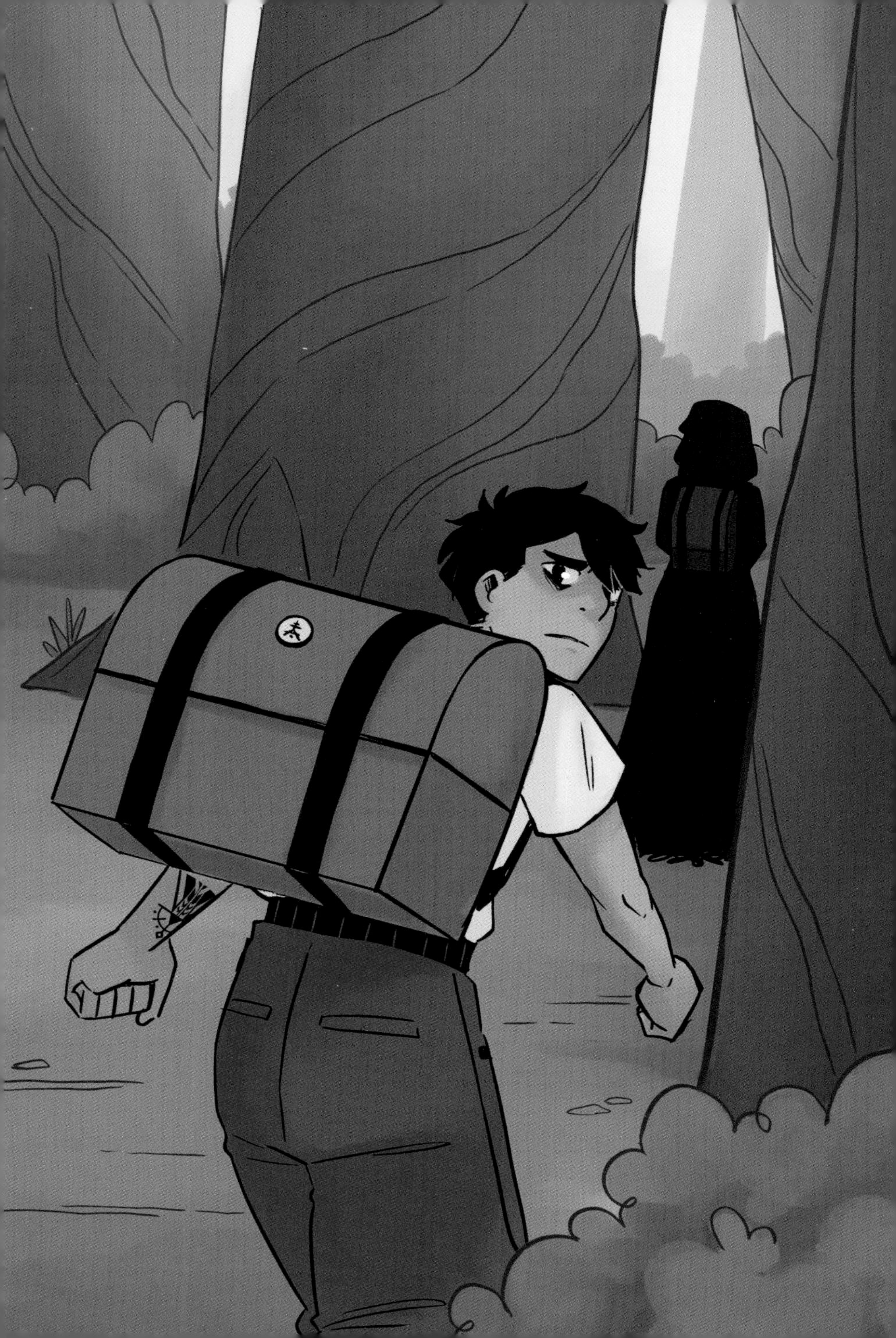

ACKNOWLEDGMENTS

If my younger self could see me now, her mouth would be gaping in awe. We made it, kiddo: we followed our heart, and now we're published!

Many, many, many thanks to:

Warren Lacaba, the love of my life, who has always believed in me and my work even before I did. Thank you for supporting me every single step of the way to get here, even making sure that I would take breaks and rest. I will forever be grateful for your patience, especially when I pushed dozens of versions of this story into your face to look over and give me feedback.

My wonderfully kind and beautiful-hearted agent, Tara Gilbert. I wouldn't be living my dream without her enthusiasm, encouragement, and gung ho attitude.

Everyone who helped make this book happen at Clarion Books, especially my editor, Elizabeth Agyemang, who helped this story blossom to be its very best; Celeste Knudsen for all of the support, design help, and hard work; and Kyla Aiko for helping bring my story to life with her amazing lettering skills. Production editors Mary Magrisso and Erika West for ensuring everything moved along smoothly and being on top of everything. Copyeditor Emily Andrukaitis for catching everything and anything that I forgot to draw, and ensuring I haven't invented a new way to spell a word. Proofreaders Romanie Rout, Anna Leuchtenberger, and Ronnie Ambrose, you're the MVPs, helping tie up this entire project in a beautiful, neat little bow. And last but not least, marketer and publicist Robby Imfeld and Kelly Haberstroh for helping bring this story to many more readers than I could have ever imagined.

To the Comics Support Group that I'm part of on Discord, thank you all for being a sounding board, a place to ask for advice, gush, and share our favorite kinds of media. This group has allowed me to wade through the US publishing world much more easily. I am so grateful to have made so many friends who I can talk to about comics, and to be a part of such an amazing, and growing, community.

To my parents, who have supported and loved me for all these years, I give you permission to brag about me to your hearts' content. I love you both! Thank you to the rest of my friends, family, and fans for cheering me on and supporting me throughout the years. I can't wait to show you all the stories that are swimming around in my head. And last but certainly not least, to my dog, Danny, for always keeping me company while I work.

—Joanna Cacao

SPELL GLOSSARY

SPELL	PRONUNCIATION	DIRECT TRANSLATION
Apoy	ah-POY	Fire
Bumalik	boo-MAH-leek	Return
Hangin	hahng-in	Wind
Ibalik ang kalusugan	e-bah-lick ahng kah-loo-soo-gahn	Restore health
Ilaw	ee-lau	Light
Ingay	ing-eye	Loud
Isipin	e-SEE-pihn	Think
Isipin ang lugar	e-SEE-pihn ahng loo-gahr	Imagine the place
Itulak	e-TOO-lack	Push
Kalasag	kah-LAH-sahg	Shield
Magpahinga	mahg-pah-HING-ah	Rest
Magyelo	mahg-YELL-oh	Ice

WHAT IT DOES	INGREDIENTS
Creates a small blast of fire and smoke, similar to sumabog but not as strong	1 chili pepper, 1 ball of cotton, pine tree sap
In combination with a transportation vessel, this sends an object back through the vessel's magic seal	Needs a specific magic circle to be drawn.
Creates a gust of wind, similar to itulak but not as strong	1 mushroom stem, 2 flower heads
Saves a target from death	1 black lily flower head, ground into a powder
Creates an intense bright light	4 sunflower seeds, 1 carnation flower head, 1 slice of lemon
Waves of an extremely loud sound emanate from the caster's hand	3 tree twigs, 1 pine cone, 2 bay leaves
Allows the caster to see a memory of their target by touching their head	1 sprig of honeysuckle, 2 ivy leaves, 3 blueberries
Allows teleportation using a memory of the target or caster	1 sprig of honeysuckle, 2 ivy leaves, 3 blueberries, 1 sweet pea flower head
A burst of air pushes out from the caster's hands	2 mushroom stems, 1 sprig of rosemary
Creates a circular shield to protect the caster from explosions	2 acorns, 1 sprig of white heather, 1 fern leaf, coconut hair
Rests the target's body, makes blood flow slower than normal	1 ginger, 1 kava root, 1 aloe vera stem, lemon juice
Freezes water	2 pansy heads, 3 winterberries

SPELL GLOSSARY

SPELL	PRONUNCIATION	DIRECT TRANSLATION
Mahulog ka sa malalim na tulog	mah-hoo-hoo-lohg kah sah mah-lah-lim nah too-lohg	You fall into a deep sleep
Makunan	mah-COO-nahn	Captured
Matulin	mah-TOO-lin	Swift
Pader ng apoy	pah-dehr nang ah-poy	Wall of fire
Pakawalan	pah-kah-wah-lahn	Release
Palutangin	pah-loo-TAHNG-ihn	Float
Pangako ng kamatayan	pahng-ah-koh nahng kah-mah-tie-ahn	Promise of death
Paputok	pah-poo-toak	Fireworks
Selyo	sell-yoh	seal
Sumabog	sue-MAH-bohg	Explode
Sundan	soon-dahn	Follow

WHAT IT DOES	INGREDIENTS
Forces the target into a deep slumber.	Requires 2 casters with the same amount of ingredients. 2 poppy seed heads, 1 chamomile flower head, 5 inches of an ivy vine
Creates a magical net to capture a target	Silk thread, 2 sprigs of thyme, 1 morning glory flower head
Makes the target move quickly	3 coffee beans, 1 foxtail plant
Creates a large wall of fire	1 acorn, 1 rose leaf, 2 chili peppers, 1 ball of cotton, pine tree sap
Releases a seal	Needs a specific magic circle to be drawn.
Allows the caster or target to float, defying gravity.	2 sycamore seeds, 1 orchid head
The Death Oath, a vow to protect the caster even at the cost of your own life. Failure results in the most excruciating death imaginable	Requires a specific symbol to be tattooed on to the target, using powdered bones, and the blood of the caster.
A burst of fireworks shoots out from the caster's hands.	2 white dandelion heads, handful of peppercorns
Creates a magical seal on a target that conceals a hidden message	Requires a magic seal to be drawn onto target while thinking of the message simultaneously.
An explosion will occur, similar to a bomb.	2 chili peppers, 3 white dandelion heads, 1 ball of cotton
Allows the caster to follow the target after attaching a spell container to said target	A container for the ingredients to attach to the target. 5 sunflower seeds, 1 sprig of creeping Charlie, 1 sweet clover

THE EVOLUTION OF THE TITAN SNAKE BATTLE

FIRST SAMPLE SPREAD

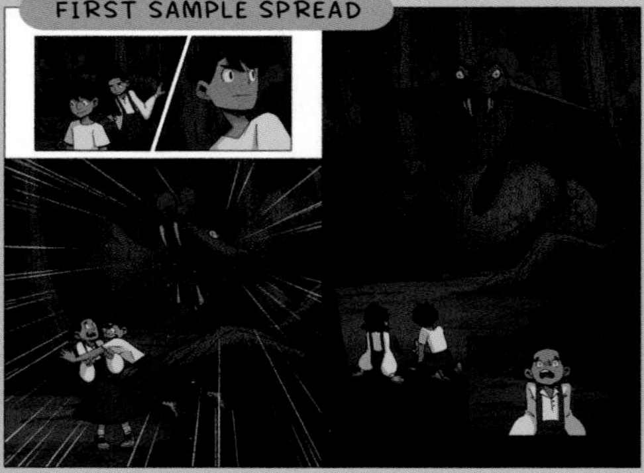

SECOND SAMPLE SPREAD

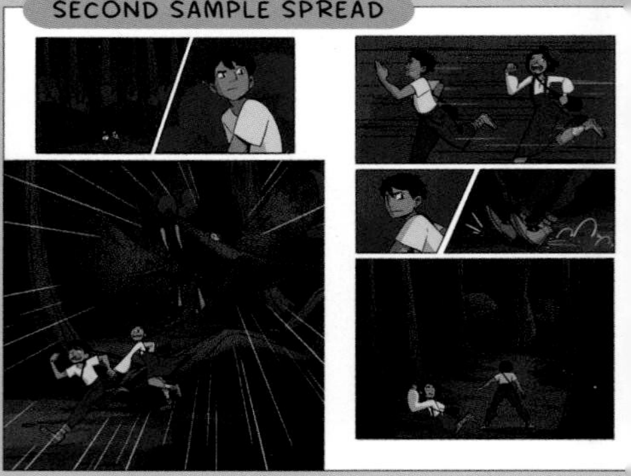

A lot of work goes into making a graphic novel!

This first sample spread is what I sent to my agent for review. After I received some feedback, I redrew the spread for better pacing for the narrative and scene, so that I could confidently send it out to editors that would hopefully pick up my story.

FINAL SPREAD FROM START TO FINISH

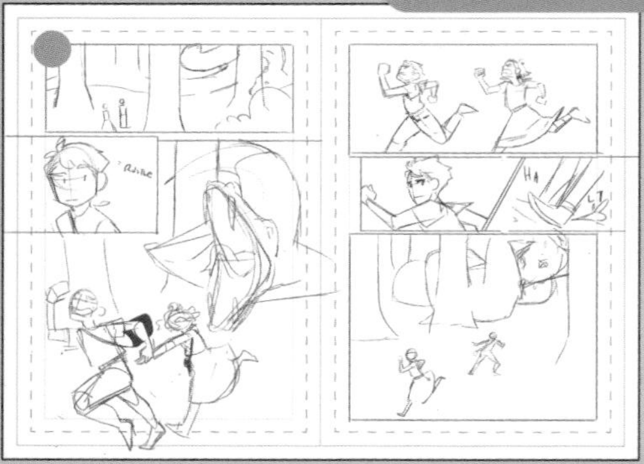
HA
LT

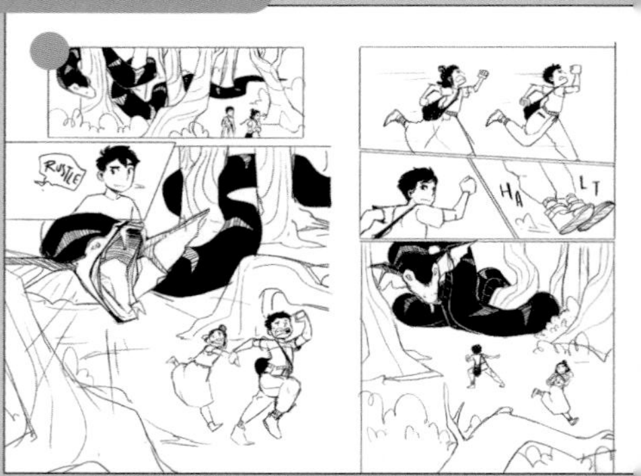
RUSTLE
HA
LT

Once I finalized the script with my editor, I worked on drawing the final pages.

Every single page of this book went through a series of approval phases:

1. Thumbnails
2. Pencils
3. Inks
4. Colors

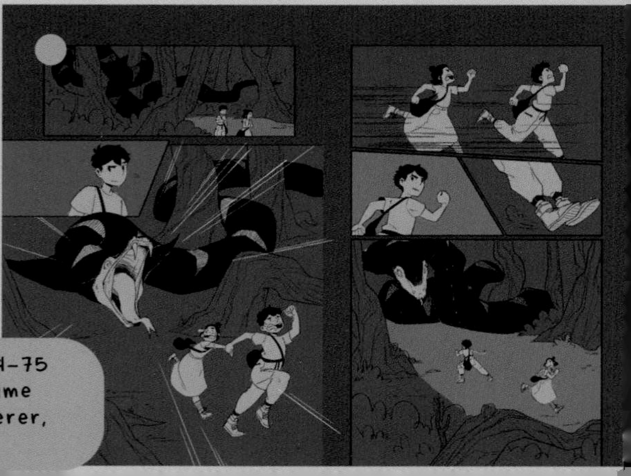

Make sure to go back to pages 74–75 to see what the final spread became after I added colors and the letterer, Kyla, added text!